PENGUIN BOOKS

THE WINTER KING

Before becoming a full-time writer Bernard Cornwell worked as a television producer in London and Belfast. He now lives in Massachusetts with his American wife. He is the author of the hugely successful *Sharpe* series of historical novels.

Penguin publish his bestselling contemporary thrillers *Sea Lord*, *Wildtrack*, *Crackdown*, *Stormchild* and *Scoundrel*, and the historical novel *Redcoat*. Penguin also publish his myth-imbued Arthurian romance, *The Warlord Chronicles*, which consists of *The Winter King*, *Enemy of God* and *Excalibur*.

For more information about Bernard Cornwell's books, please visit his official website: www.bernardcornwell.net

D1390395

05232271

The Warlord Chronicles: I

The Winter King

A Novel of Arthur

BERNARD CORNWELL

PENGUIN BOOKS

PENGUIN BOOKS

Published by the Penguin Group
Penguin Books Ltd, 80 Strand, London WC2R ORL, England
Penguin Group (USA) Inc., 375 Hudson Street, New York, New York 10014, USA
Penguin Group (Canada), 90 Eglinton Avenue East, Suite 700, Toronto, Ontario, Canada M4P 2Y3
(a division of Pearson Penguin Canada Inc.)
Penguin Ireland, 25 St Stephen's Green, Dublin 2, Ireland (a division of Penguin Books Ltd)
Penguin Group (Australia), 250 Camberwell Road,
Camberwell, Victoria 3124, Australia (a division of Pearson Australia Group Pty Ltd)
Penguin Books India Pvt Ltd, 11 Community Centre, Panchsheel Park, New Delhi – 110 017, India
Penguin Group (NZ), 67 Apollo Drive, Rosedale, Auckland 0632, New Zealand
(a division of Pearson New Zealand Ltd)
Penguin Books (South Africa) (Pty) Ltd, 24 Sturdee Avenue, Rosebank, Johannesburg 2196, South Africa

Penguin Books Ltd, Registered Offices: 80 Strand, London WC2R ORL, England

www.penguin.com

First published by Michael Joseph 1995
Published in Penguin Books 1996
Reissued in this edition 2011

001

Copyright © Bernard Cornwell, 1995
All rights reserved

The moral right of the author has been asserted

Printed in Great Britain by Clays Ltd, St Ives plc

ISBN: 978-1-405-93142-7

www.greenpenguin.co.uk

Characters

AELLE	A Saxon king
AGRICOLA	Warlord of Gwent, who serves King Tewdric
AILLEANN	Arthur's mistress, mother of his twin sons Amhar and Loholt
AMHAR	Bastard son of Arthur
ANNA	Sister of Arthur, married to King Budic of Broceliande
ARTHUR	Bastard son of Uther and protector of Mordred
BALISE	An ancient Dumnonian Druid
BAN	King of Benoic, father of Lancelot and Galahad
BEDWIN	Bishop in Dumnonia, chief counsellor to the King
BLEIDDIG	A chieftain of Benoic
BORS	Champion of Benoic
BROCHVAEL	King of Powys after Arthur's time
CADWALLON	King of Gwynedd
CADWY	Client king in Dumnonia, who guards the border with Kernow
CALEDDIN	A Druid, long dead, who compiled Merlin's scroll
CAVAN	Derfel's second-in-command
CEI	Arthur's childhood companion, now one of his warriors
CEINWYN	Princess of Powys, sister of Cuneglas, daughter of Gorfyddyd
CELWIN	A priest studying in Ynys Trebes
CERDIC	A Saxon king
CULHWCH	Arthur's cousin, one of his warriors

v

CUNEGLAS	Edling (Crown Prince) of Powys, son of Gorfyddyd
DAFYDD ap GRUFFUD	The clerk who translates Derfel's story
DERFEL CADARN	The narrator, born a Saxon, ward of Merlin and one of Arthur's warriors
DIWRNACH	Irish King of Lleyn, a country previously called Henis Wyren
DRUIDAN	A dwarf, commander of Merlin's guard
ELAINE	Queen of Benoic, Lancelot's mother
GALAHAD	Prince of Benoic, Lancelot's half-brother
GEREINT	Client prince of Dumnonia, Lord of the Stones
GORFYDDYD	King of Powys, father of Cuneglas and Ceinwyn
GRIFFID ap ANNAN	Owain's second-in-command
GUDOVAN	Merlin's scribe
GUENDOLOEN	Merlin's discarded wife
GUINEVERE	Princess of Henis Wyren
GUNDLEUS	King of Siluria
GWLYDDYN	Carpenter at Ynys Wydryn
HELLEDD	Princess of Elmet, who marries Cuneglas of Powys
HYGWYDD	Arthur's servant
HYWEL	Merlin's steward
IGRAINE	Queen of Powys, married to Brochvael, Derfel's patroness at Dinnewrac
IGRAINE of GWYNEDD	Arthur's mother (also mother of Morgan, Anna and Morgause)
IORWETH	A Druid in Powys
ISSA	One of Derfel's spearmen
LADWYS	Gundleus's lover
LANCELOT	Edling (Crown Prince) of Benoic, son of Ban
LANVAL	One of Arthur's warriors, chief of Guinevere's bodyguard

LEODEGAN	Exiled King of Henis Wyren, father of Guinevere
LIGESSAC	First commander of Mordred's bodyguard, who later serves Gundleus
LLYWARCH	Second commander of Mordred's bodyguard
LOHOLT	Arthur's bastard son, twin to Amhar
LUNETE	Derfel's early companion, later attendant to Guinevere
LWELLWYN	A clerk of the Dumnonian treasury
MAELGWYN	Monk at Dinnewrac
MARK	King of Kernow, father of Tristan
MELWAS	King of the Belgae, a client of Dumnonia
MERLIN	Lord of Avalon, a Druid
MEURIG	Edling (Crown Prince) of Gwent, son of Tewdric
MORDRED	Child King of Dumnonia
MORFANS	'The Ugly', one of Arthur's warriors
MORGAN	Arthur's sister, one of Merlin's priestesses
MORGAUSE	Arthur's sister, married to King Lot of Lothian
NABUR	Christian magistrate in Durnovaria, Mordred's legal guardian
NIMUE	Merlin's lover, a priestess
NORWENNA	Uther's daughter-in-law, mother of Mordred
OENGUS Mac AIREM	Irish King of Demetia, King of the Blackshields
OWAIN	Uther's champion, a warlord of Dumnonia
PELLINORE	Mad king imprisoned at Ynys Wydryn
RALLA	Gwlyddyn's wife, wet nurse to Mordred
SAGRAMOR	Arthur's Numidian commander

SANSUM	Christian priest and bishop, Derfel's superior at Dinnewrac
SARLINNA	A child who survives the Dartmoor massacre
SEBILE	Morgan's Saxon slave-woman
TANABURS	A Druid of Siluria
TEWDRIC	King of Gwent
TRISTAN	Edling (Crown Prince) of Kernow
TUDWAL	Novice monk at Dinnewrac
UTHER	King of Dumnonia, High King of Britain, the Pendragon
VALERIN	A chieftain of Powys, once betrothed to Guinevere

Places

Place names marked * are recorded in history

ABONA*	Avonmouth, Avon
AQUAE SULIS*	Bath, Avon
BRANOGENIUM*	Roman fort. Leintwardine, Hereford & Worcester
BURRIUM*	Tewdric's capital. Usk, Gwent
CAER CADARN	Dumnonia's royal hill. South Cadbury Hill, Somerset
CAER DOLFORWYN*	Powys's royal hill. Near Newtown, Powys
CAER LUD*	Ludlow, Shropshire
CAER MAES	White Sheet Hill, Mere, Wiltshire
CAER SWS*	Gorfyddyd's capital. Caersws, Powys
CALLEVA*	Frontier fortress. Silchester, Hampshire
COEL´S HILL*	Cole's Hill, Hereford & Worcester
CORINIUM*	Cirencester, Gloucestershire
CUNETIO*	Mildenhall, Wiltshire
DINNEWRAC	A monastery in Powys
DURNOVARIA*	Dorchester, Dorset
DUROCOBRIVIS*	Dunstable, Bedfordshire
GLEVUM*	Gloucester

ISCA*	Exeter, Devon
ISLE of the DEAD*	Portland Bill, Dorset
LINDINIS*	Roman town. Ilchester, Somerset
LUGG VALE*	Mortimer's Cross, Hereford & Worcester
MAGNIS*	Roman fort. Kenchester, Hereford & Worcester
MAI DUN*	Maiden Castle, Dorchester, Dorset
RATAE*	Leicester
THE STONES*	Stonehenge
VENTA*	Winchester, Hampshire
YNYS MON*	Anglesey
YNYS TREBES	Capital of Benoic. Mont St Michel, France
YNYS WAIR*	Lundy Island
YNYS WYDRYN*	Glastonbury, Somerset

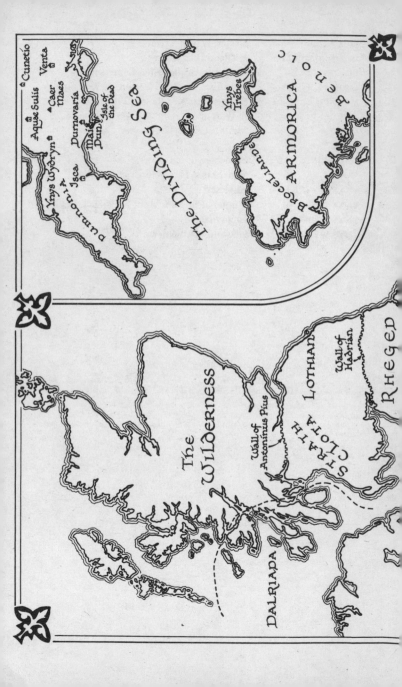

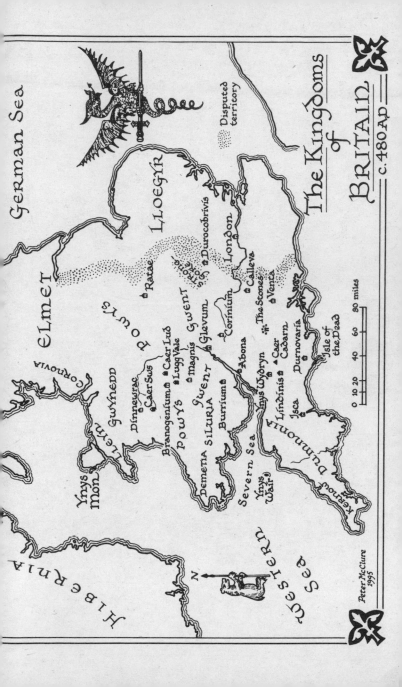

The Kingdoms of BRITAIN

c. 480 AD

German Sea

Western Sea

Hibernia

Elmet

Corfovia

Lloegyr

Powys

Ynys Mon

Llein

Gwynedd

Dinnewrac
Caer Sws

Branogenium
Caer Lud

Lugg Vale

Magnis
Glevum

Gwent
Burrium

Demetia Silura

Ynys Wair

Severn Sea

Abona

Ynys Wydryn

Lindinis

Caer Cadarn

Isca

Kernow

Dumnonia

Durnovaria

Isle of the Dead

The Stones

Venta

Corinium

Calleva

London

Durocobrivis

Corinium

Ratae

Disputed territory

0 10 20   40   60   80 miles

Peter McClure
1995

PART ONE

A Child in Winter

O NCE UPON A TIME, in a land that was called Britain, these things happened. Bishop Sansum, whom God must bless above all the saints living and dead, says these memories should be cast into the bottomless pit with all the other filth of fallen mankind, for these are the tales of the last days before the great darkness descended on the light of our Lord Jesus Christ. These are the tales of the land we call Lloegyr, which means the Lost Lands, the country that was once ours but which our enemies now call England. These are the tales of Arthur, the Warlord, the King that Never Was, the Enemy of God and, may the living Christ and Bishop Sansum forgive me, the best man I ever knew. How I have wept for Arthur.

It is cold today. The hills are deathly pale and the clouds dark. We shall have snow before nightfall, but Sansum will surely refuse us the blessing of a fire. It is good, the saint says, to mortify the flesh. I am old now, but Sansum, may God grant him many years yet, is older still so I cannot use my age as an argument to unlock the woodstore. Sansum will just say that our suffering is an offering to God who suffered more than all of us, and so we six brethren shall shiver in our half-sleep and tomorrow the well will be frozen and Brother Maelgwyn will have to climb down the chain and hammer the ice with a stone before we can drink.

Yet cold is not the worst affliction of our winter, but rather that the icy paths will stop Igraine visiting the monastery. Igraine is our Queen, married to King Brochvael. She is dark and slender, very young, and has a quickness that is like the sun's warmth on a winter's day. She comes here to pray that

3

she will be granted a son, yet she spends more time talking with me than praying to Our Lady or to her blessed son. She talks to me because she likes to hear the stories of Arthur, and this past summer I told her all that I could remember and when I could remember no more she brought me a heap of parchment, a horn flask of ink and a bundle of goose feathers for quills. Arthur wore goose feathers on his helmet. These quills are not so big, nor so white, but yesterday I held the sheaf of quills up to the winter sky and for a glorious guilty moment I thought I saw his face beneath that plume. For that one moment the dragon and the bear snarled across Britain to terrify the heathen again, but then I sneezed and saw I clutched nothing but a handful of feathers clotted with goose droppings and scarcely adequate for writing. The ink is just as bad; mere lamp-black mixed with gum from apple-bark. The parchments are better. They are made from lambs' skins left over from the Roman days and were once covered with a script none of us could read, but Igraine's women scraped the skins bare and white. Sansum says it would be better if so much lambskin were made into shoes, but the scraped skins are too thin to cobble, and besides, Sansum dare not offend Igraine and thus lose the friendship of King Brochvael. This monastery is no more than a half-day's journey from enemy spearmen and even our small storehouse could tempt those enemies across the Black Stream, up into the hills and so to Dinnewrac's valley if Brochvael's warriors were not ordered to protect us. Yet I do not think that even Brochvael's friendship would reconcile Sansum to the idea of Brother Derfel writing an account of Arthur, Enemy of God, and so Igraine and I have lied to the blessed saint by telling him that I am writing down a translation of the Gospel of our Lord Jesus Christ in the tongue of the Saxons. The blessed saint does not speak the enemy tongue, nor can he read, and so we should be able to deceive him long enough for this tale to be written.

And he will need to be deceived for, not long after I had begun writing on this very skin, the holy Sansum came into the room. He stood at the window, peered at the bleak sky

4

and rubbed his thin hands together. 'I like the cold,' he said, knowing that I do not.

'I feel it worst,' I responded gently, 'in my missing hand.' It is my left hand that is missing and I am using the wrist's knobbly stump to steady the parchment as I write.

'All pain is a blessed reminder of our dear Lord's Passion,' the Bishop said, just as I had expected, then he leaned on the table to look at what I had written. 'Tell me what the words say, Derfel,' he demanded.

'I am writing,' I lied, 'the story of the Christ-child's birth.'

He stared at the skin, then placed a dirty fingernail on his own name. He can decipher some letters and his own name must have stood out from the parchment as stark as a raven in the snow. Then he cackled like a wicked child and twisted a hank of my white hair in his fingers. 'I was not present at our Lord's birth, Derfel, yet that is my name. Are you writing heresy, you toad of hell?'

'Lord,' I said humbly as his grip kept my face bowed close over my work, 'I have started the Gospel by recording that it is only by the grace of Our Lord Jesus Christ and with the permission of His most holy saint, Sansum' –and here I edged my finger toward his name – 'that I am able to write down this good news of Christ Jesus.'

He tugged at my hair, pulling some free, then stepped away. 'You are the spawn of a Saxon whore,' he said, 'and no Saxon could ever be trusted. Take care, Saxon, not to offend me.'

'Gracious Lord,' I said to him, but he did not stay to hear more. There was a time when he bowed his knee to me and kissed my sword, but now he is a saint and I am nothing but the most miserable of sinners. And a cold sinner too, for the light beyond our walls is hollow, grey and full of threat. The first snow will fall very soon.

And there was snow when Arthur's tale began. It was a lifetime ago, in the last year of High King Uther's reign. That year, as the Romans used to reckon time, was 1233 years after the founding of their city, though we in Britain usually date our years from the Black Year which was when the Romans cut down the Druids on Ynys Mon. By that reckoning Arthur's story begins in the year 420, though Sansum, may God bless him, numbers our era from the date of our Lord Jesus Christ's birth which he believes happened 480 winters before these things began. But however you count the years it was long ago, once upon a time, in a land called Britain, and I was there.

And this is how it was.

It began with a birth.

On a bitter night, when the kingdom lay still and white beneath a waning moon.

And in the hall, Norwenna screamed.

And screamed.

It was midnight. The sky was clear, dry and brilliant with stars. The land was frozen hard as iron, its streams gripped by ice. The waning moon was a bad omen and in its sullen light the long western lands seemed to glow with a pale cold shimmer. No snow had fallen for three days, nor had there been any thaw, so all the world was white except where the trees had been windblown free of snow and now stood black and intricate against the winter-bleak land. Our breath misted, but did not blow away for there was no wind in this clear midnight. The earth seemed dead and still, as if she had been abandoned by Belenos the Sun God and left to drift in the endless cold void between the worlds. And cold it was; a bitter, deadly cold. Icicles hung long from the eaves of Caer Cadarn's great hall and from the arched gateway where, earlier that day, the High King's entourage had struggled through drifted snow to bring our Princess to this high place of kings. Caer Cadarn was where the royal stone was kept; it was the place of acclamation and thus the only place, the High King insisted, where his heir could be born.

Norwenna screamed again.

I have never seen a child's birth, nor, God willing, will I ever see one. I have seen a mare foal and watched calves slither into the world, and I have heard the soft whining of a whelping

6

bitch and felt the writhing of a birthing cat, but never have I seen the blood and mucus that accompanies a woman's screams. And how Norwenna screamed, even though she was trying not to, or so the women said afterwards. Sometimes the shrieking would suddenly stop and leave a silence hanging over the whole high fort and the High King would lift his great head from among the furs and he would listen as carefully as though he were in a thicket and the Saxons were close by, only now he was listening in hope that the sudden silence marked the moment of birth when his kingdom would have an heir again. He would listen, and in the stillness across the frozen compound we would hear the harsh noise of his daughter-in-law's terrible breathing and once, just once, there was a pathetic whimper, and the High King half turned as though to say something, but then the screams began again and his head sank down into the heavy pelts so that only his eyes could be seen glinting in the shadowed cave formed by the heavy fur hood and collar.

'You should not be on the ramparts, High Lord,' Bishop Bedwin said.

Uther waved a gloved hand as if to suggest that Bedwin was welcome to go inside where the fires burned, but High King Uther, the Pendragon of Britain, would not move. He wanted to be on Caer Cadarn's ramparts so he could gaze across the icy land and up into the middle air where the demons lurked, but Bedwin was right, the High King should not have been standing guard against demons on this hard night. Uther was old and sick, yet the kingdom's safety depended on his bloated body and on his slow, sad mind. He had been vigorous only six months before, but then had come the news of his heir's death. Mordred, the most beloved of his sons and the only one of those born to his bride still living, had been cut down by a Saxon broad-axe and had then bled to death beneath the hill of the White Horse. That death had left the kingdom without an heir, and a kingdom without an heir is a cursed kingdom, but this night, if the Gods willed, Uther's heir would be born to Mordred's widow. Unless the child was a girl, of course, in which case all the pain was for nothing and the kingdom doomed.

Uther's great head raised itself from the pelts that were crusted with ice where his breath had settled on the fur. 'All is being done, Bedwin?' Uther asked.

'All, High Lord, all,' Bishop Bedwin said. He was the King's most trusted counsellor and, like the Princess Norwenna, a Christian. Norwenna, protesting at being moved from the warm Roman villa in nearby Lindinis, had screamed at her father-in-law that she would only go to Caer Cadarn if he promised to keep the old Gods' witches away. She had insisted on a Christian birth, and Uther, desperate for an heir, had agreed to her demands. Now Bedwin's priests were chanting their prayers in a chamber beside the hall where holy water had been sprinkled, a cross had been hung over the birth bed and another put beneath Norwenna's body. 'We are praying to the blessed Virgin Mary,' Bedwin explained, 'who, without soiling her sacred body by any carnal knowledge, became Christ's holy mother and –'

'Enough,' Uther growled. The High King was no Christian and did not like any man attempting to make him one, though he did accept that the Christian God probably had as much power as most other Gods. The events of this night were testing that toleration to the limit.

Which was why I was there. I was a child on the edge of manhood, a beardless errand-runner who crouched frozen beside the King's chair on the ramparts of Caer Cadarn. I had come from Ynys Wydryn, Merlin's hall, which lay on the northern horizon. My task, if ordered, was to fetch Morgan and her helpers who waited in a pig-herder's mud hovel at the foot of Caer Cadarn's western slope. The Princess Norwenna might want Christ's mother as her midwife, but Uther was ready with the older Gods if that newer one failed.

And the Christian God did fail. Norwenna's screams became fewer, but her whimpering more desperate until at last Bishop Bedwin's wife came from the hall and knelt shivering beside the High King's chair. The baby, Ellin said, would not come and the mother, she feared, was dying. Uther waved that last comment aside. The mother was nothing, only the child mattered, and only then if it was a boy.

'High Lord . . .' Ellin began nervously, but Uther was no longer listening.

He tapped my head. 'Go, boy,' he said, and I twisted out of his shadow, leaped down to the fort's interior and raced across the moon-shadowed whiteness between the buildings. The guards on the western gate watched me run by, then I was sliding and falling on the ice-chute of the western road. I slithered through snow, tore my cloak on a tree stump and fell heavily into some ice-laden brambles, but I felt nothing, except the huge weight of a kingdom's fate on my young shoulders. 'Lady Morgan!' I shouted as I neared the hovel. 'Lady Morgan!'

She must have been waiting, for the hovel door was immediately flung open and her gold-masked face shone in the moonlight. 'Go!' she screeched at me, 'go!' and I turned and started back up the hill while around me a pack of Merlin's orphans scrambled through the snow. They were carrying kitchen pots which they clashed together as they ran, though when the slope grew too steep and treacherous they were forced to hurl the pots on ahead and scramble up behind. Morgan followed more slowly, attended by her slave Sebile who carried the necessary charms and herbs. 'Set the fires, Derfel!' Morgan called up to me.

'Fire!' I shouted breathlessly as I scrambled through the gateway. 'Fire on the ramparts! Fire!'

Bishop Bedwin protested at Morgan's arrival, but the High King turned on his counsellor in a rage and the Bishop meekly surrendered to the older faith. His priests and monks were ordered out of their makeshift chapel and told to carry firebrands to all parts of the ramparts and there pile the burning brands with wood and wattle torn out of the huts that clustered inside the fort's northern walls. The fires crackled, then blazed huge in the night and their smoke hung in the air to make a canopy that would confuse the evil spirits and so keep them from this place where a princess and her child were dying. We young

9

ones raced around the ramparts banging pots to make the great noise that would further dizzy the evil ones. 'Shout,' I ordered the children from Ynys Wydryn, and still more children came from the fortress hovels to add their noise to ours. The guards beat their spear-shafts against their shields, and the priests piled more wood on to a dozen flaming pyres while the rest of us screamed our noisy challenges against the evil wraiths that had slithered through the night to curse Norwenna's labour.

Morgan, Sebile, Nimue and one girl child went into the hall. Norwenna screamed, though whether she cried aloud in protest at the coming of Merlin's women or because the stubborn child was tearing her body in two, we could not tell. More screams sounded as Morgan expelled the Christian attendants. She threw the two crosses into the snow and tossed a handful of mugwort, the woman's herb, on to the fire. Nimue later told me that they put iron nuggets into the damp bed to scare away the evil spirits already lodged there and laid seven eagle stones around the writhing woman's head to bring the good spirits down from the Gods.

Sebile, Morgan's slave, put a birch branch over the hall door and waved another over the writhing body of the hurting Princess. Nimue crouched in the door and urinated on the threshold to keep the evil fairies away from the hall, then she cupped some of her urine and carried it to Norwenna's bed where she sprinkled it on the straw as a further precaution against the child's soul being stolen away at the moment of birth. Morgan, her gold mask bright in the flamelight, slapped Norwenna's hands away so she could force a charm of rare amber between the Princess's breasts. The small girl, one of Merlin's foundlings, waited in terror at the foot of the bed.

Smoke from the newly set fires blurred the stars. Creatures woken in the woods at the foot of Caer Cadarn howled at the noise which had erupted above them while High King Uther raised his eyes to the dying moon and prayed that he had not fetched Morgan too late. Morgan was Uther's natural daughter, the first of the four bastards the High King had whelped on Igraine of Gwynedd. Uther would doubtless have preferred Merlin to be there, but Merlin had been gone for months, gone into nowhere, gone, it sometimes seemed to us, for ever, and Morgan, who had learned her skills from Merlin, must take his place on this cold night in which we clashed pots and shouted until we were hoarse to drive the malevolent fiends away from Caer Cadarn. Even Uther joined in the noise-making, though the sound of his staff beating on the rampart's edge was very feeble. Bishop Bedwin was on his knees, praying, while his wife, expelled from the birth-room, wept and wailed and called on the Christian God to forgive the heathen witches.

But the witchcraft worked, for a child was born alive.

The scream Norwenna gave at the moment of birth was worse than any that had preceded it. It was the shriek of an animal in torment, a lament to make the whole night sob. Nimue told me later that Morgan had caused that pain by thrusting her hand into the birth canal and wrenching the baby into this world by brute force. The child came bloody from the tormented mother and Morgan shouted at the frightened girl to pick the child up while Nimue tied and bit the cord. It was important that the baby should first be held by a virgin, which is why the girl child had been taken to the hall, but she was frightened and would not come close to the blood-wet straw on which Norwenna now panted and where the new-born, blood-smeared child lay as though stillborn. 'Pick it up!' Morgan yelled, but the girl fled in tears and so Nimue plucked the baby from the bed and cleared its mouth so that it could snatch its first choking breath.

The omens were all so very bad. The haloed moon was waning and the virgin had fled from the babe that now began to cry aloud. Uther heard the noise and I saw him close his eyes as he prayed to the Gods that he had been given a boy child.

'Shall I?' Bishop Bedwin asked hesitantly.

'Go,' Uther snapped, and the Bishop scrambled down the wooden ladder, hitched up his robe and ran across the trampled snow to the hall's door. He stood there for a few seconds, then ran back towards the rampart waving his hands.

'Good news, High Lord, good news!' Bedwin called as he clambered awkwardly up the ladder. 'Most excellent news!'

'A boy.' Uther anticipated the news by breathing the words.

'A boy!' Bedwin confirmed, 'a fine boy!'

I was crouching near the High King and I saw tears show at his eyes that were gazing toward the sky. 'An heir,' Uther said in a tone of wonder as though he had not really dared to hope that the Gods would favour him. He dabbed at the tears with a fur-gloved hand. 'The kingdom is safe, Bedwin,' he said.

'Praise God, High Lord, it is safe,' Bedwin agreed.

'A boy,' Uther said, then his huge body was suddenly racked with a terrible cough. It left him panting. 'A boy,' he said again when his breathing was steady.

Morgan came after a while. She climbed the ladder and prostrated her stocky body in front of the High King. Her gold mask gleamed, hiding the horror beneath. Uther touched her shoulder with his staff. 'Rise, Morgan,' he said, then he fumbled beneath his robe to find a gold brooch with which to reward her.

But Morgan would not take it. 'The boy,' she said ominously, 'is crippled. He has a twisted foot.'

I saw Bedwin make a sign of the cross for a crippled prince was the worst omen of this cold night.

'How bad?' Uther asked.

'Just the foot,' Morgan said in her harsh voice. 'The leg is properly formed, High Lord, but the Prince will never run.'

From deep inside his swathing fur cloak Uther chuckled. 'Kings don't run, Morgan,' he said, 'they walk, they rule, they ride and they reward their good, honest servants. Take the gold.' He held the brooch towards her again. It was a piece of thick gold, marvellously wrought into the shape of Uther's talisman, a dragon.

But still Morgan would not accept it. 'And the boy is the last child Norwenna will ever bear, High Lord,' she warned Uther. 'We burned the afterbirth and it did not sound once.' The afterbirth was always put on the fire so that the popping sound

12

it made would tell how many more children the mother would bear. 'I listened close,' Morgan said, 'and it was silent.'

'The Gods wanted it silent,' Uther said angrily. 'My son is dead,' he went on bleakly, 'so who else could give Norwenna a boy child fit to be a King?'

Morgan paused. 'You, High Lord?' she said at last.

Uther chuckled at the thought, then the chuckle turned into laughter and finally into another racking cough that bent him forward in lung-aching pain. The coughing passed at last and he drew in a shuddering breath as he shook his head. 'Norwenna's only duty was to drop one boy child, Morgan, and that she has done. Our duty is to protect him.'

'With all the strength of Dumnonia,' Bedwin added eagerly.

'Newborns die easily,' Morgan warned the two men in her bleak voice.

'Not this one,' Uther said fiercely, 'not this one. He will come to you, Morgan, at Ynys Wydryn and you will use your skills to make certain he lives. Here, take the brooch.'

Morgan at last accepted the dragon brooch. The maimed babe was still crying and the mother was whimpering, but around the ramparts of Caer Cadarn the pot-beaters and fire-tenders were celebrating the news that our kingdom had an heir again. Dumnonia had an edling, and an edling's birth meant a great feast and lavish gifts. The bloody birth-straw of the bed was brought from the hall and dumped on a fire so that the flames crackled high and bright. A child had been born; all that child now needed was a name and of that name there could be no doubt. None. Uther eased himself out of his chair and stood huge and grim on Caer Cadarn's wall to pronounce the name of his new-born grandson, the name of his heir and the name of his kingdom's edling. The winter-born babe would be named after his father.

He would be called Mordred.

NORWENNA AND THE BABY came to us at Ynys Wydryn. They were brought in an ox-cart across the eastern land bridge to the Tor's foot and I watched from the windy summit as the sick mother and the maimed child were lifted from their bed of fur cloaks and carried in a cloth litter up the path to the stockade. It was cold that day; a bitter, snow-bright cold that ate at the lungs, chapped the skin and made Norwenna whimper as she was carried with her swaddled babe through the land gate of Ynys Wydryn's Tor.

Thus did Mordred, Edling of Dumnonia, enter Merlin's realm.

Ynys Wydryn, despite its name, which means the Isle of Glass, was not a true island, but rather a promontory of high ground that jutted into a waste of sea-marsh, creeks and willow-edged bogs where sedge and reeds grew thick. It was a rich place, made so by wildfowl, fish, clay and the limestone that could easily be quarried from the hills edging the tidal wastes that were crossed by wooden trackways on which unwary visitors were sometimes drowned when the wind came hard from the west and blew a high tide fast across the long, green wetlands. To the west, where the land rose, there were apple orchards and wheat fields, and to the north, where pale hills edged the marshes, cattle and sheep were herded. It was all good land, and at its heart was Ynys Wydryn.

This was all Lord Merlin's land. It was called Avalon and had been ruled by his father and his father's father, and every serf and slave within sight of the Tor's summit worked for Merlin. It was this land with its produce trapped and netted in the tidal creeks or grown on the rich soil of the inland river valleys that gave Merlin the wealth and freedom to be a Druid. Britain had once been the land of Druids, but the Romans had first slaughtered them, then tamed the religion so that even now, after two generations without Rome's rule, only a handful of the old priests remained. The Christians had taken their place, and Christianity now lapped around the old faith like a wind-driven high tide splashing through the demon-haunted reed-beds of Avalon.

Avalon's isle, Ynys Wydryn, was a cluster of grassy hills, all of them bare except for the Tor which was the steepest and highest. At its summit was a ridge where Merlin's hall was built, and beneath the hall was a spread of lesser buildings protected by a wooden stockade perched precariously at the top of the Tor's steep grassy slopes which were scraped into a pattern of terraces left from the Old Days before the Romans came. A narrow path followed the ancient terraces, winding its intricate way towards the peak, and those who visited the Tor in search of healing or prophecy were forced to follow that path which served to baffle the evil spirits who might otherwise come to sour Merlin's stronghold. Two other paths ran straight down the Tor's slopes, one to the east where the land bridge led to Ynys Wydryn, the other westward from the sea gate down to the settlement at the Tor's foot where fishermen, wildfowlers, basket-weavers and herdsmen lived. Those paths were the everyday entrances to the Tor and Morgan kept them free of evil spirits by constant prayers and charms.

Morgan gave special attention to the western path for it led not only to the settlement, but also to Ynys Wydryn's Christian shrine. Merlin's great-grandfather had let the Christians come to the isle in Roman times and nothing had been able to dislodge them since. We children of the Tor were encouraged to throw stones at the monks and toss animal dung over their wooden stockade or laugh at the pilgrims who scuttled through the wicket gate to worship a thorn tree that grew next to the impressive stone church which had been built by the Romans and still dominated the Christian compound. One year Merlin had a similar thorn tree enthroned on the Tor and we all worshipped it by singing, dancing and bowing. The village's Christians said we would be struck down by their God, but nothing happened. We burned our thorn in the end and mixed its ashes with the pig feed, but still the Christian God ignored us. The Christians claimed that their thorn was magic and that it had been brought to Ynys Wydryn by a foreigner who had seen the Christian God nailed to a tree. May God forgive me, but in those distant days I mocked such stories. I never understood then what the thorn had to do with a God's killing, but now I do, though I can tell you that the Sacred Thorn, if it still grows in Ynys Wydryn, is not the tree sprung from the staff of Joseph of Arimathaea. I know that, for one dark winter's night when I had been sent to fetch Merlin a flask of clean water from the sacred spring at the Tor's southern foot, I saw the Christian monks digging up a small thorn bush to replace the tree that had just died inside their stockade. The Holy Thorn was always dying, though whether that was because of the cow dung we threw at it or simply because the poor tree was overwhelmed by the cloth strips tied to it by pilgrims, I cannot tell. The monks of the Holy Thorn became rich anyway, fattened by the generous gifts of the pilgrims.

The monks of Ynys Wydryn were delighted that Norwenna had come to our stockade for now they had a reason to climb the steep path and bring their prayers into the heart of Merlin's stronghold. The Princess Norwenna was still a fierce and sharp-tongued Christian despite the failure of the Virgin Mary to deliver her child and she demanded that the monks be admitted every morning. I do not know if Merlin would have allowed them into the compound, and Nimue certainly cursed Morgan for granting her permission, but Merlin was not at Ynys Wydryn in those days. We had not seen our master for more than a year, but life in his strange fastness went on without him.

And strange it was. Merlin was the oddest of all Ynys Wydryn's inhabitants, but around him, for his pleasure, he had assembled a tribe of maimed, disfigured, twisted and half-mad creatures. The captain of the household and commander of its guard was Druidan, a dwarf. He stood no higher than a five-year-old child, yet he had the fury of a full-grown warrior and dressed each day in greaves, breastplate, helmet, cloak and weapons. He railed against the fate that had stunted him and took his revenge on the only creatures smaller still: the orphans whom Merlin gathered so carelessly. Few of Merlin's girls were not fanatically pursued by Druidan, though when he had tried to drag Nimue into his bed he had received an angry beating for his pains. Merlin had hit him about the head, breaking Druidan's ears, splitting his lips and blacking his eyes while the children and the stockade's guards cheered. The guards Druidan commanded were all lame or blind or mad, and some of them were all three, but none was mad enough to like Druidan.

Nimue, my friend and childhood companion, was Irish. The Irish were Britons, but they had never been ruled by the Romans and for that reason counted themselves better than the mainland Britons whom they raided, harried, enslaved and colonized. If the Saxons had not been such terrible enemies then we would have considered the Irish the worst of all the Gods' creatures, though from time to time we made alliances with them against some other tribe of Britons. Nimue had been snatched from her family in a raid Uther made against the Irish settlements in Demetia that lay across the wide sea fed by the River Severn. Sixteen captives were taken in that raid and all were sent back to become slaves in Dumnonia, but while the ships were crossing the Severn Sea a great storm blew from the west and the ship carrying the captives foundered on Ynys Wair. Nimue alone survived, walking out of the sea, it was said, without even being wet. It was a sign, Merlin claimed, that she was loved by Manawydan, the Sea God, though Nimue herself insisted that it had been Don, the most powerful Goddess, who had saved her life. Merlin wanted to call her Vivien, a name dedicated to Manawydan, but Nimue ignored the name and kept her own. Nimue almost always got her own way. She grew up in Merlin's mad household with a sharp curiosity and a self-possessed confidence and when, after

17

maybe thirteen or fourteen of her summers had passed, Merlin ordered her to his own bed, she went as though she had known all along that her fate was to become his lover and thus, in the order of these things, the second most important person in all Ynys Wydryn.

Although Morgan did not yield that post without a struggle. Morgan, of all the weird creatures in Merlin's house, was the most grotesque. She was a widow and thirty summers old when Norwenna and Mordred came to be her wards, and the appointment was appropriate for Morgan was high born herself. She was the first of the four bastards, three girls and a boy, fathered on Igraine of Gwynedd by High King Uther. Her brother was Arthur and with such a lineage and such a brother it might be thought ambitious men would have beaten down the walls of the Otherworld itself to claim the widow's hand, yet as a young bride Morgan had been trapped in a burning house that had killed her new husband and scarred Morgan horribly. The flames had taken her left ear, blinded her left eye, seared the hair from the left side of her scalp, maimed her left leg and twisted her left arm so that naked, Nimue told me, the whole left side of Morgan's body was wrinkled, raw-red and distorted, shrivelled in some places, stretched in others, gruesome everywhere. Just like a rotted apple, Nimue told me, only worse. Morgan was a creature from nightmare, but to Merlin she was a lady fit for his high hall and he had trained her to be his prophetess. He had ordered one of the High King's goldsmiths to fashion her a mask that fitted over her ravaged head like a helmet. The gold mask had a hole for her one eye and a slit for her twisted mouth and was made out of thin fine gold that was chased in spirals and dragons, and fronted with an image of Cernunnos, the Horned God, who was Merlin's protector. Gold-faced Morgan always dressed in black, had a glove on her withered left hand, and was widely famed for her healing touch and gifts of prophecy. She was also the worst-tempered woman I ever met.

Sebile was Morgan's slave and companion. Sebile was that rarity, a great beauty with hair the colour of pale gold. She was

18

a Saxon captured in a raid and after the war-band had raped her for a season she had come gibbering to Ynys Wydryn where Morgan had healed her mind. Even so she was still crazed, though not wicked mad, just foolish beyond the dreams of foolishness. She would lie with any man, not because she wanted to, but because she feared not to, and nothing Morgan did could ever stop her. She gave birth year after year, though few of the fair-haired children ever lived and those that did Merlin sold as slaves to men who prized golden-haired children. He was amused by Sebile, though nothing in her madness spoke of the Gods.

I liked Sebile for I too was a Saxon and Sebile would speak to me in my mother's tongue so that I grew up in Ynys Wydryn speaking both Saxon and the speech of the Britons. I should have been a slave, but when I was a little child, shorter even than the dwarf Druidan, a raiding party had come to Dumnonia's northern coast from Siluria and had taken the settlement where my mother was enslaved. King Gundleus of Siluria led the raid. My mother, who I think looked something like Sebile, was raped while I was carried to the death-pit where Tanaburs, Siluria's Druid, sacrificed a dozen captives as thanks to the High God Bel for the great plunder the raid had yielded. Dear God, how I remember that night. The fires, the screams, the drunken rapes, the wild dancing, and then the moment when Tanaburs hurled me into the black pit with its sharpened stake. I lived, untouched, and came from the death-pit as calmly as Nimue had come from the killing sea and Merlin, finding me, had called me a child of Bel. He named me Derfel, gave me a home, and let me grow free.

The Tor was filled with such children who had been snatched from the Gods. Merlin believed we were special and that we might grow into a new order of Druids and Priestesses who could help him re-establish the old true religion in Rome-blighted Britain, but he never had time to teach us, and so most of us grew to become farmers, fishermen or wives. During my time on the Tor only Nimue seemed marked by the Gods and was growing into a priestess. I wanted nothing more than to be a warrior.

Pellinore gave me that ambition. Pellinore was the favourite of all Merlin's creatures. He was a king, but the Saxons had taken his land and his eyes, and the Gods had taken his mind. He should have been sent to the Isle of the Dead, where the dangerous mad went, but Merlin ordered him kept on the Tor locked in a small compound like the one where Druidan kept his pigs. He lived naked with long white hair that reached to his knees and with empty eye-sockets that wept. He raved constantly, haranguing the universe about his troubles, and Merlin would listen to the madness and draw from it messages of the Gods. Everyone feared Pellinore. He was utterly crazy and ungovernably wild. He once cooked one of Sebile's children on his fire. Yet, oddly, I do not know why, Pellinore liked me. I would slip between the bars of his compound and he would pet me and tell me tales of fighting and wild hunts. He never sounded mad to me and he never hurt me, nor Nimue, but then, as Merlin always said, we two children were especially beloved of Bel.

Bel might have loved us, but Guendoloen hated us. She was Merlin's wife, now old and toothless. Like Morgan she had great skills with herbs and charms, but Merlin had cast her off when her face became disfigured by a sickness. It had happened long before I reached the Tor, during a period everyone called the Bad Time when Merlin had come back from the north mad and weeping, but even when he recovered his wits he did not take Guendoloen back, though he did allow her to live in a small hut beside the stockade fence where she spent her days casting spells against her husband and screaming insults at the rest of us. She hated Druidan most of all. Sometimes she would attack him with a fire spit and Druidan would scamper through the huts with Guendoloen chasing after him. We children would urge her on, screaming for dwarfish blood, but he always got away.

Such, then, was the strange place to which Norwenna came with the Edling Mordred, and though I may have made it sound a place of horrors it was, in truth, a good refuge. We were the privileged children of Lord Merlin, we lived free, we did little work, we laughed, and Ynys Wydryn, the Isle of Glass, was a happy place.

Norwenna arrived in wintertime when Avalon's marshes were glossed with ice. There was a carpenter in Ynys Wydryn called Gwlyddyn, whose wife had a boy child the same age as Mordred, and Gwlyddyn made us sledges and we rang the air with shrieks as we slid down the Tor's snowy slopes. Ralla, Gwlyddyn's wife, was appointed Mordred's wet nurse and the Prince, despite his maimed foot, grew strong on her milk. Even Norwenna's health improved as the bitter cold abated and the winter's first snowdrops bloomed in the thorn thickets about the sacred spring at the Tor's foot. The Princess was never strong, but Morgan and Guendoloen gave her herbs, the monks prayed, and it seemed her birth-sickness was at last passing. Each week a messenger carried news of the Edling's health to his grandfather, the High King, and each piece of good news was rewarded with a piece of gold or maybe a horn of salt or a flask of rare wine that Druidan would steal.

We waited for Merlin's return, but he did not come and the Tor seemed empty without him, though our daily life hardly changed. The store-rooms had to be kept filled and the rats had to be killed and the firewood and spring water had to be carried uphill three times a day. Gudovan, Merlin's scribe, kept a tally of the tenants' payments while Hywel, the steward, rode the estates to make certain no family cheated their absent lord. Gudovan and Hywel were both sober, hard-headed, hard-working men; proof, Nimue told me, that Merlin's eccentricities ended where his income began. It was Gudovan who had taught me to read and write. I did not want to learn such un-warriorlike skills, but Nimue had insisted. 'You are fatherless,' she had told me, 'and you'll have to make your way on your own skills.'

'I want to be a soldier.'

'You will be,' she promised me, 'but not unless you learn to read and write,' and such was her youthful authority over me

21

that I believed her and learned the clerkly skills long before I discovered that no soldier needed them.

So Gudovan taught me letters and Hywel, the steward, taught me to fight. He trained me with the single-stick, the countryman's cudgel that could crack a skull open, but which could also mimic the strokeplay of a sword or the thrust of a spear. Hywel, before he lost a leg to a Saxon axe, had been a famous warrior in Uther's band and he made me exercise until my arms were strong enough to wield a heavy sword with the same speed as a single-stick. Most warriors, Hywel said, depended on brute force and drink instead of skill. He told me I would face men reeling with mead and ale whose only talent was to give giant blows that might kill an ox, but a sober man who knew the nine strokes of the sword would always beat such a brute. 'I was drunk,' he admitted, 'when Octha the Saxon took my leg. Now faster, lad, faster! Your sword must dazzle them! Faster!' He taught me well, and the first to know it were the monks' sons in Ynys Wydryn's lower settlement. They resented we privileged children of the Tor, for we idled when they worked and ran free while they laboured, and as revenge they would chase us and try to beat us. I took my single-stick to the village one day and hammered three of the Christians bloody. I was always tall for my age and the Gods had made me strong as an ox and I ascribed my victory to their honour even though Hywel whipped me for it. The privileged, he said, should never take advantage of their inferiors, but I think he was pleased all the same for he took me hunting the next day and I killed my first boar with a man's spear. That was in a misty thicket by the River Cam and I was just twelve summers old. Hywel smeared my face with the boar's blood, gave me its tusks to wear as a necklace, then carried the corpse away to his Temple of Mithras where he gave a feast to all the old warriors who worshipped that soldiers' God. I was not allowed to attend the feast, but one day, Hywel promised me, when I had grown a beard and slain my first Saxon in battle, he would initiate me into the Mithraic mysteries.

Three years later I still dreamed of killing Saxons. Some

might have thought it odd that I, a Saxon youth with Saxon-coloured hair, was so fervently British in my loyalty, but since my earliest childhood I had been raised among the Britons and my friends, loves, daily speech, stories, enmities and dreams were all British. Nor was my colouring so unusual. The Romans had left Briton peopled with all manner of strangers, indeed mad Pellinore once told me of two brothers who were both black as charcoal and until I met Sagramor, Arthur's Numidian commander, I thought his words were mere lunacy weaving romance.

The Tor became crowded once Mordred and his mother arrived for Norwenna brought not only her women attendants, but also a troop of warriors whose task was to protect the Edling's life. We all slept four or five to a hut, though none but Nimue and Morgan were allowed into the hall's inner chambers. They were Merlin's own and Nimue alone was permitted to sleep there. Norwenna and her court lived in the hall itself, which was filled with smoke from the two fires that burned day and night. The hall was supported by twenty oak posts and had walls of plastered wattle and a thatched roof. The floor was of earth covered by rushes that sometimes caught fire and caused a panic until the flames had been stamped out. Merlin's chambers were separated from the hall by an internal wall of wattles and plaster pierced by a single small wooden door. We knew that Merlin slept, studied and dreamed in those rooms that culminated in a wooden tower built at the Tor's highest point. What happened inside the tower was a mystery to everyone but Merlin, Morgan and Nimue and none of those three would ever tell, though the country people, who could see Merlin's Tower for miles around, swore it was crammed with treasures taken from the grave mounds of the Old People.

The chief of Mordred's guard was a Christian named Ligessac, a tall, thin, greedy man whose great skill was with the bow. He could split a twig at fifty paces when he was sober, though he rarely was. He taught me some of his skill, but he became easily bored with a boy's company and preferred to gamble with his men. He did, however, tell me the true tale of Prince

Mordred's death and thus the reason why High King Uther had cursed Arthur. 'It wasn't Arthur's fault,' Ligessac said as he tossed a pebble on to his throwboard. All the soldiers had throwboards, some of them beautifully made out of bone. 'A six!' he said while I waited to hear the story of Arthur.

'Double you,' Menw, one of the Prince's guards, said, then rolled his own stone. It rattled over the board's ridges and settled on a one. He had only needed a two to win so now he scooped his pebbles off the board and cursed.

Ligessac sent Menw to fetch his purse to pay his winnings, then told me how Uther had summoned Arthur from Armorica to help defeat a great army of Saxons that had thrust deep into our land. Arthur had brought his warriors, Ligessac said, but none of his famous horses for the summons had been urgent and there had been no time to find enough ships for both men and horses. 'Not that he needed horses,' Ligessac said admiringly, 'because he trapped those Saxon bastards in the Valley of the White Horse. Then Mordred decided he knew better than Arthur. He wanted all the credit, you see.' Ligessac cuffed at his running nose, then glanced about to make sure no one was listening. 'Mordred was drunk by then,' he went on in a lower voice, 'and half his men were raving naked and swearing they could slaughter ten times their number. We should have waited for Arthur, but the Prince ordered us to charge.'

'You were there?' I asked in adolescent wonder.

He nodded. 'With Mordred. Dear God, but how they fought. They surrounded us and suddenly we were fifty Britons getting dead or sober very quick. I was shooting arrows as fast as I could, our spearmen were making a shield-wall, but their warriors were hacking in on us with sword and axe. Their drums were going bang bang, their wizards were howling and I thought I was a dead man. I'd run out of arrows and was using the spear and there can't have been more than twenty of us left alive, and all of us were at the end of our strength. The dragon banner had been captured, Mordred was bleeding his life away and the rest of us were just huddling together waiting for the end, and then Arthur's men arrived.' He paused, then shook his head ruefully. 'The bards tell you that Mordred glutted the ground with Saxon blood that day, lad, but it wasn't Mordred, it was Arthur. He killed and killed. He took the banner back, he slew the wizards, he burned the war drums, he chased the survivors till dusk and he killed their warlord at Edwy's Hangstone by the light of the moon. And that's why the Saxons are being cautious neighbours, boy, not because Mordred beat them, but because they think Arthur has come back to Britain.'

'But he hasn't,' I said bleakly.

'The High King won't have him back. The High King blames him.' Ligessac paused and looked around again in case he was being overheard. 'The High King reckons Arthur wanted Mordred dead so he could be king himself, but that's not true. Arthur's not like that.'

'What is he like?' I asked.

Ligessac shrugged as if to suggest the answer was difficult, but then, before he could answer anything, he saw Menw returning. 'Not a word, boy,' he warned me, 'not a word.'

We had all heard similar tales, though Ligessac was the first man I met who claimed to be at the Battle of the White Horse. Later I decided he had not been there at all, but was merely spinning a tale to earn a credulous boy's admiration, yet his account was accurate enough. Mordred had been a drunken fool, Arthur had been the victor, but Uther had still sent him back across the sea. Both men were Uther's sons, but Mordred was the beloved heir and Arthur the upstart bastard. Yet Arthur's banishment could not stop every Dumnonian believing that the bastard was their country's brightest hope; the young warrior from across the seas who would save us from the Saxons and take back the Lost Lands of Lloegyr.

The second half of the winter was mild. Wolves were seen beyond the earth wall that guarded Ynys Wydryn's land bridge, but none came close to the Tor, though some of the younger children made wolf charms that they hid beneath Druidan's hut in hope that a slavering great beast would leap the stockade and carry the dwarf off for supper. The charms did not work and as the winter receded we all began to prepare for the great spring festival of Beltain with its massive fires and midnight feasting, but then a greater excitement struck the Tor.

Gundleus of Siluria came.

Bishop Bedwin arrived first. He was Uther's most trusted counsellor and his arrival promised excitement. Norwenna's attendants were moved out of the hall and woven carpets were laid over the rushes, a sure sign that a great person was coming to visit. We all thought it must be Uther himself, but the banner which appeared on the land bridge a week before Beltain showed Gundleus's fox, not Uther's dragon. It was bright morning when I watched the horsemen dismount at the Tor's foot. The wind snatched at their cloaks and snapped their frayed banner on which I saw the hated fox-mask that made me cry out in protest and make the sign against evil.

'What is it?' Nimue asked. She was standing beside me on the eastern guard platform.

'That's Gundleus's banner,' I said. I saw the surprise in Nimue's eyes for Gundleus was King of Siluria and allied with King Gorfyddyd of Powys, Dumnonia's sworn enemy.

'You're sure?' Nimue asked me.

'He took my mother,' I said, 'and his Druid threw me into the death-pit.' I spat over the stockade towards the dozen men who had begun to walk up the Tor that was too steep for horses. And there, among them, was Tanaburs, Gundleus's Druid and my evil spirit. He was a tall old man with a plaited beard and long white hair that was shaved off the front half of his skull in the tonsure adopted by Druids and Christian priests. He cast his cloak aside halfway up the hill and began a protective dance in case Merlin had left spirits to guard the gate. Nimue, seeing the old man caper unsteadily on one leg on the steep slope, spat into the wind and then ran towards Merlin's chambers. I ran after her, but she thrust me aside saying that I would not understand the danger.

'Danger?' I asked, but she had gone. There seemed to be no danger for Bedwin had ordered the land gate thrown wide open and was now trying to organize a welcome out of the excited chaos on the Tor's summit. Morgan was away that day, interpreting in the dream temple in the eastern hills, but everyone else on the Tor was hurrying to see the visitors. Druidan and Ligessac were arraying their guards, naked Pellinore was baying at the clouds, Guendoloen was spitting toothless curses at Bishop Bedwin while a dozen children scrambled to get the best view of the visitors. The reception was supposed to be dignified, but Lunete, an Irish foundling a year younger than Nimue, released a pen of Druidan's pigs so that Tanaburs, who was first through the stockade gate, was greeted by a squealing frenzy.

It would take more than panicking piglets to frighten a Druid. Tanaburs, dressed in a dirty grey robe embroidered with hares and crescent moons, stood in the entranceway and raised both hands above his tonsured head. He carried a moon-tipped staff that he turned sunwise three times, then he howled at Merlin's Tower. A piglet whipped past his legs, then scrabbled for a footing in the muddy gateway before dashing downhill. Tanaburs howled again, motionless, testing the Tor for unseen enemies.

For a few seconds there was silence except for the snapping of the banner and the heavy breathing of the warriors who had climbed the hill behind the Druid. Gudovan, Merlin's scribe, had come to stand beside me, his hands wrapped in ink-stained cloth strips as a protection against the chill. 'Who is it?' he asked, then he shuddered as a wailing shriek answered Tanaburs's challenge. The shriek came from within the hall and I knew it was Nimue.

Tanaburs looked angry. He barked like a fox, touched his genitals, made the evil sign, and then began hopping on one leg towards the hall. He stopped after five paces, howled his challenge again, but this time no answering shriek sounded from the hall so he put his second foot on the ground and beckoned his master through the gate. 'It is safe!' Tanaburs called. 'Come, Lord King, come!'

'King?' Gudovan asked me. I told him who the visitors

were, then asked why Gundleus, an enemy, had come to the Tor. Gudovan scratched at a louse under his shirt, then shrugged. 'Politics, boy, politics.'

'Tell me,' I said.

Gudovan sighed as if my question was evidence of an incurable stupidity, his usual response to any query, but then offered me an answer. 'Norwenna is marriageable, Mordred is a baby who must be protected, and who protects a prince better than a king? And who better than an enemy king who can become a friend to Dumnonia? It's really very simple, boy, a moment's thought would have yielded the answer without you needing to trouble my time.' He gave me a feeble blow on the ear as retribution. 'Mind you,' he cackled, 'he'll have to give up Ladwys for a time.'

'Ladwys?' I asked.

'His lover, you stupid boy. You think any king sleeps alone? But some folk say that Gundleus is so passionate for Ladwys that he actually married her! They say he took her to Lleu's Mound and had his Druid bind them, but I can't believe he'd be such a fool. She's not of the blood. Aren't you supposed to be tallying the rents for Hywel today?'

I ignored the question and watched as Gundleus and his guards stepped carefully through the treacherous mud-slide in the gateway. The Silurian King was a tall, well-made man of perhaps thirty years. He had been a young man when his raiders had captured my mother and cast me into the death-pit, but the dozen or so years that had passed since that dark and bloody night had been kind to him for he was still handsome, with long black hair and a forked beard that showed no trace of grey. He wore a fox-fur cloak, leather boots which reached to his knee, a russet tunic and carried a sword sheathed in a red scabbard. His guards were similarly dressed, and all were tall men who towered over Druidan's sorry collection of crippled spear-carriers. The Silurians wore swords, but none carried a spear or shield, evidence that they had come in peace.

I shrank away as Tanaburs passed. I had been a toddling child when he had thrown me into the pit and there was no chance that the old man would recognize me as a death-cheater nor, after his failure to kill me, did I need to fear him, yet still I shrank from the Silurian Druid. He had blue eyes, a long nose and a slack dribbling mouth. He had hung small bones at the end of his long, lank white hair and the bones clattered together as he shuffled ahead of his king. Bishop Bedwin fell into step beside Gundleus, proclaiming a welcome and saying how honoured the Tor was by this royal visit. Two of the Silurian guards carried a heavy box that must have contained presents for Norwenna.

The delegation disappeared into the hall. The fox banner was thrust into the earth outside the door where Ligessac's men barred anyone else from entering, but those of us who had grown up on the Tor knew how to wriggle into Merlin's hall. I raced round the south side and scrambled up the log pile and pushed aside one of the leather curtains that protected the windows. Then I dropped to the floor and hid behind the wicker chests that held the feasting cloths. One of Norwenna's slaves saw my arrival, and probably some of Gundleus's men did too, but no one cared enough to eject me.

Norwenna was sitting on a wooden chair in the hall's centre. The widowed Princess was no beauty: her face was moon round with small piggish eyes and a thin, sour-lipped mouth and skin that had been pocked by some childhood disease, but none of that mattered. Great men do not marry princesses for their looks, but for the power they bring in their dowries. Yet Norwenna had still prepared herself carefully for this visit. Her attendants had dressed her in a fine woollen cloak dyed pale blue that fell to the floor all around her and they had plaited her dark hair and wound it in circles about her head before wreathing sloe blossom into the tresses. She wore a heavy gold torque about her neck, three golden bracelets on her wrist and a plain wooden cross that hung between her breasts. She was plainly nervous for her free hand was fidgeting with the wooden cross, while in her other arm, swaddled in yards of fine linen and wrapped in a cloak dyed a rare golden colour with water impregnated by the gum of bee-hives, was the Edling of Dumnonia, Prince Mordred.

King Gundleus gave Norwenna scarcely a glance. He sprawled in the chair facing her and looked as though he was utterly bored by the proceedings. Tanaburs scuttled from pillar to pillar, muttering charms and spitting. When he passed close to my hiding place I crouched low until the smell of him had faded. Flames crackled on the fire-stones at the hall's two ends, their smoke mingling and churning in the soot-blackened roof space. There was no sign of Nimue.

Wine, smoked fish and oatcakes were served to the visitors, then Bishop Bedwin made a speech explaining to Norwenna that Gundleus, King of Siluria, while on a mission of friendship to the High King, had happened to be passing close to Ynys Wydryn and had thought it courteous to pay this visit to the Prince Mordred and his mother. The King had brought the Prince some gifts, Bedwin said, upon which Gundleus carelessly waved the gift-bearers forward. The two guards carried the chest to Norwenna's feet. The Princess had not spoken, nor did she speak now as the gifts were laid on the carpet at her feet. There was a fine wolf fur, two otter pelts, a beaver fur and a hart's skin, a small gold torque, some brooches, a drinking horn wrapped in a silver wicker pattern and a Roman flask of pale green glass with a wonderfully delicate spout and a handle shaped as a wreath. The empty chest was carried away and there was an awkward silence in which no one quite knew what to say. Gundleus gestured carelessly at the gifts, Bishop Bedwin beamed happiness, Tanaburs hawked a protective gobbet of spit at a pillar while Norwenna looked dubiously at the King's gifts which were not, in truth, over generous. The hart's skin might make a fine pair of gloves, the pelts were good, though Norwenna probably had a score of better ones in her wicker baskets, while the torque around her neck was four times as heavy as the one lying at her feet. Gundleus's brooches were of thin gold and the drinking horn was chipped at its rim. Only the green Roman flask was truly precious.

30

Bedwin broke the embarrassing silence. 'The gifts are magnificent! Rare and magnificent. Truly generous, Lord King.'

Norwenna nodded obedient agreement. The child began to cry and Ralla, the wet nurse, carried him off to the shadows beyond the pillars where she bared a breast and so silenced him.

'The Edling is well?' Gundleus spoke for the first time since entering the hall.

'Praise God and His Saints,' Norwenna answered, 'he is.'

His left foot?' Gundleus asked untactfully. 'Does it mend?'

'His foot will not stop him from riding a horse, wielding a sword or sitting upon a throne,' Norwenna answered firmly.

'Of course not, of course not,' Gundleus said and glanced across at the hungry babe. He smiled, then stretched his long arms and looked about the hall. He had said nothing of marriage, but he would not in this company. If he wanted to marry Norwenna then he would ask Uther, not Norwenna. This visit was merely an opportunity for him to inspect his bride. He spared Norwenna a brief disinterested look, then gazed again about the shadowed hall. 'So this is Lord Merlin's lair, eh?' Gundleus said. 'Where is he?'

No one answered. Tanaburs was scrabbling beneath the edge of one of the carpets and I guessed he was burying a charm in the earth of the hall floor. Later, when the Silurian delegation was gone, I searched the spot and found a small bone carving of a boar that I threw on the fire. The flames burned blue and spat fiercely, and Nimue said I had done the right thing.

'Lord Merlin, we think, is in Ireland,' Bishop Bedwin at last answered. 'Or maybe in the northern wilderness,' he added vaguely.

'Or maybe dead?' Gundleus suggested.

'I pray not,' the Bishop said fervently.

'You do?' Gundleus twisted in his chair to stare into Bedwin's aged face. 'You approve of Merlin, Bishop?'

'He is a friend, Lord King,' Bedwin said. He was a dignified, plump man who was ever eager to keep the peace between the various religions.

'Lord Merlin is a Druid, Bishop, who hates Christians.' Gundleus was trying to provoke Bedwin.

'There are many Christians in Britain now,' Bedwin said, 'and few Druids. I think we of the true faith have nothing to fear.'

'You hear that, Tanaburs?' Gundleus called to his Druid. 'The Bishop doesn't fear you!'

Tanaburs did not answer. In his questing around the hall he had come to the ghost-fence that guarded the door to Merlin's chambers. The fence was a simple one: merely two skulls placed on either side of the door, but only a Druid would dare cross their invisible barrier and even a Druid would fear a ghost-fence placed by Merlin.

'Will you rest here tonight?' Bishop Bedwin asked Gundleus, trying to change the subject away from Merlin.

'No,' Gundleus said rudely, rising. I thought he was about to take his leave, but instead he looked past Norwenna to the small, black, skull-guarded door in front of which Tanaburs was quivering like a hound smelling an unseen boar. 'What's through the door?' the King asked.

'My Lord Merlin's chambers, Lord King,' Bedwin said.

'The place of secrets?' Gundleus asked wolfishly.

'Sleeping quarters, nothing more,' Bedwin said dismissively.

Tanaburs raised his moon-tipped staff and held it quivering towards the ghost-fence. King Gundleus watched his Druid's performance, then drained his wine and tossed the drinking horn on to the floor. 'Maybe I shall sleep here after all,' the King said, 'but first let us inspect the sleeping quarters.' He waved Tanaburs forward, but the Druid was nervous. Merlin was the greatest Druid in Britain, feared even beyond the Irish Sea, and no one meddled in his life lightly, yet the great man had not been seen for many a long month and some folk whispered that Prince Mordred's death had been a sign that Merlin's power was waning. And Tanaburs, like his master, was surely fascinated by what lay behind the door for secrets could

32

lie there that would make Tanaburs as mighty and learned as the great Merlin himself. 'Open the door!' Gundleus ordered Tanaburs.

The butt of the moon staff moved tremulously towards one of the skulls, hesitated, then touched the yellowing bone dome. Nothing happened. Tanaburs spat on the skull, then tipped it over before snatching his staff back like a man who has prodded a sleeping snake. Again nothing happened and so he reached his free hand towards the door's wooden latch.

Then he stopped in terror.

A howl had echoed in the hall's smoking dark. A ghastly screech, like a girl being tortured, and the awful sound drove the Druid back. Norwenna cried aloud with fear and made the sign of the cross. The baby Mordred began wailing and nothing Ralla could do would quiet him. Gundleus first checked at the noise, then laughed as the howl faded. 'A warrior,' he announced to the nervous hall, 'is not frightened of a girl's scream.' He walked towards the door, ignoring Bishop Bedwin who was fluttering his hands as he tried to restrain the King without actually touching him.

A crash sounded from the ghost-guarded door. It was a violent, splintering noise and so sudden that everyone jumped with alarm. At first I thought the door had fallen before the King's advance, then I saw that a spear had been thrust clean through it. The silver-coloured spearhead stood proud of the old, fire-blackened oak and I tried to imagine what inhuman force had been needed to drive that sharpened steel through so thick a barrier.

The spear's sudden appearance made even Gundleus check, but his pride was threatened and he would not back down in the face of his warriors. He made the sign against evil, spat at the spearhead, then walked to the door, lifted its latch and pushed it open.

And immediately stepped back with horror on his face. I was watching him and I saw the raw fear in his eyes. He took a second pace away from the open door, then I heard Nimue's keening cry as she advanced into the hall. Tanaburs was making urgent motions with his staff, Bedwin was praying, the baby was crying while Norwenna had turned in her chair with a look of anguish.

Nimue came through the door and, seeing my friend, even I shivered. She was naked and her thin white body was raddled with blood that had dripped down from her hair to run in rivulets past her small breasts and on to her thighs. Her head was crowned with a death-mask, the tanned face-skin of a sacrificed man that was perched above her own face like a snarling helmet and held in place by the skin of the dead man's arms knotted about her thin neck. The mask seemed to have a dreadful life of its own for it twitched as she walked towards the Silurian King. The dead man's dry and yellow body-skin hung loose down Nimue's back as she stuttered forward in small irregular steps. Only the whites of her eyes were showing in her bloody face, and as she twitched forward she called out imprecations in a language fouler than any soldier's tongue, while in her hands were two vipers, their dark bodies gleaming and their flickering heads questing towards the King.

Gundleus retreated, making the sign against evil, then he remembered that he was a man, a king and a warrior and so he put his hand on his sword hilt. It was then that Nimue jerked her head and the death mask fell back from the hair that was piled high on her scalp, then we all saw that it was not her hair that was piled there, but a bat that suddenly stretched its black, crinkling wings and snarled its red mouth at Gundleus.

The bat made Norwenna scream and run to fetch her baby while the rest of us stared in horror at the creature which was trapped in Nimue's hair. It jerked and flapped, tried to fly, snarled and struggled. The snakes twisted and suddenly the hall emptied. Norwenna ran first, Tanaburs followed, then everyone, even the King, was running for the morning daylight at the eastern door.

Nimue stood motionless as they fled, then her eyes rolled and she blinked. She walked to the fire and carelessly tossed the two snakes into the flames where they hissed, whiplashed, then sizzled as they died. She freed the bat, which flew up into the rafters, then untied the death-mask from around her neck and rolled it into a bundle before picking up the delicate Roman flask from among the gifts that Gundleus had brought. She stared at the flask for a few seconds, then her wiry body twisted as she hurled the treasure against an oak pillar where it shattered into a scatter of pale green shards. 'Derfel?' she snapped into the sudden silence that followed. 'I know you're here.'

'Nimue?' I said nervously, then stood up from behind my wicker screen. I was terrified. Snake fat was hissing in the fire and the bat was rustling in the roof.

Nimue smiled at me. 'I need water, Derfel,' she said.

'Water?' I asked stupidly.

'To wash off the chicken blood,' Nimue explained.

'Chicken?'

'Water,' she said again. 'There's a jar by the door. Bring some.'

'In there?' I asked, astonished because her gesture seemed to imply that I should bring the water into Merlin's rooms.

'Why not?' she asked, then walked through the door that was still impaled with the great boar spear while I lifted the heavy jar and followed to find her standing in front of a sheet of beaten copper that reflected her nude body. She was un-embarrassed, perhaps because we had all run naked as chil-dren, but I was uncomfortably aware that the two of us were children no longer.

'Here?' I asked.

Nimue nodded. I put the jar down and backed towards the door. 'Stay,' she said, 'please stay. And shut the door.'

I had to prise the spear out of the door before I could close it. I did not like to ask how she had driven that spearhead through the oak for she was in no mood for questions, so I stayed silent as I worked the weapon free and Nimue washed the blood off her white skin, then wrapped herself in a black cloak. 'Come here,' she said when she had finished. I crossed obediently to a bed of furs and woollen blankets that was piled on a low wooden platform where she evidently slept at nights.

The bed was tented with a dark, musty cloth and in its darkness I sat and cradled her in my arms. I could feel her ribs through the cloak's woollen softness. She was crying. I did not know why, so I just held her clumsily and stared about Merlin's room.

It was an extraordinary place. There were scores of wooden chests and wicker baskets piled up to make nooks and corridors through which a tribe of skinny kittens stalked. In places the piles had collapsed as though someone had sought an object in a lower box and could not be bothered to dismantle the pile, so had just heaved the whole heap over. Dust lay everywhere. I doubted that the rushes on the floor had been changed in years, though in most places they had been overlaid with carpets or blankets that had been allowed to rot. The stench of the room was overpowering; a smell of dust, cat urine, damp, decay and mould all mixed with the more subtle aromas of the herbs hanging from the beams. A table stood at one side of the door and was piled with curling, crumbling parchments. Animal skulls occupied a dusty shelf over the table, and, as my eyes grew accustomed to the sepulchral gloom, I saw there were at least two human skulls among them. Faded shields were stacked against a vast clay pot in which a sheaf of cobwebbed spears was thrust. A sword hung against a wall. A smoking brazier stood in a heap of grey fire-ash close to the big copper mirror on which, extraordinarily, there hung a Christian cross with its twisted figure of their dead God nailed to its arms. The cross was draped with mistletoe as a precaution against its inherent evil. A great tangle of antlers hung from a rafter alongside bunches of dried mistletoe and a dangling clutch of roosting bats whose droppings made small heaps on the floor. Bats in a house were the worst omen, but I supposed that people as powerful as Merlin and Nimue had no need to worry about such prosaic threats. A second table was crowded with bowls, mortars, pestles, a metal balance, flasks and wax-sealed pots which I later discovered held dew collected from murdered men's graves, the powder from crushed skulls and infusions of belladonna, mandrake and thorn-apple, while in a curious stone urn next to the table was heaped a jumble of eagle stones, fairy loaves, elf bolts, snake stones and hag stones, all mixed up with feathers, sea shells and pine cones. I had never seen a room so crowded, so filthy or so fascinating and I wondered if the chamber next door, Merlin's Tower, was just as dreadfully wonderful.

Nimue had stopped crying and now lay motionless in my arms. She must have sensed my wonder and revulsion at the room. 'He throws nothing away,' she said wearily, 'nothing.' I did not speak, but just soothed and stroked her. For a while she lay exhausted, but then, when my hand explored the cloak over one of her small breasts, she twisted angrily away. 'If that's what you want,' she said, 'go and see Sebile.' She clutched the cloak tight about her as she climbed off the platform bed and crossed to the table cluttered with Merlin's instruments.

I stammered some kind of embarrassed apology.

'It's not important,' she dismissed my apologies. We could hear voices on the Tor outside, and more voices in the great hall next door, but no one tried to disturb us. Nimue was searching among the bowls and pots and ladles on the table and found what she wanted. It was a knife made from black stone, its blade feathered into bone-white edges. She came back to the fusty bed and knelt beside its platform so that she could look straight into my face. Her cloak had fallen open and I was nervously aware of her naked, shadowed body, but she was staring fixedly into my eyes and I could do nothing but return that gaze.

She did not speak for a long time and in the silence I could almost hear my heart thumping. She seemed to be making a decision, one of those decisions so ominous that it will change the balance of a life for ever, and so I waited, fearful, helpless to move from my awkward stance. Her black hair was tousled, framing her wedge-shaped face. Nimue was neither beautiful nor plain, but her face possessed a quickness and life that did not need formal beauty. Her forehead was broad and high, her eyes dark and fierce, her nose sharp, her mouth wide and her chin narrow. She was the cleverest woman I ever knew, but even in those days, when she was scarcely more than a child, she was filled with a sadness born of that cleverness. She knew so much. She was born knowing, or else the Gods had given her that knowledge when they had spared her from drowning. As a child she had often been full of nonsense and mischief, but now, bereft of Merlin's guidance but with his responsibilities thrust on her thin shoulders, she was changing. I was changing too, of course, but my change was predictable: a bony boy turning into a tall young man. Nimue was flowing from childhood into authority. That authority sprang from her dream, a dream she shared with Merlin, but one that she would never compromise as Merlin would. Nimue was for all or she was for nothing. She would rather have seen the whole earth die in the cold of a Godless void than yield one inch to those who would dilute her image of a perfect Britain devoted to its own British Gods. And now, kneeling before me, she was, I knew, judging whether I was worthy to be a part of that fervent dream.

She made her decision and moved closer to me. 'Give me your left hand,' she said.

I held it out.

She held my hand palm uppermost in her left hand, then spoke a charm. I recognized the names of Camulos, the War God, of Manawydan fab Llyr, Nimue's own Sea God, of Agrona, the Goddess of Slaughter, and of Aranrhod the Golden, the Goddess of the Dawn, but most of the names and words were strange and they were spoken in such an hypnotic voice that I was lulled and comforted, careless of what Nimue said or did until suddenly she slashed the knife across my palm and then, startled, I cried out. She hushed me. For a second the knife-cut lay thin across my hand, then blood welled up.

She cut her own left palm in the same way that she had cut mine, then placed the cut over mine and gripped my nerveless fingers with her own. She dropped the knife and hitched up a corner of her cloak which she wrapped hard around the two bleeding hands. 'Derfel,' she said softly, 'so long as your hand is scarred and so long as mine is scarred, we are one. Agreed?'

I looked into her eyes and knew this was no small thing, no childhood game, but an oath that would bind me throughout this world and maybe into the next. For a second I was terrified of all that was to come, then I nodded and somehow managed to speak. 'Agreed,' I said.

'And so long as you carry the scar, Derfel,' she said, 'your life is mine, and so long as I carry the scar, my life is yours. Do you understand that?'

'Yes,' I said. My hand throbbed. It felt hot and swollen while her hand felt tiny and chill in my bloody grip.

'One day, Derfel,' Nimue said, 'I will call on you, and if you do not come then the scar will mark you to the Gods for a false friend, a traitor and an enemy.'

'Yes,' I said.

She looked at me in silence for a few seconds, then crawled up on to the pile of furs and blankets where she curled herself into my arms. It was awkward to lie together for our two left hands were still bound, but somehow we made ourselves comfortable and then lay still. Voices sounded outside and dust drifted in the high dark chamber where the bats slept and the kittens hunted. It was cold, but Nimue pulled a pelt over the two of us and then she slept with her body's small weight numbing my right arm. I lay awake, filled with awe and confusion over what the knife had caused between us.

She woke in the middle of the afternoon. 'Gundleus has gone,' she said sleepily, though how she knew I do not know, then she extricated herself from my grip and from the tangled furs before unwrapping the cloak that was still twisted around our hands. The blood had crusted and the scabs tore painfully away from our wounds as we pulled apart. Nimue crossed to the sheaf of spears and scooped up a handful of cobwebs that she slapped on to my bleeding palm. 'It'll heal soon,' she said carelessly, and then, with her own cut hand wrapped in a scrap of cloth, she found some bread and cheese. 'Aren't you hungry?' she asked.

'Always.'

We shared the meal. The bread was dry and hard, and the

39

cheese had been nibbled by mice. At least Nimue thought it was mice. 'Maybe the bats chewed it,' she said. 'Do bats eat cheese?'

'I don't know,' I said, then hesitated. 'Was it a tame bat?' I meant the animal that she had tied into her hair. I had seen such things before, of course, but Merlin would never talk of them, nor would his acolytes, but I suspected the odd ceremony of our bloody hands would let me into Nimue's confidence.

And it did, for she shook her head. 'It's an old trick to frighten fools,' she said dismissively. 'Merlin taught it to me. You put jesses on the bat's feet, just like falcon jesses, then tie the jesses to your hair.' She ran her hand through her black hair, then laughed. 'And it frightened Tanaburs! Imagine that! And him a Druid!'

I was not amused. I wanted to believe in her magic, not have it explained as a trick played with hawk-leashes. 'And the snakes?' I asked.

'He keeps them in a basket. I have to feed them.' She shuddered, then she saw my disappointment. 'What's wrong?'

'Is it all trickery?' I asked.

She frowned and was silent for a long time. I thought she was not going to answer at all, but finally she explained, and I knew, as I listened, that I was hearing the things that Merlin had taught her. Magic, she said, happened at the moments when the lives of the Gods and men touched, but such moments were not commanded by men. 'I can't snap my fingers and fill the room with mist,' she said, 'but I've seen it happen. I can't raise the dead, though Merlin says he has seen it done. I can't order a lightning strike to kill Gundleus, though I wish I might, because only the Gods can do that. But there was a time, Derfel, when we could do those things, when we lived with the Gods and we pleased them and we were able to use their power to keep Britain as they wanted it kept. We did their bidding, you understand, but their bidding was our desire.' She clasped her two hands to demonstrate the point, then flinched as the pressure hurt the cut on her left palm. 'But then the Romans came,' she said, 'and they broke the compact.'

'But why?' I interrupted impatiently, for I had heard much of this already. Merlin was always telling us how Rome had shattered the bond between Britain and its Gods, but he had never explained why that could happen if the Gods had such power. 'Why didn't we beat the Romans?' I asked Nimue.

'Because the Gods didn't want it. Some Gods are wicked, Derfel. And besides, they have no duty to us, only we to them. Maybe it amused them? Or maybe our ancestors broke the pact and the Gods punished them by sending the Romans. We don't know, but we do know that the Romans are gone and Merlin says we have a chance, just one chance, to restore Britain.' She was talking in a low, intense voice. 'We have to remake the old Britain, the real Britain, the land of Gods and men, and if we do it, Derfel, if we do it, then once again we will have the power of Gods.'

I wanted to believe her. How I wanted to believe that our short, disease-ridden and death-stalked lives could be given new hope thanks to the goodwill of supernatural creatures of glorious power. 'But you have to do it by trickery?' I asked, not hiding my disillusion.

'Oh, Derfel.' Nimue's shoulders slumped. 'Think about it. Not everyone can feel the presence of the Gods, so those who can have a special duty. If I show weakness, if I show a moment of disbelief, then what hope is there for the people who want to believe? They're not really tricks, they are . . .' She paused, seeking the right word. '. . . insignia. Just like Uther's crown and his torques and his banner and his stone at Caer Cadarn. Those things tell us that Uther is the High King and we treat him as such, and when Merlin walks among his people he has to wear his insignia too. It tells people that he touches the Gods and people fear him for that.' She pointed at the door with its splintered spear-rent. 'When I walked through that door, naked, with two snakes and a bat hidden under a dead man's skin, I was confronting a king, his Druid and his warriors. One girl, Derfel, against a king, a Druid and a royal guard. Who won?'

'You.'

'So the trick worked, but it wasn't my power that made it work. It was the power of the Gods, but I had to believe in that power to make it work. And to believe, Derfel, you must devote your life to it.' She was speaking with a rare and intense passion now. 'Every minute of every day and every moment of every night you must be open to the Gods, and if you are, then they will come. Not always when you want them, of course, but if you never ask, they'll never answer; but when they do answer, Derfel, oh, when they do, it is so wonderful and so terrifying, like having wings that lift you high into glory.' Her eyes shone as she spoke. I had never heard her speak of these things. Not long ago she had been a child, but now she had been to Merlin's bed and taken on his teaching and his power, and I resented that. I was jealous and angry and I did not understand. She was growing away from me and I could do nothing to stop it.

'I'm open to the Gods,' I said resentfully. 'I believe them. I want their help.'

She touched my face with her bandaged hand. 'You're going to be a warrior, Derfel, and a very great one. You're a good person, you're honest, you're as foursquare as Merlin's Tower and there isn't any madness in you. Not a trace; not even a wild, desperate speck. Do you think I want to follow Merlin?'

'Yes,' I said, hurt. 'I know you do!' I meant, of course, that I was hurt because she would not devote herself to me.

She took in a deep breath and stared into the shadowed roof where two pigeons had flown through a smoke hole and were now shuffling along a rafter. 'Sometimes,' she said, 'I think I would like to marry, have children, watch them grow, grow old myself, die, but of all those things, Derfel' – she looked at me again – 'I will only have the last. I can't bear to think of what will happen to me. I can't bear to think of enduring the Three Wounds of Wisdom, but I must. I must!'

42

'The Three Wounds?' I asked, never having heard of them before.

'The Wound to the Body,' Nimue explained, 'the Wound to the Pride,' and here she touched herself between her legs, 'and the Wound to the Mind, which is madness.' She paused as a look of horror crossed her face. 'Merlin has suffered all three, and that is why he's such a wise man. Morgan had the worst Wound to the Body that anyone can imagine, but she never suffered the other two wounds which is why she will never truly belong to the Gods. I've suffered none of the three, but I will. I must!' She spoke fiercely. 'I must because I was chosen.'

'Why wasn't I chosen?' I asked.

She shook her head. 'You don't understand, Derfel. No one chose me, except me. You have to make the choice for yourself. It could happen to any of us here. That's why Merlin collects foundlings, because he believes orphaned children might have special powers, but only a very few do.'

'And you do,' I said.

'I see the Gods everywhere,' Nimue said simply. 'They see me.'

'I've never seen a God,' I said stubbornly.

She smiled at my resentment. 'You will,' she said, 'because you must think of Britain, Derfel, as though she were laced with the ribbons of a thinning mist. Just tenuous strands here and there, drifting and fading, but those strands are the Gods, and if we can find them and please them and make this land theirs again then the strands will thicken and join to make a great, wonderful mist that will cover all the land and protect us from what lies outside. That's why we live here, on the Tor. Merlin knows that the Gods love this place, and here the sacred mist is thick, but our task is to spread it.'

'Is that what Merlin is doing?'

She smiled. 'Right at this moment, Derfel, Merlin is sleeping. And I must too. Haven't you work to do?'

'Rents to count,' I said awkwardly. The lower storehouses were filling with smoked fish, smoked eels, jars of salt, willow baskets, woven cloth, pigs of lead, tubs of charcoal, even some rare scraps of amber and jet: the winter rents payable at Beltain which Hywel had to assay, record on tallies, then divide into Merlin's share and the portion which would be given to the High King's tax-collectors.

'Then go and count,' Nimue said, as if nothing odd had happened between us, though she did reach over and give me a sisterly kiss. 'Go,' she said and I stumbled out of Merlin's chamber to face the resentful, curious stares of Norwenna's attendants who had moved back into the great hall.

The equinox came. The Christians celebrated the death feast of their God while we lit the vast fires of Beltain. Our flames roared at the darkness to bring new life to the reviving world. The first Saxon raiders were seen far in the east, but none came close to Ynys Wydryn. Nor did we see Gundleus of Siluria again. Gudovan the clerk supposed that the marriage proposal had come to nothing and he gloomily forecast a new war against the northern kingdoms.

Merlin did not return, nor did we hear any news of him.

The Edling Mordred's baby teeth came. The first to show were in his lower gums, a good omen for a long life, and Mordred used the new teeth to bite Ralla's nipples bloody, though she went on feeding him so that her own plump son would suck a prince's blood along with his mother's milk. Nimue's spirits lightened as the days grew longer. The scars on our hands went from pink to white and then to shadowy lines. Nimue never spoke of them.

The High King spent a week at Caer Cadarn and the Edling was carried there for his grandfather's inspection. Uther must have approved of what he saw, and the spring omens were all propitious, for three weeks after Beltain we heard that the future of the kingdom and the future of Norwenna and the future of Mordred would all be decided at a great High Council, the first to be held in Britain for over sixty years.

It was spring, the leaves were green, and there were such high hopes in the freshening land.

THE HIGH COUNCIL WAS held at Glevum, a Roman town that lay beside the River Severn just beyond Dumnonia's northern border with Gwent. Uther was carried there in a cart drawn by four oxen, each beast decorated with sprigs of may and saddled with green cloths. The High King enjoyed his ponderous progress through his kingdom's early summer, maybe because he knew this would be his last sight of Britain's loveliness before he went through Cruachan's Cave and over the sword bridge to the Otherworld. The hedgerows between which his oxen plodded were white with hawthorn, the woods were hazed by bluebells while poppies blazed among the wheat, rye and barley and in the almost ripe fields of hay where the corncrakes were noisy. The High King travelled slowly, stopping often at settlements and villas where he inspected farmlands and halls, and advised men who knew better than he how to layer a fulling pond or geld a hog. He bathed in the hot springs at Aquae Sulis and was so recovered when he left the city that he walked a full mile before being helped once more into his fur-lined cart. He was accompanied by his bards, his counsellors, his physician, his chorus, a train of servants and an escort of warriors commanded by Owain, his champion and commander of his guard. Everyone wore flowers and the warriors slung their shields upside down to show they marched in peace, though Uther was too old and too cautious not to make certain that their spear-points were whetted bright each new day.

I walked to Glevum. I had no business there, but Uther had summoned Morgan to the High Council. Women were not normally welcome at any councils, high or low, but Uther

45

believed no one spoke for Merlin as Morgan did and so, in his despair at Merlin's absence, he called for her. She was, besides, Uther's natural daughter, and the High King liked to say that there was more sense in Morgan's gold-wrapped head than in half his counsellors' skulls put together. Morgan was also responsible for Norwenna's health and it was Norwenna's future that was being decided, though Norwenna herself was neither summoned nor consulted. She stayed at Ynys Wydryn under the care of Merlin's wife, Guendoloen. Morgan would have taken no one but her slave Sebile to Glevum, but at the last moment Nimue calmly announced that she was also travelling there and that I was to accompany her.

Morgan made a fuss, of course, but Nimue met the older woman's indignation with an irritating calm. 'I have been instructed,' she told Morgan, and when Morgan shrilly demanded by whom, Nimue just smiled. Morgan was double Nimue's size and twice her age, but when Merlin had taken Nimue to his bed the power in Ynys Wydryn passed to her and in the face of that authority the older woman was helpless. She still objected to my going. She demanded to know why did Nimue not take Lunete, the other Irish girl among Merlin's foundlings? A boy like me, Morgan said, was no company for a young woman, and when Nimue still did nothing but smile, Morgan spat that she would tell Merlin of Nimue's fondness for me and in that telling would lie the end of Nimue, at which clumsy threat Nimue simply laughed and turned away.

I cared little for the argument. I just wanted to go to Glevum and see the jousting and hear the bards and watch the dancing and, most of all, to be with Nimue.

And so we went, an ill-assorted quartet, to Glevum. Morgan, blackthorn staff in hand and gold mask glinting in the summer sun, stumped ahead, her limp making each heavy step into an emphatic gesture of disapproval at Nimue's company. Sebile, the Saxon slave, hurried two paces behind her mistress with her back stooped beneath the bundle of bedding cloaks, dried herbs and pots. Nimue and I walked behind, barefoot, bare-headed and unburdened. Nimue wore a long black cloak over a white robe that she gathered at her waist with a slave's halter. Her long black hair was pinned high and she wore no jewels, not even a bone pin to gather her cloak. Morgan's neck was circled with a heavy golden torque and her dun-coloured cloak was clasped at her breast with two golden brooches, one cast as a triple-horned deer and the other the heavy dragon ornament that Uther had given to her at Caer Cadarn.

I enjoyed the journey. We took three days, a slow pace, for Morgan was an awkward walker, but the sun shone on us and the Roman road made our journey easy. At dusk we would find the nearest chieftain's hall and sleep as honoured guests in his straw-filled barn. Other travellers were few, and all made way for the bright blazon of Morgan's gold that was her symbol of high status. We had been warned against the masterless and landless men who robbed merchants on the high roads, but none threatened us, perhaps because Uther's soldiers had pre-pared for the High Council by scouring the woods and hills in search of brigands and we passed more than a dozen rotting bodies staked at the road's sides as warnings. The serfs and slaves we met knelt to Morgan, merchants made way for her, and only one traveller dared challenge our authority, a fierce-bearded priest with his ragged following of wild-haired women. The Christian group was dancing down the road, praising their nailed God, but when the priest saw the gold mask covering Morgan's face and the triple antlers and wide-winged dragon of her brooches he ranted at her as a creature of the devil. The priest must have thought that such a disfigured, hobbling woman would prove an easy prey to his taunting, but an errant preacher accompanied by his wife and holy whores was no match for Igraine's daughter, Merlin's ward and Arthur's sister. Morgan gave the fellow a single thump on the ear with her heavy staff, a blow that knocked him sideways into a ditch thick with nettles, and then she walked on with scarce a backwards glance. The priest's women shrieked and parted. Some prayed and others spat curses, but Nimue glided through their malevolence like a spirit.

I carried no weapons, unless a staff and a knife count as a

warrior's accoutrements. I had wanted to carry both a sword and a spear, to look like a grown man, but Hywel had scoffed that a man was not made by wanting, but by doing. For my protection he gave me a bronze torque that displayed Merlin's horned God at its finials. No one, he said, would dare challenge Merlin. Yet even so, without a man's weapons, I felt useless. Why, I asked Nimue, was I there?

'Because you're my oath-friend, little one,' Nimue said. I was already taller than she, but she used the term affectionately. 'And because you and I are chosen of Bel and if He chooses us, then we must choose each other.'

'Then why are the two of us going to Glevum?' I wanted to know.

'Because Merlin wants us there, of course.'

'Will he be there?' I asked eagerly. Merlin had been away so very long, and without him Ynys Wydryn was like a sky without its sun.

'No,' she said calmly, though how she knew Merlin's desire in this matter I did not know for Merlin was still far away and the summons for the High Council had been issued long after his departure.

'And what will we do when we reach Glevum?'

'We will know when we get there,' she said mysteriously and would explain no more.

Glevum, once I had grown accustomed to the overpowering stench of nightsoil, was marvellously strange. Other than some of the villas that had become farmsteads on Merlin's estates, this was my first time in a proper Roman place and I gawked at the sights like a new-born chick. The streets were paved with fitted stones, and though they had canted in the long years since the Romans' departure, King Tewdric's men had done their best to repair the damage by pulling up the weeds and sweeping away the soil so that the city's nine streets looked like stony watercourses in the dry season. It was hard to walk on them, and it made Nimue and me laugh to see horses trying to negotiate the treacherous stones. The buildings were as weird as the streets. We made our halls and houses out of wood, thatch, clay-cob and wattle, but these Roman buildings were all joined together and made of stone and strange narrow bricks, though over the years some of them had collapsed to leave ragged gaps in the long rows of low houses that were curiously roofed with baked clay tiles. The walled city guarded a crossing of the Severn and stood between two kingdoms and near to a third, and so it was a famous trading centre. Potters worked in the houses, goldsmiths stooped over their tables and calves bellowed in a slaughter yard behind the market place that was crowded with country folk selling butter, nuts, leather, smoked fish, honey, dyed cloth and newly sheared wool. Best of all, at least to my dazzled eyes, were King Tewdric's soldiers. They were Romans, Nimue told me, or at least they were Britons taught the Roman ways, and all kept their beards clipped short and were dressed alike in sturdy leather shoes and woollen hose beneath short leather skirts. The senior soldiers had bronze plates sewn on to the skirts and when they walked the armour plates would clank together like cow bells. Each man had a breastplate polished bright, a long russet cloak, and a leather helmet that was sewn at the crown into a ridge. Some of the helmets were plumed with dyed feathers. The soldiers carried short, broad-bladed swords, long spears with polished staffs and oblong shields of wood and leather that carried Tewdric's bull symbol. The shields were all the same size, the spears all of a length and the soldiers all marched in step, an extraordinary sight that made me laugh at first though later I became used to it.

At the centre of the town, where the four streets from the four gates met in a wide open square, there stood a vast and wondrous building. Even Nimue gaped at it, for surely no one living could make such a thing; so high, so white and so sharply cornered. Pillars held the roof high, and all along the triangular space between the roof's peak and the pillars' tops were fantastic pictures carved in white stone that showed marvellous men trampling enemies beneath their horses' hooves. The stone men carried sheaves of stone spears and wore stone helmets with soaring stone crests. Some of the pictures had dropped away or had split in the frosts, yet were still a miracle to me, though Nimue, after staring at them, spat to ward off the evil.

'Don't you like it?' I asked her resentfully.

'The Romans tried to be gods,' she said, 'which is why the Gods humbled them. The Council should not meet here.'

Yet Glevum was where the High Council was summoned, and Nimue could not change it. Here, encompassed by Roman ramparts of earth and wood, the fate of Uther's kingdom was to be decided.

The High King had already arrived by the time we reached the town. He was lodging in another high building that faced the pillared hall across the square. He showed neither surprise nor displeasure that Nimue had come, perhaps because he thought she was merely a part of Morgan's retinue, and he gave us all a single room in the back of the house where the kitchens smoked and the slaves squabbled. The High King's soldiers looked drab beside Tewdric's shining men. Our soldiers wore their hair long and their beards wild, they had patched and frayed cloaks of different colours and carried long, heavy swords, rough-shafted spears and round shields on which Uther's dragon symbol looked crude beside Tewdric's carefully painted bulls.

For the first two days there were celebrations. Champions of the two kingdoms fought mock fights outside the walls, though when Owain, Uther's champion, went into the arena King Tewdric was forced to pit two of his best men against him. Dumnonia's famous hero was reputed to be invincible, and he looked it as he stood with the summer sun glinting off his long sword. He was a huge man with tattooed arms, a matted bare chest and a bristling beard decorated with warrior rings forged from the weapons of defeated enemies. His fight against Tewdric's two champions was supposed to be a mock battle, but the mockery was hard to see as the two heroes of Gwent took their turns to attack him. The three men fought as though they were filled with hate and exchanged sword blows that must have rung north into distant Powys, and after a few minutes their sweat was mixed with blood, their blunt swords' edges were dented and all three men were limping, but Owain was still getting the best of the bout. Despite his size he was fast with a sword, and his blows carried crushing weight. The crowd, which had gathered from all the country thereabouts and was thus drawn from both Uther's and Tewdric's king-doms, was shouting like wild beasts to urge their men on to massacre, and Tewdric, seeing the passion, threw down his staff to end the fight. 'We are friends, remember,' he told the three men, and Uther, seated one step higher than Tewdric as befitted the High King, nodded agreement.

Uther looked gross and ill; his body was swollen with fluid, his face was yellowing and slack, his breathing laboured. He had been carried to the fighting field in a litter and was swathed on his throne in a heavy cloak that hid his jewelled belt and bright torque. King Tewdric dressed as a Roman, indeed his grandfather had been a real Roman which must have explained his foreign-sounding name. The King wore his hair clipped very short, had no beard, and was swathed in a white toga folded intricately at one shoulder. He was tall, thin and graceful in his movements, and though he was still a young man, the sad, wise look of his face made him seem much older. His Queen, Enid, wore her hair in a weird plaited spiral that was piled so precariously on top of her skull that she was forced to move with the angular awkwardness of a new-born colt. Her face was caked with a white paste that fixed her with a vacant expression of perplexed boredom. Her son Meurig, the Edling of Gwent, was a fidgety child of ten who sat at his mother's feet and was struck by his father every time he picked his nose.

After the fighting the harpists and bards had their contest. Cynyr, the Bard of Gwent, sang the great tale of Uther's victory over the Saxons at Caer Idern. Later I realized that Tewdric must have ordered it as a tribute to the High King, and certainly the performance pleased Uther who smiled as the verses rolled by and nodded whenever a particular warrior was praised. Cynyr declaimed the victory in a ringing voice, and

51

when he came to the lines which told how Owain had slaughtered Saxons by the thousand, he turned towards the tired, battered fighter and one of Tewdric's champions, who only an hour before had been trying to beat the big man down, stood and raised Owain's sword arm. The crowd roared, then they laughed as Cynyr adopted a woman's voice to describe the Saxons pleading for mercy. He began to run about the field in little, panicked steps, crouching as though hiding, and the crowd loved it. I loved it too, for you could almost see the hated Saxons cowering in terror and smell the stench of their death blood and hear the wings of the ravens coming to gorge on their flesh, and then Cynyr straightened to his full height and let his cloak drop away so that his blue-painted body was naked and he sang the tribute song of the Gods who had watched their champion, High King Uther of Dumnonia, the Pendragon of Britain, beat down the kings and chiefs and champions of the foe. Then, naked still, the bard prostrated himself before Uther's throne.

Uther fumbled beneath his shaggy cloak to find a torque of yellow gold that he tossed towards Cynyr. His throw was feeble and the torque fell on the edge of the wooden dais where the two kings sat. Nimue blanched at the bad omen, but Tewdric calmly picked up the torque and carried it to the white-haired bard whom the King raised up with his own hands.

After the bards had sung, and just as the sun was setting behind the low dark rill of western hills that marked the edge of the Silurian lands, a procession of girls brought flowers for the queens, but there was only one Queen on the dais, Enid. For a few seconds the girls carrying the heaps of flowers meant for Uther's lady did not know what to do, but Uther stirred himself and pointed at Morgan who had her own bench beside the dais, so the girls swerved aside and heaped the irises, meadowsweet and bee orchids before her. 'She looks like a dumpling,' Nimue hissed in my ear, 'garlanded with parsley.'

On the night before the High Council there was a Christian service in the big hall of the great building in the town's centre. Tewdric was an enthusiastic Christian and his followers

52

thronged the hall that was lit by flaming torches set into iron beckets on the walls. It had rained that evening and the crowded hall stank of sweat, damp wool and woodsmoke. The women stood on the left side of the hall and the men on the right, though Nimue calmly ignored the arrangement and climbed on to a pedestal that stood behind the dark crowd of cloaked, bare-headed men. There were other such pedestals, most crowned with statues, but our plinth was empty and provided ample space for the two of us to sit and stare at the Christian rites, though at first I was more astonished by the hall's vast interior that was higher, wider and longer than any feasting hall I had ever seen; so huge that sparrows lived inside and must have thought the Roman hall a whole wide world. The sparrows' heaven was a curved roof supported by squat brick pillars that had once been covered by smooth white plasterwork on which pictures had been painted. Fragments of the pictures remained: I could see a red outline of a running deer, a sea creature with horns and forked tail, and two women holding a twin-handled cup.

Uther was not in the hall, but his Christian warriors attended, and Bishop Bedwin, the High King's counsellor, helped with the ceremonies that Nimue and I watched from our eyrie like two naughty children eavesdropping on their elders. King Tewdric was there, and with him some of the client kings and princes who would be at the High Council the next day. Those great ones had seats at the front of the hall, but the mass of firelight shone not around their chairs, but on the Christian priests gathered about their table. It was the first time I had ever seen such creatures at their rites. 'What exactly is a bishop?' I asked Nimue.

'Like a Druid,' she said, and indeed like Druids all the Christian priests wore the front part of their skulls shaven clean. 'Except they have no training,' Nimue added derisively, 'and know nothing.'

'Are they all bishops?' I asked, for there were a score of shaven men coming and going, bobbing down and bobbing up, around the firelit table at the hall's far end.

'No. Some are just priests. They know even less than the bishops.' She laughed.

'No priestesses?' I asked.

'In their religion,' she said scornfully, 'women have to obey men.' She spat against that evil and some of the nearby warriors turned disapproving looks on her. Nimue ignored them. She was swathed in her black cloak with her arms clasped about her knees which were drawn tight up against her breasts. Morgan had forbidden us to attend the Christian ceremonies, but Nimue no longer took Morgan's orders. In the firelight her thin face was shadowed dark and her eyes shone.

The strange priests chanted and intoned in the Greek tongue that meant nothing to either of us. They kept bowing, upon which the whole crowd would duck down and struggle up again, and each downward plunge was marked on the right side of the hall by an untidy clatter as a hundred or more scabbarded swords clashed on the tiled floor. The priests, like Druids, held their arms straight out from their sides when they prayed. They wore strange robes that looked something like Tewdric's toga and were covered with short, decorated cloaks. They sang and the crowd sang back, and some of the women standing behind the fragile, white-faced Queen Enid began to shriek and tremble in ecstasy, but the priests ignored the commotion and went on chanting and singing. There was a plain cross on the table to which they bowed and at which Nimue made the sign of evil as she muttered a protective charm. She and I soon became bored and I wanted to slip away to make sure we were well placed to get some fragments of the great feast that was to be given after the ceremony in Uther's hall, but then the language of the night changed into the speech of Britain as a young priest harangued the crowd.

The young priest was Sansum, and that night was the first time I ever saw the saint. He was very young then, much younger than the bishops, but he was considered to be a coming man, the hope of the Christian future, and the bishops had deliberately given him the honour of preaching this sermon as a means of advancing his career.

54

Sansum was always a thin man, short of stature, with a sharp, clean-shaven chin and a receding forehead above which his tonsured hair stuck up stiff and black like a thorn hedge, though the hedge had been more closely trimmed on top than at its edges and thus had left him with a pair of black bristly tufts that stuck out just above his ears. 'He looks like Lughtigern,' Nimue whispered to me and I laughed aloud for Lughtigern is the Mouse Lord of children's stories; a creature full of boasts and bravado, but always running away when puss appears. Yet this tonsured Mouse Lord could certainly preach. I had never heard the blessed Gospel of Our Lord Jesus Christ before that night and I sometimes shiver when I think how ill I took that first sermon, but I will never forget the power of its delivery. Sansum stood on a second table so that he could see and be seen, and sometimes, in the passion of his preaching, he threatened to fall off the edge and had to be restrained by his fellow priests. I was hoping he would fall, yet somehow he always recovered his balance.

His preaching began conventionally enough. He thanked God for the presence of the great kings and mighty princes who had come to hear the Gospel, then he paid King Tewdric some pretty compliments before launching himself into a diatribe which set out the Christian view of the state of Britain. It was, I realized later, more of a political speech than a sermon.

The Isle of Britain, Sansum said, was beloved of God. It was a special land, set apart from other lands and girdled by a bright sea to defend it from pestilences, heresies and enemies. Britain, he went on, was also blessed by great rulers and mighty warriors, yet of late the island had been riven by strangers, and its fields, barns and villages had been put to the sword. The heathen Sais, the Saxons, were taking the land of our ancestors and turning it to waste. The dread Sais desecrated the graves of our fathers, they raped our wives and slaughtered our children, and such things could not happen, Sansum asserted, unless they were the will of God, and why would God so turn his back upon his special and beloved children?

Because, he said, those children had refused to hear His holy message. The children of Britain still bowed down to wood and stone. The so-called sacred groves still stood and their shrines still held the skulls of the dead and were washed with the blood of sacrifices. Such things might not be seen in the towns, Sansum said, for most towns were filled with Christians, but the countryside, he warned us, was infested with pagans. There might be few Druids left in Britain, yet in every valley and farmland there were men and women who acted like Druids, who sacrificed living things to dead stone and who used charms and amulets to beguile the simple people. Even Christians, and here Sansum scowled at his congregation, carried their sick to heathen witches and took their dreams to pagan prophetesses, and so long as those evil practices were encouraged so long would God curse Britain with rape and slaughter and Saxons. He paused there to draw breath and I touched the torque about my neck because I knew this ranting Mouse Lord was the enemy of my master Merlin and of my friend Nimue. We had sinned! Sansum suddenly shouted, spreading his arms as he teetered at the table's edge, and we all had to repent. The Kings of Britain, he said, must love Christ and His blessed Mother, and only when the whole of the British race was united in God would God unite the whole of Britain. By now the crowd was responding to his sermon, calling out agreement, praying aloud to their God for mercy and shouting for the death of the Druids and their followers. It was terrifying.

'Come,' Nimue whispered to me, 'I've heard enough.'

We slipped off the pedestal and eased our way through the crowd that filled the vestibule beneath the hall's outer pillars. To my shame I held my cloak up to my beardless chin so that no one would see my torque as I followed Nimue down the steps into the windy square that was lit on all sides by blustering torch flames. A small rain was spitting out of the west to make the stones of the square shine in the firelight. Tewdric's uniformed guards stood motionless all around the square's edge as Nimue led me into the very centre of the wide space where she stopped and suddenly began to laugh. At first it was a chuckle, then it was the laughter of jest that turned into a fierce mockery that changed into a defiant howl that beat up past the roofs of Glevum to echo out towards the heavens and end in a maniacal screech as wild as the death cry of a cornered beast. She turned around as she sounded the screech, turned sunwise from the north to the east to the south to the west and so back north again, and not one soldier stirred. Some of the Christians in the portico of the great building looked at us in anger, but did not interfere. Even Christians recognized some-one being touched by the Gods, and none of them dared lay a hand on Nimue.

When her breath was ended she sank down to the stones. She was silent; a tiny figure crouched beneath a black cape, a shapeless thing shuddering at my feet. 'Oh, little one,' she finally said in a tired voice, 'oh, my little one.'

'What is it?' I asked. I confess I was more tempted by the smell of roasting pork that came from Uther's hall than by whatever momentary trance had so exhausted Nimue.

She held out her scarred left hand and I hauled her to her feet. 'We have one chance,' she said to me in a small, frightened voice, 'just one chance, and if we lose it then the Gods will go from us. We will be abandoned by the Gods and left to the brutes. And those fools in there, the Mouse Lord and his fol-lowers, will ruin that chance unless we fight them. And there are so many of them and so very few of us.' She was looking into my face, crying desperately.

I did not know what to say. I had no skills with the spirit world, even though I was Merlin's foundling and the child of Bel. 'Bel will help us, won't He?' I asked helplessly. 'He loves us, doesn't He?'

'Loves us!' She snatched her hand away from mine. 'Loves us!' she repeated scornfully. 'It is not the task of Gods to love us. Do you love Druidan's pigs? Why, in Bel's name, should a God love us? Love! What do you know of love, Derfel, son of a Saxon?'

'I know I love you,' I said. I can blush now when I think of a

57

young boy's desperate lunges at a woman's affection. It had taken every nerve in my body to make that statement, every ounce of courage I hoped I possessed, and after I had blurted out the words I blushed in the rain-swept firelight and wished I had kept silent.

Nimue smiled at me. 'I know,' she said, 'I know. Now come. A feast for our supper.'

These days, these my dying days that I spend writing in this monastery in Powys's hills, I sometimes close my eyes and see Nimue. Not as she became, but as she was then: so full of fire, so quick, so confident. I know I have gained Christ and through His blessing I have gained the whole world too, but for what I have lost, for what we have all lost, there is no end to the reckoning. We lost everything.

The feast was wonderful.

The High Council began in mid-morning, after the Christians had held yet another ceremony. They held a terrible number of them, I thought, for every hour of the day seemed to demand some new genuflection to the cross, but the delay served to give the princes and warriors time to recover from their night of drinking, boasting and fighting. The High Council was held in the great hall that was again lit by torches, for although the spring sun was shining brightly the hall's few windows were high and small, less suited for letting the light in than the smoke out, though even that they did badly.

Uther, the High King, sat on a platform raised above the dais reserved for the kings, edlings and princes. Tewdric of Gwent, the Council's host, sat below Uther and on either side of Tewdric's throne were a dozen other thrones filled this day by client kings or princes who paid tribute to Uther or Tewdric. Prince Cadwy of Isca was there, and King Melwas of the Belgae and Prince Gereint, Lord of the Stones, while distant Kernow, the savage kingdom at Britain's western tip, had sent its edling, Prince Tristan, who sat swathed in wolf fur at the dais's edge next to one of the two vacant thrones.

In truth the thrones were nothing more than chairs fetched

from the feasting hall and tricked out with saddlecloths, and in front of each chair, resting on the floor and leaning against the dais, were the shields of the kingdoms. There had been a time when thirty-three shields might have rested against the dais, but now the tribes of Britain fought amongst themselves and some of the kingdoms had been buried in Lloegyr by Saxon blades. One of the purposes of this High Council was to make peace between the remaining British kingdoms, a peace that was already threatened because Powys and Siluria had not come to the Council. Their thrones were empty, mute witness to those kingdoms' continuing enmity towards Gwent and Dumnonia.

Directly before the kings and princes, and beyond a small open space that had been left for the speech-making, sat the counsellors and chief magistrates of the kingdoms. Some of the councils, like those of Gwent and Dumnonia, were huge, while others comprised only a handful of men. The magistrates and counsellors sat on the floor that I now saw was decorated with thousands of tiny coloured stones arranged into a huge picture that showed between the seated bodies. The counsellors had all fetched blankets to make themselves pillows for they knew that the High Council's deliberations could last well beyond nightfall. Behind the counsellors, and present only as observers, stood the armed warriors, some with their favourite hunting dogs leashed at their side. I stood with those armed warriors, my bronze Cernunnos-headed torque all the authority I needed to be present.

Two women were at the Council, only two, yet even their presence had caused murmurs of protest among the waiting men until a flicker of Uther's eyes had stilled the grumbling.

Morgan sat directly in front of Uther. The counsellors had edged away from her so that she had sat alone until Nimue had walked boldly through the hall door and threaded her way through the seated men to take a place beside her. Nimue had entered with such calm assurance that no one had tried to stop her. Once seated she stared up at High King Uther as though daring him to eject her, but the King ignored her arrival.

59

Morgan also ignored her young rival who sat very still and very straight-backed. She was dressed in her white linen shift with its thin leather slave belt and among the heavy-caped, grey-haired men she looked slight and vulnerable.

The High Council began, as all councils did, with a prayer. Merlin, if he had been present, would have called on the Gods, but instead Bishop Conrad of Gwent offered a prayer to the Christian God. I saw Sansum sitting in the ranks of the Gwent counsellors and noted the fierce look of hatred he shot at the two women when they did not bow their heads as the Bishop prayed. Sansum knew the women came in Merlin's place.

After the prayer the challenge was given by Owain, Dumnonia's champion who had taken on Tewdric's best men two days before. A brute, Merlin always called Owain, and he looked like a brute as he stood before the High King with his face still blood-scabbed from the fight, with his sword drawn and with a thick wolf-fur cloak draped around the humped muscles of his huge shoulders. 'Does any man here,' he growled, 'dispute Uther's right to the High Throne?'

No one did. Owain, looking somewhat disappointed at being denied the chance to slaughter a challenger, sheathed his sword and sat uncomfortably among the counsellors. He would much rather have stood with his warriors.

News of Britain was given next. Bishop Bedwin, speaking for the High King, reported that the Saxon threat to the east of Dumnonia had been diminished, though at a price too heavy for contemplation. Prince Mordred, Edling of Dumnonia and a warrior whose fame had reached to the ends of the earth, had been killed in the hour of victory. Uther's face showed nothing as he listened to the oft-told tale of his son's death. Arthur's name was not mentioned, even though it had been Arthur who had snatched the victory from Mordred's clumsy generalship and everyone in the hall knew it. Bedwin reported that the defeated Saxons had come from the lands once governed by the Catuvelan tribe and that, although they had not been ejected from all that ancient territory, they had agreed to pay a yearly tribute to the High King of gold, wheat and oxen. Pray God, he added, that the peace would last.

'Pray God,' King Tewdric intervened, 'that the Saxons will be ejected from those lands!' His words prompted the warriors at the back and sides of the hall to rap their spear-shafts against the pavement and at least one spear broke through the small mosaic tiles. Dogs howled.

To the north of Dumnonia, Bedwin continued calmly when the rough applause had ended, peace reigned, thanks to the all-wise treaty of friendship that existed between the great High King and the noble King Tewdric. To the west, and here Bedwin paused to bestow a smile on the handsome young Prince Tristan, there was also peace. 'The kingdom of Kernow,' Bedwin said, 'keeps itself to itself. We understand King Mark has taken a new wife and we pray that she, like her distinguished predecessors, will keep her master fully occupied.' That provoked a murmur of laughter.

'What wife is this?' Uther demanded suddenly. 'His fourth or fifth?'

'I believe my father has lost count himself, High Lord,' Tristan said, and the hall bellowed with laughter. More tiles broke under spear-butts and one of the small fragments skittered over the floor to lodge against my foot.

Agricola spoke next. His was a Roman name and he was famous for his adhesion to Roman ways. Agricola was Tewdric's commander and, though an old man now, he was still feared for his skill in battle. Age had not stooped his tall figure, though it had turned his close-cropped hair as grey as a sword blade. His scarred face was clean-shaven and he wore Roman uniform, but far grander than the outfits of his men. His tunic was scarlet, his breastplate and leg-greaves silver, and under his arm was a silver helmet plumed with dyed horsehair cut into a stiff scarlet comb. He too reported that the Saxons to the east of his Lord's kingdom had been defeated, but the news from the Lost Lands of Lloegyr was troubling for he had heard that more boats had come from the Saxon lands across the German Sea and in time, he warned, more boats on the Saxon shore meant more warriors pressing west into Britain. Agricola also warned us about a new Saxon leader named Aelle who was struggling for ascendancy among the Sais. That was the first time I ever heard Aelle's name and only the Gods then knew how it would come to haunt us down the years.

The Saxons, Agricola went on, might be temporarily quiet, but that had not brought peace to the kingdom of Gwent. British war-bands had come south from Powys while others had marched west out of Siluria to attack Tewdric's land. Messengers had gone to both kingdoms, inviting their monarchs to attend this council, but alas, and here Agricola gestured at the two empty chairs on the royal platform, neither Gorfyddyd of Powys nor Gundleus of Siluria had come. Tewdric could not hide his disappointment, for plainly he had been hoping that Gwent and Dumnonia could make their peace with their two northern neighbours. That hope of peace, I assumed, had also been the motive behind Uther's invitation to Gundleus to visit Norwenna in the spring, but the vacant thrones seemed to speak only of continuing enmity. If there was to be no peace, Agricola warned sternly, then the King of Gwent would have no choice but to go to war against Gorfyddyd of Powys and his ally, Gundleus of Siluria. Uther nodded, giving his consent to the threat.

From further north, Agricola reported, there came news that Leodegan, King of Henis Wyren, had been driven from his kingdom by Diwrnach, the Irish invader who had given the name Lleyn to his newly conquered lands. The dispossessed Leodegan, Agricola added, had taken shelter with King Gorfyddyd of Powys because Cadwallon of Gwynedd would not accept him. There was more laughter at that news for King Leodegan was famous for his foolishness. 'I hear too,' Agricola went on when the laughter had subsided, 'that more Irish invaders have come into Demetia and are pressing hard on the western borders of Powys and Siluria.'

'I shall speak for Siluria,' a strong voice intervened from the doorway, 'and no one else.'

There was a huge stir as every man in the hall turned to gaze at the doorway. Gundleus had come.

The Silurian King entered the room like a hero. There was no hesitation and no apology in his demeanour even though his warriors had raided Tewdric's land again and again, just as they had raided south across the Severn Sea to harass Uther's country. He looked so confident that I had to remind myself how he had fled from Nimue in Merlin's hall. Behind Gundleus, shuffling and dribbling, came Tanaburs the Druid and once again I hid myself as I remembered the death-pit. Merlin had once told me that Tanaburs's failure to kill me had put his soul into my keeping, but I still shuddered with fear as I watched the old man come into the hall with his hair clicking from the small bones tied to its tight little pigtails.

Behind Tanaburs, their long swords scabbarded in sheaths wrapped in red cloth, strode Gundleus's retinue. Their hair and moustaches were plaited and their beards long. They stood with the other warriors, edging them aside to make a solid phalanx of proud men come to their enemies' High Council while Tanaburs, draped in his dirty grey robe embroidered with crescent moons and running hares, found a space among the counsellors. Owain, scenting blood, had stood to bar Gundleus's path, but Gundleus offered the High King's champion the hilt of his sword to show that he came in peace, then he prostrated himself on the mosaic floor in front of Uther's throne.

'Rise, Gundleus ap Meilyr, King of Siluria,' Uther commanded, then held out a hand in welcome. Gundleus climbed the dais and kissed the hand before unslinging the shield with its blazon of a fox's mask from his back. He placed it with the other shields, then took his throne and proceeded to look brightly about the hall as though he were very pleased to be present. He nodded to acquaintances, mouthing surprise at seeing some and smiling at others. All the men he greeted were his enemies, yet he slouched in the chair as though he sat by his own hearth. He even hooked a long leg over the chair's arm. He raised an eyebrow when he saw the two women and I thought I detected a flicker of a scowl as he recognized Nimue, but the scowl vanished as his eyes flicked on through the crowd. Tewdric cordially invited him to give the High Council news of his kingdom, but Gundleus just smiled and said all was well in Siluria.

I will not weary you with most of the day's business. Clouds gathered over Glevum as disputes were settled, marriages agreed and judgments given. Gundleus, though never admitting his trespasses, consented to pay Tewdric a fee of cattle, sheep and gold, with the same compensation to the High King, and many lesser complaints were similarly resolved. The arguments were long and the pleadings tangled, but one by one the matters were decided. Tewdric did most of the work, though never without a sideways glance at the High King to detect any minute gesture which hinted at Uther's decision. Other than those gestures Uther hardly moved except to stir himself when a slave brought him water, bread or a medicine that Morgan had made from coltsfoot steeped in mead to calm his cough. He left the dais only once to piss against the hall's rear wall while Tewdric, ever patient and ever careful, considered a border dispute between two chiefs of his own kingdom. Uther spat into his urine to avert its evil, then limped back to the dais as Tewdric gave his judgment which, like all the others, was recorded on parchment by three scribes sitting at a table behind the dais.

Uther was saving his small energy for the most important business of the day, which came after dusk. It was a dark twilight and Tewdric's servants had fetched a dozen more blazing torches into the hall. It had also begun to rain hard and the hall became chill as streams of water found holes in the roof and dripped on to the floor or ran in rivulets down the rough brick walls. It was suddenly so cold that a brazier, an iron basket full four feet across, was filled with logs and set ablaze close to the High King's feet. The royal shields were moved and Tewdric's throne shifted aside so that the brazier's warmth could reach Uther. The woodsmoke drifted about the room, eddying in the high shadows as it searched for a way out to the beating rain.

Uther at last stood to address the High Council. He was un-steady and so leaned on a great boar-spear as he spoke his mind about his kingdom. Dumnonia, he said, had a new edling and the Gods must be thanked for that mercy, but the Edling was weak, a baby and had a crippled foot. Murmurs greeted the confirmation of that rumoured ill omen, but subsided as Uther lifted a hand for silence. The smoke wreathed about him, giving him a spectral look as though his soul was already clad in his Otherworld's shadow-body. Gold glinted at his neck and on his wrists, and a thin fillet of gold, the High King's crown, circled his straggling white hairs.

'I am old,' he said, 'and I will not live long.' He calmed the protests with another feeble wave of his hand. 'I do not claim my kingdom to be above any other in this land, but I do say that if Dumnonia falls to the Saxons then all Britain will fall. If Dumnonia falls then we lose our links to Armorica and our brethren beyond the sea. If Dumnonia falls then the Saxon will have divided the land of Britain and a divided land cannot survive.' He paused, and for a second I thought he was too tired to continue, but then that great bull's head reared up and he spoke on. 'The Saxons must not reach the Severn Sea!' he shouted that creed, which had been at the very heart of his ambitions all these years. So long as the Saxons were hemmed in by Britons then there was a chance that they could one day be driven back into the German Sea, but if they once reached our western coast then they would have divided Dumnonia from Gwent and the Britons of the south from the Britons of the north. 'The men of Gwent,' Uther went on, 'are our great-est warriors,' and here he nodded in tribute to Agricola, 'but it is no secret that Gwent lives on Dumnonian bread. Dumnonia must be held or Britain will be lost. I have a grandson and the kingdom is his! The kingdom is Mordred's to rule when I die. That is my law!' And here he stamped his spear on the plat-form and for a moment the old hard force of the Pendragon shone from his eyes. Whatever else would be decided here the kingdom would not pass from Uther's line, for that was Uther's law and everyone in the hall now knew it. All that remained was to decide how the crippled child should be protected until he was old enough to assume the kingship for himself.

And so the talking began, although everyone knew what had already been decided. Why else was Gundleus slouching so cocksure in his throne? Yet some men still advanced other candidates for Norwenna's hand. Prince Gereint, the Lord of the Stones who held Dumnonia's Saxon borderlands, proposed Meurig ap Tewdric, Gwent's Edling, but everyone in the hall knew that the proposal was merely a way of flattering Tewdric and would never be accepted because Meurig was a mere nose-picking child who had no chance of holding Dumnonia against the Saxons. Gereint, his duty done, sat and listened as one of Tewdric's counsellors proposed Prince Cuneglas, Gorfyddyd's eldest son and thus the Edling of Powys. A marriage to the enemy's crown prince, the counsellor claimed, would forge a peace between Powys and Dumnonia, the two most powerful British kingdoms, but the suggestion was ruthlessly beaten down by Bishop Bedwin who knew his master would never bequeath his kingdom to the care of a man who was the son of Tewdric's bitterest enemy.

Tristan, Prince of Kernow, was another candidate, but he demurred, knowing full well that no one in Dumnonia would trust his father, King Mark. Meriadoc, Prince of Stronggore, was suggested, but Stronggore, a kingdom east of Gwent, was already half lost to the Saxons and if a man could not hold his own kingdom how could he hold another? What of the royal houses in Armorica, someone asked, but no one knew whether the princes across the sea would abandon their new land of Brittany to defend Dumnonia.

Gundleus. It all came back to Gundleus.

But then Agricola spoke the name that almost every man in the hall both wanted to hear and feared to hear. The old soldier stood, his Roman armour bright and his shoulders braced, and he looked Uther the Pendragon straight in his rheumy eyes. 'Arthur,' Agricola said. 'I propose Arthur.'

Arthur. The name resounded in the hall, then the dying

echo was drowned by the sudden clatter of staves thumping on the floor. The applauding spearmen were warriors of Dumnonia, men who had followed Arthur into battle and knew his worth, but their rebellion was brief.

Uther the Pendragon, High King of Britain, raised his own spear and brought it down once. There was an immediate silence in which only Agricola still dared to challenge the High King. 'I propose that Arthur marries Norwenna,' he said respectfully, and even I, young as I was, knew that Agricola must be speaking for his master, King Tewdric, and that puzzled me for I had thought that Gundleus was Tewdric's candidate. If Gundleus could be detached from his friendship with Powys then the new alliance of Dumnonia, Gwent and Siluria would hold all the land on either bank of the Severn Sea and that triple alliance would be a bulwark against both Powys and the Saxons. I should have known, of course, that Tewdric, in suggesting Arthur, was inviting a refusal that would have to be recompensed by a favour.

'Arthur ap Neb,' Uther said – and that last word was greeted with a gasp of horrified surprise – 'is not of the blood.' There could be no argument with such a decree and Agricola, accepting his defeat, bowed and sat. Neb meant nobody, and Uther was denying that he was Arthur's father, thereby stating that Arthur had no royal blood and could not therefore marry Norwenna. A Belgic bishop argued for Arthur by protesting that kings had ever been chosen from the nobility and that customs which had served in the past should serve in the future, but his querulous objection was stilled by one fierce look from Uther. Rain whirled in through one of the high windows and hissed in the fire.

Bishop Bedwin stood again. It might have seemed that until this moment all talk of Norwenna's future had been so much wasted breath, yet at least the alternatives had been aired and men of sense could thus understand the reasoning behind the announcement Bedwin now made.

Gundleus of Siluria, Bedwin said mildly, was a man without a wife. There was a murmur in the hall as men remembered the rumours of Gundleus's scandalous marriage to his low-born lover, Ladwys, but Bedwin blithely ignored the disturbance. Some weeks before, the Bishop continued, Gundleus had visited Uther and made his peace with the High King and it was now Uther's pleasure that Gundleus should marry Norwenna and be a protector, he repeated the word, a protector to Mordred's kingdom. As an earnest of his good intention Gundleus had already paid a price in gold to King Uther and that price had been accepted as fitting. There were those, Bishop Bedwin admitted airily, who might not trust a man who had until so recently been an enemy, but as a further earnest of his change of heart Gundleus of Siluria had agreed to abandon Siluria's ancient claim to the kingdom of Gwent and, further, he would become a Christian by being publicly baptised in the River Severn beneath Glevum's walls the very next morning. The Christians who were present all called out hallelujah, but I was watching the Druid Tanaburs and wondered why the wicked old fool showed no sign of disapproval as his master so publicly disavowed the old religion.

I wondered too why these grown men were so quick to welcome a former enemy, but of course they were desperate. A kingdom was being passed to a crippled child and Gundleus, for all his treacherous past, was a famous warrior. If he proved true then the peace of Dumnonia and Gwent was assured. Yet Uther was no fool and so he did his best to protect his grandson should Gundleus prove false. Dumnonia, Uther decreed, would be ruled by a council until Mordred was of age to pick up the sword. Gundleus would preside over the council and a half dozen men, chief of them Bishop Bedwin, would serve as his counsellors. Tewdric of Gwent, Dumnonia's firm ally, was invited to send two men, and the council, so composed, would have the final governance of the land. Gundleus was not pleased at the decision. He had not paid two baskets of gold to sit in a council of old men, but he knew better than to protest. He held his peace as his new bride and his stepson's kingdom were bound about with rules.

And still more rules were laid down. Mordred, Uther said,

would have three sworn protectors; men bound by death-oaths to defend the boy's life with their own. If any man harmed Mordred then the oath-takers would revenge the harm or else sacrifice their own lives. Gundleus sat motionless as the edict was made, but he stirred uncomfortably when the oath-takers were named. King Tewdric of Gwent was one, Owain, the Champion of Dumnonia, was the second and Merlin, Lord of Avalon, the third.

Merlin. Men had been waiting for that name just as they had waited for the name of Arthur. Uther usually made no great decision without Merlin's counsel, yet Merlin was not present. Merlin had not been seen in Dumnonia for months. Merlin, for all any man knew, might be dead.

It was then that Uther looked at Morgan for the first time. She must have squirmed when her brother's paternity was denied, and with it her own, but she had not been commanded to the High Council as Uther's bastard daughter, but as Merlin's trusted prophetess. After Tewdric and Owain had sworn their death-oaths Uther gazed at the one-eyed, crippled woman. The Christians in the hall made the sign of the cross, which was their way of guarding against the evil spirits. 'Well?' Uther prompted Morgan.

Morgan was nervous. What was needed of her was an assurance that Merlin, her companion in mystery, would accept the high charge imposed by the oath. She was there as a priestess, not as a counsellor, and should have answered like a priestess. She did not, and her answer was insufficient. 'My Lord Merlin will be honoured by the appointment, High Lord,' she said.

Nimue screamed. The sound was so sudden and so eerie that all about the hall men shivered and gripped their spear-shafts. Hair stiffened on the spines of the hunting dogs. Then the scream faded to leave a silence among the men. Smoke gusted in great firelit shapes in the hall's dark roof where the rain beat on the tiles and then, in the scream's wake and far off in the storm-shaken night, there was the sound of thunder.

Thunder! Christians made the sign of the cross again, but no man there could have doubted the sign. Taranis, the God of

Thunder, had spoken, proof that the Gods had come to the High Council, had come, moreover, at the bidding of a young girl who, despite the cold that made men draw their cloaks about them, wore nothing but a white shift and a slave's leash.

No one moved, no one spoke, no one even fidgeted. The horns of mead rested and men left lice unscratched. There were no kings here any more, nor warriors. There were no bishops, no tonsured priests, nor old wise men. There was only a hushed, scared crowd who stared in awe as a young girl stood and unpinned her hair to let it fall black and long against her slim white back. Morgan gazed at the floor, Tanaburs gaped and Bishop Bedwin mouthed silent prayers as Nimue walked to the speech space beside the brazier. She held her arms out to her side and turned very slowly, sunwise, so that every man in the room could see her face. It was a face of horror. Her eyes showed white, nothing more, and her tongue protruded from a distorted mouth. She turned, and turned again, turning ever faster, and I swear a communal shudder went through the crowd. She was shaking now as she spun, and edging ever nearer to that great seething fire until she threatened to fall into its flames, but suddenly she leaped into the air and gave a shriek before collapsing on to the small tiles. Then, like a beast, she scuttled on all fours, questing her way back and forth along the line of shields that had been split to let the fire's heat warm the High King's legs, and when she reached the fox shield of Gundleus she reared up like a striking snake and spat once.

The spittle landed on the fox.

Gundleus started up from his throne, but Tewdric checked him. Tanaburs struggled to his feet also, but Nimue turned on him, her eyes still showing white, and screamed. She pointed at him, her shriek ululating and echoing in the vast Roman hall, and the power of her magic made Tanaburs sink down again to the floor.

Then Nimue shuddered, her eyes rolled and we could see their brown pupils again. She blinked at the crowded hall as if surprised to find herself in such a place, and then, with her back to the High King, she went utterly still. The stillness denoted that she was in the grip of the Gods and when she now spoke she would be speaking for them.

'Does Merlin live?' Tewdric asked respectfully.

'Of course he lives.' Nimue's voice was filled with scorn and she offered no title to the King who questioned her. She was with the Gods and had no need to pay respect to mere mortals.

'Where is he?'

'Gone,' Nimue said, and turned around to look at the toga-clad King on the platform.

'Gone where?' Tewdric asked.

'To seek the Knowledge of Britain,' Nimue said. Every man listened hard for this, at last, was real news. I could see Sansum the Mouse Lord wriggling in his desperate need to make a pro-test at this pagan interference with the High Council, but so long as King Tewdric questioned the girl there was no way that a mere priest could interfere.

'What is the Knowledge of Britain?' High King Uther asked.

Nimue turned around again, one full turn sunwise, but she turned only so she could gather her thoughts for the answer which, when it came, was delivered in a chanting, hypnotic voice. 'The Knowledge of Britain is the lore of our ancestors, the gifts of our Gods, the Thirteen Properties of the Thirteen Treasures which, when gathered, will give us back the power to claim our land.' She paused, and when she spoke again her voice was back to its normal timbre. 'Merlin strives to knit this land as one again, a British land,' and here Nimue whirled round so that she was staring straight into Sansum's small, bright, indignant eyes, 'with British Gods.' She turned back to the High King. 'And if Lord Merlin fails, Uther of Dumnonia, we all die.'

A murmur sounded in the room. Sansum and the Christians were yelping their protests now, but Tewdric, the Christian King, waved them to silence. 'Are those Merlin's words?' he demanded of Nimue.

Nimue shrugged as though the question was irrelevant. 'They are not my words,' she said insolently.

Uther had no doubt that Nimue, a mere child on the edge of womanhood, spoke not for herself but for her master and so he leaned his great bulk forward and frowned at her. 'Ask Merlin if he will take my oath? Ask him! Will he protect my grandson?'

Nimue paused a long time. I think she sensed the truth of Britain before any of us, before even Merlin and certainly long before Arthur, if, indeed, Arthur ever knew, but some instinct would not let her speak that truth to this old, dying and stubborn man. 'Merlin, my Lord King,' she finally said in a tired voice that implied she merely discharged a necessary but timewasting duty, 'promises at this moment, upon his soul's life, that he will take the death-oath to protect your grandchild.'

'So long!' Morgan astonished us all by interjecting. She scrambled to her feet, looking squat and dark beside Nimue. Firelight glinted off her gold helm. 'So long!' she cried again, then remembered to sway to and fro in the brazier's smoke as if to suggest the Gods were taking over her body. 'So long, Merlin says, as Arthur shares the oath. Arthur and his men should be your grandson's protector. Merlin has spoken!' She spoke the words with all the dignity of someone accustomed to being an oracle and prophetess, but I, if no one else, noticed that no thunder sounded in the rainswept night.

Gundleus was on his feet protesting Morgan's pronouncement. He had already suffered a council of six and a trio of oath-takers to be imposed upon his power, but now it was proposed that his new kingdom was to support a war-band of possible enemy warriors. 'No!' he cried again, but Tewdric ignored the protest as he stepped down from the dais to stand beside Morgan and face the High King. It was thus made plain to most of us in the hall that Morgan, even if she had been uttering in Merlin's voice, had nevertheless spoken what Tewdric had wanted her to speak. King Tewdric of Gwent might have been a good Christian, but he was a better politician and knew exactly when to have the old Gods support his demands.

'Arthur ap Neb and his warriors,' Tewdric now said to the

High King, 'will be a better surety for your grandson's life than any oath of mine, though God knows my oath is solemn.'

Prince Gereint, who was Uther's nephew and, after Owain, the second most powerful warlord in Dumnonia, might have protested Arthur's appointment, but the Lord of the Stones was an honest man of limited ambition who doubted his ability to lead all Dumnonia's armies and so he stood beside Tewdric and added his support. Owain, who was the leader of Uther's Royal Guard as well as the High King's champion, seemed less happy at the appointment of a rival, but eventually he too stood with Tewdric and growled his assent.

Uther still hesitated. Three was a lucky number and three oath-takers should have sufficed, and the addition of a fourth might risk the Gods' displeasure, but Uther owed Tewdric a favour for having dismissed his proposal of Arthur as Norwenna's husband and now the High King paid his debt. 'Arthur shall take the oath,' he agreed, and the Gods alone knew how hard it was for him thus to appoint the man he believed to be responsible for his beloved son's death, but appoint him he did and the hall rang with acclamation. Gundleus's Silurians alone were silent as the spears splintered the pavement and the warrior cheers echoed in the smoky cavernous dark.

Thus, as the High Council ended, was Arthur, son of nobody, chosen to be one of Mordred's sworn protectors.

NORWENNA AND GUNDLEUS were married two weeks after the High Council ended. The ceremony was performed at a Christian shrine in Abona, a harbour town on our northern shore that faced across the Severn Sea towards Siluria, and it cannot have been a joyful occasion for Norwenna returned to Ynys Wydryn that very same evening. None of us from the Tor went to the ceremony, though a pack of Ynys Wydryn's monks and their wives accompanied the Princess. She returned to us as Queen Norwenna of Siluria, though the honour brought her neither new guards nor added attendants. Gundleus sailed back to his own country where, we heard, there were skirmishes against the Ui Liatháin, the Blackshield Irish who had colonized the old British kingdom of Dyfed that the Blackshields called Demetia.

Our life hardly changed by having a queen among us. We of the Tor might have seemed idle compared to the folk down the hill, but we still had our duties. We cut hay and spread it in rows to dry, we finished shearing the sheep and laid the newly cut flax into stinking retting ponds to make linen. The women in Ynys Wydryn all carried distaffs and spindles on which they wound the newly sheared wool and only the Queen, Morgan and Nimue were spared that unending task. Druidan gelded pigs, Pellinore commanded imaginary armies and Hywel the steward prepared his tally sticks to count the summer rents. Merlin did not come home to Avalon, nor did we receive any news of him. Uther rested at his palace in Durnovaria while Mordred, his heir, grew under Morgan and Guendoloen's care.

Arthur stayed in Armorica. He would eventually come to

Dumnonia, we were told, but only after he had discharged his duty to Ban whose kingdom of Benoic neighboured Broceliande, the realm of King Budic who was married to Arthur's sister, Anna. Those kingdoms in Brittany were a mystery to us, for no one from Ynys Wydryn had ever crossed the sea to explore the places where so many Britons displaced by the Saxons had taken refuge. We did know that Arthur was Ban's warlord, and that he had ravaged the country west of Benoic to keep the Frankish enemy at bay, for our winter evenings had been enlivened by travellers' tales of Arthur's prowess, just as they were filled with envy by the stories about King Ban. The King of Benoic was married to a queen named Elaine and the two of them had made a wondrous kingdom where justice was swift and fair, and where even the poorest serf was fed in wintertime from the Royal storehouses. It all sounded too good to be true, though much later I visited Ban's kingdom and found the tales were not exaggerated. Ban had made his capital on an island fortress, Ynys Trebes, which was famous for its poets. The King lavished affection and money on the town that was reputed to be more beautiful than Rome itself. There were said to be springs in Ynys Trebes that Ban had channelled and dammed so that every householder could find clean water not far from his door. The merchants' scales were tested for accuracy, the King's palace lay open day and night to petitioners seeking redress of grievance, and the various religions were commanded to live in peace or else have their temples and churches pulled down and pounded into dust. Ynys Trebes was a haven of peace, but only so long as Ban's soldiers kept the enemy far away from its walls, which was why King Ban was so reluctant to let Arthur leave for Britain. Nor, perhaps, did Arthur want to come to Dumnonia while Uther still lived.

In Dumnonia that summer was blissful. We gathered the dry hay into great stacks that we built on thick foundations of bracken that would keep the damp from rising and the rats at bay. The rye and barley ripened in the strip fields that quilted all the land between Avalon's marshes and Caer Cadarn, apples grew thick in the eastern orchards, while eels and pike grew fat in our meres and creeks. There was no plague, no wolves and few Saxons. Once in a while we would see a distant pyre of smoke on the south-eastern horizon and we would guess that a shipborne raid of Saxon pirates had burned a settlement, but after the third such fire Prince Gereint led a war-band to take Dumnonia's revenge and the Saxon raids ceased. The Saxon chief even paid his tribute on time, though that was the last tribute we received from a Saxon for many a year and doubtless much of the payment had been plundered from our own border villages. Even so that summer was a good time and Arthur, men said, would die of boredom if he brought his famed horse soldiers to peaceful Dumnonia. Even Powys was calm. King Gorfyddyd had lost the alliance of Siluria, but instead of turning on Gundleus he ignored the Dumnonian marriage and concentrated his spears against the Saxons who threatened his northern territory. Gwynedd, the kingdom to the north of Powys, was embroiled with the fearsome Irish soldiers of Diwrnach of Lleyn, but in Dumnonia, the most blessed of all Britain's realms, there was plump peace and warm skies.

Yet it was in that summer, that warm idyllic summer, that I killed my first enemy and so became a man.

For peace never lasts, and ours was broken most cruelly. Uther, High King and Pendragon of Britain, died. We had known he was ill, we had known he must die soon, indeed we knew he had done all he could to prepare for his own death, yet somehow we had thought this moment would never come. He had been king for so long and under his rule Dumnonia had prospered; it had seemed to us that nothing could ever change. But then, just before the harvest, the Pendragon died. Nimue claimed she heard a hare scream in the midday sun at the very moment, while Morgan, bereft of a father, shut herself in her hut and wailed like a child.

Uther's body was burned in the ancient manner. Bedwin would have preferred to give the High King a Christian burial, but the rest of the council refused to sanction such sacrilege and so his swollen corpse was laid on a pyre on the summit of

Caer Maes and there put to the flames. His sword was melted by the smith Ystrwth and the molten steel was poured into a lake so that Gofannon, the Blacksmith God of the Otherworld, could forge the sword anew for Uther's reborn soul. The burning metal hissed as it struck the water and its steam flew like a thick cloud as the seers stooped over the lake to foretell the kingdom's future in the tortured shapes adopted by the cooling metal. They reported good news, despite which Bishop Bedwin was careful to send his swiftest messengers south to Armorica to summon Arthur while slower men travelled north into Siluria to tell Gundleus that his stepson's kingdom was now in need of its official protector.

Uther's balefire burned for three nights. Only then were the flames allowed to die, a process hastened by a mighty storm that swept in from the Western Sea. Great clouds heaped the sky, lightning harrowed the dead man's land and heavy rain beat across a broad swathe of growing crops. In Ynys Wydryn we crouched in the huts and listened to the drumming rain and the bellowing thunder and watched the water cascade in streams from the thatched roofs. It was during that storm that Bishop Bedwin's messenger brought the kingdom's great dragon banner to Mordred. The messenger had to shout like a mad thing to attract the attention of anyone inside the stockade, but finally Hywel and I opened the gate and once the storm had passed and the wind had died we planted the flag before Merlin's hall as a sign that Mordred was now king over Dumnonia. The baby was not the High King, of course, for that was an honour which was only granted to a king acknowledged by other kings as one above them all, nor was Mordred the Pendragon, for that title only went to a High King who had won his position in battle. Indeed, Mordred was not even the proper King of Dumnonia yet, nor would he be until he had been carried to Caer Cadarn and there proclaimed with sword and shout above the kingdom's royal stone, but he was the banner's owner and so the red dragon flew before Merlin's high hall.

The banner was a square of white linen as broad and high as

the shaft of a warrior's spear. It was held spread by willow withies threaded into its hems and was attached to a long elm staff that was crowned with a golden figure of a dragon. The dragon embroidered on the banner itself was made of red wool that leeched its dye in the rain to smear the lower linen pink. The arrival of the banner was followed within days by the King's Guard, a hundred men led by Owain, the champion, whose task was to protect Mordred, King of Dumnonia. Owain brought a suggestion from Bishop Bedwin that Norwenna and Mordred should move south to Durnovaria, a suggestion Norwenna eagerly adopted for she wanted to raise her son in a Christian community rather than in the Tor's blatantly pagan air, but before the arrangements could be made there came bad news from the north country. Gorfyddyd of Powys, hearing of the High King's death, had sent his spearmen to attack Gwent and the men of Powys were now burning, looting and taking captives deep inside Tewdric's territory. Agricola, Tewdric's Roman commander, was fighting back, but the treacherous Saxons, undoubtedly in league with Gorfyddyd, had brought their own war-bands into Gwent and suddenly our oldest ally was fighting for his kingdom's very existence. Owain, who would have escorted Norwenna and the babe south to Durnovaria, took his warriors north to help King Tewdric instead and Ligessac, who was once again the commander of Mordred's guard, insisted that the baby would be safer behind Ynys Wydryn's easily defended land bridge than in Caer Cadarn or Durnovaria, and so Norwenna reluctantly remained at the Tor.

We held our breath to see whose side Gundleus of Siluria would choose and the answer came swiftly. He would fight for Tewdric against his old ally Gorfyddyd. Gundleus sent a message to Norwenna saying that his levies would cross the mountain passes to attack Gorfyddyd's men from the rear and that as soon as the war-bands of Powys had been defeated he would come south to protect his bride and her royal son.

We waited for news, watching the distant hills day and night for the beacons that would tell us of disaster or the approach of enemies, and yet, despite the war's uncertainties, those were happy days. The sun healed the storm-beaten land and dried the grain while Norwenna, even though she was mired in the pagan Tor, seemed more confident now that her son was King. Mordred was always a grim child, with red hair and a stubborn heart, but in those gentle days he seemed happy enough as he played with his mother or with Ralla, his wet nurse, and her dark-haired son. Ralla's husband, Gwlyddyn the carpenter, carved Mordred a set of animals: ducks, hogs, cows and deer, and the King loved to play with them even though he was still too young to know just what they were. Norwenna was happy when her son was happy. I used to watch her tickling Mordred to make him laugh, cradling him when he was hurt and loving him always. She called him her little King, her ever-loving-lover-boy, her miracle, and Mordred chuckled back and warmed her unhappy heart. He crawled naked in the sun and we could all see how his left foot was clubbed and grown in-wards like a clenched fist, but otherwise he grew strong on Ralla's milk and his mother's love. He was baptized in the stone church beside the Holy Thorn.

News of the war came and it was all good. Prince Gereint had broken a Saxon war-band on Dumnonia's eastern border, while further north Tewdric had destroyed another force of Saxon raiders. Agricola, leading the rest of Gwent's army in al-liance with Owain of Dumnonia, had driven Gorfyddyd's in-vaders back into Powys's hills. Then a messenger came from Gundleus which said that Gorfyddyd of Powys was seeking peace, and the messenger threw two captured Powysian swords at Norwenna's feet as a token of her husband's victory. Better still, the man reported, Gundleus of Siluria was even now on his way south to collect his bride and her precious son. It was time, Gundleus said, that Mordred was proclaimed King on Caer Cadarn. Nothing could have been sweeter to Norwenna's ears and, in her gladness, she gave the messenger a heavy gold bracelet before sending him south to pass on her husband's message to Bedwin and the council. 'Tell Bedwin,' she ordered the messenger, 'that we shall acclaim Mordred before the harvest. God speed your horse!'

The messenger rode south and Norwenna began preparing for the acclamation ceremony at Caer Cadarn. She ordered the monks of the Holy Thorn to be ready to travel with her, though she peremptorily forbade either Morgan or Nimue to attend because from this day on, she declared, Dumnonia would be a Christian kingdom and its heathen witches would be kept far from her son's throne. Gundleus's victory had emboldened Norwenna, encouraging her to exercise an authority that Uther would never have allowed her to wield.

We waited for Morgan or Nimue to protest their exclusion from the ceremony of acclamation, but both women took the prohibition with a surprising calm. Morgan, indeed, simply shrugged her black shoulders, though at dusk that night she carried a bronze cauldron into Merlin's chambers and there secluded herself with Nimue. Norwenna, who had invited the head monk of the Holy Thorn and his wife to dine on the Tor, commented that the witches were brewing evil and everyone in the hall laughed. The Christians were victorious.

I was not so sure of their victory. Nimue and Morgan disliked each other, yet now they were closeted together and I suspected that only a matter of the direst importance could bring about such a reconciliation. But Norwenna had no doubts. Uther's death and her husband's victories were bringing her a blessed freedom and soon she would leave the Tor and assume her rightful place as the King's mother in a Christian court where her son would grow in Christ's image. She was never so happy as on that night when she ruled supreme; a Christian in the heart of Merlin's pagan hall.

But then Morgan and Nimue reappeared.

There was silence in the hall as the two women walked to Norwenna's chair where, with due humility, they knelt. The head monk, a small fierce man with a bristling beard who had been a tanner before converting to Christ and who still stank of the dung needed by his former trade, demanded to know their business. His wife defended herself from evil by making the sign of the cross, though she spat as well just to be sure.

Morgan answered the monk from behind her golden mask. She spoke with unaccustomed deference as she claimed that Gundleus's messenger had lied. She and Nimue, Morgan said, had peered into the cauldron and seen the truth reflected in its watery mirror. There was no victory in the north, nor was there defeat there either, but Morgan warned that the enemy was closer to Ynys Wydryn than any of us knew and that we should all be ready to leave the Tor at first light and seek safety deeper inside southern Dumnonia. Morgan spoke the words soberly and heavily, and when she had finished she bowed to the Queen, then bent awkwardly forward to kiss the hem of Norwenna's blue robe.

Norwenna snatched the robe away. She had listened in silence to the dour prophecy, but now she began to cry and with the sudden tears came a wash of anger. 'You're just a crippled witch!' she screamed at Morgan, 'and want your bastard brother to be King. It won't happen! You hear me! It will not happen. My baby is King!'

'High Lady –' Nimue tried to intervene, but was immediately interrupted.

'You're nothing!' Norwenna turned on Nimue savagely. 'You're nothing but an hysterical, wicked child of the devil. You've put a curse on my child! I know you have! He was born crooked because you were present at his birth. Oh God! My child!' She was screaming and weeping, beating her fist on the table as she spat her hatred at Nimue and Morgan. 'Now go! Both of you! Go!' There was silence in the hall as Nimue and Morgan went into the night.

And next morning it seemed Norwenna must be right for no beacons blazed on the northern hills. It was, indeed, the most beautiful day of that beautiful summer. The land was heavy as it neared harvest, the hills were hazed by the somnolent heat and the sky almost cloudless. Cornflowers and poppies grew in the thorn thickets at the Tor's foot and white butterflies sailed the warm air currents that ghosted up our patterned green slopes. Norwenna, oblivious to the day's beauty, chanted her morning prayers with the visiting monks, then decreed she would move from the Tor and wait for her husband's arrival in the pilgrims' chambers in the shrine of the Holy Thorn. 'I have lived among the wicked too long,' she announced very grandly, as a guard shouted a warning from the eastern wall.

'Horsemen!' the guard cried. 'Horsemen!'

Norwenna ran to the fence where a crowd was gathering to watch a score of armed horsemen crossing the land bridge that led from the Roman road to the green hills of Ynys Wydryn. Ligessac, commander of Mordred's guard, seemed to know who was coming for he sent orders to his men to allow the horsemen through the earth wall. The riders spurred through the wall's gate and came towards us beneath a bright banner that showed the red badge of the fox. It was Gundleus himself and Norwenna laughed with delight to see her husband riding victorious from the war with the dawn of a new Christian kingdom bright upon his spear-point. 'You see?' she turned on Morgan. 'You see? Your cauldron lied. There is victory!'

Mordred began to cry at all the commotion and Norwenna brusquely ordered him given to Ralla, then she demanded that her best cloak be fetched and a gold circlet placed upon her head and thus, dressed as a queen, she waited for her King before the doors of Merlin's hall.

Ligessac opened the Tor's land gate. Druidan's ramshackle guard formed a crude line while poor mad Pellinore shrieked in his cage for news. Nimue ran towards Merlin's chamber while I went to fetch Hywel, Merlin's steward, who I knew would want to welcome the King.

The twenty Silurian horsemen dismounted at the Tor's foot. They had come from the war and so they carried spears, shields and swords. One-legged Hywel, buckling on his own great sword, frowned when he saw that the Druid Tanaburs was among the Silurian party. 'I thought Gundleus had abandoned the old faith?' the steward said.

'I thought he'd abandoned Ladwys!' Gudovan, the scribe, cackled, then jerked his chin towards the horsemen who had begun to climb the Tor's steep narrow path. 'See?' Gudovan said, and sure enough there was one woman among the leather-armoured men. The woman was dressed as a man, but had her long black hair flowing free. She carried a sword, but no shield, and Gudovan chuckled to see her. 'Our little Queen will have her work cut out competing with that imp of Satan.'

'Who's Satan?' I asked, and Gudovan gave me a buffet on the head for wasting his time with stupid questions.

Hywel was frowning and his hand was clasped about his sword's hilt as the Silurian warriors neared the last steep steps that climbed to the gate where our motley guards waited in two ragged files. Then some instinct that was still as sharp as when he had been a warrior tugged at Hywel's fears. 'Ligessac!' he roared. 'Close the gate! Close it! Now!'

Ligessac drew his sword instead. Then he turned and cupped an ear as though he had not heard Hywel properly.

'Shut the gate!' Hywel roared. One of Ligessac's men moved to obey the order, but Ligessac checked the man and stared at Norwenna for orders instead.

Norwenna turned to Hywel and scowled her displeasure at his order. 'This is my husband coming,' she said, 'not an enemy.' She looked back to Ligessac. 'Leave the gate open,' she commanded imperiously, and Ligessac bowed his obedience.

Hywel cursed, then clambered awkwardly down from the rampart and limped on his crutch towards Morgan's hut while I just stared at that empty, sunlit gate and wondered what was about to happen. Hywel had scented some trouble in the summer air, but how I never did discover.

Gundleus reached the open gate. He spat on the threshold, then smiled at Norwenna who was waiting a dozen paces away. She raised her plump arms to greet her Lord who was sweating and breathless, and no wonder for he had climbed the steep Tor dressed in his full war gear. He had a leather breastplate, padded leggings, boots, an iron helmet crested with a fox's tail and a thick red cloak draped about his shoulders. His fox-blazoned shield hung at his left side, his sword was at his hip and he carried a heavy battle-spear in his right hand. Ligessac

knelt and offered the King the hilt of his drawn sword and
Gundleus stepped forward to touch the weapon's pommel
with a leather-gloved hand.

Hywel had gone into Morgan's hut, but now Sebile ran out
of the hut clutching Mordred in her arms. Sebile? Not Ralla? I
was puzzled by that, and Norwenna must also have been puzzled as the Saxon slave ran to stand beside her with little Mordred draped in his rich robe of golden cloth, but Norwenna
had no time to question Sebile for Gundleus was now striding
towards her. 'I offer you my sword, dear Queen!' he said in a
ringing voice, and Norwenna smiled happily, perhaps because
she had not yet noticed either Tanaburs or Ladwys who had
come through Merlin's open gate with Gundleus's band of
warriors.

Gundleus thrust his spear into the turf and drew his sword,
but instead of offering it to Norwenna hilt first he held the
blade's sharp tip towards her face. Norwenna, unsure what to
do, reached tentatively to touch that glittering point. 'I rejoice
at your return, my dear Lord,' she said dutifully, then knelt at
his feet as custom demanded.

'Kiss the sword that will defend your son's kingdom,'
Gundleus commanded, and Norwenna bent awkwardly forward to touch her thin lips to the proffered steel.

She kissed the sword as she had been commanded, and just
as her lips touched the grey steel Gundleus rammed the blade
hard down. He was laughing as he killed his bride, laughing as
he slid the sword down past her chin into the hollow of her
throat and still laughing as he forced the long blade down
through the choking resistance of her writhing body. Norwenna had no time to scream, nor any voice left to scream with
as the blade ripped through her throat and was rammed down
to her heart. Gundleus grunted as he drove the steel home. He
had slung his heavy war shield so that both his leather-gloved
hands were on the hilt as he pushed and twisted the blade
downwards. There was blood on the sword and blood on the
grass and blood on the dying Queen's blue cloak, and still more
blood as Gundleus jerked the long blade violently free. Nor-

wenna's body, bereft of the sword's support, flopped sideways, quivered for a few seconds, and then was still.

Sebile dropped the baby and fled screaming. Mordred cried aloud in protest, but Gundleus's sword cut the baby's cries short. He stabbed the red blade down just once and suddenly the golden cloth was drenched with scarlet. So much blood from so small a child.

It had all happened so fast. Gudovan, next to me, was gaping in disbelief while Ladwys, who was a tall beauty with long hair, dark eyes and a sharply fierce face, laughed at her lover's victory. Tanaburs had closed one eye, raised one hand to the sky and was hopping on one leg, all signs that he was in sacred communion with the Gods as he cast his spells of doom and as Gundleus's guards spread into the compound with levelled spears to make that doom reality. Ligessac had joined the Silurian ranks and helped the spearmen massacre his own men. A few of the Dumnonians tried to fight, but they had been arrayed to do Gundleus honour, not oppose him, and the Silurian spearmen made brief work of Mordred's guards and briefer work still of Druidan's sorry soldiers. For the very first time in my adult life I saw men die on spearheads and heard the terrible screams a man makes when his soul is spear-sent into the Otherworld.

For a few seconds I was helpless with panic. Norwenna and Mordred were dead, the Tor was screaming and the enemy was running towards the hall and Merlin's Tower. Morgan and Hywel appeared beside the tower, but as Hywel limped forward with sword in hand, Morgan fled towards the sea gate. A host of women, children and slaves ran with her; a terrified mass of people whom Gundleus seemed content to let escape. Ralla, Sebile and those of Druidan's misshapen guard who had managed to avoid the grim Silurian warriors ran with them. Pellinore leaped up and down in his cage, cackling and naked, loving the horror.

I jumped from the ramparts and ran to the hall. I was not being brave, I was simply in love with Nimue and I wanted to make sure she was safe before I fled the Tor myself. Ligessac's guards were dead and Gundleus's men were beginning to plunder the huts as I dived through the door and ran towards Merlin's chambers, but before I could reach the small black door a spear-shaft tripped me. I fell heavily, then a small hand gripped my collar and, with astounding strength, dragged me towards my old hiding place behind the baskets of feasting cloths. 'You can't help her, fool,' Druidan's voice said in my ear. 'Now, be quiet!'

I reached safety just seconds before Gundleus and Tanaburs entered the hall and all I could do was watch as the King, his Druid and three helmed men marched to Merlin's door, I knew what was to happen and I could not stop it for Druidan was holding his little hand hard over my mouth to stop me shouting. I doubted that Druidan had run into the hall to save Nimue, probably he had come to snatch what gold he could before fleeing with the rest of his men, but his presence had at least saved my life. But it saved Nimue from nothing.

Tanaburs kicked the ghost-fence aside, then thrust the door open. Gundleus ducked inside, followed by his spearmen.

I heard Nimue scream. I do not know if she used tricks to defend Merlin's chamber, or whether she had already abandoned hope. I do know that pride and duty had made her stay to protect her master's secrets and now she paid for that pride. I heard Gundleus laugh, then I heard little except for the sound of the Silurians raking through Merlin's boxes, bales and baskets. Nimue whimpered, Gundleus shouted in triumph, and then she screamed again in sudden, terrible pain. 'That'll teach you to spit on my shield, girl,' Gundleus said as Nimue sobbed helplessly.

'She's well raped now,' Druidan said in my ear with a wicked relish. More of Gundleus's spearmen ran through the hall to enter Merlin's rooms. Druidan had forced a hole in the wattle wall with his spear and now ordered me to wriggle through and follow him down the hill, but I would not leave while Nimue still lived. 'They'll be searching these baskets soon,' the dwarf warned me, but still I would not go with him. 'More fool you, boy,' Druidan said, and he scrambled through the hole and scuttled towards the shadowed space between a nearby hut and a chicken pen.

I was saved by Ligessac. Not because he saw me, but because he told the Silurians there was nothing in the baskets that hid me except for banquet cloths. 'All the treasure's inside,' he told his new allies, and I crouched, not daring to move, as the victorious soldiers plundered Merlin's chambers. The Gods alone know what they found: dead men's skins, old bones, new charms and ancient elf bolts, but precious little treasure. And the Gods alone know what they did to Nimue, for she would never tell, though no telling was needed. They did what soldiers always do to captured women, and when they had finished they left her bleeding and half mad.

They also left her to die, for when they had ransacked the treasure chamber and found it filled with musty nonsense and only a little gold, they took a brand from the hall fire and tossed it among the broken baskets. Smoke billowed from the door. Another burning brand was thrown into the baskets where I was hidden, then Gundleus's men retreated from the hall. Some carried gold, a few had found some silver baubles, but most fled empty handed. When the last man was gone I covered my mouth with a corner of my jerkin and ran through the choking smoke towards Merlin's door and found Nimue just inside the room. 'Come on!' I said to her desperately. 'The air was filling with smoke while flames were leaping wildly up the boxes where cats screamed and bats flapped in panic.

Nimue would not move. She was lying belly down, hands clasped to her face, naked, with blood thick on her legs. She was weeping.

I ran to the door which led into Merlin's Tower, thinking there might be some escape that way, but when I opened the door I found the walls unbreached. I also discovered that the tower, far from being a treasure chamber, was almost empty. There was a bare earthen floor, four timber walls and an open roof. It was a chamber open to the sky, but halfway up the open funnel, suspended on a pair of beams and reached by a stout ladder, I could see a wooden platform that was swiftly being obscured by smoke. The tower was a dream chamber, a hollow place in which the Gods' whispers would echo to Merlin. I looked up at the dream platform for a second, then more smoke surged out behind me to funnel up the dream tower and I ran back to Nimue, seized her black cloak off the disordered bed and rolled her in the wool like a sick animal. I grabbed the corners of the cloak and then, with her light body bundled inside, I struggled into the hall and headed towards the far door. The fire was roaring now with the hunger of flames feasting on dry wood, my eyes were streaming and my lungs were soured by the smoke that lay thickest by the hall's main door, so I dragged Nimue, her body bumping on the earth floor behind me, to where Druidan had made his rat hole in the wall. My heart thumped in terror as I peered through, but I could see no enemies. I kicked the hole larger, bending back the willow wattles and breaking off chunks of the plaster daub, then I struggled through, hauling Nimue after me. She made small noises of protest as I jerked her body through the crude gap, but the fresh air seemed to revive her for she at last tried to help herself and I saw, as she took her hands away from her face, just why her last scream had been so terrible. Gundlcus had taken one of her eyes. The socket was a well of blood over which she again clapped a bloody hand. The tussle in the ragged hole had left her naked so I snatched the cloak free from a splintered wattle and draped it around her shoulders before clasping her free hand and running towards the nearest hut.

One of Gundleus's men saw us, then Gundleus himself recognized Nimue and he shouted that the witch should be taken alive and thrown back into the flames. The cry of the chase went up, great whoops like the sound of hunters pursuing a wounded boar to its death, and the two of us would surely have been caught if some of the other fugitives had not already ripped a gap in the stockade on the Tor's southern side. I ran towards the new gap only to discover Hywel, good Hywel, lying dead in the breach with his crutch beside him, his head half severed and his sword still in his hand. I plucked up the sword and hauled Nimue onwards. We reached the steep southern slope and tumbled down, both of us screaming as we slithered down the precipitous grass. Nimue was half blind and utterly maddened by her pain while I was frantic with terror, yet somehow I clutched on to Hywel's war sword, and somehow I made Nimue get to her feet at the Tor's foot and stumble on past the sacred well, past the Christians' orchard, through a grove of alders and so down to where I knew Hywel's marsh boat was moored beside a fisherman's hut. I threw Nimue into the small boat of bundled reeds, slashed the painter with my new sword and pushed the boat away from the wooden stage only to realize I had no quant pole to drive the clumsy craft out into the intricate maze of channels and lakes that laced the marsh. I used the sword instead; Hywel's blade made a sorry punting pole, yet it was all I had until the first of Gundleus's pursuers reached the reedy bank and, unable to wade out to us because of the glutinous marsh mud, hurled his spear at us instead.

The spear whistled as it flew towards me. For a second I could not move, transfixed by the sight of that heavy pole with its glittering steel head hurtling towards us, but then the weapon thumped past me to bury its blade in the punt's reed gunwale. I grabbed the quivering ash staff and used it as my quant pole to drive the boat hard and quick out into the waterways. We were safe there. Some of Gundleus's men ran along a wooden trackway that paralleled our course, but I soon turned away from them. Others leaped into coracles and used their spears as paddles, but no coracle could match a reed punt for speed and so we left them far behind. Ligessac fired an arrow, but we were already out of range and his missile plunged soundlessly into the dark water. Behind our frustrated pursuers, high on the green Tor, the flames leaped hungrily at huts and hall and tower so that grey churning smoke rose high in the blue summer sky.

'Two wounds.' Nimue spoke for the first time since I had snatched her from the flames.

'What?' I turned to her. She was huddled in the bow, the

black cloak wrapped about her thin body and with one hand clasped over her empty eye.

'I've suffered two Wounds of Wisdom, Derfel,' she said in a voice of crazed wonderment. 'The Wound to the Body and the Wound to the Pride. Now all I face is madness and then I shall be as wise as Merlin.' She tried to smile, but there was a hysterical wildness in her voice that made me wonder whether she was not already under the spell of madness.

'Mordred's dead,' I told her, 'and so are Norwenna and Hywel. The Tor is burning.' Our whole world was being destroyed, yet Nimue seemed strangely unmoved by the disaster. Instead she almost seemed elated because she had endured two of the three tests of wisdom.

I poled past a line of willow fish traps, then turned into Lissa's Mere, a great black lake that lay on the southern edge of the marshes. I was aiming towards Ermid's Hall, a wooden settlement where Ermid, a chieftain of a local tribe, kept his household. I knew Ermid would not be at the hall for he had marched north with Owain, but his people would help us, and I also knew that our boat would reach the hall long before the swiftest of Gundleus's horsemen could gallop around the lake's long, reed-thick and marshy banks. They would have to go almost as far as the Fosse Way, the great Roman road that ran east of the Tor, before they could turn around the lake's eastern extremity and gallop towards Ermid's Hall, and by then we would be long gone south. I could see other boats far ahead of me on the mere and guessed that the Tor's fugitives were being carried to safety by Ynys Wydryn's fishermen.

I told Nimue my plan to reach Ermid's Hall and then keep going southwards until the night fell or we met friends. 'Good,' she said dully, though I was not really sure she had understood anything I had said. 'Good Derfel,' she added. 'Now I know why the Gods made me trust you.'

'You trust me,' I said bitterly, and thrust the spear into the muddy lake bottom to push the boat forward, 'because I'm in love with you, and that gives you power over me.'

'Good,' she said again, and said nothing more until our reed

boat glided into the tree-shaded landing beneath Ermid's stockade where, as I pushed the boat still deeper into the creek's
shadows, I saw the other fugitives from the Tor. Morgan
was there with Sebile, and Ralla was weeping with her baby
safe in her arms next to Gwlyddyn her husband. Lunete, the
Irish girl, was there, and she ran crying to the waterside to
help Nimue. I told Morgan of Hywel's death, and she said she
had seen Guendoloen, Merlin's wife, cut down by a Silurian.
Gudovan was safe, but no one knew what had happened to
poor Pellinore or to Druidan. None of Norwenna's guards had
survived, though a handful of Druidan's wretched soldiers had
reached the dubious safety of Ermid's Hall, as had three of
Norwenna's weeping attendants and a dozen of Merlin's
frightened foundlings.

'We have to go soon,' I told Morgan. 'They're chasing
Nimue.' Nimue was being bandaged and clothed by Ermid's
servants.

'It's not Nimue they're after, you fool,' Morgan snapped at
me, 'but Mordred.'

'Mordred's dead!' I protested, but Morgan answered by
turning and snatching at the baby that lay in Ralla's arms. She
tugged the rough brown cloth away from the child's body and I
saw the clubbed foot.

'Do you think, fool,' Morgan said to me, 'that I would
permit our King to be killed?'

I stared at Ralla and Gwlyddyn, wondering how they could
ever have conspired to let their own son die. It was Gwlyddyn
who answered my mute look. 'He's a king,' he explained
simply, pointing to Mordred, 'while our boy was just a carpenter's son.'

'And soon,' Morgan said angrily, 'Gundleus will discover
that the baby he killed has two good feet, and then he'll bring
every man he can to search for us. We go south.' There was no
safety in Ermid's Hall. The chief and his warriors had gone to
war, leaving only a handful of servants and children in the
settlement.

We left a little before midday, plunging into the green woods south of Ermid's holdings. One of Ermid's huntsmen led us on narrow paths and secret ways. There were thirty of us, mostly women and children, with only a half dozen men capable of bearing arms and of those only Gwlyddyn had ever killed a man in battle. Druidan's few surviving fools would be no use, and I had never fought in anger, though I walked as a rearguard with Hywel's naked sword thrust into my rope belt and the heavy Silurian war spear clasped in my right hand.

We passed slowly beneath the oaks and hazels. From Ermid's Hall to Caer Cadarn was no more than a four-hour walk, though it would take us much longer for we travelled on secret, circuitous paths and were slowed by the children. Morgan had not said she would try to reach Caer Cadarn, but I knew the royal sanctuary was her probable destination for it was there that we were likely to find Dumnonian soldiers, but Gundleus would surely have made that same deduction and he was just as desperate as we were. Morgan, who had a shrewd grasp of this world's wickedness, surmised that the Silurian King had been planning this war ever since the High Council, just waiting for Uther's death to launch an attack in alliance with Gorfyddyd. We had all been fooled. We had thought Gundleus a friend and so no one had guarded his borders and now Gundleus was aiming at nothing less than the throne of Dumnonia itself. But to gain that throne, Morgan told us, he would need more than a score of horsemen, and so his spearmen would surely even now be hurrying to catch up with their King as they marched down the long Roman road that led from Dumnonia's northern coast. The Silurians were loose in our country, but before Gundleus could be sure of victory he had to kill Mordred. He had to find us or else his whole daring enterprise would fail.

The great wood muffled our steps. Occasionally a pigeon would clatter through the high leaves, and sometimes a woodpecker would rattle a trunk not far off. Once there was a great crashing and trampling in the nearby underbrush and we all stopped, motionless, fearing a Silurian horseman, but it was only a tusked boar that blundered into a clearing, took one look at us and turned away. Mordred was crying and would not take Ralla's breast. Some of the smaller children were also weeping out of fear and tiredness, but they fell silent when Morgan threatened to turn them all into stink-toads.

Nimue limped ahead of me. I knew she was in pain, but she would not complain. Sometimes she wept silently and nothing Lunete could say would comfort her. Lunete was a slender, dark girl, the same age as Nimue and not unlike her in looks, but she lacked Nimue's knowledge and fey spirit. Nimue could look at a stream and know it as the dwelling place of water spirits, whereas Lunete would simply see it as a good place for washing clothes. After a while Lunete dropped back to walk beside me. 'What happens to us now, Derfel?' she asked.

'I don't know.'

'Will Merlin come?'

'I hope so,' I said, 'or perhaps Arthur will.' I spoke in fervent but disbelieving hope, because what we needed was a miracle. Instead we seemed trapped in a midday nightmare for when, after a couple of hours walking, we were forced to leave the woods to cross a deep, winding stream that looped through grassy pastures bright with flowers, we saw more smoke pyres on the distant eastern skyline, though whether the fires had been set by Silurian raiders or by Saxons taking advantage of our weakness, none could tell.

A deer ran out of the woods a quarter mile to the east. 'Down!' the huntsman's voice hissed and we all sank into the grass at the edge of the wood. Ralla forced Mordred on to her breast to silence him and he retaliated by biting her so hard that the blood trickled down to her waist, but neither he nor she made a sound as the horseman who had startled the deer appeared at the trees' edge. The horseman was also to the east of us, but much closer than the pyres, so close that I could see the fox mask on his round shield. He carried a long spear and a horn that he sounded after he had stared for a long time in our direction. We all feared that its signal meant that the rider had seen us and that soon a whole pack of Silurian horsemen would come into view, but when the man urged his horse back into

93

the trees we guessed that the horn's dull note meant that he had not seen us at all. Far away another horn sounded, then there was silence.

We waited long minutes. Bees buzzed through the pastures edging the stream. We were all watching the treeline, fearing to see more armed horsemen, but no enemy showed there and after a while our guide whispered that we were to creep down to the stream, cross it, and crawl up to the trees on its far bank.

It was a long, difficult crawl, especially for Morgan with her twisted left leg, though at least we all had a chance to lap at the water as we splashed through the stream. Once in the far woods we walked with soaking clothes, but also with the relieved feeling that perhaps we had left our enemies behind us. But not, alas, our troubles. 'Will they make us slaves?' Lunete asked me. Like many of us Lunete had originally been captured for Dumnonia's slave market and only Merlin's intervention had kept her free. Now she feared that the loss of Merlin's protection would doom her.

'I don't think so,' I said. 'Not unless Gundleus or the Saxons capture us. You'd be taken for a slave, but they'd probably kill me.' I felt very brave saying it.

Lunete put her arm into mine for comfort and I felt flattered by her touch. She was a pretty girl and till today she had treated me with disdain, preferring the company of the wild fisherboys in Ynys Wydryn. 'I want Merlin to come back,' she said. 'I don't want to leave the Tor.'

'There's nothing left there now,' I said. 'We'll have to find a new place to live. Or else we'll have to go back and rebuild the Tor, if we can.' But only, I thought, if Dumnonia survived. Maybe even now, in this smoke-haunted afternoon, the kingdom was dying. I wondered how I had been so blind as not to see what horrors Uther's death would bring. Kingdoms need kings, and without them they are nothing but empty land inviting a conqueror's spears.

In mid-afternoon we crossed a wider stream, almost a river, so deep that the water came up to my chest as I waded through. Once on the far bank I dried off Hywel's sword as best I could. It was a lovely blade, made by the famous smiths in Gwent and decorated with curling designs and interlocking circles. Its steel blade was straight and stretched from my throat to my fingertips when I held my arm straight out. The crosspiece was made of thick iron with plain round finials, while the hilt was of apple wood that had been riveted to the tang and then bound about with strips of long, thin leather that were oiled smooth. The pommel was a round ball wrapped with silver wire that kept breaking free and in the end I took the wire off and fashioned it into a crude bracelet for Lunete.

South of the river was another wide pasture, this one grazed by bullocks that lumbered over to inspect our draggled passing. Maybe it was their movement that attracted the trouble, for it was not long after we had entered the woods on the far side of the pasture that I heard the hoofbeats sound loud behind us. I sent a warning forward, then turned, spear and sword in my hands, to watch the path.

The tree branches grew low here, so low that a horseman could not ride down the path. Whoever pursued us would be forced to abandon their horses and follow us on foot. We had not been using the wood's wider paths, but taking hidden trackways that threaded narrowly through the trees, so narrow that our pursuers, like us, would have to adopt a single file. I feared they were Silurian scouts sent far ahead of Gundleus's small force. Who else would be interested in whatever had caused the cattle on the river bank to stir themselves in this lazy afternoon?

Gwlyddyn arrived beside me and took the heavy spear out of my hand. He listened to the distant footfalls, then nodded as though satisfied. 'Only two of them,' he said calmly. 'They've left their horses and are coming on foot. I'll take the first, and you hold the second man till I can kill him.' He sounded extraordinarily calm, which helped soothe my fears. 'And remember, Derfel,' he added, 'they're frightened too.' He pushed me into the shadows, then crouched on the path's far side behind the upended root mass of a fallen beech tree. 'Get down,' he hissed at me. 'Hide!'

I crouched and suddenly all the terror welled back inside me. My hands were sweating, my right leg was twitching, my throat was dry, I wanted to vomit, and my bowels were liquid. Hywel had taught me well, but I had never faced a man wanting to kill me. I could hear the approaching men, but I could not see them and my strongest instinct was to turn and run after the women. But I stayed. I had no choice. Since childhood I had been hearing tales of warriors and had been taught again and again that a man never turned and ran. A man fought for his Lord and a man stood up to his enemy and a man never fled. Now my Lord was sucking at Ralla's breast and I was facing his enemies, but how I wanted to be a child and just run! Suppose there were more than two enemy spearmen? And even if there were only two they were bound to be experienced warriors; skilled and hardened and careless in their killing.

'Calm, boy, calm,' Gwlyddyn said softly. He had fought in Uther's battles. He had faced the Saxon and carried a spear against the men of Powys. Now, deep in his native land, he stooped in the tangle of earthy root-suckers with a half-grin on his face and my long spear in his sturdy brown hands. 'This is revenge for my child,' he told me grimly, 'and the Gods are on our side.'

I was crouched behind brambles and flanked by ferns. My damp clothes felt heavy and uncomfortable. I stared at the trees that were thick with lichens and tangled with leaves. A woodpecker rattled nearby and I jumped with alarm. My hiding place was better than Gwlyddyn's, but even so I felt exposed, and never more so than when at last our two pursuers appeared just a dozen paces beyond my leafy screen.

They were two lithe young spearmen with leather breastplates, strapped leggings and long russet cloaks thrown back over their shoulders. Their plaited beards were long and their dark hair was bound behind by leather thongs. Both men carried long spears and the second man also had a sword at his belt, though he had not yet drawn it. I held my breath.

The leading man raised a hand and both men stopped and

listened for a while before coming on again. The nearest man's face was scarred from an old fight, his mouth was open and I could see the gaps in his yellowed teeth. He looked immensely tough, experienced and frightening, and I was suddenly over-whelmed with a terrible desire to flee, but then the scar on my left palm, the scar that Nimue had put there, throbbed and that warm pulse gave me a jolt of courage.

'We heard a deer,' the second man said disparagingly. The two men were advancing at a stealthy walk now, placing their feet carefully and watching the leaves ahead for the smallest flicker of movement.

'We heard a baby,' the first man insisted. He was two paces ahead of the other who looked, to my scared eyes, to be even taller and grimmer than his companion.

'Bastards have disappeared,' the second man said and I saw the sweat dripping off his face and I noticed how he gripped and regripped his ash spear-shaft and I knew he was nervous. I was saying Bel's name over and over in my head, begging the God for courage, begging him to make me a man. The enemy was six paces away now and still coming, and all around us the greenwood lay warm and breathless and I could smell the two men, smell their leather and the lingering scent of their horses as sweat dripped into my eyes and I almost whimpered aloud in terror, but then Gwlyddyn leaped out of his ambush and screamed a war cry as he ran forward.

I ran with him and suddenly I was released from fear as the mad, God-given joy of battle came to me for the very first time. Later, much later, I learned that the joy and the fear are the exact same things, the one merely transformed into the other by action, but on that summer afternoon I was suddenly elated. May God and His angels forgive me, but that day I discovered the joy that lies in battle and for a long time afterwards I craved it like a thirsty man seeking water. I ran forward, screaming like Gwlyddyn, but I was not so crazed as to follow him blindly. I moved over to the right side of the narrow path so that I could run past him when he struck the closer Silurian. That man tried to parry Gwlyddyn's spear, but the carpenter expected the low sweep of the ash staff, and raised his own weapon above it as he thrust his weapon home. It all happened so fast. One moment the Silurian was a threatening figure in war gear, then he was gasping and twitching as Gwlyddyn rammed the heavy spearhead through the leather armour and deep into his chest. And I was already past him, yelling as I swung Hywel's sword. At that moment I felt no fear, perhaps because the soul of dead Hywel came back from the Otherworld to fill me, for suddenly I knew exactly what I had to do and my war scream was a cry of triumph.

The second man had a heartbeat's more warning than his dying companion and so he had dropped into a spearman's crouch from which he could spring forward with killing force. I leaped at him, and as the spear came at me in a bright, sun-touched lunge of steel I twisted aside and parried with my blade, not so hard as to lose control of the steel, but just enough to slide the man's weapon past my right side as I whirled the sword around. 'It's all in the wrists, boy, all in the wrists,' I heard Hywel say and I shouted his name as I brought the sword hard down on to the side of the Silurian's neck.

It was all so quick, so very quick. The wrist manoeuvres the sword, but the arm gives it force, and my arm held Hywel's great strength that afternoon. My steel buried itself in the Silurian's neck like an axe biting into rotten wood. At first, so green was I, I thought he had not died and I wrenched the sword free to strike at him again. I struck that second time and was aware of blood brightening the day and the man falling sideways and I could hear his choking breath and see his dying effort to pull the spear back for a second thrust, but then his life rattled in his throat and another great wash of blood ran down his leather-covered chest as he slumped on to the leaf mould.

And I stood there shaking. I suddenly wanted to cry. I had no idea what I had done. I had no sense of victory, only of guilt, and I stood shocked and motionless with my sword still embedded in the dead man's throat on which the first flies were already settling. I could not move.

A bird screamed in the high leaves, then Gwlyddyn's strong arm was around my shoulders and tears were streaming down my face. 'You're a good man, Derfel,' Gwlyddyn said and I turned to him and held him like a child clinging to a father. 'Well done,' he said again and again, 'well done.' He patted me clumsily until at last I sniffed back my tears.

'I'm sorry,' I heard myself saying.

'Sorry?' he laughed. 'For what? Hywel always said you were the best he ever trained and I should have believed him. You're fast. Now come, we have to see what we've won.'

I took my victim's sword scabbard that was made of willow-stiffened leather and found it fitted Hywel's sword tolerably well, then we searched the two bodies for what little plunder we could find: an unripe apple, an old coin worn smooth, two cloaks, the weapons, some leather thongs and a bone-handled knife. Gwlyddyn debated whether we should go back and fetch the two horses, then decided we did not have the time. I did not care. My vision might be blurred by tears, but I was alive and I had killed a man and I had defended my King and suddenly I was deliriously happy as Gwlyddyn led me back to the frightened fugitives and raised my arm as a sign that I had fought well.

'You made enough noise, the two of you,' Morgan snarled. 'We'll have half Siluria on our heels soon. Now come! Move!'

Nimue did not seem interested in my victory, but Lunete wanted to hear all about it and in the telling I exaggerated both the enemy and the fight, and Lunete's admiration engendered even more exaggeration. She had her arm in mine again and I glanced at her dark-eyed face and wondered why I had never really noticed just how beautiful she was. Like Nimue she had a wedge-shaped face, but where Nimue's was full of a wary knowledge Lunete's was soft with a teasing warmth, and her closeness gave me new confidence as we walked on through the long afternoon until at last we turned east towards the hills of which Caer Cadarn stood like an outrider.

One hour later we stood at the edge of the woods that faced Caer Cadarn. It was late in the day, but we were in midsummer and the sun was still high in the sky and its lovely gentle light was flooding the western ramparts of Caer Cadarn with a green glow. We were a mile away from the fortress, but still close enough to see the yellow palisades atop the ramparts, close enough to see that no guards stood on those walls and no smoke rose from the small settlement inside.

But nor was there any enemy in sight, and that decided Morgan to cross the open land and climb the western path to the King's fortress. Gwlyddyn argued that we should stay in the forest till nightfall, or else go to the nearby settlement of Lindinis, but Gwlyddyn was a carpenter and Morgan a high-born lady, so he surrendered to her wishes.

We moved out into the pastureland and our shadows stretched long in front of us. The grass had been cropped short by deer or cattle, yet it was soft and lush underfoot. Nimue, who still seemed to be in a pain-haunted trance, slipped off her borrowed shoes and paced barefoot. A hawk sailed overhead and then a hare, startled by our sudden appearance, sprang out of a grassy hollow and raced nimbly away.

We followed a path edged with cornflowers, ox-eyes, rag-weed and dogwood. Behind us, shadowed by the sun's western slant, the woods looked dark. We were tired and ragged, but journey's end was in sight and some among us even appeared cheerful. We were bringing Mordred back to his birthplace, back to Dumnonia's royal hill, but before we were even halfway to that glorious green refuge, the enemy appeared behind us.

Gundleus's war-band appeared. Not just the horsemen who had ridden to Ynys Wydryn in the morning, but his spearmen too. Gundleus must have known all along where we would go and so he had brought his surviving cavalrymen and over a hundred spearmen to this sacred place of Dumnonia's kings. And even if he had not been forced to pursue the baby King, then Gundleus would still have come to Caer Cadarn, for he wanted nothing less than the crown of Dumnonia, and Caer Cadarn was where that crown was bestowed upon the ruler's head. Who held Caer Cadarn held Dumnonia, the old saying went, and who held Dumnonia held Britain.

The Silurian horsemen spurred ahead of their spearmen. It would take them only a few minutes to reach us and I knew that none of us, not even the swiftest runners, could reach the long slopes of the fortress before those horsemen swept around us with slashing steel and stabbing spears. I went to Nimue's side and saw that her thin face was drawn and tired, and her remaining eye bruised and tearful. 'Nimue?' I said.

'It's all right, Derfel.' She seemed annoyed that I wanted to take care of her.

She was mad, I decided. Of all the living who had survived this terrible day, she had survived the worst experience of all and it had driven her to a place I could neither follow nor understand. 'I do love you,' I said, trying to touch her soul with tenderness.

'Me? Not Lunete?' Nimue said angrily. She was not looking at me, but towards the fortress, while I turned and stared at the approaching horsemen who had spread into a long line like men intent on flushing game. Their cloaks lay on their horses' rumps, their scabbards hung down beside their dangling boots, and the sun glinted on spear-points and lit the banner of the fox. Gundleus rode beneath the banner, the iron helmet with its fox-tail crest on his head. Ladwys was beside him, a sword in her hand, while Tanaburs, his long robe flapping, rode a grey horse close beside his King. I was going to die, I thought, on the day that I had become a man. That realization seemed very cruel.

'Run!' Morgan suddenly shouted, 'run!' I thought she had panicked, and I did not want to obey her for I thought it would be nobler to stand and die like a man than be cut down from behind as a fugitive. Then I saw she was not panicking and that Caer Cadarn was not deserted after all, but that the gates had opened and a stream of men was running and riding down the path. The horsemen were dressed like Gundleus's riders, only these men bore the dragon shields of Mordred on their arms.

We ran. I dragged Nimue along by the arm while the handful of Dumnonian horse spurred towards us. There were a dozen riders, not many, but enough to check the advance of Gundleus's men, while behind the horsemen came a band of Dumnonian spearmen.

'Fifty spears,' Gwlyddyn said. He had been counting the rescue party. 'We can't beat them with fifty,' he added grimly, 'but we might make safety.'

Gundleus was making the same deduction and now he led his horsemen in a wide curve that would lead them behind the approaching Dumnonian spearmen. He wanted to cut off our retreat for once he had assembled his enemies in one place he could kill us all whether we numbered seventy or seven. Gundleus had the advantage of numbers and, by coming down from their fortress, the Dumnonians had sacrificed their one advantage of height.

The Dumnonian horsemen thundered past us, their horses' hooves cutting great chunks of turf from the lush pasture. These were not the fabled horsemen of Arthur, the armoured men who struck home like thunderbolts, but lightly armed scouts who would normally dismount before going into battle, but now they formed a protective screen between us and the Silurian spearmen. A moment later our own spearmen arrived and made their shield-wall. That wall gave us all a new confidence, a confidence that veered towards recklessness when we saw who led the rescue party. It was Owain, mighty Owain, king's champion and the greatest fighter in all Britain. We had thought Owain was far to the north, fighting alongside the men of Gwent in the mountains of Powys, yet here he was at Caer Cadarn.

Yet, in sober truth, Gundleus still held the advantage. We were twelve horsemen, fifty spearmen and thirty tired fugitives who were gathered in an open place where Gundleus had gathered almost twice as many horsemen and twice as many spearmen.

The sun was still bright. It would be two hours before twilight and four before it was full dark and that gave Gundleus more than enough time to finish his slaughter, though first he tried to persuade us with words. He rode forward, splendid on his sweat-foamed horse and with his shield held upside down as a sign of truce. 'Men of Dumnonia,' he called, 'give me the child and I will go!' No one answered. Owain had hidden himself in the centre of our shield-wall so that Gundleus, seeing no leader, addressed us all. 'It's a maimed child!' the Silurian King called. 'Cursed by the Gods. You think any good fortune can attend a country ruled by a crippled king? You want your harvests blighted? You want your children born sick? You want your cattle to die of a murrain? You want the Saxons to be lords of this land? What else does a crippled king bring but ill fortune?'

Still no one answered though, God knows, enough men in our hastily aligned ranks must have feared that Gundleus spoke the truth.

The Silurian King lifted the helmet from his long hair and smiled at our plight. 'You may all live,' he promised, 'so long as you give me the child.' He waited for an answer that did not come. 'Who leads you?' he finally asked.

'I do!' Owain at last pushed through the ranks to take his place in front of our shield-line.

'Owain.' Gundleus recognized him, and I thought I saw a flicker of fear in Gundleus's eyes. Like us he had not known that Owain had returned to the heart of Dumnonia. Yet Gundleus was still confident of victory even though he must have known that with Owain among his enemies that victory would be much harder. 'Lord Owain,' Gundleus said giving Dumnonia's champion his proper title, 'son of Eilynon and grandson of Culwas. I salute you!' Gundleus raised his speartip towards the sun. 'You have a son, Lord Owain.'

'Many men have sons,' Owain answered carelessly. 'What is it to you?'

'Do you want your boy to be fatherless?' Gundleus asked. 'Do you want your lands wasted? Your home burned? Do you want your wife to be my men's plaything?'

'My wife,' Owain said, 'could outfight all your men, and you too. You want playthings, Gundleus? Go back to your whore' – he jerked his chin towards Ladwys – 'and if you won't share

103

your whore with your men then Dumnonia can spare Siluria a few lonely ewes.' Owain's defiance cheered us. He looked indomitable with his massive spear, long sword and iron-plated shield. He always fought bare headed, disdaining a helmet, and his hugely muscled arms were tattooed with Dumnonia's dragon and his own symbol of a long-tusked boar.

'Yield me the child.' Gundleus ignored the insults, knowing they were merely the defiance expected of a man facing battle. 'Give me the crippled King!'

'Give me your whore, Gundleus,' Owain retorted. 'You're not man enough for her. Give her to me and you can go in peace.'

Gundleus spat. 'The bards will sing of your death, Owain. The song of the pig-sticking.'

Owain thrust his huge spear butt-first into the soil. 'Here the pig stands, Gundleus ap Meilyr, King of Siluria,' he shouted, 'and here the pig will either die or piss on your corpse. Now go!'

Gundleus smiled, shrugged and turned his horse away. He also turned his shield the right side up, letting us know that we would have a fight.

It was my first battle.

The Dumnonian horsemen formed behind our line of spears to protect the women and children so long as they could. The rest of us arrayed ourselves in the battle line and watched as our enemies did the same. Ligessac, the traitor, was among the Silurian ranks. Tanaburs performed the rites, hopping on one leg and with one hand raised and one eye closed in front of Gundleus's shield-wall as it advanced slowly across the grassland. Only when Tanaburs had cast his protective spell did the Silurians begin to shout insults at us. They warned us of the massacre to come and boasted how many of us they would kill, yet even so I noticed how slowly they came and, when they were only fifty paces away, how they stopped altogether. Some of our men jeered at their timidity, but Owain growled at us to be silent.

The battle lines stared at each other. Neither moved.

It takes extraordinary courage to charge into a line of shields and spears. That is why so many men drink before the fight. I have seen armies pause for hours while they summon the courage to charge, and the older the warrior the more courage is needed. Young troops will charge and die, but older men know how terrible an enemy shield-wall can be. I had no shield, yet I was covered by the shields of my neighbours, and their shields touched others and so on down our small line so that any man charging home would be met by a wall of leather-covered wood bristling with razor-sharp spears.

The Silurians began beating their shields with their spear-staffs. The rattling sound was meant to unsettle us, and it did, though none on our side showed the fear. We just huddled together, waiting for the charge. 'There'll be some false charges first, lad,' my neighbour warned me, and no sooner had he spoken than a group of Silurians ran screaming from their line and hurled their long spears at the centre of our defence. Our men crouched and the long spears banged home into our shields and suddenly the whole Silurian line was moving forward, but Owain immediately ordered our line to stand and march forward too and that deliberate motion checked the enemy's threatened attack. Those of our men whose shields were cumbered with the enemy spears wrenched the weapons loose, then made the shield-wall whole again.

'Edge back!' Owain ordered us. He would try to shuffle slowly backwards across the half-mile of grassland to Caer Cadarn, hoping that the Silurians would not raise the courage to make their charge while we completed that pitifully slow journey. To give us more time Owain strode ahead of our line and shouted at Gundleus to fight him man to man. 'Are you a woman, Gundleus?' our King's champion called. 'Lost your courage? Not enough mead? Why don't you go back to your weaving loom, woman? Go back to your embroidery! Go back to your spindle!'

We shuffled back, shuffled back, shuffled back, but suddenly a charge of the enemy made us stand firm and duck behind our shields as the spears were hurled. One whipped over my head, its passage sounding like a sudden rush of wind, but again the attack was a feint intended to panic us. Ligessac was firing arrows, but he must have been drunk for his shots went wildly overhead. Owain was a target for a dozen spears, but most missed and the others he swept contemptuously aside with spear or shield before mocking the throwers. 'Who taught you spear-craft? Your mothers?' He spat towards the enemy. 'Come Gundleus! Fight me! Show your scullions you're a king, not a mouse!'

The Silurians beat spear-shafts on their shields to drown Owain's taunts. He turned his back to show them his scorn and walked slowly back to our shield-line. 'Back,' he called to us softly, 'back.'

Then two of the Silurians threw down their shields and weapons and tore off their clothes to fight naked. My neighbour spat. 'There'll be trouble now,' he warned me grimly.

The naked men were probably drunk, or else so intoxicated by the Gods that they believed no enemy blade could hurt them. I had heard of such men and knew that their suicidal example was usually the signal for a real attack. I gripped my sword and tried to make a vow to die well, but in truth I could have wept for the pity of it all. I had become a man this day, and now I would die. I would join Uther and Hywel in the Otherworld and there wait through the shadowed years until my soul found another human body in which to return to this green world.

The two men unbound their hair, took up their spears and swords, then danced in front of the Silurian line. They howled as they worked themselves into the battle frenzy; that state of mindless ecstasy that will let a man try any feat. Gundleus, sitting his horse beneath his banner, smiled at the two men whose bodies were intricately tattooed with blue patterns. The children were crying behind us and our women were calling to the Gods as the men danced nearer and nearer, their spears and swords whirling in the evening sun. Such men had no need of shields, clothes or armour. The Gods were their protection and glory was their reward, and if they succeeded in killing Owain then the bards would sing of their victory for years to come. They advanced one on each side of our champion who hefted his spear as he prepared to meet their frenzied attack which would also mark the moment when the whole enemy line would charge.

And then the horn sounded.

The horn gave a clear, cold note like none I had ever heard before. There was a purity to that horn, a chill hard purity like nothing else on all the earth. It sounded once, it sounded twice, and the second call was enough to give even the naked men pause and make them turn towards the east from where the sound had come.

I looked too.

And I was dazzled. It was as though a new bright sun had risen on that dying day. The light slashed over the pastures, blinding us, confusing us, but then the light slid on and I saw it was merely the reflection of the real sun glancing from a shield polished bright as a mirror. But that shield was held by such a man as I had never seen before; a man magnificent, a man lifted high on a great horse and accompanied by other such men; a horde of wondrous men, plumed men, armoured men, men sprung from the dreams of the Gods to come to this murderous field, and over the men's plumed heads there floated a banner I would come to love more than any banner on all God's earth. It was the banner of the bear.

The horn sounded a third time, and suddenly I knew I would live, and I was weeping for joy and all our spearmen were half crying and half shouting and the earth was shuddering with the hooves of those Godlike men who were riding to our rescue.

For Arthur, at last, had come.

PART TWO

The Princess Bride

IGRAINE IS UNHAPPY. She wants tales of Arthur's childhood. She has heard of a sword in the stone and wants me to write of it. She tells me he was sired by a spirit on a queen and that the skies were filled with thunder on the night of his birth and maybe she is right and the skies were noisy that night, but everyone I ever talked to slept through it, and as for the sword in the stone, well, there was a sword and there was a stone, but their place in the tale is still far ahead. The sword was called Caledfwlch, which means 'hard lightning' though Igraine prefers to call it Excalibur and I shall call it so as well because Arthur never cared what name his longsword carried. Nor did he care about his childhood, for certainly I never heard him speak of it. I once questioned him about his early days and he would not answer. 'What is the egg to the eagle?' he asked me, then said that he had been born, he had lived and he had become a soldier, and that was all I needed to know.

But for my most fair and generous protector, Igraine, let me set down what little I did learn. Arthur, despite Uther's denial at Glevum, was the son of the High King, though there was small advantage to be gained from that patronage for Uther fathered as many bastards as a tom cat makes kittens. Arthur's mother was, like my most precious queen, called Igraine. She came from Caer Gei in Gwynedd and is said to have been the daughter of Cunedda, King of Gwynedd and High King before Uther, though Igraine was no princess for her mother was not Cunedda's wife, but was instead married to a chieftain of Henis Wyren. All that Arthur would ever say of Igraine of Gwynedd, who died when he was on the verge of manhood, is that she was the most wonderful and clever and beautiful mother any boy could ever wish for, though according to Cei, who knew Ígraine well, her beauty was sharpened by a rancorous wit. Cei is the son of Ector ap Ednywain, the chieftain at Caer Gei who took Igraine and her four bastard children into his household when Uther rejected them. That rejection occurred in the same year Arthur was born, and Igraine never forgave her son for it. She used to say that Arthur was one child too many, and somehow she believed that she would always have ruled as Uther's mistress had Arthur not been born.

Arthur was the fourth of Igraine's children to survive infancy. The other three were all girls and Uther evidently liked his bastards to be female for they were less likely to make demands on his patrimony when they grew. Cei and Arthur were raised together and Cei says, though never in Arthur's hearing, that both he and Arthur were frightened of Igraine. Arthur, he told me, was a dutiful, hard-working boy who strove to be the best at every lesson, whether in reading or sword-fighting, but nothing he could ever achieve gave his mother pleasure, though Arthur always worshipped her, defended her, and wept inconsolably when she died of a fever. Arthur was then thirteen, and Ector, his protector, appealed to Uther to help Igraine's four impoverished orphans. Uther brought them to Caer Cadarn, probably because he thought the three daughters would be useful throwpieces in the game of dynastic marriages. Morgan's marriage to a Prince of Kernow was short-lived thanks to fire, but Morgause married King Lot of Lothian and Anna was wed to King Budic ap Camran across the water in Brittany. These last two were not important marriages, for neither king was close enough to send reinforcements to Dumnonia in time of war, but both served their small purposes. Arthur, being a boy, had no such usefulness and so he went to Uther's court and learned to use a sword and spear. He also met Merlin, though neither man talked much of what passed between them in those months before Arthur, despairing of ever being given preferment by Uther, followed his sister Anna to Brittany. There, in the turmoil of Gaul, he grew into a great soldier and Anna, ever conscious that a warrior brother was a valued relative, kept his exploits known to Uther. That was why Uther brought Arthur back to Britain for the campaign which ended in his son's death. The rest you know.

And now I have told Igraine all I know of Arthur's childhood and doubtless she will embellish the tale with the legends that are already being told of Arthur among the common folk. Igraine is taking away these skins one by one and having them transcribed into the proper tongue of Britain by Dafydd ap Gruffud, the clerk of the justice who speaks the Saxon tongue, and I do not trust him or Igraine to leave these words untouched by their own fancies. There are times when I wish that I dared to set this tale down in the British tongue, but Bishop Sansum, whom God cherishes above all the saints, still suspects what I write. At times he has tried to stop this work, or else has commanded the imps of Satan to impede me. One day I found my quills all gone, and on another there was urine in the inkhorn, but Igraine restores everything and Sansum, unless he learns to read and masters the Saxon tongue, cannot confirm his suspicions that this work is not, in truth, a Saxon Gospel.

Igraine urges me to write more and faster, and pleads with me to tell the truth about Arthur, but then complains when that truth does not match the fairy-tales she hears in the Caer's kitchen or in her robing chamber. She wants shape-changing and questing beasts, but I cannot invent what I did not see. It is true, God forgive me, that I have changed some things, but nothing important. Thus, when Arthur saved us in the battle before Caer Cadarn, I realized he was coming long before he actually appeared, for Owain and his men knew all along that Arthur and his horsemen, newly arrived from Brittany, were concealed in the woodlands north of Caer Cadarn, just as they knew that Gundleus's war-band was approaching. Gundleus's mistake was to fire the Tor, for the smoke pyre served as a warning beacon to all the south country and Owain's mounted scouts had been watching Gundleus's men since midday. Owain, having helped Agricola defeat Gorfyddyd's invasion, had hurried south to greet Arthur, not out of friendship, but rather to be present when a rival warlord appeared in the kingdom, and it was fortunate for us that Owain had returned. Yet even so, the battle could never have happened as I described it. If Owain had not known that Arthur was nearby he would have given the baby Mordred to his swiftest horseman and sent the child galloping to safety, even if the rest of us did go down beneath Gundleus's spears. I could have written that truth, of course, but the bards showed me how to shape a tale so that the listeners are kept waiting for the part they want to hear, and I think the tale is better for keeping the news of Arthur's arrival until the very last minute. It is a small sin, this tale-shaping, though God knows Sansum would never forgive it.

It is still winter here in Dinnewrac, and bitter cold, but King Brochvael ordered Sansum to light our fires after Brother Aron was found frozen dead in his cell. The saint refused until the King sent firewood from his Caer, and so we do now have fires, though not many and never great. Still, even a small fire makes the writing easier, and of late the blessed Saint Sansum has been less meddlesome. Two novices have joined our small flock, mere boys with unbroken voices, and Sansum has taken it upon himself to train them in the ways of Our Most Precious Saviour. Such is the saint's care for their immortal souls that he even insists the boys must share his sleeping cell and he seems a happier man for their company. God be thanked for that, and for the gift of fire, and for the strength to go on with this tale of Arthur, the King that Never Was, the Enemy of God and our Lord of Battles.

I shall not weary you with the details of that fight before Caer Cadarn. It was a rout, not a battle, and only a handful of Silurians escaped. Ligessac, the traitor, was one who escaped, but most of Gundleus's men were captured. A score of the enemy died, including the two naked fighters who went down to Owain's war spear. Gundleus, Ladwys and Tanaburs were all taken alive. I killed no one. I did not even dent my sword's edge.

Nor do I even remember much about the rout, for all I wanted to do was stare at Arthur.

He was mounted on Llamrei, his mare, a great black beast with shaggy fetlocks and flat iron shoes tied to her hooves with leather straps. All Arthur's men rode such big horses that had their nostrils slit into flaring holes so that they could breathe more easily. The beasts were made even more alarming by extraordinary shields of stiffened leather that hung to protect the animals' chests from spear thrusts. The shields were so thick and cumbersome that the horses could not lower their heads to graze at the battle's end and Arthur ordered one of his grooms to unstrap the device so Llamrei could feed. Each of the horses needed two grooms apiece, one to look after the horse shield, body cloth and saddle, the other to lead the horse by the bridle, while still a third servant carried the warrior's spear and shield. Arthur had a long, heavy spear named Rhongomyniad while his shield, Wynebgwrthucher, was made of willow boards covered with a skin of beaten silver that was polished until it dazzled. At his hip hung the knife called Carnwenhau and the famous sword Excalibur in its black scabbard that was cross-hatched with golden thread.

I could not see his face at first for his head was enclosed in a helmet with broad cheek pieces that shadowed his features. The helmet, with its gash for eyes and dark hole for a mouth, was made of polished iron decorated with swirling patterns of silver and had a high plume of white goose feathers. There was something deathly about that pale helmet; it had a fearsome, skull-like appearance which suggested its wearer was one of the walking dead. His cloak, like his plume, was white. The cloak, which he was fastidious about keeping clean, hung from his shoulders to keep the sun off his long coat of scale armour. I had never seen scale armour before, though Hywel had told me of it, and seeing Arthur's I was overwhelmed with a desire to possess such a coat myself. The armour was Roman and made from hundreds of iron plates, each no bigger than a thumbprint, sewn in overlapping rows on to a knee-length coat of leather. The plates were square at the top, where two holes were left for the sewing thread, and pointed at their base, and the scales overlapped in such a manner that a spear head would always encounter at least two layers of iron before striking the stout leather beneath. The stiff armour chinked when Arthur moved, and it was not just iron sounding for his smiths had added a row of golden plates around the neck and scattered silver scales among the polished iron so that the whole coat seemed to shimmer. It took hours of polishing each day to prevent the iron rusting, and after every battle a few plates would be missing and would need to be reforged. Few smiths could make such a coat, and very few men could afford to buy one, but Arthur had taken his from a Frankish chieftain he had killed in Armorica. Besides the helmet, cloak and scale coat, he wore leather boots, leather gloves and a leather belt from which Excalibur hung in its cross-hatched scabbard that was supposed to protect its wearer against all harm.

To me, dazzled by his coming, he appeared as a white, shining God come to earth. I could not take my eyes from him.

He embraced Owain and I heard the two men laugh. Owain was a tall man, but Arthur could look him in the eye, though he was nowhere near as heavily built as Owain. Owain was all muscle and bulk, while Arthur was a lean and wiry man. Owain thumped Arthur's back and Arthur returned the affectionate gesture before the two men walked, their arms about each other's shoulders, to where Ralla was holding Mordred.

Arthur fell to his knees before his King and, with a surprising delicacy for a man in stiff, heavy armour, lifted a gloved hand to take the hem of the baby's robe. He pushed his helmet's hinged cheek pieces aside, then kissed the robe. Mordred responded by screaming and struggling.

Arthur stood and held his arms towards Morgan. She was older than her brother, who was still only twenty-five or twenty-six years old, but when he offered to embrace her she began to cry behind her gold mask that clashed lightly against Arthur's helmet as they clasped each other. He held her tight and patted her back. 'Dear Morgan,' I heard him say, 'dear, sweet Morgan.'

I had never realized how lonely Morgan was until I saw her weep in her brother's arms.

He pulled gently away from her grip then used both his gloved hands to lift the silver-grey helmet from his head. 'I have a gift for you,' he told Morgan, 'at least I think I do, unless Hygwydd's stolen it. Where are you, Hygwydd?'

The servant Hygwydd ran forward and was given the white-plumed helmet in exchange for a necklace of bears' teeth that were set in gold sockets on a gold chain that Arthur hung around his sister's neck. 'Something beautiful for my lovely sister,' he said, and then he insisted on knowing who Ralla was, and when he heard about her baby's death his face showed such pain and sympathy that Ralla began to weep and Arthur impulsively hugged her and almost crushed the baby King against his scale-armoured chest. Then Gwlyddyn was introduced, and Gwlyddyn told Arthur how I had killed a Silurian to protect Mordred and so Arthur swung round to thank me.

And, for the first time, I looked full into his face.

It was a face of kindness. That was my first impression. No, that is what Igraine wants me to write. In truth my first impression was of sweat, lots of sweat come from wearing metal armour on a summer's day, but after the sweat I noticed how kind he looked. You trusted Arthur on sight. That was why women always liked Arthur, not because he was good-looking, for he was not overly handsome, but because he looked at you with genuine interest and an obvious benevolence. He had a strong, bony face that was full of enthusiasm, and a full head of dark brown hair that when I first saw him was sweat-plastered tight to his skull, thanks to his helmet's leather liner. His eyes were brown, he had a long nose and a heavy, clean-shaven jaw, but his most noticeable feature was his mouth. It was unnaturally large and had a full set of teeth. He was proud of his teeth and cleaned them every day with salt when he could find it, and with plain water when he could not. It was a big face and a strong one, yet what impressed me most about him was that look of kindness and the impish humour in his eyes. There was an air of enjoyment about Arthur, something in his face

117

radiated a happiness that embraced you in its aura. I noticed then, and ever after, how men and women became more cheerful when Arthur was in their company. Everyone became more optimistic, there was more laughter, and when he departed a dullness would ensue, yet Arthur was no great wit, nor a storyteller, he was simply Arthur, a good man of infectious confidence, impatient will and iron-hard resolve. You did not notice that hardness at first, and even Arthur himself pretended it was not there, yet it was. A slew of battlefield graves bear witness to it.

'Gwlyddyn tells me you're a Saxon!' he teased me.

'Lord,' was all I could say as I dropped to my knees.

He stooped and lifted me by the shoulders. His touch was firm. 'I'm no King, Derfel,' he said, 'you don't kneel to me, but I should kneel to you for risking your life to save our King.' He smiled. 'For that I thank you.' He had the knack of making you feel that no one else in the world mattered to him as much as you did and I was already lost in worship of him. 'How old are you?' he asked me.

'Fifteen, I think.'

'But big enough for twenty years.' He smiled. 'Who taught you to fight?'

'Hywel,' I said, 'Merlin's steward.'

'Ah! The best teacher! He taught me too, and how is good Hywel?' The question was asked eagerly, but I had neither the words nor courage to answer.

'Dead,' Morgan answered for me. 'Slain by Gundleus.' She spat through the mouth-slit of her mask towards the captured King who was being held a few paces away.

'Hywel dead?' Arthur asked the question of me, his eyes on mine, and I nodded and blinked back tears and Arthur instantly hugged me. 'You are a good man, Derfel,' he said, 'and I owe you a reward for saving our King's life. What do you want?'

'To be a warrior, Lord,' I said.

He smiled and stepped away from me. 'You're a lucky man, Derfel, because you are what you want to be. Lord Owain?' He turned to the burly, tattooed champion. 'Can you use this good Saxon warrior?'

'I can use him.' Owain agreed readily enough.

'Then he's your man,' Arthur said, and he must have sensed my disappointment for he turned back and rested a hand on my shoulder. 'For the moment, Derfel,' he said softly, 'I employ horsemen, not spearmen. Let Owain be your lord, for there's no one better to teach you the soldier's trade.' He gripped my shoulder with his gloved hand, then turned and waved the two guards away from Gundleus's side. A crowd had gathered close to the captured King who stood beneath the victors' banners. Arthur's horsemen, helmed with iron, armoured in iron-clad leather and cloaked in linen or wool, mingled with Owain's spearmen and the Tor's fugitives about the grassy space where Arthur now faced Gundleus.

Gundleus straightened his back. He had no weapons, but he would not let go of his pride, nor did he flinch as Arthur approached.

Arthur walked in silence until he stood two paces from the captured King. The crowd held its breath. Gundleus was shadowed by Arthur's standard that showed a black bear on a white field. The bear was flying between Mordred's recaptured dragon banner and Owain's boar standard, while at Gundleus's feet was his own fallen fox banner that had been spat on, pissed on and trampled by the victors. Gundleus stared as Arthur drew Excalibur from its scabbard. The blade had a bluish tinge to its steel that was polished as brightly as Arthur's scale coat, helmet or shield.

We waited for the fatal stroke, but instead Arthur dropped to one knee and held Excalibur's hilt to Gundleus. 'Lord King,' he said humbly and the crowd, who had been anticipating Gundleus's death, gasped.

Gundleus hesitated for a heartbeat, then reached out to touch the sword's pommel. He said nothing. Perhaps he was too astonished to speak.

Arthur stood and sheathed the sword. 'I took an oath to protect my King,' he said, 'not to kill kings. What happens to you,

Gundleus ap Meilyr, is not mine to decide, but you will be held captive till the decision is made.'

'Who makes that decision?' Gundleus demanded. Arthur hesitated, plainly unsure of the answer. Many of our warriors were shouting for Gundleus's death, Morgan was urging her brother to avenge Norwenna while Nimue was shrieking for the captive King to be given to her revenge, but Arthur shook his head. Much later he explained to me that Gundleus was a cousin of Gorfyddyd, King of Powys, and that made Gundleus's death a matter of state, not revenge. 'I wanted to make peace, and peace rarely comes out of revenge,' he admitted to me, 'but I probably should have killed him. Not that it would have made much difference.' Now though, facing Gundleus in the slanting sun outside Caer Cadarn, he merely said that Gundleus's fate was in the hands of Dumnonia's council.

'And what of Ladwys?' Gundleus asked, gesturing towards the tall, pale-faced woman who stood close behind him with a look of terror on her face. 'I ask that she be allowed to stay with me,' he added.

'The whore is mine,' Owain said harshly. Ladwys shook her head and moved closer to Gundleus.

'She is my wife!' Gundleus protested to Arthur, thereby confirming the old rumour that he had indeed married his low-born lover. Which also meant that he had married Norwenna falsely, though that sin, considering what else he did to her, was small indeed.

'Wife or whatever,' Owain insisted, 'she is mine.' He saw Arthur's hesitation. 'Until the council decides otherwise,' he added in a deliberate echo of Arthur's invocation of that higher authority.

Arthur seemed troubled by Owain's claim, but his position in Dumnonia was still uncertain, for though he had been named as Mordred's protector and one of the kingdom's warlords, that only gave him an authority equal to Owain's. All of us had noted how, in the wake of the Silurian rout, Arthur had taken charge, but Owain, by demanding Ladwys as his slave, was reminding Arthur that he held equal power. The moment was awkward until Arthur sacrificed Ladwys to Dumnonian unity. 'Owain has decided the matter,' he said to Gundleus, then turned away so he would not have to witness the effect of his words on the lovers. Ladwys screamed her protest, then went silent as one of Owain's men dragged her away.

Tanaburs laughed at Ladwys's distress. He was a Druid, so no harm would be done to him. He was no prisoner, but free to go, though he would have to leave the field without food, blessing or company. Yet, emboldened by the day's events, I could not let him go without speaking and so I followed him across the pasture that was littered with the Silurian dead. 'Tanaburs!' I called after him.

The Druid turned and watched me draw my sword. 'Careful, boy,' he said and made a sign of warning with his moon-tipped staff.

I should have felt fear, but a new warrior spirit filled me as I stepped close to him and placed the sword in the tangled white hairs of his beard. His head jerked back at the touch of the steel, rattling the yellow bones tied to his hair. His old face was lined, brown and blotchy, his eyes red and his nose twisted. 'I ought to kill you,' I said.

He laughed. 'And the curse of Britain will follow you. Your soul will never reach the Otherworld, you will have torments unknown and unnumbered, and I will be their author.' He spat towards me, then tried to push the sword blade out of his beard, but I tightened my grip on the hilt and he suddenly looked alarmed as he realized my strength.

A few curious onlookers had followed me and some tried to warn me of the dreadful fate that would torment me if I killed a Druid, but I had no intention of killing the old man. I just wanted to frighten him. 'Ten or more years ago,' I said, 'you came to Madog's holding.' Madog was the man who had enslaved my mother, and whose homestead the young Gundleus had raided.

Tanaburs nodded as he remembered the raid. 'So we did, so we did. A good day! We took much gold,' he said, 'and many slaves!'

'And you made a death-pit,' I said.

'So?' He shrugged, then leered at me. 'The Gods must be thanked for good fortune.'

I smiled and let the sword point tickle his scrawny throat. 'So I lived, Druid. I lived.'

It took Tanaburs a few seconds to understand just what I had said, but then he blanched and trembled, for he knew that I, alone of all in Britain, possessed the power to kill him. He had sacrificed me to the Gods, but his carelessness in not making sure of his gift meant that the Gods had granted the power of his life into my keeping. He screamed in terror, thinking my blade was about to lunge into his gullet, but instead I pulled the steel away from his ragged beard and laughed at him as he turned and stumbled away across the field. He was desperate to escape me, but just before he reached the woodland into which the handful of Silurian survivors had fled, he turned and pointed a bony hand towards me. 'Your mother lives, boy!' he shouted. 'She lives!' Then he was gone.

I stood there with my mouth open and my sword hanging in my hand. It was not that I was overcome by any particular emotion for I could hardly remember my mother and had no real recollection of any love between us, but the very thought that she lived wrenched my whole world as violently as that morning's destruction of Merlin's hall. Then I shook my head. How could Tanaburs remember one slave among so many? His claim was surely false, mere words to unsettle me, nothing more, and so I sheathed the sword and walked slowly back towards the fortress.

Gundleus was placed under guard in a chamber off the great hall at Caer Cadarn. There was a feast of sorts that night, though because so many people were in the fortress the helpings of meat were small and hastily cooked. Much of the night was spent by old friends exchanging news of Britain and Brittany, for many of Arthur's followers had originally come from Dumnonia or from the other British kingdoms. The names of Arthur's men blurred in my mind, for there were over seventy horsemen in his band, as well as grooms, servants, women and a tribe of children. In time the names of Arthur's warriors became so familiar, but that night they meant nothing: Dagonet, Aglaval, Cei, Lanval, the brothers Balan and Balin, Gawain and Agravain, Blaise, Illtyd, Eiddilig, Bedwyr. I did notice Morfans, for he was the ugliest man I ever saw, so ugly that he took pride in his twisted looks, goitred neck, hare lip and misshapen jaw. I also noticed Sagramor, for he was black and I had never seen, let alone believed in, such men. He was a tall, thin and sourly laconic man, though when he could be persuaded to tell a story in his horribly accented British he could put a whole hall under his spell.

And, of course, I noticed Ailleann. She was a slender, black-haired woman, a few years older than Arthur, with a thin, grave and gentle face that gave her a look of great wisdom. She was dressed in royal finery that night. Her robe was of linen dyed a rusty red with iron-soil, girdled by a heavy silver chain, and had long loose sleeves that were fringed with otter fur. She wore a gleaming torque of heavy gold about her long neck, bracelets of gold around her wrists and an enamelled brooch showing Arthur's symbol of the bear at her breast. She moved gracefully, spoke little and watched Arthur protectively. I thought she had to be a queen, or at least a princess, except that she was carrying bowls of food and flasks of mead like any common servant.

'Ailleann's a slave, lad,' Morfans the Ugly said. He was squatting opposite me on the hall floor and had seen me watching the tall woman as she moved from the patches of firelight into the hall's flickering shadows.

'Whose slave?' I asked.

'Whose do you think?' he asked, then put a rib of pork in his mouth and used his two remaining teeth to strip the bone of its succulent flesh. 'Arthur's,' he said after he had tossed the bone to one of the many dogs in the hall. 'And she's his lover as well as his slave, of course.' He belched, then drank from a horn cup. 'She was given to him by his brother-in-law, King Budic. That was a long time ago. She's a good few years older than Arthur and I don't suppose Budic thought he'd keep her long, but once Arthur takes a fancy to someone they seem to stay for ever. Those are her twin boys.' He jerked a greasy beard towards the back of the hall where a pair of sullen boys of about nine squatted in the dirt with their bowls of food.

'Arthur's sons?' I asked.

'No one else's,' Morfans said derisively. 'Amhar and Loholt, they're called, and their father worships them. Nothing's too good for those little bastards, and that's exactly what they are, lad, bastards. Real good-for-nothing little bastards.' There was a genuine hatred in his voice. 'I tell you, son, Arthur ap Uther is a great man. He's the best soldier I've ever known, the most generous man and the most fair lord, but when it comes to breeding children I could do better with a sow for a mother.'

I looked back to Ailleann. 'Are they married?'

Morfans laughed. 'Of course not! But she's kept him happy these ten years. Mind you, the day will come when he'll send her away just like his father sent his mother away. Arthur will marry something royal and she won't be half as gentle as Ailleann, but that's what men like Arthur have to do. They have to marry well. Not like you and me, boy. We can marry what we want, so long as it isn't royal. Listen to that!' He grinned as a woman screamed in the night outside the hall.

Owain had left the hall and Ladwys was evidently being taught her new duties. Arthur flinched at the sound, and Ailleann raised her elegant head and frowned at him, but the only other person in the hall who seemed to notice Ladwys's distress was Nimue. Her bandaged face was drawn and sad, but the scream made her smile because of the torment she knew the sound would give to Gundleus. There was no forgiveness in Nimue, not one drop. She had already begged Arthur and Owain for permission to kill Gundleus herself, and had been refused, but so long as Nimue lived Gundleus would know fear.

Arthur led a party of horsemen to Ynys Wydryn the next day and returned that evening to report that Merlin's settlement had been burned to the ground. The horsemen also returned with poor mad Pellinore and an indignant Druidan who had taken shelter in a well belonging to the monks of the Holy Thorn. Arthur declared his intention of rebuilding Merlin's hall, though how it was to be done without money and an army of labourers, none of us knew, and Gwlyddyn was formally appointed as Mordred's royal builder and instructed to start felling trees to remake the Tor's buildings. Pellinore was locked into an empty stone-built store-room attached to the Roman villa at Lindinis, which was the settlement nearest to Caer Cadarn and the place where the women, children and slaves who followed Arthur's men found themselves roofs. Arthur organized everything. He was always a restless man who hated to be idle and in those first few days after Gundleus's capture he worked from dawn until long after dusk. Most of his time was spent in arranging for his followers' livelihoods; royal land had to be allotted to them and houses enlarged for their families, all without offending the people already living at Lindinis. The villa itself had belonged to Uther and Arthur now took it for himself. No task was too trivial for him and I even found him wrestling with a great sheet of lead one morning. 'Give me some help, Derfel!' he called. I was flattered that he remembered my name and hurried to help him lift the unwieldy mass. 'Rare stuff, this!' he said cheerfully. He was stripped to the waist and his skin was stained with the lead that he planned to cut into strips to line the stone gutter that had once carried water from a spring into the villa's interior. 'The Romans took all the lead away with them when they left,' he explained, 'and that's why the water conduits don't work. We should get the mines working again.' He dropped his end of the lead and wiped his brow. 'Get the mines working, rebuild the bridges, pave the fords, dig out the sluices and find a way of persuading the Sais to go back home. That's enough work for one man's life, don't you think?'

'Yes, Lord,' I said nervously, and wondered why a warlord would busy himself repairing water conduits. The council was to meet later in the day and I thought Arthur would be busy enough preparing for that business, but he seemed more concerned with the lead than with matters of state.

'I don't know if you saw lead, or cut it with a knife,' he said ruefully. 'I ought to know. I'll ask Gwlyddyn. He seems to know everything. Did you know that you always put tree trunks upside down if you use them for pillars?'

'No, Lord.'

'It stops the damp from rising, you see, and keeps the timber from rotting. That's what Gwlyddyn tells me. I like that sort of knowledge. It's good, practical knowledge, the kind that makes the world work.' He grinned at me. 'So how are you liking Owain?' he asked.

'He's good to me, Lord,' I said, embarrassed by the question. In truth I was still nervous of Owain, though he never showed me any unkindness.

'He should be good to you,' Arthur said. 'Every leader depends on having good men for his reputation.'

'But I'd rather serve you, Lord,' I blurted out with youthful indiscretion.

He smiled. 'You will, Derfel, you will. In time. If you pass the test of fighting for Owain.' He made the remark casually enough, but later I wondered if he foresaw what was to come. In time I did pass Owain's test, but it was hard, and perhaps Arthur wanted me to learn that lesson before I joined his band of men. He stooped again to the lead sheet, then straightened as a howl sounded through the shabby building. It was Pellinore, protesting his imprisonment. 'Owain says we should send poor Pell' to the Isle of the Dead,' Arthur said, referring to the island where the violent mad were put away. 'What do you think?'

I was so astonished at being asked that at first I did not reply, then I stammered that Pellinore was beloved of Merlin and Merlin had wanted him kept among the living and I thought Merlin's wishes should be respected. Arthur listened gravely and even seemed grateful for my advice. He did not need it, of course, but was just trying to make me feel valued. 'Then Pellinore can stay here, lad,' he said. 'Now get hold of the other end. Lift!'

Lindinis emptied next day. Morgan and Nimue returned to

Ynys Wydryn where they planned to rebuild the Tor. Nimue brushed aside my farewell; her eye still hurt, she was bitter, and she wanted nothing from life except revenge on Gundleus which was denied her. Arthur went north with all his horsemen to reinforce Tewdric on Gwent's northern border while I stayed with Owain who had taken up residence in Caer Cadarn's great hall. I might be a warrior, but in that high summer it was more important to gather in the harvest than stand guard on the fort's ramparts, so for days at a time I gave up my sword and the helmet, shield and leather breastplate I had inherited from a dead Silurian and went to the King's fields to help the serfs bring in the rye, barley and wheat. It was hard work done with a short sickle that had to be sharpened constantly on a strickle: a wooden baton that was first dipped in pig's grease, then coated with fine sand that put a keen edge on the sickle's blade, though the edge never seemed sharp enough for me and, fit as I was, the constant stooping and tugging left my back aching and my muscles sore. I had never worked so hard when I lived on the Tor, but I had now left Merlin's privileged world and was a part of Owain's troop.

We stooked the cut grain in the fields, then carted vast heaps of rye straw to Caer Cadarn and Lindinis. The straw was used to repair the thatched roofs and to restuff the mattresses so that for a few blissful days our beds were free of lice and fleas, though that blessing did not last long. It was at that time I grew my first beard, a wispy gold affair of which I was inordinately proud. I spent my days doing backbreaking work in the fields but I still had to endure two hours of military training each night. Hywel had taught me well, but Owain wanted better. 'That Silurian you killed,' Owain said to me one evening when I was sweating on Caer Cadarn's ramparts after a bout of single-stick with a warrior named Mapon, 'I'll wager you a month's wages to a dead mouse that you killed him with your sword's edge.' I did not take the wager, but confirmed that I had indeed sliced the sword down like an axe. Owain laughed, then dismissed Mapon with a wave of his hand. 'Hywel always taught people to fight with the edge,' Owain said. 'Watch

Arthur the next time he fights. Slash, slash, like a haymaker trying to finish before the rain comes.' He drew his own sword. 'Use the point, boy,' he told me. 'Always use the point. It kills quicker.' He lunged at me, making me parry desperately. 'If you're using the sword's edge,' he said, 'it means you're in the open field. The shield-wall has broken, and if it's your shield-wall that's broken then you're a dead man, however good a swordsman you are. But if the shield-wall holds firm then it means you're standing shoulder to shoulder and you don't have room to swing a sword, only to stab.' He thrust again, making me parry. 'Why do you think the Romans had short swords?' he asked me.

'I don't know, Lord.'

'Because a short sword stabs better than a long one, that's why,' he said, 'not that I'll ever persuade any of you to change your swords, but even so, remember to stab. The point always wins, always.' He turned away then suddenly whipped back to stab at me and somehow I managed to knock his blade aside with the clumsy single-stick. Owain grinned. 'You're fast,' he said, 'and that's good. You'll make it, boy, so long as you stay sober.' He sheathed his sword and stared eastwards. He was looking for those distant grey smears of smoke that betrayed the presence of a raiding party, but this was harvest time for the Saxons as well as for ourselves and their soldiers had better things to do than cross our distant frontier. 'So what do you think of Arthur, boy?' Owain asked me suddenly.

'I like him,' I said awkwardly, as nervous of his question as I had been of Arthur's about Owain.

Owain's great shaggy head, so much like his old friend Uther's, turned to me. 'Oh, he's likeable enough,' he said grudgingly. 'I've always liked Arthur. Everyone likes Arthur, but the Gods alone know if anyone understands him. Except Merlin. You think Merlin's alive?'

'I know he is,' I said fervently, knowing nothing of the sort.

'Good,' Owain said. I came from the Tor and Owain assumed I had a magical knowledge denied to other men. The word had also spread among his warriors that I had cheated a

Druid's death-pit, and that made me both lucky and auspicious in their eyes. 'I like Merlin,' Owain went on, 'even though he did give Arthur that sword.'

'Caledfwlch?' I asked, using Excalibur's proper name.

'You didn't know?' Owain asked in astonishment. He had heard the surprise in my voice, and no wonder, for Merlin had never spoken of making such a great gift. He sometimes talked of Arthur whom he had known in the brief time Arthur spent at Uther's court, but Merlin always used a fondly disparaging tone as if Arthur was a slow but willing pupil whose later exploits were greater than Merlin had ever expected, but the fact that he had given Arthur the famous sword suggested that Merlin's opinion of him was a great deal higher than he pretended it to be.

'Caledfwlch,' Owain explained to me, 'was forged in the Otherworld by Gofannon.' Gofannon was the God of Smithcraft. 'Merlin found it in Ireland,' Owain went on, 'where the sword was called Cadalcholg. He won it off a Druid in a dream contest. The Irish Druids say that when Cadalcholg's wearer is in desperate trouble he can thrust the sword into the soil and Gofannon will leave the Otherworld and come to his help.' He shook his head, not in disbelief, but in wonderment. 'Now why did Merlin give such a gift to Arthur?'

'Why not?' I asked carefully for I sensed the jealousy in Owain's question.

'Because Arthur doesn't believe in the Gods,' Owain said, 'that's why not. He doesn't even believe in that milksop God the Christians worship. So far as I can make out Arthur doesn't believe in anything, except big horses, and the Gods alone know what earthly use they are.'

'They're frightening,' I said, wanting to be loyal to Arthur.

'Oh, they're frightening,' Owain agreed, 'but only if you've never seen one before. But they're slow, they take two or three times the amount of feed of a proper horse, they need two grooms, their hooves split like warm butter if you don't strap those clumsy shoes on to their feet, and they still won't charge home into a shield-wall.'

'They won't?'

'No horse will!' Owain said scornfully. 'Stand your ground and every horse in the world will swerve away from a line of steady spears. Horses are no use in war, boy, except to carry your scouts far and wide.'

'Then why –' I began.

'Because,' Owain anticipated my question, 'the whole point of battle, boy, is to break the enemy's shield-wall. Everything else is easy, and Arthur's horses scare battle lines into flight, but the time will come when an enemy will stand firm, and the Gods help those horses then. And the Gods help Arthur too if he's ever knocked off his lump of horseflesh and tries to fight on foot wearing that suit of fish-armour. The only metal a warrior needs is his sword and the lump of iron at the end of his spear, the rest's just weight, lad, dead weight.' He stared down into the fort's compound where Ladwys was clinging to the fence that surrounded Gundleus's prison. 'Arthur won't last here,' he said confidently. 'One defeat and he'll sail back to Armorica where they're impressed by big horses, fish suits and fancy swords.' He spat, and I knew that despite Owain's professed liking for Arthur there was something else there, something deeper than jealousy. Owain knew he had a rival, but he was biding his time as, I guessed, Arthur was biding his, and the mutual enmity worried me for I liked both men. Owain smiled at Ladwys's distress. 'She's a loyal bitch, I'll say that for her,' the big man said, 'but I'll break her yet. Is that your woman?' He nodded towards Lunete who was carrying a leather bag of water towards the warriors' huts.

'Yes,' I said and blushed at the confession. Lunete, like my new beard, was a sign of manhood and I wore both clumsily. Lunete had decided to stay with me instead of going back to what was left of Ynys Wydryn with Nimue. The decision really had been Lunete's and I was still nervous of everything about our relationship, though Lunete seemed to have no doubts about the arrangement. She had taken over a corner of the hut, swept it, screened it with some withy hurdles, and now talked confidently about our joint future. I had thought she would want to stay with Nimue, but since her rape Nimue had been quiet and withdrawn. Indeed, she had become hostile, speaking to no one except to turn away their conversation. Morgan was tending her eye and the same smith who had made Morgan's mask was offering to make a gold ball to replace the lost eyeball. Lunete, like the rest of us, had become a little frightened of this new, sour, spitting Nimue.

'She's a pretty girl,' Owain said grudgingly of Lunete, 'but girls live with warriors for one reason only, boy, to get rich. So make sure you keep her happy, or sure as eggs she'll make you miserable.' He fished in his coat's pockets and found a small gold ring. 'Give it to her,' he said.

I stammered my thanks. Warrior leaders were supposed to grant their followers gifts, yet even so the ring was a generous gift for I had yet to fight as one of Owain's men. Lunete liked the ring which, with the silver wire I had unwrapped from my sword's pommel, was the beginning of her treasure hoard. She incised a cross on the ring's worn surface, not because she was a Christian, but because the cross made it into a lover's ring and showed that she had passed from girlhood into womanhood. Some men also wore lovers' rings, but I craved after the simple iron hoops that victorious warriors hammered from the spearheads of their defeated enemies. Owain wore a score of such rings in his beard, and his fingers were dark with others. Arthur, I had noticed, wore none.

Once our own harvest was gathered from the fields around Caer Cadarn we marched all over Dumnonia to collect the tax crops. We visited client kings and chiefs, and were always accompanied by a clerk from Mordred's treasury who tallied the revenue. It was strange to think that Mordred was now King and that it was no longer Uther's treasury we filled, but even a baby king needed money to pay for Arthur's troops as well as all the other soldiers who were keeping Dumnonia's borders secure. Some of Owain's men were sent to reinforce the permanent guard in Gereint's frontier fortress at Durocobrivis while the rest of us became taxmen for a while.

I was surprised that Owain, that famous lover of battle, did not go to Durocobrivis nor back to Gwent, but instead stayed with the commonplace work of assessing tax. To me such work seemed menial, but I was just a wispy-bearded boy who did not understand Owain's mind.

Tax, to Owain, was more important than any Saxon. Taxes, as I was to learn, were the best source of wealth for men who did not want to work, and this tax season, now that Uther was dead, was Owain's opportunity. At hall after hall he reported a bad harvest, and thus levied a low tax payment, and all the while he was lining his own purse with the bribes offered in return for making just such a false report. He was quite guileless about it. 'Uther would never have let me get away with it,' he told me one day as we walked along the southern coast towards the Roman town of Isca. He spoke fondly of the dead king. 'Uther was a fly old bastard, and always had a shrewd idea of what he should get, but what does Mordred know?' He looked to his left. We were crossing a wide, bare heath atop a great hill and the view to the south was of the glittering empty sea where a wind blew strong to fleck the grey waves white. Way off to the east, where a long sweeping shingle bank ended, there was a mighty headland on which the waves shattered into foam. The headland was almost an island, joined to the mainland only by a narrow causeway of stone and shingle. 'Know what that is?' Owain asked me, jutting his chin towards the headland.

'No, Lord.'

'The Isle of the Dead,' he said, then spat to ward off ill luck while I stopped and stared at the awful place that was the seat of Dumnonian nightmares. The headland was the isle of the mad, the place where Pellinore belonged with all the other crazed and violent souls who were considered dead the moment they crossed the guarded causeway. The Isle was under the guardianship of Crom Dubh, the dark crippled God, and some men said that Cruachan's Cave, the mouth of the Otherworld, lay at the Isle's extremity. I stared at it in dread until Owain clapped my shoulder. 'You'll never need to worry about the Isle of the Dead, boy,' he said. 'You've got a rare head on your shoulders.' he walked on westwards. 'Where are we staying tonight?' he called to Lwellwyn, the treasury clerk whose mule carried the year's falsified records.

'With Prince Cadwy of Isca,' Lwellwyn answered.

'Ah, Cadwy! I like Cadwy. What did we take from the ugly rogue last year?'

Lwellwyn did not need to look at his wooden tally sticks with their recording notches, but reeled off a list of hides, fleeces, slaves, tin ingots, dried fish, salt and milled corn. 'He paid most in gold, though,' he added.

'I like him even more!' Owain said. 'What will he settle for, Lwellwyn?'

Lwellwyn estimated an amount half of what Cadwy had paid the previous year, and that was precisely the amount agreed before the evening meal in Prince Cadwy's hall. It was a grand place, built by the Romans, with a pillared portico that faced down a long wooded valley towards the sea reach of the River Exe. Cadwy was a Prince of the Dumnonii, the tribe which had given our country its name, and Cadwy's princedom made him of the second rank in the kingdom. Kings were of the highest rank, princes like Gereint and Cadwy and client kings like Melwas of the Belgae came next, and after them were the chiefs like Merlin, though Merlin of Avalon was also a Druid which put him outside the hierarchy altogether. Cadwy was both a prince and a chief and he ruled a sprawling tribe that inhabited all the land between Isca and the border of Kernow. There had been a time when all the tribes of Britain were separate and a man of the Catuvellani would look quite different from a man of the Belgae, but the Romans had left us all much alike. Only some tribes, like Cadwy's, still retained their distinct appearance. His tribe believed themselves to be superior to other Britons, in mark of which they tattooed their faces with the symbols of their tribe and sept. Each valley had its own sept, usually of no more than a dozen families. Rivalry between the septs was keen, but nothing compared to the rivalry between Prince Cadwy's tribe and the rest of Britain.

The tribal capital was Isca, the Roman town, which had fine walls and stone buildings as great as any in Glevum, though Cadwy preferred to live outside the town on his own estate. Most of the townspeople followed Roman ways and eschewed tattoos, but beyond the walls, in the valleys of Cadwy's land where Roman rule had never lain heavily, every man, woman and child bore the blue tattoo marks on their cheeks. It was also a wealthy area, but Prince Cadwy had a mind to make it wealthier still.

'Been on the moor lately?' he asked Owain that night. It was a warm, sweet night and supper had been served on the open portico that faced Cadwy's estates.

'Never,' Owain said.

Cadwy grunted. I had seen him at Uther's High Council, but this was my first chance to look closely at the man whose responsibility was to guard Dumnonia against raids from Kernow or distant Ireland. The Prince was a short, bald, middle-aged man, heavily built, with tribal marks on his cheeks, arms and legs. He wore British dress, but liked his Roman villa with its paving and pillars and channelled water that ran in stone troughs through the central courtyard and out to the portico where it made a small foot-washing pool before running over a marble dam to join the stream further down the valley. Cadwy, I decided, had a good life. His crops were plentiful, his sheep and cows fat, and his many women happy. He was also far from the threat of Saxons, yet still he was discontented. 'There's money on the moor,' he told Owain. 'Tin.'

'Tin?' Owain sounded scornful.

Cadwy nodded solemnly. He was fairly drunk, but so were most of the men around the low table on which the meal had been served. They were all warriors, either Cadwy's or Owain's men, though I, being junior, had to stand behind Owain's couch as his shield-bearer. 'Tin,' Cadwy said again, 'and gold, maybe. But plenty of tin.' Their conversation was private, for the meal was almost over and Cadwy had provided slave girls for the warriors. No one had any attention for the two leaders, except for me and Cadwy's shield-holder, who was a dozy lad staring slack-jawed and dull-eyed at the slave girls' antics. I was listening to Owain and Cadwy, but kept so still and straight that they probably forgot I was even standing there. 'You may not want tin,' Cadwy said to Owain, 'but there's plenty who do. Can't make bronze without tin, and they pay a fancy price for the stuff in Armorica, let alone up country.' He jerked a dismissive fist towards the rest of Dumnonia, then gave a belch that seemed to surprise him. He calmed his belly with a draught of good wine, then frowned as though he could not remember what he had been talking about. 'Tin,' he finally said, remembering.

'So tell me about it,' Owain said. He was watching one of his men who had stripped a slave girl naked and was now smearing butter on her belly.

'It isn't my tin,' Cadwy said forcefully.

'Must be someone's,' Owain said. 'You want me to ask Lwellwyn? He's a clever bastard when it comes to money and ownership.' His man slapped the girl's belly hard, splattering butter all over the low table and causing a gust of laughter. The girl complained, but the man told her to be quiet and started scooping butter and pork grease on to the rest of her body.

'The fact of the matter is,' Cadwy said forcefully to get Owain's attention off the naked girl, 'that Uther let in a pack of men from Kernow. They came to work the old Roman mines, because none of our people had the skills. The bastards are supposed, mark that, supposed to send their rent to your treasury, but the buggers are sending tin back to Kernow. I know that for a fact.'

Owain's ears had pricked up now. 'Kernow?'

'Making money off our land, they are. Our land!' Cadwy said indignantly.

Kernow was a separate kingdom, a mysterious place at the very end of Dumnonia's western peninsula that had never been ruled by the Romans. Most of the time it lived in peace with us, but every now and then King Mark would stir himself from his latest wife's bed and send a raiding party over the

135

River Tamar. 'What are men of Kernow doing here?' Owain asked in a voice every bit as indignant as his host's.

'I told you. Stealing our money. And not just that. I've been missing good cattle, sheep, even a few slaves. Those miners are getting above themselves, and they're not paying you like they should. But you'll never prove it. Never. Not even your clever fellow Lwellwyn can look at a hole in the moor and tell me how much tin is supposed to come out in a year.' Cadwy swiped at a moth, then shook his head moodily. 'They think they're above the law. That's the problem. Just because Uther was their patron they think they're above the law.'

Owain shrugged. His attention was back on the butter-smothered girl who was now being chased about the lower terrace by a half dozen drunken men. The grease on her body made her hard to catch and the grotesque hunt was making some of the watching men helpless with laughter. I was having a hard time stopping myself from giggling. Owain looked back to Cadwy. 'So go up there and kill a few of the bastards, Lord Prince,' he said as though it was the easiest solution in the world.

'I can't,' Cadwy said.

'Why not?'

'Uther gave them protection. If I attack them they'll complain to the council and to King Mark and I'll be forced to pay *sarhaed*.' *Sarhaed* was the blood price put on a man by law. A King's *sarhaed* was unpayable, a slave's was cheap, but a good miner probably had a high enough price to hurt even a wealthy prince like Cadwy.

'So how will they know it's you who attacked them?' Owain asked scornfully.

For answer Cadwy just tapped his cheek. The blue tattoos, he was suggesting, would betray his men.

Owain nodded. The buttered girl had at last been pinned down and was now surrounded by her captors among some shrubs that grew on the lower terrace. Owain crumbled some bread, then looked up at Cadwy again. 'So?'

'So,' Cadwy said slyly, 'if I could find a bunch of men who

could thin these bastards out a little, it would help. It'll make them look to me for protection, see? And my price will be the tin they're sending to King Mark. And your price . . .' He paused to make sure Owain was not shocked by the implication, '. . . will be half that tin's value.'

'How much?' Owain asked quickly. The two men were speaking softly and I had to concentrate to hear their words over the warriors' laughter and cheers.

'Fifty gold pieces a year? Like this,' said Cadwy and took a gold ingot the size of a sword handle from a pouch and slid it along the table.

'That much?' Even Owain was surprised.

'It's a rich place, the moor,' Cadwy said grimly. 'Very rich.'

Owain stared down Cadwy's valley to where the moon's reflection lay on the distant river as flat and silver as a sword blade. 'How many of these miners are there?' he finally asked the Prince.

'The nearest settlement,' Cadwy said, 'has got seventy or eighty men. And there are a deal of slaves and women, of course.'

'How many settlements?'

'Three, but the other two are a way off. I'm just worried about the one.'

'Only twenty of us,' Owain said cautiously.

'Night-time?' Cadwy suggested. 'And they've not been attacked ever, so they won't be keeping watch.'

Owain sipped wine from his horn. 'Seventy gold pieces,' he said flatly, 'not fifty.'

Prince Cadwy thought for a second, then nodded his acceptance of the price.

Owain grinned. 'Why not, eh?' he said. He palmed the gold ingot, then turned fast as a snake to look up at me. I did not move, nor took my eyes from one of the girls who was wrapping her naked body round one of Cadwy's tattooed warriors. 'Are you awake, Derfel?' Owain snapped.

I jumped as though startled. 'Lord?' I said, pretending my mind had been wandering for the last few minutes.

'Good lad,' Owain said, satisfied I had heard nothing. 'Want one of those girls, do you?'

I blushed. 'No, Lord.'

Owain laughed. 'He's just got himself a pretty little Irish girl,' he told Cadwy, 'so he's staying true to her. But he'll learn. When you get to the Otherworld, boy' – he had turned back to me – 'you won't regret the men you never killed, but you will regret the women you passed up.' He spoke gently. In my first days in his service I had been frightened of him, but for some reason Owain liked me and treated me well. Now he looked back at Cadwy. 'Tomorrow night,' he said softly. 'Tomorrow night.'

I had gone from Merlin's Tor to Owain's band, and it was like leaping from this world to the next. I stared at the moon and thought of Gundleus's long-haired men massacring the guards on the Tor, and I thought of the people on the moor who would face the same savagery the very next night and I knew I could do nothing to stop it, even though I knew it should be stopped, but fate, as Merlin always taught us, is inexorable. Life is a jest of the Gods, Merlin liked to claim, and there is no justice. You must learn to laugh, he once told me, or else you'll just weep yourself to death.

Our shields had been smeared with boat-builder's pitch so they would look like the black shields of Oengus Mac Airem's Irish raiders whose long, sharp-prowed boats raided Dumnonia's northern coast. A local guide with tattooed cheeks led us all afternoon through deep, lush valleys that climbed slowly towards the great bleak loom of the moor that was occasionally visible through some break in the heavy trees. It was good woodland, full of deer and cut with fast, cold streams running seaward off the moor's high plateau.

By nightfall we were on the moor's edge, and after dark we followed a goat track up to the heights. It was a mysterious place. The Old People had lived here and left their sacred stone circles in its valleys while the peaks were crowned with jumbled masses of grey rock and the low places were filled

138

with treacherous swamps through which our guide led us unerringly.

Owain had told us that the people of the moor were in rebellion against King Mordred, and that their religion had taught them to fear men with black shields. It was a good tale, and I might have believed it had I not eavesdropped on his conversation with Prince Cadwy the night before. Owain had also promised us gold if we did our task properly, then warned us that this night's killing would have to stay secret for we had no orders from the council to mete out this punishment. Deep in the thick woods on our way to the moor we had come to an old shrine built beneath a grove of oaks and Owain had made us each swear the death-oath of secrecy in front of the moss-grown skulls that were lodged in niches of the shrine's wall. Britain was full of such ancient, hidden shrines – evidence of how widespread the Druids had been before the Romans came – where countryfolk still came to seek the Gods' help. And that afternoon, under the great lichen-hung oaks, we had knelt before the skulls and touched the hilt of Owain's sword and those men who were initiates in the secrets of Mithras had received Owain's kiss. Then, thus blessed by the Gods and sworn to the killing, we moved on towards the night.

It was a filthy place we came to. Great smelting fires spewed sparks and smoke towards the heavens. A sprawl of huts lay between the fires and around the gaping black maws that showed where men delved into the earth. Huge mounds of charcoal looked like black tors, while the valley smelt like no other I had ever seen; indeed, to my heated imagination that upland mining village seemed more like Annawn's realm, the Other-world, than any human settlement.

Dogs barked as we approached, but no one in the settlement took any notice of their noise. There was no fence, not even an earth bank to protect the place. Ponies were picketed close to rows of carts and they began to whinny as we edged down the valley's side, but still no one came out of the low huts to find the cause of the unrest. The huts were circles made of stone

139

and roofed with turf, but in the settlement's centre was a pair of old Roman buildings; square, tall and solid.

'Two men apiece, if not more,' Owain hissed at us, reminding us how many men we were each expected to kill. 'And I'm not counting slaves or women. Go fast, kill fast and always watch your backs. And stay together!'

We divided into two groups. I was with Owain whose beard glinted from the fire that reflected off his iron warrior rings. The dogs barked, the ponies whinnied, then at last a cockerel crowed and a man crawled from a hut to discover what had disturbed the livestock, but it was already too late. The killing had begun.

I saw many such killings. In Saxon villages we would have burned the huts before we began the slaughter, but these crude stone and turf circles would not take the fire and so we were forced to go inside with spears and swords. We snatched burning wood from a nearby fire and hurled it inside the huts before entering so that the interior would be light enough for the killing, and sometimes the flames were enough to drive the inhabitants out to where the waiting swords chopped down like butchers' axes. If the fire did not drive the family out then Owain would order two of us to go inside while the others stood guard outside. I dreaded my turn, but knew it would come and knew, too, that I dared not disobey the command. I was oath-bound to this bloody work and to refuse it would have been my death warrant.

The screaming began. The first few huts were easy enough for the people were asleep or only just waking, but as we moved deeper into the settlement the resistance became fiercer. Two men attacked us with axes and were cut down with contemptuous ease by our spearmen. Women fled with children in their arms. A dog leaped at Owain and died whimpering with its spine broken. I watched a woman run with a baby in one arm and holding a bleeding child's hand with the other, and I suddenly remembered Tanaburs's parting shout that my mother still lived. I shuddered as I realized that the old Druid must have laid a curse on me when I had threatened his life, and though my good fortune was holding the curse at bay, I could feel its malevolence circling me like a hidden dark enemy. I touched the scar on my left hand and prayed to Bel that Tanaburs's curse would be defeated.

'Derfel! Licat! That hut!' Owain shouted and, like a good soldier, I obeyed my orders. I dropped my shield, flung a fire-brand through the door, then crouched double to get through the tiny entrance. Children screamed as I entered, and a half-naked man leaped at me with a knife that forced me to twist desperately aside. I fell on a child as I lunged at her father with my spear. The blade slid off the man's ribs and he would have landed on top of me and stabbed the knife down through my throat if Licat had not killed him. The man doubled over, clasping his belly, then he gasped as Licat wrenched the spearhead free and drew his own knife to begin killing the screaming children. I ducked back outside, blood on my spearhead, to tell Owain there had only been the one man inside.

'Come on!' Owain shouted. 'Demetia! Demetia!' That was our war cry of the night; the name of Oengus Mac Airem's Irish kingdom to the west of Siluria. The huts were all empty now and we began hunting miners down in the dark spaces of the settlement. Fugitives were running everywhere, but some men stayed behind and tried to fight us. One brave group even formed a crude battle line and attacked us with spears, picks and axes, but Owain's men met the crude charge with a terrible efficiency, letting their black shields soak up the impact, then using their spears and swords to cut down their attackers. I was one of those efficient men. May God forgive me, but I killed my second man that night, and perhaps a third too. The first I speared in the throat, the second in the groin. I did not use my sword, for I did not think Hywel's blade a fit instrument for that night's purpose.

It ended quickly enough. The settlement was suddenly empty of all but the dead, the dying and a few men, women and children trying to hide. We killed all we found. We killed their animals, we burned the carts they used to fetch the charcoal up from the valleys, we stove in the turf roofs of their huts, we trampled their vegetable gardens, and then we ransacked the settlement for treasure. A few arrows flickered down from the skyline, but none of us was hit.

There was a tub of Roman coins, gold ingots and silver bars in their chief's hut. It was the biggest hut, full twenty feet across, and inside the hut the light of our fire-brands showed the dead chief sprawling with a yellowish face and a slit belly. One of his women and two of his children lay dead in his blood. A third child, a girl, lay under a blood-soaked pelt and I thought I saw her hand twitch when one of our men stumbled on her body, but I pretended she was dead and left her alone. Another child screamed in the night as her hiding place was found and a sword hacked down.

God forgive me, God and his angels forgive me, but I only ever confessed that night's sin to one person, and she was not a priest and had no power to grant me Christ's absolution. In purgatory, or maybe hell, I know I will meet those dead children. Their fathers and mothers will be given my soul for their plaything, and I shall deserve the punishment.

But what choice did I have? I was young; I wanted to live; I had taken the oath; I followed my leader. I killed no man who did not attack me, but what plea is that in the face of those sins? To my companions it seemed no sin at all: they were merely killing creatures of another tribe, another nation indeed, and that was justification enough for them; but I had been raised on the Tor where we came from all races and all tribes, and though Merlin was himself a tribal chief and fierce-ly protective of anyone who could boast the name of Briton, he did not teach a hatred of other tribes. His teaching made me unfit for the unthinking slaughter of strangers for no reason other than their strangeness.

Yet, unfit or not, I killed, and may God forgive me that, and all the other sins too numerous to remember.

We left before dawn. The valley was smoking, blood-sodden and horrid. The moor stank from the killing and was haunted with the wailing cries of widows and orphans. Owain gave me a gold ingot, two silver bars and a handful of coins and, God forgive me, I kept them.

AUTUMN BRINGS BATTLE, for all through spring and summer the boats ferry new Saxons to our eastern shore, and the autumn is when those newcomers try to find their own land. It is war's last fling before winter locks the land.

And it was in the autumn of the year of Uther's death that I first fought the Saxons, for no sooner had we come back from our tax collecting in the west than we heard of Saxon raiders in the east. Owain put us under the command of his captain, a man named Griffid ap Annan, and sent us to aid Melwas, King of the Belgae, a client monarch of Dumnonia. Melwas's responsibility was to defend our southern shore against the Sais invaders who, in that grim year of Uther's balefire, had found a new belligerence. Owain stayed at Caer Cadarn for there was a sharp squabble in the kingdom's council about who should be responsible for Mordred's upbringing. Bishop Bedwin wanted to raise the King in his household, but the non-Christians, who were the majority on the council, did not want Mordred raised as a Christian, just as Bedwin and his party objected to the child-King being raised as a pagan. Owain, who claimed to worship all Gods equally, proposed himself as a compromise. 'Not that it matters what God a king believes in,' he told us before we marched, 'because a king should be taught how to fight, not how to pray.' We left him arguing his case while we went to kill Saxons.

Griffid ap Annan, our captain, was a lean, lugubrious man who reckoned that what Owain really wanted was to prevent Arthur from raising Mordred. 'It isn't that Owain doesn't like Arthur,' he hastened to add, 'but if the King belongs to Arthur, then so does Dumnonia.'

'Is that so bad?' I asked.

'It's better for you and me, boy, if the land belongs to Owain.' Griffid fingered one of the gold torques around his neck to show what he meant. They all called me boy or lad, but only because I was the youngest in the troop and still un-blooded by proper battle against other warriors. They also be-lieved that my presence in their ranks brought them good luck because I had once escaped from a Druid's death-pit. All Owain's men, like soldiers everywhere, were mightily super-stitious. Every omen was considered and debated; every man carried a hare's foot or a lightning stone; and every action was ritualized, so that no man would pull on a right boot be-fore a left or sharpen a spear in his own shadow. There were a handful of Christians in our ranks and I had thought they might show less fear of the Gods, spirits and ghosts, but they proved every bit as superstitious as the rest of us.

King Melwas's capital, Venta, was a poor frontier town. Its workshops had long closed down and the walls of its large Roman buildings showed great scorch marks from the times when the town had been sacked by raiding Saxons. King Melwas was terrified that the town was about to be sacked again. The Saxons, he said, had a new leader who was hungry for land and dreadful in battle. 'Why didn't Owain come?' he demanded petulantly, 'or Arthur? They want to destroy me, is that it?' He was a fat and suspicious man with the foulest breath of anyone I ever met. He was the king of a tribe, rather than of a country, which made him of the second rank, though to look at him you would have thought Melwas was a serf and a querulous serf at that. 'There aren't many of you, are there?' he complained to Griffid. 'It's a good thing I raised the levy.'

The levy was Melwas's citizen army and every able-bodied man in his Belgic tribe was supposed to serve, though a good few had made themselves scarce and most of the richer tribes-men had sent slaves as substitutes. Nevertheless Melwas had managed to assemble a force of more than three hundred men, each carrying his own food and bringing his own weapons. Some of the levy had once been warriors and came equipped with fine war spears and carefully preserved shields, but most had no armour and a few had nothing but single-sticks or sharpened mattocks for weapons. A lot of women and children accompanied the levy, unwilling to stay alone in their homes when the Saxons were threatening.

Melwas insisted that he and his own warriors would stay to defend the crumbling ramparts of Venta, which meant that Griffid had to lead the levy against the enemy. Melwas had no idea where the Saxons were and so Griffid blundered helplessly into the deep woods east of Venta. We were more of a rabble than a war-band, and the sight of a deer would start a mad whooping pursuit that would have alerted any enemy within a dozen miles, and the pursuit would always finish with the levy scattered across a swathe of woodland. We lost nearly fifty men that way, either because their careless pursuit led them into Saxon hands, or else because they simply became lost and decided to go home.

There were plenty of Saxons in those woods, though at first we saw none. Sometimes we found their campfires still warm and once we found a small Belgic settlement that had been raided and burned. The men and the old people were still there, all of them dead, but the young and the women had been taken as slaves. The smell of the dead dampened the high spirits of the remaining levy and made them stay together as Griffid edged on eastwards.

We encountered our first Saxon war-band in a wide river valley where a group of the invaders was making a settlement. By the time we arrived they had built half a wooden stockade and planted the wood pillars of their main hall, but our appearance at the edge of the woods made them drop their tools and pick up their spears. We outnumbered them three to one, yet even so Griffid could not persuade us to charge their well-knit, fierce-speared shield-line. We younger men were keen enough and some of us pranced like fools in front of the Saxons, but there were never enough of us to charge home and the Saxons ignored our taunts while the rest of Griffid's men drank their mead and cursed our eagerness. To me, desperate

146

to earn a warrior ring made from Saxon iron, it seemed madness that we did not attack, but I had yet to experience the butchery of two locked shield-walls, nor had I learned how hard it is to persuade men to offer their bodies to that grisly work. Griffid did make some half-hearted efforts to encourage an attack; then was content to drink his mead and shout insults; and thus we faced the enemy for three hours or more without ever advancing more than a few steps.

Griffid's timidity at least gave me a chance to examine the Saxons who, in truth, did not look so very different from ourselves. Their hair was fairer, their eyes palely blue, their skins ruddier than ours, and they liked to wear a lot of fur about their clothes, but otherwise they dressed like us and the only differences in weapons were that most Saxons carried a long-bladed knife that was wicked for close-quarter work, and many of them used huge broad-bladed axes that could split a shield with one stroke. Some of our own men were so impressed by the axes that they carried such weapons themselves, but Owain, like Arthur, disdained them as clumsy. You cannot parry with an axe, Owain used to say, and a weapon that does not defend as well as attack was no good in his eyes. The Saxon priests were quite different from our own holy men, for these foreign sorcerers wore animal skins and caked their hair with cow dung so that it stood in spikes about their heads. On that day in the river valley one such Sais priest sacrificed a goat to discover whether or not they should fight us. The priest first broke one of the animal's back legs, then stabbed it in the neck and let it run away with its broken leg trailing. It lurched bleeding and crying along their battle line, then turned towards us before collapsing on the grass, and that was evidently a bad omen for the Saxon shield-line lost its defiance and summarily retreated through their half-built compound, across a ford, and back into the trees. They took their women, children, slaves, pigs and herd with them. We called it a victory, ate the goat and pulled down their stockade. There was no plunder.

Our levy was now hungry, for in the manner of all levies

they had eaten their whole supply of food in the first few days and now had nothing to eat except for the hazelnuts they stripped from the wood's trees. That lack of food meant we had no choice but to retreat. The hungry levy, eager to be home, went first while we warriors followed more slowly. Griffid was dour, for he was returning with neither gold nor slaves, though in truth he had accomplished as much as most warbands that roamed the disputed lands. But then, when we were almost back in familiar country, we met a Saxon war-band returning the other way. They must have encountered part of our retreating levy for they were burdened with captured weapons and women.

The meeting was a surprise to both sides. I was at the rear of Griffid's column and only heard the beginning of the fight which started when our vanguard emerged from the trees to find a half dozen Saxons crossing a stream. Our men attacked, then spearmen from both sides rushed to join the haphazard fight. There was no shield-wall, just a bloody brawl across a shallow stream, and once again, just like that day when I had killed my first enemy in the woods south of Ynys Wydryn, I experienced the joy of battle. It was, I decided, the same feeling that Nimue felt when the Gods filled her; like having wings, she had said, that lift you high into glory, and that was just how I felt that autumn day. I met my first Saxon at a flat run, my spear levelled, and I saw the fear in his eyes and I knew he was dead. The spear stuck fast in his belly, so I drew Hywel's sword, that now I called Hywelbane, and finished him with a sideways cut, then waded into the stream itself and killed two more. I was screaming like an evil spirit, shouting at the Saxons in their own tongue to come and taste death, and then a huge warrior accepted my invitation and charged me with one of the big axes that look so terrifying. Except an axe has too much dead weight. Once swung it cannot be reversed, and I put the big man down with a straight sword thrust that would have warmed Owain's heart. I took three gold torques, four brooches and a jewelled knife off that one axeman alone and I kept his axe blade to make my first battle rings.

The Saxons fled, leaving eight dead and as many again wounded. I had killed no fewer than four of the enemy, a feat which was noticed by my companions. I basked in their respect, though later, when I was older and wiser, I ascribed my day's disproportionate killing to mere youthful stupidity. The young will often rush in where the wise go steadily. We lost three men, one of them Licat, the man who had saved my life on the Moor. I retrieved my spear, collected two more silver torques from the men I had killed in the stream, then watched as the enemy wounded were despatched to the Otherworld where they would become the slaves of our own dead fighters. We found six British captives huddled in the trees. They were women who had followed our levy to war and been captured by these Saxons, and it was one of those women who discovered the single enemy warrior still hiding in some brambles at the stream's edge. She screamed at him, and tried to stab him with a knife, but he scrambled away into the stream where I captured him. He was only a beardless youngster, perhaps my own age, and he was shaking with fear. 'What are you called?' I asked him with my bloody spear-blade at his throat.

He was sprawling in the water. 'Wlenca,' he answered, and then he told me he had come to Britain just weeks before, though when I asked him where he had come from he could not really answer except to say from home. His language was not quite the same as mine, but the differences were slight and I understood him well enough. The King of his people, he told me, was a great leader called Cerdic who was taking land on the south coast of Britain. Cerdic, he said, had needed to fight Aesc, a Saxon king who now ruled the Kentish lands, to establish his new colony, and that was the first time I realized that the Saxons fought amongst themselves just as we British did. It seems that Cerdic had won his war against Aesc and was now probing into Dumnonia.

The woman who had discovered Wlenca was squatting close by and hissing threats at him, but another of the women declared that Wlenca had taken no part in the raping that had followed their capture. Griffid, feeling relief at having some booty to take home, declared that Wlenca could live and so the Saxon was stripped naked, put under a woman's guard and marched west towards slavery.

That was the last expedition of the year and though we declared it a great victory it paled beside Arthur's exploits. He had not only driven Aelle's Saxons out of northern Gwent, but had then defeated the forces of Powys and in the process had chopped off King Gorfyddyd's shield arm. The enemy King had escaped, but it was a great victory all the same and all of Gwent and Dumnonia rang with Arthur's praises. Owain was not happy.

Lunete, on the other hand, was delirious. I had brought her gold and silver, enough so she could wear a bearskin robe in winter and employ her own slave, a child of Kernow whom Lunete purchased from Owain's household. The child worked from dawn to dusk, and at night wept in the corner of the hut we now called home. When the girl cried too much Lunete hit her, and when I tried to defend the girl Lunete hit me. Owain's men had all moved from Caer Cadarn's cramped warrior quarters to the more comfortable settlement at Lindinis where Lunete and I had a thatched, wattle-walled hut inside the low earth ramparts built by the Romans. Caer Cadarn was six miles away and was occupied only when an enemy came too close, or when a great royal occasion was celebrated. We had one such occasion that winter on the day when Mordred turned one year old and when, by chance, Dumnonia's troubles came to their head. Or perhaps it was not chance at all, for Mordred was ever ill-omened and his acclamation was doomed to be touched by tragedy.

The ceremony happened just after the Solstice. Mordred was to be acclaimed king and the great men of Dumnonia gathered at Caer Cadarn for the occasion. Nimue came a day early and visited our hut, which Lunete had decorated with holly and ivy for the solstice. Nimue stepped over the hut's threshold that was scored with patterns to keep the evil spirits away, then sat by our fire and pushed back the hood of her cloak.

I smiled because she had a golden eye. 'I like it,' I said.

'It's hollow,' she said, and disconcertingly tapped the eye with a fingernail. Lunete was shouting at the slave for burning the pottage of sprouted barley seeds and Nimue flinched at the display of anger. 'You're not happy,' she said to me.

'I am,' I insisted, for the young hate to admit making mistakes.

Nimue glanced about the untidy and smoke-blackened interior of our hut as though she was scenting the mood of its inhabitants. 'Lunete's wrong for you,' she said calmly as she idly picked from the littered floor half an empty egg-shell and crunched it into fragments so that no evil spirit could lurk in its shelter. 'Your head is in the clouds, Derfel,' she went on as she tossed the shell fragments on to the flames, 'while Lunete is earth-bound. She wants to be rich and you want to be honourable. It won't mix.' She shrugged, as though it was not really important, then gave me her news of Ynys Wydryn. Merlin had not come back and no one knew where he was, but Arthur had sent money captured from the defeated King Gorfyddyd to pay for the Tor's reconstruction and Gwlyddyn was supervising the building of a new and grander hall. Pellinore was alive, as were Druidan and Gudovan the scribe. Norwenna, Nimue told me, had been buried in the shrine of the Holy Thorn where she was revered as a saint.

'What's a saint?' I asked.

'A dead Christian,' she said flatly. 'They should all be saints.'

'And what about you?' I asked her.

'I'm alive,' she said tonelessly.

'Are you happy?'

'You always ask such stupid things. If I wanted to be happy, Derfel, I'd be down here with you, baking your bread and keeping your bedding clean.'

'Then why aren't you?'

She spat in the fire to ward off my stupidity. 'Gundleus lives,' she said flatly, changing the subject.

'Imprisoned in Corinium,' I said, as though she did not already know where her enemy was.

'I've buried his name on a stone,' she said, then gave me a golden-eyed glance. 'He made me pregnant when he raped me, but I killed the foul thing with ergot.' Ergot was a black blight that grew on rye and women used it to abort their young. Merlin also used it as a means of going into the dream-state and talking with the Gods. I had tried it once and was sick for days.

Lunete insisted on showing Nimue all her new possessions: the trivet, cauldron and sieve, the jewels and cloak, the fine linen shift and the battered silver jug with the naked Roman horseman chasing a deer about its belly. Nimue made a bad pretence of being impressed, then asked me to walk her to Caer Cadarn where she would spend the night. 'Lunete's a fool,' she told me. We were walking along the edge of a stream that flowed into the River Cam. Brown brittle leaves crunched underfoot. There had been a frost and the day was bitterly cold. Nimue looked angrier than ever and, because of that, more beautiful. Tragedy suited Nimue, she knew it and so she sought it. 'You're making a name for yourself,' she said, glancing at the plain iron warrior rings on my left hand. I kept my right hand free of the rings so I could keep a firm grip of a sword or spear, but I now wore four iron rings on my left hand.

'Luck.' I explained the rings.

'No, not luck.' She raised her left hand so I could see the scar. 'When you fight, Derfel, I fight with you. You're going to be a great warrior, and you'll need to be.'

'Will I?'

She shivered. The sky was grey, the same grey as an un-polished sword, though the western horizon was streaked with a sour, yellow light. The trees were winter black, the grass sullenly dark, and the smoke from the settlement's fires clung to the ground as though it feared the cold, empty sky. 'Do you know why Merlin left Ynys Wydryn?' she asked me suddenly, surprising me with the question.

'To find the Knowledge of Britain,' I answered, repeating what she had told the High Council in Glevum.

'But why now? Why not ten years ago?' Nimue asked me,

then answered her own question. 'He has gone now, Derfel, because we are coming into the bad time. Everything good will get bad, everything bad will get worse. Everyone in Britain is gathering their strength because they know the great struggle is coming. Sometimes I think the Gods are playing with us. They are heaping all the throwpieces at once to see how the game will end. The Saxons are getting stronger and soon they'll attack in hordes, not war-bands. The Christians' – she spat into the stream to avert evil – 'say that very soon it will be five hundred winters since their wretched God was born and claim that means the time for their triumph is coming.' She spat again. 'And for us Britons? We fight each other, we steal from each other, we build new feasting halls when we should be forging swords and spears. We are going to be put to the test, Derfel, and that's why Merlin is gathering his strength, for if the kings will not save us then Merlin must persuade the Gods to come to our aid.' She stopped beside a pool of the stream and stared into the black water that had the gelid still-ness that comes just before freezing. The water in the cattle hoofprints at the pool's edge was already frozen.

'What of Arthur?' I asked. 'Won't he save us?'

She gave me a flicker of a smile. 'Arthur is to Merlin what you are to me. Arthur is Merlin's sword, but neither of us can control you. We give you power' – she reached out her scarred left hand and touched the bare pommel of my sword – 'and then we let you go. We have to trust that you will do the right thing.'

'You can trust me,' I said.

She sighed as she always did when I made such a statement, then shook her head. 'When the Test of Britain comes, Derfel, and it will, none of us will know how strong our sword will prove.' She turned and looked at the ramparts of Caer Cadarn that were bright with the banners of all the lords and chiefs come to witness Mordred's acclamation on the morrow. 'Fools,' she said bitterly, 'fools.'

Arthur arrived the next day. He came shortly after dawn, having ridden with Morgan from Ynys Wydryn. He was accompanied by only two warriors, the three men all mounted on their big horses, though they carried no armour or shields, just spears and swords. Arthur did not even bring his banner. He was very relaxed, almost as though this ceremony had no interest for him other than curiosity. Agricola, Tewdric's Roman warlord, had come in place of his master who had a fever, and Agricola too seemed aloof from the ceremony, but everyone else in Caer Cadarn was tense, worried that the day's omens might prove bad. Prince Cadwy of Isca was there, his cheeks blue with tattoos. Prince Gereint, Lord of the Stones, had come from the Saxon frontier and King Melwas had come from decaying Venta. All the nobility of Dumnonia, more than a hundred men, waited in the fort. There had been sleet in the night that had left Caer Cadarn's compound slick and muddy, but first light brought a brisk westerly wind and by the time Owain emerged from the hall with the royal baby the sun was actually showing on the hills which circled Caer Cadarn's eastern approaches.

Morgan had decided on the hour of the ceremony, divining it from auguries of fire, water and earth. It was, predictably, a morning ceremony, for nothing good comes of endeavours undertaken when the sun is in decline, but the crowd had to wait until Morgan was satisfied that the exact hour was imminent before the proceedings could begin in the stone circle that crowned Caer Cadarn's peak. The stones of the circle were not large, none was bigger than a stooping child while in the very centre, where Morgan fussed as she took her alignments on the pale sun, was the royal stone of Dumnonia. It was a flat, grey boulder, indistinguishable from a thousand others, yet it had been on that stone, we were taught, that the God Bel had anointed his human child Beli Mawr who was the ancestor of all Dumnonia's kings. Once Morgan was satisfied with her calculation, Balise was ushered to the circle's centre. He was an ancient Druid who lived in the woods west of Caer Cadarn and, in Merlin's absence, had been persuaded to attend and invoke the Gods' blessings. He was a stooped, lice-ridden creature, draped in goatskin and rags, so dirty that it was impossible to tell where his rags began and his beard ended, yet it was Balise, I had been told, who had taught Merlin many of his skills. The old man raised his staff to the watery sun, mumbled some prayers, then spat in a sunwise circle before succumbing to a terrible coughing fit. He stumbled to a chair at the edge of the circle where he sat panting as his companion, an old woman almost indistinguishable in appearance from Balise himself, feebly rubbed his back.

Bishop Bedwin said a prayer to the Christian God, then the baby King was paraded around the outside of the stone circle. Mordred had been laid upon a war shield and swathed in fur and it was thus he was shown to all the warriors, chiefs and princes who, as the baby passed, dropped to their knees to pay him homage. A grown king would have walked about the circle, but two Dumnonian warriors carried Mordred, while behind the child, his longsword drawn, paced Owain, the King's champion. Mordred was carried against the sun, the only time in all a king's life when he would so go against the natural order, but the unlucky direction was deliberately chosen to show that a king descended from the Gods was above such petty rules as always going sunwise in a circle.

Mordred was then laid in his shield upon the central stone while gifts were brought to him. A child laid a loaf of bread before him as a symbol of his duty to feed his people, then a second child brought him a scourge to show that he had to be a magistrate to his country, and afterwards a sword was laid at his feet to symbolize his role as a defender of Dumnonia. Mordred screamed throughout, and kicked so lustily that he almost tipped himself out of his shield. His kicking bared his maimed foot and that, I thought, had to be a bad omen, but the celebrants ignored the clubbed limb as the great men of the kingdom approached one by one and added their own gifts. They brought gold and silver, precious stones, coins, jet and amber. Arthur gave the child a golden statue of a hawk, a present that made the onlookers gasp with its beauty, but Agricola brought the most valuable gift of all. He laid the royal war gear of King Gorfyddyd of Powys at the baby's feet. Arthur had captured

155

the gold-trimmed armour after rousting Gorfyddyd from his encampment and had, in turn, presented the armour to King Tewdric who now, through his warlord, gave the treasure back to Dumnonia.

The fretful baby was at last lifted from the stone and given to his new nurse, a slave of Owain's household. Now came Owain's moment. Every other great man had come cloaked and furred against the day's cold, but Owain strode forward dressed in nothing but his trews and boots. His tattooed chest and arms were as bare as the drawn sword that, with due ceremony, he laid flat upon the royal stone. Then, deliberately, and with scorn on his face, he walked around the outer circle and spat towards all present. It was a challenge. If any man there deemed that Mordred should not be King then all he needed to do was step forward and pluck the naked sword from the stone. Then he must fight Owain. Owain strutted, sneered and invited a challenge, but no one moved. Only when Owain had made two full circuits did he go back to the stone and pick up the sword.

Upon which everyone cheered, for Dumnonia had a king again. The warriors who ringed the ramparts beat their spear-staffs against their shields.

One last ritual was needed. Bishop Bedwin had tried to forbid it, but the council had over-ridden him. Arthur, I noticed, walked away, but everyone else, even Bishop Bedwin, stayed as a captive was led, naked and frightened, to the royal stone. It was Wlenca, the Saxon lad I had captured. I doubt he knew what was happening, but he must have feared the worst.

Morgan tried to rouse Balise, but the old Druid was too weak to do his part, so Morgan herself walked up to the shivering Wlenca. The Saxon was unbound and could have tried to run, though the Gods know there could have been no escape through the armed crowd that circled him, but in the event he stood quite still as Morgan approached him. Maybe the sight of her gold mask and limping walk froze him, and he did not move until she had dipped her maimed and gloved left hand in a dish and then, after a moment's deliberation, touched him high on his belly. At that touch Wlenca jumped in alarm, but then went still again. Morgan had dipped her hand into a dish of newly drawn goat's blood that now made its wet red mark on Wlenca's thin, pale belly.

Morgan walked away. The crowd was very still, silent and apprehensive, for this was an awesome moment of truth. The Gods were about to speak to Dumnonia.

Owain entered the circle. He had discarded his sword and was instead carrying his black-shafted war spear. He kept his eyes on the frightened Saxon lad who seemed to be praying to his own Gods, but they had no power at Caer Cadarn.

Owain moved slowly. He took his eyes off Wlenca's gaze for only a second, just the time he needed to place the tip of his spear directly over the marked spot on the Saxon's belly, then he looked again into the captive's eyes. Both men were still. There were tears in Wlenca's eyes and he gave a tiny shake of his head in a mute appeal for mercy, but Owain ignored the plea. He waited until Wlenca was still again. The spear-tip rested on the blood mark and neither man moved. The wind stirred their hair and lifted the damp cloaks of the spectators.

Owain thrust. He gave one hard-muscled lunge that drove the spear deep into Wlenca's body and then wrenched the blade free and ran backwards to leave the bleeding Saxon alone in the royal circle.

Wlenca screamed. The wound was a terrible one, deliberately inflicted to give a slow, pain-crazed death, but from the dying man's death-throes a trained augurer like Balise or Morgan could tell the kingdom's future. Balise, stirred from his torpor, watched as the Saxon staggered with one hand clutched to his belly and his body bent over against the awful pain. Nimue leaned eagerly forward, for this was the first time she had witnessed the most powerful of all divinations and she wanted to learn its secrets. I confess I grimaced, not for the horror of the ceremony, but because I had liked Wlenca and seen in his broad, blue-eyed face an idea of what I myself probably looked like, yet I consoled myself with the knowledge that his sacrifice meant he would be offered a warrior's place in the Otherworld where, one day, he and I would meet again.

Wlenca's screaming had subsided into a desperate panting. His face had gone yellow, he was shaking, but somehow he kept his feet as he tottered towards the east. He reached the circle of stones and for a second it seemed he must collapse, then a spasm of pain made him arch his back, then snap forward again. He whirled in a wild circle, spattering blood, and took a few steps to the north. And then, at last, he fell. He was jerking in agony, and each spasm meant something to Balise and Morgan. Morgan scuttled forward to watch him more closely as he twisted, shivered and twitched. For a few seconds his legs shuddered, then his bowels broke, his head went back and a choking rattle sounded in his throat. A great wash of blood spilt almost to Morgan's feet as the Saxon died.

Something in Morgan's stance told us that the augury was bad and her sour mood spread to the crowd who waited for the dreaded pronouncement. Morgan went back to stoop beside Balise who gave a raucous, irreverent cackle. Nimue had gone to inspect the blood trail and then the body, and afterwards she joined Morgan and Balise as the crowd waited. And waited.

Morgan at last went back to the body. She addressed her words to Owain, the King's champion who stood beside the baby King, but everyone in the crowd leaned forward to hear her speak. 'King Mordred,' she said, 'will have a long life. He will be a leader of battle, and he will know victory.'

A sigh went through the crowd. The augury could be translated as favourable, though I think everyone knew how much had been left unsaid and a few present could remember Uther's acclamation when the dying man's blood trail and agonized twitches had truthfully predicted a reign of glory. Still, even without glory, there was some hope in the augury of Wlenca's death.

That death ended Mordred's acclamation. Poor Norwenna, buried beneath Ynys Wydryn's Holy Thorn, would have done it all so differently, yet even if a thousand bishops and a myriad of saints had gathered to pray Mordred on to his throne, the auguries would still have been the same. For Mordred, our King, was crippled and neither Druid nor bishop could ever change that.

Tristan of Kernow arrived that afternoon. We were in the great hall at Mordred's feast, an event remarkable for its lack of cheer, but Tristan's arrival made it even less cheerful. No one even noticed his arrival until he drew near to the big central fire and the flames glinted off his leather breastplate and iron helmet. The Prince was known as a friend of Dumnonia and Bishop Bedwin greeted him as such, but Tristan's only response was to draw his sword.

The gesture commanded instant attention for no man was supposed to carry a weapon into a feasting hall, let alone a hall that celebrated a king's acclamation. Some men in the hall were drunk, but even they went silent as they gazed at the young, dark-haired Prince.

Bedwin tried to ignore the drawn sword. 'You came for the acclamation, Lord Prince? Doubtless you were delayed? Travel is so difficult in winter. Come, a seat here? Next to Agricola of Gwent? There's venison.'

'I come with a quarrel,' Tristan said loudly. He had left his six guards just outside the hall door where a cold sleet was spitting across the hilltop. The guards were grim men in wet armour and dripping cloaks whose shields were the right way up and whose war spears were whetted bright.

'A quarrel!' Bedwin said as though the very thought was remarkable. 'Not on this auspicious day, surely not!'

Some of the warriors in the hall growled challenges. They were drunk enough to enjoy a quarrel, but Tristan ignored them. 'Who speaks for Dumnonia?' he demanded.

There was a moment's hesitation. Owain, Arthur, Gereint and Bedwin all had authority, but none was pre-eminent. Prince Gereint, never a man to put himself forward, shrugged the question away, Owain stared balefully at Tristan, while Arthur respectfully deferred to Bedwin who suggested, very diffidently, that as the kingdom's chief counsellor he could speak as well as any man on behalf of King Mordred.

'Then tell King Mordred,' Tristan said, 'that there will be blood between my country and his unless I receive justice.'

Bedwin looked alarmed and his hands fluttered with calming motions as he tried to think what to say. Nothing suggested itself to him and in the end it was Owain who responded. 'Say what you have to say,' he said flatly.

'A group of my father's people,' Tristan said, 'were given protection by High King Uther. They came to this country at Uther's request to work the mines and to live in peace with their neighbours, yet late last summer some of those neighbours came to their mine and gave them sword, fire and slaughter. Fifty-eight dead, tell your King, and their *sarhaed* will be the value of their lives plus the life of the man who ordered them killed, or else we shall come with our own swords and shields to take the price ourselves.'

Owain roared with laughter. 'Little Kernow? We're so frightened!'

The warriors all around me shouted scorn. Kernow was a small country and no match for Dumnonia's forces. Bishop Bedwin tried to stop the noise, but the room was full of men drunk into boastfulness and they refused to calm down until Owain himself called for silence. 'I heard, Prince,' Owain said, 'that it was the Blackshield Irish of Oengus Mac Airem who attacked the moor.'

Tristan spat on the floor. 'If they did,' he said, 'then they flew across country to do it, for no man saw them pass and they did not steal so much as an egg from any Dumnonian.'

'That's because they fear Dumnonia, but not Kernow,' Owain said, and the hall burst into jeering laughter again.

Arthur waited until the laughter had subsided. 'Do you know of any man other than Oengus Mac Airem who might have attacked your people?' he asked courteously.

Tristan turned and searched the men squatting on the hall floor. He saw Prince Cadwy of Isca's bald head and pointed at it with his sword. 'Ask him. Or better still' – he raised his voice to quieten the jeers – 'ask the witness I have outside.' Cadwy was on his feet and shouting to be allowed to fetch his sword while his tattooed spearmen were threatening all Kernow with massacre.

Arthur slapped his hand on the high table. The sound echoed in the hall, drawing silence. Agricola of Gwent, sitting next to Arthur, kept his eyes down, for this quarrel was none of his business, but I doubt if a single nuance of the confrontation was escaping his shrewd wits. 'If any man draws blood tonight,' Arthur said, 'he is my enemy.' He waited until Cadwy and his men subsided, then looked again to Tristan. 'Bring your witness, Lord.'

'Is this a court of law?' Owain objected.

'Let the witness come in,' Arthur insisted.

'This is a feast!' Owain protested.

'Let the witness come, let him come.' Bishop Bedwin wanted the whole distasteful business over, and agreeing with Arthur seemed the quickest way to settle it. Men at the hall's edges shuffled closer to hear the drama, but laughed when Tristan's witness appeared, for she was just a small child, perhaps nine years old, who walked calmly and stiff-backed to stand beside her Prince who put an arm about her shoulder. 'Sarlinna ferch Edain.' He gave the child's name, then squeezed her shoulder reassuringly. 'Speak.'

Sarlinna licked her lips. She chose to speak direct to Arthur, perhaps because he had the kindest face of the men sitting at the high table. 'My father was killed, my mother was killed, my brothers and sisters were killed . . .' She spoke as though she had been rehearsed in her words, though no man present doubted the truth of them. 'My baby sister was killed,' she went on, 'and my kitten was killed' – a first tear showed – 'and I saw it done.'

Arthur shook his head in sympathy. Agricola of Gwent ran a hand across his close-cropped grey hair, then stared up into the soot-blackened rafters. Owain leaned back in his chair and drank from a horn beaker while Bishop Bedwin looked troubled. 'Did you really see the killers?' the Bishop asked the child.

'Yes, Lord.' Sarlinna, now that she was no longer saying words she had prepared and practised, was more nervous.

'But it was night, child,' Bedwin objected. 'Wasn't the raid at night, Lord Prince?' he demanded of Tristan. The Lords of Dumnonia had all heard about the raid on the moor, but they had believed Owain's assertion that the massacre was the work of Oengus's Blackshield Irish. 'How could the child see at night?' Bedwin asked.

Tristan encouraged the child by patting her shoulder. 'Tell the Lord Bishop what happened,' he instructed her.

'The men threw fire into our hut, Lord,' Sarlinna said in a small voice.

'Not enough fire,' a man growled from the shadows and the hall laughed.

'How did you live, Sarlinna?' Arthur asked her gently when the laughter had faded.

'I hid, Lord, under a pelt.'

Arthur smiled. 'You did well. But did you see the man who killed your mother and father?' He paused. 'And your kitten?'

She nodded. Her eyes were bright with tears in the dim hall. 'I saw him, Lord,' she said quietly.

'So tell us about him,' Arthur said.

Sarlinna was wearing a small grey shift under a black woollen cloak and now she lifted her thin arms and pushed the shift's sleeves back to bare her pale skin. 'The man's arms had pictures, Lord, of a dragon. And of a boar. Here.' She showed where the tattoos might be on her own small arms, then looked at Owain. 'And there were rings in his beard,' the girl added, and then she went silent, but she had no need to say more. Only one man wore warrior rings in his beard, and every man present had watched Owain's arms drive the spear into Wlenca's midriff that morning, and everyone knew those arms were tattooed with Dumnonia's dragon and with his own symbol of a long-tusked boar.

There was silence. A log crackled in the fire, sending a puff of smoke into the rafters. A gust of wind pattered sleet on the thick thatch and fluttered the rush–light flames that were scat-

162

tered about the hall. Agricola was examining the silver-chased holder of his drinking horn as though he had never seen such an object before. Somewhere in the hall a man belched, and the noise seemed to prompt Owain to turn his great shaggy head to stare at the child. 'She lies,' he said harshly, 'and children who lie should be beaten bloody.'

Sarlinna began to cry, then buried her face in the wet folds of Tristan's cloak. Bishop Bedwin frowned. 'It is true, Owain, is it not, that you visited Prince Cadwy late in the summer?'

'So?' Owain bristled. 'So?' He roared the word again, this time as a challenge to the whole assembly. 'Here are my warriors!' He gestured at us, sitting together on the right-hand side of the hall. 'Ask them! Ask them! The child lies! On my oath, she lies!'

The hall was in sudden uproar as men spat their defiance at Tristan. Sarlinna was weeping so much that the Prince stooped, picked her up and held her in his arms and continued to hold her while Bedwin tried to regain control over the hall. 'If Owain swears on his oath,' the Bishop shouted, 'then the child does lie.' The warriors growled agreement.

Arthur, I saw, was watching me. I looked down at my wooden bowl of venison.

Bishop Bedwin was wishing he had not invited the child into the hall. He dragged his fingers through his beard, then shook his head wearily. 'A child's word carries no weight in law,' he said plaintively. 'A child is not among the Tongued-ones.' The Tongued-ones were the nine witnesses whose word carried the weight of truth in law: a Lord, a Druid, a priest, a father speaking of his children, a magistrate, a gift-giver speaking of his gift, a maiden speaking of her virginity, a herdsman speaking of his animals and a condemned man speaking his final words. Nowhere in the list was there any mention of a child speaking of her family's massacre. 'Lord Owain,' Bishop Bedwin pointed out to Tristan, 'is a Tongued-one.'

Tristan was pale, but he would not back down. 'I believe the child,' he said, 'and tomorrow, after sunrise, I shall come for

Dumnonia's answer, and if that answer denies Kernow justice then my father will take justice for himself.'

'What's the matter with your father?' Owain jeered. 'Lost interest in his latest wife, has he? So he wants to take a beating in battle instead?'

Tristan walked out amidst laughter, a laughter that grew as men tried to imagine little Kernow declaring war on mighty Dumnonia. I did not join in the laughter, but finished my stew instead, telling myself I needed the food if I was to keep warm during my spell of guard duty that would start at the feast's end. Nor did I drink any mead, so I was still sober when I fetched my cloak, spear, sword and helmet and went to the north wall. The sleet had stopped and the clouds were passing to reveal a bright half-moon sailing amidst a shimmer of stars, though more clouds were heaping in the west above the Severn Sea. I shivered as I paced the rampart.

Where Arthur found me.

I had known he was coming. I had wanted him to come and yet I felt a fear of him as I watched him cross the compound and climb the short flight of wooden steps that led to the low wall of earth and stone. At first he said nothing, but just leaned on the wood palings and stared towards the distant speck of flamelight that lit Ynys Wydryn. He was dressed in his white cloak, which he had gathered up so that its hem would not drag in the mud. He had tied the cloak's corners about his waist just above his cross-hatched scabbard. 'I'm not going to ask you,' he spoke at last, his breath misting in the night air, 'what happened on the moor, because I don't want to invite any man, least of all a man I like, to break a death-oath.'

'Yes, Lord,' I said, and wondered how he had known it was a death-oath that had bound us on that dark night.

'So instead, let us walk.' He smiled at me, and gestured along the rampart. 'A walking sentry stays warm,' he said. 'I hear you're a good soldier?'

'I try, Lord.'

'And I hear you succeed, so well done.' He fell silent as we passed one of my comrades who was huddled against the palings. The man looked up at me as I passed and his face showed alarm that I might betray Owain's troop. Arthur pushed the cloak's hood back off his face. He had a long, firm stride and I had to hurry to keep pace with him. 'What do you think a soldier's job is, Derfel?' he asked me in that intimate manner that made you feel he was more interested in you than anyone else in the world.

'To fight battles, Lord,' I said.

He shook his head. 'To fight battles, Derfel,' he corrected me, 'on behalf of people who can't fight for themselves. I learned that in Brittany. This miserable world is full of weak people, powerless people, hungry people, sad people, sick people, poor people, and it's the easiest thing in the world to despise the weak, especially if you're a soldier. If you're a warrior and you want a man's daughter, you just take her; you want his land, you just kill him; after all, you're a soldier and you have a spear and a sword, and he's just a poor weak man with a broken plough and a sick ox and what's to stop you?' He did not expect an answer to the question, but just paced on in silence. We had come to the western gateway and the split-log steps that climbed to the platform over the gate were whitening with a new frost. We climbed them side by side. 'But the truth is, Derfel,' Arthur said when we reached the high platform, 'that we are only soldiers because that weak man makes us soldiers. He grows the grain that feeds us, he tans the leather that protects us and he polls the ash trees that make our spear-shafts. We owe him our service.'

'Yes, Lord,' I said and stared with him across the wide, flat land. It was not so cold as the night on which Mordred had been born, but it was still bitter, and the wind made it more so.

'There is a purpose to all things,' Arthur said, 'even being a soldier.' He smiled at me, as though apologizing for being so earnest, yet he had no need to be apologetic for I was drinking in his words. I had dreamed of becoming a soldier because of a warrior's high status and because it had always seemed to me that it was better to carry a spear than a rake, but I had never thought beyond those selfish ambitions. Arthur had thought far beyond and he brought to Dumnonia a clear vision of where his sword and spear must take him.

'We have a chance' – Arthur leaned on the high rampart as he spoke – 'to make a Dumnonia in which we can serve our people. We can't give them happiness, and I don't know how to guarantee a good harvest that will make them rich, but I do know that we can make them safe, and a safe man, a man who knows that his children will grow without being taken for slaves and his daughter's bride price won't be ruined by a soldier's rape, is a man more likely to be happy than a man living under the threat of war. Is that fair?'

'Yes, Lord,' I said.

He rubbed his gloved hands against the cold. My hands were wrapped in rags that made holding my spear difficult, especially as I was also trying to keep them warm beneath my cloak. Behind us, in the feasting hall, a great roar of men's laughter gusted. The food had been as bad as any at a winter feast, but there had been plenty of mead and wine, though Arthur was as sober as I was myself. I looked at his profile as he gazed west towards the building clouds. The moon shadowed his lantern jaw and made his face seem bonier than ever. 'I hate war,' Arthur said suddenly.

'You do?' I sounded surprised, but then I was young enough to enjoy war.

'Of course!' He smiled at me. 'I happen to be good at it, maybe you are too, and that just means we have to use it wisely. Do you know what happened in Gwent last autumn?'

'You wounded Gorfyddyd,' I said eagerly. 'You took his arm.'

'So I did,' he said, almost in a tone of surprise. 'My horses aren't much use in hilly country, and no use at all in wooded land, so I took them north into Powys's flat farmlands. Gorfyddyd was trying to knock down Tewdric's walls so I started burning Gorfyddyd's haystacks and grain-stores. We burned, we killed. We did it well, not because we wanted to, but because it needed to be done. And it worked. It brought Gorfyddyd back from Tewdric's walls to the flat farmland where my horses could break him. And they did. We attacked him at dawn, and he fought well, but he lost the battle along with his left arm, and that, Derfel, was the end of the killing. It had served its purpose, do you understand? The purpose of the killing was to persuade Powys that it would be better for them to be at peace with Dumnonia than at war. And now there will be peace.'

'There will?' I asked dubiously. Most of us believed the spring thaw could bring only a fresh attack from Powys's embittered King Gorfyddyd.

'Gorfyddyd's son is a sensible man,' Arthur said. 'His name is Cuneglas and he wants peace, and we must give Prince Cuneglas time to persuade his father that he'll lose more than one arm if he goes to war with us again. And once Gorfyddyd is persuaded that peace is better than war he'll call a council and we'll all go and make a lot of noise and at the end of it, Derfel, I shall marry Gorfyddyd's daughter, Ceinwyn.' He gave me a swift and somehow embarrassed look. '*Seren*, they call her, the star! The star of Powys. They say she's very beautiful.' He was pleased by that prospect and his pleasure somehow surprised me, but back then I had still not recognized the vanity in Arthur. 'Let's hope she is as beautiful as a star,' he went on, 'but beautiful or not, I'll marry her and we'll pacify Siluria, and then the Saxons will face a united Britain. Powys, Gwent, Dumnonia and Siluria, all embracing each other, all fighting the same enemy, and all at peace with one another.'

I laughed, not at him, but with him, for his ambitious prophecy had been so matter of fact. 'How do you know?' I asked.

'Because Cuneglas has offered the peace terms, of course, and you're not to tell that to anyone, Derfel, otherwise it might not happen. Even his father doesn't know yet so this is a secret between you and me.'

'Yes, Lord,' I said, and I felt hugely privileged to be told such an important secret, but of course that was just how Arthur wanted me to feel. He always knew how to manipulate men, and he especially knew how to manipulate young, idealistic men.

'But what use is peace,' Arthur asked me, 'if we're fighting amongst ourselves? Our task is to give Mordred a rich, peaceful kingdom, and to do that we have to make it a good and just kingdom.' He was looking at me now, and speaking very earnestly in his deep, soft voice. 'We cannot have peace if we break our treaties, and the treaty that let the men of Kernow mine our tin was a good one. I've no doubt they were cheating us, all men cheat when it comes to giving their money to kings, but was that reason to kill them and their children and their children's kittens? So next spring, Derfel, unless we finish this nonsense now, we shall have war instead of peace. King Mark will attack. He won't win, but his pride will ensure that his men kill a lot of our farmers and we shall have to send a war-band into Kernow and that's a bad country to fight in, very bad, but we'll win in the end. Pride will be settled, but at what price? Three hundred dead farmers? How many dead cattle? And if Gorfyddyd sees that we're fighting a war on our western frontier he'll be tempted to take advantage of our weakness by attacking in the north. We can make peace, Derfel, but only if we're strong enough to make war. If we look weak then our enemies will swoop like hawks. And how many Saxons will we face next year? Can we really spare men to cross the Tamar to kill a few farmers in Kernow?'

'Lord,' I began, and was about to confess the truth, but Arthur hushed me. The warriors in the hall were chanting the War Song of Beli Mawr, beating the earth floor with their feet as they proclaimed the great slaughter and doubtless anticipated more slaughter in Kernow.

'You mustn't say a word about what happened on the moor,' Arthur warned me. 'Oaths are sacred, even to those of us who wonder if any God cares enough to enforce them. Let us just assume, Derfel, that Tristan's little girl was telling the truth. What does that mean?'

I gazed into the frosted night. 'War with Kernow,' I said bleakly.

'No,' Arthur said. 'It means that tomorrow morning, when Tristan returns, someone has to challenge for the truth. The

Gods, people tell me, always favour the honest in such encounters.'

I knew what he was saying and I shook my head. 'Tristan won't challenge Owain,' I said.

'Not if he has as much sense as he seems to have,' Arthur agreed. 'Even the Gods would find it hard to make Tristan beat down Owain's sword. So if we want peace, and if we want all those good things that follow peace, someone else must be Tristan's champion. Isn't that right?'

I looked at him, horrified at what I thought he was saying. 'You?' I finally asked.

He shrugged under his white cloak. 'I'm not sure who else will do it,' he said gently. 'But there is one thing you can do for me.'

'Anything, Lord,' I said, 'anything.' And at that moment I think I would even have agreed to fight Owain for him.

'A man going into battle, Derfel,' Arthur said carefully, 'should know that his cause is right. Perhaps the Blackshield Irish did carry their shields across the land unseen by anyone. Or maybe their Druids did make them fly? Or maybe, tomorrow, the Gods, if they take an interest, will think I fight for a good cause. What do you think?'

He asked the question as innocently as if he was merely enquiring about the weather. I stared at him, overwhelmed by him and desperately wanting him to avoid this challenge against the best swordsman in Dumnonia.

'Well?' he prompted me.

'The Gods . . .' I began, but then had difficulty speaking for Owain had been good to me. The champion was not an honest man, but I could count on my fingers how many honest men I had met, yet despite his roguery, I liked him. Yet I liked this honest man much more. I also paused to determine whether or not my words broke any oath, then decided they did not. 'The Gods will support you, Lord,' I said at last.

He smiled sadly. 'Thank you, Derfel.'

'But why?' I blurted out.

He sighed and looked back to the moon-glossed land.

'When Uther died,' he said after a long time, 'the land fell into chaos. That happens to a land without a king, and we are without a king now. We have Mordred, but he is a child, so someone has to hold the power until he is of age. One man must hold the power, Derfel, not three or four or ten, just one. I wish it were not so. With all my heart, believe me, I would rather leave things as they are. I would rather grow old with Owain as my dear friend, but it cannot be. The power must be held for Mordred, and it must be held properly and justly and given to him intact, and that means we cannot afford perpetual squabbles between men who want the king's power for themselves. One man has to be a king who is no king, and that one man must relinquish the powers of the kingdom when Mordred is of age. And that's what soldiers do, remember? They fight the battles for people who are too weak to fight for themselves. They also,' he smiled, 'take what they want, and tomorrow I want something of Owain; I want his honour, so I shall take it.' He shrugged. 'Tomorrow I fight for Mordred and for that child. And you, Derfel' – he poked me hard in the chest – 'will find her a kitten.' He stamped his feet against the cold, then peered westward. 'You think those clouds will bring rain or snow in the morning?' he asked.

'I don't know, Lord.'

'Let us hope so. Now, I hear you had a conversation with that poor Saxon they killed to learn the future. So tell me all he told you. The more we know of our enemies, the better.'

He walked me back to my post, listened to what I had to say about Cerdic, the new Saxon leader on the south coast, then went to his bed. He seemed untroubled by what must happen in the morning, but I was terrified for him. I remembered Owain beating back the combined attack of both Tewdric's champions and I tried to say a prayer to the stars which are the homes of the Gods, but I could not see them because my eyes were watering.

The night was long and bitterly cold. But I wished the dawn would never come.

*

Arthur's wish was granted for at dawn it began to rain. It soon became a hard pelting storm of winter rain that swept in grey veils across the long, wide valley between Caer Cadarn and Ynys Wydryn. The ditches overflowed; water poured off the ramparts and puddled under the great hall's eaves. Smoke leaked from the holes in damp thatched roofs and sentries hunched their shoulders beneath their soaking cloaks.

Tristan, who had spent the night in the small village just east of Caer Cadarn, struggled up the fort's muddy approach path. His six guards and the orphaned child accompanied him, all of them slipping in the steep mud whenever they could not find a foothold on the tufts of grass growing at the path's sides. The gate was open and no sentry moved to stop the Prince of Kernow as he splashed through the compound's mud to the door of the great hall.

Where no one waited to receive him. The hall's interior was a damp chaos of men sleeping off a night's drunkenness, of discarded food, scavenging dogs, soggy grey embers and vomit congealing in the floor rushes. Tristan kicked one of the sleeping men awake and sent him to find Bishop Bedwin or some other person in authority. 'If anyone,' he called after the man, 'has any authority in this country.'

Bedwin, heavily cloaked against the seething rain, slipped and staggered his way through the treacherous mud. 'My Lord Prince,' he gasped as he dashed out of the weather into the hall's dubious shelter, 'my apologies. I had not expected you so early. Inclement weather, is it not?' He wrung water from the skirts of his cloak. 'Still, rather rain than snow, I think, don't you?'

Tristan said nothing.

Bedwin was flustered by his guest's silence. 'Some bread, perhaps? And warm wine? There will be a porridge cooking, I'm sure.' He looked about for someone to despatch to the kitchens, but the sleeping men lay snoring and immovable. 'Little girl?' Bedwin winced because of an aching head as he leaned towards Sarlinna, 'you must be hungry, yes?'

'We came for justice, not food,' Tristan said harshly.

'Ah, yes. Of course. Of course.' Bedwin pushed the hood away from his white tonsured hair and scratched in his beard for a troublesome louse. 'Justice,' he said vaguely, then nodded vigorously. 'I have thought on the matter, Lord Prince, indeed I have, and I have decided that war is not a desirable thing. Won't you agree?' He waited, but Tristan's face showed no response. 'Such a waste,' Bedwin said, 'and while I cannot find my Lord Owain to be at fault I do confess we failed in our duty to protect your countrymen on the moor. We did indeed. We failed sadly, and so, Lord Prince, if it pleases your father, we shall, of course, make payment of *sarhaed*, though not,' and here Bedwin chuckled, 'for the kitten.'

Tristan grimaced. 'What of the man who did the killing?'

Bedwin shrugged. 'What man? I know of no such man.'

'Owain,' Tristan said. 'Who almost certainly took gold from Cadwy.'

Bedwin shook his head. 'No. No. No. It cannot be. No. On my oath, Lord Prince, I have no knowledge of any man's guilt.' He gave Tristan a pleading look. 'My Lord Prince, it would hurt me deeply to see our countries at war. I have offered what I can offer, and I shall have prayers said for your dead, but I cannot countermand a man's oath of innocence.'

'I can,' Arthur said. He had been waiting behind the kitchen screen at the hall's far end. I was with him as he stepped into the hall where his white cloak looked bright in the damp gloom.

Bedwin blinked at him. 'Lord Arthur?'

Arthur stepped between the stirring, groaning bodies. 'If the man who killed Kernow's miners is not punished, Bedwin, then he may murder again. Do you not agree?'

Bedwin shrugged, spread his hands, then shrugged again. Tristan was frowning, not sure where Arthur's words were leading.

Arthur stopped by one of the hall's central pillars. 'And why should the kingdom pay *sarhaed* when the kingdom did not do the killing?' he demanded. 'Why should my Lord Mordred's treasury be depleted for another man's offence?'

Bedwin gestured Arthur to silence. 'We do not know the murderer!' he insisted.

'Then we must prove his identity,' Arthur said simply.

'We can't!' Bedwin protested irritably. 'The child is not a Tongued-one! And Lord Owain, if he is the man you speak of, has sworn on oath that he is innocent. He is a Tongued-one, so why go through the farce of a trial? His word is enough.'

'In a court of words, yes,' Arthur said, 'but there is also the court of swords, and by my sword, Bedwin,' here he paused and drew Excalibur's glittering length into the half-light, 'I maintain that Owain, Champion of Dumnonia, has caused our cousins of Kernow harm and that he, and no other, must pay the price.' He thrust Excalibur's tip through the filthy rushes into the earth and left it there, quivering. For a second I wondered if the Gods of the Otherworld would suddenly appear to aid Arthur, but there was only the sound of wind and rain and newly woken men gasping.

Bedwin gasped too. For a few seconds he was speechless. 'You . . .' he finally managed to say, but then could say no more.

Tristan, his handsome face pale in the wan light, shook his head. 'If anyone should contend in the court of swords,' he said to Arthur, 'let it be me.'

Arthur smiled. 'I asked first, Tristan,' he said lightly.

'No!' Bedwin found his tongue. 'It cannot be!'

Arthur gestured at the sword. 'You wish to pluck it, Bedwin?'

'No!' Bedwin was in distress, foreseeing the death of the kingdom's best hope, but before he could say another word Owain himself burst through the hall door. His long hair and thick beard were wet and his bare chest gleamed with rain.

He looked from Bedwin to Tristan to Arthur, then down to the sword in the earth. He seemed puzzled. 'Are you mad?' he asked Arthur.

'My sword,' Arthur said mildly, 'maintains your guilt in the matter between Kernow and Dumnonia.'

'He is mad,' Owain said to his warriors who were crowding

173

in behind him. The champion was red-eyed and tired. He had drunk for much of the night, then slept badly, but the challenge seemed to give him a new energy. He spat towards Arthur. 'I'm going back to that Silurian bitch's bed,' he said, 'and when I wake up I want this to prove a dream.'

'You are a coward, a murderer and a liar,' Arthur said calmly as Owain turned away and the words made the men in the hall gasp once more.

Owain turned back into the hall. 'Whelp,' he said to Arthur. He strode up to Excalibur and knocked the blade over, the formal acceptance of the challenge. 'So your death, whelp, will be part of my dream. Outside.' He jerked his head towards the rain. The fight could not be held indoors, not unless the feasting hall was to be cursed with abominable luck, so the men had to fight in the winter rain.

The whole fort was stirring now. Many of the folk who lived at Lindinis had slept in Caer Cadarn that night and the compound seethed as people were woken to witness the fight. Lunete was there, and Nimue and Morgan; indeed all Caer Cadarn hurried to watch the battle that took place, as tradition demanded, within the royal stone circle. Agricola, a red cloak over his gorgeous Roman armour, stood between Bedwin and Prince Gereint while King Melwas, a hunk of bread in his hand, watched wide-eyed among his guards. Tristan stood on the circle's far side where I, too, took my place. Owain saw me there and assumed I had betrayed him. He roared that my life would follow Arthur's to the Otherworld, but Arthur proclaimed my life was under his surety.

'He broke his oath!' Owain shouted, pointing at me.

'On my oath,' Arthur said, 'he broke none.' He took off his white cloak and folded it carefully on to one of the stones. He was dressed in trews, boots and a thin leather jerkin over a woollen vest. Owain was bare chested. His trews were criss-crossed with leather and he had massive nailed boots. Arthur sat on the stone and pulled his own boots off, preferring to fight barefoot.

'This is not necessary,' Tristan said to him.

'It is, sadly,' Arthur said, then stood and pulled Excalibur from its scabbard.

'Using your magic sword, Arthur?' Owain jeered. 'Afraid to fight with a mortal weapon, are you?'

Arthur sheathed Excalibur again and laid the sword on top of his cloak. 'Derfel,' he turned to me, 'is that Hywel's sword?'

'Yes, Lord.'

'Would you lend it me?' he asked. 'I promise to return it.'

'Make sure you live to keep that promise, Lord,' I said, taking Hywelbane from her scabbard and handing it to him hilt first. He gripped the sword, then asked me to run to the hall and fetch a handful of gritty ash that, when I returned, he rubbed into the oiled leather of the hilt.

He turned to Owain. 'If, Lord Owain,' he said courteously, 'you would rather fight when you are rested, then I can wait.'

'Whelp!' Owain spat. 'Sure you don't want to put on your fish armour?'

'It rusts in the rain,' Arthur answered very calmly.

'A fair-weather soldier,' Owain sneered, then gave his long-sword two practice cuts that whistled in the air. In the shield-line he preferred to fight with a short sword, but with any length of blade Owain was a man to fear. 'I'm ready, whelp,' he called.

I stood with Tristan and his guards as Bedwin made one last futile effort to stop the fight. No one doubted the outcome. Arthur was a tall man, but slender compared with Owain's muscled bulk, and no one had ever seen Owain bested in a fight. Yet Arthur seemed remarkably composed as he took his place at the circle's western edge and faced Owain who stood, uphill of him, at the east.

'Do you submit judgment to the court of swords?' Bedwin asked the two men, and both nodded their assent.

'Then God bless you, and God give the truth victory,' Bedwin said. He made the sign of the cross and then, his old face heavy, he walked out of the circle.

Owain, as we had expected, rushed at Arthur, but halfway across the circle, right by the King's royal stone, his foot slipped in the mud, and suddenly Arthur was charging. I had expected Arthur to fight calmly, using the skills Hywel had taught him, but that morning, as the rains poured from the winter skies, I saw how Arthur changed in battle. He became a fiend. His energy was poured into just one thing, death, and he laid at Owain with massive, fast strokes that drove the big man back and back. The swords rang harsh. Arthur was spitting at Owain, cursing him, taunting him, and cutting again and again with the edge of the sword and never giving Owain a chance to recover from a parry.

Owain fought well. No other man could have sustained that opening, slaughterous assault. His boots slipped in the mud, and more than once he had to beat off Arthur's attacks from his knees, but he always managed to recover his footing even if he was still driven backwards. When Owain slipped a fourth time I understood part of Arthur's confidence. He had wanted rain to make the footing treacherous and I think he knew that Owain would be bloated and tired from a night's feasting. Yet he could not break through that dogged guard, even though he did drive the champion clean back to the place where Wlenca's blood was still just visible as a darker patch of soaking mud.

And there, by the Saxon's blood, Owain's luck changed. Arthur slipped, and though he recovered the falter was all the opening Owain needed. He lunged whip-fast. Arthur parried, but Owain's sword slit through the leather jerkin to draw the fight's first blood from Arthur's waist. Arthur parried again, then again, this time stepping back before the hard, quick lunges that would have gored an ox to its heart. Owain's men roared their support as the champion, scenting victory, tried to throw his whole body on to Arthur to drive his lighter opponent down into the mud, but Arthur had been ready for the manoeuvre and he sidestepped on to the royal stone and gave a back-cut of his sword that slashed open the back of Owain's skull. The wound, like all scalp wounds, bled copiously so that the blood matted in Owain's hair and trickled down his broad back to be diluted by the rain. His men went silent.

Arthur leaped from the stone, attacking again, and once

again Owain was on the defensive. Both men were panting, both were mud-spattered and bloody, and both too tired to spit any more insults at the other. The rain made their hair hang in long, soaking hanks as Arthur cut left and right in the same fast rhythm with which he had opened the fight. It was so fast that Owain had no chance to do anything but counter the strokes. I remembered Owain's scornful description of Arthur's fighting style, slashing like a haymaker, Owain had said, hurrying to beat bad weather. Once, and only once, did Arthur whip his blade past Owain's guard, but the blow was half parried, robbing it of force, and the sword was checked by the iron warrior rings in Owain's beard. Owain threw the blade off, then tried again to drive Arthur down on to the ground with the weight of his body. Both fell and for a second it looked as though Owain would trap Arthur, but somehow Arthur scrambled away and climbed to his feet.

Arthur waited for Owain to rise. Both men were breathing hard and for a few seconds they watched each other, judging their chances, and then Arthur moved forward into the attack again. He swung again and again, just as he had before, and again and again Owain parried the wild blows, then Arthur slipped for a second time. He called in fear as he fell, and his cry was answered by a shout of triumph as Owain drew back his arm for the killing blow. Then Owain saw that Arthur had not slipped at all, but had merely pretended it to make Owain open his guard and now it was Arthur who lunged. It was his first lunge of the battle, and his last. Owain had his back to me and I was half hiding my eyes so that I would not have to see Arthur's death, but instead, right before me, I saw the shining tip of Hywelbane come clean out through Owain's wet and blood-streaked back. Arthur's lunge had gone straight through the champion's body. Owain seemed to freeze, his sword arm suddenly powerless. Then, from nerveless fingers, his sword dropped into the mud.

For a second, for a heartbeat, Arthur left Hywelbane in Owain's belly, then, with a huge effort that took every muscle in his body, he twisted the blade and ripped it free. He shouted as he tore that steel out of Owain, shouted as the blade broke the flesh's suction and ripped through bowel and muscle and skin and flesh, and still shouted as he dragged the sword out into the day's grey light. The force needed to drag the steel from Owain's heavy body meant that the sword kept going in a wild backswing that sprayed blood far across the mud-churned circle.

While Owain, disbelief on his face and with his guts spilling into the mud, fell.

Then Hywelbane thrust down once into the champion's neck.

And there was silence in Caer Cadarn.

Arthur stepped back from the corpse. Then he turned sun-wise to look into the faces of every man around the circle. Arthur's own face was hard as stone. There was not a scrap of kindness there, only the face of a fighter come to triumph. It was a terrible face, his big jaw set in a rictus of hate so that those of us who only knew Arthur as a painstakingly thought-ful man were shocked by the change in him. 'Does any man here,' he called in a loud voice, 'dispute the judgment?'

None did. Rain dripped from cloaks and diluted Owain's blood as Arthur walked to face the fallen champion's spear-men. 'Now's your chance,' he spat at them, 'to avenge your Lord, otherwise you are mine.' None could meet his eye, so he turned away from them, stepped over the fallen warlord and faced Tristan. 'Does Kernow accept the judgment, Lord Prince?'

Tristan, pale-faced, nodded. 'It does, Lord.'

'*Sarhaed*,' Arthur decreed, 'will be paid from Owain's estate.' He turned again to look at the warriors. 'Who com-mands Owain's men now?'

Griffid ap Annan stepped nervously forward. 'I do, Lord.'

'You will come to me for orders in one hour. And if any man of you touches Derfel, my comrade, then all of you will burn in a fire-pit.' They lowered their gaze rather than meet his eyes.

Arthur used a handful of mud to clean the sword of its blood, then handed it to me. 'Dry it well, Derfel.'

'Yes, Lord.'

'And thank you. A good sword.' He closed his eyes suddenly. 'God help me,' he said, 'but I enjoyed that. Now' – his eyes opened – 'I've done my part, what about yours?'

'Mine?' I gaped at him.

'A kitten,' he said patiently, 'for Sarlinna.'

'I have one, Lord,' I said.

'Then fetch it,' he said, 'and come to the hall for breakfast. Do you have a woman?'

'Yes, Lord.'

'Tell her we leave tomorrow when the council has finished its business.'

I stared at him, hardly believing my luck. 'You mean –' I began.

'I mean,' he interrupted me impatiently, 'that you will serve me now.'

'Yes, Lord!' I said. 'Yes, Lord!'

He picked up his sword, cloak and boots, took Sarlinna's hand and walked away from the rival he had killed.

And I had found my Lord.

LUNETE DID NOT WANT to travel north to Corinium where Arthur was wintering with his men. She did not want to leave her friends and besides, she added almost as an afterthought, she was pregnant. I greeted the announcement with disbelieving silence.

'You heard me,' she snapped, 'pregnant. I can't go. And why should we go? We were happy here. Owain was a good lord, then you had to spoil it. So why don't you go by yourself?' She was squatting by our hut's fire, trying to take what warmth she could from its feeble flames. 'I hate you,' she said and she vainly tried to pull our lovers' ring from her finger.

'Pregnant?' I asked in a shocked voice.

'But maybe not by you!' Lunete screamed, then gave up trying to tug the ring off her swollen finger and hurled a billet of firewood at me instead. Our slave howled in misery at the back of the hut and Lunete threw a log at her for good measure.

'But I have to go,' I said, 'I have to go with Arthur.'

'And abandon me?' she shrieked. 'You want me to be a whore? Is that it?' She hurled another piece of wood and I abandoned the fight. It was the day after Arthur's contest with Owain and we were all back in Lindinis where the council of Dumnonia was meeting in Arthur's villa, which was consequently surrounded by petitioners with their relatives and friends. Those eager people waited at the villa's front gates. At the back a huddle of armouries and storehouses stood where the villa's garden had once grown. Owain's old war-band was waiting for me there. They had chosen the site of their ambush well, at a place where holly trees hid us from the buildings. Lunete was still screaming at me as I walked up the path, call-

180

ing me a traitor and a coward. 'She's got you right, Saxon,' Griffid ap Annan said, then spat towards me.

His men blocked my path. There were a dozen spearmen there, all old comrades, but all now with implacably hostile faces. Arthur might have placed my life under his protection, but here, hidden from the villa windows, no one would know how I had ended up dead in the mud.

'You broke your oath,' Griffid accused me.

'I did not,' I claimed.

Minac, an old warrior whose neck and wrists were heavy with the gold given him by Owain, levelled his spear. 'Don't worry about your girl,' he said nastily, 'there's plenty of us who know how to look after young widows.'

I drew Hywelbane. Behind me the women had come from their huts to see their men avenge the death of their Lord. Lunete was among them and jeering at me like the rest.

'We've taken a new oath,' Minac said, 'and unlike you, we keep our oaths.' He advanced down the path with Griffid beside him. The other spearmen crowded in behind their leaders, while at my back the women pressed closer and some of them put aside their ever-present distaffs and spindles to begin throwing stones to drive me forward on to Griffid's spear. I hefted Hywelbane, its edge still dented from Arthur's fight with Owain, and I said a prayer that the Gods would give me a good death.

'Saxon,' Griffid said, using the worst insult he could find. He was advancing very cautiously for he knew my skill with a sword. 'Saxon traitor,' he said, then recoiled as a heavy stone splashed into the mud on the path between us. He looked past me and I saw the fear come on to his face and the blade of his spear drop.

'Your names,' Nimue's voice hissed from behind me, 'are on the stone. Griffid ap Annan, Mapon ap Ellchyd, Minac ap Caddan . . .' She recited the spearmen's names and ancestry one by one, and each time she pronounced a name she spat towards the curse stone that she had lobbed into their path. The spears dropped.

I stood aside to let Nimue pass. She was dressed in a black hooded cloak that cast her face into a shadow out of which her golden eye glittered malevolently. She stopped beside me, then suddenly turned and pointed a staff dressed with a sprig of mistletoe towards the women who had been throwing stones. 'You want your children turned into rats?' Nimue called to the onlookers. 'You want your milk to dry and your urine to burn like fire? Go!' The women seized their children and ran to hide themselves in the huts.

Griffid knew Nimue was Merlin's beloved and possessed of the Druid's power and he was shaking with fear of her curse. 'Please,' he said as Nimue turned back to face him.

She walked past his lowered spear-point and struck him hard on the cheek with her staff. 'Down,' she said. 'All of you! Down! Flat! On your faces! Flat!' She struck Minac. 'Get down!'

They lay on their bellies in the mud and, one by one, she stepped on their backs. Her tread was light, but her curse heavy. 'Your deaths are in my hand,' she told them, 'your lives are all mine. I will use your souls as gaming-pieces. Each dawn that you wake alive you will thank me for my mercy, and each dusk you will pray that I do not see your filthy faces in my dreams. Griffid ap Annan: swear allegiance to Derfel. Kiss his sword. On your knees, dog! On your knees!'

I protested that these men owed me no allegiance, but Nimue turned on me in anger and ordered me to hold out the sword. Then, one by one, with mud and terror on their faces, my old companions shuffled on their knees to kiss the tip of Hywelbane. The oath gave me no rights of lordship over these men, but it did make it impossible for any of them to attack me without endangering their souls, for Nimue told them that if they broke this oath their souls were doomed to stay for ever-more in the dark Otherworld, never to find new bodies on this green, sunlit earth again. One of the spearmen, a Christian, defied Nimue by saying the oath meant nothing, but his cour-age failed when she prised the golden eye from its socket and held it towards him, hissing a curse, and in abject terror he dropped to his knees and kissed my sword like the others. Nimue, once their oaths were sworn, ordered them to lie flat again. She worked the golden ball back into her eye socket and then we left them in the mud.

Nimue laughed as we climbed out of their sight. 'I enjoyed that!' she said, and there was a flash of the old, childish mischief in her voice. 'I did enjoy that! I do so hate men, Derfel.'

'All men?'

'Men in leather, carrying spears.' She shuddered. 'Not you. But the rest I hate.' She turned and spat back down the path. 'How the gods must laugh at little strutting men.' She pushed back her hood to look at me. 'Do you want Lunete to go to Corinium with you?'

'I swore to protect her,' I said unhappily, 'and she tells me she's pregnant.'

'Does that mean you do want her company?'

'Yes,' I said, meaning no.

'I think you're a fool,' Nimue said, 'but Lunete will do as I tell her. But I tell you, Derfel, that if you don't leave her now, she'll leave you in her own good time.' She put her hand on my arm to check me. We had come close to the villa's porch where the crowd of petitioners was waiting to see Arthur. 'Did you know,' Nimue asked me in a low voice, 'that Arthur is thinking of releasing Gundleus?'

'No.' I was shocked by the news.

'He is. He thinks Gundleus will keep the peace now, and he thinks Gundleus is the best man to rule Siluria. Arthur won't release him without Tewdric's agreement, so it won't happen yet, but when it does, Derfel, I'll kill Gundleus.' She spoke with the terrible simplicity of truth and I thought how ferocity gave her a beauty that nature had denied her. She was staring across the wet, cold land towards the distant mound of Caer Cadarn. 'Arthur,' she said, 'dreams of peace, but there never will be peace. Never! Britain is a cauldron, Derfel, and Arthur will stir it to horror.'

'You're wrong,' I said loyally.

Nimue mocked that assertion with a grimace and then,

without another word, she turned and walked back down the path towards the warriors' huts.

I pushed through the petitioners into the villa. Arthur glanced up as I came in, waved a casual welcome, then returned his attention to a man who was complaining that his neighbour had moved their boundary stones. Bedwin and Gereint sat at the table with Arthur, while to one side Agricola and Prince Tristan stood like guards. A number of the kingdom's counsellors and magistrates sat on the floor, which was curiously warm thanks to the Roman way of making a space beneath that could be filled with warm smoky air from a furnace. A crack in the tiles was allowing wisps of the smoke to drift across the big chamber.

The petitioners were seen one by one and justice was pronounced. Almost all of the cases could have been dealt with in Lindinis's magistrates' court that stood just a hundred paces from the villa, but many folk, especially the pagan country dwellers, reckoned that a decision given in Royal Council was more binding than a judgment made in a court established by the Romans, and so they stored their grudges and feuds until the council was conveniently close by. Arthur, representing the baby Mordred, dealt with them patiently, but he was relieved when the real business of the day could commence. That business was to dispose of the tangled ends left by the previous day's fight. Owain's warriors were given to Prince Gereint with Arthur's recommendation that they be split between various troops. One of Gereint's captains, a man called Llywarch, was appointed in Owain's place as the new commander of the King's guard, then a magistrate was given the task of tallying Owain's wealth and sending to Kernow the portion that was owed in *sarhaed*. I noted how brusquely Arthur conducted the business, though never without giving each man present a chance to speak his mind. Such consultation could lead to interminable argument, but Arthur had the happy talent of understanding complicated matters swiftly and proposing compromises that pleased everyone. I noticed, too, how Gereint and Bedwin were content to let Arthur take the first place. Bedwin had placed all his hopes for Dumnonia's future on Arthur's sword and Bedwin was thus Arthur's strongest supporter, while Gereint, who was Uther's nephew, could have been an opponent, but the Prince had none of his uncle's ambition and was happy that Arthur was willing to take the responsibility of government. Dumnonia had a new King's champion, Arthur ab Uther, and the relief in the room was palpable.

Prince Cadwy of Isca was ordered to contribute to the *sarhaed* owed to Kernow. He protested against the decision, but quailed before Arthur's anger and meekly agreed to pay one quarter of Kernow's price. Arthur, I suspect, would have preferred to inflict a sterner punishment, but I was oath-bound not to reveal Cadwy's part in the attack on the moor and there was no other evidence of his complicity, so Cadwy escaped a heavier judgement. Prince Tristan acknowledged Arthur's decisions with a nod of his head.

The next business of the day was arranging the future of our King. Mordred had been living in Owain's household and now he needed a new home. Bedwin proposed a man named Nabur who was the chief magistrate in Durnovaria. Another counsellor immediately protested, condemning Nabur for being a Christian.

Arthur rapped on the table to end a bitter argument before it began. 'Is Nabur here?' he demanded.

A tall man stood at the back of the room. 'I'm Nabur.' He was clean shaven and dressed in a Roman toga. 'Nabur ap Lwyd,' he introduced himself formally. He was a young man with a narrow, grave face and receding hair that gave him the appearance of a bishop or a Druid.

'You have children, Nabur?' Arthur asked.

'Three living, Lord. Two boys and a girl. The girl is our Lord Mordred's age.'

'And is there a Druid or Bard in Durnovaria?'

Nabur nodded. 'Derella the Bard, Lord.'

Arthur spoke privately with Bedwin, who nodded, then Arthur smiled at Nabur. 'Would you take the King into your care?'

'Gladly, Lord.'

'You may teach him your religion, Nabur ap Lwyd, but only when Derella is present, and Derella must become the boy's tutor when he is five years of age. You will receive half a king's allowance from the treasury and will be required to keep twenty guards about our Lord Mordred at all times. The price of his life is your soul and the souls of your whole family. Do you agree?'

Nabur blanched when he was told that his wife and children would die if he let Mordred be killed, but he still nodded acceptance. And no wonder. To be the King's guardian gave Nabur a place very close to the centre of Dumnonia's power. 'I agree, Lord,' he said.

The last business of the council was the fate of Ladwys, Gundleus's wife and lover, and slave to Owain. She was brought into the room where she stood defiantly in front of Arthur. 'This day,' Arthur told her, 'I ride north to Corinium where your husband is our captive. Do you wish to come?'

'So you can humiliate me further?' Ladwys asked. Owain, for all his brutality, had never managed to break her spirit.

Arthur frowned at her hostile tone. 'So you can be with him, Lady,' he said gently. 'Your husband's imprisonment is not harsh, he has a house like this, though admittedly it is guarded. But you may live with him in privacy and peace, if that is what you want.'

Tears showed at Ladwys's eyes. 'He may not want me. I've been soiled.'

Arthur shrugged. 'I can't speak for Gundleus, I just want your decision. If you choose to stay here then you may. Owain's death means you are free.'

She seemed bemused by Arthur's generosity, but managed to nod. 'I will come, Lord.'

'Good!' Arthur stood and carried his chair to the side of the room where he courteously invited Ladwys to sit. Then he faced the assembled counsellors, spearmen and chiefs. 'I have one thing to say, just one, but you must all understand this one thing and you must repeat it to your men, your families, your

186

tribes and your septs. Our King is Mordred, no one but Mordred, and it is to Mordred we owe our allegiance and our swords. But in the next years the kingdom will face enemies, as all kingdoms do, and there will be a need, as there always is, for strong decisions, and when those decisions are taken there will be men among you who will whisper that I am usurping the King's power. You will even be tempted to think I want the King's power. So in front of you now, and in front of our friends from Gwent and Kernow' – here Arthur gestured courteously towards Agricola and Tristan – 'let me swear upon whatever oath you hold most dear that I shall use the power you give me for one end only, and that one end is to see Mordred take his kingdom from me when he is of age. That I swear.' He stopped abruptly.

There was a stir in the room. Until that moment no one had fully understood how swiftly Arthur had taken power in Dumnonia. The fact that he sat at the table with Bedwin and Prince Gereint suggested that the three men were equals in power, but Arthur's speech proclaimed that there was only one man in charge, and Bedwin and Gereint, by their silence, gave support to Arthur's claim. Neither Bedwin nor Gereint were stripped of their power, but rather they now exercised it at Arthur's pleasure and his pleasure decreed that Bedwin would stay to be the arbiter of disputes within the kingdom, Gereint would guard the Saxon frontier while Arthur went north to face the forces of Powys. I knew, and maybe Bedwin knew, that Arthur had high hopes of peace with Gorfyddyd's kingdom, but until that peace was agreed he would continue a posture of war.

A large party went north that afternoon. Arthur, with his two warriors and his servant Hygwydd, rode ahead with Agricola and his men. Morgan, Ladwys and Lunete rode in a cart while I walked with Nimue. Lunete was subdued, overwhelmed by Nimue's anger. We spent the night at the Tor where I saw the good work Gwlyddyn was doing. The new stockade was in place and a new tower rising on the foundations of the old. Ralla was pregnant. Pellinore did not know me, but just walked about his new cage as though he was on guard and barked orders at unseen spearmen. Druidan ogled Ladwys. Gudovan, the clerk, showed me Hywel's grave north of the Tor, then took Arthur to the shrine of the Holy Thorn where Saint Norwenna was buried close beside the miraculous tree.

Next morning I said farewell to Morgan and to Nimue. The sky was blue again, the wind was cold, and I went north with Arthur.

In the spring my son was born. He died three days later. For days afterwards I would see that small wrinkled red face and tears would come to my eyes at the memory. He had seemed healthy, but one morning, hung in his swaddling clothes on the wall of the kitchen so he would be out of the way of the dogs and piglets, he simply died. Lunete, like me, wept, but she also blamed me for her baby's death, saying the air at Corinium was pestilential, though she was, in fact, happy enough in the town. She liked the clean Roman buildings and her small brick house that faced on to a stone-paved street, and she had struck up an unlikely friendship with Ailleann, Arthur's lover, and with Ailleann's twin sons, Amhar and Loholt. I liked Ailleann well enough, but the two boys were fiends. Arthur indulged them, perhaps because he felt guilty that they, like him, were not proper sons born to inherit, but bastards who would need to make their own way in a hard world. They received no discipline that I ever saw, except once when I found them prying at a puppy's eyes with a knife and I struck them both hard. The puppy was blinded and I did the merciful thing of killing it quickly. Arthur sympathized with me, but said it was not my place to strike his boys. His warriors applauded me, and Ailleann, I think, approved.

She was a sad woman. She knew her days as Arthur's companion were numbered for her man had become the effective ruler of Britain's strongest kingdom and he would need to marry a bride who could buttress his power. I knew that bride was Ceinwyn, star and Princess of Powys, and I suspect Ailleann knew it too. She wanted to return to Benoic, but Arthur would not allow his precious sons to leave the country. Ailleann knew that Arthur would never let her starve, but nor would he disgrace his royal wife by keeping his lover close. As the spring put leaves on trees and spread blossom across the land her sadness deepened.

The Saxons attacked in the spring, but Arthur did not go to war. King Melwas defended the southern border from his capital at Venta while Prince Gereint's war-bands sallied out of Durocobrivis to oppose the Saxon levies of the dreaded King Aelle. Gereint had the harder time of it and Arthur reinforced him by sending him Sagramor with thirty horsemen, and Sagramor's intervention tipped the balance in our favour. Aelle's Saxons, we were told, believed Sagramor's black face made him a monster sent from the Kingdom of the Night and they had neither the sorcerers nor the swords that could oppose him. The Numidian drove Aelle's men so far back that he made a new frontier a full day's march beyond the old and he marked his new boundary with a row of severed Saxon heads. He pillaged deep into Lloegyr, once even leading his horsemen as far as London, a city that had been the greatest in Roman Britain, but which was now decaying behind fallen walls. The surviving Britons there, Sagramor told us, were timid and begged him not to disturb the fragile peace they had made with their Saxon overlords.

There was no news of Merlin.

In Gwent they waited for Gorfyddyd of Powys to attack, but no attack came. Instead a messenger rode south from Gorfyddyd's capital at Caer Sws and two weeks later Arthur rode north to meet the enemy King. I went with him, one of twelve warriors who marched with swords, but no shields or war spears. We went on a mission of peace, and Arthur was excited at the prospect. We took Gundleus of Siluria with us, and first marched east to Tewdric's capital of Burrium that was a walled Roman town filled with armouries and the reeking smoke of blacksmiths' forges, and from there we went north accompanied by Tewdric and his attendants. Agricola was defending

Gwent's Saxon frontier and Tewdric, like Arthur, took only a handful of guards, though he was accompanied by three priests, among them Sansum, the angry little black-tonsured priest whom Nimue had nicknamed Lughtigern, the Mouse Lord.

We made a colourful party. King Tewdric's men were cloaked in red above their Roman uniforms while Arthur had outfitted each of his warriors with new green cloaks. We travelled beneath four banners: Mordred's dragon for Dumnonia, Arthur's bear, Gundleus's fox and Tewdric's bull. With Gundleus rode Ladwys, the only woman in our party. She was happy again and Gundleus seemed content to have her back at his side. He was still a prisoner, but he wore a sword again and he rode in the place of honour alongside Arthur and Tewdric. Tewdric was still suspicious of Gundleus, but Arthur treated him like an old friend. Gundleus, after all, was a part of his plan to bring peace among the Britons, a peace that would allow Arthur to turn his swords and spears against the Saxons.

At the border of Powys we were met by a guard come to do us honour. Rushes were laid on the road and a bard sang a song telling of Arthur's victory over the Saxons in the Valley of the White Horse. King Gorfyddyd had not come to greet us, but instead sent Leodegan, the King of Henis Wyren whose lands had been taken by the Irish and who was now an exile in Gorfyddyd's court. Leodegan had been chosen because his rank did us honour, though he himself was a notorious fool. He was an extraordinarily tall man, very thin and with a long neck, wispy dark hair and a slack wet mouth. He could never keep still, but darted and jerked and blinked and scratched and fussed all the time. 'The King would be here,' he told us, 'yes indeed, but cannot be here. You understand? But all the same, greetings from Gorfyddyd!' He watched enviously as Tewdric rewarded the bard with gold. Leodegan, we were to learn, was a much impoverished man and spent most of his days trying to recoup the vast losses that had been inflicted on him when Diwrnach, the Irish conqueror, had taken his lands. 'Shall we move on? There are lodgings at . . .' Leodegan paused. 'Bless me, I've forgotten, but the guard commander knows. Where is he? There. What's his name? Never mind, we'll get there.'

The eagle flag of Powys and Leodegan's own stag banner joined our standards. We followed a Roman road that lay spear-straight across good country, the same country that Arthur had laid waste the previous autumn, though only Leodegan was tactless enough to mention the campaign. 'You've been here before, of course,' he called up to Arthur. Leodegan had no horse and so was forced to walk alongside the royal party.

Arthur frowned. 'I'm not sure I know this land,' he said diplomatically.

'Indeed you do, yes indeed. See? The burned farm? Your work!' Leodegan beamed up at Arthur. 'They underestimated you, didn't they? I told Gorfyddyd so, told him straight to his face. Young Arthur's good, I said, but Gorfyddyd has never been a man to hear sense. A fighter, yes, a thinker, no. The son is better, I think. Cuneglas is definitely better. I rather hoped young Cuneglas might marry one of my daughters, but Gorfyddyd won't hear of it. Never mind.' He tripped on a tussock of grass. The road, just like the Fosse Way near Ynys Wydryn, was embanked so that the surface would drain into the edging ditches, but the years had filled in the ditches and drifted soil on to the road's stones that were now thick with weed and grass. Leodegan persisted in pointing out other places that Arthur had laid waste, but after a while he gave up trying to provoke any response and so fell back to where we guards walked behind Tewdric's three priests. Leodegan attempted to talk to Agravain, the commander of Arthur's guard, but Agravain was in a sullen mood and Leodegan finally decided that I was the most sympathetic of Arthur's entourage and so questioned me eagerly about Dumnonia's nobility. He was trying to discover who was and who was not married. 'Prince Gereint, now? Is he? Is he?'

'Yes, Lord,' I said.

'And she's in health?'

'So far as I know, Lord.'

'King Melwas, then? He has a queen?'

'She died, Lord.'

'Ah!' He brightened immediately. 'I have daughters, you see?' he explained very earnestly. 'Two daughters, and daughters must be wed, must they not? Unwed daughters are no use to man or beast. Mind you, to be fair, one of my two darlings is to be married. Guinevere is spoken for. She's to marry Valerin. You know of Valerin?'

'No, Lord.'

'A fine man, a fine man, a fine man, but no . . .' He paused, seeking the right word. 'No wealth! No real land, you see. Some scrubby stuff west, I think, but no money worth counting. He has no rents, no gold, and a man can't go far without rents or gold. And Guinevere's a princess! Then there's Gwenhwyvach, her sister, and she has no prospects of marriage at all, none! She lives off my purse only, and the Gods know that's thin enough. But Melwas keeps an empty bed, does he? That's a thought! Though it's a pity about Cuneglas.'

'Why, Lord?'

'He doesn't seem to want to marry either girl!' Leodegan said indignantly. 'I suggested it to his father. Solid alliance, I said, adjoining kingdoms, an ideal arrangement! But no. Cuneglas has his eye set on Helledd of Elmet and Arthur, we hear, is to marry Ceinwyn.'

'I wouldn't know, Lord,' I said innocently.

'Ceinwyn's a pretty girl! Oh yes! But so's my Guinevere, only she's to marry Valerin. Dear me. What a waste! No rents, no gold, no money, nothing but some drowned pasture and a handful of sickly cows. She won't like it! She likes her comfort, Guinevere does, but Valerin doesn't know what comfort means! Lives in a pig hut, so far as I can make out. Still, he is a chief. Mind you, the deeper you go into Powys the more men call themselves chiefs.' He sighed. 'But she's a princess! I thought one of Cadwallon's boys in Gwynedd might marry her, but Cadwallon's a strange fellow. Never liked me much. Didn't help me when the Irish came.'

He fell silent as he brooded on that great injustice. We had travelled far enough north now for the land and the people to be unfamiliar. In Dumnonia we were surrounded by Gwent, Siluria, Kernow and the Saxons, but here men spoke of Gwynedd and Elmet, of Lleyn and Ynys Mon. Lleyn had once been Henis Wyren, Leodegan's kingdom, of which Ynys Mon, the island of Mona, had been a part. Both were now ruled by Diwrnach, one of the Irish Lords Across the Sea who were carving out kingdoms for themselves in Britain. Leodegan, I reflected, must have been easy meat for a grim man like Diwrnach whose cruelty was famous. Even in Dumnonia we had heard how he painted the shields of his war-band with the blood of the men they killed in battle. It was better to fight the Saxons, men said, than take on Diwrnach.

But we travelled to Caer Sws to make peace not to contemplate war. Caer Sws proved to be a small muddy town surrounding a drab Roman fort set in a wide, flat-bottomed valley beside a deep ford across the Severn that was here called the River Hafren. The real capital of Powys was Caer Dolforwyn, a fine hill topped by a royal stone, but Caer Dolforwyn, like Caer Cadarn, had neither the water nor the space to accommodate a kingdom's law court, treasury, armouries, kitchens and storehouses, and so just as Dumnonia's day-to-day business was conducted from Lindinis, so the government of Powys functioned out of Caer Sws and only in times of danger or at high royal festivals did Gorfyddyd's court move down the river to Caer Dolforwyn's commanding summit.

Caer Sws's Roman buildings had all but vanished, though Gorfyddyd's feasting hall was built on one of their old stone foundations. He had flanked that hall with two new halls built specially for Tewdric and Arthur. Gorfyddyd greeted us inside his own hall. The Powysian King was a sour man whose left sleeve hung empty thanks to Excalibur. He was middle-aged, heavily built and had a suspicious, small-eyed face that showed no warmth as he embraced Tewdric and growled a reluctant welcome. He went sullenly silent as Arthur, no king, knelt before him. His chiefs and warriors all had long plaited moustaches and heavy cloaks dripping from the rain that had fallen all day long. The hall smelled of wet dogs. There were no women present except for two slaves who carried jars out of which Gorfyddyd scooped frequent hornfuls of mead. We learned later that he had taken to the drink in the long weeks after he had lost his arm to Excalibur; weeks in which he was fevered and men doubted his survival. The mead was brewed thick and strong, and its effect was to transfer the care of Powys from the embittered and befuddled Gorfyddyd on to the shoulders of his son Cuneglas, the Edling of Powys.

Cuneglas was a young man with a round, clever face and long dark moustaches. He was quick to laugh, relaxed and friendly. He and Arthur, it was plain, were twin souls. For three days they hunted deer in the mountains and at night they feasted and listened to the bards. There were few Christians in Powys, but once Cuneglas learned that Tewdric was a Christian he turned a storehouse into a church and invited the priests to preach. Cuneglas even listened to one of the sermons himself, though afterwards he shook his head and said he preferred his own Gods. King Gorfyddyd called the church a nonsense, but did not forbid his son from indulging Tewdric's religion, though Gorfyddyd took care that his Druid surrounded the makeshift church with a ring of charms. 'Gorfyddyd is not wholly convinced we mean to keep the peace,' Arthur warned us on the second night, 'but Cuneglas has persuaded him. So for God's sake stay sober, keep your swords in your scabbards and don't pick a fight. One spark here and Gorfyddyd will throw us out and make war again.'

On the fourth day the council of Powys met in the great hall. The main business of the day was to make peace, and that, despite Gorfyddyd's reservations, was done swiftly. The Powysian King slouched in his chair and watched as his son gave the proclamation. Powys, Gwent and Dumnonia, Cuneglas said, would be allies, blood of each other's blood, and an attack on any one of the three would be construed as an attack on the others. Gorfyddyd nodded his assent, though without enthusiasm. Better still, Cuneglas continued, once his own marriage with Helledd of Elmet was achieved, Elmet too would join the pact and so the Saxons would be surrounded by a united front of British kingdoms. That alliance was the great advantage Gorfyddyd gained from making peace with Dumnonia: the chance to make war on the Saxons, and Gorfyddyd's price for that peace was a recognition that Powys would be the leader of that war. 'He wants to be High King,' Agravain growled to us at the back of the hall. Gorfyddyd also demanded the restoration of his cousin, Gundleus of Siluria. Tewdric, who had suffered more than any from Siluria's raids, was reluctant to put Gundleus back on his throne and we Dumnonians were unwilling to forgive him for Norwenna's murder, while I hated the man for what he had done to Nimue, but Arthur had persuaded us that Gundleus's freedom was a small enough price to pay for peace and so the treacherous Gundleus was duly restored.

Gorfyddyd may have seemed reluctant to conclude the treaty, yet he must have been persuaded of its advantages for he was willing to pay the greatest price of all for its successful conclusion. He was willing for his daughter Ceinwyn, the star of Powys, to marry Arthur. Gorfyddyd was a dour man, suspicious and harsh, yet he loved his seventeen-year-old daughter and he poured on to her all the remnants of affection and kindness that were left in his soul, and the fact that he was willing for her to marry Arthur, who was no king and did not even possess the title of prince, was evidence of Gorfyddyd's conviction that his warriors had to be turned away from fighting fellow Britons. The betrothal was also evidence that Gorfyddyd, like his son Cuneglas, recognized that Arthur was the real power in Dumnonia and so, at the great feast that followed the council, Ceinwyn and Arthur were formally betrothed.

The betrothal ceremony was deemed sufficiently important for the whole assembly to decamp from Caer Sws to the more auspicious feasting hall on the summit of Caer Dolforwyn that was named after Dolforwyn, a meadow at the hill's base which, appropriately enough, meant the Maiden's Meadow. We arrived at sunset when the hilltop was smoky from the great fires on which deer and swine were being roasted. Far beneath us the silvery Severn twisted in its valley, while to the north the great hill ranges stretched dim towards darkening Gwynedd. It was said that on a clear day Cadair Idris could be seen from Caer Dolforwyn's peak, but that evening the horizon was misted by a distant rain. The lower slopes of the hill were thick with great oaks out of which a pair of red kites climbed as the sun turned the western clouds scarlet and we all agreed that the sight of the two birds flying so late in the dying day was a wonderful omen for what was about to happen. Inside the hall the bards were singing the tale of Hafren, the human maid who had given Dolforwyn its name and who had turned into a Goddess when her stepmother tried to drown her in the river at the foot of the hill. They sang until the sun dropped.

The betrothal was performed at night so that the Moon Goddess would bless the pair. Arthur prepared for it first, leaving the hall for a whole hour before returning in all his glory. Even hardened warriors gasped as he re-entered the hall, for he came in his full armour. The scale coat, with its gold and silver plates, glittered in the flamelight and the goose feathers on his high, silver-chased, death's-head helmet brushed the hall rafters as he strode up the central passage. His silver-covered shield dazzled in the light while his white cloak swept the ground behind. Men did not carry weapons in a feasting hall, but that night Arthur chose to wear Excalibur and he stalked to the high table like a conqueror making peace and even Gorfyddyd of Powys gaped as his erstwhile enemy strode towards the dais. Till now Arthur had been a peacemaker, but that night he wanted to remind his future father-in-law of his power.

Ceinwyn entered the hall a few moments later. Ever since our arrival at Caer Sws she had been hidden in the women's quarters and that concealment had only heightened the expectations among those of us who had never seen Gorfyddyd's daughter. I confess that most of us expected to be disappointed in this star of Powys, but in truth she outshone any star. She came into the hall with her attendant ladies and the sight of the Princess took men's breath away. It took mine. She had the fair colouring more common in Saxons, but in Ceinwyn that fairness was turned into a pale, delicate loveliness. She looked very young, with a shy face and a demure manner. She was dressed in a robe of linen dyed yellow-gold with hive-gum, and the dress was embroidered with white stars about its neck and hem. Her hair was gold and so light that it seemed to shine as brightly as Arthur's armour. She was so slender that Agravain, who was sitting next to me on the feasting floor, commented that she would be no good for breeding children. 'Any decent baby will die trying to struggle through those hips,' he said sourly, yet even so I pitied Ailleann who must surely have hoped that Arthur's wife would prove to be nothing more than a dynastic convenience.

The moon sailed high above Caer Dolforwyn's summit as Ceinwyn paced slowly and shyly towards Arthur. In her hands she carried a halter, the gift she brought to her future husband as a symbol that she was passing from her father's authority to his. Arthur fumbled and almost dropped the halter when Ceinwyn gave it to him, and that was surely a bad omen, but everyone, even Gorfyddyd, laughed the moment away, and then Iorweth, Powys's Druid, formally betrothed the couple. The torches flickered as their hands were bound in a knotted chain of grass. Arthur's face was hidden behind the silver-grey helmet, but Ceinwyn, sweet Ceinwyn, looked so full of joy. The Druid gave his blessing, enjoining Gwydion the God of Light and Aranrhod the Golden Goddess of the Dawn to be their special deities and to bless all Britain with their peace. A harpist played, men applauded and Ceinwyn, lovely silver Ceinwyn, wept and laughed for the joy in her soul. I lost my heart to Ceinwyn that night. Many men did. She looked so happy, and no wonder, for in Arthur she was escaping the nightmare of all princesses, which is to marry for their country rather than their heart. A princess will be bedded with any stinking, slack-bellied old goat if it will secure a frontier or make an alliance, but Ceinwyn had found Arthur and in his youth and kindness she doubtless saw an escape from her fears.

Leodegan, the exiled King of Henis Wyren, arrived at the feasting hall at the climax of the ceremony. The exiled King had not been with us since our arrival, but had instead gone to his own home north of Caer Sws. Now, eager to share in the largesse that always followed a betrothal ceremony, he stood at the back of the hall and joined in the applause that greeted the distribution of Arthur's gold and silver. Arthur had also gained the permission of Dumnonia's council to bring back Gorfyddyd's war gear that he had captured the previous year, but that treasure had been returned privately so that no man present need be reminded of the Powysian defeat.

Once the gifts were given Arthur took off the helmet and sat beside Ceinwyn. He talked to her, bending close as he always did so that she doubtless felt she was the most important person in all his firmament as, indeed, she had a right to feel. Many of us in the hall were jealous of a love that looked so perfect, and even Gorfyddyd, who must have been bitter at losing his daughter to a man who had beaten and maimed him in battle, seemed happy in Ceinwyn's joy.

But it was on that happy night, when peace had come at last, that Arthur broke Britain.

None of us knew it then. The distribution of the betrothal gifts was followed by drinking and singing. We watched jugglers, we listened to Gorfyddyd's royal bard and we roared our own songs. One of our men forgot Arthur's warning and fell into a fight with a Powysian warrior and the two drunken men were dragged outside and drenched with water, and half an hour later they were clasped in each other's arms swearing undying friendship. And some time in that period, when the fires roared high and the drink flowed fast, I saw Arthur staring fixedly towards the back of the hall and, being curious, I turned to see what had trapped his gaze.

I turned and saw a young woman who stood head and shoulders above the crowd and who carried a bold defiant look on her face. If you can master me, that look seemed to say, then you can master whatever else this wicked world might bring. I can see her now, standing amidst her deerhounds that had the same thin, lean bodies, and the same long nose and the same huntress eyes as their mistress. Green eyes, she had, with a kind of cruelty deep inside them. It was not a soft face, any more than her body was soft. She was a woman of strong lines and high bones, and that made for a good face and a handsome one, but hard, so hard. What made her beautiful was her hair and her carriage, for she stood as straight as a spear and her hair fell around her shoulders like a cascade of tumbling red tangles. That red hair softened her looks, while her laughter snared men like salmon caught in basket traps. There have been many more beautiful women, and thousands who were better, but since the world was weaned I doubt there have been many so unforgettable as Guinevere, eldest daughter of Leodegan, the exiled King of Henis Wyren.

And it would have been better, Merlin always said, had she been drowned at birth.

The royal party hunted deer next day. Guinevere's hounds brought down a pricket, a young male without antlers, though to hear Arthur praise the dogs you would have thought they had chased down the Wild Stag of Dyfed itself.

The bards sing of love and men and women yearn for it, but none knows what love is until, like a spear thrown from the dark, it strikes. Arthur could not take his eyes from Guinevere, though the Gods know he tried. In the days after the betrothal feast, when we were back at Caer Sws, he walked and talked with Ceinwyn, but he could not wait to see Guinevere and she, knowing just what game she played, tantalized him. Her betrothed, Valerin, was at the court and she would walk with her arm in Valerin's arm, laughing, then cast a sudden, modest sidelong glance at Arthur for whom the world would suddenly stop in its turning. He burned for Guinevere.

Would it have made a difference if Bedwin had been there? I think not. Not even Merlin could have stopped what happened. A man might as well call on the rain to go back to the clouds or command a river to curl back to its source.

On the second night after the feast Guinevere came to Arthur's hall in the dark and I, who was standing guard, heard the ring of their laughter and the murmur of their talk. All night they talked and maybe they did more than talk, I wouldn't know, but talk they did, and that I do know for I was posted outside the room and could hardly help but listen. Sometimes the talk was too low to hear, but at other times I heard Arthur explaining and cajoling, pleading and urging. They must have spoken of love, but that I did not hear, instead I heard Arthur talk of Britain and of the dream that had brought him over the sea from Armorica. He spoke of the Saxons and how they were a plague that must be cured if the land was ever to be happy. He spoke of war, and of the terrible joy it was to ride an armoured horse into battle. He spoke as he had spoken to me on the ice-cold ramparts of Caer Cadarn, describing a land at peace in which the common folk did not fear the coming of spearmen in the dawn. He talked passionately, urgently, and Guinevere listened so willingly and assured him his dream was inspired. Arthur spun a future from his dream and Guinevere was deep inside the thread. Poor Ceinwyn, she had only her beauty and her youth, while Guinevere saw the loneliness in Arthur's soul and promised to heal it. She left before the dawn, a dark figure gliding across Caer Sws with a sickle moon trapped in her tangling hair.

Next day, full of remorse, Arthur walked with Ceinwyn and her brother. Guinevere wore a new torque of heavy gold that day and some of us felt a sorrow for Ceinwyn, but Ceinwyn was a child, Guinevere was a woman and Arthur was helpless.

It was a madness that love. Mad as Pellinore. Mad enough to doom Arthur to the Isle of the Dead. Everything vanished for Arthur: Britain; the Saxons; the new alliance; all the great, careful, balanced structure of peace for which he had worked ever since he had sailed from Armorica, was set whirling into destruction for the possession of that penniless, landless, red-haired Princess. He knew what he was doing, but he could no more stop himself than he could stop the sun from rising. He was possessed, he thought about her, talked about her, dreamed of her, could not live without her, yet somehow, agonizingly, he kept up the pretence of his betrothal to Ceinwyn. The marriage arrangements were being made. As a mark of Tewdric's contribution to the peace treaty the marriage was to be at Glevum and Arthur would travel there first and make his preparations. The wedding could not take place until the moon was waxing. It was now on the wane and no marriage could be risked in a time of such ill-omen, but in two weeks the auguries would be right and Ceinwyn would come south with flowers in her hair.

But Arthur wore Guinevere's hair about his neck. It was a narrow red braid that he hid beneath his collar, but which I saw when I brought him water one morning. He was barechested, sharpening his shaving knife on a stone, and he shrugged when he saw me notice the woven braid. 'You think red hair is unlucky, Derfel?' he asked when he saw my expression.

'Everyone says so, Lord.'

'But is everyone right?' he asked the bronze mirror. 'To make a sword blade hard, Derfel, you don't quench it in water, but in urine passed by a red-headed boy. That must be lucky, must it not? And what if red hair is unlucky?' He paused, spat on the stone and worked the knife blade to and fro. 'Our task, Derfel, is to change things, not let them stand. Why not make red hair lucky?'

'You can do anything, Lord,' I said with unhappy loyalty.

He sighed. 'I hope that's true, Derfel. I do hope that's true.' He peered into the bronze mirror, then flinched as he laid the knife against his cheek. 'Peace is more than a marriage, Derfel. It has to be! You don't make war over a bride. If peace is so desirable, and it is, then you don't abandon it because a marriage doesn't happen, do you?'

'I don't know, Lord,' I said. I only knew that my Lord was rehearsing arguments in his head, repeating them over and over until he believed them. He was mad with love, so mad that north was south and heat was cold. This, to me, was an Arthur I had not seen before; a man of passion and, dare I say it, self-ishness. Arthur had risen so fast. It is true he had been born with a king's blood in his veins, but he had not been given his patrimony and so he considered that all his achievements were his alone. He was proud of that and convinced by those achievements that he knew better than any other man save perhaps Merlin, and because that knowledge was so often what other men incoherently wished, his selfish ambitions were usu-ally seen as noble and far-seeing, but at Caer Sws the ambitions clashed with what other men wanted.

I left him shaving and went outside into the new sunshine where Agravain was sharpening a boar spear. 'Well?' he asked me.

'He's not going to marry Ceinwyn,' I said. We were out of earshot of the hall, but even if we had been closer Arthur would not have heard us. He was singing.

Agravain spat. 'He'll marry who he's told to marry,' he said, then rammed the spear-butt into the turf and stalked across to Tewdric's quarters.

Whether Gorfyddyd and Cuneglas knew what was happen-ing I could not tell, for they were not in constant touch with Arthur as we were. Gorfyddyd, if he suspected, probably thought it did not matter. He doubtless believed, if he believed anything, that Arthur would take Guinevere as a lover and Ceinwyn as a wife. It was bad manners, of course, to come to such an arrangement in the week of the betrothal, but bad manners had never worried Gorfyddyd of Powys. He had no manners himself and knew, as all kings know, that wives are for making dynasties and lovers for making pleasure. His own wife was long dead, but a succession of slave girls kept his bed warm and, to him, impoverished Guinevere would never rank much above a slave and was thus no threat to his beloved daughter. Cuneglas was more perspicacious, and I am sure he must have scented trouble, but he had invested all his energies into this new peace and he must have hoped that Arthur's ob-session with Guinevere would blow away like a summer squall. Or maybe neither Gorfyddyd nor Cuneglas suspected anything, for certainly they did not send Guinevere away from Caer Sws, though whether that would have achieved anything, the Gods alone know. Agravain thought the madness might pass. He told me that Arthur had been obsessed like this once before. 'It was a girl in Ynys Trebes,' Agravain told me, 'can't think of her name. Mella? Messa? Something like that. Pretty little thing. Arthur was besotted, trailing after her like a dog behind a corpse cart. But mind you, he was young then, so young that her father reckoned he'd never amount to anything so he packed his Mella-Messa off to Broceliande and married her to a magistrate fifty years older than her. She died giving birth, but Arthur was over her by then. And these things do pass, Derfel. Tewdric will hammer some brains back into Arthur, you watch.'

Tewdric spent the whole morning closeted with Arthur, and I thought perhaps he had succeeded in hammering some brains back into my Lord for Arthur seemed chastened for the rest of the day. He did not look at Guinevere once, but forced himself to be solicitous of Ceinwyn, and that night, perhaps to please Tewdric, he and Ceinwyn listened to Sansum preach in the little makeshift church. I thought Arthur must have been pleased with the Mouse Lord's sermon for he invited Sansum back to his hall afterwards and was closeted alone with the priest for a long time.

Next morning Arthur appeared with a set, stern face and announced that we would all leave that very same morning. That very same hour, indeed. We were not due to depart for another two days and Gorfyddyd, Cuneglas and Ceinwyn must have been surprised, but Arthur persuaded them he needed more time to prepare for his wedding and Gorfyddyd accepted the excuse placidly enough. Cuneglas may have believed Arthur was going early to remove himself from Guinevere's temptation and so he made no protest, but instead ordered bread, cheese, honey and mead packed for our journey. Ceinwyn, pretty Ceinwyn, said her farewells, starting with us, the guard. We were all in love with her, and that made us resent Arthur's madness, though there had been little any of us could do about our resentment. Ceinwyn gave us each a small gift of gold, and each of us tried to refuse her gift, but she insisted. She gave me a brooch of interlocking patterns and I tried to thrust it back into her hands, but she just smiled and folded my fingers over the gold. 'Look after your Lord,' she said earnestly.

'And after you, Lady,' I answered fervently.

She smiled and moved on to Arthur, presenting him with a spray of may blossom that would give him a swift and safe journey. Arthur fixed the blossom in his sword belt and kissed his betrothed's hand before clambering on to Llamrei's broad back. Cuneglas wanted to send guards to escort us, but Arthur declined the honour. 'Let us leave, Lord Prince,' he said, 'the sooner to arrange our happiness.'

Ceinwyn was pleased by Arthur's words and Cuneglas, ever gracious, ordered the gates opened and Arthur, like a man released from an ordeal, galloped Llamrei madly out of Caer Sws and through the Severn's deep ford. We guards followed on foot to find a spray of may lying on the river's far bank. Agravain plucked the may from the ground so that Ceinwyn should not find it.

Sansum came with us. His presence was not explained, though Agravain surmised that Tewdric had ordered the priest to counsel Arthur against his madness, a madness we all prayed was passing, but we were wrong. The madness had been hopeless from the very first moment Arthur had looked down Gorfyddyd's hall and seen Guinevere's red hair. Sagramor used to tell us an ancient tale of a battle in the old world; a battle over a great city of towers and palaces and temples, and the whole sorry thing was all started because of a woman, and for that woman ten thousand bronze-clad warriors died in the dust.

The story was not so ancient after all.

For just two hours after we had left Caer Sws, in a stretch of lonely woodland where no farms stood, but only steep-sided hills and fast streams and thick, heavy trees, we found Leodegan of Henis Wyren waiting beside the track. He led us without a word down a path that twisted between the roots of great oaks to a clearing beside a pool made by a beaver-dammed stream. The woods were thick with dog mercury and lilies while the last bluebells made a dancing shimmer in the shadows. Sunlight fell on the grass where primroses, cuckoo pints and dog violets grew and where, shining brighter than any flower, Guinevere waited in a robe of cream linen. She had cowslips woven into her red hair. She wore Arthur's golden torque, bracelets of silver and a cape of lilac-coloured wool. The sight of her was enough to catch a man's throat. Agravain cursed quietly.

Arthur threw himself off his horse and ran to Guinevere. He caught her in his arms and we heard her laugh as he whirled her about. 'My flowers!' she cried, putting a hand to her head, and Arthur let her gently down, then knelt to kiss the hem of her robe.

Then he stood and turned. 'Sansum!'

'Lord?'

'You can marry us now.'

Sansum refused. He folded his arms over his dirty black robe and tilted up his stubborn mouse face. 'You are betrothed, Lord,' he insisted nervously.

I thought Sansum was being noble, but in truth it had all been arranged. Sansum had not come with us at Tewdric's bidding, but at Arthur's, and now Arthur's face turned angry at the priest's stubborn change of heart. 'We agreed!' Arthur said, and when Sansum just shook his tonsured head, Arthur touched the hilt of Excalibur. 'I could take the skull off your shoulders, priest.'

'Martyrs are ever made by tyrants, Lord,' Sansum said, dropping to his knees in the flowery grass where he bent his head to bare the grubby nape of his neck. 'I'm coming to you, O Lord,' he bawled towards the grass, 'Thy servant! Coming to Thy glory, oh praise Thee! I see the gates of heaven open! I see the angels waiting for me! Receive me, Lord Jesus, into Thy blessed bosom! I'm coming! I'm coming!'

'Be quiet and get up,' Arthur said tiredly.

205

Sansum squinted slyly up at Arthur. 'You won't give me the bliss of heaven, Lord?'

'Last night,' Arthur said, 'you agreed to marry us. Why do you refuse now?'

Sansum shrugged. 'I have wrestled with my conscience, Lord.'

Arthur understood and sighed. 'So what is your price, priest?'

'A bishopric,' Sansum said hurriedly, struggling to his feet.

'I thought you had a Pope who grants bishoprics,' Arthur said. 'Simplicius? Isn't that his name?'

'The most blessed and holy Simplicius, may he still live in health,' Sansum agreed, 'but give me a church, Lord, and a throne in the church, and men will call me bishop.'

'A church and a chair?' Arthur asked. 'Nothing more?'

'And the appointment to be King Mordred's chaplain. I must have that! His sole and personal chaplain, you under-stand? With an allowance from the treasury sufficient for me to keep my own steward, doorkeeper, cook and candleman.' He brushed grass off his black gown. 'And a laundress,' he added hastily.

'Is that all?' Arthur asked sarcastically.

'A place on Dumnonia's council,' Sansum said as though it were trivial. 'That's all.'

'Granted,' Arthur said carelessly. 'So what do we do to get married?'

While these negotiations were being consummated I was watching Guinevere. There was a look of triumph on her face, and no wonder for she was marrying far above her poor father's hopes. Her father, slack mouth trembling, was watch-ing in abject terror in case Sansum should refuse to perform the ceremony, while behind Leodegan stood a dumpy wee girl who seemed to be in charge of Guinevere's quartet of leashed deerhounds and what little baggage the exiled royal family possessed. The dumpy girl, it turned out, was Gwenhwyvach, Guinevere's younger sister. There was a brother, too, though he had long since retired to a monastery on the wild coast of

Strath Clota where strange Christian hermits competed to grow their hair, starve on berries and preach salvation to the seals.

There was little enough ceremony to the marriage. Arthur and Guinevere stood beneath his banner while Sansum spread his arms to say some prayers in the Greek tongue, then Leodegan drew his sword and touched his daughter's back with the blade before handing the weapon to Arthur as a sign that Guinevere had passed from her father's authority to her husband's. Sansum then scooped some water from the stream and sprinkled it over Arthur and Guinevere, saying that thereby he was cleansing them of sin and receiving them into the family of the Holy Church that hereby recognized their union as one and indissoluble, sacred before God and dedicated to the procreation of children. Then he stared at each of us guards in turn and demanded that we declare that we had witnessed the solemn ceremony. We all made the declaration and Arthur was so happy that he did not hear the reluctance in our voices, though Guinevere did. Nothing escaped Guinevere. 'There,' Sansum said when the paltry ritual was done, 'you're married, Lord.'

Guinevere laughed. Arthur kissed her. She was as tall as he was, maybe a finger's breadth taller, and I confess as I watched them that they looked a splendid pair. More than splendid, for Guinevere was truly striking. Ceinwyn was beautiful, but Guinevere dulled the sun with her presence. We guards were in shock. There was nothing we could have done to stop this consummation of our Lord's madness, but the haste of it seemed as indecent as it was deceitful. Arthur, we knew, was a man of impulse and enthusiasm, but he had taken our breath away by the speed of this decision. Leodegan, though, was jubilant, babbling to his younger daughter how the family finances would now recover and how, sooner than anyone knew, Arthur's warriors would sweep the Irish usurper Diwrnach out of Henis Wyren. Arthur heard the boast and turned quickly. 'I doubt that's possible, Father,' he said.

'Possible! Of course it's possible!' Guinevere intervened.

'You shall make it my wedding gift, Lord, the return of my dear father's kingdom.'

Agravain spat his disapproval. Guinevere chose to ignore the gesture, and instead walked along the row of guards and gave us each a cowslip from the diadem she had worn in her hair. Then, like criminals fleeing a lord's justice, we hurried south to leave the kingdom of Powys before Gorfyddyd's retribution followed.

Fate, Merlin always said, is inexorable. So much followed from that hurried ceremony in the flower-speckled clearing beside the stream. So many died. There was so much heartache, so much blood and so many tears that they would have made a great river; yet, in time, the eddies smoothed, new rivers joined, and the tears went down to the great wide sea and some people forgot how it ever began. The time of glory did come, yet what might have been never did, and of all those who were hurt by that moment in the sun, Arthur was hurt the most.

But on that day he was happy. We hurried home.

The news of the marriage rang in Britain like a God's spear clanging against a shield. At first the sound stunned, and in that calm period, while men tried to understand the consequences, an embassy came from Powys. One of that embassy was Valerin, the chief who had been betrothed to Guinevere. He challenged Arthur to a fight, but Arthur refused, and when Valerin tried to draw his sword we guards had to drive him out of Lindinis. Valerin was a tall, vigorous man with black hair and a black beard, deep-set eyes and a broken nose. His pain was terrible, his anger worse and his attempt at revenge thwarted.

Iorweth the Druid was chief of Powys's delegation, which had been sent by Cuneglas rather than Gorfyddyd. Gorfyddyd was drunk with mead and rage, while his son still hoped there was a chance to retrieve peace from the disaster. The Druid Iorweth was a grave and sensible man and he talked long with Arthur. The marriage, the Druid said, was not valid for it had been conducted by a Christian priest and the Gods of Britain did not recognize the new religion. Take Guinevere for your lover, Iorweth urged Arthur, and Ceinwyn for your wife.

'Guinevere is my wife.' We all heard Arthur shout that statement.

Bishop Bedwin added his support to Iorweth, but Bedwin could not change Arthur's mind. Not even the prospect of war would change Arthur's mind. Iorweth raised that possibility, saying that Dumnonia had insulted Powys and the insult would needs be washed clean with blood if Arthur did not change his mind. Tewdric of Gwent had sent Bishop Conrad to plead for peace, begging Arthur to renounce Guinevere and marry Ceinwyn, and Conrad even threatened that Tewdric might make a separate peace with Powys. 'My Lord King will not fight against Dumnonia,' I heard Conrad reassure Bedwin as the two bishops paced up and down on the terrace in front of Lindinis's villa, 'but nor will he fight for that whore of Henis Wyren.'

'Whore?' Bedwin asked, alarmed and shocked by the word.

'Maybe not,' Conrad allowed. 'But I tell you one thing, my brother, Guinevere's never had a whip taken to her. Never!'

Bedwin shook his head at such laxity on Leodegan's part, then the two men walked out of my earshot. Next day both Bishop Conrad and the Powysian embassy left for their homes and took no good news with them.

But Arthur believed the time of his happiness had come. There would be no war, he insisted, for Gorfyddyd had already lost one arm and would not risk the other. Cuneglas's good sense, Arthur claimed, would ensure peace. For a time, he said, there would be grudges and mistrust, but it would all pass. He thought his happiness must embrace the world.

Labourers were hired to extend and repair Lindinis's villa to make it into a palace fit for a princess. Arthur sent a messenger to Ban of Benoic, beseeching his former lord to send him masons and plasterers who knew how to restore Roman buildings. He wanted an orchard, a garden, a pool of fish; he wanted a bath with heated water; he wanted a courtyard where harpists would play. Arthur wanted a heaven on earth for his bride, but other men wanted revenge and that summer we heard that Tewdric of Gwent had met with Cuneglas and made a treaty of peace, and part of that treaty was an agreement that Powys's armies could march freely across the Roman roads that crossed Gwent. Those roads led only to Dumnonia.

Yet, as that summer passed, no attack came. Sagramor held Aelle's Saxons at bay while Arthur spent a summer in love. I was a member of his guard, so I was with him day in and day out. I should have carried a sword, shield and spear, but as often as not I was burdened with flasks of wine and hampers of food for Guinevere liked to take her meals in hidden glades and by secret streams and we spearmen were required to carry silver plate, horn cups, food and wine to the designated spot. She gathered a company of ladies to be her court and, so help me, my Lunete was one of them. Lunete had grumbled bitterly at having to abandon her brick house in Corinium, but it took her only a few days to decide that a better future lay with Guinevere. Lunete was beautiful and Guinevere declared that she would only be surrounded by people and objects that were pretty, and so she and her ladies dressed in the finest linens decorated with gold, silver, jet and amber, and she paid harpists, singers, dancers and poets to amuse her court. They played games in the woods where they chased each other, hid and paid forfeits if they broke one of the elaborate rules that Guinevere devised. The money for these games, like the money being spent on Lindinis's villa, was provided by Leodegan who had been appointed the treasurer of Arthur's household. Leodegan swore the money all came from back rents and maybe Arthur believed his father-in-law, though the rest of us heard dark tales of Mordred's treasury being lightened of gold and filled with Leodegan's worthless promises of repayment. Arthur seemed not to care. That summer was his foretaste of Britain at peace, but for the rest of us it was a fool's heaven.

Amhar and Loholt were brought to Lindinis, though their mother Ailleann was not summoned. The twins were presented to Guinevere, and Arthur, I think, hoped they would live in the pillared palace that was rising around the heart of the old villa. Guinevere kept the twins company for one day, then said their presence upset her. They were not amusing. They were not pretty, she said, just as her sister Gwenhwyvach was not pretty, and if they were not pretty, nor amusing, they had no place in Guinevere's life. Besides, she said, the twins belonged to Arthur's old life, and that was dead. She did not want them, nor did she care that she made that announcement publicly. She touched Arthur's cheek. 'If we want children, my Prince, we shall make our own.'

Guinevere always called Arthur a prince. At first Arthur claimed he was no prince, but Guinevere insisted he was Uther's son and therefore royal. Arthur, to humour her, allowed her to call him by the title, but soon the rest of us were ordered to use it too. Guinevere ordered it and we obeyed.

No one had ever challenged Arthur about Amhar and Loholt and won the argument, but Guinevere did and so the twins were sent back to their mother in Corinium. The harvest was poor that year for the crops were blighted by late rain that left them blackened and wilting. Rumour claimed that the Saxon harvest had been better, for the rains had spared their lands and so Arthur led a war-band east beyond Durocobrivis to find and capture their stores of grain. He was happy, I think, to escape the songs and dances of Caer Cadarn, and we were happy that he was at our head again and that we were carrying spears instead of feasting cloths. It was a successful raid, filling Dumnonia with captured grain, plundered gold and Saxon slaves. Leodegan, now a member of Dumnonia's council, was given the task of distributing the free grain to every part of the kingdom, but there were horrid rumours that much of it was being sold instead and that the resultant gold found its way to the new house Leodegan was building across the stream from Guinevere's damp-plastered palace.

Madness ends sometimes. The Gods decree it, not man. Arthur had been mad for love all summer, and it was a good summer despite our menial occupations, for a happy Arthur was a beguiling and generous Lord, but as autumn swept the land with wind, rain and golden leaves, he seemed to wake from his summer dream. He was still in love – indeed I do not think he was ever out of love with Guinevere – but that autumn he saw the damage he had done to Britain. Instead of peace there was a sullen truce, and he knew it could not last.

We cut ash pollards for spears and the blacksmiths' huts rang with the sound of hammer on anvil. Sagramor was called back from the Saxon frontier to be nearer to the kingdom's heart. Arthur sent a messenger to King Gorfyddyd, acknowledging the hurt he had done to the King and to his daughter, apologizing for it, but pleading that there must be peace in Britain. He sent a necklace of pearls and gold to Ceinwyn, but Gorfyddyd returned the necklace draped about the messenger's severed head. We heard that Gorfyddyd had stopped drinking and taken his kingdom's reins back from his son, Cuneglas. That news confirmed that there would never be peace until the insult done to Ceinwyn had been avenged by Powys's long spears.

Travellers brought tales of doom from everywhere. The Lords Across the Sea were bringing new Irish warriors into their coastal kingdoms. The Franks were massing war-bands on the edge of Brittany. Powys's harvest was stored and its levies were being trained to fight with spears instead of cutting corn with sickles. Cuneglas had married Helledd of Elmet and men of that northern country were now coming to swell the ranks of Powys's army. Gundleus, restored in Siluria, was forging swords and spears in the deep valleys of his kingdom, while to the east, more Saxon boats were grounding on their captured shores.

Arthur donned his scale armour, only the third time I had seen it since his arrival in Britain, and then, with two score of his armoured horsemen, he rode in progress around Dumnonia. He wanted to show the kingdom his power, and he wanted the travellers who carried their goods across the kingdoms' frontiers to carry a tale of his prowess. Then he came back to Lindinis where Hygwydd, his servant, scoured the new rust from the armour's scales.

The first defeat came that autumn. There had been a plague in Venta, weakening King Melwas's men, and Cerdic, the new Saxon leader, defeated the Belgic war-band and captured a great swathe of good river land. King Melwas pleaded for reinforcements, but Arthur knew Cerdic to be the least of his problems. The war drums were beating throughout the Saxon-held Lloegyr and throughout the northern British kingdoms and no spears could be spared for Melwas. Besides, Cerdic seemed fully occupied with his new holdings and did not threaten Dumnonia further, so Arthur would let the Saxon stay for the time being. 'We'll give peace a chance,' Arthur told the council.

But there was no peace.

In late autumn, when most armies are thinking of greasing their weapons and storing them through the cold months, the might of Powys marched. Britain was at war.

PART THREE

The Return of Merlin

IGRAINE TALKS TO ME of love. It is spring here in Dinnewrac and the sun infuses the monastery with a feeble warmth. There are lambs on the southern slopes, though yesterday a wolf killed three of them and left a blood trail past our gate. Beggars gather at the gate for food and hold out their diseased hands when Igraine comes to visit. One of the beggars stole the maggoty remains of a lamb carcass from the scavenging ravens and sat there gnawing at the pelt as Igraine arrived this morning.

Was Guinevere really beautiful, she asks me. No, I say, but many women would exchange their beauty for Guinevere's looks. Igraine, of course, wanted to know if she herself was beautiful and I assured her she was, but she said the mirrors in her husband's Caer were very old and battered and it was so hard to tell. 'Wouldn't it be lovely,' she said, 'to see ourselves as we really are?'

'God does that,' I said, 'and only God.'

She wrinkled her face at me. 'I do hate it when you preach at me, Derfel. It doesn't suit you. If Guinevere wasn't beautiful, then why did Arthur fall in love with her?'

'Love is not only for the beautiful,' I said reprovingly.

'Did I say it was?' Igraine asked indignantly, 'but you said Guinevere attracted Arthur from the very first moment, so if it wasn't beauty, what was it?'

'The very sight of her,' I answered, 'turned his blood to smoke.'

Igraine liked that. She smiled. 'So she was beautiful?'

'She challenged him,' I answered, 'and he thought he would be less than a man if he failed to capture her. And maybe the

Gods were playing games with us?' I shrugged, unable to come up with more reasons. 'And besides,' I said, 'I never meant to say she was not beautiful, just that she was more than beautiful. She was the best-looking woman I ever saw.'

'Including me?' my Queen immediately demanded.

'Alas,' I said, 'my eyes are dim with age.'

She laughed at the evasion. 'Did Guinevere love Arthur?' she asked.

'She loved the idea of him,' I said. 'She loved that he was the champion of Dumnonia, and she loved him as he was when she first saw him. He was in his armour, the great Arthur, the shining one, the lord of war, the most feared sword in all of Britain and Armorica.'

Igraine ran the tasselled cord of her white robe through her hands. She was thoughtful for a while. 'Do you think I turn Brochvael's blood to smoke?' she asked wistfully.

'Nightly,' I said.

'Oh, Derfel,' she sighed and slipped off the window-sill to walk to the door from where she could stare down into our little hall. 'Were you ever in love like that?' she asked.

'Yes,' I admitted.

'Who was it?' she demanded instantly.

'Never mind,' I said.

'I do mind! I insist. Was it Nimue?' she asked.

'It wasn't Nimue,' I said firmly. 'Nimue was different. I loved her, but I wasn't mad with desire for her. I just thought she was infinitely . . .' I paused, looking for the word and failing to find it. 'Wonderful,' I offered lamely, not looking at Igraine so she would not see my tears.

She waited a while. 'So who were you in love with? Lunete?'

'No! No!'

'Who, then?' she persisted.

'The story will come in time,' I said, 'if I live.'

'Of course you'll live. We shall send you special foods from the Caer.'

'Which my Lord Sansum,' I told her, not wanting her to

218

waste the effort, 'will take from me as unworthy fare for a mere brother.'

'Then come and live in the Caer,' she said eagerly. 'Please!'

I smiled. 'I would do that most willingly, Lady, but alas, I took an oath to stay here.'

'Poor Derfel.' She went back to the window and watched Brother Maelgwyn digging. He had our surviving novice, Brother Tudwal, with him. The second novice died of a fever in the late winter, but Tudwal still lives and shares the saint's cell. The saint wants the boy taught his letters, mainly, I think, so he can discover whether I really am translating the Gospel into Saxon, but the lad is not bright and seems better suited to digging than to reading. It is time we had some real scholars here in Dinnewrac for this feeble spring has brought our usual rancorous arguments about the date of Easter and we shall have no peace until the argument is done. 'Did Sansum really marry Arthur and Guinevere?' Igraine interrupted my gloomy thoughts.

'Yes,' I said, 'he really did.'

'And it wasn't in a great church? With trumpets playing?'

'It was in a clearing beside a stream,' I said, 'with frogs croaking and willow catkins piling up behind the beaver dam.'

'We were married in a feasting hall,' Igraine said, 'and the smoke made my eyes water.' She shrugged. 'So what did you change in the last part?' she asked accusingly. 'What story-shaping did you do?'

I shook my head. 'None.'

'But at Mordred's acclamation,' she asked disappointedly, 'the sword was only laid on the stone? Not thrust into it? Are you sure?'

'It was laid flat on top. I swear it' – I made the sign of the cross – 'on Christ's blood, my Lady.'

She shrugged. 'Dafydd ap Gruffud will translate the tale any way I want him to, and I like the idea of a sword in the stone. I'm glad you were kind about Cuneglas.'

'He was a good man,' I said. He was also Igraine's husband's grandfather.

'Was Ceinwyn really beautiful?' Igraine asked.

I nodded. 'She was, she truly was. She had blue eyes.'

'Blue eyes!' Igraine shuddered at such Saxon features. 'What happened to the brooch she gave you?'

'I wish I knew,' I said, lying. The brooch is in my cell, hidden there safe from even Sansum's vigorous searches. The saint, whom God will surely exalt above all men living and dead, does not allow us to possess any treasures. All our goods must be surrendered to his keeping, that is the rule, and though I surrendered everything else to Sansum, including Hywelbane, God forgive me, I have Ceinwyn's brooch still. The gold has been smoothed by the years, yet still I see Ceinwyn when, in the darkness, I take the brooch from its hiding place and let the moonlight gloss its intricate pattern of interlocking curves. Sometimes – no, always – I touch it to my lips. What a foolish old man I have become. Perhaps I shall give the brooch to Igraine, for I know she will value it, but I shall keep it a while for the gold is like a scrap of sunshine in this chill grey place. Of course, when Igraine reads this she will know the brooch exists, but if she is as kind as I know her to be, she will let me keep it as a small remembrance of a sinful life.

'I don't like Guinevere,' Igraine said.

'Then I have failed,' I said.

'You make her sound very hard,' Igraine said.

I said nothing for a while, but just listened to the sheep bleating. 'She could be wonderfully kind,' I said after the pause. 'She knew how to make the sad happy, but she was impatient with the commonplace. She had a vision of a world that did not hold cripples or bores or ugly things, and she wanted to make that world real by banishing such inconveniences. Arthur had a vision, too, only his vision offered help to the cripples, and he wanted to make his world just as real.'

'He wanted Camelot,' Igraine said dreamily.

'We called it Dumnonia,' I said severely.

'You try to suck all the joy out of it, Derfel,' Igraine said crossly, though she was never truly angry with me. 'I want it to be the poet's Camelot: green grass and high towers and ladies in gowns and warriors strewing their paths with flowers. I want minstrels and laughter! Wasn't it ever like that?'

'A little,' I said, 'though I don't remember many flowery paths. I do recall the warriors limping out of battle, and some of them crawling and weeping with their guts trailing behind in the dust.'

'Stop it!' Igraine said. 'So why do the bards call it Camelot?' she challenged me.

'Because poets were ever fools,' I said, 'otherwise why would they be poets?'

'No, Derfel! What was special about Camelot? Tell me.'

'It was special,' I answered, 'because Arthur gave the land justice.'

Igraine frowned. 'Is that all?'

'It is more, child,' I said, 'than most rulers ever dream of doing, let alone do.'

She shrugged the topic away. 'Was Guinevere clever?' she asked.

'Very,' I said.

Igraine played with the cross she wore about her neck. 'Tell me about Lancelot.'

'Wait!'

'When does Merlin come?'

'Soon.'

'Is Saint Sansum being horrid to you?'

'The saint has the fate of our immortal souls on his conscience. He does what he must do.'

'But did he really fall to his knees and scream for martyrdom before he married Arthur to Guinevere?'

'Yes,' I said and could not help smiling at the memory.

Igraine laughed. 'I shall ask Brochvael to make the Mouse Lord into a real martyr,' she said, 'then you can be in charge of Dinnewrac. Would you like that, Brother Derfel?'

'I would like some peace to carry on with my tale,' I chided her.

'So what happens next?' Igraine asked eagerly.

Armorica is next. The Land across the Sea. Beautiful Ynys

Trebes, King Ban, Lancelot, Galahad and Merlin. Dear Lord, what men they were, what days we had, what fights we gave and dreams we broke. In Armorica.

Later, much later, when we looked back on those times we simply called them the 'bad years', but we rarely discussed them. Arthur hated to be reminded of those early days in Dumnonia when his passion for Guinevere tore the land into chaos. His betrothal to Ceinwyn had been like an elaborate brooch that held together a fragile gown of gossamer, and when the brooch went the garment fell into shreds. Arthur blamed himself and did not like to talk about the bad years.

Tewdric, for a time, refused to fight on either side. He blamed Arthur for the broken peace and in retribution he allowed Gorfyddyd and Gundleus to lead their war-bands through Gwent into Dumnonia. The Saxons pressed from the east, the Irish raided out of the Western Sea and, as if those enemies were not enough, Prince Cadwy of Isca rebelled against Arthur's rule. Tewdric tried to stay aloof from it all, but when Aelle's Saxons savaged Tewdric's frontier the only friends he could call on for help were Dumnonians and so, in the end, he was forced into the war on Arthur's side, but by then the spearmen of Powys and Siluria had used his roads to capture the hills north of Ynys Wydryn and when Tewdric declared for Dumnonia they occupied Glevum as well.

I grew up in those years. I lost count of the men I killed and the warrior rings I forged. I received a nickname, Cadarn, which means 'the mighty'. Derfel Cadarn, sober in battle and with a dreadful quick sword. At one time Arthur invited me to become one of his horsemen, but I preferred to stay on firm ground and so remained a spearman. I watched Arthur during that time and began to appreciate just why he was such a great soldier. It was not merely his bravery, though he was brave, but how he outfoxed his enemies. Our armies were clumsy instruments, slow to march and sluggish to change direction once they were marching, but Arthur forged a small force of men who learned to travel quickly. He led those men, some on foot, some in the saddle, on long marches that looped about the enemies' flanks so they always appeared where they were least expected. We liked to attack at dawn, when the enemy was still fuddled from a night's drinking, or else we lured them on with false retreats and then slashed into their unprotected flanks. After a year of such battles, when we had at last driven the forces of Gorfyddyd and Gundleus out of Glevum and northern Dumnonia, Arthur made me a captain and I began handing my own followers gold. Two years later I even received the ultimate accolade of a warrior, an invitation to defect to the enemy. Of all people it came from Ligessac, Norwenna's traitorous guard commander, who spoke to me in a temple of Mithras, where his life was protected, and offered me a fortune if I would serve Gundleus as he did. I refused. God be thanked, but I was always loyal to Arthur.

Sagramor was also loyal, and it was he who initiated me into Mithras's service. Mithras was a God the Romans had brought to Britain and He must have liked our climate for He still has power. He is a soldiers' God and no women can be initiated into His mysteries. My initiation took place in late winter, when soldiers have time to spare. It happened in the hills. Sagramor took me alone into a valley so deep that even by late afternoon the morning frost still crisped the grass. We stopped by a cave entrance where Sagramor instructed me to lay my weapons aside and strip naked. I stood there shivering as the Numidian tied a thick cloth about my eyes and told me I must now obey every instruction and that if I flinched or spoke once, just once, I would be brought back to my clothes and weapons and sent away.

The initiation is an assault on a man's senses, and to survive he must remember one thing only: to obey. That is why soldiers like Mithras. Battle assaults the senses, and that assault ferments fear, and obedience is the narrow thread that leads out of fear's chaos into survival. In time I initiated many men into Mithras and came to know the tricks well enough, but that first time, as I stepped into the cave, I had no idea what would be inflicted on me. When I first entered the God's cave

Sagramor, or perhaps some other man, turned me about and about, sunwise, so quickly and so violently that my mind reeled into dizziness and then I was ordered to walk forward. Smoke choked me, but I kept going, following the downwards slope of the rock floor. A voice shouted at me to stop, another ordered me to turn, a third to kneel. Some substance was thrust at my mouth and I recoiled from the stench of human dung that made my head reel. 'Eat!' a voice snapped and I almost spewed the mouthful out until I realized I merely chewed on dried fish. I drank some vile liquid that made me light-headed. It was probably thorn-apple juice mixed with mandrake or fly-agaric for though my eyes were tight covered I saw visions of bright creatures coming with crinkled wings to snap at my flesh with beaked mouths. Flames touched my skin, burning the small hairs on my legs and arms. I was ordered to walk forward again, then to stop and I heard logs being heaped on a fire and felt the vast heat grow in front of me. The fire roared, the flames roasted my bare skin and manhood, and then the voice commanded me to step forward into the fire and I obeyed, only to have my foot sink into a pool of icy water that almost made me cry aloud from fear that I had stepped into a vat of molten metal.

A sword point was held to my manhood, pressed there, and I was ordered to step into it, and as I did the sword point went away. All tricks, of course, but the herbs and fungi put into the drink were enough to magnify the tricks into miracles and by the time I had followed the tortuous course down to the hot, smoky and echoing chamber at the heart of the ceremony I was already in a trance of terror and exaltation. I was taken to a stone the height of a table and a knife was put into my right hand, while my left was placed palm downwards on a naked belly. 'It's a child under your hand, you miserable toad,' the voice said, and a hand moved my right hand until the blade was poised over the child's throat, 'an innocent child that has harmed no one,' the voice said, 'a child that deserves nothing but life, and you will kill it. Strike!' The child cried aloud as I plunged the knife downwards to feel the warm blood spurt over my wrist and hand. The heart-pulsing belly beneath my left hand gave a last spasm and was still. A fire roared nearby, the smoke choking my nostrils.

I was made to kneel and drink a warm, sickly fluid that clogged in my throat and soured my stomach. Only then, when that horn of bull's blood was drained, was my blindfold taken away and I saw I had killed an early lamb with a shaven belly. Friends and enemies clustered about me, full of congratulations for I had now entered the service of the soldiers' God. I had become part of a secret society that stretched clear across the Roman world and even beyond its edges; a society of men who had proved themselves in battle, not as mere soldiers, but as true warriors. To become a Mithraist was a real honour, for any member of the cult could forbid another man's initiation. Some men led armies and were never selected, others never rose above the ranks and were honoured members.

Now, one of that elect, my clothes and weapons were brought to me, I dressed, and then was given the secret words of the cult that would allow me to identify my comrades in battle. If I found I was fighting a fellow Mithraist I was enjoined to kill him swiftly, with mercy, and if such a man became my prisoner I was to do him honour. Then, the formalities over, we went into a second huge cave lit by smoking torches and by a great fire where a bull's carcass was being roasted. I was done high honour by the rank of the men who attended that feast. Most initiates must be content with their own comrades, but for Derfel Cadarn the mighty of both sides had come to the winter cave. Agricola of Gwent was there, and with him were two of his enemies from Siluria, Ligessac and a spearman called Nasiens who was Gundleus's champion. A dozen of Arthur's warriors were present, some of my own men and even Bishop Bedwin, Arthur's counsellor, who looked unfamiliar in a rusty breastplate, sword belt and warrior's cloak. 'I was a warrior once,' he explained his presence, 'and was initiated, oh, when? Thirty years ago? That was long before I became a Christian, of course.'

'And this' – I waved about the cave where the bull's severed head had been hoisted on a tripod of spears to drip blood on to the cave's floor – 'is not contrary to your religion?'

Bedwin shrugged. 'Of course it is,' he said, 'but I would miss the companionship.' He leaned towards me and lowered his voice to a conspiratorial whisper. 'I trust you will not tell Bishop Sansum that I am here?' I laughed at the thought of ever confiding in the angry Sansum who buzzed about war-shrunken Dumnonia like a worker-bee. He was forever condemning his enemies and he had no friends. 'Young Master Sansum,' Bedwin said, his mouth full of beef and his beard dripping with the meat's bloody juice, 'wants to replace me, and I think he will.'

'He will?' I sounded aghast.

'Because he wants it so badly,' Bedwin said, 'and he works so hard. Dear God, how that man works! Do you know what I discovered just the other day? He can't read! Not a word! Now, to be a senior churchman a fellow must be able to read, so what does Sansum do? He has a slave read aloud to him and learns it all by heart.' Bedwin nudged me to make certain I understood Sansum's extraordinary memory. 'Learns it all by heart! Psalms, prayers, liturgy, writings of the fathers, all by heart! Dear me.' He shook his head. 'You're not a Christian, are you?'

'No.'

'You should consider it. We may not offer too many earthly delights, but our lives after death are certainly worth having. Not that I could ever persuade Uther of that, but I have hopes of Arthur.'

I glanced round the feast. 'No Arthur,' I said, disappointed that my Lord was not of the cult.

'He was initiated,' Bedwin said.

'But he doesn't believe in the Gods,' I said, repeating Owain's assertion.

Bedwin shook his head. 'Arthur does believe. How can a man not believe in God or Gods? You think Arthur believes that we made ourselves? Or that the world simply appeared by chance? Arthur's no fool, Derfel Cadarn. Arthur believes, but he keeps his beliefs very silent. That way the Christians think he is one of them, or might be, and the pagans believe the same, and so both serve him the more willingly. And remember, Derfel, Arthur is loved of Merlin, and Merlin, believe me, does not love unbelievers.'

'I miss Merlin.'

'We all miss Merlin,' Bedwin said calmly, 'but we can take comfort in his absence, for he would not be otherwise if Britain was threatened with destruction. Merlin will come when he is needed.'

'You think he isn't needed now?' I asked sourly.

Bedwin wiped his beard with the sleeve of his coat, then drank wine. 'Some say,' he said, dropping his voice, 'that we would be better off without Arthur. That without Arthur there would be peace, but if there's no Arthur, who protects Mordred? Me?' He smiled at the thought. 'Gereint? He's a good man, few better, but he's not clever and he can't make up his mind and he doesn't want to rule Dumnonia either. It's Arthur or no one, Derfel. Or rather it's Arthur or Gorfyddyd. And this war is not lost. Our enemies fear Arthur and so long as he lives, Dumnonia is safe. No, I don't think Merlin is needed yet.'

The traitor Ligessac, who was another Christian who saw no conflict between his avowed faith and Mithras's secret rituals, spoke with me at the feast's end. I was cold towards him, even though he was a fellow Mithraist, but he ignored my hostility and plucked me by the elbow into a dark corner of the cave. 'Arthur's going to lose. You know that, don't you?' he said.

'No.'

Ligessac pulled a shred of meat from between the remains of his teeth. 'More men from Elmet will come into the war,' he said. 'Powys, Elmet and Siluria' – he ticked the names off on his fingers – 'united against Gwent and Dumnonia. Gorfyddyd will be the next Pendragon. First we drive the Saxons out of the land east of Ratae, then we come south and finish off Dumnonia. Two years?'

'The feast has gone to your head, Ligessac,' I told him.

'And my Lord will pay for the services of a man like you.'

Ligessac was delivering a message. 'My Lord King Gundleus is generous, Derfel, very generous.'

'Tell your Lord King,' I said, 'that Nimue of Ynys Wydryn shall have his skull for her drinking vessel, and that I will provide it for her.' I walked away.

That spring the war flared again, though less destructively at first. Arthur had paid gold to Oengus Mac Airem, the Irish King of Demetia, to attack the western reaches of Powys and Siluria, and those attacks drained enemies from our northern frontiers. Arthur himself led a war-band to pacify western Dumnonia where Cadwy had declared his tribal lands an independent kingdom, but while he was there Aelle's Saxons launched a mighty attack on Gereint's lands. Gorfyddyd, we later learned, had paid the Saxons as we had paid the Irish and Powys's cash was probably better spent for the Saxons came in a flood that brought Arthur hurrying back from the west where he left Cei, his childhood companion, in charge of the fight against Cadwy's tattooed tribesmen.

It was then, with Aelle's Saxon army threatening to capture Durocobrivis and with Gwent's forces occupied against both Powys and the northern Saxons and with Cadwy's undefeated rebellion being encouraged by King Mark of Kernow, that Ban of Benoic sent his summons.

We all knew that King Ban had only ever permitted Arthur to come to Dumnonia on condition that he returned to Armorica if Benoic was ever in jeopardy. Now, Ban's messenger claimed, Benoic was in dire danger and King Ban, insisting that Arthur fulfil his oath, was demanding Arthur's return.

The news came to us in Durocobrivis. The town had once been a prosperous Roman settlement with lavish baths, a marble justice hall and a fine market place, but now it was an impoverished frontier fort, forever watching east towards the Saxons. The buildings beyond the town's earth wall had all been burnt by Aelle's raiders and were never rebuilt, while inside the wall the great Roman structures crumbled to ruin. Ban's messenger came to us in what remained of the arched hall of the Roman baths. It was night and a fire burned in the pit of the old plunge bath, its smoke churning about the arched ceiling where the wind caught and sucked the smoke out of a small window. We had been eating our evening meal, seated in a circle on the cold floor, and Arthur led Ban's messenger into the circle's centre where he scratched a crude map of Dumnonia in the dirt, then scattered red and white mosaic scraps to show where our enemies and friends were placed. Everywhere the red tiles of Dumnonia were being squeezed by the white stone scraps. We had fought that day and Arthur had taken a spear cut on his right cheekbone, not a dangerous wound, but deep enough to crust his cheek in blood. He had been fighting without his helmet, claiming he saw better without the enclosing metal, but if the Saxon had thrust an inch higher and to one side he would have rammed his steel through Arthur's brain. He had fought on foot, as he usually did, because he was saving his heavy horses for the more desperate battles. A half dozen of his horsemen were mounted each day, but most of the expensive, rare war horses were kept deep in Dumnonia where they were safe from enemy raids. This day, after Arthur had been wounded, our handful of heavy cavalrymen had scattered the Saxon line, killing their chief and sending the survivors back east, but Arthur's narrow escape had left us all uneasy. King Ban's messenger, a chief called Bleiddig, only deepened that gloom.

'You see,' Arthur said to Bleiddig, 'why I cannot leave?' He gestured at the red and white scraps.

'An oath is an oath,' Bleiddig answered bluntly.

'If the Prince leaves Dumnonia,' Prince Gereint intervened, 'Dumnonia falls.' Gereint was a heavy, dull-witted man, but loyal and honest. As Uther's nephew he had a claim on Dumnonia's throne, but he never made the claim and was always true to Arthur, his bastard cousin.

'Better that Dumnonia fall than Benoic,' Bleiddig said, and ignored the angry murmur that followed his words.

'I took an oath to defend Mordred,' Arthur pointed out.

'You took an oath to defend Benoic,' Bleiddig answered,

shrugging away Arthur's objection. 'Bring the child with you.'

'I must give Mordred his kingdom,' Arthur insisted. 'If he leaves the kingdom loses its king and its heart. Mordred stays here.'

'And who threatens to take the kingdom from him?' Bleiddig demanded angrily. The Benoic chieftain was a big man, not unlike Owain and with much of Owain's brute force. 'You!' He pointed scornfully at Arthur. 'If you had married Ceinwyn there would be no war! If you had married Ceinwyn then not only Dumnonia, but Gwent and Powys would be sending troops to aid my King!'

Men were shouting and swords were drawn, but Arthur bellowed for silence. A trickle of blood escaped from beneath his wound's scab and ran down his long, hollow cheek. 'How long,' he asked Bleiddig, 'before Benoic falls?'

Bleiddig frowned. It was clear he could not guess the answer, but he suggested six months or maybe a year. The Franks, he said, had brought new armies into the east of his country and Ban could not fight them all. Ban's own army, led by his champion, Bors, was holding the northern border while the men Arthur had left behind, led by his cousin Culhwch, held the southern frontier.

Arthur was staring at his map of red and white tiles. 'Three months,' he said, 'and I will come. If I can! Three months. But in the meanwhile, Bleiddig, I shall send you a war-band of good men.'

Bleiddig argued, protesting that Arthur's oath demanded Arthur's immediate presence in Armorica, but Arthur would not be budged. Three months, he said, or not at all, and Bleiddig had to accept the compromise.

Arthur gestured for me to walk with him in the colonnaded courtyard that lay next to the hall. There were vats in the small courtyard that stank like a latrine, but he appeared not to notice the stench. 'God knows, Derfel,' he said, and I knew he was under strain for using the word 'God', just as I noticed he used the singular Christian word though he immediately balanced the score, 'the Gods know I don't want to lose you, but I need to send someone who isn't afraid to break a shield-wall. I need to send you.'

'Lord Prince –' I began.

'Don't call me prince,' he interrupted angrily. 'I'm not a prince. And don't argue with me. I have everyone arguing with me. Everyone knows how to win this war except me. Melwas is screaming for men, Tewdric wants me in the north, Cei says he needs another hundred spears, and now Ban wants me! If he spent more money on his army and less on his poets he wouldn't be in trouble!'

'Poets?'

'Ynys Trebes is a haven of poets,' he said bitterly, referring to King Ban's island capital. 'Poets! We need spearmen, not poets.' He stopped and leaned against a pillar. He looked more tired than I had ever seen him. 'I can't achieve anything,' he said, 'until we stop fighting. If I could just talk to Cuneglas, face to face, there might be hope.'

'Not while Gorfyddyd lives,' I said.

'Not while Gorfyddyd lives,' he agreed, then went silent and I knew he was thinking of Ceinwyn and Guinevere. Moonlight came through a gap in the colonnade's roof to touch his bony face with silver. He closed his eyes and I knew he was blaming himself for the war, but what was done could not be undone. A new peace would have to be made and there was only one man who could force that peace on Britain, and that was Arthur himself. He opened his eyes and grimaced. 'What's the smell?' he asked, noticing it at last.

'They bleach cloth here, Lord,' I explained, and gestured toward the wooden vats that were filled with urine and washed chicken dung to produce the valuable white fabric like the cloaks Arthur himself favoured.

Arthur would usually have been encouraged at such evidence of industry in a decayed town like Durocobrivis, but that night he just shrugged away the smell and touched the trickle of fresh blood on his cheek. 'One more scar,' he said ruefully. 'I'll soon have as many as you, Derfel.'

'You should wear your helmet, Lord,' I said.

'I can't see right and left when I do,' he said dismissively. He pushed away from the pillar and gestured for me to walk with him round the arcade. 'Now listen, Derfel. Fighting Franks is just like fighting Saxons. They're all Germans, and there's nothing special about the Franks except that they like to carry throwing spears as well as the usual weapons. So keep your head down when they first attack, but after that it's just shield-wall against shield-wall. They're hard fighters, but they drink too much so you can usually out-think them. That's why I'm sending you. You're young, but you can think which is more than most of our soldiers do. They just believe it's enough to get drunk and hack away, but no one will win wars that way.' He paused and tried to hide a yawn. 'Forgive me. And for all I know, Derfel, Benoic isn't in danger at all. Ban is an emotional man' – he used the description sourly – 'and he panics easily, but if he loses Ynys Trebes then he'll break his heart and I'll have to live with that guilt too. You can trust Culhwch, he's good. Bors is capable.'

'But treacherous.' Sagramor spoke from the shadows beside the bleaching vats. He had come from the hall to watch over Arthur.

'Unfair,' said Arthur.

'He's treacherous,' Sagramor insisted in his harsh accent, 'because he's Lancelot's man.'

Arthur shrugged. 'Lancelot can be difficult,' he admitted. 'He's Ban's heir and he likes to have things his own way, but then, so do I.' He smiled and glanced at me. 'You can write, can't you?'

'Yes, Lord,' I said. We had walked on past Sagramor who stayed in the shadows, his eyes never leaving Arthur. Cats slunk past us, and bats wheeled next to the smoking gable of the big hall. I tried to imagine this stinking place filled with robed Romans and lit by oil-lamps, but it seemed an impossible idea.

'You must write and tell me what's happening,' Arthur said, 'so I don't have to rely on Ban's imagination. How's your woman?'

'My woman?' I was startled by the question and for a second I thought Arthur was referring to Canna, a Saxon slave girl who kept me company and who was teaching me her dialect that differed slightly from my mother's native Saxon, but then I realized Arthur had to mean Lunete. 'I don't hear from her, Lord.'

'And you don't ask, eh?' He shot me an amused grin, then sighed. Lunete was with Guinevere who, in turn, had gone to distant Durnovaria to occupy Uther's old winter palace. Guinevere had not wanted to leave her pretty new palace near Caer Cadarn, but Arthur had insisted she go deeper into the country to be safer from enemy raiding parties. 'Sansum tells me Guinevere and her ladies all worship Isis,' Arthur said.

'Who?' I asked.

'Exactly.' He smiled. 'Isis is a foreign Goddess, Derfel, with her own mysteries; something to do with the moon, I think. At least that's what Sansum tells me. I don't think he knows either, but he still says I must stop the cult. He says the mysteries of Isis are unspeakable, but when I ask him what they are, he doesn't know. Or he won't say. You've heard nothing?'

'Nothing, Lord.'

'Of course,' Arthur said rather too forcefully, 'if Guinevere finds solace in Isis then it cannot be bad. I worry about her. I promised her so much, you see, and am giving her nothing. I want to put her father back on his throne, and we will, we will, but it will all take longer than we think.'

'You want to fight Diwrnach?' I asked, appalled at the idea.

'He's just a man, Derfel, and can be killed. One day we'll do it.' He turned back towards the hall. 'You're going south. I can't spare you more than sixty men – God knows it isn't enough if Ban really is in trouble – but take them over the sea, Derfel, and put yourself under Culhwch's command. Maybe you can travel through Durnovaria? Send me news of my dear Guinevere?'

'Yes, Lord,' I said.

'I shall give you a gift for her. Maybe that jewelled collar the Saxon leader was wearing? You think she'd like that?' He asked the question anxiously.

'Any woman would,' I said. The collar was Saxon work, crude and heavy, but still beautiful. It was a necklace of golden plates that were splayed like the sun's rays and studded with gems.

'Good! Take it to Durnovaria for me, Derfel, then go and save Benoic.'

'If I can,' I said grimly.

'If you can,' Arthur echoed, 'for my conscience's sake.' He added the last words quietly, then kicked a scrap of clay tile that skittered away from his booted foot and startled a cat that arched its back and hissed at us. 'Three years ago,' he said softly, 'it all seemed so easy.'

But then came Guinevere.

Next day, with sixty men, I went south.

'Did he send you to spy on me?' Guinevere demanded with a smile.

'No, Lady.'

'Dear Derfel,' she mocked me, 'so like my husband.'

That surprised me. 'Am I?'

'Yes, Derfel, you are. Only he's much cleverer. Do you like this place?' She gestured about the courtyard.

'It's beautiful,' I said. The villa in Durnovaria was, of course, Roman, though in its day it had served as Uther's winter palace. God knows it would not have been beautiful when he occupied it, but Guinevere had restored the building to something of its former elegance. The courtyard was colonnaded like the one in Durocobrivis, but here all the roof tiles were in place and all the columns were lime-washed. Guinevere's symbol was painted on the walls inside the arcade in a repeating pattern of stags crowned with crescent moons. The stag was her father's symbol, the moon her addition, and the painted roundels made a pretty show. White roses grew in beds where small tiled channels ran with water. Two hunting falcons stood on perches, their hooded heads twitching as we walked around the Roman arcade. Statues stood about the courtyard, all of naked men and women, while on plinths beneath the colonnade were bronze heads festooned with flowers. The heavy Saxon necklace I had brought from Arthur now hung about the neck of one of those bronze heads. Guinevere had toyed with the gift for a few seconds, then frowned. 'It's clumsy work, is it not?' she had asked me.

'Prince Arthur thinks it beautiful, Lady, and worthy of you.'

'Dear Arthur.' She had said it carelessly, then selected the ugly bronze head of a scowling man and placed the necklace around its neck. 'That'll improve him,' she said of the bronze head. 'I call him Gorfyddyd. He looks like Gorfyddyd, don't you think so?'

'He does, Lady,' I said. The bust did have something of Gorfyddyd's dour, unhappy face.

'Gorfyddyd is a beast,' Guinevere said. 'He tried to take my virginity.'

'He did?' I managed to say when I had recovered from the shock of the revelation.

'Tried and failed,' she said firmly. 'He was drunk. He slobbered all over me. I was reeking with slobber, all down here.' She brushed her breasts. She was wearing a simple white linen shift that fell in straight folds from her shoulders to her feet. The linen must have been breathtakingly expensive for the fabric was so tantalizingly thin that if I stared at her, which I tried not to do, it was possible to see hints of her nakedness beneath the fine cloth. A golden image of the moon-crowned stag hung around her neck, her earrings were amber drops set in gold while on her left hand was a gold ring crowned with Arthur's bear and cut with a lover's cross. 'Slobber, slobber,' she said delightedly, 'so when he'd finished, or to be exact when he'd finished trying to begin and was sobbing about how he meant to make me his Queen and how he would make me the richest queen in Britain, I went to Iorweth and had him make me a spell against an unwanted lover. I didn't tell the Druid it was the King, of course, though it probably wouldn't have mattered if I had because Iorweth would do anything if you smiled at him, so he made the charm and I buried it, then I made my father tell Gorfyddyd that I'd buried a death-charm against the daughter of a man who'd tried to rape me. Gorfyddyd knew who I meant and he dotes on that insipid little Ceinwyn, so he avoided me after that.' She laughed. 'Men are such fools!'

'Not Prince Arthur,' I said firmly, being careful to use the title on which Guinevere insisted.

'He is a fool about jewellery,' she had said tartly, and then had asked me if Arthur had sent me to spy on her.

We walked on around the colonnade. We were alone. A warrior named Lanval was the commander of the Princess's guard and he had wanted to leave his men inside the courtyard, but Guinevere insisted they leave. 'Let them start a rumour about us,' she told me happily, but then had scowled. 'I sometimes think Lanval is ordered to spy on me.'

'Lanval merely watches over you, Lady,' I told her, 'for upon your safety depends Prince Arthur's happiness, and upon his happiness rests a kingdom.'

'That is pretty, Derfel. I like that.' She spoke half mockingly. We walked on. A bowl of rose petals soaking in water wafted a pretty scent under the colonnade that offered welcome shade from the hot sun. 'Do you want to see Lunete?' Guinevere suddenly asked me.

'I doubt she wants to see me.'

'Probably not. But you're not married, are you?'

'No, Lady, we never married.'

'Then it doesn't matter, does it?' she asked, though what did not matter she did not say and I did not ask. 'I wanted to see you, Derfel,' Guinevere said earnestly.

'You flatter me, Lady,' I said.

'Your words get prettier and prettier!' She clapped her hands, then wrinkled her nose. 'Tell me, Derfel, do you ever wash?'

I blushed. 'Yes, Lady.'

'You stink of leather and blood and sweat and dust. It can be quite a nice aroma, but not today. It's too hot. Would you like my ladies to give you a bath? We do it the Roman way, with lots of sweat and scraping. It's quite tiring.'

I deliberately moved a step away from her. 'I'll find a stream, Lady.'

'But I did want to see you,' she said. She stepped back next to me and even put her arm into mine. 'Tell me about Nimue.'

'Nimue?' I was surprised by the question.

'Can she really do magic?' Guinevere asked eagerly. The Princess was as tall as I was and her face, so handsome and high-boned, was close to mine. Proximity to Guinevere was overpowering, like the heavy disturbance of the senses given by the drink of Mithras. Her red hair was scented with perfume and her startling green eyes were lined with a gum that had been mixed with lamp black so that they seemed larger. 'Can she do magic?' Guinevere asked again.

'I think so.'

'Think!' She stepped away from me, disappointed. 'Only think?'

The scar on my left hand throbbed and I did not know what to say.

Guinevere laughed. 'Tell me the truth, Derfel. I need to know!' She put her arm back into mine and walked me on beneath the arcade's shade. 'That horrible man Bishop Sansum is trying to make us all Christians and I won't put up with it! He wants us to feel guilty all the time and I keep telling him I've nothing to be guilty about, but the Christians are getting more powerful. They're building a new church here! No, they're doing worse than that. Come!' She turned impulsively and clapped her hands. Slaves ran into the courtyard and Guinevere ordered her cloak and dogs brought to her. 'I'll show you something, Derfel, so you can see for yourself what that wretched little Bishop is doing to our kingdom.'

She donned a mauve woollen cloak to hide the thin linen shift, then took the leashes of a brace of deerhounds that panted beside her with their long tongues lolling between sharp teeth. The villa's gates were thrown open and with two slaves following and a quartet of Lanval's guards hastily forming post on either side of us, we went down Durnovaria's main street which was handsomely paved with wide stones and

237

guttered to take the rain down to the river that ran to the east of the town. The open-fronted shops were full of goods: shoes, a butchery, salt, a potter. Some houses had collapsed, but most were in good repair, perhaps because the presence of Mordred and Guinevere had brought the town a new prosperity. There were beggars, of course, who shuffled close on stumps, risking the guards' spear-staves in order to grab the copper coins distributed by Guinevere's two slaves. Guinevere herself, her red hair bared to the sun, strode down the hill with barely a glance at the commotion her presence caused. 'See that house?' Guinevere gestured towards a handsome two-storey building on the northern side of the street. 'That's where Nabur lives, and where our little King farts and vomits.' She shuddered. 'Mordred is a particularly unpleasant child. He limps and he never stops screaming. There! Can you hear him?' I could indeed hear a child wailing, though whether it was Mordred I could not tell. 'Now, come through here,' Guinevere commanded and she plunged through a small crowd who stared at her from the side of the street then climbed over a pile of broken stone that stood next to Nabur's handsome house.

I followed her to find that we had reached a building site, or rather a place where one building was being torn down and another erected on its ruins. The building that was being destroyed had been a Roman temple. 'It was where people worshipped Mercury,' Guinevere said, 'but now we're to have a shrine for a dead carpenter instead. And how will a dead carpenter give us good crops, tell me that!' These last words, ostensibly spoken to me, were said loud enough to disturb the dozen Christians who were labouring at their new church. Some were laying stones, some adzing doorposts, while others were pulling down the old walls to provide the material for the new building. 'If you must have a hovel for your carpenter,' Guinevere said in a ringing voice, 'why not just take over the old building? I asked Sansum that, but he says it must all be new so that his precious Christians don't have to breathe air once used by pagans, in which nonsensical belief we pull down the old, which was exquisite, and throw up a nasty building full of ill-dressed stone and without any grace at all!' She spat into the dust to ward off evil. 'He says it's a chapel for Mordred! Can you believe it? He's determined to make the wretched child into a whining Christian and this abomination is where he'll do it.'

'Dear Lady!' Bishop Sansum appeared from behind one of the new walls which were indeed ill-dressed compared with the careful masonry of the old temple's remains. Sansum was in a black gown which, like his stiffly tonsured hair, was whitened with stone dust. 'You do us a striking honour by your gracious presence, Lady,' he said as he bowed to Guinevere.

'I'm not doing you honour, you worm. I came to show Derfel what carnage you're making. How can you worship in that?' She threw a hand towards the half-built church. 'You might as well take over a cow shed!'

'Our dear Lord was born in a cattle shed, Lady, so I rejoice that our humble church reminds you of one.' He bowed again to her. Some of his workers had gathered at the far end of their new building where they began to sing one of their holy songs to ward off the baleful presence of pagans.

'It certainly sounds like a cow shed,' Guinevere said tartly, then pushed past the priest and strode over the masonry-littered ground to where a wooden hut leaned against the stone-and-brick wall of Nabur's house. She released her hounds' leashes to let them run free. 'Where's that statue, Sansum?' She threw the question over her shoulder as she kicked the hut door open.

'Alas, gracious Lady, though I tried to save it for you, our blessed Lord commanded that it be melted down. For the poor, you understand?'

She turned on the Bishop savagely. 'Bronze! What use is bronze to the poor? Do they eat it?' She looked at me. 'A statue of Mercury, Derfel, the height of a tall man and beautifully worked. Beautiful! Roman work, not British, but now it's gone, melted in a Christian furnace because you people' – she was staring at Sansum again with loathing on her strong face – 'cannot stand beauty. You're frightened of it. You're like grubs pulling down a tree, and you have no idea what you do.' She ducked into the hut, which was evidently where Sansum stored the valuable objects he discovered in the temple remains. She emerged with a small stone statuette that she tossed to one of her guards. 'It isn't much,' she said, 'but at least it's safe from a carpenter-grub born in a cow shed.'

Sansum, still smiling despite all the insults, enquired of me how the fighting in the north went. 'We win slowly,' I said.

'Tell my Lord the Prince Arthur that I pray for him.'

'Pray for his enemies, you toad,' Guinevere said, 'and maybe we'd win more quickly.' She stared at her two dogs that were pissing against the new church walls. 'Cadwy raided this way last month,' she told me, 'and came close.'

'Praise God we were spared,' Bishop Sansum added piously.

'No thanks to you, you pitiful worm,' Guinevere said. 'The Christians ran away. Plucked up their skirts and scampered east. The rest of us stayed, and Lanval, the Gods be thanked, saw Cadwy off.' She spat towards the new church. 'In time,' she said, 'we'll be free of enemies, and when that happens, Derfel, I shall pull down that cattle shed and build a temple fit for a real God.'

'For Isis?' Sansum enquired slyly.

'Careful,' Guinevere warned him, 'for my Goddess rules the night, toad, and she might snatch your soul for her amusement. Though the Gods alone know what use your miserable soul would be to anyone. Come, Derfel.'

The two deerhounds were collected and we strode back up the hill. Guinevere shook with anger. 'You see what he's doing? Pulling down the old! Why? So he can impose his tawdry little superstitions on us. Why can't he leave the old alone? We don't care if fools want to worship a carpenter, so why does he care who we worship? The more Gods the better, I say. Why offend some Gods to exalt your own? It doesn't make sense.'

'Who is Isis?' I asked her as we turned into the gate of her villa.

She shot me an amused look. 'Is that my dear husband's question I hear?'

'Yes,' I said.

She laughed. 'Well done, Derfel. The truth is always astonishing. So Arthur is worried by my Goddess?'

'He's worried,' I said, 'because Sansum worries him with tales of mysteries.'

She shrugged off the cloak, letting it fall on the courtyard tiles to be picked up by a slave. 'Tell Arthur,' she said, 'that he has nothing to worry about. Does he doubt my affection?'

'He adores you,' I said tactfully.

'And I him.' She smiled at me. 'Tell him that, Derfel,' she added warmly.

'I shall, Lady.'

'And tell him he has nothing to worry about with Isis.' She reached impulsively for my hand. 'Come,' she said, just as she had when she had led me down to the new Christian shrine, but this time she hurried me across the courtyard, jumping the small water channels, to a small door set into the far arcade. 'This,' she said, letting go of my hand and pushing the door open, 'is the shrine of Isis that so worries my dear Lord.'

I hesitated. 'Are men allowed to enter?'

'By day, yes. By night? No.' She ducked through the door and pulled aside a thick woollen curtain that was hung immediately inside. I followed, pushing through the curtain to find myself in a black, lightless room. 'Stay where you are,' she warned me, and at first I thought that I was obeying some rule of Isis, but as my eyes grew accustomed to the thick gloom, I saw that she had made me stop so I did not stumble into a pool of water that was set into the floor. The only light in the shrine came around the edges of the curtain at the door, but as I waited I became aware of a grey light seeping into the room's far end; then I saw that Guinevere was pulling down layer after layer of black wall hangings, each one supported on a pole carried by brackets and each woven so thick that no light could come through the layered cloths. Behind the hangings, that now lay crumpled on the floor, were shutters that Guinevere threw open to let in a dazzling flood of light.

'There,' she said, standing to one side of the big, arched window, 'the mysteries!' She was mocking Sansum's fears, yet in truth the room was truly mysterious for it was entirely black. The floor was of black stone, the walls and arched ceiling were painted with pitch. In the black floor's centre was the shallow pool of black water and behind it, between the pool and the newly opened window, was a low black throne made of stone.

'So what do you think, Derfel?' Guinevere asked me.

'I see no Goddess,' I said, looking for a statue of Isis.

'She comes with the moon,' Guinevere said, and I tried to imagine the full moon flooding through that window to gloss the pool and shimmer on the deep black walls. 'Tell me about Nimue,' Guinevere ordered, 'and I will tell you about Isis.'

'Nimue is Merlin's priestess,' I said, my voice echoing hollow from the black painted stone, 'and she's learning his secrets.'

'What secrets?'

'The secrets of the old Gods, Lady.'

She frowned. 'But how does he find such secrets? I thought the old Druids wrote nothing down. They were forbidden to write, were they not?'

'They were, Lady, but Merlin searches for their knowledge anyway.'

Guinevere nodded. 'I knew we'd lost some knowledge. And Merlin's going to find it? Good! That might settle that bitter toad Sansum.' She had walked to the centre of the window and was now staring across the tiled and thatched roofs of Durno-varia and over the southern ramparts and the mounded grass of the amphitheatre beyond, towards the vast earth walls of Mai Dun that reared on the horizon. White clouds heaped in the blue sky, but what made the breath catch in my throat was that the sunlight was now flooding through Guinevere's white linen shift so that my Lord's Lady, this Princess of Henis Wyren, might just as well have been naked and, for those moments, as the blood pounded in my ears, I was jealous of my Lord. Was Guinevere aware of that sun's treachery? I thought not, but I might have been wrong. She had her back to me, but suddenly half turned so she could look at me. 'Is Lunete a magician?'

'No, Lady,' I said.

'But she learned with Nimue, did she not?'

'No,' I said. 'She was never allowed in Merlin's rooms. She had no interest.'

'But you were in Merlin's rooms?'

'Only twice,' I said. I could see her breasts and I deliberately dropped my gaze to the black pool, but that only mirrored her beauty and added a sultry sheen of dark mystery to her long, lithe body. A heavy silence fell and I realized, thinking about our last exchange, that Lunete must have claimed some knowledge of Merlin's magic and that I had undoubtedly just spoiled that claim. 'Maybe,' I said feebly, 'Lunete knows more than she ever told me?'

Guinevere shrugged and turned away. I raised my eyes again. 'But Nimue, you say, is more skilled than Lunete?' she asked me.

'Infinitely, Lady.'

'I have twice demanded that Nimue come to me,' Guinevere said sharply, 'and twice she has refused. How do I make her come to me?'

'The best way,' I said, 'of making Nimue do anything is to forbid her to do it.'

There was silence in the room again. The sounds of the town were loud enough; the cry of hawkers in the market, the clatter of cart wheels on stone, dogs barking, a rattle of pots in a nearby kitchen, but in the room it was silent. 'One day,' Guinevere broke our silence, 'I shall build a temple to Isis up there.' She pointed to the ramparts of Mai Dun that filled the southern sky. 'Is it a sacred place?'

'Very.'

'Good.' She turned towards me again, the sun filling her red hair and glowing on her smooth skin beneath the white shift. 'I do not want to play childish games, Derfel, by trying to out-guess Nimue. I want her here. I need a priestess of power. I need a friend of the old Gods if I am to fight that grub Sansum. I need Nimue, Derfel, so for the love you have for Arthur, tell me what message will bring her here. Tell me that and I will tell you why I worship Isis.'

I paused, thinking what lure could possibly attract Nimue. 'Tell her,' I finally said, 'that Arthur will give her Gundleus if she obeys you. But make sure he does,' I added.

'Thank you, Derfel.' She smiled, then sat in the black, polished stone throne. 'Isis,' she told me, 'is a woman's Goddess and the throne is her symbol. A man might sit on a kingdom's throne, but Isis can determine who that man is. That is why I worship her.'

I smelt the hint of treason in her words. 'The throne of this kingdom, Lady,' I said, repeating Arthur's frequent claim, 'is filled by Mordred.'

Guinevere mocked that assertion with a sneer. 'Mordred could not fill a pissing pot! Mordred is a cripple! Mordred is a badly behaved child who already scents power like a hog snuffling to rut a sow.' Her voice was whip-hard and scornful. 'And since when, Derfel, was a throne handed from father to son? It was never thus in the old days! The best man of the tribe took the power, and that is how it should be today.' She closed her eyes as though she suddenly regretted her outburst. 'You are a friend of my husband?' she asked after a while, her eyes open again.

'You know I am, Lady.'

'Then you and I are friends, Derfel. We are one, because we both love Arthur, and do you think, my friend Derfel Cadarn, that Mordred will make a better king than Arthur?'

I hesitated for she was inviting me to speak treason, but she was also inviting me to speak honestly in a sacred place and so I gave her the truth. 'No, Lady. Prince Arthur would make the better king.'

'Good.' She smiled at me. 'So tell Arthur he has nothing to fear and much to gain by my worship of Isis. Tell him it is for his future that I worship here, and that nothing that happens in this room can cause him injury. Is that plain enough?'

'I shall tell him, Lady.'

She stared at me for a long time. I stood soldier straight, my cloak touching the black floor, Hywelbane at my side and my full beard gold in the shrine's sun. 'Are we going to win this war?' Guinevere asked after a while.

'Yes, Lady.'

She smiled at my confidence. 'Tell me why.'

'Because Gwent stands like a rock to our north,' I said, 'because the Saxons fight amongst themselves like we do and so they never combine against us. Because Gundleus of Siluria is terrified of another defeat. Because Cadwy is a slug who will be squashed when we have time to spare. Because Gorfyddyd knows how to fight, but not how to lead armies. Most of all, Lady, because we have Prince Arthur.'

'Good,' she said again, then stood so that the sun flooded through that fine white linen shift. 'You must go, Derfel. You've seen enough.' I blushed and she laughed. 'And find a stream!' she called as I pushed through the curtain at the door. 'Because you stink like a Saxon!'

I found a stream, washed myself, then took my men south to the sea.

I do not like the sea. It is cold and treacherous, and its grey shifting hills run endlessly from the far west where the sun dies each day. Somewhere beyond that empty horizon, the seamen told me, the fabled land of Lyonesse lies, but no one has seen it, or certainly no one has ever returned from Lyonesse, and so it has become a blessed haven to all poor seamen; a land of earthly delights where there is no war, no famine and, above all, no ships to cross the grey lumpy sea with its wind-scoured white-caps whipping down the grey-green slopes that heaved our small wooden boats so mercilessly. The coast of Dumnonia looked so green. I had not realized how much I loved the place till first I left it.

My men travelled in three ships, all rowed by slaves, though once we were out of the river a wind came from the west and the oars were shipped as the ragged sails dragged the clumsy ships down the long waves' swooping sides. Many of my men were sick. They were young, mostly younger than myself, for war is truly a boys' game, but a few were older. Cavan, who was my second-in-command, was close to forty and had a grizzled beard and a face cross-hatched with scars. He was a dour Irishman who had taken service with Uther and who now found nothing strange in being commanded by a man only half his age. He called me Lord, assuming that because I came from the Tor I was Merlin's heir, or at least the magician's lordly child whelped on a Saxon slave. Arthur had given me Cavan, I think, in case my authority should prove no greater than my years, but in all honesty I never had trouble commanding men. You tell soldiers what they must do, do it yourself, punish them when they fail, but otherwise reward them well and give them victory. My spearmen were all volunteers and were going to Benoic either because they wanted to serve me or, more likely, because they believed there would be greater plunder and glory south of the sea. We travelled without women, horses or servants. I had given Canna her freedom and sent her to the Tor, hoping Nimue would look after her, but I doubted I would see my little Saxon again. She would find herself a husband soon enough, while I would find the new Britain, Brittany, and see for myself the fabled beauty of Ynys Trebes.

Bleiddig, the chief sent by King Ban, travelled with us. He grumbled at my lack of years, but after Cavan growled that I had probably killed more men than Bleiddig himself Bleiddig decided to keep his reservations about me private. He still complained that our numbers were too few. The Franks, he said, were land-hungry, well armed and numerous. Two hundred men, he now claimed, might make a difference, but not sixty.

We anchored that first night in the bay of an island. The seas roared past the bay's mouth while on the shore a ragged band of men shouted at us and sometimes fired feeble arrows that fell far short of our three ships. Our shipmaster feared a storm was coming and he sacrificed a kid that was on board for just that purpose. He drizzled the dying animal's blood on the bow of his ship and by morning the winds had calmed, though a great fog had crept over the sea instead. None of the ships' captains would sail in the fog so we waited a full day and night, and then, under a clear sky, rowed southwards. It was a long day. We skirted some dreadful rocks that were crowned with the bones of ships that had foundered, and then, in a warm evening, with a small wind and a rising tide helping our tired rowers, we slid into a wide river where, beneath the lucky wings of a flight of swans, we beached our craft. There was a fort nearby and armed men came to the river bank to challenge us, but Bleiddig shouted that we were friends. The men called back in British, welcoming us. The setting sun was gilding the river's swirls and eddies. The place smelt of fish and salt and tar. Black nets hung on racks beside beached fishing boats, fires blazed under the salt pans, dogs ran in and out of the small waves barking at us and a group of children came from some nearby huts to watch as we splashed ashore.

I went first, carrying my shield, with its symbol of Arthur's bear, upside down, and when I had gone beyond the wrack-littered line of the high tide I plunged the butt of my spear into the sand and said a prayer to Bel, my protector, and to Manawydan, the Sea God, that one day they would float me back from Armorica, back to my Lord's side, back to Arthur in blessed Britain.

Then we went to war.

I HAVE HEARD MEN say that no town, not even Rome or Jerusalem, was as beautiful as Ynys Trebes, and maybe those men spoke true for though I never saw those others, I did see Ynys Trebes and it was a place of marvels, a wondrous town, the most beautiful place I ever saw. It was built on a steep granite island set in a wide and shallow bay that could be riven with foam and howling with wind, yet inside Ynys Trebes all would be calm. In summer the bay would shimmer with heat, but inside Benoic's capital it always seemed cool. Guinevere would have loved Ynys Trebes, for everything old was treasured and nothing ugly was allowed to mar its grace.

The Romans had been to Ynys Trebes, of course, but they had not fortified it, only built a pair of villas on its summit. The villas were still there: King Ban and Queen Elaine had joined them together and then added to them by pillaging Roman buildings on the mainland for new pillars and pedestals, mosaics and statues, so that the island's summit was now crowned with an airy palace, full of light, where white linen curtains billowed with every breath of wind that gusted off the glittering sea. The island was best reached by boat, though there was a causeway of sorts that was covered by every high tide and at low tide could become treacherous with quicksands. Withies marked the causeway, but the surge of the bay's huge tides washed the markers away and only a fool attempted the passage without hiring the services of a local guide to steer him through the sucking sands and trembling creeks. At the lowest tides Ynys Trebes would emerge from the sea to stand amidst a wilderness of rippled sand cut through with gullies and tide-pools, while at the highest tides, when the wind blew strong from the west, the city was like some monstrous ship crashing her dauntless way through tumultuous seas.

Beneath the palace was a huddle of lesser buildings that clung to the steep granite slopes like sea-birds' nests. There were temples, shops, churches and houses, all lime-washed, all built of stone, all tricked out with whatever carvings and decorations had not been wanted in Ban's high palace, and all fronting on to the stone-paved road that climbed in steps around the steep island towards the royal house. There was a small stone quay on the island's eastern side where boats could land, though only in the calmest weather was the landing comfortable, which was why our ships had landed us at a safe place a day's march to the west. Beyond the quay was a small harbour which was nothing but a tidal pool protected by sandbanks. At low tide the pool was cut off from the sea while at the tide's height the holding was poor whenever the wind was in the north. All around the island's base, except in those places where the granite itself was too steep to climb, a stone wall tried to keep the outer world at bay. Outside Ynys Trebes was turmoil, Frankish enemies, blood, poverty and disease, while inside the wall lay learning, music, poetry and beauty.

I did not belong in King Ban's beloved island capital. My task was to defend Ynys Trebes by fighting on the mainland of Benoic where the Franks were pushing into the farmlands that supported the lavish capital, but Bleiddig insisted I met the king, so I was guided across the causeway, through the city gate that was decorated with a carved merman brandishing a trident, and up the steep road that led to the lofty palace. My men had all stayed on the mainland and I wished I had brought them to see the wonders of the city: the carved gates; the steep stone stairs that plunged up and down the granite island between the temples and shops; the balconied houses decorated with urns of flowers; the statues; and the springs that poured clean fresh water into carved marble troughs where anyone could dip a pail or stoop to drink. Bleiddig was my guide and he growled how the city was a waste of good money that should have been spent on defences ashore, but I was awestruck. This, I thought, was a place worth fighting for.

Bleiddig led me through the final merman-decorated gate into the palace courtyard. The palace's vine-clad buildings filled three sides of the court, while the fourth was bounded by a series of white-painted arches that opened on to a long view of the sea. Guards in white cloaks stood at every door, their spear-shafts polished and spearheads shining. 'They're no earthly use,' Bleiddig muttered to me. 'Couldn't fight off a puppy, but they look pretty.'

A courtier in a white toga met us at the palace door and escorted us through room after room, each one filled with rare treasures. There were alabaster statues, golden dishes, and a room lined with speculum mirrors that made me gasp as I saw myself reflected into an unending distance: a bearded, dirty, russet-cloaked soldier getting ever smaller in the mirrors' crinkling diminutions. In the next room, which was painted white and was filled with the scent of flowers, a girl played a harp. She wore a short tunic and nothing else. She smiled as we passed and went on playing. Her breasts were golden from the sun, her hair was short and her smile easy. 'Looks like a whorehouse,' Bleiddig confided in a hoarse whisper, 'and I wish it was. It might be of some use then.'

The toga-clad courtier thrust open the last pair of bronze-handled doors and bowed us into a wide room that overlooked the glittering sea. 'Lord King' – he bowed to the room's only occupant – 'Chief Bleiddig and Derfel, a captain of Dumnonia.'

A tall thin man with a worried face and a thinning head of white hair stood up from behind a table where he had been writing on parchment. A catspaw of wind stirred his work and he fussed until he had weighted the parchment's corners with inkhorns and snake stones. 'Ah, Bleiddig!' the King said as he advanced towards us. 'You're back, I see. Good, good. Some people never come back. The ships don't survive. We should ponder that. Is the answer bigger ships, do you think? Or do we build them wrong? I'm not sure we have the proper boat-building skills, though our fishermen swear we do, but some of them never come back either. A problem.' King Ban stopped halfway across the room and scratched his temple, transferring yet more ink on to his sparse hair. 'No immediate solution suggests itself,' he finally announced, then peered at me. 'Drivel, is it?'

'Derfel, Lord King,' I said, dropping to one knee.

'Derfel!' He said my name with astonishment. 'Derfel! Let me think now! Derfel. I suppose, if that name means anything, it means "pertaining to a Druid". Do you so pertain, Derfel?'

'I was reared by Merlin, Lord.'

'Were you? Were you, indeed! My, my! That is something. I see we must talk. How is my dear Merlin?'

'He hasn't been seen these five years, Lord.'

'So he's invisible! Ha! I always thought that might be one of his tricks. A useful one, too. I must ask my wise men to investigate. Do stand up, do stand up. I can't abide people kneeling to me. I'm not a God, at least I don't think I am.' The King inspected me as I stood and seemed disappointed by what he saw. 'You look like a Frank!' he observed in a puzzled voice.

'I am a Dumnonian, Lord King,' I said proudly.

'I'm sure you are, and a Dumnonian, I pray, who precedes dear Arthur, yes?' he asked eagerly.

I had not been looking forward to this moment. 'No, Lord,' I said. 'Arthur is besieged by many enemies. He fights for our kingdom's existence and so he has sent me and a few men, all we can spare, and I am to write and tell him if more are needed.'

'More will be needed, indeed they will,' Ban said as fiercely as his thin, high-pitched voice allowed. 'Dear me, yes. So you've brought a few men, have you? How few, pray, is few, precisely?'

'Sixty, Lord.'

King Ban abruptly sat on a wooden chair inlaid with ivory. 'Sixty! I had hoped for three hundred! And for Arthur himself. You look very young to be a captain of men,' he said dubiously, then suddenly brightened. 'Did I hear you correctly? Did you say you can write?'

'Yes, Lord.'

'And read?' he insisted anxiously.

'Indeed, Lord King.'

'You see, Bleiddig!' the King cried in a triumphant voice as he sprang from the chair. 'Some warriors can read and write! It doesn't unman them. It does not reduce them to the petty status of clerks, women, kings or poets as you so fondly believe. Ha! A literate warrior. Do you, by any happy chance, write poetry?' he asked me.

'No, Lord.'

'How sad. We are a community of poets. We are a brother-hood! We call ourselves the *fili*, and poetry is our stern mistress. It is, you might say, our sacred task. Maybe you will be inspired? Come with me, my learned Derfel.' Ban, Arthur's absence forgotten, scurried excitedly across the room, beckoning me to follow through a second set of great doors and across another small room where a second harpist, half-naked like the first and just as beautiful, touched her strings, and then into a great library.

I had never seen a proper library before and King Ban, delighted to show the room off, watched my reaction. I gaped, and no wonder, for scroll after scroll was bound in ribbon and stored in custom-made open-ended boxes that stood one on top of the other like the cells of a honeycomb. There were hundreds of such cells, each with its own scroll and each cell labelled in a carefully inked hand. 'What languages do you speak, Derfel?' Ban asked me.

'Saxon, Lord, and British.'

'Ah.' He was disappointed. 'Rude tongues only. I, now, have a command of Latin, Greek, British, of course, and some small Arabic. Father Celwin there speaks ten times as many languages, isn't that so, Celwin?'

The King spoke to the library's only occupant, an old white-bearded priest with a grotesquely humped back and a black monkish cowl. The priest raised a thin hand in acknowledgement, but did not look up from the scrolls that were weighted down on his table. I thought for a moment that the priest had a

252

fur scarf draped about the back of his monk's hood, then I saw it was a grey cat that lifted its head, looked at me, yawned, then went back to sleep. King Ban ignored the priest's rudeness, and instead conducted me past the racks of boxes and told me about the treasures he had collected. 'What I have here,' he said proudly, 'is anything the Romans left, and anything my friends think to send me. Some of the manuscripts are too old to handle any more, so those we copy. Let's see now, what's this? Ah, yes, one of Aristophanes's twelve plays. I have them all, of course. This one is *The Babylonians*. A comedy in Greek, young man.'

'And not at all funny,' the priest snapped from his table.

'And mightily amusing,' King Ban said, unruffled by the priest's rudeness, to which he was evidently accustomed. 'Maybe the *fili* should build a theatre and perform it?' he added. 'Ah, this you'll enjoy. Horace's *Ars Poetica*. I copied this one myself.'

'No wonder it's illegible,' Father Celwin interjected.

'I make all the *fili* study Horace's maxims,' the King told me.

'Which is why they're such execrable poets,' the priest put in, but still did not look up from his scrolls.

'Ah, Tertullian!' The King slid a scroll from its box and blew dust from the parchment. 'A copy of his *Apologeticus*!'

'All rubbish,' Celwin said. 'Waste of precious ink.'

'Eloquence itself!' Ban enthused. 'I'm no Christian, Derfel, but some Christian writing is full of good moral sense.'

'No such thing,' the priest maintained.

'Ah, and this is a work you must already know,' the King said, drawing another scroll from its box. 'Marcus Aurelius's *Meditations*. It is an unparalleled guide, my dear Derfel, to the manner in which a man should live his life.'

'Platitudes in bad Greek written by a Roman bore,' the priest growled.

'Probably the greatest book ever written,' the King said dreamily, replacing the Marcus Aurelius and drawing out another work. 'And this is a curiosity, indeed it is. The great treatise of Aristarchus of Samos. You know it, I'm sure?'

'No, Lord,' I confessed.

'It is not perhaps on everyone's reading list,' the King admitted sadly, 'but it has a certain quaint amusement. Aristarchus maintains – do not laugh – that the earth revolves around the sun and not the sun around the earth.' He illustrated this cantankerous notion with extravagant wheeling gestures with his long arms. 'He got it backwards, do you see?'

'Sounds sensible to me,' Celwin said, still without looking up from his work.

'And Silius Italicus!' The King gestured at a whole group of honeycomb cells filled with scrolls. 'Dear Silius Italicus! I have all eighteen volumes of his history of the Second Punic War. All in verse, of course. What a treasure!'

'The second turgid war,' the priest cackled.

'Such is my library,' Ban said proudly, conducting me from the room, 'the glory of Ynys Trebes! That and our poets. Sorry to have disturbed you, Father!'

'Is a camel disturbed by a grasshopper?' Father Celwin demanded, then the door was closed on him and I followed the King past the bare-breasted harpist back to where Bleiddig waited.

'Father Celwin is conducting research,' Ban announced proudly, 'into the wingspan of angels. Maybe I should ask him about invisibility? He does seem to know everything. But do you see now, Derfel, why it is so important that Ynys Trebes does not fall? In this small place, my dear fellow, is stored the wisdom of our world, gathered from its ruins and held in trust. I wonder what a camel is. Do you know what a camel is, Bleiddig?'

'A kind of coal, Lord. Blacksmiths use it for making steel.'

'Do they indeed? How interesting. But coal wouldn't be bothered by a grasshopper, would it? The contingency would scarcely arise, so why suggest it? How perplexing. I must ask Father Celwin when he's in a mood to be asked, which is not often. Now, young man, I know you've come to save my kingdom and I'm sure you're eager to be about that business, but first you must stay for supper. My sons are here, warriors both! I had hoped they might devote their lives to poetry and scholarship, but the times demand warriors, do they not? Still, my dear Lancelot values the *fili* as highly as I do myself, so there is hope for our future.' He paused, wrinkled his nose and offered me a kindly smile. 'You will, I think, want a bath?'

'Will I?'

'Yes,' Ban said decisively. 'Leanor will take you to your chamber, prepare your bath and provide you with clothes.' He clapped his hands and the first harpist came to the door. It seemed she was Leanor.

I was in a palace by the sea, full of light and beauty, haunted by music, sacred to poetry and enchanted by its inhabitants who seemed to me to come from another age and another world.

And then I met Lancelot.

'You're hardly more than a child,' Lancelot said to me.

'True, Lord,' I said. I was eating lobster soaked in melted butter and I do not think before or since I have ever eaten anything so delicious.

'Arthur insults us by sending a mere child,' Lancelot insisted.

'Not true, Lord,' I said, butter dripping into my beard.

'You accuse me of lying?' Prince Lancelot, the Edling of Benoic, demanded.

I smiled at him. 'I accuse you, Lord Prince, of being mistaken.'

'Sixty men?' he sneered. 'Is that all Arthur can manage?'

'Yes, Lord,' I said.

'Sixty men led by a child,' Lancelot said scornfully. He was only a year or two older than I yet he possessed the world-weariness of a much older man. He was savagely handsome, tall and well built, with a narrow, dark-eyed face that was as striking in its maleness as Guinevere's was in its femininity, though there was something disconcertingly serpent-like in Lancelot's aloof looks. He had black hair that he wore in oiled

255

loops pinned with gold combs, his moustache and beard were neatly trimmed and oiled to a gloss, and he wore a scent that smelled of lavender. He was the best-looking man I ever saw and, worse, he knew it, and I had disliked him from the very first moment I saw him. We met in Ban's feasting hall, which was unlike any feasting hall I was ever in. This one had marble pillars, white curtains that misted the sea view, and smooth plastered walls on which were paintings of Gods, Goddesses and fabulous animals. Servants and guards lined the walls of the gracious room that was lit by a myriad of small bronze dishes in which wicks floated in oil, while thick beeswax candles burned on the long table covered by a white cloth which I was constantly soiling with drips of butter, just as I was smearing the awkward toga that King Ban had insisted I wore to the feast.

I was loving the food and hating the company. Father Celwin was present and I would have welcomed a chance to talk with him, but he was annoying one of the three poets at the table, all of them members of King Ban's beloved band of *fili*, while I was marooned at the table's end with Prince Lancelot. Queen Elaine, who was seated beside her husband, the King, was defending the poets against Celwin's barbs, which seemed much more amusing than Prince Lancelot's bitter conversation. 'Arthur does insult us,' Lancelot insisted again.

'I am sorry you should think so, Lord,' I answered.

'Do you never argue, child?' he demanded of me.

I looked into his flat, hard eyes. 'I thought it unwise for warriors to argue at a feast, Lord Prince,' I said.

'So you're a timid child!' he sneered.

I sighed and lowered my voice. 'Do you really want an argument, Lord Prince?' I asked, my patience at last nearing its end, 'because if you do then just call me a child again and I'll tear your skull off.' I smiled.

'Child,' he said after a heartbeat.

I gave him another puzzled look, wondering if he played a game the rules of which I could not guess, but if he did then the game was in deadly earnest. 'Ten times the black sword,' I said.

'What?' He frowned, not recognizing the Mithraic formula which meant he was not my brother. 'Have you gone mad?' he asked, and then, after a pause, 'Are you a mad child, as well as a timid one?'

I hit him. I should have kept my temper, but my discomfort and anger overcame all prudence. I gave him a backswing with my elbow that bloodied his nose, cracked his lip and spilt him backwards off the chair. He sprawled on the floor and tried to swing the fallen chair at me, but I was too fast and too close for the blow to have any force. I kicked the chair aside, hauled him upright then rammed him backwards against a pillar where I smashed his head against the stone and put my knee into his groin. He flinched. His mother was screaming, while King Ban and his poetic guests just gaped at me. A nervous white-cloaked guard put his spear-point at my throat. 'Take it away,' I told the guard, 'or you're a dead man.' He took it away.

'What am I, Lord Prince?' I asked Lancelot.

'A child,' he said.

I put my forearm across his throat, half choking him. He struggled, but he could not shift me. 'What am I, Lord?' I asked again.

'A child,' he croaked.

A hand touched my arm and I turned to see a fair-haired man of my own age smiling at me. He had been sitting at the table's opposite end and I had assumed he was another poet, but that assumption was wrong. 'I've long wanted to do what you're doing,' the young man said, 'but if you want to stop my brother insulting you then you'll have to kill him and family honour will insist I shall have to kill you and I'm not sure I want to do that.'

I eased my arm from Lancelot's throat. For a few seconds he stood there, trying to breathe, then he shook his head, spat at me, and walked back to the table. His nose was bleeding, his lips swelling and his carefully oiled hair hung in sad disarray. His brother seemed amused by the fight. 'I'm Galahad,' he said, 'and proud to meet Derfel Cadarn.'

I thanked him, then forced myself to cross to King Ban's

chair where, despite his avowed dislike of respectful gestures, I knelt down. 'For the insult to your house, Lord King,' I said, 'I apologize and submit to your punishment.'

'Punishment?' Ban said in a surprised voice. 'Don't be so silly. It's just the wine. Too much wine. We should water our wine as the Romans did, shouldn't we, Father Celwin?'

'Ridiculous thing to do,' the old priest said.

'No punishment, Derfel,' Ban said. 'And do stand up, I can't abide being worshipped. And what was your offence? Merely to be avid in argument, and where is the fault in that? I like argument, isn't that so, Father Celwin? A supper without argument is like a day without poetry' – the King ignored the priest's acid comment about how blessed such a day would be – 'and my son Lancelot is a hasty man. He has a warrior's heart and a poet's soul, and that, I fear, is a most combustible mix. Stay and eat.' Ban was a most generous monarch, though I noted that his Queen, Elaine, was anything but pleased at his decision. She was grey-haired, yet her face was unlined and contained a grace and calm that suited Ynys Trebes's serene beauty. At that moment, though, the Queen was frowning at me in severe disapproval.

'Are all Dumnonian warriors so ill-mannered?' she asked the table at large in an acid voice.

'You want warriors to be courtiers?' Celwin retorted brusquely. 'You'd send your precious poets to kill the Franks? And I don't mean by reciting their verses at them, though come to think of it that might be quite effective.' He leered at the Queen and the three poets shuddered. Celwin had somehow evaded the prohibition on ugly things in Ynys Trebes for, without the cowl he had worn in the library, he appeared as an astonishingly ill-favoured man with one sharp eye, a mildewed eyepatch on the other, a sour twisted mouth, lank hair that grew behind a ragged tonsure line, a filthy beard half hiding a crude wooden cross hanging on his hollow chest, and with a bent, twisted body that was distorted by its stupendous hump. The grey cat that had been draped about his neck in the library was now curled on his lap eating scraps of lobster.

'Come to my end of the table,' Galahad said, 'and don't blame yourself.'

'But I do,' I said. 'It's my fault. I should have kept my temper.'

'My brother,' Galahad said when the seating had been re-arranged, 'my half-brother, rather, delights in goading people. It's his sport, but most daren't fight back because he's the Edling and that means one day he'll have powers of life and death. But you did the right thing.'

'No, the wrong thing.'

'I won't argue. But I will get you ashore tonight.'

'Tonight?' I was surprised.

'My brother does not take defeat lightly,' Galahad said softly. 'A knife in the ribs while you're sleeping? If I were you, Derfel Cadarn, I should join your men ashore and sleep safe in their ranks.'

I looked down the table to where the darkly handsome Lancelot was now being consoled by his mother as she dabbed at the blood on his face with a napkin dampened by wine. 'Half-brother?' I asked Galahad.

'I was born to the King's lover, not to his wife,' Galahad leaned close to me and explained softly. 'But Father has been good to me and insists on calling me prince.'

King Ban was now arguing with Father Celwin about some obscure point of Christian theology. Ban was debating with courteous enthusiasm while Celwin was spitting insults and both men were enjoying themselves hugely. 'Your father tells me you and Lancelot are both warriors,' I said to Galahad.

'Both?' Galahad laughed. 'My dear brother employs poets and bards to sing his praises as the greatest warrior of Armorica, but I've yet to see him in the shield-line.'

'But I have to fight,' I said sourly, 'to preserve his inheritance.'

'The kingdom's lost,' Galahad said carelessly. 'Father has spent his money on buildings and manuscripts, not soldiers, and here in Ynys Trebes we're too far from our people so they'd rather retreat to Broceliande than look to us for help.

The Franks are winning everywhere. Your job, Derfel, is to stay alive and get safe home.'

His honesty made me look at him with a new interest. He had a broader, blunter face than his brother, and a more open one; the kind of face you would be glad to see on your right-hand side in the shield-line. A man's right side was the one defended by his neighbour's shield, so it served to be on good terms with that man, and Galahad, I felt instinctively, would be an easy man to like. 'Are you saying we shouldn't fight the Franks?' I asked him quietly.

'I'm saying the fight is lost, but yes, you're oath-bound by Arthur to fight, and every moment that Ynys Trebes lives is a moment of light in a dark world. I'm trying to persuade Father to send his library to Britain, but I think he'd rather cut his own heart out first. But when the time comes, I'm sure, he'll send it away. Now' – he pushed his gilded chair away from the table – 'you and I must leave. Before,' he added softly, 'the *fili* recite. Unless, of course, you have a taste for unending verses about the glories of moonlight on reed beds?'

I stood and rapped the table with one of the special eating knives that King Ban provided his guests. Those guests now eyed me warily. 'I have an apology to make,' I said, 'not just to you all, but to my Lord Lancelot. Such a great warrior as he deserved a better companion for supper. Now, forgive me, I need to sleep.'

Lancelot did not respond. King Ban smiled, Queen Elaine looked disgusted and Galahad hurried me first to where my own clothes and weapons waited, then down to the flamelit quay where a boat waited to take us ashore. Galahad, still dressed in his toga, was carrying a sack that he slung on to the small boat's deck. It fell with a clang of metal. 'What is it?' I asked.

'My weapons and armour,' he said. He untied the boat's painter, then leaped aboard. 'I'm coming with you.'

The boat glided from the quay under a dark sail. The water rippled at the bow and splashed gently down the hull's length as we drew off into the bay. Galahad was stripping himself of the toga, which he tossed to the boatman, before dressing in war gear, while I stared back at the palace on the hill. It hung in the sky like a skyship sailing into clouds, or maybe like a star come down to earth; a place of dreams; a refuge where a just King and a beautiful Queen ruled and where poets sang and old men could study the wingspan of angels. It was so beautiful, Ynys Trebes, so utterly beautiful.

And, unless we could save it, doomed utterly.

Two years we fought. Two years against all odds. Two years of splendour and vileness. Two years of slaughter and feast, of broken swords and shattered shields, of victory and disaster, and in all those months and in all those sweated fights when brave men choked on their own life blood and ordinary men did deeds they never dreamed possible, I never saw Lancelot once. Yet the poets said he was the hero of Benoic, the most perfect warrior, the fighter of fighters. The poets said that preserving Benoic was Lancelot's fight, not mine, not Galahad's, not Culhwch's, but Lancelot's. But Lancelot spent the war in bed, begging his mother to bring him wine and honey.

No, not always in bed. Lancelot was sometimes at a fight, but always a mile behind so that he could be first back to Ynys Trebes with his news of victory. He knew how to tear a cloak, batter a sword edge, rumple his oiled hair and even cut his face so that he staggered home looking the hero, and then his mother would have the *fili* compose a new song and the song would be carried to Britain by traders and seamen so that even in distant Rheged, north of Elmet, they believed that Lancelot was the new Arthur. The Saxons feared his coming, while Arthur sent him the gift of an embroidered sword belt with a richly enamelled buckle.

'You think life should be fair?' Culhwch asked me when I complained about the gift.

'No, Lord,' I said.

'Then don't waste breath on Lancelot,' Culhwch said. He was the cavalry leader left behind in Armorica when Arthur went to Britain, and also a cousin of Arthur's, though he bore no resemblance to my Lord. Culhwch was a squat, fiercely bearded, long-armed brawler who asked nothing of life but a plentiful supply of enemies, drink and women. Arthur had left him in command of thirty men and horses, but the horses were all dead and half the men were gone so that now Culhwch fought on foot. I joined my men to his and so accepted his command. He could not wait for the war in Benoic to end so that he could fight again at Arthur's side. He adored Arthur.

We fought a strange war. When Arthur had been in Armorica the Franks were still some miles to the east where the land was flat and cleared of trees and thus ideal for his heavy horsemen, but now the enemy was deep inside the woods that cloaked the hills of central Benoic. King Ban, like Tewdric of Gwent, had put his faith in fortifications, but where Gwent was ideally placed for massive forts and high walls, the woods and hills of Benoic offered the enemy too many paths that passed by the hilltop fortresses garrisoned by Ban's dispirited forces. Our job was to give those forces hope again and we did it by using Arthur's own tactics of hard marches and surprise attacks. The wooded hills of Benoic were made for such battles and our men were peerless. There are few joys to compare with the fight that follows an ambush well sprung, when the enemy is strung out and has his weapons sheathed. I put new scars on Hywelbane's long edge.

The Franks feared us. They called us forest wolves and we adopted the insult as our symbol and wore grey wolf-tails on our helmets. We howled to frighten them, kept them awake night after night, stalked them for days and sprang our ambushes when we wanted and not when they were ready, yet the enemy was many and we were few, and month by month our numbers shrank.

Galahad fought with us. He was a great fighter, yet he was also a scholar who had delved into his father's library and he would talk at night of old Gods, new religions, strange countries and great men. I remember one night when we camped in a ruined villa. A week before it had been a thriving settlement with its own fulling mill, pottery and dairy, but the Franks had been there and now the villa was a smoking ruin, splashed by blood, its walls tumbled and its spring poisoned with the corpses of women and children. Our sentries were guarding the paths in the woods so we had the luxury of a fire on which we roasted a brace of hares and a kid. We drank water and pretended it was wine.

'Falernian,' Galahad said dreamily, holding his clay cup to the stars as though it were a golden flask.

'Who's he?' Culhwch asked.

'Falernian, my dear Culhwch, is a wine, a most pleasant Roman wine.'

'I never did like wine,' Culhwch said, then yawned hugely. 'A woman's drink. Now Saxon ale! There's a drink for you.' Within minutes he was asleep.

Galahad could not sleep. The fire flickered low while above us the stars shone bright. One fell, cutting its swift white path through the heavens and Galahad made the sign of the cross for he was a Christian and to him a falling star was the sign of a demon falling from paradise. 'It was on earth once,' he said.

'What was?' I asked.

'Paradise.' He leaned back on the grass and rested his head on his arms. 'Sweet paradise.'

'Ynys Trebes, you mean?'

'No, no. I mean, Derfel, that when God made man He gave us a paradise in which to live, and it occurs to me that we have been losing that paradise, inch by inch, ever since. And soon, I think, it will be gone. Darkness descends.' He went silent for a while, then sat up as his thoughts gave him a new energy. 'Just think of it,' he said, 'not a hundred years ago this land was peaceful. Men built great houses. We can't build like they did. I know Father has made a fine palace, but it's just broken pieces of old palaces cobbled together and patched with stone. We can't build like the Romans. We can't build as high, or as beautifully. We can't make roads, we can't make canals, we can't make aqueducts.' I did not even know what an aqueduct was, but kept silent as Culhwch snored contentedly beside me. 'The Romans built whole cities,' Galahad went on, 'places so vast, Derfel, it would take a whole morning to walk from one side of the city to the other and all of your footsteps would fall on trimmed, dressed stone. And in those days you could walk for weeks and still be on Rome's land, subject to Rome's laws and listening to Rome's language. Now look at it.' He waved at the night. 'Just darkness. And it spreads, Derfel. The dark is creeping into Armorica. Benoic will go, and after Benoic, Broceliande, and after Broceliande, Britain. No more laws, no more books, no more music, no more justice, only vile men round smoky fires planning on who they'll kill next day.'

'Not while Arthur lives,' I said stubbornly.

'One man against the dark?' Galahad asked sceptically.

'Wasn't your Christ one man against the dark?' I asked.

Galahad thought for a second, staring into the fire that shadowed his strong face. 'Christ,' he said finally, 'was our last chance. He told us to love one another, to do good to each other, to give alms to the poor, food to the hungry, cloaks to the naked. So men killed Him.' He turned and looked at me. 'I think Christ knew what was coming and that was why He promised us that if we lived as He lived then one day we'd be with Him in paradise. Not on earth, Derfel, but in paradise. Up there' – he pointed to the stars – 'because He knew the earth was finished. We're in the last days. Even your Gods have fled from us. Isn't that what you tell me? That your Merlin is scouring strange lands to find clues to the old Gods, but what use will the clues be? Your religion died long ago when the Romans ravaged Ynys Mon and all you have left are disconnected scraps of knowledge. Your Gods are gone.'

'No,' I said, thinking of Nimue who felt their presence, though to me the Gods were always distant and shadowy. Bel, to me, was like Merlin, only far away and indescribably huge and far more mysterious. I thought of Bel as somehow living in the far north, while Manawydan must live in the west where the waters tumbled endlessly.

'The old Gods are gone,' Galahad insisted. 'They abandoned us because we are not worthy.'

'Arthur is worthy,' I said stubbornly, 'and so are you.'

He shook his head. 'I am a sinner so vile, Derfel, that I cringe.'

I laughed at his abject tone. 'Nonsense,' I said.

'I kill, I lust, I envy.' He was truly miserable, but then Galahad, like Arthur, was a man who was for ever judging his own soul and finding it wanting and I never met such a man who was happy for long.

'You only kill men who would kill you,' I defended him.

'And, God help me, I enjoy it.' He made the sign of the cross.

'Good,' I said. 'And what's wrong with lust?'

'It overcomes reason.'

'But you're reasonable,' I pointed out.

'But I lust, Derfel, how I lust. There is a girl in Ynys Trebes, one of my father's harpists.' He shook his head hopelessly.

'But you control your lust,' I said, 'so be proud of that.'

'I am proud of it, and pride is another sin.'

I shook my head at the hopelessness of arguing with him. 'And envy?' I offered him the last of his trinity of sins. 'Whom do you envy?'

'Lancelot.'

'Lancelot?' I was surprised.

'Because he is Edling, not I. Because he takes what he wants, when he wants, and does not seem to regret it. That harpist? He took her. She screamed, she fought, but no one dared stop him for he was Lancelot.'

'Not even you?'

'I would have killed him, but I was far from the city.'

'Your father didn't stop him?'

'My father was with his books. He probably thought the girl's screams were a gull calling into the sea wind or two of his *fili* having a squabble about a metaphor.'

I spat into the fire. 'Lancelot is a worm,' I said.

'No,' Galahad insisted, 'he is, simply, Lancelot. He gets what he wants and he spends his days plotting how to get it. He can be very charming, very plausible and he could even be a great king.'

'Never,' I said firmly.

'Truly. If power is what he wants, and it is, and if he receives it, then perhaps his appetites will be slaked? He does want to be liked.'

'He goes a strange way about it,' I said, remembering how Lancelot had taunted me at his father's table.

'He knew, from the first, that you were not going to like him and so he challenged you. That way, when he makes an enemy of you, he can explain to himself why you don't like him. But with people who don't threaten him he can be kind. He might be a great king.'

'He's weak,' I said scornfully.

Galahad smiled. 'Strong Derfel. Derfel the Doubtless. You must think we're all weak.'

'No,' I said, 'but I think we're all tired and tomorrow we have to kill Franks, so I'll sleep.'

And next day we did kill Franks, and afterwards we rested in one of Ban's hilltop forts before, with our wounds bandaged and our battered swords sharpened, we went back into the woods. Yet week by week, month by month, we fought closer to Ynys Trebes. King Ban called on his neighbour, Budic of Broceliande, to send troops, but Budic was fortifying his own frontier and declined to waste men on defending a lost cause. Ban appealed to Arthur, and though Arthur did send one small shipload of men, he did not come himself. He was too busy fighting Saxons. We did get news from Britain, though such news was infrequent and often vague, but we heard that new hordes of Saxons were trying to colonize the middle lands and pressing hard on Dumnonia's borders. Gorfyddyd, who had been such a threat when I left Britain, had been quieter of late, thanks to a terrible plague that had afflicted his country. Travellers told us that Gorfyddyd himself was ill and many thought he would not last the year. The same sickness that had afflicted Gorfyddyd had killed Ceinwyn's betrothed, a prince of Rheged. I had not even known she was betrothed again and I confess that I felt a selfish pleasure that the dead prince of Rheged would not marry the star of Powys. Of Guinevere, Nimue or Merlin I heard nothing.

Ban's kingdom crumbled. There were no men to gather the harvest in the last year and that winter we huddled in a fortress on the southern edge of the kingdom where we lived on venison, roots, berries and wildfowl. We still made an occasional raid into Frankish territory, but now we were like wasps trying to sting a bull to death for the Franks were everywhere. Their axes rang through the winter forests as they cleared land for their farms while their new-built stockades of brightly split logs shone in the pale wintry sun.

Early in the new spring we fell back before an army of Frankish warriors. They came with drums beating and under banners made of bull horns mounted on poles. I saw one shield-wall of over two hundred men and knew our fifty survivors could never break it and so, with Culhwch and Galahad either side of me, we retreated. The Franks jeered and pursued us with a hail of their light throwing spears.

The kingdom of Benoic was stripped of people now. Most had gone to the kingdom of Broceliande that promised them land in return for war service. The old Roman settlements were deserted and their fields were tangled with couch grass. We Dumnonians walked north with our spears trailing as we went to defend the last fortress of Ban's kingdom: Ynys Trebes itself.

The island city was crowded with fugitives. Every house slept twenty. Children cried and families squabbled. Fishing boats carried some of the fugitives west to Broceliande or north to Britain, but there were never enough boats, and when the Frankish armies appeared on the shore facing the island, Ban ordered the remaining boats to stay anchored in Ynys Trebes's awkward little harbour. He wanted them there so they could supply the garrison once the siege started, but shipmasters are a stubborn breed and when the order came for them to stay many hauled their anchors instead and ran north empty. Only a handful of boats remained.

Lancelot was made commander of the city and women cheered as he walked down the city's circling street. All would be well now, the citizens believed, for the greatest of soldiers was in command. He took the adulation gracefully and made speeches in which he promised to build Ynys Trebes a new causeway from the skulls of dead Franks. The Prince certainly looked the part of a hero for he wore a suit of scale armour on which every metal plate had been enamelled a dazzling white so that the suit shone in the early spring sunshine. Lancelot claimed the armour had belonged to Agamemnon, a hero of antiquity, though Galahad assured me it was Roman work. Lancelot's boots were made of red leather, his cloak was dark blue, and at his hip, hanging from the embroidered sword belt that had been Arthur's gift, he wore Tanlladwyr, 'bright-killer', his sword. His helmet was black, crested with the spread wings of a sea-eagle. 'So he can fly away,' Cavan, my dour Irishman, commented sourly.

Lancelot convened a council of war in the high, wind-kissed chamber next to Ban's library. It was low tide and the sea had fled from the bay's sandbanks where groups of Franks were trying to find a safe path to the city. Galahad had planted false withies all across the bay, trying to lead the enemy into quick-sands or else on to firm banks that would be the first to be cut off when the tide turned and seethed across the bay. Lancelot, his back to the enemy, told us his strategy. His father sat on one side of him, his mother on the other, and both nodded at their son's wisdom.

The defence of Ynys Trebes was simple, Lancelot an-nounced. All we needed to do was hold the island's walls. Nothing else. The Franks had few boats, they could not fly, so they must walk to Ynys Trebes and that was a journey they could only make at low tide and after they had discovered the safe route across the tidal plain. Once at the city they would be tired and never able to scale the stone walls. 'Hold the walls,' Lancelot said, 'and we stay safe. Boats can supply us. Ynys Trebes need never fall!'

'True! True!' King Ban said, cheered by his son's optimism.

'How much food do we have?' Culhwch growled the question.

Lancelot gave him a pitying look. 'The sea,' he said, 'is full of fish. They're the shiny things, Lord Culhwch, with tails and fins. You eat them.'

'I didn't know,' Culhwch said straight-faced, 'I've been too busy killing Franks.'

A murmur of laughter went through some of the warriors summoned to the meeting. A dozen of them, like us, had been fighting on the mainland, but the remainder were intimates of Prince Lancelot and had been newly promoted into captains for this siege. Bors, Lancelot's cousin, was Benoic's champion and commander of the palace guard. He, at least, had seen some fighting and had earned a reputation as a warrior, though now, sprawling long-legged in a Roman uniform and with his black hair, like his cousin Lancelot's, oiled flat against his skull, he looked jaded.

'How many spears do we have?' I asked.

Lancelot had ignored me till then. I knew he had not forgotten our meeting of two years before, but he nevertheless smiled at my question. 'We have four hundred and twenty men under arms and each of them has a spear. Can you work out the answer?'

I returned the silky smile. 'Spears break, Lord Prince, and men defending walls throw their spears like javelins. When four hundred and twenty spears are thrown, what do we throw next?'

'Poets,' Culhwch growled, luckily too softly for Ban to hear.

'There are spares,' Lancelot said airily, 'and besides, we shall use the spears the Franks throw at us.'

'Poets, for sure,' Culhwch said.

'You spoke, Lord Culhwch?' Lancelot asked.

'I belched, Lord Prince. But while I have your gracious attention, do we have archers?'

'Some.'

'Many?'

'Ten.'

'The Gods help us,' Culhwch said and slid down in his chair. He hated chairs.

Elaine spoke next, reminding us that the island was

sheltering women, children and the world's greatest poets. 'The safety of the *fili* is in your hands,' she told us, 'and you know what will happen to them if you fail.' I kicked Culhwch to stop him from making a comment.

Ban stood and gestured towards his library. 'Seven thousand, eight hundred and forty-three scrolls are in there,' he said solemnly, 'the accumulated treasures of human knowledge, and if the city falls, so will civilization.' He then told us an ancient tale of a hero going into a labyrinth to kill a monster and trailing behind him a woollen thread with which he could find his way out of the darkness. 'My library,' he finally explained the point of the long tale, 'is that thread. Lose it, gentlemen, and we stay in eternal darkness. So I beg you, I beg you, fight!' He paused, smiling. 'And I have summoned help. Letters are gone to Broceliande and to Arthur, and I think the day is not far off when our horizon will be thick with friendly sails! And Arthur, remember, is oath-bound to help us!'

'Arthur,' Culhwch intervened, 'has his hands full of Saxons.'

'An oath is an oath!' Ban said reprovingly.

Galahad enquired whether we planned to make our own raids on the Frankish encampments ashore. We could easily go by boat, he said, landing east or west of their positions, but Lancelot turned down the idea. 'If we leave the walls,' he said, 'we die. It is that simple.'

'No sallies?' Culhwch asked in disgust.

'If we leave the walls,' Lancelot repeated, 'we die. Your orders are simple: you stay behind the walls.' He announced that Benoic's best warriors, a hundred veterans of the war on the mainland, would guard the main gate. We fifty surviving Dumnonians were given the western walls, while the city's levies, bolstered by fugitives from the mainland, guarded the rest of the island. Lancelot himself, with a company of the white-cloaked palace guard, would form the reserve that would watch the fighting from the palace and come down to intervene wherever their help was needed.

'Might as well call on the fairies,' Culhwch growled to me.

'Another belch?' Lancelot enquired.

'It's all the fish I eat, Lord Prince,' Culhwch said.

King Ban invited us to inspect his library before we left, perhaps wanting to impress us with the value of what we defended. Most of the men who had been at the council of war shuffled in, gaped at the pigeon-holed scrolls, then went to stare at the bare-breasted harpist who played in the library's antechamber. Galahad and I lingered longer among the books where the hump-backed Father Celwin was still bent over his old table where he was trying to keep his grey cat from playing with his quill. 'Still working out the wingspan of angels, Father?' I asked him.

'Someone must,' he said, then turned to scowl at me with his one eye. 'Who are you?'

'Derfel, Father, of Dumnonia. We met two years ago. I'm surprised you're still here.'

'Your surprise is of no interest to me, Derfel of Dumnonia. Besides, I did leave for a while. I went to Rome. Filthy place. I thought the Vandals might have cleaned it up, but the place is still full of priests and their plump little boys, so I came back here. Ban's harpists are much prettier than Rome's catamites.' He gave me an unfriendly look. 'Do you care about my safety, Derfel of Dumnonia?'

I could hardly answer no, though I was tempted to. 'My job is to protect lives,' I said rather pretentiously, 'including yours, Father.'

'Then I put my life in your hands, Derfel of Dumnonia,' he said as he turned his ugly face back to the table and pushed the cat away from his quill. 'I lay my life on your conscience, Derfel of Dumnonia, and now you can go and fight and leave me to do something useful.'

I tried to ask the priest about Rome, but he waved my questions away and so I went down to the storehouse on the western wall that would be our home for the rest of the siege. Galahad, who considered himself an honorary Dumnonian now, was with us and he and I tried to count the Franks who were retreating from the incoming tide after another attempt to

271

discover the track across the sands. The bards, singing of Ynys Trebes's siege, say the enemy outnumbered the grains of sand in the bay. They were not quite that many, but still they were formidable. Every Frankish war-band in western Gaul had combined to help capture Ynys Trebes, the jewel of Armorica which, it was rumoured, was crammed with the treasures of Rome's fallen Empire. Galahad estimated we were faced by three thousand Franks, my guess was two thousand, while Lancelot assured us there were ten thousand. But by anyone's count there was a terrible lot of them.

The first attacks brought the Franks nothing but disaster. They found a way across the sand and assaulted the main gate and were repelled bloodily, then the next day they attacked our part of the wall and were given the same treatment, only this time they stayed too long and a large part of their force was cut off by the incoming tide. Some tried to wade to the mainland and were drowned, others retreated to the shrinking stretch of sand before our walls where they were slaughtered by a sally of spearmen led from the gate by Bleiddig, the chief who had fetched me to Benoic and who was now the leader of Benoic's veterans. Bleiddig's sortie across the sand was in direct disobedience to Lancelot's rule that we must stay inside the city's wall, but the dead were so many that Lancelot pretended to have ordered the attack and later, after Bleiddig's death, he even claimed to have led the sally. The *fili* made a song telling how Lancelot had dammed the bay with Frankish dead, but in truth the Prince stayed in the palace while Bleiddig attacked. For days afterwards the bodies of Frankish warriors swilled around the island's base, carried by the tide and providing rich carrion for the gulls.

The Franks then began to build a proper causeway. They cut hundreds of trees and laid them on the sand, then weighted the trunks with rocks carried to the shore by slaves. The tides in Ynys Trebes's wide bay were fierce, sometimes rising forty feet, and the new causeway was ripped by the currents so that at low tide the flats were littered with floating logs, but always the Franks brought more trees and stone and so plugged the gaps. They had captured thousands of slaves and did not care how many died in building the new road. The causeway became longer as our food supplies grew shorter. Our few remaining boats still went fishing, and others carried grain from Broceliande, but the Franks launched their own boats from the shore and after two of our fishing boats were captured and their crews disembowelled, our shipmasters stayed at home. The poets on the hilltop, posturing with their spears, lived off the palace's rich stores, but we warriors scraped barnacles off the rocks, ate mussels and razor clams or stewed the rats we trapped in our storehouse that was still filled with pelts, salt and barrels of nails. We did not starve. We had willow fish traps at the base of the rocks and most days they yielded a few small fish though at low tide the Franks would send raiding parties to destroy the traps.

At high tide the Frankish boats rowed round the island to pull up the fish traps set further from the city's shore. The bay was shallow enough for the enemy to see the traps and then to break them with spears. One such boat grounded on its return to the mainland and was left stranded a quarter-mile from the city as the tide fell. Culhwch ordered a sortie and thirty of us climbed down fishing nets suspended from the wall's top. The twelve men of the boat's crew fled as we approached, and inside the abandoned craft we found a barrel of salted fish and two dry loaves of bread that we carried back in triumph. When the tide rose we brought the boat back to the city and tied it safe beneath our wall. Lancelot watched our disobedience, but sent no reprimand though a message did come from Queen Elaine demanding to know what supplies we had fetched back from the ship. We sent some dried fish up the road and no doubt the gift was construed as an insult. Lancelot then accused us of capturing the boat so that we could desert Ynys Trebes and ordered us to deliver the ship to the island's small harbour. For answer I climbed the hill to the palace and demanded that he back up his accusation of cowardice with his sword. I shouted the challenge around the courtyard, but the

Prince and his poets stayed inside their locked doors. I spat on their threshold and left.

Galahad was happier the more desperate things became. Part of his happiness sprang from the presence of Leanor, the harpist who had welcomed me two years before, the girl for whom Galahad had confessed his lust to me, the same girl Lancelot had raped. She and Galahad lived in a corner of the store-room. We all had women. There was something about the hopelessness of our plight that eroded normal behaviour and so we crammed as much living as we could into those hours before our expected deaths. The women stood guard with us and hurled rocks whenever the Franks tried to dismantle our fragile fish traps. We had long run out of spears, except for those we had brought to Benoic ourselves and which we were saving for the main assault. Our handful of archers had no missiles except the ones shot into the city by the Franks, and that supply increased when the enemy's causeway was a short bow's shot from the city gate. The Franks erected a timber fence at the end of the causeway and their archers stood behind the fence and poured arrows on the gate's defenders. The Franks made no attempt to extend the causeway all the way to the city, for the new roadway was only ever intended to give them a dry passage to the place where their assault could begin. We knew that attack must come soon.

It was early summer when the causeway was finished. The moon was full and brought huge tides. For much of the time the causeway was under water, but at low tide the sands stretched wide about Ynys Trebes, and the Franks, who were learning the secrets of the sandflats day by day, ranged all about us. Their drums were our constant music and their threats were ever in our ears. One day brought a feast special to their tribes and instead of attacking us they lit great fires on the beach then marched a column of slaves to the causeway's end where, one by one, the captives were beheaded. The slaves were Britons, some of them with relatives watching from the city's wall, and the barbarism of the slaughter goaded some of Ynys Trebes's defenders to rush out of the gate in a vain attempt to rescue the doomed women and children. The Franks were waiting for the attack and formed a shield-wall on the sand, but the men of Ynys Trebes, crazed by anger and hunger, charged home. Bleiddig was one of the attackers. He died that day, cut down by a Frankish spear. We Dumnonians watched as a handful of survivors fled back to the city. There was nothing we could have done except add our corpses to the pile. Bleiddig's body was flayed, disembowelled, then planted on a stake at the causeway's end so that we were forced to look at him until the next high tide. Somehow, though, the body stayed on the stake despite being immersed so that next morning, in a grey dawn, the gulls were tearing at his salt-washed corpse.

'We should have charged with Bleiddig,' Galahad told me bitterly.

'No.'

'Better to have died like a man in front of a shield-wall than be starved here.'

'You'll get your chance to fight the shield-wall,' I promised him, but I also took what steps I could to help my people in defeat. We barricaded the alleys leading to our sector so that should the Franks break into the island-city we could hold them at bay while our women were taken on a narrow rock-bound path that twisted across the shoulder of the granite peak to a tiny cleft on the island's north-western shore where we had hidden our captured ship. The cleft was no kind of harbour, so we protected our ship by filling it with stones so that the tide flooded it twice a day. Under water the fragile hull was safe from being pounded against the cleft's rocky sides by the wind and waves. I guessed that the enemy assault would be made at low water and two of our wounded men were under instructions to empty the boat of its rocks as soon as the attack began so that the craft would float on the flooding tide. The idea of escaping in the boat was desperate, but it gave our people heart.

No ships came to our rescue. One morning a great sail was seen in the north and the rumour flashed about the city that

275

Arthur himself was coming, but gradually the sail hauled off and disappeared in the summer haze. We were alone. At night we sang songs and told tales, while by day we watched the Frankish war-bands gather on the shore.

Those war-bands made their assault on a summer afternoon, late on a falling tide. They came in a great swarm of leather-armoured men, iron-helmeted, with wooden shields held high. They crossed the causeway, leaped off its end and climbed the gentle slope of sand towards the city gate. The leading attackers carried a huge log as a battering ram, its end fire-hardened and sheathed in leather, while the men who followed brought long ladders. One horde came and threw their ladders against our walls. 'Let them climb!' Culhwch bellowed at our soldiers. He waited until one ladder held five men then hurled a huge boulder straight down between its uprights. The Franks screamed as they were plucked off the rungs. An arrow glanced off Culhwch's helmet as he hurled another stone. More arrows rattled on the wall or hissed over our heads while a rain of light throwing spears clattered uselessly against the stone. The Franks were a churning dark mass at the wall's foot into which we hurled rocks and sewage. Cavan managed to lift one ladder clean over the wall and we broke it into scraps that we rained down on our attackers. Four of our women struggled to the rampart with a fluted stone column taken from a city doorway and we heaved it over the wall and took pleasure in the terrible screams of the men it crushed.

'This is how the darkness comes!' Galahad shouted at me. He was exultant; fighting the last battle and spitting in death's eye. He waited for a Frank to reach a ladder's top, then gave a mighty slash with his sword so that the man's head bounded off down to the sand. The rest of the dead man's corpse stayed clinging to the ladder, obstructing the Franks behind who became easy targets for our stones. We were breaking down the store-house wall now to make our ammunition and we were winning the fight too, for fewer and fewer Franks dared try to climb the ladders. Instead they retreated from the wall's base and we jeered at them, told them they had been beaten by women, but if they attacked again we would wake our warriors to the fight. Whether they understood our taunts I cannot tell, but they hung back, fearful of our defences. The main attack still seethed at the gate where the sound of the battering ram's pounding head was like a giant drum sickening the whole bay.

The sun stretched the shadows of the bay's western headland long across the sand while high pink clouds made bars across the sky. Gulls flew to their roosts. Our two wounded men had gone to empty our boat of stones – I hoped no Franks had reached that far about the island to discover the craft – yet I did not think we would even need it. Evening was falling and the tide was rising so that soon the water would drive the attackers back to the causeway, then back to their encampments and we would celebrate a famous victory.

But then we heard the battle roar of cheering men from beyond the city's gate and we saw our defeated Franks run from before our wall to join that distant assault and we knew the city was lost. Later, talking to survivors, we discovered that the Franks had succeeded in climbing the harbour's stone quay and now they were swarming into the city.

And so the screaming began.

Galahad and I took twenty men across our nearest barricade. Women were running towards us, but seeing us they panicked and tried to climb the granite hill. Culhwch stayed to guard our wall and to protect our retreat to the boat as the first smoke of a defeated city curled into the evening sky.

We ran behind the main gate's defenders, turned down a flight of stone steps and there saw the enemy scrambling like rats into a granary. Hundreds of enemy spearmen were flooding up from the quay. Their bull-horn standards were advancing everywhere, their drums were beating while the women trapped in the city's houses were shrieking. Off to our left, at the harbour's far side where only a few attackers had gained a lodgement, a surge of white-cloaked spearmen suddenly appeared. Bors, Lancelot's cousin and the commander of the palace guard, was leading a counter-attack and for a moment I thought he would turn the day and seal off the

277

invaders' retreat, but instead of assaulting along the quay Bors led his men to the sea-steps where a fleet of small boats waited to take them all to safety. I saw Prince Lancelot hurrying amid the guard, bringing his mother by the hand and leading a clutch of panicking courtiers. The *fili* were fleeing the doomed city.

Galahad cut down two men trying to climb the steps, then I saw the street behind us fill with dark-cloaked Franks. 'Back!' I shouted, and hauled Galahad away from the alley.

'Let me fight!' He tried to pull away from me and face the next two men coming up the narrow stone steps.

'Live, you fool.' I pushed him behind me, feinted left with my spear, then brought it up and rammed its blade into a Frank's face. I let go of the shaft, took the second man's spear thrust on my shield while I drew Hywelbane, then I gave the low jab under the shield's edge that sent the man screaming to the steps with blood welling between hands that cupped his groin. 'You know how to get us safe through the city!' I shouted at Galahad. I abandoned my spear as I pushed him back from the battle-maddened enemies who were surging up the steps. There was a potter's shop at the head of the steps and despite the siege the shopkeeper's wares were still displayed on trestle tables under a canvas awning. I tipped a table full of jugs and vases into the attackers' path, then ripped down the awning and hurled it into their faces. 'Lead us!' I screamed. There were alleys and gardens that only Ynys Trebes's inhabitants knew, and we would need such secret paths if we were to escape.

The invaders had broken through the main gate now to cut us off from Culhwch and his men. Galahad led us uphill, turned left into a short tunnel that ran beneath a temple, then across a garden and up to a wall that edged a rain cistern. Beneath us the city writhed in horror. The victorious Franks broke down doors to take revenge for their dead left on the sand. Children wailed and were silenced by swords. I watched one Frankish warrior, a huge man with horns on his helmet, cut down four trapped defenders with an axe. More smoke poured up from houses. The city might have been built of stone, but there was plenty of furniture, boat-pitch and timber roofs to feed a maniacal fire. Out at sea, where the incoming tide swirled across the sandbanks, I could see Lancelot's winged helmet bright in one of the three escaping boats, while above me, pink in the setting sun, the graceful palace waited for its last moments. The evening breeze snatched at the grey smoke and softly billowed a white curtain that hung in a shadowed palace window.

'Over here!' Galahad called, pointing to a narrow path. 'Follow the path to our boat!' Our men ran for their lives. 'Come on, Derfel!' he called to me.

But I did not move. I was staring up the steep hill.

'Come on, Derfel!' Galahad insisted.

But I was hearing a voice in my head. It was an old man's voice; a dry, sardonic and unfriendly voice, and the sound of it would not let me move.

'Come on, Derfel!' Galahad screamed.

'I put my life in your hands,' the old man had said, and suddenly he spoke again inside my skull. 'I lay my life on your conscience, Derfel of Dumnonia.'

'How do I reach the palace?' I called to Galahad.

'Palace?'

'How!' I shouted angrily.

'This way,' he said, 'this way!'

We climbed.

THE BARDS SING OF love, they celebrate slaughter, they extol kings and flatter queens, but were I a poet I would write in praise of friendship.

I have been fortunate in friends. Arthur was one, but of all my friends there was never another like Galahad. There were times when we understood each other without speaking and others when words tumbled out for hours. We shared everything except women. I cannot count the number of times we stood shoulder to shoulder in the shield-wall or the number of times we divided our last morsel of food. Men took us for brothers and we thought of ourselves in the same way.

And on that broken evening, as the city smouldered into fire beneath us, Galahad understood I could not be taken to the waiting boat. He knew I was in the hold of some imperative, some message from the Gods that made me climb desperately towards the serene palace crowning Ynys Trebes. All around us horror flooded up the hill, but we stayed ahead of it, running desperately across a church roof, jumping down to an alley where we pushed through a crowd of fugitives who believed the church would give them sanctuary, then up a flight of stone steps and so to the main street that circled Ynys Trebes. There were Franks running towards us, competing to be the first into Ban's palace, but we were ahead of them along with a pitiful handful of people who had escaped the slaughter in the lower town and were now seeking a hopeless refuge in the hilltop dwelling.

The guards were gone from the courtyard. The palace doors lay open and inside, where women cowered and children cried, the beautiful furniture waited for the conquerors. The curtains stirred in the wind.

I plunged into the elegant rooms, ran through the mirrored chamber and past Leanor's abandoned harp and so to the great room where Ban had first received me. The King was still there, still in his toga, and still at his table with a quill in his hand. 'It's too late,' he said as I burst into the room with sword drawn. 'Arthur failed me.'

Screams sounded in the palace corridors. The view from the arched windows was smeared by smoke.

'Come with us, Father!' Galahad said.

'I have work to do,' Ban said querulously. He dipped his quill into the inkhorn and began to write. 'Can't you see I'm busy?'

I pushed through the door which led to the library, crossed the empty antechamber, then thrust open the library door to see the hunchbacked priest standing at one of the scroll shelves. The polished wooden floor was littered with manuscripts. 'Your life is mine,' I shouted angrily, resenting that such an ugly old man had put me to this obligation when there were so many other lives to save in the city, 'so come with me! Now!' The priest ignored me. He was frantically pulling scrolls from the shelves, tearing off their ribbons and seals and scanning the first lines before throwing them down and snatching other scrolls. 'Come on!' I snarled at him.

'Wait!' Celwin insisted, pulling down another scroll, then discarded it and ripped another open. 'Not yet!'

A crash sounded in the palace; a cheer resounded and was drowned in screams. Galahad was standing in the library's outer door, pleading with his father to come with us, but Ban just waved his son away as though his words were a nuisance. Then the door burst open and three sweating Frankish warriors rushed in. Galahad ran to meet them, but he had no time to save his father's life and Ban did not even try to defend himself. The leading Frank hacked at him with a sword and I think the King of Benoic was already dead of a broken heart before the enemy's blade ever touched him. The Frank tried to cut off the King's head, and that man died on Galahad's spear while I lunged at the second man with Hywelbane and swung his wounded body around to obstruct the third. The dying Frank's breath reeked of ale like the breath of Saxons. Smoke showed outside the door. Galahad was beside me now, his spear slashing forward to kill the third man, but more Franks were pounding down the corridor outside. I pulled my sword free and backed into the antechamber. 'Come on, you old fool!' I screamed over my shoulder at the obstinate priest.

'Old, yes, Derfel, but a fool? Never.' The priest laughed, and something about that sour laughter made me turn and I saw, as though in a dream, that the hunched back was disappearing as the priest stretched his long body to its full height. He was not ugly at all, I thought, but wonderful and majestic and so full of wisdom that even though I was in a place of death that reeked of blood and echoed with the shrieks of the dying I felt safer than I had ever felt in all my life. He was still laughing at me, delighted at having deceived me for so long.

'Merlin!' I said, and I confess there were tears at my eyes.

'Give me a few minutes,' he said, 'hold them off.' He was still plucking down scrolls, tearing at their seals and dropping them after a cursory glance. He had taken off the eyepatch, which had merely been a part of his disguise. 'Hold them off,' he said again, moving to a new rack of unexamined scrolls. 'I hear you're good at slaughter, so be very good at it now.'

Galahad put the harp and the harpist's stool into the outer doorway, then the two of us defended the passage with spear, sword and shields. 'Did you know he was here?' I asked Galahad.

'Who?' Galahad rammed his spear into a round Frankish shield and jerked it back.

'Merlin.'

'He is?' Galahad was astonished. 'Of course I didn't know.'

A screaming Frank with ringletted hair and blood on his beard rammed a spear at me. I gripped it just below the head and used it to tug him on to my sword. Another spear was thrown past me and buried its steel head in the lintel behind. A man tangled his feet in the cacophonous harp strings and stumbled forward to be kicked in the face by Galahad. I chopped the edge of my shield on to the back of the man's neck, then parried a sword cut. The palace rang with screams and was filling with an acrid smoke, but the men attacking us were losing interest in any plunder they might discover in the library, preferring easier pickings elsewhere in the hilltop building.

'Merlin's here?' Galahad asked me in disbelief.

'Look for yourself.'

Galahad turned to stare at the tall figure who was so desperately searching among Ban's doomed library. 'That's Merlin?'

'Yes.'

'How did you know he was here?'

'I didn't,' I said. 'Come on, you bastard!' This was to a big Frank, leather-cloaked and carrying a double-headed war axe, who wanted to prove himself a hero. He chanted his war hymn as he charged and was still chanting as he died. The axe buried itself in the floorboards by Galahad's feet as he pulled his spear from the man's chest.

'I have it! I have it!' Merlin suddenly shouted behind us. 'Silius Italicus, of course! He never wrote eighteen books on the Second Punic War, only seventeen. How can I have been so stupid? You're right, Derfel, I am an old fool! A dangerous fool! Eighteen books on the Second Turgid War? The merest child knows there were only ever seventeen! I have it! Come on, Derfel, don't waste my time! We can't loiter here all night!'

We ran back into the disordered library where I rammed the big work table up against the door as a temporary barrier while Galahad kicked open the shutters on the windows facing the west. A new swarm of Franks surged through the harpist's room and Merlin snatched the wooden cross from around his neck and hurled the feeble missile at the invaders who were momentarily checked by the heavy table. As the cross fell a great burst of flame engulfed the antechamber. I thought the deadly fire was mere coincidence and that the wall to the room had collapsed to let in a furnace surge just as the cross struck, but Merlin claimed it as his own triumph. 'The horrible thing had to be good for something,' he said of the cross, then cackled at the screaming, burning enemy. 'Roast, you worms, roast!' He was thrusting the precious scroll into the breast of his gown. 'Did you ever read Silius Italicus?' he asked me.

'Never heard of him, Lord,' I said, tugging him towards the open window.

'He wrote epic verse, my dear Derfel, epic verse.' He resisted my panicked tugging and placed a hand on my shoulder. 'Let me give you some advice.' He spoke very seriously. 'Shun epic verse. I speak from experience.'

I suddenly wanted to cry like a child. It was such relief to look into his wise and wicked eyes again. It was like being reunited with my own father. 'I've missed you, Lord,' I blurted out.

'Don't go sentimental on me now!' Merlin snapped, then hurried to the window as a Frankish warrior burst through the flames in the doorway and slid along the table's top, screaming defiance. The man's hair was smoking as he thrust his spear towards us. I knocked his blade aside with my shield, lunged with the sword, kicked him and lunged again. 'This way!' Galahad shouted from the garden beyond the window. I gave the dying Frank a last cut, then saw that Merlin had gone back to his work table. 'Hurry, Lord!' I shouted to him.

'The cat!' Merlin explained. 'I can't abandon the cat! Don't be absurd!'

'For the Gods' sake, Lord!' I yelled at him, but Merlin was scrabbling under the table to retrieve the frightened grey cat that he cradled in his arms as he at last scrambled over the sill into a herb garden protected by low bay hedges. The sun was splendid in the west, drenching the sky brilliant red and shivering its fiery reflection across the waters of the bay. We crossed the hedge and followed Galahad down a flight of steps that led to a gardener's hut, then on to a perilous path that ran around the breast of the granite peak. On one side of the path was a stone cliff, and on the other air, but Galahad knew these tracks from childhood and led us confidently down towards the dark water.

Bodies floated in the sea. Our boat, crowded to the point where it was a miracle it could even float at all, was already a quarter-mile off the island with its oars labouring to drag its weight of passengers to safety. I cupped my hands and shouted. 'Culhwch!' My voice echoed off the rock and faded across the sea where it was lost in the immensity of cries and wailing that marked Ynys Trebes's end.

'Let them go,' Merlin said calmly, then searched under the dirty robe he had worn as Father Celwin. 'Hold this.' He thrust the cat into my arms, then groped again under his robe until he found a small silver horn that he blew once. It gave a sweet note.

Almost immediately a small dark wherry appeared around Ynys Trebes's northern shore. A single robed man propelled the little boat with a long sweep that was gripped by an oar-lock at the stern. The wherry had a high pointed prow and room in its belly for just three passengers. A wooden chest lay on the bottom boards, branded with Merlin's seal of the Horned God, Cernunnos. 'I made these arrangements,' Merlin said airily, 'when it became apparent that poor Ban had no real idea what scrolls he possessed. I thought I would need more time, and so it proved. Of course the scrolls were labelled, but the *fili* were for ever mixing them up, not to say trying to improve them when they weren't stealing the verse and calling it their own. One wretch spent six months plagiarizing Catullus, then filed him under Plato. Good evening, my dear Caddwg!' he greeted the boatman genially. 'All is well?'

'Other than the world dying, yes,' Caddwg growled in answer.

'But you've got the chest.' Merlin gestured at the sealed box. 'Nothing else matters.'

The elegant wherry had once been a palace boat used to ferry passengers from the harbour to the larger ships anchored offshore, and Merlin had arranged for it to wait his summons. Now we stepped aboard and sank to its deck as the dour Caddwg thrust the small craft out into the evening sea. A single spear plunged from the heights to be swallowed by the water alongside us, but otherwise our departure was unnoticed and untroubled. Merlin took the cat from me and settled contentedly in the boat's bows while Galahad and I stared back at the island's death.

Smoke poured across the water. The cries of the doomed were a wailing threnody in the dying day. We could see the dark shapes of Frankish spearmen still crossing the causeway and splashing off its end towards the fallen city. The sun sank, darkening the bay and making the flames in the palace brighter. A curtain caught the fire and flared brief and vivid before crumbling to soft ash. The library burned fiercest; scroll after scroll bursting into quick flame to make that corner of the palace into an inferno. It was King Ban's balefire, burning through the night.

Galahad wept. He knelt on the deck, clutching his spear, and watched his home turn to dust. He made the sign of the cross and said a silent prayer that willed his father's soul to whatever Otherworld Ban had believed in. The sea was mercifully calm. It was coloured red and black, blood and death, a perfect mirror for the burning city where our enemy danced in ghoulish triumph. Ynys Trebes was never rebuilt in our time: the walls fell, the weeds grew, seabirds roosted there. Frankish fishermen avoided the island where so many had died. They did not call it Ynys Trebes any more, but gave it a new name in their own coarse tongue: the Mount of Death, and at night, their seamen say, when the deserted isle looms black out of an obsidian sea, the cries of women and the whimpering of children can still be heard.

We landed on an empty beach on the western side of the bay. We abandoned the boat and carried Merlin's sealed chest up through whin and gale-bent thorn to the headland's high ridge. Full night fell as we reached the summit, and I turned to see Ynys Trebes glowing like a ragged ember in the dark, then I walked on to carry my burden home to Arthur's conscience. Ynys Trebes was dead.

*

We took ship for Britain out of the same river where I had once prayed that Bel and Manawydan would see me safe home. We found Culhwch in the river, his overloaded boat grounded on the mud. Leanor was alive and so were most of our men. One ship fit to make the voyage home was left in the river, its master having waited in hope of making a fat profit from desperate survivors, but Culhwch put his sword to the man's throat and had him take us home for free. The rest of the river's people had already fled from the Franks. We waited through a night made garish by the reflected flames of Ynys Trebes's burning and in the morning we raised the ship's anchor and sailed north.

Merlin watched the shore recede and I, scarce daring to believe that the old man had really come back to us, gazed at him. He was a tall bony man, perhaps the tallest I ever knew, with long white hair that grew back from his tonsure line to be gathered in a black-ribboned pigtail. He had worn his hair loose and dishevelled when he pretended to be Celwin, but now, with the pigtail restored, he looked like the old Merlin. His skin was the colour of old, polished wood, his eyes were green and his nose a sharp bony prow. His beard and moustaches were plaited into fine cords that he liked to twist in his fingers when he was thinking. No one knew how old he was, but certainly I never met anyone older, unless it was the Druid Balise, nor did I ever know any man who seemed so ageless as Merlin. He had all his teeth, every last one, and retained a young man's agility, though he did love to pretend to be old and frail and helpless. He dressed in black, always in black, never another colour, and habitually carried a tall black staff, though now, fleeing from Armorica, he lacked that badge of office.

He was a commanding man, not just because of his height, reputation or the elegance of his frame, but because of his presence. Like Arthur, he had the ability to dominate a room and to make a crowded hall seem empty when he left, but where Arthur's presence was generous and enthusiastic, Merlin's was always disturbing. When he looked at you it seemed that he could read the secret part of your heart and, worse still, find it amusing. He was mischievous, impatient, impulsive and totally, utterly wise. He belittled everything, maligned everyone and loved a few people wholly. Arthur was one, Nimue another and I, I think, was a third, though I could never really be sure for he was a man who loved pretence and disguises. 'You're looking at me, Derfel!' he accused me from the boat's stern where he still had his back turned towards me.

'I hope never to lose sight of you again, Lord.'

'What an emotional fool you are, Derfel.' He turned and scowled at me. 'I should have thrown you back into Tanaburs's pit. Carry that chest into my cabin.'

Merlin had commandeered the shipmaster's cabin where I now stowed the wooden chest. Merlin ducked under the low door, fussed with the captain's pillows to make himself a comfortable seat, then sank down with a sigh of happiness. The grey cat leaped on to his lap as he unrolled the top few inches of the thick scroll he had risked his life to obtain on a crude table that glittered with fish-scales.

'What is it?' I asked.

'It is the one real treasure Ban possessed,' Merlin said. 'The rest was mostly Greek and Roman rubbish. A few good things, I suppose, but not much.'

'So what is it?' I asked again.

'It is a scroll, dear Derfel,' he said, as though I was a fool to have asked. He glanced up through the open skylight to see the sail bellying in a wind still soured by Ynys Trebes's smoke. 'A good wind!' he said cheerfully. 'Home by nightfall, perhaps? I have missed Britain.' He looked back to the scroll. 'And Nimue? How is the dear child?' he asked as he scanned the first lines.

'The last time I saw her,' I said bitterly, 'she'd been raped and had lost an eye.'

'These things happen,' Merlin said carelessly.

His callousness took my breath away. I waited, then again asked him what was so important about the scroll.

He sighed. 'You are an importunate creature, Derfel. Well, I shall indulge you.' He let go of the manuscript so that it rolled itself up, then leaned back on the shipmaster's damp and threadbare pillows. 'You know, of course, who Caleddin was?'

'No, Lord,' I admitted.

He threw his hands up in despair. 'Are you not ashamed of your ignorance, Derfel? Caleddin was a Druid of the Ordovicii. A wretched tribe, and I should know. One of my wives was an Ordoviciian and one such creature was sufficient for a dozen lifetimes. Never again.' He shuddered at the memory, then peered up at me. 'Gundleus raped Nimue, right?'

'Yes.' I wondered how he knew.

'Foolish man! Foolish man!' He seemed amused rather than angry at his lover's fate. 'How he will suffer. Is Nimue angry?'

'Furious.'

'Good. Fury is very useful, and dear Nimue has a talent for it. One of the things I can't stand about Christians is their admiration of meekness. Imagine elevating meekness into a virtue! Meekness! Can you imagine a heaven filled only with the meek? What a dreadful idea. The food would get cold while everyone passed the dishes to everyone else. Meekness is no good, Derfel. Anger and selfishness, those are the qualities that make the world march.' He laughed. 'Now, about Caleddin. He was a fair Druid for an Ordoviciian, not nearly as good as me, of course, but he had his better days. I did enjoy your attempt to murder Lancelot, by the way, a pity you didn't finish the job. I suppose he escaped from the city?'

'As soon as it was doomed, yes.'

'Sailors say rats are always first off the doomed ship. Poor Ban. He was a fool, but a good fool.'

'Did he know who you were?' I asked.

'Of course he knew,' Merlin said. 'It would have been monstrously rude of me to have deceived my host. He didn't tell anyone else, of course, otherwise I'd have been besieged by those dreadful poets all asking me to use magic to make their wrinkles disappear. You've no idea, Derfel, how bothersome a little magic can be. Ban knew who I was, and so did Caddwg. He's my servant. Poor Hywel's dead, yes?'

'If you already know,' I said, 'why do you ask?'

'I'm just making conversation!' he protested. 'Conversation is one of the civilized arts, Derfel. We can't all stump through life with a sword and shield, growling. A few of us do try to preserve the dignities.' He sniffed.

'So how do you know Hywel's dead?' I asked.

'Because Bedwin wrote and told me, of course, you idiot.'

'Bedwin's been writing to you all these years?' I asked in astonishment.

'Of course! He needed my advice. What do you think I did? Vanish?'

'You did,' I said resentfully.

'Nonsense. You simply didn't know where to look for me. Not that Bedwin took my advice about anything. What a mess the man has made! Mordred alive! Pure foolishness. The child should have been strangled with his own birth cord, but I suppose Uther could never have been persuaded of that. Poor Uther. He believed that virtues are handed down through a man's loins! What nonsense! A child is like a calf; if the thing is born crippled you knock it smartly on the skull and serve the cow again. That's why the Gods made it such a pleasure to engender children, because so many of the little brutes have to be replaced. There's not much pleasure in the process for women, of course, but someone has to suffer and thank the Gods it's them and not us.'

'Did you ever have children?' I asked, wondering why I had never thought to enquire before.

'Of course I did! What an extraordinary question.' He gazed at me as though he doubted my sanity. 'I never liked any of them very much and happily most of them died and the rest I've disowned. One, I think, is even a Christian.' He shuddered. 'I much prefer other people's children; they're so much more grateful. Now what were we talking about? Oh yes, Caleddin. Terrible man.' He shook his head gloomily.

'Did he write the scroll?' I asked.

'Don't be absurd, Derfel,' he snapped impatiently. 'Druids are not allowed to write anything down, it's against the rules.

You know that! Once you write something down it becomes fixed. It becomes dogma. People can argue about it, they become authoritative, they refer to the texts, they produce new manuscripts, they argue more and soon they're putting each other to death. If you never write anything down then no one knows exactly what you said so you can always change it. Do I have to explain everything to you?'

'You can explain what is written on the scroll,' I said humbly.

'I was doing precisely that! But you keep interrupting me and changing the subject! Extraordinary behaviour! And to think you grew up on the Tor. I should have had you whipped more often, that might have given you better manners. I hear Gwlyddyn is rebuilding my hall?'

'Yes.'

'A good, honest man, Gwlyddyn. I shall probably have to rebuild it all myself but he does try.'

'The scroll,' I reminded him.

'I know! I know! Caleddin was a Druid, I told you that. An Ordoviciian, too. Dreadful beasts, Ordoviciians. Whatever, cast your mind back to the Black Year and ask yourself how Suetonius knew all he did about our religion. You do know who Suetonius was, I suppose?'

The question was an insult, for all Britons know and revile the name of Suetonius Paulinus, the Governor appointed by the Emperor Nero and who, in the Black Year that occurred some four hundred years before our time, virtually destroyed our ancient religion. Every Briton grew up with the dread tale of how Suetonius's two legions had crushed the Druid sanctuary on Ynys Mon. Ynys Mon, like Ynys Trebes, was an island, the greatest sanctuary of our Gods, but the Romans had somehow crossed the straits and put all the Druids, bards and priestesses to the sword. They had cut down the sacred groves and defiled the holy lake so that all we had left was but a shadow of the old religion and our Druids, like Tanaburs and Iorweth, were just faint echoes of an old glory. 'I know who Suetonius was,' I told Merlin.

'There was another Suetonius,' he said with amusement. 'A Roman writer, and rather a good one. Ban possessed his *De Viris Illustribus* which is mainly about the lives of the poets. Suetonius was particularly scandalous about Virgil. It's extraordinary what things poets will take to their beds; mostly each other, of course. It's a pity that work burned, for I never saw another. Ban's scroll might well have been the very last copy, and it's just ashes now. Virgil will be relieved. Whatever, the point is that Suetonius Paulinus wanted to know everything there was to know about our religion before he attacked Ynys Mon. He wanted to make certain we wouldn't turn him into a toad or a poet, so he found himself a traitor, Caleddin the Druid. And Caleddin dictated everything he knew to a Roman scribe who copied it all down in what looks to be execrable Latin. But execrable or not, it is the only record of our old religion; all its secrets, all its rituals, all its meanings and all its power. And this, child, is it.' He gestured at the scroll and managed to knock it off the table.

I retrieved the manuscript from under the shipmaster's bunk. 'And I thought,' I said bitterly, 'that you were a Christian trying to discover the wingspan of angels.'

'Don't be perverse, Derfel! Everyone knows the wingspan must vary according to the angel's height and weight.' He unwound the scroll again and peered at its contents. 'I sought this treasure everywhere. Even in Rome! And all the while that silly old fool Ban had it catalogued as the eighteenth volume of Silius Italicus. It proves he never read the whole thing, even though he did claim it was wonderful. Still, I don't suppose anyone's read the whole thing. How could they?' He shuddered.

'No wonder it took you over five years to find it,' I said, thinking how many people had missed him during that time.

'Nonsense. I only learned of the scroll's existence a year ago. Before that I was searching for other things: the Horn of Bran Galed, the Knife of Laufrodedd, the Throwboard of Gwenddolau, the Ring of Eluned. The Treasures of Britain, Derfel . . .' He paused, glancing at the sealed chest, then looked back to me. 'The Treasures are the keys of power, Derfel, but without the secrets in this scroll they're just so many dead objects.' There was a rare reverence in his voice, and no wonder, for the Thirteen Treasures were the most mysterious and sacred talismans of Britain. One night in Benoic, when we had been shivering in the dark and listening for Franks among the trees, Galahad had scorned the very existence of the Treasures by doubting whether they could have survived the long years of Roman rule, but Merlin had always insisted that the old Druids, facing defeat, had hidden them so deep that no Roman would ever find them. His life's work was the collection of the thirteen talismans; his ambition was the final awesome moment when they would be put to use. That use, it seemed, was described in the lost scroll of Caleddin.

'So what does the scroll tell us?' I asked eagerly.

'How would I know? You won't give me time to read it. Why don't you go and be useful? Splice an oar or whatever it is sailors do when they're not drowning.' He waited till I had reached the door. 'Oh, and one other thing,' he added abstractedly.

I turned to see he was again gazing at the opening lines of the heavy scroll. 'Lord?' I prompted him.

'I just wanted to thank you, Derfel,' he said carelessly. 'So, thank you. I always hoped you'd be useful some day.'

I thought of Ynys Trebes burning and of Ban dead. 'I failed Arthur,' I said bitterly.

'Everyone fails Arthur. He expects too much. Now go.'

I had supposed that Lancelot and his mother Elaine would sail west to Broceliande, there to join the mass of refugees hurled from Ban's kingdom by the Franks, but instead they sailed north to Britain. To Dumnonia.

And once in Dumnonia they travelled to Durnovaria, reaching the town a full two days before Merlin, Galahad and I landed, so we were not there to see their entry, though we heard all about it for the town rang with admiring tales of the fugitives.

293

Benoic's royal party had travelled in three fast ships, all of which had been provisioned ahead of Ynys Trebes's fall and in whose holds were crammed the gold and silver that the Franks had hoped to find in Ban's palace. By the time Queen Elaine's party reached Durnovaria the treasure had been hidden away and the fugitives were all on foot, some of them shoeless, all ragged and dusty, their hair tangled and crusted with sea salt, and with blood caked on their clothes and on the battered weapons they clutched in nerveless hands. Elaine, Queen of Benoic, and Lancelot, now King of a Lost Kingdom, limped up the town's principal street to beg like indigents at Guinevere's palace. Behind them was a motley mixture of guards, poets and courtiers who, Elaine pitifully exclaimed, were the only survivors of the massacre. 'If only Arthur had kept his word,' she wailed to Guinevere, 'if only he had done just half of all that he promised!'

'Mother! Mother!' Lancelot clutched her.

'All I want to do is die, my dear,' Elaine declared, 'as you so nearly did in the fight.'

Guinevere, of course, rose splendidly to the occasion. Clothes were fetched, baths filled, food cooked, wine poured, wounds bandaged, stories heard, treasure given and Arthur summoned.

The stories were wonderful. They were told all over the town and by the time we reached Durnovaria the tales had spread to every corner of Dumnonia and were already flying over the frontiers to be retold in countless British and Irish feasting halls. It was a great tale of heroes; how Lancelot and Bors had held the Merman Gate and how they had carpeted the sands with Frankish dead and glutted the gulls with Frankish offal. The Franks, the tales said, had been shrieking for mercy, fearing that bright Tanlladwyr would flash in Lancelot's hand again, but then some other defenders, out of Lancelot's sight, gave way. The enemy was inside the city and if the fight had been grim before, now it became ghastly. Enemy after enemy fell as street after street was defended, yet not all the heroes of antiquity could have stemmed that rush of iron-helmed foes who swarmed from the encircling sea like so many demons released from Manawydan's nightmares. Back went the outnumbered heroes, leaving the streets choked with enemy dead; still more enemies came and back the heroes went, back to the palace itself where Ban, good King Ban, leaned on his terrace to search the horizon for Arthur's ships. 'They will come!' Ban had insisted, 'for Arthur has promised.'

The King, the story said, would not leave the terrace for if Arthur came and he were not there, what would men say? He insisted he would stay to greet Arthur, but first he kissed his wife, embraced his heir, then wished them both fair winds for Britain before turning to gaze for the rescue that never came.

It was a mighty tale, and next day, when it seemed that no more ships would come from far Armorica, the tale changed subtly. Now it was the men of Dumnonia, the forces led by Culhwch and Derfel, who had allowed the enemy into Ynys Trebes. 'They fought,' Lancelot assured Guinevere, 'but they could not hold.'

Arthur, who had been campaigning against Cerdic's Saxons, rode hard for Durnovaria to welcome his guests. He arrived just hours before our sad party trudged unremarked up the road that ran from the sea past the great grassy ramparts of Mai Dun. One of the guards on the city's southern gate recognized me and let us in. 'You're just in time,' he said.

'For what?' I asked.

'Arthur's here. They're going to tell the tale of Ynys Trebes.'

'Are they now?' I glanced across the town towards the palace on its western hill. 'I'd like to hear that,' I said, then I led my companions into the town. I hurried towards the crossroads in the centre, curious to inspect the chapel Sansum had built for Mordred, but to my surprise there was neither chapel nor temple on the site, just a waste space where ragweed grew. 'Nimue,' I said, amused.

'What?' Merlin asked me. He was cowled so that no one would recognize him.

'A self-important little man,' I said, 'was going to build a church here. Guinevere summoned Nimue to stop him.'

'So Guinevere is not entirely without sense?' Merlin asked.

'Did I say she was?'

'No, dear Derfel, you did not. Shall we go on?' We turned up the hill towards the palace. It was evening and the palace slaves were putting torches into beckets about the courtyard where, heedless of the damage they were causing to Guinevere's roses and water channels, a crowd had gathered to see Lancelot and Arthur. No one recognized us as we came through the gate. Merlin was hooded, while Galahad and I wore the cheek pieces of our wolf-tailed helmets closed across our faces. We squeezed with Culhwch and a dozen other men into the arcade at the very back of the crowd.

And there, as night fell, we heard the tale of Ynys Trebes's fall.

Lancelot, Guinevere, Elaine, Arthur, Bors and Bedwin stood on the eastern side of the courtyard where the pavement was elevated a few feet above the other three sides to make a natural stage; an impression heightened by the bright torches fixed to the wall beneath the terrace that had steps leading down to the courtyard. I looked for Nimue, but could not see her, nor was young Bishop Sansum there. Bishop Bedwin said a prayer and the Christians in the crowd murmured their response, crossed themselves, then settled to listen once again to the awful tale of Ynys Trebes's fall. Bors told the story. He stood at the head of the steps and he told of Benoic's fight and the listening crowd gasped as they heard of the horror and cheered when he described some particular passage of Lancelot's heroism. Once, overcome by emotion, Bors simply gestured at Lancelot who tried to quell the cheers by raising a hand thickly wrapped in bandages and when the gesture failed he shook his head as though the crowd's praise was simply too great to bear. Elaine, draped in black, wept beside her son. Bors did not dwell on Arthur's failure to reinforce the doomed garrison, instead he explained that though Lancelot knew Arthur was fighting in Britain, King Ban had clung to his unrealistic hopes. Arthur, wounded all the same, shook his head and seemed close to tears, especially when Bors told the touching tale of King Ban's farewell to his wife and son. I was close to tears too, not because of the lies I heard, but out of sheer joy at seeing Arthur again. He had not changed. The bony face was still strong and his eyes still full of care.

Bedwin asked what had happened to the men of Dumnonia and Bors, with apparent reluctance, allowed the tale of our sorry deaths to be drawn from him. The crowd groaned when they learned that it had been us, the men of Dumnonia, who had yielded the city's wall. Bors raised a gloved hand. 'They fought well!' he said, but the crowd was not consoled.

Merlin seemed to have been ignoring Bors's nonsense. Instead he had been whispering with a man at the back of the crowd, but now he shuffled forward to touch my elbow. 'I need a piss, dear boy,' he said in Father Celwin's voice. 'Old man's bladder. You deal with those fools and I'll be back soon.'

'Your men fought well!' Bors shouted to the crowd, 'and though they were defeated, they died like men!'

'And now, like ghosts, they're back from the Otherworld,' I shouted, and I clashed my shield against a pillar, shaking free a small cloud of powdered lime. I stepped into the flamelight of a torch. 'You lie, Bors!' I shouted.

Culhwch stepped up beside me. 'I say you lie, too,' he growled.

'And I say it!' Galahad appeared.

I drew Hywelbane. The scrape of the steel on the scabbard's wooden throat made the crowd shrink back to leave a path through the trampled roses that led towards the terrace. The three of us, battle weary, dusty, helmed and armed, walked forward. We walked in step, slowly, and neither Bors nor Lancelot dared speak when they saw the wolf tails hanging from our helmets. I stopped at the garden's centre and slammed Hywelbane point downwards into a rosebed. 'My sword says you lie,' I shouted. 'Derfel, son of a slave, says that Lancelot ap Ban, King of Benoic, lies!'

'Culhwch ap Galeid says so too!' Culhwch rammed his battered blade beside mine.

'And Galahad ap Ban, Prince of Benoic, also.' Galahad added his sword.

'No Franks took our wall,' I said, removing my helmet so that Lancelot could see my face. 'No Frank dared climb our wall for there were so many dead at its foot.'

'And I, brother' – Galahad also removed his helmet – 'was with our father at the last, not you.'

'And you, Lancelot,' I cried, 'had no bandage when you fled Ynys Trebes. What happened? Did a splinter from the ship's gunwale prick your thumb?'

There was uproar. Some of Bors's guards were at the side of the courtyard and they drew their swords and shouted insults, but Cavan and the rest of our men pushed through the open gate with raised spears to threaten massacre. 'None of you bastards fought at the city,' Cavan shouted, 'so fight now!'

Lanval, commander of Guinevere's guards, shouted at his archers to line the terrace. Elaine had gone white, Lancelot and Bors were both at her side and both seemed to be trembling. Bishop Bedwin was shouting, but it was Arthur who restored order. He drew Excalibur and clashed it against his shield. Lancelot and Bors had shrunk to the back of the terrace, but Arthur waved them forward, then looked at us three warriors. The crowd went silent and the archers took the arrows off their strings. 'In battle,' Arthur said gently, commanding the attention of all the courtyard, 'things are confused. Men rarely see all that happens in a battle. There is so much noise, so much chaos, so much horror. Our friends from Ynys Trebes' – and here he laid his sword arm around Lancelot's shoulders – 'are mistaken, but theirs was an honest mistake. Doubtless some poor confused man told them the tale of your deaths, and they believed it, but now, happily, they stand corrected. But not shamed! There was glory enough in Ynys Trebes for all to share. Am I not right?'

Arthur had directed the question at Lancelot, but it was Bors who answered. 'I am wrong,' he said, 'and glad to be wrong.'

'I also,' Lancelot added in a brave, clear voice.

'There!' Arthur exclaimed and smiled down at the three of us. 'Now, my friends, pick up your weapons. We will have no enmity here! You are all heroes, all of you!' He waited, but not one of us moved. The torch flames glanced off our helmets and touched the blades of our planted swords that were a challenge for a fight to establish the truth. Arthur's smile disappeared as he drew himself to his full height. 'I am ordering you to pick up your swords,' he said. 'This is my house. You, Culhwch, and you, Derfel, are oath-sworn to me. Are you breaking your oaths?'

'I am defending my honour, Lord,' Culhwch answered.

'Your honour is in my service,' Arthur snapped, and the steel in his voice was enough to make me shiver. He was a kind man, but it was easy to forget that he had not become a war-lord by mere kindness. He spoke so much of peace and re-conciliation, but in battle his soul was released from such concerns and gave itself to slaughter. He threatened slaughter now by putting his hand on Excalibur's hilt. 'Pick up the swords,' he ordered us, 'unless you wish me to pick them up for you.'

We could not fight our own Lord and so we obeyed him. Galahad followed our example. The surrender left us feeling sullen and cheated, but Arthur, the moment he had restored amity inside his house, smiled once again. He spread his arms in welcome as he strode down the steps and his joy at seeing us was so obvious that my resentment vanished instantly. He embraced his cousin Culhwch, then hugged me and I felt my Lord's tears on my cheek. 'Derfel,' he said, 'Derfel Cadarn. Is it really you?'

'None else, Lord.'

'You look older,' he said with a smile.

'You don't.'

He grimaced. 'I was not in Ynys Trebes. I wish that I had been.' He turned to Galahad. 'I've heard of your bravery, Lord Prince, and I salute you.'

'But don't insult me, Lord, by believing my brother,' Gala-had said bitterly.

'No!' Arthur said. 'I will not have quarrels. We shall be friends. I insist upon it.' And he put his arm through mine and led the three of us up the terrace steps where he decreed that we should all embrace with Bors and Lancelot. 'There is trouble enough,' he told me quietly when I held back, 'without this.'

I stepped forward and spread my arms. Lancelot hesitated, then stepped towards me. His oiled hair smelt of violets. 'Child,' he whispered in my ear after kissing my cheek.

'Coward,' I whispered back, then we drew apart, smiling.

Bishop Bedwin had tears in his eyes as he hugged me. 'Dear Derfel!'

'I have even better news for you,' I told him softly, 'Merlin is here.'

'Merlin?' Bedwin stared at me, not daring to believe my news. 'Merlin is here? Merlin!' The news spread through the crowd. Merlin was back! Great Merlin had returned. The Christians crossed themselves, but even they recognized the import of the news. Merlin had come to Dumnonia and suddenly the kingdom's troubles seemed halved.

'So where is he?' Arthur demanded.

'He went out,' I said feebly, gesturing at the gate.

'Merlin.' Arthur shouted. 'Merlin.'

But there was no answer. Guards searched for him, but none found him. Later the sentries at the western gate said that an old priest with a hunched back, an eyepatch, a grey cat and a filthy cough had left the city, but they had seen no other white-bearded sage.

'You have been through a dreadful battle, Derfel,' Arthur told me when we were in the palace's feasting hall where a meal of pork, bread and mead was served. 'Men dream strange dreams when they suffer hardships.'

'No, Lord,' I insisted, 'Merlin was here. Ask Prince Galahad.'

'I shall,' he said, 'of course I shall.' He turned to look at the high table where Guinevere leaned on an elbow to listen to Lancelot. 'You've all suffered,' he said.

'But I failed you, Lord,' I confessed, 'and for that I am sorry.'

'No, Derfel, no! I failed Ban. But what more could I do? There are so many enemies.' He fell silent, then smiled as Guinevere's laughter sounded bright in the hall. 'I am glad that at least she is happy,' he said, then went to talk to Culhwch who was single-mindedly devouring a whole suckling pig.

Lunete was at the court that night. Her hair was braided and twisted into a flower-studded circlet. She wore torques, brooches and bangles, while her dress was of red-dyed linen girdled with a silver-buckled belt. She smiled at me, brushed dirt off my sleeve then wrinkled her nose at the stink of my clothes. 'Scars suit you, Derfel,' she said, lightly touching my face, 'but you take too many risks.'

'I'm a warrior.'

'Not those sort of risks. I mean making up stories about Merlin. You embarrassed me! And announcing yourself as the son of a slave! Didn't you ever think how that might make me feel? I know we aren't together any more, but people know we were once, and how do you think it makes me feel when you say you're slave-born? You should think of others, Derfel, you really should.' I noted she no longer wore our lovers' ring, but I would hardly have expected to see it for she had long found other men who could afford to be more generous than I ever could. 'I suppose Ynys Trebes made you a little mad,' she went on. 'Why else would you challenge Lancelot to a fight? I know you're good with a sword, Derfel, but he's Lancelot, not just any warrior.' She turned to look at where the King sat beside Guinevere. 'Isn't he wonderful?' she asked me.

'Incomparably,' I said sourly.

'And unmarried, I hear?' Lunete said coquettishly.

I leaned close to her ear. 'He prefers boys,' I whispered.

She hit my arm. 'Fool. Anyone can see he doesn't. See how he looks at Guinevere?' It was Lunete's turn to put her mouth close to my ear. 'Don't tell anyone,' she whispered hoarsely, 'but she's pregnant.'

'Good,' I said.

'It isn't good at all. She's not happy. She doesn't want to be lumpy, you see. And I don't blame her. I hated being pregnant. Ah, there's someone I want to see. I do like new faces at court. Oh, and one other thing, Derfel?' She smiled sweetly. 'Take a bath, dear.' She crossed the room to accost one of Queen Elaine's poets.

'Off with the old, on with the new?' Bishop Bedwin appeared beside me.

'I'm so old I'm surprised Lunete even remembers me,' I answered dourly.

Bedwin smiled then took me into the courtyard that was now empty. 'Merlin was with you,' he said, not as a question, but as a statement.

'Yes, Lord.' And I told him how Merlin had claimed to be leaving the palace for just a few moments.

Bedwin shook his head. 'He likes these games,' he said despairingly. 'Tell me more.'

I told him all I could. We walked up and down the upper terrace through the smoke of the guttering torches and I spoke of Father Celwin and of Ban's library, and gave him the real story of the siege and the truth about Lancelot, and I ended by describing Caleddin's scroll that Merlin had snatched from the fall of the city. 'He says,' I told Bedwin, 'that it contains the Knowledge of Britain.'

'I pray God it does, may God forgive me,' Bedwin said. 'Someone has to help us.'

'Are things bad?'

Bedwin shrugged. He looked old and tired. His hair was wispy now, his beard thin and his face more haggard than I remembered. 'I suppose they could be worse,' he admitted, 'but sadly they never get better. Things are really not much different from when you left, except that Aelle grows stronger, so strong that he even dares call himself the Bretwalda now.' Bedwin shuddered at the barbarous pretension. Bretwalda was a Saxon title and meant Ruler of Britain. 'He captured all the land between Durocobrivis and Corinium,' Bedwin told me, 'and he probably would have captured both those fortresses if we hadn't purchased peace with the last of our gold. Then there's Cerdic in the south and he's proving even more vicious than Aelle.'

'Doesn't Aelle attack Powys?' I asked.

'Gorfyddyd paid him gold just like we did.'

'I thought Gorfyddyd was sick?'

'The plague passed as plagues do. He recovered, and now he leads the men of Elmet along with the forces of Powys. He's doing better than we feared,' Bedwin said bleakly, 'perhaps because he's driven by hate. He doesn't drink like he used to and he's sworn to avenge that lost arm on Arthur's head. Worse than that, Derfel, Gorfyddyd is doing what Arthur hoped to do; uniting the tribes, but sadly he's uniting them against us and not against the Saxons. He pays Gundleus's Silurians and the Blackshield Irish to raid our coasts and he bribes King Mark to help Cadwy, and I daresay he's raising the money now to pay Aelle to break our truce. Gorfyddyd rises and we fall. In Powys they call Gorfyddyd the High King now. And he has Cuneglas as an heir while we have poor little lame Mordred. Gorfyddyd collects an army and we have war-bands. And once this year's harvest is collected, Derfel, then Gorfyddyd will come south with the men of Elmet and Powys. Men say it will be the greatest army ever seen in Britain and it's hardly a wonder that there are those' – he lowered his voice – 'who say we should make peace on his terms.'

'Which are?'

'There is only one condition. Arthur's death. Gorfyddyd will never forgive Arthur for the slight to Ceinwyn. Can you blame him?' Bedwin shrugged and walked a few paces in silence. 'The real danger,' he went on, 'is if Gorfyddyd does find the money to bring Aelle back into the war. We can't pay more to the Saxons. We've nothing left. The treasury is empty. Who'll pay taxes to a dying regime? And we can't spare any spearmen to collect the taxes.'

'There's plenty of gold in there,' I said, jerking my head towards the hall where the sounds of the feast were loud. 'Lunete was wearing enough,' I added sourly.

'The Princess Guinevere's ladies,' Bedwin said bitterly 'are not expected to contribute their jewels to the war. Even if they did, I doubt there'd be enough to bribe Aelle again, and if he does attack us in the autumn, Derfel, then those men who want Arthur's life won't whisper their demand, they'll shout it from the ramparts. Arthur, of course, could simply leave. He could go to Broceliande, I suppose, then Gorfyddyd would take young Mordred into his care and we'd just be a client kingdom ruled from Powys.'

I paced in silence. I had no idea things were so desperate.

Bedwin smiled sadly. 'So it seems, my young friend, that you have jumped from the seething pot into the fire. There will be work for your sword, Derfel, and soon, never fear.'

'I had wanted time to visit Ynys Wydryn' I said.

'To find Merlin again?'

'To find Nimue,' I said.

He stopped. 'You hadn't heard?'

Something cold caressed my heart. 'I've heard nothing. I thought she might be here in Durnovaria.'

'She was,' Bedwin said. 'Princess Guinevere fetched her. I was surprised she came, but she did. You have to understand, Derfel, that Guinevere and Bishop Sansum – remember him? How could you forget him? – he and she are at odds. Nimue was Guinevere's weapon. God knows what she thought Nimue could do, but Sansum did not wait to find out. He preached against Nimue as a witch. Some of my fellow Christians, I fear, are not full of kindness and Sansum preached that she should be stoned to death.'

'No!' I protested.

'No, no!' He held up a hand to calm me. 'She fought back by bringing the pagans of the countryside into the town. They sacked Sansum's new chapel, there was a riot and a dozen people died, though neither she nor Sansum were hurt. The King's guards panicked, thinking it was an attack on Mordred. It wasn't, of course, but that didn't stop them using their spears. Then Nimue was arrested by Nabur, the magistrate responsible for the King, and he found her guilty of stirring up revolt. He would, of course, being a Christian. Bishop Sansum demanded her death, the Princess Guinevere demanded

Nimue's release, and in between those two demands Nimue rotted in Nabur's cells.' Bedwin paused and I could see from his face that the worst was still to come. 'She went mad, Derfel,' the Bishop at last continued. 'It was like caging a falcon, you see, and she rebelled against her bars. She went screaming mad. No one could restrain her.'

I knew what was coming and shook my head. 'No,' I said.

'The Isle of the Dead,' Bedwin gave the awful news. 'What else could they do?'

'No!' I protested again, for Nimue was on the Isle of the Dead, lost among the broken ones, and I could not bear to think of that fate. 'She has her Third Wound,' I said softly.

'What?' Bedwin cupped an ear.

'Nothing,' I said. 'Does she live?'

'Who knows? No living person goes there, or if they do, they cannot return.'

'But that's where Merlin must have gone!' I cried in relief. Merlin had doubtless heard the news from the man he had been whispering with at the back of the courtyard, and Merlin could do what no other man or woman dare do. The Isle of the Dead would hold no terrors for Merlin. What else would have made him vanish so precipitately? In a day or two, I thought, he would return to Durnovaria with Nimue rescued and restored. It had to be thus.

'Pray God it is,' Bedwin said, 'for her sake.'

'What happened to Sansum?' I asked vengefully.

'He wasn't punished officially,' Bedwin said, 'but Guinevere persuaded Arthur to strip him of Mordred's chaplaincy and then the old fellow who administered the shrine of the Holy Thorn at Ynys Wydryn died and I managed to persuade our young Bishop to take over there. He wasn't happy, but he knew he'd made too many enemies in Durnovaria, so he accepted.' Bedwin was plainly delighted at Sansum's fall. 'He's certainly lost his power here and I don't see him getting it back. Not unless he's a great deal more subtle than I think. He, of course, is one of those who whisper that Arthur should be sacrificed. Nabur is another. There's a Mordred faction in our kingdom,

305

Derfel, and it asks why we should fight to preserve Arthur's life.'

I stepped round a puddle of vomit thrown up by a drunken soldier come from the hall. The man groaned, looked up at me, then retched again. 'Who else could rule Dumnonia?' I asked Bedwin when we were safely out of the drunk's hearing.

'There's a good question, Derfel, who indeed? Gorfyddyd, of course, or else his son Cuneglas. Some men whisper Gereint's name, but he doesn't want it. Nabur even suggested I might take over. He said nothing specific, of course, nothing but hints.' Bedwin chuckled derisively. 'But what use would I be against our enemies? We need Arthur. No one else could have held off this ring of enemies for so long, Derfel, but folk don't understand that. They blame him for the chaos, yet if anyone else was in power the chaos would be worse. We're a kingdom without a proper king so every ambitious rogue has his eye on Mordred's throne.'

I stopped beside the bronze bust that looked so like Gorfyddyd. 'If Arthur had just married Ceinwyn –' I began.

Bedwin interrupted me. 'If, Derfel, if. If Mordred's father had lived, or if Arthur had killed Gorfyddyd instead of just taking his arm, everything would be different. History is nothing but ifs. And perhaps you're right. Perhaps if Arthur had married Ceinwyn we would be at peace now and perhaps Aelle's head would be planted on a spear-point in Caer Cadarn, but how long do you think Gorfyddyd would have endured Arthur's success? And remind yourself why Gorfyddyd agreed to the marriage in the first place.'

'For peace?' I suggested.

'Dear me, no. Gorfyddyd only allowed Ceinwyn to be betrothed because he believed her son, his grandson, would rule Dumnonia instead of Mordred. I should have thought that was obvious.'

'Not to me,' I said, for at Caer Sws, when Arthur had been struck mad by love, I had been a mere spearman in the guard, not a captain who needed to probe the motives of kings and princes.

'We need Arthur,' Bedwin said, looking up into my eyes. 'And if Arthur needs Guinevere, then so be it.' He shrugged and walked on. 'I would have preferred Ceinwyn as his wife, but the choice and the marriage-bed were not mine to make. Now, poor thing, she'll marry Gundleus.'

'Gundleus!' I said too loudly, startling the sick soldier who groaned over his vomit. 'Ceinwyn will marry Gundleus?' I asked Bedwin.

'Their betrothal ceremony is in two weeks,' Bedwin said calmly, 'during Lughnasa.' Lughnasa was the summer festival of Lleullaw, God of Light, and was dedicated to fertility, and thus any betrothal made at the feast was considered particularly auspicious. 'They'll marry in late autumn, after the war.' He paused, aware that his last three words suggested that Gorfyddyd and Gundleus would win the war, and that the marriage ceremony would thus be a part of the victor's celebrations. 'Gorfyddyd has sworn to give them Arthur's head as a wedding gift,' Bedwin added sadly.

'But Gundleus is already married!' I protested, wondering why I was so indignant. Was it because I remembered Ceinwyn's fragile beauty? I still wore her brooch inside my breastplate, but I told myself my indignation was not because of her, but simply because I hated Gundleus.

'Being married to Ladwys didn't stop Gundleus marrying Norwenna,' Bedwin said scornfully. 'He'll put Ladwys aside, go three times round the sacred rock then kiss the magic toadstool or whatever else you pagans do to get divorced these days. He's not a Christian any more, by the way. A pagan divorce, marry Ceinwyn, serve her with an heir, then hurry back to Ladwys's bed. That seems to be the way of things nowadays.' He paused, cocking an ear towards the sounds of laughter coming from the hall. 'Though maybe,' he went on, 'in years to come we shall think of these days as the last of the good times.'

Something in his voice made my spirits sink even further. 'Are we doomed?' I asked him.

'If Aelle keeps his truce we may last another year, but only if

307

we defeat Gorfyddyd. And if not? Then we must pray Merlin has brought us new life.' He shrugged, but did not seem very hopeful.

He was not a good Christian, Bishop Bedwin, though he was a very good man. Sansum now tells me that Bedwin's goodness will not prevent his soul from roasting in hell. But that summer, fresh back from Benoic, all our souls seemed doomed to perdition. The harvest was just beginning, but once it was gathered, Gorfyddyd's onslaught would come.

PART FOUR

The Isle of the Dead

IGRAINE DEMANDED TO see Ceinwyn's brooch. She held it in the window, turning it and gazing at its golden spirals. I could see the desire in her eyes. 'You have many that are more beautiful,' I told her gently.

'But none so full of story,' she said, holding the brooch against her breast.

'My story, dear Queen,' I chided her, 'not yours.'

She smiled. 'But what did you write? That if I were as kind as you know me to be, then I would let you keep it?'

'Did I write that?'

'Because you knew that would make me give it back to you. You are a cunning old man, Brother Derfel.' She held the brooch out to me, then folded her fingers over the gold before I could take it. 'Will it be mine one day?'

'No one else's, dear Lady. I promise.'

She still held it. 'And you won't let Bishop Sansum take it?'

'Never,' I said fervently.

She dropped it into my hand. 'Did you really wear it under your breastplate?'

'Always,' I said, tucking the brooch safe under my robe.

'Poor Ynys Trebes.' She was sitting in her usual place on my window-sill from where she could stare down Dinnewrac's valley towards the distant river that was swollen with an early summer rain. Was she imagining Frankish invaders crossing the ford and swarming up the slopes? 'What happened to Leanor?' she asked, surprising me with the question.

'The harpist? She died.'

'No! But I thought you said she escaped from Ynys Trebes?'

I nodded. 'She did, but she sickened her first winter in Britain and died. Just died.'

'And what about your woman?'

'Mine?'

'In Ynys Trebes. You said that Galahad had Leanor, but that the rest of you all had women too, so who was yours? And what happened to her?'

'I don't know.'

'Oh, Derfel! She can't have been nothing!'

I sighed. 'She was a fisherman's daughter. Her name was Pellcyn, only everyone called her Puss. Her husband had drowned a year before I met her. She had a baby daughter, and when Culhwch led our survivors to the boat Puss fell off the cliff path. She was holding her baby, you see, and couldn't hold on to the rocks. There was chaos and everyone was panicking and hurrying. It was no one's fault.' Though if I had been there, I have often thought, Pellcyn would have lived. She was a sturdy, bright-eyed girl with a quick laugh and an inexhaustible appetite for hard work. A good woman. But if I had saved her life Merlin would have died. Fate is inexorable.

Igraine must have been thinking the same. 'I wish I'd met Merlin,' she said wistfully.

'He'd have liked you,' I said. 'He always liked pretty women.'

'But so did Lancelot?' she asked quickly.

'Oh, yes.'

'Not boys?'

'Not boys.'

Igraine laughed. This day she was wearing an embroidered dress of blue dyed linen that suited her fair skin and dark hair. Two gold torques circled her neck and a tangle of bracelets rattled on a slim wrist. She stank of faeces, a fact I was diplomatic enough to ignore for I realized she must be wearing a pessary of a newborn baby's first motions, an old remedy for a barren woman. Poor Igraine. 'You hated Lancelot?' she suddenly accused me.

'Utterly.'

'That isn't fair!' She jumped up from the window-sill and paced to and fro in the small room. 'People's stories shouldn't be told by their enemies. Supposing Nwylle wrote mine?'

'Who is Nwylle?'

'You don't know her,' she said, frowning, and I guessed Nwylle was her husband's lover. 'But it isn't fair,' she insisted, 'because everyone knows Lancelot was the greatest of Arthur's soldiers. Everyone!'

'I don't.'

'But he must have been brave!'

I stared through the window, trying to be fair in my mind, trying to find something good to say about my worst enemy. 'He could be brave,' I said, 'but he chose not to be. He fought sometimes, but usually he avoided battle. He was frightened of his face being scarred, you see. He was very vain about his looks. He collected Roman mirrors. The mirrored room in Benoic's palace was Lancelot's room. He could sit there and admire himself on every wall.'

'I don't believe he was as bad as you make him sound,' Igraine protested.

'I think he was worse,' I said. I do not enjoy writing about Lancelot for the memory of him lies like a stain on my life. 'Above everything,' I told Igraine, 'he was dishonest. He told lies out of choice because he wanted to hide the truth about himself, but he also knew how to make people like him when he wanted. He could charm the fish from the sea, my dear.'

She sniffed, unhappy at my judgment. Doubtless, when Dafydd ap Gruffud translates these words, Lancelot will be burnished just as he would have liked. Shining Lancelot! Upright Lancelot! Handsome, dancing, smiling, witty, elegant Lancelot! He was the King without Land and the Lord of Lies, but if Igraine has her way he will shine through the years as the very paragon of kingly warriors.

Igraine peered through the window to where Sansum was driving a group of lepers from our gate. The saint was flinging clods of earth at them, screaming at them to go to the devil and summoning our other brothers to help him. The novice

313

Tudwal, who daily grows ruder to the rest of us, danced beside his master and cheered him on. Igraine's guards, lolling at the kitchen door as usual, finally appeared and used their spears to rid the monastery of the diseased beggars. 'Did Sansum really want to sacrifice Arthur?' Igraine asked.

'So Bedwin told me.'

Igraine gave me a sly look. 'Does Sansum like boys, Derfel?'

'The saint loves everyone, dear Queen, even young women who ask impertinent questions.'

She smiled dutifully, then grimaced. 'I'm sure he doesn't like women. Why won't he let any of you marry? Other monks marry, but none here.'

'The pious and beloved Sansum,' I explained, 'believes women distract us from our duty of adoring God. Just like you distract me from my proper work.'

She laughed, then suddenly remembered an errand and looked serious. 'There are two words Dafydd did not understand in the last batch of skins, Derfel. He wants you to explain them. Catamite?'

'Tell him to ask someone else.'

'I shall ask someone else, certainly,' she said indignantly. 'And camel? He says it isn't coal.'

'A camel is a mythical beast, Lady, with horns, wings, scales, a forked tail and flames for breath.'

'It sounds like Nwylle,' Igraine said.

'Ah! The Gospel writers at work! My two evangelists!' Sansum, his hands dirty from the earth he had thrown at the lepers, sidled into the room to give this present parchment a dubious look before wrinkling his nose. 'Do I smell something foul?' he asked.

I looked sheepish. 'The beans at breakfast, Lord Bishop,' I said. 'I apologize.'

'I am astonished you can abide his company,' Sansum said to Igraine. 'And shouldn't you be in the chapel, my Lady? Praying for a baby? Is that not your business here?'

'It's certainly not yours,' Igraine said tartly. 'If you must know, my Lord Bishop, we were discussing our Saviour's parables. Did you not once preach to us about the camel and the needle's eye?'

Sansum grunted and looked over my shoulder. 'And what, foul Brother Derfel, is the Saxon word for camel?'

'Nwylle,' I said.

Igraine laughed and Sansum glared at her. 'My Lady finds the words of our blessed Lord amusing?'

'I am just happy to be here,' Igraine said humbly, 'but I would love to know what a camel is.'

'Everyone knows!' Sansum said derisively. 'A camel is a fish, a great fish! Not unlike,' he added slyly, 'the salmon that your husband sometimes remembers to send to us poor monks?'

'I shall have him send more,' Igraine said, 'with the next batch of Derfel's skins, and I know he'll be sending some of those soon for this Saxon Gospel is very dear to the King.'

'It is?' Sansum asked suspiciously.

'Very dear, my Lord Bishop,' Igraine said firmly.

She is a clever girl, very clever, and beautiful too. King Brochvael is a fool if he takes a lover as well as his Queen, but men were ever fools for women. Or some men were, and chief of them, I suppose, was Arthur. Dear Arthur, my Lord, my Gift-Giver, most generous of men, whose tale this is.

It was strange to be home, especially as I had no home. I possessed some gold torques and scraps of jewellery, but those, save Ceinwyn's brooch, I sold so that my men would at least have food in their first days back in Britain. My other belongings had all been in Ynys Trebes, and now they formed a part of some Frank's hoard. I was poor, homeless, with nothing more to give to my men, not even a hall in which to feast them, but they forgave me that. They were good men and sworn to my service. Like me, they had left behind anything they could not carry when Ynys Trebes fell. Like me they were poor, yet none of them complained. Cavan simply said a soldier must take his losses like he takes his plunder, lightly. Issa, a farm boy who was an extraordinary spearman, tried to return a narrow

315

gold torque that I had given him. It was not just, he said, that a spearman should wear a gold torque when his captain did not, but I would not take it, so Issa gave it as a token to the girl he had brought home from Benoic and the next day she ran off with a tramping priest and his band of whores. The countryside was full of such travelling Christians, missionaries they called themselves, and almost all of them had a band of women believers who were supposed to assist in the Christian rituals, but who, it was rumoured, were more likely to be used for the seduction of converts to the new religion.

Arthur gave me a hall just north of Durnovaria: not for my own, since it belonged to an heiress named Gyllad, an orphan, but Arthur made me her protector; a position which usually ended with the ruination of the child and the enrichment of the guardian. Gyllad was scarcely eight years old and I could have married her had I wanted and then disposed of her property, or else I could have sold her hand in marriage to a man willing to buy the bride along with the farmland, but instead, as Arthur had intended, I lived off Gyllad's rents and allowed her to grow in peace. Even so her relatives protested at my appointment. That very same week of my return from Ynys Trebes, when I had been in Gyllad's hall scarce two days, an uncle of hers, a Christian, appealed against my protectorship to Nabur, the Christian magistrate in Durnovaria, saying that before his death Gyllad's father had promised him the guardianship, and I only managed to keep Arthur's gift by posting my spearmen all around the courthouse. They were in full war gear with spearheads whetted bright, and their presence somehow persuaded the uncle and his supporters not to press their suit. The town guards were summoned, but one look at my veterans persuaded them that maybe they had better business elsewhere. Nabur complained about returning soldiers committing thuggery in a peaceful town, but when my opponents did not appear in court he weakly awarded me the judgment. I later heard the uncle had already purchased the opposite verdict from Nabur and that he was never able to have his money refunded. I appointed one of my men, Llystan, who had lost a foot in a battle in Benoic's woods, as Gyllad's steward and he, like the heiress and her estate, prospered.

Arthur summoned me the following week. I found him in the palace hall where he was eating his midday meal with Guinevere. He ordered a couch and more food to be fetched for me. The courtyard outside was crowded with petitioners. 'Poor Arthur,' Guinevere commented, 'one visit home and suddenly every man is complaining about his neighbour or demanding a reduction in rent. Why don't they use the magistrates?'

'Because they're not rich enough to bribe them,' Arthur said.

'Or powerful enough to surround the courthouse with iron-helmed men?' Guinevere added, smiling to show that she did not disapprove of my action. She wouldn't, for she was a sworn opponent of Nabur who was a leader of the kingdom's Christian faction.

'A spontaneous gesture of support by my men,' I said blandly, and Arthur laughed.

It was a happy meal. I was rarely alone with Arthur and Guinevere, yet when I was I always saw how contented she made him. She had a barbed wit that he lacked, but liked, and she used it gently, as she knew he preferred it used. She flattered Arthur, yet she also gave him good advice. Arthur was ever ready to believe the best about people and he needed Guinevere's scepticism to redress that optimism. She looked no older than the last time I had been so close to her, though maybe there was a new shrewdness in those green huntress eyes. I could see no evidence that she was pregnant: her pale green dress lay flat over her belly where a gold-tasselled rope hung like a loose belt. Her badge of the moon-crested stag hung around her neck beneath the heavy sun-rays of the Saxon necklace that Arthur had sent her from Durocobrivis. She had scorned the necklace when I had presented it to her, but now wore it proudly.

The conversation at that midday meal was mostly light. Arthur wanted to know why the blackbirds and thrushes stopped singing in the summer, but neither of us had an answer, any more than we could tell him where the martins and swallows went in winter, though Merlin once told me they went to a great cave in the northern wilderness where they slept in huge feathered clumps until the spring. Guinevere pressed me about Merlin and I promised her, upon my life, that the Druid had indeed returned to Britain. 'He's gone to the Isle of the Dead,' I told her.

'He's done what?' Arthur asked, appalled.

I explained about Nimue and remembered to thank Guinevere for her efforts to save my friend from Sansum's revenge.

'Poor Nimue,' Guinevere said. 'But she is a fierce creature, isn't she? I liked her, but I don't think she liked us. We are all too frivolous! And I could not interest her in Isis. Isis, she'd tell me, is a foreign Goddess, and then she would spit like a little cat and mutter a prayer to Manawydan.'

Arthur showed no reaction to the mention of Isis and I supposed he had lost his fears of the strange Goddess. 'I wish I knew Nimue better,' he said instead.

'You will,' I said, 'when Merlin brings her back from the dead.'

'If he can,' Arthur said dubiously. 'No one ever has come back from the Isle.'

'Nimue will,' I insisted.

'She is extraordinary,' Guinevere said, 'and if anyone can survive the Isle, she can.'

'With Merlin's help,' I added.

Only at the meal's end did our talk turn to Ynys Trebes, and even then Arthur was careful not to mention the name Lancelot. Instead he regretted that he had no gift with which he could reward me for my efforts.

'Being home is reward enough, Lord Prince,' I said, remembering to use the title Guinevere preferred.

'I can at least call you Lord,' Arthur said, 'and so you will be called from now on, Lord Derfel.'

I laughed, not because I was ungrateful, but because the

reward of a warlord's title seemed too grand for my attainments. I was also proud: a man was called lord for being a king, a prince, a chief or because his sword had made him famous. I superstitiously touched Hywelbane's hilt so that my luck would not be soured by the pride. Guinevere laughed at me, not out of spite, but with delight at my pleasure, and Arthur, who loved nothing more than seeing others happy, was pleased for both of us. He was happy himself that day, but Arthur's happiness was always quieter than other men's joy. At that time, when he first came back to Britain, I never saw him drunk, never saw him boisterous and never saw him lose his self-possession except on a battlefield. He had a stillness about him that some men found disconcerting for they feared he read their souls, but I think that calm came from his desire to be different. He wanted admiration and he loved rewarding the admiration with generosity.

The noise of the waiting petitioners grew louder and Arthur sighed as he thought of the work awaiting him. He pushed away his wine and gave me an apologetic glance. 'You deserve to rest, Lord,' he said, deliberately flattering me with my new title, 'but alas, very soon I shall ask you to take your spears north.'

'My spears are yours, Lord Prince,' I said dutifully.

He traced a circle on the marble table top with his finger. 'We are surrounded by enemies,' he said, 'but the real danger is Powys. Gorfyddyd collects an army like Britain has never seen. That army will come south very soon and King Tewdric, I fear, has no stomach for the fight. I need to put as many spears as I can into Gwent to hold Tewdric's loyalty staunch. Cei can hold Cadwy, Melwas will have to do his best against Cerdic, and the rest of us will go to Gwent.'

'What of Aelle?' Guinevere asked meaningfully.

'He is at peace,' Arthur insisted.

'He obeys the highest price,' Guinevere said, 'and Gorfyddyd will be raising the price very soon.'

Arthur shrugged. 'I cannot face both Gorfyddyd and Aelle,' he said softly. 'It will take three hundred spears to hold Aelle's

Saxons, not defeat them, mark you, just hold them. The lack of those three hundred spears will mean defeat in Gwent.'

'Which Gorfyddyd knows,' Guinevere pointed out.

'So what, my love, would you have me do?' Arthur asked her.

But Guinevere had no better answer than Arthur, and his answer was merely to hope and pray that the fragile peace held with Aelle. The Saxon King had been bought with a cartload of gold and no further price could be paid for there was no gold left in the kingdom. 'We just have to hope Gereint can hold him,' Arthur said, 'while we destroy Gorfyddyd.' He pushed his couch back from the table and smiled at me. 'Rest till after Lughnasa, Lord Derfel,' he told me, 'then as soon as the harvest's gathered you can march north with me.'

He clapped his hands to summon servants to clear away the remains of the meal and to let in the waiting petitioners. Guinevere beckoned me as the servants hurried about their work. 'Can we talk?' she asked.

'Gladly, Lady.'

She took off the heavy necklace, handed it to a slave, then led me up a flight of stone steps that ended at a door opening into an orchard where two of her big deerhounds waited to greet her. Wasps buzzed around windfalls and Guinevere demanded that slaves clear the rotting fruit away so we could walk unmolested. She fed the hounds scraps of chicken left from the midday meal while a dozen slaves scooped the sodden, bruised fruit into the skirts of their robes, then scuttled away, well stung, to leave the two of us alone. Wicker frames of booths that would be decorated with flowers for the great feast of Lughnasa had been erected all around the orchard wall. 'It looks pretty' – Guinevere spoke of the orchard – 'but I wish I was in Lindinis.'

'Next year, Lady,' I said.

'It'll be in ruins,' she said tartly. 'Hadn't you heard? Gundleus raided Lindinis. He didn't capture Caer Cadarn, but he did pull down my new palace. That was a year ago.' She grimaced. 'I hope Ceinwyn makes him utterly miserable, but I doubt she will. She's an insipid little thing.' The leaf-filtered sun lit her red hair and cast strong shadows on her good face. 'I sometimes wish I was a man,' she said, surprising me.

'You do?'

'Do you know how hateful it is to wait for news?' she asked passionately. 'In two or three weeks you'll all go north and then we must just wait. Wait and wait. Wait to hear if Aelle breaks his word, wait to hear how huge Gorfyddyd's army really is.' She paused. 'Why is Gorfyddyd waiting? Why doesn't he attack now?'

'His levies are working on the harvest,' I said. 'Everything stops for harvest. His men will want to make sure of their harvest before they come to take ours.'

'Can we stop them?' she asked me abruptly.

'In war, Lady,' I said, 'it is not always a question of what we can do, but what we must do. We must stop them.' Or die, I thought grimly.

She walked in silence for a few paces, thrusting the excited dogs away from her feet. 'Do you know what people are saying about Arthur?' she asked after a while.

I nodded. 'That it would be better if he fled to Broceliande and yielded the kingdom to Gorfyddyd. They say the war is lost.'

She looked at me, overwhelming me with her huge eyes. At that moment, so close to her, alone with her in the warm garden and engulfed by her subtle scent, I understood why Arthur had risked a kingdom's peace for this woman. 'But you will fight for Arthur?' she asked me.

'To the end, Lady,' I said. 'And for you,' I added awkwardly.

She smiled. 'Thank you.' We turned a corner, walking towards the small spring that sprang from a rock in the corner of the Roman wall. The trickle of water irrigated the orchard and someone had tucked votive ribbons into niches of the mossy rock. Guinevere lifted the golden hem of her apple-green dress as she stepped over the rivulet. 'There's a Mordred party in the kingdom,' she told me, repeating what Bishop Bedwin had spoken of on the night of my return. 'They're Christians, mostly, and they're all praying for Arthur's defeat. If he was defeated, of course, they'd have to grovel to Gorfyddyd, but grovelling, I've noticed, comes naturally to Christians. If I were a man, Derfel Cadarn, three heads would fall to my sword. Sansum, Nabur and Mordred.'

I did not doubt her words. 'But if Nabur and Sansum are the best men the Mordred party can muster, Lady,' I said, 'then Arthur need not worry about them.'

'King Melwas too, I think,' Guinevere said, 'and who knows how many others? Almost every wandering priest in the kingdom spreads the pestilence, asking why men should die for Arthur. I'd strike all their heads off, but traitors don't reveal themselves, Lord Derfel. They wait in the dark and strike when you're not looking. But if Arthur defeats Gorfyddyd they'll all sing his praises and pretend they were his supporters all the while.' She spat to avert evil, then gave me a sharp glance. 'Tell me about King Lancelot,' she said suddenly.

I had an impression that we were at last reaching the real reason for this stroll beneath the apple and pear trees. 'I don't really know him,' I said evasively.

'He spoke well of you last night,' she said.

'He did?' I responded sceptically. I knew Lancelot and his companions were still resident in Arthur's house, indeed I had been dreading meeting him and relieved that he had not been at the midday meal.

'He said you were a great soldier,' Guinevere said.

'It's nice to know,' I answered sourly, 'that he can sometimes tell the truth.' I assumed that Lancelot, trimming his sails to a new wind, had tried to gain favour with Arthur by praising a man he knew to be Arthur's friend.

'Maybe,' Guinevere said, 'warriors who suffer a terrible defeat like the fall of Ynys Trebes always end up squabbling?'

'Suffer?' I said harshly. 'I saw him leave Benoic, Lady, but I don't remember him suffering. Any more than I remember seeing that bandage on his hand when he left.'

'He's no coward,' she insisted warmly. 'He wears warrior rings thick on his left hand, Lord Derfel.'

'Warrior rings!' I said derisively, and plunged my hand into my belt pouch and brought out a fistful of the things. I had so many now that I no longer bothered to make them. I scattered the rings on the orchard's grass, startling the deerhounds that looked to their mistress for reassurance. 'Anyone can find warrior rings, Lady.'

Guinevere stared at the fallen rings, then kicked one aside. 'I like King Lancelot,' she said defiantly, thus warning me against any more disparaging remarks. 'And we have to look after him. Arthur feels we failed Benoic and the least we can do is to treat its survivors with honour. I want you to be kind to Lancelot, for my sake.'

'Yes, Lady,' I said meekly.

'We must find him a rich wife,' Guinevere said. 'He must have land and men to command. Dumnonia is fortunate, I think, in having him come to our shores. We need good soldiers.'

'Indeed we do, Lady,' I agreed.

She caught the sarcasm in my voice and grimaced, but despite my hostility she persevered with the real reason she had invited me to this shadowed, private orchard. 'King Lancelot,' she said, 'wants to be a worshipper of Mithras, and Arthur and I do not want him opposed.'

I felt a flare of rage at my religion being taken so lightly. 'Mithras, Lady,' I said coldly, 'is a religion for the brave.'

'Even you, Derfel Cadarn, do not need more enemies,' Guinevere replied just as coldly, so I knew she would become my enemy if I blocked Lancelot's desires. And doubtless, I thought, Guinevere would deliver the same message to any other man who might oppose Lancelot's initiation into the Mithraic mysteries.

'Nothing will be done till winter,' I said, evading a firm commitment.

'But make sure it is done,' she said, then pushed open the hall door. 'Thank you, Lord Derfel.'

'Thank you, Lady,' I said, and felt another surge of anger as I ran down the steps to the hall. Ten days! I thought, just ten days and Lancelot had made Guinevere into his supporter. I cursed, vowing that I would become a miserable Christian before I ever saw Lancelot feasting in a cave beneath a bull's bloody head. I had broken three Saxon shield-walls and buried Hywelbane to her hilt in my country's enemies before I had been elected to Mithras's service, but all Lancelot had ever done was boast and posture.

I entered the hall to find Bedwin seated beside Arthur. They were hearing petitioners, but Bedwin left the dais to draw me to a quiet spot beside the hall's outer door. 'I hear you're a lord now,' he said. 'My congratulations.'

'A lord without land,' I said bitterly, still upset by Guinevere's outrageous demand.

'Land follows victory,' Bedwin told me, 'and victory follows battle, and of battle, Lord Derfel, you will have plenty this year.' He stopped as the hall door was thrown open and as Lancelot and his followers stalked in. Bedwin bowed to him, while I merely nodded. The King of Benoic seemed surprised to see me, but said nothing as he walked to join Arthur, who ordered a third chair arranged on the dais. 'Is Lancelot a member of the council now?' I asked Bedwin angrily.

'He's a King,' Bedwin said patiently. 'You can't expect him to stand while we sit.'

I noticed that the King of Benoic still had a bandage on his right hand. 'I trust the King's wound will mean he can't come with us?' I said acidly. I almost confessed to Bedwin how Guinevere had demanded that we elect Lancelot a Mithraist, but decided that news could wait.

'He won't come with us,' Bedwin confirmed. 'He's to stay here as commander of Durnovaria's garrison.'

'As what?' I asked loudly and so angrily that Arthur twisted in his chair to see what the commotion was about.

'If King Lancelot's men guard Guinevere and Mordred,' Bedwin said wearily, 'it frees Lanval's and Llywarch's men to fight against Gorfyddyd.' He hesitated, then laid a frail hand on my arm. 'There's something else I need to tell you, Lord

324

Derfel.' His voice was low and gentle. 'Merlin was in Ynys Wydryn last week.'

'With Nimue?' I asked eagerly.

He shook his head. 'He never went for her, Derfel. He went north instead, but why or where we don't know.'

The scar on my left hand throbbed. 'And Nimue?' I asked, dreading to hear the answer.

'Still on the Isle, if she even lives.' He paused. 'I'm sorry.'

I stared down the crowded hall. Did Merlin not know about Nimue? Or had he preferred to leave her among the dead? Much as I loved him I sometimes thought that Merlin could be the cruellest man in all the world. If he had visited Ynys Wydryn then he must have known where Nimue was imprisoned, yet he had done nothing. He had left her with the dead, and suddenly my fears were shrieking inside me like the cries of the dying children of Ynys Trebes. For a few cold seconds I could neither move nor speak, then I looked at Bedwin. 'Galahad will take my men north if I don't return,' I told him.

'Derfel!' He gripped my arm. 'No one comes back from the Isle of the Dead. No one!'

'Does it matter?' I asked him. For if all Dumnonia was·lost, what did it matter? And Nimue was not dead, I knew that because the scar was pounding on my hand. And if Merlin did not care about her, I did, I cared more about Nimue than I cared about Gorfyddyd or Aelle or the wretched Lancelot with his ambitions to join Mithras's elect. I loved Nimue even if she would never love me, and I was scar-sworn to be her protector.

Which meant that I must go where Merlin would not. I must go to the Isle of the Dead.

The Isle lay only ten miles south of Durnovaria, no more than a morning's gentle walk, yet for all I knew of the Isle it could have been on the far side of the moon.

I did know it was no island, but rather a peninsula of hard pale stone that lay at the end of a long narrow causeway. The Romans had quarried the isle, but we quarried their buildings rather than the earth and so the quarries had closed and the

Isle of the Dead had been left empty. It became a prison. Three walls were built across the causeway, guards were set, and to the Isle we sent those we wanted to punish. In time we sent others too; those men and women whose wits had flown and who could not live in peace among us. They were the violent mad, sent to a kingdom of the mad where no sane person lived and where their demon-haunted souls could not endanger the living. The Druids claimed the Isle was the domain of Crom Dubh, the dark crippled God, the Christians said it was the Devil's foothold on earth, but both agreed that men or women sent across its causeway's walls were lost souls. They were dead while their bodies still lived, and when their bodies did die the demons and evil spirits would be trapped on the Isle so they could never return to haunt the living. Families would bring their mad to the Isle and there, at the third wall, release them to the unknown horrors that waited at the causeway's end. Then, back on the mainland, the family would hold a death feast for their lost relative. Not all the mad were sent to the Isle. Some of them were touched by the Gods and thus were sacred, and some families kept their mad locked up as Merlin had penned poor Pellinore, but when the Gods who touched the mad were malevolent, then the Isle was the place where the captured soul must be sent.

The sea broke white about the Isle. At its seaward end, even in the calmest weather, there was a great maelstrom of whirlpools and seething water over the place where Cruachan's Cave led to the Otherworld. Spray exploded from the sea above the cave and waves clashed interminably to mark its horrid unseen mouth. No fisherman would go near that maelstrom, for any boat that did get blown into its churning horror was surely lost. It would sink and its crew would be sucked down to become shadows in the Otherworld.

The sun shone on the day I went to the Isle. I carried Hywelbane, but no other war gear since no man-made shield or breastplate would protect me from the spirits and serpents of the Isle. For supplies I carried a skin of fresh water and a pouch of oatcakes, while for my talismans against the Isle's demons I wore Ceinwyn's brooch and a sprig of garlic pinned to my green cloak.

I passed the hall where the death feasts were held. The road beyond the hall was edged with skulls, human and animal, warnings to the unwary that they approached the Kingdom of Dead Souls. To my left now was the sea, and to my right a brackish, dark marsh where no birds sang. Beyond the marsh was a great shingle bank that curved away from the coast to become the causeway that joined the Isle to the mainland. To approach the Isle by the shingle bank meant a detour of many miles, so most traffic used the skull-edged road that led to a decaying timber quay where a ferry crossed over to the beach. A sprawl of wattle guards' houses stood close to the quay. More guards patrolled the shingle bank.

The guards on the quay were old men or else wounded veterans who lived with their families in the huts. The men watched me approach, then barred my path with rusty spears.

'My name is Lord Derfel,' I said, 'and I demand passage.'

The guard commander, a shabby man in an ancient iron breastplate and a mildewed leather helmet, bowed to me. 'I am not empowered to stop you passing, Lord Derfel,' he said, 'but I cannot let you return.' His men, astonished that anyone would voluntarily travel to the Isle, gaped at me.

'Then I shall pass,' I said, and the spearmen moved aside as the guard commander shouted at them to man the small ferryboat. 'Do many ask to pass this way?' I asked the commander.

'A few,' he said. 'Some are tired of living; some think they can rule an isle of mad people. Few have ever lived long enough to beg me to let them out again.'

'Did you let them out?' I asked.

'No,' he said curtly. He watched as oars were brought from one of the huts, then he frowned at me. 'Are you sure, Lord?' he asked.

'I'm sure.'

He was curious, but dared not ask my business. Instead he helped me down the slippery steps of the quay and handed me into the pitch-blackened boat. 'The rowers will let you through the first gate,' he told me, then pointed further along the causeway that lay at the far side of the narrow channel. 'After that you'll come to a second wall, then a third at the causeway's end. There are no gates in those walls, just steps across. You'll likely meet no dead souls between the walls, but after that? The Gods only know. Do you truly want to go?'

'Have you never been curious?' I asked him.

'We're permitted to carry food and dead souls as far as the third wall and I've no wish to go farther,' he said grimly. 'I'll reach the bridge of swords to the Otherworld in my own time, Lord.' He jerked his chin towards the causeway. 'Cruachan's Cave lies beyond the Isle, Lord, and only fools and desperate men seek death before their time.'

'I have reasons,' I said, 'and I shall see you again in this world of the living.'

'Not if you cross the water, Lord.'

I stared at the isle's green and white slope that loomed above the causeway's walls. 'I was in a death-pit once,' I told the guard commander, 'and I crawled from there as I shall crawl from here.' I fished in my pouch and found a coin to give him. 'We shall discuss my leaving when the time comes.'

'You're a dead man, Lord,' he warned me one last time, 'the very moment you cross that channel.'

'Death doesn't know how to take me,' I said with foolish bravado, then ordered the oarsmen to row me across the swirling channel. It took only a few strokes, then the boat grounded on a bank of shelving mud and we climbed to the archway in the first wall where the two oarsmen lifted the bar, pulled the gates aside and stood back to let me pass. A black threshold marked the divide between this world and the next. Once over that slab of blackened timber I was counted as a dead man. For a second my fears made me hesitate, then I stepped across.

The gates crashed shut behind me. I shivered.

I turned to examine the inner face of the main wall. It was ten feet high, a barrier of smooth stone laid as clean as any Roman work and so well made that not a single handhold showed on its white face. A ghost-fence of skulls topped the wall to keep the dead souls from the world of the living.

I said prayers to the Gods. I said one to Bel, my special protector, and another to Manawydan, the Sea God who had saved Nimue in the past, and then I walked on down the causeway to where the second wall barred the road. This wall was a crude bank of sea-smoothed stones that were, like the first wall, topped with a line of human skulls. I went down the steps on the wall's farther side. To my right, the west, the great waves crashed against the shingle, while to my left the shallow bay lay calm under the sun. A few fishing boats worked the bay, but all were staying well clear of the Isle. Ahead of me was the third wall. I could see no man or woman waiting there. Gulls soared above me, their cries forlorn in the west wind. The causeway's sides were edged with tidelines of dark sea wrack.

I was frightened. In the years since Arthur had returned to Britain I had faced countless shield-walls and unnumbered men in battle, yet at none of those fights, not even in burning Benoic, had I felt a fear like the cold that gripped my heart now. I stopped and turned to stare at Dumnonia's soft green hills and the small fishing village in the eastern bay. Go back now, I thought, go back! Nimue had been here one whole year and I doubted if many souls survived that long in the Isle of the Dead unless they were both savage and powerful. And even if I found her, she would be mad. She could not leave here. This was her kingdom, death's dominion. Go back, I urged myself, go back, but then the scar on my left palm pulsed and I told myself that Nimue lived.

A cackling howl startled me. I turned to see a black, ragged figure caper on the third wall's summit, then the figure disappeared down the wall's farther side and I prayed to the Gods to give me strength. Nimue had always known she would suffer the Three Wounds, and the scar on my left hand was her surety that I would help her survive the ordeals. I walked on.

I climbed the third wall, which was another bank of smooth grey stones, and saw a flight of crude steps leading down to the Isle. At the foot of the steps lay some empty baskets; evidently

329

the means whereby the living delivered bread and salted meat to their dead relatives. The ragged figure had vanished, leaving only the towering hill above me and a tangle of brambles either side of a stony road that led to the Isle's western flank, where I could just see a group of ruined buildings at the base of the great hill. The Isle was a huge place. It would take a man two hours to walk from the third wall to where the sea seethed at the Isle's southern tip, and as much time again to climb up over the spine of the great rock to cross from the Isle's western to its eastern coast.

I followed the road. Wind rustled the sea grass beyond the brambles. A bird screamed at me then soared on outspread white wings into the sunny sky. The road turned so that I was walking directly towards the ancient town. It was a Roman town, but no Glevum or Durnovaria, merely a squalid huddle of low stone buildings where once the quarry slaves had lived. The buildings' roofs were crude thatches made from driftwood and dry seaweed, poor shelters even for the dead. Fear of what lay in the town made me falter, then a sudden voice shouted in warning and a stone sailed out of the scrub up the slope to my left and clattered on the road beside me. The warning provoked a swarm of ragged creatures to scuttle out of the huts to see who approached their settlement. The swarm was composed of men and women, mostly in rags, but some wore their rags with an air of grandeur and walked towards me as though they were the greatest monarchs on earth. Their hair was crowned with wreaths of seaweed. A few of the men carried spears and nearly all the people clutched stones. Some of them were naked. There were children among them; small, feral and dangerous children. Some of the adults shook uncontrollably, others twitched, and all watched me with bright, hungry eyes.

'A sword!' A huge man spoke. 'I'll have the sword! A sword!' He shuffled towards me and his followers advanced behind on bare feet. A woman hurled a stone, and suddenly they were all screaming with delight because they had a new soul to plunder.

I drew Hywelbane, but not one man, woman or child was checked by the sight of her long blade. Then I fled. There could be no disgrace in a warrior fleeing the dead. I ran back up the road and a clatter of stones landed at my heels, then a dog leaped to bite at my green cloak. I beat the brute off with the sword, then reached the road's turning where I plunged to my right, pushing through the brambles and scrub to reach the hillside. A thing reared in front of me, a naked thing with a man's face and a brute's body of hair and dirt. One of the thing's eyes was a running sore, its mouth was a pit of rotting gums and it lunged at me with hands made into claws by hook-like nails. Hywelbane sliced bright. I was screaming with terror, certain that I faced one of the Isle's demons, but my instincts were still as sharp as my blade that cut through the brute's hairy arm and slashed into his skull. I leaped over him and climbed the hill, aware that a horde of famished souls was clambering behind me. A stone struck my back, another hit the rock beside me, but I was scrambling fast up the pillars and platforms of quarried rock until I found a narrow path that twisted like the paths of Ynys Trebes around the hill's raw flank.

I turned on the path to face my pursuers. They checked, frightened at last by the sword waiting for them on the narrow path where only one of them could approach me at a time. The big man leered. 'Nice man,' he called in a wheedling voice, 'come down, nice man.' He held up a gull's egg to tempt me. 'Come and eat!'

An old woman lifted her skirts and thrust her loins at me. 'Come to me, my lover! Come to me, my darling. I knew you'd come!' She began to piss. A child laughed and flung a stone.

I left them. Some followed me along the path, but after a while they became bored and went back to their ghostly settlement.

The narrow path led between the sky and the sea. Every now and then it would be interrupted by an ancient quarry where the marks of Roman tools scarred baulks of stone, but beyond each quarry the path would wind on again through patches of thyme and spinneys of thorn. I saw no one until, suddenly, a voice hailed me from one of the small quarries.

'You don't look mad,' the voice said dubiously. I turned, sword raised, to see a courtly man in a dark cloak gazing gravely from the mouth of a cave. He raised a hand. 'Please! No weapons. My name is Malldynn, and I greet you, stranger, if you come in peace, and if not, then I beg you to pass us by.'

I wiped the blood from Hywelbane and thrust her back into the scabbard. 'I come in peace,' I said.

'Are you newly come to the Isle?' he asked as he approached me gingerly. He had a pleasant face, deeply lined and sad, with a manner that reminded me of Bishop Bedwin.

'I arrived this hour,' I answered.

'And you were doubtless pursued by the rabble at the gate. I apologize for them, though the Gods know I have no responsibility for those ghouls. They take the bread each week and make the rest of us pay for it. Fascinating, is it not, how even in a place of lost souls we form our hierarchies? There are rulers here. There are the strong and the weak. Some men dream of making paradises on this earth and the first requirement of such paradises, or so I understand, is that we must be unshackled by laws, but I do suspect, my friend, that any place unshackled by laws will more resemble this Isle than any paradise. I do not have the pleasure of your name.'

'Derfel.'

'Derfel?' He frowned in thought. 'A servant of the Druids?'

'I was. Now I'm a warrior.'

'No, you are not,' he corrected me, 'you are dead. You have come to the Isle of the Dead. Please, come and sit. It is not much, but it is my home.' He gestured into the cave where two semi-dressed blocks of stone served as a chair and table. An old piece of cloth, perhaps dragged from the sea, half hid his sleeping quarter where I could see a bed made from dried grass. He insisted I use the small stone block as my chair. 'I can offer you rainwater to drink,' he said, 'and some five-day-old bread to eat.'

I put an oatcake on the table. Malldynn was plainly hungry, but he resisted the impulse to snatch the biscuit. Instead he drew a small knife with a blade that had been sharpened so often that it had a wavy edge and used it to divide the oatcake into halves. 'At risk of sounding ungrateful,' he said, 'oats were never my favourite food. I prefer meat, fresh meat, but still I thank you, Derfel.' He had been kneeling opposite me, but once the oatcake was eaten and the crumbs had been delicately dabbed from his lips he stood and leaned against the cave's wall. 'My mother made oatcakes,' he told me, 'but hers were tougher. I suspect the oats were not husked properly. That one was delicious, and I shall now revise my opinion of oats. Thank you again.' He bowed.

'You don't seem mad,' I said.

He smiled. He was middle-aged, with a distinguished face, clever eyes and a white beard that he tried to keep trimmed. His cave had been swept clean with a brush of twigs that leaned against the wall. 'It is not just the mad who are sent here, Derfel,' he said reprovingly. 'Some who want to punish the sane send them here also. Alas, I offended Uther.' He paused ruefully. 'I was a counsellor,' he went on, 'a great man even, but when I told Uther that his son Mordred was a fool, I ended here. But I was right. Mordred was a fool, even at ten years old he was a fool.'

'You've been here that long?' I asked in astonishment.

'Alas, yes.'

'How do you survive?'

He offered me a self-deprecating shrug. 'The gate-keeping ghouls believe I can work magic. I threaten to re-store their wits if they offend me, and so they take good care to keep me happy. They are happier mad, believe me. Any man who possessed his wits would pray to go insane on this Isle. And you, friend Derfel, might I enquire what brings you here?'

'I search for a woman.'

'Ah! We have plenty, and most are unconstrained by modesty. Such women, I believe, are another requisite of earthly paradises, but alas, the reality proves otherwise. They are certainly immodest, but they are also filthy, their conversation is tedious, and the pleasure to be derived from them is as momentary as it is shameful. If you seek such a woman, Derfel, then you will find them here in abundance.'

'I'm searching for a woman called Nimue,' I said.

'Nimue,' he said, frowning as he tried to remember the name, 'Nimue! Yes indeed, I do recall her now! A one-eyed girl with black hair. She's gone to the sea folk.'

'Drowned?' I asked, appalled.

'No, no.' He shook his head. 'You must understand we have our own communities on the Isle. You have already made the acquaintance of the gate ghouls. We here in the quarries are the hermits, a small group who prefer our solitude and so inhabit the caves on this side of the Isle. On the far side are the beasts. You may imagine what they are like. At the southern end are the sea folk. They fish with lines of human hair using thorns for hooks and are, I must say, the best behaved of the Isle's tribes, though none are exactly famed for their hospitality. They all fight each other, of course. Do you see how we have everything here that the Land of the Living offers? Except, perhaps, religion, although one or two of our inhabitants do believe themselves to be Gods. And who is to deny them?'

'You've never tried to leave?'

'I did,' he said sadly. 'A long time ago. I once tried to swim across the bay, but they watch us, and a spear-butt on the head is an efficient reminder that we are not supposed to leave the Isle and I turned back long before they could administer such a blow. Most drown who try to escape that way. A few go along the causeway and some of them, perhaps, do get back among the living, but only if they succeed in passing the gate ghouls first. And if they survive that ordeal they have to avoid the guards waiting on the beach. Those skulls you saw as you crossed the causeway? They are all men and women who tried to escape. Poor souls.' He went silent and I thought, for a second, he was about to weep. Then he pushed himself briskly off the wall. 'What am I thinking about? Do I have no manners? I must offer you water. See? My cistern!' He gestured proudly towards a wooden barrel that stood just outside the cave mouth and which was placed to catch the water that cascaded off the quarry's sides during rainstorms. He had a ladle with which he filled two wooden cups with water. 'The barrel and ladle came from a fishing boat that was wrecked here, when? Let me see . . . two years ago. Poor people! Three men and two boys. One man tried to swim away and was drowned, the other two died under a hail of stones and the two boys were carried off. You can imagine what happened to them! There may be women aplenty, but a clean young fisherboy's flesh is a rare treat on this Isle.' He put the cup in front of me and shook his head. 'It is a terrible place, my friend, and you have been foolish to come here. Or were you sent?'

'I came by choice.'

'Then you belong here anyway, for you're plainly mad.' He drank his water. 'Tell me,' he said, 'the news of Britain.'

I told him. He had heard of Uther's death and Arthur's coming, but not much else. He frowned when I said King Mordred was maimed, but was pleased when he heard that Bedwin still lived. 'I like Bedwin,' he said. 'Liked, rather. We have to learn to talk here as though we were dead. He must be old?'

'Not so old as Merlin.'

'Merlin lives?' he asked in surprise.

'He does.'

'Dear me! So Merlin is alive!' He seemed pleased. 'I once gave him an eagle stone and he was so grateful. I have another here somewhere. Where now?' He searched among a small pile of rocks and scraps of wood that made a collection beside the cave door. 'Is it over there?' He pointed towards the bed-curtain. 'Can you see it?'

I turned away to look for the precious rattling stone and the moment I looked away Malldynn leaped on my back and tried to drag his small knife's ragged edge across my throat. 'I'll eat you!' he cried in triumph. 'Eat you!' But I had somehow caught his knife hand with my left and managed to keep the blade away from my windpipe. He wrestled me to the floor and tried to bite my ear. He was slavering above me, his appetite

335

whetted by the thought of new, clean human flesh to eat. I hit him once, twice, managed to twist around and bring up my knee, then hit him again, but the wretch had remarkable strength and the sound of our fight brought more men running from other caves. I had only a few seconds before I would be overpowered by the newcomers and so I gave one last desperate heave, then butted Malldynn's head with mine and finally threw him off. I kicked him away, scrambled desperately back from the onrush of his friends, then stood in the entrance to his bed-chamber where I at last had room to draw Hywelbane. The hermits shrank away from the sword's bright blade.

Malldynn, his mouth bleeding, lay at the side of the cave. 'Not even a scrap of fresh liver?' he begged me. 'Just a morsel? Please?'

I left him. The other hermits plucked at my cloak as I passed through the quarry, but none tried to stop me. One of them laughed as I left. 'You'll have to come back!' the man called to me, 'and we'll be hungrier then!'

'Eat Malldynn,' I told them bitterly.

I climbed to the Isle's ridge where gorse grew among rocks. I could see from the summit that the great rock hill did not extend all the way to the Isle's southern tip, but fell steeply to a long plain that was hatched by a tangle of ancient stone walls; evidence that ordinary men and women had once lived on the Isle and farmed the stony plateau that sloped towards the sea. There were settlements still on the plateau: the homes, I supposed, of the sea folk. A group of those dead souls watched me from their cluster of round huts that stood at the hill's base and their presence persuaded me to stay where I was and wait for dawn. Life creeps slow in the early morning, which is why soldiers like to attack in the first light and why I would search for my lost Nimue when the mad denizens of the Isle were still sluggish and bemused with sleep.

It was a hard night. A bad night. The stars wheeled above me, bright homes from where the spirits look down on feeble earth. I prayed to Bel, begging for strength, and sometimes I slept, though every rustle of grass or fall of stone brought me wide awake. I had sheltered in a narrow crack of rock that would restrict any attack and as a result I was confident I could protect myself, though only Bel knew how I would ever leave the Isle. Or whether I would ever find my Nimue.

I crept from my rock niche before the dawn. A fog hung over the sea beyond the sullen turmoil that marked the entrance of Cruachan's Cave and a weak grey light made the Isle look flat and cold. I could see no one as I walked downhill. The sun had still not risen as I entered the first small village of crude huts. Yesterday, I had decided, I had been too timid with the Isle's denizens. Today I would treat the dead like the carrion they were.

The huts were wattle and mud, thatched with branches and grass. I kicked in a ramshackle wooden door, stooped inside the hut and grabbed the first sleeping form I found. I hurled that creature outside, kicked another, then slashed a hole in the roof with Hywelbane. Things that had once been human untangled themselves and slithered away from me. I kicked a man in the head, slapped another with the flat of Hywelbane's blade, then dragged a third man out into the sickly light. I threw him to the ground, put my foot on his chest and held Hywelbane's tip at his throat. 'I seek a woman named Nimue,' I said.

He stammered gibberish at me. He could not speak, or rather he could only talk in a language of his own devising and so I left him and ran after a woman who was limping into the bushes. She screamed as I caught her, and screamed again as I placed the steel at her throat. 'Do you know a woman called Nimue?'

She was too terrified to speak. Instead she lifted her filthy skirts and offered me a toothless leer, so I slapped her face with the flat of the sword's blade. 'Nimue!' I shouted at her. 'A girl with one eye called Nimue. Do you know her?' The woman still could not speak, but she pointed south, jabbing her hand towards the Isle's seaward tip in a frantic effort to make me relent. I took the sword away and kicked the skirts back over her thighs. The woman scrambled away into a patch of thorns.

The other frightened souls stared from their huts as I followed the path south towards the churning sea.

I passed two other tiny settlements, but no one tried to stop me now. I had become part of the Isle of the Dead's living nightmare; a creature in the dawn with naked steel. I walked through fields of pale grass dotted with bird's-foot trefoil, blue milkwort and the crimson spikes of orchids and told myself I should have known that Nimue, a creature of Manawydan's, would have found her refuge as close to the sea as she could find it.

The Isle's southern shore was a tangle of rocks edging a low cliff. Great waves crashed into foam, sucked through gullies and shattered white into clouds of spray. The cauldron swirled and spat offshore. It was a summer morning, but the sea was grey like iron, the wind was cold and the sea birds loud with laments.

I jumped from rock to rock, going down towards that deathly sea. My ragged cloak lifted in the wind as I turned around a pillar of pale stone to see a cave that lay a few feet above the dark line of oarweed and bladderwrack stranded by the highest tides. A ledge led to the cave, and on the ledge were piled the bones of birds and animals. The piles had been made by human hands, for they were regularly spaced and each heap was braced by a careful latticework of longer bones and topped by a skull. I stopped, fear surging in me like the surge of the sea, as I stared at the refuge as close to the sea as any place could be on this Isle of doomed souls. 'Nimue?' I called as I summoned the courage to approach the ledge. 'Nimue?'

I climbed to the narrow rock platform and walked slowly between the heaped bones. I feared what I would find in the cave. 'Nimue?' I called.

Beneath me a wave roared across a spur of rock and clawed white fingers towards the ledge. The water fell back and drained in dark sluices to the sea before another roller thundered on the headland's stone and across the glistening rocks. The cave was dark and silent. 'Nimue?' I said again, my voice faltering.

The cave's mouth was guarded by two human skulls that had been forced into niches so that their broken teeth grinned into the moaning wind either side of the entrance. 'Nimue?' There was no answer except for the wind's howl and the birds' laments and the suck and shudder of the ghastly sea.

I stepped inside. It was cold in the cave and the light was sickly. The walls were damp. The shingle floor rose in front of me and forced me to stoop beneath the roof's heavy loom as I stepped cautiously forward. The cave narrowed and twisted sharply to the left. A third yellowing skull guarded the bend where I waited as my eyes settled to the gloom, then I turned past the guardian skull to see the cave dwindling towards a dead, dark end.

And there, at the cave's dark limit, she lay. My Nimue.

I thought at first she was dead for she was naked and huddled with her dark hair filthy across her face and with her thin legs drawn up to her breasts and her pale arms clutching her shins. Sometimes, in the green hills, we would risk the barrow wights to dig into the grassy mounds and seek the old people's gold, and we would find their bones in just such a huddle as they crouched in the earth to fend off the spirits through all eternity.

'Nimue?' I was forced to go on hands and knees to crawl the last few feet to where she lay. 'Nimue?' I said again. This time her name caught in my throat for I was sure she must be dead, but then I saw her ribs move. She breathed, but was otherwise still as death. I put Hywelbane down and reached a hand to touch her cold white shoulder. 'Nimue?'

She sprang towards me, hissing, teeth bared, one eye a livid red socket and the other turned so that only the white of its eyeball showed. She tried to bite me, she clawed at me, she keened a curse in a whining voice then spat it at me, and afterwards she slashed her long nails at my eyes. 'Nimue!' I yelled. She was spitting, drooling, fighting and snapping with filthy teeth at my face. 'Nimue!'

She screamed another curse and put her right hand at my throat. She had the strength of the mad and her scream rose in triumph as her fingers closed on my windpipe. Then, suddenly, I knew just what I had to do. I seized her left hand, ignored the pain in my throat, and laid my own scarred palm across her scar. I laid it there; I left it there; I did not move.

And slowly, slowly, the right hand at my throat weakened. Slowly, slowly, her good eye rolled so that I could see my love's bright soul once more. She stared at me, and then she began to cry.

'Nimue,' I said, and she put her arms around my neck and clung to me. She was sobbing now in great heaves that racked her thin ribs as I held her, stroked her and spoke her name.

The sobs slowed and at last ended. She hung on my neck for a long time; then I felt her head move. 'Where's Merlin?' she asked in a small child's voice.

'Here in Britain,' I said.

'Then we must go.' She took her arms from around my neck and settled on her haunches so she could stare into my face. 'I dreamed that you'd come,' she said.

'I do love you,' I said. I had not meant to say it, even if it was true.

'That's why you came,' she said as though it were obvious.

'Do you have clothes?' I asked.

'I have your cloak,' she said. 'I need nothing else except your hand.'

I crawled out of the cave, sheathed Hywelbane and wrapped my green cloak around her pale shivering body. She pushed an arm through a rent in the cloak's ragged wool and then, her hand in mine, we walked between the bones and climbed the hill to where the sea folk watched. They parted as we reached the cliff's top and did not follow as we walked slowly down the Isle's eastern side. Nimue said nothing. Her madness had fled the moment my hand touched hers, but it had left her horribly weak. I helped her on the steeper portions of the path. We passed through the hermits' caves without being troubled. Perhaps they were all asleep, or else the Gods had put the Isle under a spell as we two walked our way north away from the dead souls.

The sun rose. I could see now that Nimue's hair was matted with dirt and crawling with lice, her skin was filthy and she had lost her golden eye. She was so weak she could hardly walk and as we descended the hill towards the causeway I picked her up in my arms and found she weighed less than a ten-year-old child. 'You're weak,' I said.

'I was born weak, Derfel,' she said, 'and life is spent pretending otherwise.'

'You need some rest,' I said.

'I know.' She leaned her head against my chest and for once in her life she was utterly content to be looked after.

I carried her to the causeway and over the first wall. The sea broke on our left and the bay glimmered a reflection of the rising sun on our right. I did not know how I was to take her past the guards. All I knew was that we had to leave the Isle because that was her fate and I was the instrument of that fate, and so I walked content that the Gods would solve the problem when I reached the final barrier.

I carried her over the middle wall with its row of skulls and walked towards Dumnonia's dawn-green hills. I could see a single spearman silhouetted above the final wall's sheer, smooth face of stone and I supposed some of the guards had rowed across the channel when they saw me leaving the isle. More guards were standing on the shingle bank; they had stationed themselves to bar my passage to the mainland. If I have to kill, I thought, then kill I shall. This was the Gods' will, not mine, and Hywelbane would cut with a God's skill and strength.

But as I walked towards the final wall with my burden light in my arms the gates of life and death swung open to receive me. I half expected the guard commander to be there with his rusty spear, ready to turn me back; instead it was Galahad and Cavan who waited on the black threshold with their swords drawn and battle shields on their arms. 'We followed you,' Galahad said.

'Bedwin sent us,' Cavan added. I covered Nimue's awful hair with the cloak's hood so my friends would not see her degradation and she clung to me, trying to hide herself.

Galahad and Cavan had brought my men who had commandeered the ferry and were holding the Isle's guardians at
spear-point on the channel's farther bank. 'We would have
come looking for you today,' Galahad said, then made the sign
of the cross as he stared down the causeway. He gave me a
curious look as though he feared I might have come back from
the Isle a different man.

'I should have known you would be here,' I told him.

'Yes,' he said, 'you should.' There were tears in his eyes,
tears of happiness.

We rowed across the channel and I carried Nimue up the
road of skulls to the feast hall at the road's end where I found a
man loading a cart with salt to carry to Durnovaria. I laid
Nimue on his cargo and walked behind her as the cart creaked
north towards the town. I had brought Nimue out of the Isle of
the Dead, back to a land at war.

I TOOK NIMUE TO GYLLAD's farm. I did not put her in the big hall, but rather used an abandoned shepherd's cottage where the two of us could be alone. I fed her on broth and milk, but first I washed her clean; washed every inch of her, washed her twice and then washed her black hair and afterwards used a bone comb to tease the tangles free. Some of the tangles were so tight they needed to be cut, but most came free and when her hair hung wet and straight I used the comb to find and kill the lice before I washed her once again. She endured the process like a small obedient child, and when she was clean I wrapped her in a great woollen blanket and took the broth off the fire and made her eat while I washed myself and hunted down the lice that had gone from her body on to mine.

By the time I had finished it was dusk and she was fast asleep on a bed made from newly cut bracken. She slept all night and in the morning ate six eggs I had stirred in a pan over the fire. Then she slept again while I took a knife and a piece of leather and cut an eyepatch with a lace she could tie around her hair. I had one of Gyllad's slaves bring clothes and sent Issa into town to find what news he could. He was a clever lad with an easy open manner so that even strangers were happy to confide in him across a tavern's table.

'Half the town says the war's already lost, Lord,' he told me on his return. Nimue was sleeping and we spoke beside the stream which ran close beside the cottage.

'And the other half?' I asked.

He grinned. 'Looking forward to Lughnasa, Lord. They're not thinking beyond that. But the half that are thinking are all Christians.' He spat into the stream. 'They say Lughnasa's an

343

evil feast and that King Gorfyddyd is coming to punish our sins.'

'In which case,' I said, 'we'd better make sure we commit enough sins to deserve the punishment.'

He laughed. 'Some say Lord Arthur daren't leave town for fear there'd be a revolt once his soldiers are gone.'

I shook my head. 'He wants to be with Guinevere at Lughnasa.'

'Who wouldn't?' Issa asked.

'Did you see the goldsmith?' I asked.

He nodded. 'He says he can't make an eye in under two weeks because he's never done one before, but he'll find a corpse and cut out its eye to get the size right. I told him he'd better make it a child's corpse, for the lady isn't big, is she?' He jerked his head towards the cottage.

'You told him the eye had to be hollow?'

'I did, Lord.'

'You did well,' I told him. 'And now I suppose you want to do your worst and celebrate Lughnasa?'

He grinned. 'Yes, Lord.' Lughnasa was supposedly a celebration of the imminent harvest, yet the young have always made it a feast of fertility and their festivities would begin this night, the feast's eve.

'Then go,' I told him. 'I'll stay here.'

That afternoon I made Nimue her own bower for Lughnasa. I doubted somehow that she would appreciate it, but I wanted to do it and so I made a small lodge beside the stream, cutting the withies and bending them into a hooded shelter into which I wove cornflowers, poppies, ox-eyes, foxgloves and long tangling swathes of pink convolvulus. Such booths were being made all across Britain for the feast, and all across Britain, late next spring, hundreds of Lughnasa babies would be born. The spring was reckoned a good time to be born for the child would come into a world waking to summer's plenty, though whether this year's planting would lead to a lucky crop depended on the battles that must be fought after harvest.

Nimue emerged from the hut just as I was weaving the last

foxgloves into the bower's summit. 'Is it Lughnasa?' she asked in surprise.

'Tomorrow.'

She laughed shyly. 'No one ever made me a bower.'

'You never wanted one.'

'I do now,' she said, and sat under the flowery shade with such a look of delight that my heart leaped. She had found the eyepatch and donned one of the dresses Gyllad's maid had brought to the hut; it was a slave's dress of ordinary brown cloth, yet it suited her as simple things always did. She was pale and thin, but she was clean and there was a blush of colour in her cheeks. 'I don't know what happened to the golden eye,' she said ruefully, touching her new patch.

'I'm having another eye made,' I told her, but did not add that the goldsmith's deposit had taken the last of my coins. I desperately needed a battle's plunder, I thought, to replenish my purse.

'And I'm hungry,' Nimue said with a touch of her old mischievousness.

I put some birch twigs in the bottom of the pan so the broth would not stick, then poured in the last of the broth and set it on the fire. She ate it all, and afterwards she stretched out in the Lughnasa bower and watched the stream. Bubbles showed where an otter swam underwater. I had seen him earlier, an old dog with a hide scarred by battle and near misses from hunters' spears. Nimue watched his bubble trail disappear beneath a fallen willow and then began to talk.

She always had an appetite for talk, but that evening it was insatiable. She wanted news and I gave it to her, but then she wanted more detail, always more detail, and every detail she obsessively fitted inside a scheme of her own devising so that the story of the last year became, at least for her, like a great tiled floor where any one tile might seem insignificant, but added to the others it became a part of an intricate and meaningful whole. She was most interested in Merlin and the scroll he had snatched from Ban's doomed library. 'You didn't read it?' she asked.

'No.'

'I will,' she said fervently.

I hesitated a moment, then spoke my mind. 'I thought Merlin would come to the Isle to fetch you,' I said. I was risking offending her twice, first by implicitly criticizing Merlin and secondly by mentioning the one subject she did not talk about, the Isle of the Dead, but she did not seem to mind.

'Merlin would reckon I can look after myself,' she said, then smiled. 'And he knows I have you.'

It was dark by then and the stream rippled silver under Lughnasa's moon. There were a dozen questions I wanted to ask, but dared not, but suddenly she began to answer them anyway. She spoke of the Isle, or rather she spoke of how one tiny part of her soul had always been aware of the Isle's horror even as the rest of her had abandoned itself to its doom. 'I thought madness would be like death,' she said, 'and that I wouldn't know there was an alternative to being mad, but you do know. You really do. It's as though you watch yourself and cannot help yourself. You forsake yourself,' she said, then stopped and I saw the tears at her one good eye.

'Don't,' I said, suddenly not wanting to know.

'And sometimes,' she went on, 'I would sit on my rock and watch the sea and I would know I was sane, and I would wonder what purpose was being served, and then I knew I would have to be mad because if I was not then it was all to no purpose.'

'There was no purpose,' I said angrily.

'Oh, Derfel, dear Derfel. You have a mind like a stone falling off a cliff.' She smiled. 'It is the same purpose that made Merlin find Caleddin's scroll. Don't you understand? The Gods play games with us, but if we open ourselves then we can become a part of the game instead of its victims. Madness has a purpose! It's a gift from the Gods, and like all their gifts it comes with a price, but I've paid it now.' She spoke passionately, but suddenly I felt a yawn threatening me and try as I might I could not check it. I did try to hide it, but she saw anyway. 'You need some sleep,' she said.

'No,' I protested.

'Did you sleep last night?'

'A little.' I had sat at the cottage door and dozed fitfully as I listened to the mice scrabbling in the thatch.

'Then go to bed now,' she said firmly, 'and leave me here to think.'

I was so tired I could scarcely undress, but at last I lay on the bracken bed where I slept like the dead. It was a great, deep sleep like the rest that comes in safety after battle when the bad sleep, the one interrupted by nightmare reminders of near spear thrusts and sword blows, has been washed away from the soul. Thus I slept, and in the night Nimue came to me and at first I thought it was a dream, but then I woke with a start to find her chill naked skin next to mine. 'It's all right, Derfel,' she whispered, 'go to sleep,' and I slept again with my arms around her thin body.

We woke in Lughnasa's perfect dawn. There have been times in my life of pure happiness, and that was one. They are times, I suppose, when love is in step with life or perhaps when the Gods want us to be fools, and nothing is so sweet as Lughnasa's foolishness. The sun shone, filtering its light through the flowers in our bower where we made love, then afterwards we played like children in the stream where I tried to make otter bubbles under water and came up choking to find Nimue laughing. A kingfisher raced between the willows, its colours bright as a dream cloak. The only people we saw all day were a pair of horsemen who rode up the stream's far bank with falcons on their wrists. They did not see us, and we lay quietly and watched as one of their birds struck down a heron: a good omen. For that one perfect day Nimue and I were lovers, even though we were denied the second pleasure of love which is the certain knowledge of a shared future spent in a happiness as great as love's beginning. But I had no future with Nimue. Her future lay in the paths of the Gods, and I had no talent for those roads.

Yet even Nimue was tempted from those paths. In Lughnasa's evening, when the long light was shadowing the trees on the western slopes, she lay curled in my arms beneath the bower and spoke of all that might be. A small house, a piece of land, children and flocks. 'We could go to Kernow,' she said dreamily. 'Merlin always says Kernow is the blessed place. It's a long way from the Saxons.'

'Ireland,' I said, 'is further.'

I felt the shake of her head on my chest. 'Ireland is cursed.'

'Why?' I asked.

'They owned the Treasures of Britain,' she said, 'and let them go.'

I did not want to talk of the Treasures of Britain, nor of the Gods, nor of anything that would spoil this moment. 'Kernow, then,' I agreed.

'A small house,' she said, then listed all the things a small house needed: jars, pans, spits, winnowing sheets, sieves, yew pails, reaping hooks, croppers, a spindle, a skein winder, a salmon net, a barrel, a hearth, a bed. Had she dreamed of such things in her damp, cold cave above the cauldron? 'And no Saxons,' she said, 'and no Christians either. Maybe we should go to the isles in the Western Sea? To the isles beyond Kernow. To Lyonesse.' She spoke the lovely name softly. 'To live and love in Lyonesse,' she added, then laughed.

'Why do you laugh?'

She lay silent for a while, then shrugged. 'Lyonesse is for another life,' she said, and with that bleak statement she broke the spell. At least she did for me, because I thought I heard Merlin's mocking laughter cackling in the summer leaves, and so I let the dream fade as we lay unmoving in the long, soft light. Two swans flew north up the valley, going towards the great phallic image of the God Sucellos that was carved in the chalk hillside just north of Gyllad's land. Sansum had wanted to obliterate the bold image. Guinevere had stopped him, though she had not been able to prevent him from building a small shrine at the foot of the hill. I had a mind to buy the land when I could, not to farm, but to stop the Christians grassing over the chalk or digging up the God's image.

'Where is Sansum?' Nimue asked. She had been reading my thoughts.

'He's the guardian of the Holy Thorn now.'

'May it prick him,' she said vengefully. She uncurled from my arms and sat up, pulling the blanket up to our necks. 'And Gundleus is betrothed today?'

'Yes.'

'He won't live to enjoy his bride,' she said, more in hope, I feared, than in prophecy.

'He will if Arthur can't beat their army,' I said.

And next day the hopes of that victory seemed gone for ever. I was making things ready for Gyllad's harvest; sharpening the sickles and nailing the wooden threshing flails to their leather hinges, when a messenger arrived in Durnovaria from Duro-cobrivis. Issa brought us the messenger's news from town and it was dreadful. Aelle had broken the truce. On Lughnasa's Eve a swarm of Saxons had attacked Gereint's fortress and overrun its walls. Prince Gereint was dead, Durocobrivis had fallen, and Dumnonia's client Prince Meriadoc of Stronggore was a fugitive and the last remnants of his kingdom had become a part of Lloegyr. Now, as well as facing Gorfyddyd's army, Arthur must fight the Saxon war host. Dumnonia was surely doomed.

Nimue scorned my pessimism. 'The Gods won't end the game this soon,' she claimed.

'Then the Gods had better fill our treasury,' I said sharply, 'because we can't defeat both Aelle and Gorfyddyd, which means we have to buy the Saxon off or else go down to death.'

'Little minds worry about money,' Nimue said.

'Then thank the Gods for little minds,' I retorted. I worried about money endlessly.

'There's money in Dumnonia if you need it,' Nimue said carelessly.

'Guinevere's?' I said, shaking my head. 'Arthur won't touch it.' At that time none of us knew how big was the treasure Lancelot had fetched back from Ynys Trebes; that treasure might have sufficed to buy Aelle's peace, but the exiled King of Benoic was keeping it well hidden.

349

'Not Guinevere's gold,' Nimue said, and then she told me where a Saxon's blood-price might be found and I cursed myself for not thinking of it sooner. There was a chance after all, I thought, just a chance, so long as the Gods gave us time and Aelle's price was not impossibly high. I reckoned it would take Aelle's men a week to sober up after their sack of Durocobrivis so we had just that one week to work our miracle.

I took Nimue to Arthur. There would be no idyll in Lyonesse, no sieve or winnowing sheet and no bed beside the sea. Merlin had gone north to save Britain, now Nimue must work her own sorcery in the south. We went to buy a Saxon's peace while behind us, on the bank of our summer stream, the flowers of Lughnasa wilted.

Arthur and his guard rode north on the Fosse Way. Sixty horsemen, caparisoned in leather and iron, were going to war and with them were fifty spearmen, six mine and the rest led by Lanval, Guinevere's erstwhile guard commander, whose job and purpose had been usurped by Lancelot, King of Benoic, who, with his men, was now the protector of all the high people living in Durnovaria. Galahad had taken the rest of my men north to Gwent and it was a measure of our urgency that we all marched before the harvest, but Aelle's treachery gave us no choice. I marched with Arthur and Nimue. She had insisted on accompanying me even though she was still far from strong, but nothing would have kept her away from the war that was about to begin. We marched two days after Lughnasa and, perhaps as a portent of what was to come, the sky had clouded over to threaten a heavy rain.

The horsemen, with their grooms and pack-mules, together with Lanval's spearmen, waited on the Fosse Way while Arthur crossed the land bridge to Ynys Wydryn. Nimue and I went with him, taking only my six spearmen as an escort. It was strange to be back beneath the Tor's looming peak where Gwlyddyn had rebuilt Merlin's halls so that the Tor's summit looked almost as it had on the day when Nimue and I had fled from Gundleus's savagery. Even the tower had been rebuilt and

I wondered if, like the first tower, it was a dream chamber in which the whispers of the Gods would echo to the sleeping wizard.

But our business was not with the Tor, but with the shrine of the Holy Thorn. Five of my men stayed outside the shrine's gates while Arthur, Nimue and I walked into the compound. Nimue's head was shrouded with a hood so that her face with its leather eye-patch could not be seen. Sansum hurried to meet us. He looked in fine condition for a man who was ostensibly in disgrace for rousing Durnovaria to deadly riot. He was plumper than I remembered and wore a new black gown that was half covered with a cope lavishly embroidered with golden crosses and silver thorns. A heavy golden cross hung on a golden chain at his breast, while a torque of thick gold shone at his neck. His mouse-like face with its stiffly tonsured brush offered us a smirk that was intended as a smile. 'The honour you do us!' he cried, his hands flying apart in welcome. 'The honour! Dare I hope, Lord Arthur, that you come to worship our dear Lord? That is His Sacred Thorn! A reminder of the thorns that pricked His head as He suffered for your sins.' He gestured towards the drooping tree with its small sad leaves. A group of pilgrims surrounding the tree had draped its pathetic limbs with votive offerings. Seeing us, those pilgrims shuffled away, not realizing that the poorly dressed farm boy who worshipped with them was one of our men. It was Issa, whom I had sent on ahead with a small offering of coins for the shrine. 'Some wine, perhaps?' Sansum now offered us. 'And food? We have cold salmon, new bread, some strawberries even.'

'You live well, Sansum,' Arthur said, looking around the shrine. It had grown since I had last been in Ynys Wydryn. The stone church had been extended and two new buildings constructed, one a dormitory for the monks and the other a house for Sansum himself. Both buildings were of stone and had roofs made of tiles taken from Roman villas.

Sansum raised his eyes to the threatening clouds. 'We are merely humble servants of the great God, Lord, and our life on earth is all due to His grace and providence. Your esteemed wife is well, I pray?'

'Very, thank you.'

'The news brings joy to us, Lord,' Sansum lied. 'And our King, he is well too?'

'The boy grows, Sansum.'

'And in the true faith, I trust.' Sansum was backing away as we advanced. 'So what, Lord, brings you to our small settlement?'

Arthur smiled. 'Need, Bishop, need.'

'Of spiritual grace?' Sansum enquired.

'Of money.'

Sansum threw up his hands. 'Would a man searching for fish climb to a mountain top? Or a man panting for water go to a desert? Why come to us, Lord Arthur? We brothers are vowed to poverty and what meagre crumbs the dear Lord does permit to fall into our laps we give to the poor.' He closed his hands gracefully together.

'Then I am come, dear Sansum,' Arthur said, 'to make certain that you are keeping your vows of poverty. The war goes hard, it needs money, the treasury is empty, and you will have the honour of making your King a loan.' Nimue, who now shuffled humbly behind us like a cowled servant, had reminded Arthur of the church's wealth. How she must have been enjoying Sansum's discomfort.

'The church had been spared these enforced loans,' Sansum said sharply and putting a scornful bite on the last word. 'High King Uther, may his soul rest in peace, exempted the church from all such exactions, just as the pagan shrines' – he crossed himself – 'are shamefully and sinfully exempted.'

'King Mordred's council,' Arthur said, 'has rescinded the exemption, and your shrine, Bishop, is known as the wealthiest in Dumnonia.'

Sansum raised his eyes to the sky again. 'If we possessed so much as one gold coin, Lord, I would take pleasure in giving it to you as an outright gift. But we are poor. You should seek your loan on the hill.' He gestured to the Tor. 'The pagans there, Lord, have been hoarding infidel gold for centuries!'

'The Tor,' I intervened coldly, 'was raided by Gundleus

when Norwenna was killed. What little gold was there, and it was little, was stolen.'

Sansum pretended to have just noticed me. 'It's Derfel, isn't it? I thought so. Welcome home, Derfel!'

'Lord Derfel,' Arthur corrected Sansum.

Sansum's small eyes opened wide. 'Praise God! Praise Him! You rise in the world, Lord Derfel, and what satisfaction that gives me, a humble churchman who will now be able to boast that he knew you when you were but a common spearman. A lord now? What a blessing! And what honour your presence does us! But even you know, my dear Lord Derfel, that when King Gundleus raided the Tor he also raided the poor monks here. Alas, what depredations he made! The shrine suffered for Christ and it has never recovered.'

'Gundleus went to the Tor first,' I said. 'I know, because I was there. And by so doing he gave the monks here time to hide their treasures.'

'Such fantasies you pagans hold about we Christians! Do you still claim we eat babies at our love feasts?' Sansum laughed.

Arthur sighed. 'Dear Bishop Sansum,' he said, 'I know my request is hard for you. I know it is your job to preserve the wealth of your church so that it can grow and reflect the glory of God. All that I know, but I also know that if we do not have the money to fight our enemies then the enemy will come here and there will be no church, there will be no Holy Thorn, and the shrine's Bishop' – he prodded a finger into Sansum's ribs – 'will be nothing but dry bones pecked clean by ravens.'

'There are other ways to keep the enemy from our gates,' Sansum said, unwisely hinting that Arthur was the cause of the war and that if Arthur simply left Dumnonia then Gorfyd-dyd would be satisfied.

Arthur did not become angry. He simply smiled. 'Your treasury is needed for Dumnonia, Bishop.'

'We have no treasury. Alas!' Sansum made the sign of the cross. 'As God is my witness, Lord, we possess nothing.'

I strolled across to the thorn. 'The monks of Ivinium,' I

said, referring to a monastery some miles to the south, 'are better gardeners than you, Bishop.' I scraped Hywelbane from her scabbard and prodded her tip into the soil beside the sorry tree. 'Maybe we should dig up the Holy Thorn and take it to Ivinium's care? I am sure their monks would pay highly for the privilege.'

'And the Thorn would be further from the Saxons!' Arthur said brightly. 'Surely you approve of our plan, Bishop?'

Sansum was waving his hands desperately. 'The monks at Ivinium are ignorant fools, Lord, mere mumblers of prayers. If your Lordships would wait in the church, maybe I can find some few coins for your purpose?'

'Do,' Arthur said.

The three of us were ushered into the church. It was a plain building with a stone floor, stone walls and a beamed roof. It was a gloomy place for only a little light came through the small high windows where sparrows bickered and wallflowers grew. At the church's far end was a stone table on which stood a crucifix. Nimue, the hood thrown back from her hair, spat at the crucifix while Arthur strolled to the table, then hitched himself up so he could sit on its edge. 'I take no pleasure in this, Derfel,' he said.

'Why should you, Lord?'

'It does not do to offend Gods,' Arthur said gloomily.

'This God,' Nimue said contemptuously, 'is said to be a forgiving one. Better offend that kind than any other.'

Arthur smiled. He was wearing a simple jerkin, trousers, boots, a cloak and Excalibur. He wore no gold, nor armour, but there was no mistaking his authority, nor, at that moment, his unease. He sat in silence for a time, then looked up at me. Nimue was exploring the small rooms at the back of the church and we were alone together. 'Perhaps I should leave Britain?' Arthur said.

'And yield Dumnonia to Gorfyddyd?'

'Gorfyddyd will enthrone Mordred in time,' Arthur said, 'and that is all that matters.'

'He says as much?' I asked.

'He does.'

'And what else would he say?' I argued, appalled that my Lord should even contemplate exile. 'But the truth,' I added forcefully, 'is that Mordred will be Gorfyddyd's client and why should Gorfyddyd enthrone a client? Why not put one of his own relatives on the throne? Why not put his son Cuneglas on our throne?'

'Cuneglas is honourable,' Arthur insisted.

'Cuneglas will do whatever his father tells him,' I said scornfully, 'and Gorfyddyd wants to be High King, which means he certainly won't want the old High King's heir growing to be a rival. Besides, do you think Gorfyddyd's Druids will let a maimed king live? If you go, Lord, I number Mordred's days.'

Arthur did not respond. He sat there, his hands on the table's edge and his head down as he stared at the floor. He knew I was right, just as he knew that he alone of Britain's warlords fought for Mordred. The rest of Britain wanted their own man on Dumnonia's throne, while Guinevere wanted Arthur himself to sit there. He looked up at me. 'Did Guinevere –' he began.

'Yes,' I interrupted him bleakly. I had supposed he was referring to Guinevere's ambition to place him on Dumnonia's throne, but he had been thinking of another matter entirely.

He jumped off the table and began pacing up and down. 'I understand your feelings for Lancelot,' he said, surprising me, 'but consider this, Derfel. Suppose that Benoic had been your kingdom, and supposing that you believed I would save it for you, indeed you knew that I was oath-bound to save it, and then I did not. And Benoic was destroyed. Would that not make you bitter? Would it not make you distrustful? King Lancelot has suffered greatly, and the suffering was at my hands! Mine! And I want, if I can, to make his losses good. I can't recapture Benoic, but I can, perhaps, give him another kingdom.'

'Which?' I asked.

He smiled slyly. He had the whole scheme worked out and

355

he was taking an immense pleasure in revealing it to me. 'Siluria,' he said. 'Let us suppose we can defeat Gorfyddyd, and with him, Gundleus. Gundleus has no heir, Derfel, so if we can kill Gundleus a throne is vacant. We have a king without a throne, they have a throne without a king. More, we have an unmarried king! Offer Lancelot as husband to Ceinwyn and Gorfyddyd will have his daughter as a queen and we shall have our friend on the Silurian throne. Peace, Derfel!' He spoke with all his old enthusiasm, building a wonderful vision with his words. 'A union! The marriage union I never made, but now we can make it again. Lancelot and Ceinwyn! And to achieve it we only need to kill one man. Just one.'

And as many other men who needed to die in battle, I thought, but said nothing. Somewhere to the north a rumble of thunder sounded. The God Taranis was aware of us, I thought, and I hoped he was on our side. The sky through the tiny high windows was black as night.

'Well?' Arthur pressed me.

I had not spoken because the thought of Lancelot wedding Ceinwyn was so bitter that I could not trust myself to speak, but now I forced myself to sound civil. 'We have to buy off the Saxons and defeat Gorfyddyd first,' I said sourly.

'But if we do?' he asked impatiently, as though my objections were trivial obstacles.

I shrugged as though the idea of the marriage was far beyond my competency to judge.

'Lancelot likes the idea,' Arthur said, 'and his mother does too. Guinevere approves as well, but then she would because it was her idea to marry Ceinwyn to Lancelot in the first place. She's a clever girl. Very clever.' He smiled as he always did when he thought of his wife.

'But even your clever wife, Lord,' I dared to say, 'cannot dictate Mithras's adherents.'

He jerked his head as though I had struck him. 'Mithras!' he said angrily. 'Why can't Lancelot join?'

'Because he's a coward,' I snarled, unable to hide my bitterness any longer.

'Bors says not, so do a dozen other men,' Arthur challenged me.

'Ask Galahad,' I said, 'or your cousin Culhwch.' Rain sounded sudden on the roof and a moment later began to drip from the high window-sills. Nimue had reappeared in the small arched door beside the stone table where she pulled the hood over her face again.

'If Lancelot proves himself, will you relent?' Arthur asked me after a while.

'If Lancelot shows himself to be a fighter, Lord, I shall relent. But I thought he was your palace guard now?'

'His wish is to command in Durnovaria only until his wounded hand heals,' Arthur explained, 'but if he does fight, Derfel, then you will elect him?'

'If he fights well,' I promised reluctantly, 'yes.' I was fairly sure it was a promise I would never have to keep.

'Good,' Arthur said, pleased as always to have found a measure of agreement, then he turned as the church door banged open with a gust of rainy wind and Sansum ran inside followed by two monks. The two monks were carrying leather bags. Very small leather bags.

Sansum shook water off his robe as he hurried up the church. 'We have searched, Lord,' he said breathlessly, 'we have hunted, we have pecked high and low, and we have assembled what little treasures our paltry house possesses, which treasures we now lay before you in humble but reluctant duty.' He shook his head sadly. 'We shall go hungry this season as a result of our generosity, but where a sword commands, we mere servants of God must obey.'

His monks poured the contents of the two bags on to the flagstones. A coin rolled across the floor until I trapped it with my foot.

'Gold from the Emperor Hadrian!' Sansum said of the coin.

I picked it up. It was a brass sesterce with the Emperor Hadrian's head on one side and an image of Britannia with her trident and shield on the other. I bent the coin double between my finger and thumb and tossed it to Sansum. 'Fool's gold, Bishop,' I said.

357

The rest of the treasure was not much better. There were some worn coins, mostly copper with a few of silver, some iron bars that were commonly used as currency, a brooch of poor gold and some thin golden links from a broken chain. The whole collection was perhaps worth a dozen gold pieces. 'Is this all?' Arthur asked.

'We give to the poor, Lord!' Sansum said, 'though if your needs are pressing then maybe I could add this.' He lifted the golden cross from around his neck. The heavy cross and its thick chain were easily worth forty or fifty gold pieces and now, reluctantly, the Bishop held them out to Arthur. 'My personal loan for your war, Lord?' he suggested.

Arthur reached for the chain and Sansum immediately jerked it back. 'Lord,' he dropped his voice so that only Arthur and I could hear him. 'I was unjustly treated last year. For the loan of this chain,' he twitched it so that the heavy links clinked together, 'I would demand that my appointment as King Mordred's personal chaplain be honoured. My place is at the King's side, Lord, not here in this pestilential marshland.' Before Arthur could respond the door of the church opened once again and a rainsoaked Issa shambled inside. Sansum turned furiously on the newcomer. 'The church is not open to pilgrims!' the Bishop snapped. 'There are regular services. Now get out! Out!'

Issa pushed wet hair away from his face, grinned and spoke to me. 'They hide all their goods beside the pond behind the big house, Lord, all of it under a pile of rocks. I watched them put today's tribute there.'

Arthur plucked the heavy chain from Sansum's hand. 'You may keep those other treasures' – he gestured at the shabby collection on the floor – 'to feed your paltry house through the winter, Bishop. And keep your torque as a reminder that your neck is in my gift.' He strode towards the door.

'Lord!' Sansum shouted in protest. 'I beg you –'

'Beg,' Nimue interrupted him, pushing the hood back from her face. 'Beg, you dog.' She turned and spat on the crucifix, then on to the church floor, then a third time at Sansum. 'Beg, you piece of dirt,' she snarled at him.

'Dear God!' Sansum blanched at the sight of his enemy. He reeled backward, making the sign of the cross on his thin chest. For a moment he seemed too terrified to even speak. He must have thought Nimue lost for ever on the Isle of the Dead, yet here she was, spitting in triumph. He crossed himself a third time, then wheeled on Arthur. 'You dare bring a witch into God's house!' he screamed. 'This is sacrilege! Oh sweet Christ!' He dropped to his knees and gazed up at the rafters. 'Cast fire from heaven! Cast it now!'

Arthur ignored him, plunging instead into the pelting rain that was bedraggling the pathetic votive ribbons draped on the Holy Thorn. 'Call the other spearmen inside,' Arthur ordered Issa. My men had waited outside the shrine in case Sansum had attempted to hide his treasures beyond the encircling wall, but now the spearmen came into the enclosure to help drive the frantic monks away from the pile of rocks that hid their secret treasury. Some of the monks dropped to their knees as they saw Nimue. They knew who she was.

Sansum ran from the church and threw himself on to the rocks, dramatically decreeing that he would sacrifice his life to preserve God's money. Arthur shook his head sadly. 'Are you sure of this sacrifice, Lord Bishop?'

'Dear sweet God!' Sansum bellowed. 'Thy servant comes, slaughtered by wicked men and their foul witch! All I did was obey Your word. Receive me, Lord! Receive Thy humble servant!' This was followed by a scream as he anticipated his death, but it was only Issa lifting him by the scruff of his neck and the seat of his robe and carrying him gently away from the stone pile to the pond where he dropped Sansum into the shallow, muddy water. 'I'm drowning, Lord!' Sansum shouted. 'Cast into mighty waters like Jonah into the ocean! A martyr for Christ! As Paul and Peter were martyred, Lord, so now I come!' He blew some urgent bubbles, but no one beside his God was taking any notice and so he slowly dragged himself out of the muddy duckweed to spit curses at my men who were eagerly dragging the stones aside.

Beneath the rock pile was a cover of wooden boards that

lifted to reveal a stone cistern crammed with leather sacks, and in the sacks was gold. Thick gold coins, gold chains, gold statues, gold torques, gold brooches, gold bracelets, gold pins; the gold fetched here by hundreds of pilgrims seeking the blessing of the Thorn, that Arthur now insisted a monk count and weigh so that a proper receipt could be issued to the monastery. He left my men to supervise the tally while he led a damp and protesting Sansum across the compound to the Holy Thorn. 'You must learn to grow thorn trees before you meddle in the affairs of kings, my Lord Bishop,' Arthur said. 'You are not restored to the King's chaplaincy, but will stay here and learn husbandry.'

'Mulch the next tree,' I advised him. 'Let the roots stay damp while it settles in. And don't transplant a tree in flower, Bishop, they don't like it. That's been the trouble with the last few thorns you planted here; you dug them out of the woods at the wrong time. Bring them across in winter and dig them a good hole with some dung and mulch and you might get a real miracle.'

'Forgive them, Lord!' Sansum said, dropping to his knees and gazing into the damp heavens.

Arthur wanted to visit the Tor, though first he stood beside Norwenna's grave that had become a place of veneration for Christians. 'She was an ill-used woman,' he told me.

'All women are,' Nimue said. She had followed us to the grave that stood close beside the Holy Thorn.

'No,' Arthur insisted. 'Maybe most people are, but not all women any more than all men. But this woman was, and we still have to avenge her.'

'You had your chance of vengeance once,' Nimue accused him harshly, 'and you let Gundleus live.'

'Because I hoped for peace,' Arthur said. 'But next time he dies.'

'Your wife,' Nimue said, 'promised him to me.'

Arthur shuddered, knowing what cruelty lay behind Nimue's desire, but he nodded. 'He is yours,' he said, 'I promise it.' He turned and led the two of us through the pouring rain to the Tor's summit. Nimue and I were going home, Arthur to see Morgan.

He embraced his sister in the hall. Morgan's gold mask shone dully in the stormy light, while round her neck she wore the bear claws set in gold that Arthur had brought her from Benoic so very long ago. She clung to him, desperate for affection, and I left them alone. Nimue, almost as though she had never been away from the Tor, ducked through the small door into Merlin's rebuilt chambers while I ran through the rain to Gudovan's hut. I found the old clerk sitting at his desk, but not working for he was blinded with cataracts, though he said he could still make out light and dark. 'And mostly it's dark now,' he said sadly, then smiled. 'I suppose you're too big to hit now, Derfel?'

'You can try, Gudovan,' I said, 'but it won't do much good any more.'

'Did it ever?' He chuckled. 'Merlin spoke of you when he was here last week. Not that he stayed long. He came, he talked with us, he left us another cat as if we didn't have enough cats already, and then he left. He didn't even stay the night, he was in such a hurry.'

'Do you know where he went?' I asked.

'He wouldn't say, but where do you think he went?' Gudovan asked with a touch of his old asperity. 'Chasing Nimue. At least I suppose that's what he's doing, though why he should chase that silly girl, I don't know. He should take a slave!' He paused and suddenly seemed on the edge of tears. 'You know Sebile died?' he went on. 'Poor woman. She was murdered, Derfel! Murdered! Had her throat slit. No one knows who did it. Some traveller, I assume. The world goes to the dogs, Derfel, to the dogs.' For a moment he seemed lost, then he found the thread of his thoughts again. 'Merlin should use a slave. Nothing wrong with a willing slave and there are plenty in town who oblige for a small coin. I use the house down by Gwlyddyn's old workshop. There's a nice woman there, though these days we tend to talk more than we bump about the bed. I get old, Derfel.'

361

'You don't look old. And Merlin isn't chasing Nimue. She's here.'

Thunder sounded again and Gudovan's hand found a small piece of iron that he stroked for protection against evil. 'Nimue here?' he asked in amazement. 'But we heard she was on the Isle!' He touched the iron again.

'She was,' I said flatly, 'but isn't now.'

'Nimue . . .' He said the name almost in disbelief. 'Is she staying?'

'No, we all go east today.'

'And leaving us alone?' he asked petulantly. 'I miss Hywel.'

'So do I.'

He sighed. 'Times change, Derfel. The Tor isn't what it was. We're all old now and there are no children left. I miss them, and poor Druidan has no one to chase. Pellinore rants to emptiness, while Morgan is bitter.'

'Wasn't she always?' I asked lightly.

'She has lost her power,' he explained. 'Not her power to tell dreams or heal the sick, but the power she enjoyed when Merlin was here and Uther was on the throne. She resents that, Derfel, just as she resents your Nimue.' He paused, thinking. 'She was especially angry when Guinevere sent for Nimue to fight Sansum about that church in Durnovaria. Morgan believes she should have been summoned, but we hear that the Lady Guinevere wants no one but the beautiful around her and where does that leave Morgan?' He chuckled at the question. 'But she's still a strong woman, Derfel, and she has her brother's ambition so she won't be content to stay here listening to the dreams of peasants and grinding herbs to cure the milk-fever. She's bored! So bored that she even plays throwboard with that wretched Bishop Sansum from the shrine. Why did they send him to Ynys Wydryn?'

'Because they didn't want him in Durnovaria. Does he really come here to play games with Morgan?'

Gudovan nodded. 'He says he needs intelligent company and that she has the cleverest mind in Ynys Wydryn, and I dare say he's right. He preaches to her, of course, endless non-sense about a virgin whelping a God who gets nailed to a cross, but Morgan just lets it roll past her mask. At least I hope she does.' He paused and sipped from a horn of mead in which a wasp was struggling as it drowned. When he put the horn down I fished the wasp out and squashed it on his desk. 'Christianity gains converts, Derfel,' Gudovan went on. 'Even Gwlyddyn's wife, that nice woman Ralla, has converted, which probably means that Gwlyddyn and the two children will follow her. I don't mind, but why do they have to sing so much?'

'You don't like singing?' I teased him.

'No one loves a good song better than I!' he said stoutly. 'The Battle Song of Uther or the Slaughter Chant of Taranis, that's what I call a song, not this whining and moaning about being sinners in need of grace.' He sighed and shook his head. 'I hear you were in Ynys Trebes?' he asked.

I told him the tale of the city's fall. It seemed an appropriate story as we sat there with the rain falling on the fields outside and a gloom lowering over all Dumnonia. When the tale was told Gudovan stared sightlessly through the door, saying nothing. I thought he might have fallen asleep, but when I rose from the stool, he waved me down. 'Are things as bad as Bishop Sansum claims?' he asked.

'They're bad, my friend,' I admitted.

'Tell me.'

I told him how the Irish and the Cornish were raiding in the west where Cadwy still pretended to rule an independent kingdom. Tristan did his best to restrain his father's soldiers, but King Mark could not resist enriching his poor kingdom by stealing from a weakened Dumnonia. I told him how Aelle's Saxons had broken the truce, but added that Gorfyddyd's army still posed the greatest threat. 'He's assembled the men of Elmet, Powys and Siluria,' I told Gudovan, 'and once the harvest is gathered he'll lead them all south.'

'And Aelle doesn't fight against Gorfyddyd?' the old scribe asked.

'Gorfyddyd has purchased peace from Aelle.'

'And will Gorfyddyd win?' Gudovan asked.

I paused a long time. 'No,' I finally said, not because it was the truth, but because I did not want this old friend to worry that his last glimpse of this life would be a flash of light as a warrior's sword swung towards his blinded eyes. 'Arthur will fight them,' I said, 'and Arthur has yet to be beaten.'

'You'll fight them too?'

'It's my job now, Gudovan.'

'You would have made a good clerk,' he said sadly, 'and it is an honourable and useful profession, even though no one makes us lords because of it.' I thought he had not known of my honour and I suddenly felt ashamed of being so proud of it. Gudovan groped for his mead and took another sip. 'If you see Merlin,' he said, 'tell him to come back. The Tor is dead without him.'

'I'll tell him.'

'Goodbye, Lord Derfel,' Gudovan said, and I sensed he knew we would never meet again in this world. I tried to embrace the old man, but he waved me away for fear of betraying his emotions.

Arthur was waiting at the sea gate where he stared westward across the marshes that were being storm-swept by great pale waves of rain. 'This will be bad for the harvest,' he said bleakly. Lightning flickered above the Severn Sea.

'There was a storm like this after Uther died,' I said.

Arthur pulled his cloak tight around his body. 'If Uther's son had lived . . .' he said, then fell silent rather than finish the thought. His mood was as dark and bleak as the weather.

'Uther's son could not have fought Gorfyddyd, Lord,' I said, 'nor Aelle.'

'Nor Cadwy,' he added bitterly, 'nor Cerdic. So many enemies, Derfel.'

'Then be glad you have friends, Lord.'

He acknowledged that truth with a smile, then turned to gaze northwards. 'I worry about one friend,' he said softly. 'I worry that Tewdric won't fight. He's tired of war, and I can't blame him for that. Gwent has suffered much worse than

Dumnonia.' He looked at me and there were tears in his eyes, or maybe it was just the rain. 'I wanted to do such great things, Derfel,' he said, 'such great things. And in the end it was I who betrayed them, wasn't it?'

'No, Lord,' I said firmly.

'Friends should speak the truth,' he chided me gently.

'You needed Guinevere,' I said, embarrassed to be speaking thus, 'and you were meant to be with her, else why would the Gods have brought her to the feasting hall on the night of your betrothal? It isn't for us, Lord, to read the minds of Gods, just to live our fate fully.'

He grimaced at that, for he liked to believe he was master of his own fate. 'You think we should all rush madly down the paths of destiny?'

'I think, Lord, that when fate grips you, you do well to put reason aside.'

'And I did,' he said quietly, then smiled at me. 'Do you love someone, Derfel?' he asked.

'The only women I love, Lord, are not for me,' I answered in self-pity.

He frowned, then shook his head in commiseration. 'Poor Derfel,' he said softly and something about his tone made me look at him. Could he believe I had meant to include Guinevere among those women? I blushed and wondered what I should say, but Arthur had already turned to watch as Nimue came from the hall. 'You must tell me about the Isle of the Dead sometime,' he said, 'when we have the time.'

'I shall tell you, Lord, after your victory,' I said, 'when you need good tales to fill long winter evenings.'

'Yes,' he said, 'after our victory.' Though he did not sound hopeful. Gorfyddyd's army was so huge and ours so small.

But before we could fight Gorfyddyd we had to buy a Saxon's peace with God's money. And so we travelled towards Lloegyr.

We smelt Durocobrivis long before we came near the town. That smell came on our second day of travel and we were still a half-day's journey from the captured town, but the wind was in the east and it carried the sour reek of death and smoke far across the deserted farmlands. The fields were ready for harvest, but the people had fled in terror of the Saxons. At Cunetio, a small Roman-built town where we had spent the night, refugees filled the streets and their livestock had been crowded into hastily re-erected winter sheep pens. No one had cheered Arthur in Cunetio, and no wonder, for he was blamed for both the war's length and its disasters. Men grumbled that there had been peace under Uther and nothing but war under Arthur.

Arthur's horsemen led our silent column. They wore their armour, they carried spears and swords, but their shields were slung upside down and green branches were tied to their spear-tips as signs that we came in peace. Behind the vanguard marched Lanval's spearmen, and after them came two score of baggage mules that were loaded with Sansum's gold and with all the heavy leather shields that Arthur's horses wore in battle. A second smaller contingent of horsemen formed the rearguard. Arthur himself walked with my wolf-tailed spearmen just behind his banner holder who rode with the leading group of horsemen. Arthur's black mare Llamrei was led by Hygwydd, his servant, and with him was a stranger I took to be another servant. Nimue walked with us and, like Arthur, tried to learn some Saxon from me, but neither was a good pupil. Nimue was soon bored by the coarse tongue while Arthur had too much on his mind, though he duly learned a few words: peace, land, spear, food, mother, father. I was to be his interpreter, the first of many times that I spoke for Arthur and returned his enemy's words.

We met the enemy at midday as we descended a long gentle hill where woods grew on either side of the road. An arrow suddenly flickered from the trees and slashed into the turf just ahead of our leading man, Sagramor. He raised a hand and Arthur shouted at every man in the column to be still. 'No swords!' he ordered. 'Just wait!'

The Saxons must have been watching us all morning for

they had assembled a small war-band to face us. Those men, sixty or seventy strong, trailed out of the trees behind their leader, a broad-chested man who walked beneath a chieftain's banner of deer-antlers from which hung shreds of tanned human skin.

The chieftain had the Saxon's love of fur; a sensible affection for few things stop a sword stroke so well as a thick rich pelt. This man had a collar of heavy black fur about his neck and strips of fur around his upper arms and thighs. The rest of his clothing was leather or wool: a jerkin, trousers, boots, and a leather helmet crested with a tuft of black fur. At his waist hung a long sword, while in his hand was that favourite Saxon weapon, the broad-bladed axe.

'Are you lost, *wealhas*?' he shouted. *Wealhas* was their word for us Britons. It means foreigners and has a derisive ring, just as our word Sais does for them. 'Or are you just tired of life?' He stood firmly in our road, feet apart, head up and with his axe resting on his shoulder. He had a brown beard and a mass of brown hair that jutted sharply out from under his helmet's rim. His men, some in iron helmets, some in leather, and almost all carrying axes, formed a shield-wall across the road. A few had huge leashed dogs, beasts the size of wolves, and of late, we had heard, the Sais had been using such dogs as weapons, releasing them against our shield-walls just a few seconds before they struck with axe and spear. The dogs frightened some of our men far more than the Saxons did.

I walked with Arthur, stopping a few paces short of the defiant Saxon. Neither of us carried spear or shield and our swords rested in their scabbards. 'My Lord,' I said in Saxon, 'is Arthur, Protector of Dumnonia, who comes to you in peace.'

'For the moment,' the man said, 'peace is yours, but only for the moment.' He spoke defiantly, but he had been impressed by Arthur's name and he gave my Lord a long curious inspection before glancing back to me. 'Are you Saxon?' he asked.

'I was born one. Now I am British.'

'Can a wolf become a toad?' he asked with a scowl. 'Why not become a Saxon again?'

'Because I am sworn to Arthur's service,' I said, 'and that service is to bring your King a great gift of gold.'

'For a toad,' the man said, 'you howl well. I am Therdig.'

I had never heard of him. 'Your fame,' I said, 'gives nightmares to our children.'

He laughed. 'Well spoken, toad. So who is our King?'

'Aelle,' I said.

'I didn't hear you, toad.'

I sighed. 'The Bretwalda Aelle.'

'Well said, toad,' Therdig said. We Britons did not recognize the title Bretwalda, but I used it to placate the Saxon chief. Arthur, who understood nothing of our talk, patiently waited until I was ready to translate something. He had trust in those he appointed and would not hurry me or intervene.

'The Bretwalda,' Therdig said, 'is some hours from here. Can you give me some reason, toad, why I should disturb his day with news that a plague of rats, mice and grubs have crawled into his land?'

'We bring the Bretwalda more gold, Therdig,' I said, 'than you can dream of. Gold for your men, for your wives, for your daughters, even enough for your slaves. Is that reason enough?'

'Show me, toad.'

It was a risk, but Arthur willingly took it, taking Therdig and six of his men back to the mules and there revealing the great hoard stowed in the sacks. The risk was that Therdig might decide the fortune was worth a fight there and then, but we outnumbered him, and the sight of Arthur's men on their big horses was a fearsome deterrent, so he merely took three gold coins and said he would report our presence to the Bretwalda. 'You will wait at the Stones,' he ordered us. 'Be there by evening and my King shall come to you in the morning.' The command told us that Aelle must have been warned of our approach and must also have guessed what our business was. 'You may stay at the Stones in peace,' Therdig told us, 'until the Bretwalda decides your fate.'

That evening, for it took us all afternoon to reach the Stones, was the first time I ever saw the great ring. Merlin had often spoken of them, and Nimue had heard of their power, but no one knew who had made them or why the great dressed boulders were arrayed in their towering circle. Nimue was sure that only the Gods could have made such a place and so she chanted prayers as we approached the grey, lonely monoliths whose evening shadows stretched dark and long across the pale grassland. A ditch surrounded the Stones that were formed into a great circle of pillars with other stones forming lintels above, while inside that massive and crude arcade were more vast upright rocks that stood close around a slablike altar. There were plenty of other stone circles in Britain, some even larger in their circumference, but none of such mystery and majesty and all of us were awed and silent as we approached.

Nimue cast her spells, then told us it was safe to cross the ditch and so we wandered in wonder among these boulders of the Gods. Lichens grew thick on the Stones, some of which had canted or even fallen over the long years, while others were deeply carved with Roman names and numerals. Gereint had held the lordship of these Stones, an office devised by Uther to reward the man responsible for holding our eastern border against the Saxons, though now a new man would have to take the title and try to thrust Aelle back beyond burned Durocobrivis. It was shameful, Nimue told me, that Aelle had demanded to meet us here, so deep inside Dumnonia.

There were woods in a valley a mile to the south and we used the mules to fetch enough timber to make a fire that burned bright through all that ghost-haunted night. More fires burned just beyond our eastern skyline, evidence that the Saxons had followed us. It was a nervous night. Our fire burned like a blaze of Beltain, but the flame-shadows on the stones still unnerved us. Nimue cast spells of safety around the ditch and that precaution calmed our men, but the picketed horses whinnied and trampled the turf all night long. Arthur suspected they could smell the Saxon war dogs, but Nimue was certain that the spirits of the dead were whirling all about us. Our sentries gripped their spear-shafts and challenged every wind that sighed across the grave mounds surrounding the Stones, but no dog, ghoul or warrior disturbed us, though few of our number slept.

Arthur slept not at all. At one point in the night he asked me to walk with him and I paced beside him around the outer circle of big stones. He walked without speaking for a while, his head bare to the stars. 'I was here once before,' he broke his silence abruptly.

'When, Lord?' I asked.

'Ten years ago. Maybe eleven.' He shrugged as though the number of years was not important. 'Merlin brought me here.' He fell silent again and I said nothing for I sensed from his last words that this place held a special place in his memory. It did too, for he at last stopped pacing and pointed toward the grey rock that lay like an altar at the heart of the Stones. 'It was there, Derfel, that Merlin gave me Caled-fwlch.'

I glanced down at the sword's cross-hatched scabbard. 'A noble gift, Lord,' I said.

'A heavy one, Derfel. It came with a burden.' He plucked my arm so that we continued walking. 'He gave it to me on condition that I did what he ordered me to do, and I obeyed him. I went to Benoic and I learned from Ban what a king's duties are. I learned that a king is only as good as the poorest man under his rule. That was Ban's lesson.'

'It wasn't a lesson that Ban learned himself,' I said bitterly, thinking how Ban had ignored his people to enrich Ynys Trebes.

Arthur smiled. 'Some men are better at knowing than doing, Derfel. Ban was very wise, but not practical. I have to be both.'

'To be a king?' I dared to ask, for stating such an ambition was counter to everything Arthur claimed about his destiny.

But Arthur took no offence at my words. 'To be a ruler,' he said. He had stopped again and was staring over the dark cloaked shapes of his sleeping men at the stone in the circle's centre, and to me it seemed as if the slab of rock shimmered in the moonlight, or perhaps that was just my heightened imagination. 'Merlin made me strip naked and stand on that stone all night long,' Arthur went on. 'There was rain on the wind and it was cold. He chanted spells and made me hold the sword at arm's length and keep it there. I remember my arm was like fire and then at last it went numb, but still he would not let me drop Caledfwlch. "Hold it!" he shouted at me, "hold it," and I stood there, quivering while he summoned the dead to witness his gift. And they came, Derfel, rank on rank of the dead, warriors with empty eyes and rusted helmets who rose from the Otherworld to see the sword given to me.' He shook his head at the memory. 'Or perhaps I just dreamed those worm-eaten men. I was young, you see, and very impressionable, and Merlin does know how to put the fear of the Gods into young minds. Once he'd scared me with the throng of dead witnesses, though, he told me how to lead men, how to find warriors who need leaders and how to fight battles. He told me my destiny, Derfel.' He fell silent again, his long face very grim in the moonlight. Then he smiled ruefully. 'All nonsense.'

His last two words had been spoken so softly that I had almost not heard them. 'Nonsense?' I asked, unable to hide my disapproval.

'I am to yield Britain back to her Gods,' Arthur said, mocking the duty by the tone of his voice.

'You will, Lord,' I said.

He shrugged. 'Merlin wanted a strong arm to hold a good sword,' he said, 'but what the Gods want, Derfel, I do not know. If they want Britain, why do they need me? Or Merlin? Do Gods need men? Or are we like dogs barking for masters who don't want to listen?'

'We aren't dogs,' I said. 'We're the creatures of the Gods. They must have a purpose for us.'

'Must they? Maybe we just make them laugh.'

'Merlin says we've lost touch with the Gods,' I said stubbornly.

'Just as Merlin has lost touch with us,' Arthur said firmly. 'You saw how he ran from Durnovaria that night you returned from Ynys Trebes. Merlin is too busy, Derfel. Merlin is chasing his Treasures of Britain and what we do in Dumnonia is of no consequence to him. I could make a great kingdom for Mordred, I could establish justice, I could bring peace, I could have Christians and pagans dancing in the moonlight together and none of that would interest Merlin. Merlin only yearns for the moment when all of it is given back to the Gods, and when that moment comes he'll demand I give Caledfwlch back to him. That was his other condition. I could take the sword of the Gods, he said, so long as I gave it back when he needed it.'

He had spoken with a trace of mockery that had disturbed me. 'Don't you believe in Merlin's dream?' I asked.

'I believe Merlin is the wisest man in Britain,' Arthur said seriously, 'and that he knows more than I might ever hope to know. I also know that my fate is twisted into his, just as yours, I think, is twisted into Nimue's, but I also think that Merlin was bored from the moment he was born, so Merlin is doing what the Gods do. He is amusing himself at our expense. Which means, Derfel, that when the moment comes to return Caledfwlch it will be at a time when I need the sword most.'

'So what will you do?'

'I have no idea. None.' He seemed to find that thought amusing for he smiled, then put a hand on my shoulder. 'Go and sleep, Derfel. I need your tongue tomorrow and I don't want it slurred by tiredness.'

I left him, and somehow I did snatch a few moments' sleep in the moon-cast shadow of a looming stone, though before I slept I lay thinking about that far-off night when Merlin had made Arthur's arm ache with the weight of the sword and his soul heavy with the greater burden of fate. Why had Merlin chosen Arthur, I wondered, for it seemed to me now that Arthur and Merlin were opposed. Merlin believed that chaos could only be defeated by harnessing the powers of mystery, while Arthur believed in the powers of men. It could be, I thought, that Merlin had trained Arthur to rule men so as to leave himself free to rule the dark powers, but I also realized, however dimly, that the moment might come when we would all have to choose between them and I feared that moment. I prayed it would never come. Then I slept until the sun rose to lance the shadow of a single stone pillar that stood isolated outside the circle straight into the very heart of the Stones where we tired warriors guarded a kingdom's ransom.

We drank water, ate hard bread, then buckled on our swords before spreading the gold on the dew-wet grass beside the altar stone. 'What's to stop Aelle taking the gold and continuing his war?' I asked Arthur as we waited for the Saxon's arrival. Aelle, after all, had taken gold from us before and that had not stopped him from burning Durocobrivis.

Arthur shrugged. He was wearing his spare armour, a coat of Roman mail that was dented and scarred from frequent fights. He wore the heavy mail under one of his white cloaks. 'Nothing,' he answered, 'except what little honour he might have. Which is why we might have to offer him more than gold.'

'More?' I asked, but Arthur did not reply because, on the dawn-blazoned eastern skyline, the Saxons had appeared.

They came in a long line spread across the horizon with their war drums beating and their spearmen arrayed for battle, though their weapons were tipped by leaves to show that they meant us no immediate harm. Aelle led them. He was the first of the two men I ever met who claimed the title Bretwalda. The other came later and was to give us more trouble, but Aelle was trouble enough. He was a tall man with a flat, hard face and dark eyes that revealed none of his thoughts. His beard was black, his cheeks were scarred from battle and two fingers were missing from his right hand. He wore a coat of black cloth that was belted with leather, boots of leather, an iron helmet on which bull horns were mounted, and over it all a bearskin cloak that he dropped when the heat of the day became too much for such a flamboyant garment. His banner was a blood-daubed bull's skull held aloft on a spear-shaft.

His war-band numbered two hundred men, maybe a few

more, and over half those men had great war dogs leashed with leather ropes. Behind the warriors was a horde of women, children and slaves. There were more than enough Saxons to overwhelm us now, but Aelle had given his word that we were at peace, at least until he had decided our fate, and his men made no hostile show. Their line stopped outside the circling ditch while Aelle, his council, an interpreter and a pair of wizards came to meet Arthur. The wizards had hair stiffened into spikes with dung and wore ragged cloaks of wolfskin. When they whirled around to say their charms, the legs, tails and faces of the wolves flared out from their painted bodies. They shouted those charms as they came closer, nullifying any magic we might be working against their leader. Nimue crouched behind us and chanted her own countercharms.

The two leaders weighed each other up. Arthur was taller and Aelle broader. Arthur's face was striking, but Aelle's was terrifying. It was implacable, the face of a man who had come from beyond the sea to carve out a kingdom in a strange land, and he had made that kingdom with a savage and direct brutality. 'I should kill you now, Arthur,' he said, 'and have one less enemy to destroy.'

His wizards, naked beneath their moth-eaten skins, crouched behind him. One chewed a mouthful of earth, the other rolled his eyes while Nimue, her empty eye-socket bared, hissed at them. The struggle between Nimue and the wizards was a private war that the two leaders ignored.

'The time will come, Aelle,' Arthur said, 'when maybe we shall meet in battle. But for now I offer you peace.' I had half expected Arthur to bow to Aelle who was, unlike Arthur, a king, but Arthur treated the Bretwalda as an equal and Aelle accepted the treatment without protest.

'Why?' Aelle asked bluntly. Aelle used no circumlocutions like we British favoured. I came to notice that difference between ourselves and the Saxons. The British thought in curves, like the intricate whorls of their jewellery, while Saxons were blunt and straight, as crude as their heavy gold brooches and chunky neck chains. Britons rarely broached a subject

374

headlong, but talked around it, wrapping it with hints and allusions, always looking for manoeuvre, but Saxons thrust subtlety aside. Arthur once claimed I had that same Saxon straightforwardness and I think he meant it as a compliment.

Arthur ignored Aelle's question. 'I thought we had peace already. We had an agreement sealed with gold.'

Aelle's face betrayed no shame at having broken the truce. He merely shrugged, as though a broken peace was a small thing. 'So if one truce fails, why buy another?' he asked.

'Because I have a quarrel with Gorfyddyd,' Arthur replied, adopting the Saxon's blunt manner, 'and I seek your help in that quarrel.'

Aelle nodded. 'But if I help you destroy Gorfyddyd I make you stronger. Why should I do that?'

'Because if you do not then Gorfyddyd will destroy me and he will then be stronger.'

Aelle laughed, displaying a mouth of rotting teeth. 'Does a dog care which of two rats it kills?' he asked.

I translated that as does a dog care which stag it pulls down. It seemed more tactful and I noted that Aelle's interpreter, a British slave, did not tell his master.

'No,' Arthur allowed, 'but the stags are not equal.' Aelle's interpreter said the rats were not equal and I did not tell Arthur. 'At best, Lord Aelle,' Arthur went on, 'I preserve Dumnonia and make Powys and Siluria my allies. But if Gorfyddyd wins he will unite Elmet, Rheged, Powys, Siluria and Dumnonia against you.'

'But you will also have Gwent on your side,' Aelle said. He was a shrewd man, and quick.

'True, but so will Gorfyddyd if it comes to a war between the British and the Saxons.'

Aelle grunted. The present situation, with the British fighting amongst themselves, served him best, but he knew that the British wars would eventually cease. Since it now seemed Gorfyddyd must win those wars soon, Arthur's presence gave him a way of prolonging his enemies' conflict. 'So what do you want of me?' he asked. His wizards were now leaping up and down on all fours like human grasshoppers while Nimue was arranging pebbles on the ground. The pebbles' pattern must have disturbed the Saxon sorcerers for they began to utter small yelps of distress. Aelle ignored them.

'I want you to give Dumnonia and Gwent three moons of peace,' Arthur said.

'You're only buying peace?' Aelle roared the words and even Nimue was startled. The Saxon threw a gloved hand towards his war-band that squatted with their women, dogs and slaves beyond the shallow ditch. 'What does an army do in peace? Tell me that! I promised them more than gold. I promised them land! I promised them slaves! I promised them *wealhas* blood, and you give me peace?' He spat. 'In the name of Thor, Arthur, I will give you peace, but the peace will be across your bones and my men will take turns with your wife. That's my peace!' He spat on the turf, then looked at me. 'Tell your master, dog,' he said, 'that half my men have just arrived in boats. They have no harvest gathered and no means to feed their folk through winter. We cannot eat gold. If we don't take land and grain, then we starve. What good is peace to a starved man?'

I translated for Arthur, leaving out the more egregious insults.

A look of pain crossed Arthur's face. Aelle saw the look, translated it as weakness and so turned scornfully away. 'I will give you two hours' start, vermin,' he called over his shoulder, 'then I shall pursue you.'

'Ratae,' Arthur said, without even waiting for me to translate Aelle's threat.

The Saxon turned back. He said nothing, but just stared into Arthur's face. The stench of his bearskin robe was appalling; a mix of sweat, dung and grease. He waited.

'Ratae,' Arthur said again. 'Tell him it can be taken. Tell him it is full of all the things he desires. Tell him the land it guards will be his.'

Ratae was the fortress that protected Gorfyddyd's easternmost border with the Saxons and if Gorfyddyd lost that fortress then the Saxons moved twenty miles closer to Powys's heartland.

I translated. It took me some time to identify Ratae to Aelle, but at last he understood. He was not happy for it seemed Ratae was a formidable Roman fortress that Gorfyddyd had strengthened with a massive earth wall.

Arthur explained that Gorfyddyd had taken the garrison's best spearmen to add to the army he had collected for his invasion of Gwent and Dumnonia. He did not need to explain that Gorfyddyd had only risked that move because of the peace he believed he had purchased from Aelle, a peace that Arthur was now outbidding. Arthur revealed that a Christian community at Ratae had built a monastery just outside the fort's earth walls and the comings and goings of the monks had worn a passage through the ramparts. The fortress commander, he explained, was one of Gorfyddyd's rare Christians and had given his blessing to the monastery.

'How does he know?' Aelle demanded of me.

'Tell him I have a man with me, a man from Ratae, who knows how the monastery can be approached and who is willing to serve as a guide. Tell him I ask only that the man be rewarded with his life.' I realized then who the stranger must be who had been walking with Hygwydd. I realized, too, that Arthur had known he would have to sacrifice Ratae even before he left Durnovaria.

Aelle demanded to know more about the traitor and Arthur told how the man had deserted Powys and come to Dumnonia seeking revenge because his wife had abandoned him for one of Gorfyddyd's chieftains.

Aelle spoke with his council while the two wizards gibbered at Nimue. One of them pointed a human thigh bone at her, but Nimue merely spat. That gesture seemed to conclude their war of sorcery for the two wizards shuffled backwards as Nimue stood up and brushed her hands. Aelle's council haggled with us. At one point they insisted that we yield all the big war horses to them, but Arthur demanded all their war dogs in return, and finally, in the afternoon, the Saxons accepted the

377

offer of Ratae and Arthur's gold. It was maybe the greatest hoard of gold ever paid from a Briton to a Saxon, but Aelle also insisted on taking two hostages who, he promised, would be released if the attack on Ratae did not prove to be a trap laid by Gorfyddyd and Arthur together. He chose at random, picking two of Arthur's warriors: Balin and Lanval.

That night we ate with the Saxons. I was curious to meet these men who were my birth-brothers and even feared I might feel some kinship with them, but in truth I found their company repellent. Their humour was coarse, their manners loutish and the smell of their fur-wrapped flesh sickening. Some of them mocked me by saying I resembled their King Aelle, but I could see no likeness between his flat hard features and what I believed my own face to be. Aelle finally snarled at my mockers to be silent, then gave me a cold stare before bidding me to invite Arthur's men to share an evening meal of huge cuts of roasted meat which we ate with gloved hands, gnawing into the scalding flesh until the bloody juices dripped from our beards. We gave them mead, they gave us ale. A few drunken fights started, but no one was killed. Aelle, like Arthur, stayed sober, though the Bretwalda's two wizards became foully drunk and after they fell asleep beside their own vomit Aelle explained that they were madmen in touch with the Gods. He possessed other priests, he said, who were sane, but the lunatics were thought to possess a special power that the Saxons might need. 'We feared you would bring Merlin,' he explained.

'Merlin is his own master,' Arthur answered, 'but this is his priestess.' He gestured at Nimue who stared one-eyed at the Saxon.

Aelle made a gesture that must have been his way of averting evil. He feared Nimue because of Merlin, and that was good to know. 'But Merlin is in Britain?' Aelle asked fearfully.

'Some men say so,' I answered for Arthur, 'and some say not. Who knows? Maybe he is out there in the dark.' I jerked my head towards the blackness beyond the fire-lit stones.

Aelle used a spear-shaft to prod one of his mad wizards

awake. The man yowled piteously, and Aelle seemed content that the sound would avert any mischief. The Bretwalda had hung Sansum's cross about his neck, while others of his men wore Ynys Wydryn's heavy gold torques. Later in the night, when most of the Saxons were snoring, some of their slaves told us the tale of Durocobrivis's fall, and how Prince Gereint had been taken alive and then tortured to death. The tale made Arthur weep. None of us had known Gereint well, but he had been a modest, unambitious man who had tried his best to hold back the growing Saxon forces. Some of the slaves begged us to take them away with us, but we dared not offend our hosts by granting the request. 'We shall come for you one day,' Arthur promised the slaves. 'We shall come.'

The Saxons left next afternoon. Aelle insisted we wait another whole night before leaving the Stones to make certain we did not follow him, and he took Balin, Lanval and the man from Powys with his war-band. Nimue, consulted by Arthur on whether Aelle would keep his word, nodded and said she had dreamed of the Saxon's compliance and of the safe return of our hostages. 'But Ratae's blood is on your hands,' she said ominously.

We packed and made ready for our own journey, which would not begin until the next day's dawn. Arthur was never happy when forced to idleness and as evening came he asked that Sagramor and I walk with him to the southern woods. For a time it seemed that we wandered aimlessly, but at last Arthur stopped beneath a huge oak hung with long beards of grey lichen. 'I feel dirty,' he said. 'I failed to keep my oath to Benoic, now I am buying the death of hundreds of Britons.'

'You could not have saved Benoic,' I insisted.

'A land that buys poets instead of spearmen does not deserve to survive,' Sagramor added.

'Whether I could have saved it or not,' Arthur said, 'does not matter. I took an oath to Ban and did not keep it.'

'A man whose house is burning to the ground does not carry water to his neighbour's fire,' Sagramor said. His black face, as impenetrably tough as Aelle's, had fascinated the Saxons. Many had fought against him in the last years and believed him to be some kind of demon summoned by Merlin, and Arthur had played on those fears by hinting that he would leave Sagramor to defend the new frontier. In truth Arthur would take Sagramor to Gwent, for he needed all his best men to fight Gorfyddyd. 'You weren't able to keep your oath to Benoic,' Sagramor went on, 'so the Gods will forgive you.' Sagramor had a robustly pragmatic view of Gods and man; it was one of his strengths.

'The Gods may forgive me,' Arthur said, 'but I don't. And now I pay Saxons to kill Britons.' He shuddered at the very thought. 'I found myself wishing for Merlin last night,' he said, 'to know that he would approve of what we are doing.'

'He would,' I said. Nimue might not have approved of sacrificing Ratae, but Nimue was always purer than Merlin. She understood the necessity of paying Saxons, but revolted at the thought of paying with British blood even if that blood did belong to our enemies.

'But it doesn't matter what Merlin thinks,' Arthur said angrily. 'It wouldn't matter if every priest, Druid and bard in Britain agreed with me. To ask another man's blessing is simply to avoid taking the responsibility. Nimue is right, I shall be responsible for all the deaths in Ratae.'

'What else could you do?' I asked.

'You don't understand, Derfel,' Arthur accused me bitterly, though in truth he was accusing himself. 'I always knew Aelle would want something more than gold. They're Saxons! They don't want peace, they want land! I knew that, why else would I have brought that poor man from Ratae? Before Aelle ever asked I was ready to give, and how many men will die for that foresight? Three hundred? And how many women taken into slavery? Two hundred? How many children? How many families will be broken apart? And for what? To prove I'm a better leader than Gorfyddyd? Is my life worth so many souls?'

'Those souls,' I said, 'will keep Mordred on his throne.'

'Another oath!' Arthur said bitterly. 'All these oaths that

bind us! I am oath-bound to Uther to put his grandson on the throne, oath-bound to Leodegan to retake Henis Wyren.' He stopped abruptly and Sagramor looked at me with an alarmed face for it was the first either of us had ever heard about an oath to fight Diwrnach, the dread Irish King of Lleyn who had taken Leodegan's land. 'Yet of all men,' Arthur said miserably, 'I break oaths so easily. I broke the oath to Ban and I broke my oath to Ceinwyn. Poor Ceinwyn.' It was the first time any of us had ever heard him so openly lament that broken promise. I had thought Guinevere was a sun so bright in Arthur's firmament that she had dimmed Ceinwyn's paler lustre into invisibility, but it seemed the memory of Powys's Princess could still gall Arthur's conscience like a spur. Just as the thought of Ratae's doom galled him now. 'Maybe I should send them a warning,' he said.

'And lose the hostages?' Sagramor asked.

Arthur shook his head. 'I'll exchange myself for Balin and Lanval.'

He was thinking of doing just that. I could tell. The agony of remorse was biting at him and he was seeking a way out of that tangle of conscience and duty, even at the price of his own life. 'Merlin would laugh at me now,' he said.

'Yes,' I agreed, 'he would.' Merlin's conscience, if he possessed one at all, was merely a guide to how lesser men thought, and thus served as a goad for Merlin to behave in the contrary manner. Merlin's conscience was a jest to amuse the Gods. Arthur's was a burden.

Now he stared at the mossy ground beneath the oak's shadow. The day was settling into twilight as Arthur's mind sank into gloom. Was he truly tempted to abandon everything? To ride to Aelle's fastness and exchange his existence for the lives of Ratae's souls? I think he was, but then the insidious logic of his ambition rose to overcome his despair like a tide flooding Ynys Trebes's bleak sands. 'A hundred years ago,' he said slowly, 'this land had peace. It had justice. A man could clear land in the happy knowledge that his grandsons would live to tell it. But those grandsons are dead, killed by Saxons or their own kind. If we do nothing then the chaos will spread until there's nothing left but prancing Saxons and their mad wizards. If Gorfyddyd wins he'll strip Dumnonia of its wealth, but if I win I shall embrace Powys like a brother. I hate what we are doing, but if we do it, then we can put things right.' He looked up at us both. 'We are all of Mithras,' he said, 'so you can witness this oath made to Him.' He paused. He was learning to hate oaths and their duties, but such was his state after that meeting with Aelle that he was willing to burden himself with a new one. 'Find me a stone, Derfel,' he ordered.

I kicked a stone out of the soil and brushed the earth from it, then, at Arthur's bidding, I scratched Aelle's name on the stone with the point of my knife. Arthur used his own knife to dig a deep hole at the foot of the oak, then stood. 'My oath is this,' he said, 'that if I survive this battle with Gorfyddyd then I shall avenge the innocent souls I have condemned at Ratae. I will kill Aelle. I shall destroy him and his men. I shall feed them to the ravens and give their wealth to the children of Ratae. You two are my witnesses, and if I fail in this oath you are both released from all the bonds you owe me.' He dropped the stone into the hole and the three of us kicked earth over it. 'May the Gods forgive me,' Arthur said, 'for the deaths I have just caused.'

Then we went to cause some more.

WE TRAVELLED TO GWENT through Corinium. Ailleann still lived there and though Arthur saw his sons he did not receive their mother so that no word of any such meeting could hurt his Guinevere, though he did send me with a gift for Ailleann. She received me with kindness, but shrugged when she saw Arthur's present, a small brooch of enamelled silver depicting an animal very like a hare though with shorter legs and ears. It had come from the treasures of Sansum's shrine, though Arthur had punctiliously replaced the cost of the brooch with coins from his pouch. 'He wishes he had something better to send you,' I said, delivering Arthur's message, 'but alas, the Saxons must have our best jewels these days.'

'There was a time,' she said bitterly, 'when his gifts came from love, not guilt.' Ailleann was still a striking woman, though her hair was now touched with grey and her eyes clouded with resignation. She was clothed in a long blue woollen dress and wore her hair in twin coils above her ears. She peered at the strange enamelled animal. 'What do you think it is?' she asked me. 'It's not a hare. Is it a cat?'

'Sagramor says it's called a rabbit. He's seen them in Cappadocia, wherever that is.'

'You mustn't believe everything Sagramor tells you,' Ailleann chided me as she pinned the small brooch to her gown. 'I have jewellery enough for a queen,' she added as she led me to the small courtyard of her Roman house, 'but I am still a slave.'

'Arthur didn't free you?' I asked, shocked.

'He worries I would move back to Armorica. Or to Ireland,

and so take the twins away from him.' She shrugged. 'On the day the boys are of age Arthur will give me my freedom and do you know what I shall do? I shall stay right here.' She gestured me to a chair that stood in the shade of a vine. 'You look older,' she said as she poured a straw-coloured wine from a wicker-wrapped flask. 'I hear Lunete has left you?' she added as she handed me a horn beaker.

'We left each other, I think.'

'I hear she is now a Priestess of Isis,' Ailleann said mockingly. 'I hear a lot from Durnovaria and dare not believe the half of it.'

'Such as what?' I asked.

'If you don't know, Derfel, then you're best left in ignorance.' She sipped the wine and grimaced at its taste. 'So is Arthur. He never wants to hear bad news, only good. He even believes there is goodness in the twins.'

It shocked me to hear a mother speak of her sons in such a way. 'I'm sure there is,' I said.

She gave me a level, amused look. 'The boys are no better, Derfel, than they ever were, and they were never good. They resent their father. They think they should be princes and so behave like princes. There is no mischief in this town which they don't begin or encourage, and if I try to control them they call me a whore.' She crumbled a fragment of cake and threw its scraps to some scavenging sparrows. A servant swept the courtyard's far side with a bundle of broom twigs until Ailleann ordered the man to leave us alone, then she asked me about the war and I tried to hide my pessimism about Gorfyddyd's huge army. 'Can't you take Amhar and Loholt with you?' Ailleann asked me after a while. 'They might make good soldiers.'

'I doubt their father thinks they're old enough,' I said.

'If he thinks about them at all. He sends them money. I wish he didn't.' She fingered her new brooch. 'The Christians in the town all say that Arthur is doomed.'

'Not yet, Lady.'

She smiled. 'Not for a long time, Derfel. People underestimate Arthur. They see his goodness, hear his kindness, listen to his talk of justice, and none of them, not even you, knows what burns inside him.'

'Which is?'

'Ambition,' she said flatly, then thought for a second. 'His soul,' she went on, 'is a chariot drawn by two horses; ambition and conscience, but I tell you, Derfel, the horse of ambition is in the right-hand harness and it will always outpull the other. And he's able, so very able.' She smiled sadly. 'Just watch him, Derfel, when he seems doomed, when everything is at its darkest, and then he will astonish you. I've seen it before. He'll win, but then the horse of conscience will tug at its reins and Arthur will make his usual mistake of forgiving his enemies.'

'Is that bad?'

'It isn't a question of bad or good, Derfel, but of practicality. We Irish know one thing above all others: an enemy forgiven is an enemy who will have to be fought over and over again. Arthur confuses morality with power, and he worsens the mix by always believing that people are inherently good, even the worst of them, and that is why, mark my words, he will never have peace. He longs for peace, he talks of peace, but his own trusting soul is the reason he will always have enemies. Unless Guinevere manages to put some flint into his soul? And she may. Do you know who she reminds me of?'

'I didn't think you'd met her,' I said.

'I never met the person she reminds me of either, but I hear things, and I do know Arthur very well. She sounds like his mother; very striking and very strong, and I suspect he will do anything to please her.'

'Even at the price of his conscience?'

Ailleann smiled at the question. 'You should know, Derfel, that some women always want their men to pay an exorbitant price. The more the man pays, the greater the woman's worth, and I suspect Guinevere is a lady who values herself very highly. And so she should. So should we all.' She said the last words sadly, then rose from her chair. 'Give him my love,' she told me as we walked back through the house, 'and tell him please to take his sons to war.'

Arthur would not take them. 'Give them another year,' he told me as we marched away next morning. He had dined with the twins and given them small gifts, but all of us had noted the sullenness with which Amhar and Loholt had received their father's affection. Arthur had noticed it too, which was why he was unnaturally dour as we marched west. 'Children born to unwed mothers,' he said after a long silence, 'have parts of their souls missing.'

'What about your soul, Lord?' I asked.

'I patch it every morning, Derfel, piece by piece.' He sighed. 'I shall have to give time to Amhar and Loholt, and the Gods only know where I shall find it because in four or five months I shall be a father again. If I live,' he added bleakly.

So Lunete had been right and Guinevere was pregnant. 'I'm happy for you, Lord,' I said, though I was thinking of Lunete's comment on how unhappy Guinevere was at her condition.

'I'm happy for me!' He laughed, his black mood abruptly vanquished. 'And happy for Guinevere. It'll be good for her, and in ten years' time, Derfel, Mordred will be on the throne and Guinevere and I can find some happy place to rear our cattle, children and pigs! I shall be happy then. I shall train Llamrei to pull a cart and use Excalibur as a goad for my plough-oxen.'

I tried to imagine Guinevere as a farm wife, even as a rich farm wife, and somehow I could not conjure the image, but I kept my peace.

From Corinium we went to Glevum, then crossed the Severn and marched through Gwent's heartland. We made a fine sight, for Arthur deliberately rode with banners flying and his horsemen armoured for combat. We marched in that high style for we wanted to give the local people a new confidence. They had none now. Everyone assumed that Gorfyddyd would be victorious and even though it was harvest-time the country-side was sullen. We passed a threshing floor and the chanter was singing the Lament of Essylt instead of the usual cheerful song that gave rhythm to the flails. We also noted how every villa, house and cottage was strangely bare of anything valuable. Possessions were being hidden, buried probably, so that Gorfyddyd's invaders would not strip the populace bare. 'The moles are getting rich again,' Arthur said sourly.

Arthur alone did not ride in his best armour. 'Morfans has the scale armour,' he told me when I asked why he was wearing his spare coat of mail. Morfans was the ugly warrior who had befriended me at the feast that had followed Arthur's arrival at Caer Cadarn so many years before.

'Morfans?' I asked, astonished. 'How did he earn such a gift?'

'It's not a gift, Derfel. Morfans is just borrowing it, and every day for the past week he has been riding close to Gorfyddyd's men. They think I'm already there, and maybe that has given them pause? So far, at least, we have no news of any attack.'

I had to laugh at the thought of Morfans's ugly face being concealed behind the cheek pieces of Arthur's helmet, and maybe the deception worked for when we joined King Tewdric at the Roman fort of Magnis the enemy had still not sallied from their strongholds in Powys's hills.

Tewdric, dressed in his fine Roman armour, looked almost an old man. His hair had gone grey and there was a stoop in his carriage that had not been there when I had last seen him. He greeted the news about Aelle with a grunt, then made an effort to be more complimentary. 'Good news,' he said curtly, then rubbed his eyes, 'though God knows Gorfyddyd never needed Saxon help to beat us. He has men to spare.'

The Roman fort seethed. Armourers were making spear-heads, and every pollard ash for miles had been stripped for shafts. Carts of newly harvested grain arrived hourly and the bakers' ovens burned as fierce as the blacksmiths' furnaces so that a constant pyre of smoke hung above the palisaded walls. Yet despite the new harvest the gathering army was hungry. Most of the spearmen were camped outside the walls, some were miles away, and there were constant arguments about the distribution of the hard-baked bread and dried beans. Other contingents complained of water fouled by the latrines of men camped upstream. There was disease, hunger and desertion; evidence that neither Tewdric nor Arthur had ever had to grapple with the problems of commanding an army so large. 'But if we have difficulties,' Arthur said optimistically, 'imagine Gorfyddyd's troubles.'

'I would rather have his problems than mine,' Tewdric said gloomily.

My spearmen, still under Galahad's command, were camped eight miles to the north of Magnis where Agricola, Tewdric's commander, kept a close watch on the hills that marked the frontier between Gwent and Powys. I felt a pang of happiness at seeing their wolf-tail helmets again. After the defeatism of the countryside it was suddenly good to think that here, at least, were men who would never be beaten. Nimue came with me and my men clustered about her so she could touch their spearheads and sword blades to give them power. Even the Christians, I noted, wanted her pagan touch. She was doing Merlin's business, and because she was known to have come from the Isle of the Dead she was thought to be almost as powerful as her master.

Agricola received me inside a tent, the first I had ever seen. It was a wondrous affair with a tall central pole and four corner staffs holding up a linen canopy that filtered the sunlight so that Agricola's short grey hair looked oddly yellow. He was in his Roman armour and sitting at a table covered in scraps of parchment. He was a stern man and his greeting was perfunctory, though he did add a compliment about my men. 'They're confident. But so are the enemy, and there are many more of them than there are of us.' His tone was grim.

'How many?' I asked.

Agricola seemed offended by my bluntness, but I was no longer the boy I had been when I had first seen Gwent's warlord. I was a lord myself now, a commander of men, and I had a right to know what odds those men faced. Or maybe it was not my directness that irritated Agricola, but rather that he did not want to be reminded of the enemy's preponderance. Finally, however, he gave me the tally. 'According to our spies,' he said,

'Powys has assembled six hundred spearmen from their own land. Gundleus has brought another two hundred and fifty from Siluria, maybe more. Ganval of Elmet has sent two hundred men, and the Gods alone know how many masterless men have gone to Gorfyddyd's banner for a share of the spoils.' Masterless men were rogues, exiles, murderers and savages who were drawn to an army for the plunder they could gain in battle. Such men were feared for they had nothing to lose and everything to gain. I doubted we had many such on our side, not just because we were expected to lose, but because both Tewdric and Arthur were ill disposed towards such lordless creatures. Curiously, though, many of Arthur's best horsemen had once been just such men. Warriors like Sagramor had fought in the Roman armies that had been shattered by the heathen invaders of Italy and it had been Arthur's youthful genius to harness such lordless mercenaries into a war-band.

'There's more,' Agricola went on ominously. 'The kingdom of Cornovia has donated men and just yesterday we heard that Oengus Mac Airem of Demetia has come with a war-band of his Blackshields; maybe a hundred strong? And another report says the men of Gwynedd have joined Gorfyddyd.'

'Levies?' I asked.

Agricola shrugged. 'Five, six hundred? Maybe even a thousand. But they won't come until the harvest's finished.'

I was beginning to wish I had not asked. 'And our numbers, Lord?'

'Now that Arthur has arrived . . .' He paused. 'Seven hundred spears.'

I said nothing. It was no wonder, I thought, that men in Gwent and Dumnonia buried their treasures and whispered that Arthur should leave Britain. We were faced by a horde.

'I would be grateful,' Agricola said acidly, as though the thought of gratitude was utterly alien to his thinking, 'if you did not bruit the numbers about? We've had desertions enough already. More, and we might as well dig our own graves.'

'No deserters from my men,' I insisted.

'No,' he allowed, 'not yet.' He stood and took his short Roman sword from where it hung on a tent pole, then paused in the doorway from where he cast a baleful eye towards the enemy hills. 'Men say you're a friend of Merlin.'

'Yes, Lord.'

'Will he come?'

'I don't know, Lord.'

Agricola grunted. 'I pray he does. Someone needs to talk sense into this army. All commanders are summoned to Magnis tonight. A council of war.' He said it bitterly, as though he knew that such councils produced more quarrels than comradeship. 'Be there by sunset.'

Galahad came with me. Nimue stayed with my men for her presence gave them confidence and I was glad she did not come for the council was opened by a prayer from Bishop Conrad of Gwent who seemed imbued with defeatism as he begged his God to give us strength to face the over-mighty foe. Galahad, his arms spread in the Christian pose of prayer, murmured along with the Bishop while we pagans grumbled that we should not pray for strength, but victory. I wished we had some Druids among us, but Tewdric, a Christian, employed none, and Balise, the old man who had attended Mordred's acclamation, had died during the first winter I was in Benoic. Agricola was right to hope that Merlin would come, for an army without Druids was giving away an advantage to its enemy.

There were some forty or fifty men at the council, all of us chieftains or leaders. We met in the bare stone hall of Magnis's bath house that reminded me of Ynys Wydryn's church. King Tewdric, Arthur, Agricola and Tewdric's son, the Edling Meurig, sat at a table on a stone dais. Meurig had grown into a pale thin creature who looked unhappy in his ill-fitting Roman armour. He was just old enough to fight, but with his nervous air he looked very unfit for battle. He blinked constantly, as if he had just come into sunlight from a very dark room, and he kept fidgeting with a heavy gold cross that hung around his neck. Arthur alone of the commanders was not in war gear, but looked relaxed in his countryman's clothes.

The warriors cheered and stamped their spear-butts when King Tewdric announced that the Saxons were believed to have withdrawn from the eastern frontier, but that was the last cheering for a long while that night, because Agricola then stood and gave his blunt assessment of the two armies. He did not list all the enemy's smaller contingents, but even without those additions it was clear that Gorfyddyd's army would out-number ours by two to one. 'We'll just have to kill twice as fast!' Morfans shouted from the back. He had returned the scale armour to Arthur, swearing that only a hero could wear that amount of metal and still fight. Agricola ignored the inter-ruption, adding instead that the harvest should be complete in a week and the levies of Gwent would then swell our numbers. No one seemed too cheered by that news.

King Tewdric proposed that we should fight Gorfyddyd under the walls of Magnis. 'Give me a week,' he said, 'and I will so fill this fortress with the new harvest that Gorfyddyd will never pitch us out. Fight here' – he gestured towards the dark beyond the hall doors – 'and if the battle goes ill we pull inside the gates and let them waste their spears on wooden pal-isades.' It was the way of war Tewdric preferred and had long perfected: siege warfare, where he could use the work of long-dead Roman engineers to frustrate spears and swords. A murmur of agreement sounded in the room, and that murmur swelled when Tewdric told the council that Aelle might well be planning to attack Ratae.

'Hold Gorfyddyd here,' one man said, 'and he'll run back north when he hears Aelle's coming through his back door.'

'Aelle will not fight my battle.' Arthur spoke for the first time, and the room became still. Arthur seemed embarrassed at having spoken so firmly. He smiled apologetically at King Tewdric and asked exactly where the enemy forces were gath-ered. Arthur already knew, of course, but he was asking the question so that the rest of us would hear the answer.

Agricola answered for Tewdric. 'Their forward men are

strung between Coel's Hill and Caer Lud,' he said, 'while the main army gathers at Branogenium. More men are marching from Caer Sws.'

The names meant little to us, but Arthur seemed to understand the geography. 'So they guard the hills between us and Branogenium?'

'Every pass,' Agricola confirmed, 'and every hilltop.'

'How many at Lugg Vale?' Arthur asked.

'At least two hundred of their best spearmen. They're not fools, Lord,' Agricola added sourly.

Arthur stood. He was at his best at these councils, easily dominating crowds of fractious men. He smiled at us. 'The Christians will understand this best,' he said, subtly flattering the men most likely to oppose him. 'Imagine a Christian cross. Here at Magnis we are at the foot of the cross. The cross's shaft is the Roman road that runs north from Magnis to Branogenium, and the crosspiece is made by the hills that bar that road. Coel's Hill is at the left of the crosspiece, Caer Lud at the right, and Lugg Vale is at the cross's centre. The vale is where the road and river pass through the hills.'

He walked out from behind the table and perched himself on its front so he was closer to his audience. 'I want you to think about something,' he said. The flamelight from the becketed torches cast shadows on his long cheeks, but his eyes were bright and his tone energetic. 'Everyone knows we must lose this battle,' he said. 'We are outnumbered. We wait here for Gorfyddyd to attack us. We wait and some of us become dispirited and carry our spears home. Others fall ill. And all of us brood on that great army gathering in the bowl of the hills around Branogenium and we try not to imagine our shield-wall outflanked and the enemy coming at us from three sides at once. But think of the enemy! They wait too, but as they wait they get stronger! Men come from Cornovia, from Elmet, from Demetia, from Gwynedd. Landless men come to gain land and masterless men to take plunder. They know they will win and they know we wait like mice trapped by a tribe of cats.'

He smiled again and stood up. 'But we're not mice. We have some of the greatest warriors ever to lift a spear. We have champions!' The cheering began. 'We can kill cats! And we know how to skin them too! But.' That last word stopped the next cheer just as it began. 'But,' Arthur went on, 'not if we wait here to be attacked. Wait here behind Magnis's walls and what happens? The enemy will march around us. Our homes, our wives, our children, our lands, our flocks and our new harvest become theirs, and all we become are mice in a trap. We must attack, and attack soon.'

Agricola waited for the Dumnonian cheers to die. 'Attack where?' he asked sourly.

'Where they least expect it, Lord, in their strongest place. Lugg Vale. Straight up the cross! Straight to the heart!' He held up a hand to stop any cheering. 'The vale is a narrow place,' he said, 'where no shield-line can be outflanked. The road fords the river north of the valley.' He was frowning as he spoke, trying to remember a place he had seen only once in his life, but Arthur had a soldier's memory for terrain and only needed to see a place once. 'We would need to put men on the western hill to stop their archers raining arrows down, but once in the vale I swear we cannot be moved.'

Agricola objected. 'We can hold there,' he agreed, 'but how do we fight our way in? They have two hundred spearmen there, maybe more, but even one hundred men can hold that valley all day. By the time we've fought to the vale's far end Gorfyddyd will have brought his horde down from Branogenium. Worse, the Blackshield Irish who garrison Coel's Hill can march south of the hills and take our rear. We might not be moved, Lord, but we'll be killed where we stand.'

'The Irish on Coel's Hill don't matter,' Arthur said carelessly. He was excited and could not stay still; he began pacing up and down the dais, explaining and cajoling. 'Think, I beg you, Lord King' – he spoke to Tewdric – 'what happens if we stay here. The enemy will come, we shall retreat behind impregnable walls and they will raid our lands. By midwinter we'll be alive, but will anyone else in Gwent or Dumnonia still live? No. Those hills south of Branogenium are Gorfyddyd's walls. If we breach those walls he has to fight us, and if he fights in Lugg Vale he is a defeated man.'

'His two hundred men in Lugg Vale will stop us,' Agricola insisted.

'They will vanish like the mist!' Arthur proclaimed confidently. 'They are two hundred men who have never faced armoured horse in battle.'

Agricola shook his head. 'The vale is barred by a wall of felled trees. Armoured horse will be stopped' – he paused to ram his fist into an upraised palm – 'dead.' He said the word flatly and the finality of his tone made Arthur sit. There was the smell of defeat in the hall. From outside the baths, where the blacksmiths worked day and night, I heard the hiss of a newly forged blade being quenched in water.

'Perhaps I might be permitted to speak?' The speaker was Meurig, Tewdric's son. He had a strangely high voice, almost petulant in its tone, and he was evidently short-sighted for he screwed up his eyes and cocked his head whenever he wanted to look at a man in the main part of the hall. 'What I would like to ask,' he said when his father had given him permission to address the council, 'is why we fight at all?' He blinked rapidly when the question was asked.

No one answered. Maybe we were all too astonished at the question.

'Let me, permit me, allow me to explain,' Meurig said in a pedantic tone. He might have been young, but he possessed the confidence of a prince, though I found the false modesty with which he cloaked his pronouncements irritating. 'We fight Gorfyddyd – correct me if I am wrong – out of our long-standing alliance with Dumnonia. That alliance has served us well, I doubt not, but Gorfyddyd, as I understand it, has no designs upon the Dumnonian throne.'

A growl came from we Dumnonians, but Arthur held up his hand for silence, then gestured for Meurig to continue. Meurig blinked and tugged at his cross. 'I just wonder why we fight? What, if I might phrase it thus, is our *casus belli*?'

'Cow's belly?' Culhwch shouted. Culhwch had seen me when I arrived and had crossed the hall to welcome me. Now he put his mouth close to my ear. 'Bastards have got thin shields, Derfel,' he said, 'and they're looking for a way out.'

Arthur stood again and spoke courteously to Meurig. 'The cause of the war, Lord Prince, is your father's oath to preserve King Mordred's throne, and King Gorfyddyd's evident desire to take that throne from my King.'

Meurig shrugged. 'But – correct me, please, I beg you – but as I understand these things Gorfyddyd does not seek to dethrone King Mordred.'

'You know that?' Culhwch shouted.

'There are indications,' Meurig said irritably.

'Bastards have been talking to the enemy,' Culhwch whispered in my ear. 'Ever had a knife in the back, Derfel? Arthur's getting one now.'

Arthur stayed calm. 'What indications?' he asked mildly.

King Tewdric had stayed silent as his son spoke, evidence that he had given his permission for Meurig to suggest, however delicately, that Gorfyddyd should be appeased rather than confronted, but now, looking old and tired, the King took control of the hall. 'There are no indications, Lord, upon which I would want to depend my strategy. Nevertheless' – and when Tewdric pronounced that word so emphatically we all knew Arthur had lost the debate – 'nevertheless, Lord, I am convinced that we need not provoke Powys unnecessarily. Let us see whether we cannot have peace.' He paused, almost as if he feared the word would anger Arthur, but Arthur said nothing. Tewdric sighed. 'Gorfyddyd fights,' he said slowly and carefully, 'because of an insult done to his family.' Again he paused, fearing that his bluntness might have offended Arthur, but Arthur was never a man to evade responsibility and he nodded his reluctant agreement with Tewdric's frankness. 'While we,' Tewdric continued, 'fight to keep the oath we gave to High King Uther. An oath by which we promised to preserve Mordred's throne. I, for one, will not break that oath.'

'Nor I!' Arthur said loudly.

'But what, Lord Arthur, if King Gorfyddyd has no designs on that throne?' King Tewdric asked. 'If he means to keep Mordred as King, then why do we fight?'

There was uproar in the hall. We Dumnonians smelled treachery, the men of Gwent smelled an escape from the war, and for a time we shouted at each other until at last Arthur regained order by slapping his hand on the table. 'The last envoy I sent to Gorfyddyd,' Arthur said, 'had his head sent back in a sack. Are you suggesting, Lord King, we send another?'

Tewdric shook his head. 'Gorfyddyd is refusing to receive my envoys. They are turned back at the frontier. But if we wait here and let his army waste its efforts against our walls then I believe he will become discouraged and will then negotiate.' His men murmured agreement.

Arthur tried one more time to dissuade Tewdric. He conjured a picture of our army rooted behind walls while Gorfyddyd's horde ravaged the newly harvested farms, but the men of Gwent would not be moved by his oratory or his passion. They only saw outflanked shield-walls and fields of dead men, and so they seized on their King's belief that peace would come if only they retreated into Magnis and let Gorfyddyd weary his men by battering its strong walls. They began to demand Arthur's agreement for their strategy and I saw the hurt on his face. He had lost. If he waited here then Gorfyddyd would demand his head. If he ran to Armorica he would live, but he would be abandoning Mordred and his own dream of a just, united Britain. The clamour in the hall grew louder, and it was then that Galahad stood and shouted for a chance to be heard.

Tewdric pointed at Galahad, who first introduced himself. 'I am Galahad, Lord King,' he said, 'a Prince of Benoic. If King Gorfyddyd will receive no envoys from Gwent or Dumnonia, then surely he will not refuse one from Armorica? Let me go, Lord King, to Caer Sws and enquire what Gorfyddyd intends to do with Mordred. And if I do go, Lord King, will you accept my word as to his verdict?'

Tewdric was happy to accept. He was happy with anything that might avert war, but he was still anxious for Arthur's agreement. 'Suppose Gorfyddyd decrees that Mordred is safe,' he suggested to Arthur. 'What will you do then?'

Arthur stared at the table. He was losing his dream, but he could not tell a lie to save that dream and so he looked up with a rueful smile. 'In that case, Lord King, I would leave Britain and I would entrust Mordred to your keeping.'

Once again we Dumnonians shouted our protests, but this time Tewdric silenced us. 'We do not know what answer Prince Galahad will bring,' he said, 'but this I promise. If Mordred's throne is threatened then I, King Tewdric, will fight. If not? I see no reason to fight.'

And with that promise we had to be content. The war, it seemed, hung on Gorfyddyd's answer. To find it, next morning, Galahad rode north.

I rode with Galahad. He had not wanted me to come, saying that my life would be in danger, but I argued with him as I had never argued before. I also pleaded with Arthur, saying that at least one Dumnonian should hear Gorfyddyd declare his intentions about our King, and Arthur pleaded my case with Galahad who at last relented. We were friends, after all, though for my own safety Galahad insisted that I travel as his servant and that I carry his symbol on my shield. 'You have no symbol,' I told him.

'I do now,' he said, and ordered that our shields be painted with crosses. 'Why not?' he asked me, 'I'm a Christian.'

'It looks wrong,' I said. I was accustomed to warriors' shields being blazoned with bulls, eagles, dragons and stags, not with some desiccated piece of religious geometry.

'I like it,' he said, 'and besides, you are now my humble servant, Derfel, so your opinion is of no interest to me. None.' He laughed and skipped away from a blow I aimed at his arm.

I was forced to ride to Caer Sws. In all my years with Arthur I never did accustom myself to sitting on a horse's back. To me it always seemed a natural thing to sit well back on a horse, but sitting thus it was impossible to grip the animal's flanks with your knees, for which you had to slide forward until you were perched just behind its neck with your feet dangling in the air behind its forelegs. In the end I used to tuck one foot into the saddle girth to give me an anchoring point, a shift that offended Galahad who was proud of his horsemanship. 'Ride it properly!' he would say.

'But there's nowhere to put my feet!'

'The horse has got four. How many more do you want?'

We rode to Caer Lud, Gorfyddyd's major fortress in the border hills. The town stood on a hill in a river bend and we reckoned its sentries would be less wary than those who guarded the Roman road at Lugg Vale. Even so we did not state our real business in Powys, but simply declared ourselves as landless men from Armorica seeking entry into Gorfyddyd's country. The guards, discovering Galahad was a prince, insisted on escorting him to the town's commander and so led us through the town that was filled with armed men whose spears were stacked at every door and whose helmets were piled under all the tavern benches. The town commander was a harassed man who plainly hated the responsibilities of governing a garrison swollen by the imminence of war. 'I knew you must be from Armorica when I saw your shields, Lord Prince,' he told Galahad. 'An outlandish symbol to our provincial eyes.'

'An honoured one in mine,' Galahad said gravely, not catching my eye.

'To be sure, to be sure,' the commander said. His name was Halsyd. 'And of course you are welcome, Lord Prince. Our High King is welcoming all . . .' He paused, embarrassed. He had been about to say that Gorfyddyd was welcoming all landless warriors, but that phrase cut too close to insult when uttered to a dispossessed prince of an Armorican kingdom. 'All brave men,' the commander said instead. 'You were not thinking of staying here, by any chance?' He was worried that we would prove two more hungry mouths in a town already hard pressed to feed its existing garrison.

'I would ride to Caer Sws,' Galahad announced. 'With my servant.' He gestured towards me.

'May the Gods speed your path, Lord Prince.'

398

And thus we entered the enemy country. We rode through quiet valleys where newly stooked corn patterned the fields and orchards hung heavy with ripening apples. The next day we were among the hills, following an earth road that wound through great tracts of damp woodland until, at last, we climbed above the trees and crossed the pass that led down to Gorfyddyd's capital. I felt a shudder of nerves as I saw Caer Sws's raw earth walls. Gorfyddyd's army might be gathering in Branogenium, some forty miles away, but still the land around Caer Sws was thick with soldiers. The troops had thrown up crude shelters with walls of stone roofed with turf, and the shelters surrounded the fort that flew eight banners from its walls to show that the men of eight kingdoms served in Gorfyddyd's growing ranks. 'Eight?' Galahad asked. 'Powys, Siluria, Elmet, but who else?'

'Cornovia, Demetia, Gwynedd, Rheged and Demetia's Blackshields,' I said, finishing off the grim list.

'No wonder Tewdric wants peace,' Galahad said softly, marvelling at the host of men camped on either side of the river that ran beside the enemy's capital.

We rode down into that hive of iron. Children followed us, curious about our strange shields, while their mothers watched us suspiciously from the shadowed openings of their shelters. The men gave us brief glances, taking in our strange insignia and noting the quality of our weapons, but none challenged us until we reached the gates of Caer Sws where Gorfyddyd's royal guard barred our way with polished spearheads. 'I am Galahad, Prince of Benoic,' Galahad announced grandly, 'come to see my cousin the High King.'

'Is he a cousin?' I whispered.

'It's how we royalty talk,' he whispered back.

The scene inside the compound went some way to explaining why so many soldiers were gathered at Caer Sws. Three tall stakes had been driven into the earth and now waited for the formal ceremonies that preceded war. Powys was one of the least Christian kingdoms and the old rituals were done carefully here, and I suspected that many of the soldiers

camped outside the walls had been fetched back from Branogenium specifically to witness the rites and so to inform their
comrades that the Gods had been placated. There was to be
nothing hasty about Gorfyddyd's invasion, everything would
be done methodically, and Arthur, I thought, was probably
right in thinking that such a pedestrian endeavour could be
tipped off balance by a surprise attack.

Our horses were taken by servants, then, after a counsellor
had questioned Galahad and determined that he was, indeed,
who he claimed to be, we were ushered into the great feasting
hall. The doorkeeper took our swords, shields and spears and
added them to the stacks of similar weapons belonging to the
men already gathered in Gorfyddyd's hall.

Over a hundred men were assembled between the squat oak
pillars that were hung with human skulls to show that the
kingdom was at war. The men beneath those grinning bones
were the kings, princes, lords, chiefs and champions of the assembled armies. The only furniture in the hall was the row of
thrones placed on a dais at the far dark end where Gorfyddyd
sat beneath his symbol of the eagle, while next to him, but on a
lower throne, sat Gundleus. The very sight of the Silurian
King made the scar on my left hand pulse. Tanaburs squatted
beside Gundleus, while Gorfyddyd had Iorweth, his own
Druid, at his right side. Cuneglas, Powys's Edling, sat on a
third throne and was flanked by kings I did not recognize. No
women were present. This was doubtless a council of war, or at
least a chance for men to gloat over the victory that was about
to be theirs. The men were dressed in mail coats and leather
armour.

We paused at the back of the hall and I saw Galahad mouth a
silent prayer to his God. A wolfhound with a chewed ear and
scarred haunches sniffed our boots, then loped back to its
master who stood with the other warriors on the rush-covered
earth floor. In a far corner of the hall a bard softly chanted a
war song, though his staccato recitation was ignored by the
men who were listening to Gundleus describing the forces he
expected to come from Demetia. One chief, evidently a man

who had suffered from the Irish in the past, protested that Powys had no need of the Blackshields' help to defeat Arthur and Tewdric, but his protest was stilled by an abrupt gesture from Gorfyddyd. I half expected that we would be forced to linger while the council finished its other business, but we did not have to wait more than a minute before we were conducted down the hall's centre to the open space in front of Gorfyddyd. I looked at both Gundleus and Tanaburs but neither recognized me.

We fell to our knees and waited.

'Rise,' Gorfyddyd said. We obeyed and once again I looked into his bitter face. He had not changed much in the years since I had seen him last. His face was as pouchy and suspicious as when Arthur had come to claim Ceinwyn's hand, though his sickness in the last few years had turned his hair and beard white. The beard was skimpy and could not hide a goitre that now disfigured his throat. He looked at us warily. 'Galahad,' he said in a hoarse voice, 'Prince of Benoic. We have heard of your brother, Lancelot, but not of you. Are you, like your brother, one of Arthur's whelps?'

'I am oath-bound to no man, Lord King,' Galahad said, 'except to my father whose bones were trampled by his enemies. I am landless.'

Gorfyddyd shifted in his throne. His empty left sleeve hung beside the armrest, an ever-present reminder of his hated foe, Arthur. 'So you come to me for land, Galahad of Benoic?' he asked. 'Many others have come for the same purpose,' he warned, gesturing about the crowded hall. 'Though I daresay there is land enough for all in Dumnonia.'

'I come to you, Lord King, with greetings, freely carried, from King Tewdric of Gwent.'

That caused a stir in the hall. Men at the back who had not heard Galahad's announcement asked for it to be repeated and the murmur of conversation went on for several seconds. Cuneglas, Gorfyddyd's son, looked up sharply. His round face with its long dark moustaches looked worried, and no wonder, I thought, for Cuneglas was like Arthur, a man who craved peace, but when Arthur spurned Ceinwyn he had also destroyed Cuneglas's hopes and now the Edling of Powys could only follow his father into a war that threatened to lay waste the southern kingdoms.

'Our enemies, it seems, are losing their hunger for battle,' Gorfyddyd said. 'Why else does Tewdric send greetings?'

'King Tewdric, High King, fears no man, but loves peace more,' Galahad said, carefully using the title Gorfyddyd had bestowed on himself in anticipation of his victory.

Gorfyddyd's body heaved and for a second I thought he was about to vomit, then I realized he was laughing. 'We Kings only love peace,' Gorfyddyd said at last, 'when war becomes inconvenient to us. This gathering, Galahad of Benoic' – he gestured at the throng of chiefs and princes – 'will explain Tewdric's new love of peace.' He paused, gathering breath. 'Till now, Galahad of Benoic, I have refused to receive Tewdric's messages. Why should I receive them? Does an eagle listen to a lamb bleating for mercy? In a few days I intend to listen to all Gwent's men bleating to me for peace, but for now, since you have come this far, you may amuse me. What does Tewdric offer?'

'Peace, Lord King, just peace.'

Gorfyddyd spat. 'You are landless, Galahad, and empty-handed. Does Tewdric think peace is for the asking? Does Tewdric think I have expended my kingdom's gold on an army for no cause? Does he think I am a fool?'

'He thinks, Lord King, that blood shed between Britons is wasted blood.'

'You talk like a woman, Galahad of Benoic.' Gorfyddyd spoke the insult in a deliberately loud voice so that the raftered hall echoed with jeers and laughter. 'Still,' he went on when the laughter had subsided, 'you must take some answer to Gwent's King, so let it be this.' He paused to compose his thoughts. 'Tell Tewdric that he is a lamb sucking at Dumnonia's dry teat. Tell him my quarrel is not with him, but with Arthur, so tell Tewdric that he may have his peace on these two conditions. First, that he lets my army pass through his land without hindrance and second that he gives me enough grain to feed a thousand men for ten days.' The warriors in the hall gasped, for they were generous terms, but also clever. If Tewdric accepted then he would avoid the sack of his country and make Gorfyddyd's invasion of Dumnonia easier. 'Are you empowered, Galahad of Benoic,' Gorfyddyd asked, 'to accept these terms?'

'No, Lord King, only to enquire what terms you would offer and to ask what you intend to do with Mordred, King of Dumnonia, whom Tewdric is sworn to protect.'

Gorfyddyd adopted a hurt look. 'Do I look like a man who makes war on children?' he asked, then stood and advanced to the edge of the throne dais. 'My quarrel is with Arthur,' he said, not just to us, but to the whole hall, 'who preferred to marry a whore out of Henis Wyren rather than wed my daughter. Would any man leave such an insult unavenged?' The hall roared its answer. 'Arthur is an upstart,' Gorfyddyd shouted, 'whelped on a whore mother, and to a whore he has returned! So long as Gwent protects the whore-lover, so long is Gwent our enemy. So long as Dumnonia fights for the whore-lover, so long is Dumnonia our enemy. And our enemy will be the generous provider of our gold, our slaves, our food, our land, our women and our glory! Arthur we will kill, and his whore we shall put to work in our barracks.' He waited until the cheers had died away, then stared imperiously down on Galahad. 'Tell that to Tewdric, Galahad of Benoic, and after that tell it to Arthur.'

'Derfel can tell it to Arthur.' A voice spoke from the hall and I turned to see Ligessac, sly Ligessac, once commander of Norwenna's guard and now a traitor in Gundleus's service. He pointed to me. 'That man is Arthur's sworn man, High King. I swear it on my life.'

The hall seethed with noise. I could hear men shouting that I was a spy and others demanding my death. Tanaburs was staring at me intently, trying to see past my long, fair beard and thick moustaches, then suddenly he recognized me and screamed, 'Kill him! Kill him!'

Gorfyddyd's guards, the only armed men in the hall, ran

towards me. Gorfyddyd checked his spearmen with his raised hand that slowly silenced the noisy crowd. 'Are you oath-bound to the whore-lover?' the King asked me in a dangerous voice.

'Derfel is in my service, High King,' Galahad insisted.

Gorfyddyd pointed at me. 'He will answer,' he said. 'Are you oath-bound to Arthur?'

I could not lie about an oath. 'Yes, Lord King,' I admitted.

Gorfyddyd stepped heavily off the platform and stretched his one arm towards a guard, though he still stared at me. 'Do you know, you dog, what we did to Arthur's last messenger?'

'You killed him, Lord King,' I said.

'I sent his maggot-ridden head to your whore-lover, that is what I did. Come on, hurry!' he snapped at the nearest guard who had not known what to put in his King's outstretched hand. 'Your sword, fool!' Gorfyddyd said, and the guard hastily drew his sword and gave it hilt first to the King.

'Lord King.' Galahad stepped forward, but Gorfyddyd whirled the blade so that it quivered just inches from Gala-had's eyes.

'Be careful what you say in my hall, Galahad of Benoic,' Gorfyddyd growled.

'I plead for Derfel's life,' Galahad said. 'He is not here as a spy, but as an emissary of peace.'

'I don't want peace!' Gorfyddyd shouted at Galahad. 'Peace is not my pleasure! I want to see Arthur weeping as my daughter once wept. Do you understand that? I want to see his tears! I want to see him pleading as she pleaded with me. I want to see him grovel, I want to see him dead and his whore pleasuring my men. No emissary from Arthur is welcome here and Arthur knows that! And you knew that!' He shouted the last four words at me as he turned the sword towards my face.

'Kill him! Kill him!' Tanaburs, in his raggedly embroidered robe, leaped up and down so that the bones in his hair rattled like dried beans in a pot.

'Touch him, Gorfyddyd,' said a new voice in the hall, 'and your life is mine. I shall bury it in the dungheap of Caer Idion and call the dogs to piss on it. I shall give your soul to the spirit children who lack playthings. I shall keep you in darkness till the last day is done and then I shall spit on you till the next era begins, and even then, Lord King, your torments will hardly have begun.'

I felt the tension sweep out of me like a rush of water. Only one man would dare speak to a High King thus. It was Merlin. Merlin! Merlin who now walked slow and tall up the hall's central aisle, Merlin who walked past me and with a gesture more royal than anything Gorfyddyd could manage, used his black staff to thrust the King's sword aside. Merlin, who now walked to Tanaburs and whispered in his ear so that the lesser Druid screamed and fled from the hall.

It was Merlin, who could change like no other man. He loved to pretend, to confuse and to deceive. He could be abrupt, mischievous, patient or lordly, but this day he had chosen to appear in stark, cold majesty. There was no smile on his dark face, no hint of joy in his deep eyes, just a look of such arrogant authority that the men closest to him instinctively sank to their knees and even King Gorfyddyd, who a moment before had been ready to thrust the sword into my neck, lowered the blade. 'You speak for this man, Lord Merlin?' Gorfyddyd asked.

'Are you deaf, Gorfyddyd?' Merlin snapped. 'Derfel Cadarn shall live. He shall be your honoured guest. He shall eat of your food and drink of your wine. He shall sleep in your beds and take your slave women if he desires. Derfel Cadarn and Galahad of Benoic are under my protection.' He turned to stare at the whole hall, daring any man to oppose him. 'Derfel Cadarn and Galahad of Benoic are under my protection!' he repeated, and this time he raised his black staff and you could feel the warriors quake beneath its threat. 'Without Derfel Cadarn and Galahad of Benoic,' Merlin said, 'there would be no Knowledge of Britain. I would be dead in Benoic and you would all be doomed to slavery under Saxon rule.' He turned back to Gorfyddyd. 'They need food. And stop staring at me, Derfel,' he added without even looking at me.

I had been staring at him, as much with astonishment as with relief, but I was also wondering just what Merlin was doing in this citadel of the enemy. Druids, of course, were free to travel where they liked, even in enemy territory, but his presence at Caer Sws at such a time seemed strange and even dangerous, for though Gorfyddyd's men were cowed by the Druid's presence they were also resentful of his interference and some, safe at the hall's rear, growled that he should mind his own business.

Merlin turned on them. 'My business,' he said in a low voice that nevertheless stopped the small protest dead, 'is the care of your souls and if I care to drown those souls in misery then you will wish your mothers had never given birth. Fools!' This last word was snapped loudly and accompanied by a gesture from the staff that made the armoured men struggle down to their knees. None of the kings dared to intervene as Merlin swept the staff to give one of the skulls hanging from a pillar a sharp crack. 'You pray for victory!' Merlin said. 'But over what? Over your kin and not your enemies! Your enemies are Saxons. For years we suffered under Roman rule, but at last the Gods saw fit to take the Roman vermin away and what do we do? We fight among ourselves and let a new enemy take our land, rape our women and harvest our corn. So fight your war, fools, fight it and win, and still you shall not have victory.'

'But my daughter will be avenged,' Gorfyddyd said behind Merlin.

'Your daughter, Gorfyddyd,' Merlin said, turning, 'will avenge her own hurt. You want to know her fate?' He asked the question mockingly, but answered it soberly and in a voice that had the lilt of a prophetic utterance. 'She will never be high and she will never be low, but she will be happy. Her soul, Gorfyddyd, is blessed, and if you had the sense of a flea you would be content with that.'

'I shall be content with Arthur's skull,' Gorfyddyd said defiantly.

'Then go and fetch it,' Merlin said scornfully, then plucked me by the elbow. 'Come, Derfel, and enjoy your enemy's hospitality.'

He led us out of the hall, walking unconcernedly through the iron and leather ranks of the enemy. The warriors watched us resentfully, but there was nothing they could do to stop us leaving nor to prevent us taking one of Gorfyddyd's guest chambers that Merlin had evidently been using himself. 'So Tewdric wants peace, does he?' he asked us.

'Yes, Lord,' I answered.

'Tewdric would. He's a Christian so he thinks he knows better than the Gods.'

'And you know the minds of the Gods, Lord?' Galahad asked.

'I believe the Gods hate to be bored, so I do my best to amuse them. That way they smile on me. Your God,' Merlin said sourly, 'despises amusement, demanding grovelling worship instead. He must be a very sorry creature. He's probably rather like Gorfyddyd, endlessly suspicious and foully jealous of his reputation. Aren't you both lucky that I was here?' He grinned at us, suddenly and mischievously, and I saw how much he had enjoyed his public humiliation of Gorfyddyd. Part of Merlin's reputation was made by his performances; some Druids, like Iorweth, worked quietly, others, like Tanaburs, relied on a sinister wiliness, but Merlin liked to dominate and dazzle, and humbling an ambitious king was as pleasurable to him as it was instinctive.

'Is Ceinwyn really blessed?' I asked him.

He looked astonished at the unexpected question. 'Why should it matter to you? But she's a pretty girl, and I confess that pretty girls are a weakness of mine so I shall weave her a charm of bliss. I did the same for you once, Derfel, though not because you are pretty.' He laughed, then glanced through the window to judge the length of the sun's shadows. 'I must be on my way soon.'

'What brought you here, Lord?' Galahad asked.

'I needed to talk to Iorweth,' Merlin said, looking around to make sure that he had collected all his belongings. 'He might be a bumbling idiot, but he does possess the odd scrap of knowledge I might have momentarily forgotten. He proved knowledgeable about the Ring of Eluned. I have it somewhere.' He patted the pockets sewn into the lining of his robe. 'Well, I did have it,' he said carelessly, though I suspected the indifference was merely a pretence.

'What is the Ring of Eluned?' Galahad asked.

Merlin scowled at my friend's ignorance, then decided to indulge it. 'The Ring of Eluned,' he announced grandly, 'is one of the Thirteen Treasures of Britain. We've always known about the Treasures, of course – at least, those of us who recognize the true Gods,' he added pointedly, glancing at Galahad, 'but none of us were sure what their real power was.'

'And the scroll told you?' I asked.

Merlin smiled wolfishly. His long white hair was neatly bound in black ribbon at the back of his neck while his beard was plaited in tight pigtails. 'The scroll,' he said, 'confirmed everything I either suspected or knew, and it even suggested one or two new scraps of knowledge. Ah, here it is.' He had been searching his pockets for the Ring which he now produced. To me the treasure looked like any ordinary warrior's ring made of iron, but Merlin held it in his palm as though it was the greatest jewel of Britain. 'The Ring of Eluned,' Merlin said, 'forged in the Otherworld at the beginning of time. Piece of metal really, nothing special.' He tossed it to me and I made a hasty catch. 'By itself,' Merlin said, 'the Ring has no power. None of the Treasures has power by themselves. The Mantle of Invisibility won't make you invisible, any more than the Horn of Bran Galed sounds any better than any other hunting horn. By the way, Derfel, did you fetch Nimue?'

'Yes.'

'Well done. I thought you would. Interesting place, the Isle of the Dead, don't you think? I go there when I need some stimulating company. Where was I? Oh, yes, the Treasures. Worthless rubbish, really. You wouldn't give the Coat of Padarn to a beggar, not if you were kind, yet it's still one of the Treasures.'

'Then what use are they?' Galahad asked. He had taken the Ring from me, but now handed it back to the Druid.

'They command the Gods, of course,' Merlin snapped, as though the answer should have been obvious. 'By themselves they're tawdry nothings, but put them all together and you can have the Gods hopping like frogs. It isn't enough just to gather the Treasures, of course,' he added hastily, 'there are one or two other rituals that are needed. And who knows if it will all work? No one has ever tried, so far as I know. Is Nimue well?' he asked me earnestly.

'She is now.'

'You sound resentful! You think I should have gone to fetch her? My dear Derfel, I am quite busy enough without running around Britain after Nimue! If the girl can't cope with the Isle of the Dead then what earthly use is she?'

'She could have died,' I accused him, thinking of the ghouls and cannibals of the Isle.

'Of course she could! What's the point of an ordeal if there's no danger? You do have infantile ideas, Derfel.' Merlin shook his head pityingly, then slipped the Ring on to one of his long bony fingers. He stared solemnly at us, and we each waited awestruck for some manifestation of supernatural power, but after a few ominous seconds Merlin just laughed at our expressions. 'I told you!' he said, 'the Treasures are nothing special.'

'How many of the Treasures do you have?' Galahad asked.

'Several,' Merlin answered evasively, 'but even if I had twelve of the thirteen I would still be in trouble unless I could find the thirteenth. And that, Derfel, is the missing Treasure. The Cauldron of Clyddno Eiddyn. Without the Cauldron we are lost.'

'We're lost anyway,' I said bitterly.

Merlin peered at me as though I was being particularly obtuse. 'The war?' he said after a few seconds. 'Is that why you came here? To plead for peace! What fools the two of you are! Gorfyddyd doesn't want peace. The man's a brute. He has the brains of an ox and a not very clever ox at that. He wants to be High King, which means he has to rule Dumnonia.'

'He says he'll leave Mordred on the throne,' Galahad said.

'Of course he says that!' Merlin said scornfully. 'What else would he say? But the minute he gets his hands on that wretched child's neck he'll wring it like a chicken, and a good thing too.'

'You want Gorfyddyd to win?' I asked, appalled.

He sighed. 'Derfel, Derfel,' he said, 'you're so like Arthur. You think the world is simple, that good is good and bad is bad, that up is up and down is down. You ask what I want? I tell you what I want. I want the Thirteen Treasures, and I shall use them to bring the Gods back to Britain and then I shall command them to restore Britain to the blessed condition it enjoyed before the Romans came. No more Christians' – he pointed a finger at Galahad – 'and no Mithraists either' – he pointed at me – 'just the people of the Gods in the country of the Gods. That, Derfel, is what I want.'

'Then what of Arthur?' I asked.

'What of him? He's a man, he's got a sword, he can look after himself. Fate is inexorable, Derfel. If fate means Arthur to win this war then it doesn't matter if Gorfyddyd masses the armies of the world against him. If I had nothing better to do then I confess I would help Arthur, because I like him, but fate has decreed that I am an old man, increasingly feeble and possessed of a bladder like a leaking waterskin, and I must therefore husband my waning energies.' He proclaimed this pathetic state in a vigorous tone. 'Even I cannot win Arthur's wars, heal Nimue's mind and discover the Treasures all at the same time. Of course, if I find that saving Arthur's life helps me find the Treasures, then be assured I shall come to the battle. But otherwise?' He shrugged, as though the war was of no importance to him. Nor, I suppose, was it. He turned to the small window and peered at the three stakes that had been erected in the compound. 'You'll stay to see the formalities, I hope?'

'Should we?' I asked.

'Of course you should, if Gorfyddyd allows you. All experience is useful, however ugly. I've performed the rites often enough, so I won't stay to be amused, but be assured you will be safe here. I shall turn Gorfyddyd into a slug if he touches a hair of your foolish heads, but for now I have to go. Iorweth thinks there's an old woman on the Demetian border who might remember something useful. If she's alive, of course, and kept her memory. I do hate talking to old women; they're so grateful for company that they never stop chattering and never keep to the subject either. What a prospect. Tell Nimue I look forward to seeing her!' And with those words he was out of the door and striding across the fort's inner compound.

The sky clouded that afternoon and a grey ugly drizzle soaked the fort before evening. The Druid Iorweth came to us and assured us we were safe, but tactfully suggested that we would strain Gorfyddyd's reluctant hospitality if we attended the evening's feast that marked the last gathering of Gorfyddyd's allies and chiefs before the men at Caer Sws marched south to join the rest of the army at Branogenium. We assured Iorweth we had no wish to attend the feast. The Druid smiled his thanks, then sat on a bench beside the door. 'You're friends of Merlin?' he asked.

'Lord Derfel is,' Galahad said.

Iorweth rubbed his eyes tiredly. He was old, with a friendly, mild face and a bald head on which a ghost of a tonsure showed just above each ear. 'I cannot help thinking,' he said, 'that my brother Merlin expects too much of the Gods. He believes the world can be made anew and that history can be rubbed out like a line drawn in the mud. Yet it isn't so.' He scratched at a louse in his beard, then looked at Galahad, who wore a cross about his neck. He shook his head. 'I envy your Christian God. He is three and He is one, He is dead and He is alive, He is everywhere and He is nowhere, and He demands that you worship Him, but claims nothing else is worthy of worship. There's room in those contradictions for a man to believe in anything or nothing, but not with our Gods. They are like kings, fickle and powerful, and if they want to forget us, they do. It doesn't matter what we believe, only what they want. Our spells only work when the Gods permit. Merlin disagrees, of course. He thinks that if we shout loud enough we'll get their attention, but what do you do to a child who shouts?'

'Give it attention?' I suggested.

'You hit it, Lord Derfel,' Iorweth said. 'You hit it until it is quiet. I fear Lord Merlin may shout too loud for too long.' He stood and picked up his staff. 'I apologize that you cannot eat with the warriors tonight, but the Princess Helledd says you are very welcome to dine with her household.'

Helledd of Elmet was the wife of Cuneglas and her invitation was not necessarily a compliment. Indeed, the invitation could have been a measured insult devised by Gorfyddyd to imply that we were only fit to dine with women and children, but Galahad said we would be honoured to accept.

And there, in Helledd's small hall, was Ceinwyn. I had wanted to see her again, I had wanted it ever since Galahad had first ventured the suggestion that he make an embassy to Powys, and that was why I had made such strenuous efforts to accompany him. I had not come to Caer Sws to make peace, but to see Ceinwyn's face again, and now, in the flickering rushlight of Helledd's hall, I saw her.

The years had not changed her. Her face was as sweet, her manner as demure, her hair as bright and her smile as lovely. When we entered the room she was fussing with a small child, trying to feed him scraps of apple. The child was Cuneglas's son, Perddel. 'I've told him if he won't eat his apple then the horrid Dumnonians will take him away,' she said with a smile. 'I think he must want to go with you, for he won't eat a thing.'

Helledd of Elmet, Perddel's mother, was a tall woman with a heavy jaw and pale eyes. She made us welcome, ordering a maidservant to pour us mead, then introduced us to two of her aunts, Tonwyn and Elsel, who looked at us resentfully. We had evidently interrupted a conversation they were relishing and the aunts' sour glances suggested we should leave, but Helledd was more gracious. 'Do you know the Princess Ceinwyn?' she asked us.

Galahad bowed to her, then squatted beside Perddel. He

always liked children who, in turn, trusted him on sight. Before a moment had passed the two Princes were playing with the apple scraps as though they were foxes, with Perddel's mouth the foxes' den and Galahad's fingers the hounds chasing the fox. The pieces of apple disappeared. 'Why didn't I think of that?' Ceinwyn asked.

'Because you weren't raised by Galahad's mother, Lady,' I said, 'who doubtless fed him in the same way. To this day he can't eat unless someone sounds a hunting horn.'

She laughed, then caught sight of the brooch I wore. She caught her breath, coloured, and for an instant I thought I had made a huge mistake. Then she smiled. 'I should remember you, Lord Derfel?'

'No, Lady. I was very young.'

'And you kept it?' she asked, apparently astonished that anyone should treasure one of her gifts.

'I kept it, Lady, even when I lost everything else.'

The Princess Helledd interrupted us by asking what business had brought us to Caer Sws. I am sure she already knew, but it was politic for a princess to pretend that she was outside men's council. I answered by saying we had been sent to determine whether war was inevitable. 'And is it?' the Princess asked with understandable worry, for on the morrow her husband would go south towards the enemy.

'Sadly, Lady,' I answered, 'it seems so.'

'It's all Arthur's fault,' Princess Helledd said firmly and her aunts nodded vigorously.

'I think Arthur would agree with you, Lady,' I said, 'and he regrets it.'

'Then why does he fight us?' Helledd wanted to know.

'Because he is sworn to keep Mordred on the throne, Lady.'

'My father-in-law would never dispossess Uther's heir,' Helledd said fiercely.

'Lord Derfel almost lost his head through having this conversation this morning,' Ceinwyn said mischievously.

'Lord Derfel,' Galahad intervened, looking up from the

latest fox-chase, 'kept his head because he is beloved by his Gods.'

'Not by yours, Lord Prince?' Helledd asked sharply.

'My God loves everyone, Lady.'

'He is indiscriminate, you mean?' She laughed.

We ate goose, chicken, hare and venison, and were served a villainous wine that must have been stored too long since it was brought to Britain. After the meal we moved to cushioned couches and a harpist played for us. The couches were furniture for a woman's hall and both Galahad and I were uncomfortable on their low, soft beds, but I was happy enough for I had made sure I took the couch next to Ceinwyn. For a time I sat straight up, but then leaned on one elbow so I could talk softly to her. I complimented her on her betrothal to Gundleus.

She gave me an amused glance. 'That sounds like a courtier speaking,' she said.

'I am forced to be a courtier at times, Lady. Would you prefer me to be the warrior?'

She leaned back on an elbow so we could talk without disturbing the music, and her proximity made it seem as though my senses floated in smoke. 'My Lord Gundleus,' she said softly, 'demanded my hand as the price of his army in this coming war.'

'Then his army, Lady,' I said, 'is the most valuable in Britain.'

She did not smile at the compliment, but kept her eyes steadily on mine. 'Is it true,' she asked very quietly, 'that he killed Norwenna?'

The bluntness of the question unsettled me. 'What does he say, Lady?' I asked instead of answering directly.

'He says' – and her voice was even lower so that I could scarcely hear her words – 'that his men were attacked and that in the confusion, she died. It was an accident, he says.'

I glanced at the young girl playing the harp. The aunts were glaring at the two of us, but Helledd seemed unworried by our talking. Galahad was listening to the music, one arm around the sleeping Perddel. 'I was on the Tor that day, Lady,' I said, turning back to Ceinwyn.

'And?'

I decided her bluntness deserved a blunt answer. 'She knelt to him in welcome, Lady,' I said, 'and he ran his sword down her throat. I saw it done.'

Her face hardened for a second. The glimmering rushlight burnished her pale skin and made soft shadows on her cheeks and under her lower lip. She was wearing a rich dress of pale blue linen that was trimmed with the black-flecked silver-white fur of a winter-stoat. A silver torque encircled her neck, silver rings were in her ears and I thought how well silver suited her bright hair. She gave a small sigh. 'I feared to hear that truth,' she said, 'but being a princess means I must marry where it is most useful for me to do so and not where I might want to.' She turned her head to the musician for a time, then leaned close to me again. 'My father,' she said nervously, 'says this is a war about my honour. Is it?'

'For him, Lady, yes, though I can tell you Arthur regrets the hurt he did you.'

She grimaced slightly. The subject was clearly painful, but she could not let it go, for Arthur's rejection had changed Ceinwyn's life much more subtly and sadly than it had ever changed his. Arthur had gone on to happiness and marriage while she had been left to suffer the long regrets and find the painful answers which, evidently, had not been found. 'Do you understand him?' she asked after a while.

'I did not understand him back then, Lady,' I said. 'I thought he was a fool. So did we all.'

'And now?' she asked, her blue eyes on mine.

I thought for a few seconds. 'I think, Lady, that for once in his life Arthur was struck by a madness that he could not control.'

'Love?'

I looked at her and told myself that I was not in love with her and that her brooch was a talisman snatched randomly from chance. I told myself that she was a Princess and I the son of a slave. 'Yes, Lady,' I said.

'Do you understand that madness?' she asked me.

I was aware of nothing in the room except Ceinwyn. The Princess Helledd, the sleeping Prince, Galahad, the aunts, the harpist, none of them existed for me, any more than did the woven wall hangings or the bronze rushlight holders. I was aware only of Ceinwyn's large sad eyes and of my own beating heart.

'I do understand that you can look into someone's eyes,' I heard myself saying, 'and suddenly know that life will be impossible without them. Know that their voice can make your heart miss a beat and that their company is all your happiness can ever desire and that their absence will leave your soul alone, bereft and lost.'

She said nothing for a while, but just looked at me with a slightly puzzled expression. 'Has that ever happened to you, Lord Derfel?' she asked at last.

I hesitated. I knew the words my soul wanted to say and I knew the words my station should make me say, but then I told myself that a warrior did not thrive on timidity and I let my soul have government of my tongue. 'It has never happened until this moment, Lady,' I said. It took more bravery to make that declaration than I had ever needed to break a shield-wall.

She immediately looked away and sat up, and I cursed myself for offending her with my stupid clumsiness. I stayed back on the couch, my face red and my soul hurting with embarrassment as Ceinwyn applauded the harpist by throwing some silver coins on to the rug beside the instrument. She asked for the Song of Rhiannon to be played.

'I thought you were not listening, Ceinwyn,' one of the aunts said cattily.

'I am, Tonwyn, I am, and I am taking a great pleasure in all I hear,' Ceinwyn said and I felt suddenly like a man feels when the enemy's shield-wall collapses. Except I dared not trust her words. I wanted to; I dared not. Love's madness, swinging from ecstasy to despair in one wild second.

The music began again, its background the raucous cheers coming from the great hall where the warriors anticipated battle. I leaned all the way back on the cushions, my face still red as I tried to work out whether Ceinwyn's last words had referred to our conversation or to the music, and then Ceinwyn lay back and leaned close to me again. 'I do not want a war fought over me,' she said.

'It seems inevitable, Lady.'

'My brother agrees with me.'

'But your father rules in Powys, Lady.'

'That he does,' she said flatly. She paused, frowning, then looked up at me. 'If Arthur wins, who will he want me to marry?'

Once again the directness of her question surprised me, but I gave her the true answer. 'He wants you to be Queen of Siluria, Lady,' I said.

She looked at me with sudden alarm. 'Married to Gundleus?'

'To King Lancelot of Benoic, Lady,' I said, giving away Arthur's secret hope. I watched for her reaction.

She gazed into my eyes, apparently trying to judge whether I had spoken the truth. 'They say Lancelot is a great warrior,' she said after a while and with a lack of enthusiasm that warmed my heart.

'They do say that, Lady, yes,' I said.

She was silent again. She leaned on her elbow and watched the harpist's hands flicker across the strings, and I watched her. 'Tell Arthur,' she said after a while and without looking at me, 'that I hold no grudge. And tell him something else.' She stopped suddenly.

'Yes, Lady?' I encouraged her.

'Tell him that if he wins,' she said, then turned to me and reached a slender finger across the gap between our couches to touch the back of my hand to show how important her words were, 'that if he wins,' she said again, 'I shall beg for his protection.'

'I shall tell him, Lady,' I said, then paused with my heart full. 'And I swear you mine too, in all honour.'

She kept her finger on my hand, her touch as light as the sleeping Prince's breath. 'I might hold you to that oath, Lord Derfel,' she said, her eyes on mine.

'Till time ends and evermore, that oath will be true, Lady.'

She smiled, took her hand away and sat up straight.

And that night I went to my bed in a daze of confusion, hope, stupidity, apprehension, fear and delight. For, just like Arthur, I had come to Caer Sws and been stricken by love.

PART FIVE

The Shield-wall

'So IT WAS HER!' Igraine accused me. 'The Princess Cein-wyn who turned your blood to smoke, Brother Derfel.'

'Yes, Lady, it was,' I confessed, and I confess now that there are tears in my eyes as I remember Ceinwyn. Or perhaps it is the weather that is making my eyes water, for autumn has come to Dinnewrac and a cold wind is stealing through my window. I must soon make a pause in this writing, for we shall have to be busy storing our foodstuffs for the winter and making the log pile that the blessed Saint Sansum will take pleasure in not burning so that we can share our dear Saviour's suffering.

'No wonder you hate Lancelot so much!' Igraine said. 'You were rivals. Did he know how you felt for Ceinwyn?'

'In time,' I said, 'yes.'

'So what happened?' she asked eagerly.

'Why don't we leave the story in its proper order, Lady?'

'Because I don't want to, of course.'

'Well I do,' I said, 'and I am the storyteller, not you.'

'If I didn't like you so much, Brother Derfel, I would have your head cut off and your body fed to our hounds.' She frowned, thinking. She looks very pretty today in a cloak of grey wool edged with otter fur. She is not pregnant, so either the pessary of baby's faeces did not work or else Brochvael is spending too much time with Nwylle. 'There was always talk in my husband's family about Great-aunt Ceinwyn,' she said, 'but no one ever really explained what the scandal was about.'

'There is no one I have ever known, Lady,' I said sternly, 'about whom there was less scandal.'

'Ceinwyn never married,' Igraine said, 'I know that much.'

'Is that so scandalous?' I asked.

'It is if she behaved as though she were married,' Igraine said indignantly. 'That's what your church preaches. Our church,' she hastily corrected herself. 'So what happened? Tell me!'

I pulled my monk's sleeve over the stump of my hand, always the first part of me to feel a chill wind. 'Ceinwyn's tale is too long to tell now,' I said, and refused to add any more, despite my Queen's importunate demands.

'So did Merlin find the Cauldron?' Igraine demanded instead.

'We shall come to that in its proper time,' I insisted.

She threw up her hands. 'You infuriate me, Derfel. If I behaved like a proper queen I really would demand your head.'

'And if I was anything but an ancient and feeble monk, Lady, I would give it to you.'

She laughed, then turned to look out of the window. The leaves of the small oak trees that Brother Maelgwyn planted to make a windbreak have turned brown early and the woods in the combe below us are thick with berries, both signs that a harsh winter is coming. Sagramor once told me there were places where winter never comes and the sun shines warm all year, but maybe, like the existence of rabbits, that was another of his fanciful tales. I once hoped that the Christian heaven would be a warm place, but Saint Sansum insists heaven must be cold because hell is hot and I suppose the saint is right. There is so little to look forward to. Igraine shivered and turned back towards me. 'No one ever made me a Lughnasa bower,' she said wistfully.

'Of course they did!' I said. 'Every year you have one!'

'But that's the Caer's bower. The slaves make it because they have to, and naturally I sit there, but it isn't the same as having your own young man make you a bower out of foxgloves and willow. Was Merlin angry about you and Nimue making love?'

'I should never have confessed that to you,' I said. 'If he knew he never said anything. It wouldn't have mattered to him. He was not jealous.' Not like the rest of us. Not like Arthur,

422

not like me. How much of our earth has been wet by blood because of jealousy! And at the end of life, what does it all matter? We grow old and the young look at us and can never see that once we made a kingdom ring for love.

Igraine adopted her mischievous look. 'You say Gorfyddyd called Guinevere a whore. Was she?'

'You should not use that word.'

'All right, was Guinevere what Gorfyddyd said she was, which I'm not allowed to say for fear of offending your innocent ears?'

'No,' I said, 'she was not.'

'But was she faithful to Arthur?'

'Wait,' I said.

She stuck her tongue out at me. 'Did Lancelot become a Mithraist?' she asked.

'Wait and see,' I insisted.

'I hate you!'

'And I am your most worshipping servant, dear Lady,' I said, 'but I am also tired and this cold weather makes the ink clog. I shall write the rest of the story, I promise you.'

'If Sansum lets you,' Igraine said.

'He will,' I answered. The saint is happier these days, thanks to our remaining novice who is no longer a novice, but consecrated a priest and a monk and already, Sansum insists, a saint like himself. Saint Tudwal, we must now call him, and the two saints share a cell and glorify God together. The only thing I can find wrong with such a blessed partnership is that the holy Saint Tudwal, now twelve years old, is making yet another effort to learn how to read. He cannot speak this Saxon tongue, of course, but even so I fear what he might decipher from these writings. But that fear must wait till Saint Tudwal masters his letters, if he ever does, and for the moment, if God wills it, and to satisfy the impatient curiosity of my most lovely Queen, Igraine, I shall continue this tale of Arthur, my dear lost Lord, my friend, my lord of war.

I noticed nothing the next day. I stood with Galahad as an

unwelcome guest of my enemy Gorfyddyd while Iorweth made the propitiation to the Gods, and the Druid could have been blowing dandelion seeds for all the note I took of the ceremonies. They killed a bull, they tied three prisoners to the three stakes, strangled them, then took the war's auguries by stabbing a fourth prisoner in the midriff. They sang the Battle Song of Maponos as they danced about the dead, and then the kings, princes and chieftains dipped their spearheads in the dead men's blood before licking the blood off the blades and smearing it on their cheeks. Galahad made the sign of the cross while I dreamed of Ceinwyn. She did not attend the ceremonies. No women did. The auguries, Galahad told me, were favourable to Gorfyddyd's cause, but I did not care. I was blissfully remembering that silver-light touch of Ceinwyn's finger on my hand.

Our horses, weapons and shields were brought to us and Gorfyddyd himself walked us to Caer Sws's gate. Cuneglas, his son, came also; he might well have intended a courtesy by accompanying us, but Gorfyddyd had no such niceties in mind. 'Tell your whore-lover,' the King said, his cheeks still smeared with blood, 'that war can be avoided by one thing only. Tell Arthur that if he presents himself in Lugg Vale for my judgment and verdict I shall consider the stain on my daughter's honour cleansed.'

'I shall tell him, Lord King,' Galahad answered.

'Is Arthur still beardless?' Gorfyddyd asked, making the question sound like an insult.

'He is, Lord King,' Galahad said.

'Then I can't plait a prisoner's leash from his beard,' Gorfyddyd growled, 'so tell him to cut off his whore's red hair before he comes and have it woven ready for his own leash.' Gorfyddyd clearly enjoyed demanding that humiliation of his enemies, though Prince Cuneglas's face betrayed an acute embarrassment for his father's crudeness. 'Tell him that, Galahad of Benoic,' Gorfyddyd continued, 'and tell him that if he obeys me, then his shaven whore can go free so long as she leaves Britain.'

'The Princess Guinevere can go free,' Galahad restated the offer.

'The whore!' Gorfyddyd shouted. 'I lay with her often enough, so I should know. Tell Arthur that!' He spat the demand into Galahad's face. 'Tell him she came to my bed willingly, and to other beds too!'

'I shall tell him,' Galahad lied to stem the bitter words. 'And what, Lord King,' Galahad went on, 'of Mordred?'

'Without Arthur,' Gorfyddyd said, 'Mordred will need a new protector. I shall take responsibility for Mordred's future. Now go.'

We bowed, we mounted and we rode away, and I looked back once in hope of seeing Ceinwyn, but only men showed on Caer Sws's ramparts. All around the fortress the shelters were being pulled down as men prepared to march on the direct road to Branogenium. We had agreed not to use that road, but to go home the longer way through Caer Lud so we would not be able to spy on Gorfyddyd's gathering host.

Galahad looked grim as we rode eastwards, but I could not restrain my happiness and once we had ridden clear of the busy encampments I began to sing the Song of Rhiannon.

'What is the matter with you?' Galahad asked irritably.

'Nothing. Nothing! Nothing! Nothing!' I shouted in joy and kicked back my heels so that the horse bolted down the green path and I fell into a patch of nettles. 'Nothing at all,' I said when Galahad brought the horse back to me. 'Absolutely nothing.'

'You're mad, my friend.'

'You're right,' I said as I clambered awkwardly back on to the horse. I was indeed mad, but I was not going to tell Galahad the reason for my madness, so for a time I tried to behave soberly. 'What do we tell Arthur?' I asked him.

'Nothing about Guinevere,' Galahad said firmly. 'Besides, Gorfyddyd was lying. My God! How could he tell such lies about Guinevere?'

'To provoke us, of course,' I said. 'But what do we tell Arthur about Mordred?'

'The truth. Mordred is safe.'

'But if Gorfyddyd lied about Guinevere,' I said, 'why shouldn't he lie about Mordred? And Merlin didn't believe him.'

'We weren't sent for Merlin's answer,' Galahad said.

'We were sent to find the truth, my friend, and I say Merlin spoke it.'

'But Tewdric,' Galahad answered firmly, 'will believe Gorfyddyd.'

'Which means Arthur has lost,' I said bleakly, but I did not want to talk about defeat, so instead I asked Galahad what he had thought of Ceinwyn. I was letting the madness take hold of me again and I wanted to hear Galahad praise her and say she was the most beautiful creature between the seas and the mountains, but he simply shrugged. 'A neat little thing,' he said carelessly, 'and pretty enough if you like those frail-looking girls.' He paused, thinking. 'Lancelot will like her,' he went on. 'You do know Arthur wants them to marry? Though I don't suppose that will happen now. I suspect Gundleus's throne is safe and Lancelot will have to look elsewhere for a wife.'

I said nothing more about Ceinwyn. We rode back the way we had come and reached Magnis on the second night where, just as Galahad had predicted, Tewdric put his faith in Gorfyddyd's promise while Arthur preferred to believe Merlin. Gorfyddyd, I realized, had used us to separate Tewdric and Arthur, and it seemed to me that Gorfyddyd had done well, for as we listened to the two men wrangle in Tewdric's quarters it was plain that the King of Gwent had no stomach for the coming war. Galahad and I left the two men arguing while we walked on Magnis's ramparts that were formed by a great earthen wall flanked by a flooded ditch and topped with a stout palisade. 'Tewdric will win the argument,' Galahad told me bleakly. 'He doesn't trust Arthur, you see.'

'Of course he does,' I protested.

Galahad shook his head. 'He knows Arthur's an honest man,' he allowed, 'but Arthur's also an adventurer. He's land-less, have you ever thought of that? He defends a reputation, not property. He holds his rank because of Mordred's age, not through his own birth. For Arthur to succeed he must be bolder than other men, but Tewdric doesn't want boldness right now. He wants security. He'll accept Gorfyddyd's offer.' He was silent for a while. 'Maybe our fate is to be wandering warriors,' he continued gloomily, 'deprived of land, and always being driven back towards the Western Sea by new enemies.'

I shivered and drew my cloak tighter. The night was clouding over and bringing a chill promise of rain on the western wind. 'You're saying Tewdric will desert us?'

'He already has,' Galahad said bluntly. 'His only problem now is getting rid of Arthur gracefully. Tewdric has too much to lose and he won't take risks any more, but Arthur has nothing to lose except his hopes.'

'You two!' A loud voice called us from behind and we turned to see Culhwch hurrying along the ramparts. 'Arthur wants you.'

'For what?' Galahad asked.

'What do you think, Lord Prince? He's lacking for throw-board players?' Culhwch grinned. 'These bastards may not have the belly for a fight' – he gestured towards the fort that was thronged with Tewdric's neatly uniformed men – 'but we have. I suspect we're going to attack all on our own.' He saw our surprise and laughed. 'You heard Lord Agricola the other night. Two hundred men can hold Lugg Vale against an army. Well? We've got two hundred spearmen and Gorfyddyd possesses an army, so why do we need anyone from Gwent? Time to feed the ravens!'

The first rain fell, hissing in the smithy fires, and it seemed we were going to war.

I sometimes think that was Arthur's bravest decision. God knows he took other decisions in circumstances just as desperate, but never was Arthur weaker than on that rainy night in Magnis where Tewdric was drawing up patient orders that would withdraw his forward men back to the Roman walls in preparation for a truce between Gwent and the enemy.

Arthur gathered five of us in a soldier's house close to those walls. The rain seethed on the roof while under the thatch a log fire smoked to light us with a lurid glare. Sagramor, Arthur's most trusted commander, sat beside Morfans on the hut's small bench, Culhwch, Galahad and I squatted on the floor while Arthur talked.

Prince Meurig, Arthur allowed, had spoken an uncomfortable truth, for the war was indeed of his own making. If he had not spurned Ceinwyn there would be no enmity between Powys and Dumnonia. Gwent was involved by being Powys's most ancient enemy and Dumnonia's traditional friend, but it was not in Gwent's interest to continue the war. 'If I had not come to Britain,' Arthur said, 'then King Tewdric would not be foreseeing the rape of his land. This is my war and, just as I began it, so I must end it.' He paused. He was a man to whom emotion came easily, and he was, at that moment, overcome with feeling. 'I am going to Lugg Vale tomorrow,' he finally spoke and for a dreadful second I thought he meant to give himself up to Gorfyddyd's awful revenge, but then Arthur offered us his open generous smile, 'and I would like it if you came with me, but I have no right to demand it.'

There was silence in the room. I suppose we were all thinking that the fight in the vale had seemed a risky prospect when the combined armies of Gwent and Dumnonia were to be employed, but how were we to win with only Dumnonia's men? 'You have a right to demand that we come,' Culhwch broke the silence, 'for we took oaths to serve you.'

'I release you from those oaths,' Arthur said, 'asking only that if you live you stand by my promise to see Mordred grow into our King.'

There was silence again. None of us, I think, wavered in our loyalty, but nor did we know how to express it until Galahad spoke. 'I swore you no oath,' he said to Arthur, 'but I do now. Where you fight, Lord, I fight, and he who is your enemy is mine, and he who is your friend is my friend also. I swear that on the precious blood of the living Christ.' He leaned forward, took Arthur's hand and kissed it. 'May my life be forfeit if I break my word.'

'It takes two to make an oath,' Culhwch said. 'You might release me, Lord, but I don't release myself.'

'Nor I, Lord,' I added.

Sagramor looked bored. 'I'm your man,' he said to Arthur, 'no one else's.'

'Bugger the oath,' ugly Morfans said, 'I want to fight.'

Arthur had tears in his eyes. For a time he could not speak, so instead he busied himself ramming at the fire with a log until he had succeeded in halving its warmth and doubling its smoke. 'Your men are not oath-bound,' he said thickly, 'and I want none but willing men in Lugg Vale tomorrow.'

'Why tomorrow?' Culhwch asked. 'Why not the day after? The more time we have to prepare, the better, surely?'

Arthur shook his head. 'We'll be no better prepared if we wait a whole year. Besides, Gorfyddyd's spies will already be going north with news that Tewdric is accepting Gorfyddyd's terms, so we must attack before those same spies discover that we Dumnonians have not retreated. We attack at dawn to-morrow.' He looked at me. 'You will attack first, Lord Derfel, so tonight you must reach your men and talk to them, and if they prove unwilling, then so be it, but if they are willing then Morfans can tell you what they must do.'

Morfans had ridden the whole enemy line, flaunting himself in Arthur's armour but also reconnoitring the enemy positions. Now he took handfuls of grain from a pot and piled them on his outspread cloak to make a rough model of Lugg Vale. 'It's not a long valley,' he said, 'but the sides are steep. The barricade is here at the southern end.' He pointed to a spot just inside the modelled valley. 'They felled trees and made a fence. It's big enough to stop a horse, but it won't take long for a few men to haul those trees aside. Their weakness is here.' He indicated the western hill. 'It's steep at the northern end of the valley, but where they built their barricade you can easily run down that slope. Climb the hill in the dark and in the dawn you attack downhill and dismantle their tree fence while they're still waking up. Then the horses can come through.' He grinned, relishing the thought of surprising the enemy.

'Your men are used to marching by night,' Arthur told me, 'so at dawn tomorrow you take the barricade, destroy it, then hold the vale long enough for our horse to arrive. After the horse our spearmen will come. Sagramor will command the spearmen in the vale while I and fifty horsemen attack Branogenium.' Sagramor showed no reaction to the announcement which gave him command of most of Arthur's army.

The rest of us could not hide our astonishment, not at Sagramor's appointment, but at Arthur's tactics. 'Fifty horsemen attacking Gorfyddyd's whole army?' Galahad asked dubiously.

'We won't capture Branogenium,' Arthur admitted, 'we may not even get close, but we shall stir them into a pursuit and that pursuit will bring them down to the vale. Sagramor will meet that pursuit at the vale's northern end, where the road fords the river, and when they attack, you retreat.' He looked at us in turn, making sure we understood his instructions. 'Retreat,' he said again, 'always retreat. Let them think they win! And when you have sucked them deep into the valley, I shall attack.'

'From where?' I asked.

'From behind, of course!' Arthur, energized by the prospect of battle, had regained all his enthusiasm. 'When my horsemen retreat from Branogenium we won't go back into the vale, but hide outside its northern end. The place is smothered in trees. And once you've sucked the enemy in, we'll come from their rear.'

Sagramor stared at the piles of grain. 'The Blackshield Irish at Coel's Hill,' he said in his execrable accent, 'can march south of the hills to take us in the rear,' he pushed a finger through the scattered grains at the Vale's southern end to show what he meant. Those Irish, we all knew, were the fearsome warriors of Oengus Mac Airem, King of Demetia, who had been our ally until Gorfyddyd had changed his loyalty with gold. 'You want us to hold an army in front and the Blackshields behind?' Sagramor asked.

'You see,' Arthur said with a smile, 'why I offer to release you from your oaths. But once Tewdric knows we're embattled, he'll come. As the day passes, Sagramor, you will find your shield-line thickening by the minute. Tewdric's men will deal with the enemy from Coel's Hill.'

'And if they don't?' Sagramor asked.

'Then we will probably lose,' Arthur admitted calmly, 'but with my death will come Gorfyddyd's victory and Tewdric's peace. My head will go to Ceinwyn as a present for her wedding and you, my friends, will be feasting in the Otherworld where, I trust, you will keep a place at table for me.'

There was silence again. Arthur seemed sure that Tewdric would fight, though none of us could be so certain. It seemed to me that Tewdric might well prefer to let Arthur and his men perish in Lugg Vale and thus rid himself of an inconvenient alliance, but I also told myself that such high politics were not my concern. My concern was surviving the next day and, as I looked at Morfans's crude model of the battlefield, I worried about the western hill down which we would attack in the dawn. If we could attack there, I thought, so could the enemy. 'They'll outflank our shield-line,' I said, describing my concern.

Arthur shook his head. 'The hill's too steep for a man in armour to climb at the vale's northern end. The worst they'll do is send their levies there, which means archers. If you can spare men, Derfel, put a handful there, but otherwise pray that Tewdric comes quickly. To which end,' he said, turning to Galahad, 'though it hurts me to ask you to stay away from the shield-wall, Lord Prince, you will be of most value to me tomorrow if you ride as my envoy to King Tewdric. You are a prince, you speak with authority and you, above all men, can persuade him to take advantage of the victory I intend to give him by my disobedience.'

Galahad looked troubled. 'I would rather fight, Lord.'

'On balance,' Arthur smiled, 'I would rather win than lose. For that, I need Tewdric's men to come before the day's end and you, Lord Prince, are the only fit messenger I can send to an aggrieved king. You must persuade him, flatter him, plead with him, but above all, Lord Prince, convince him that we win the war tomorrow or else fight for the rest of our days.'

Galahad accepted the choice. 'Though I have your permission to return and fight at Derfel's side when the message is delivered?' he added.

'You will be welcome,' Arthur said. He paused, staring down at the piles of grain. 'We are few,' he said simply, 'and they are a host, but dreams do not come true by using caution, only by braving danger. Tomorrow we can bring peace to the Britons.' He stopped abruptly, struck perhaps by the thought that his ambition of peace was also Tewdric's dream. Maybe Arthur was wondering whether he should fight at all. I remembered how after our meeting with Aelle, when we made the oath under the oak, Arthur had contemplated giving up the fight and I half expected him to bare his soul again, but on that rainy night the horse of ambition was tugging his soul hard and he could not contemplate a peace in which his own life or exile was the price. He wanted peace, but even more he wanted to dictate that peace. 'Whatever Gods you pray to,' he said quietly, 'go with you all tomorrow.'

I had to ride a horse to get back to my men. I was in a hurry and fell off three times. As omens, the falls were dire, but the road was soft with mud and nothing was hurt but my pride. Arthur rode with me, but checked my horse when we were still a spear's throw from where my men's campfires flickered low in the insistent rain. 'Do this for me tomorrow, Derfel,' he said, 'and you may carry your own banner and paint your own shields.'

In this world or the next, I thought, but I did not speak the thought aloud for fear of tempting the Gods. Because tomorrow, in a grey, bleak dawn, we would fight against the world.

Not one of my men tried to evade their oaths. Some, a few, might have wanted to avoid battle, but none wanted to show weakness in front of their comrades and so we all marched, leaving in the night's middle to make our way across a rainsoaked countryside. Arthur saw us off, then went to where his horsemen were encamped.

Nimue insisted on accompanying us. She had promised us a spell of concealment, and after that nothing would persuade my men to leave her behind. She worked the spell before we left, performing it on the skull of a sheep she found by flame-light in a ditch close to our camp. She dragged the carcass out of the thicket where a wolf had feasted, chopped the head away, stripped away the remnants of maggoty skin, then crouched with her cloak hiding both her and the stinking skull. She crouched there a long time, breathing the ghastly stench of the decomposing head, then stood and kicked the skull scornfully aside. She watched where it came to rest and, after a moment's deliberation, declared that the enemy would look aside as we marched through the night. Arthur, who was fascinated by Nimue's intensity, shuddered when she made the pronouncement, then embraced me. 'I owe you a debt, Derfel.'

'You owe me nothing, Lord.'

'If for nothing else,' he said, 'I thank you for bringing me Ceinwyn's message.' He had taken enormous pleasure in her forgiveness, then shrugged when I had added her further words about being granted his protection. 'She has nothing to fear from any man in Dumnonia,' he had said. Now he clapped me on the back. 'I shall see you in the dawn,' he promised, then watched as we filed out from the firelight into the dark.

We crossed grassy meadows and newly harvested fields where no obstacles other than the soaking ground, the dark and the driving rain impeded us. That rain came from our left, the west, and it seemed relentless; a stinging, pelting, cold rain that trickled inside our jerkins and chilled our bodies. At first we bunched together so that no man would find himself alone in the dark, though even crossing the easy ground we were constantly calling out in low voices to find where our comrades might be. Some men tried to keep hold of a friend's cloak, but spears clashed together and men tripped until finally I stopped everyone and formed two files. Every man was ordered to sling his shield on his back, then to hold on to the spear of the man in front. Cavan was at our rear, making sure no one dropped out, while Nimue and I were in the lead. She held my hand, not out of affection, but simply so that we should stay together in the black night. Lughnasa seemed like a dream now, swept away not by time, but by Nimue's fierce refusal to acknowledge that our time in the bower had ever happened. Those hours, like her months on the Isle of the Dead, had served their purpose and were now irrelevant.

We came to trees. I hesitated, then plunged down a steep, muddy bank and into a darkness so engulfing that I despaired of ever taking fifty men through its horrid blackness, but then Nimue began to croon in a low voice and the sound acted like a beacon to beckon men safely through the stumbling dark. Both spear chains broke, but by following Nimue's voice we all somehow blundered through the trees to emerge into a meadow on their farther side. We stopped there while Cavan and I made a tally of the men and Nimue circled us, hissing spells at the dark.

My spirits, dampened by the rain and gloom, sank lower. I thought I had possessed a mental picture of this countryside that lay just north of my men's camp, but our stumbling progress had obliterated that picture. I had no idea where I was, nor where I should go. I thought we had been heading north, but without a star to guide me or moon to light my way, I let my fears overcome my resolve.

'Why are you waiting?' Nimue came to my side and whispered the words.

I said nothing, not willing to admit that I was lost. Or perhaps not willing to admit that I was frightened.

Nimue sensed my helplessness and took command. 'We have a long stretch of open pasture ahead of us,' she told my men. 'It used to graze sheep, but they've taken the flock away, so there are no shepherds or dogs to see us. It's uphill all the way, but easy enough going if we stay together. At the end of the pasture we come to a wood and there we'll wait for dawn. It isn't far and it isn't difficult. I know we're wet and cold, but

434

tomorrow we shall warm ourselves on our enemies' fires.' She spoke with utter confidence.

I do not think I could have led those men through that wet night, but Nimue did. She claimed that her one eye saw in the dark where our eyes could not, and maybe that was true, or maybe she simply possessed a better idea of this stretch of countryside than I did, but however it was done, she did it well. In the last hour we walked along the shoulder of a hill and suddenly the going became easier for we were now on the western height above Lugg Vale and our enemies' watch-fires burned in the dark beneath us. I could even see the barricade of felled pine trees and the glint of the River Lugg beyond. In the vale men threw great baulks of wood on the fires to light the road where attackers might come from the south.

We reached the woods and sank on to the wet ground. Some of us half slept in the deceptive, dream-filled, shallow slumber that seems like no sleep at all and leaves a man cold, weary and aching, but Nimue stayed awake, muttering charms and talking to men who could not sleep. It was not small-talk, for Nimue had no time for idle chatter, but fierce explanations of why we fought. Not for Mordred, she said, but for a Britain shorn of foreigners and of foreign ideas, and even the Christians in my ranks listened to her.

I did not wait for the dawn to make my attack. Instead, when the rain-soaked sky showed the first pale glimmer of steely light in the east, I woke the sleepers and led my fifty spearmen down to the wood's edge. We waited there above a grassy slope that fell down to the vale's bed as steeply as the flanks of Ynys Wydryn's Tor. My left arm was tight in the shield straps, Hywelbane was at my hip and my heavy spear was gripped in my right hand. A small mist showed where the river flowed out of the vale. A white owl flew low beside our trees and my men thought the bird an ill omen, but then a wildcat snarled behind us and Nimue said that the owl's doom-laden appearance had been nullified. I said a prayer to Mithras, giving all the next hours to His glory, then I told my men that the Franks had been far fiercer enemies than these night-fuddled Powysians in the valley beneath us. I doubted that was entirely true, but men on the edge of battle do not need truth, but confidence. I had privately ordered Issa and another man to stay close to Nimue for if she died I knew my men's confidence would vanish like a summer mist.

The rain spat from behind us, making the grassy slope slick. The sky above the vale's far side lightened further, showing the first shadows among the flying clouds. The world was grey and black, night-dark in the vale itself, but lighter on the wood's edge, a contrast that made me fear the enemy could see us while we could not see him. Their fires still blazed, but much lower than they had during the dark spirit-haunted depths of night. I could see no sentries. It was time to go.

'Move slowly,' I ordered my men. I had imagined a mad rush down the hill, but now I changed my mind. The wet grass would be treacherous and it would be better, I decided, if we crept slow and silent down the slope like wraiths in the dawn. I led the way, stepping ever more cautiously as the hill became steeper. Even nailed boots gave treacherous holding on wet ground and so we went as slow as stalking cats and the loudest noise in the half-dark was the sound of our own breathing. We used spears as staffs. Twice men fell heavily, their shields clattering against scabbards or spears, and both times we all went still and waited for a challenge. None came.

The last part of the slope was the steepest, but from the brow of that final descent we could at last see the whole bed of the vale. The river ran like a black shadow on the far side, while beneath us the Roman road passed between a group of thatched huts where the enemy had to be sheltering. I could only see four men. Two were crouching near the fires, a third was sitting under the eaves of a hut while the fourth paced up and down behind the tree fence. The eastern sky was paling towards the bright flare of dawn and it was time to release my wolf-tailed spearmen to the slaughter. 'The Gods be your shield-wall,' I told them, 'and kill well.'

We hurled ourselves down the last yards of that steep slope. Some men slid down on their backsides rather than try to stay

436

on their feet, some ran headlong and I, because I was their leader, ran with them. Fear gave us wings and made us scream our challenge. We were the wolves of Benoic come to the border hills of Powys to offer death, and suddenly, as ever in battle, the elation took over. The soaring joy flared inside our souls as all restraint and thought and decency were obliterated to leave only the feral glare of combat. I leaped down the last few feet, stumbled among raspberry bushes, kicked over an empty pail, then saw the first startled man emerge from a nearby hut. He was in trousers and jerkin, carrying a spear and blinking at the rainy dawn, and thus he died as I speared him through the belly. I was howling the wolf-howl, daring my enemies to come and be killed.

My spear stuck in the dying man's guts. I left it there and drew Hywelbane. Another man peered from the hut to see what happened and I lunged at his eyes, throwing him back. My men streamed past me, howling and whooping. The sentries were fleeing. One ran to the river, hesitated, turned back and died under two spear thrusts. One of my men seized a brand from the fire and tossed it on to the wet thatch. More firebrands followed until at last the huts caught fire to drive their inhabitants out to where my spearmen waited. A woman screamed as burning thatch fell on her. Nimue had taken a sword from a dead enemy and was plunging it into the neck of a fallen man. She was keening a weird, high sound that gave the chill dawn a new terror.

Cavan bellowed at men to start hauling the tree fence aside. I left the few enemy that still lived to the mercies of my men and went to help him. The fence was a barricade made from two dozen felled pines, and each tree needed a score of men to pull aside. We had made a gap forty feet wide where the road pierced the barricade, then Issa called a warning to me.

The men we had slaughtered had not been the whole guard force in the valley, but rather the picquet line who guarded the fence, and now the main garrison, woken by the commotion, was showing in the shadowy northern part of the valley.

'Shield-wall!' I called, 'shield-wall!'

437

We formed the line just north of the burning cottages. Two of my men had broken their ankles coming down the steep slope and a third had been killed in the first moments of the fight, but the rest of us shuffled into line and touched our shield edges together to make certain the wall was tight. I had retrieved my own spear so now I sheathed Hywelbane and pushed my spear-point out to join the other steel points that bristled five feet ahead of the shield-wall. I ordered a half-dozen men to stay behind with Nimue in case any of the enemy still lay hidden among the shadows, then we had to wait while Cavan replaced his shield. The straps of his own had broken so he picked up a Powysian shield and swiftly cut away the leather cover with its eagle symbol, then took his place at the right-hand end of the wall, the most vulnerable place because the right-hand man in a line must hold his shield to protect the man to his left and thus expose his own right side to enemy thrusts. 'Ready, Lord!' he called to me.

'Forward!' I shouted. It was better to advance, I thought, than let the enemy form and attack us.

The vale's sides grew higher and steeper as we marched north. The slope on our right, beyond the river, was a thick tangle of trees, while to our left the hill was grassy at first, but then turned to scrub. The valley narrowed as we advanced, though it never narrowed sufficiently to be called a gorge. There was room for a war-band to manoeuvre in Lugg Vale, though the marshy river bank did help to constrict the dry level ground needed for battle. The first clouded light was illuminating the western hills, but that light had yet to flood into the valley's depths where the rain had at last stopped, though the wind gusted cold and damp to flicker the flames of the campfires that burned in the upper vale. Those campfires revealed a thatched village around a Roman building. The shadows of hurrying men flickered in front of the fires, a horse whinnied, then suddenly, as at last the dawn's ghostly light sifted down to the road, I saw a shield-wall forming.

I could also see that the shield-wall held at least a hundred men, and more were hurrying into its ranks. 'Hold!' I called to my men, then stared into the bad light and guessed that nearer two hundred men were forming the enemy wall. The grey light glinted from their spearheads. This was the elite guard Gorfyddyd had set to hold the vale.

The vale was certainly too broad for my fifty men to hold. The road ran close to the western slope and left a wide meadow to our right where the enemy could easily outflank us and so I ordered my men back. 'Slowly back!' I called, 'slow and sure! Back to the fence!' We could guard the gap we had ripped in the tree fence, though even so it would only be a matter of moments before the enemy clambered over the remaining trees and so surrounded us. 'Slowly back!' I called again, then stood still as my men retreated. I waited because a single horseman had ridden out from the enemy ranks and was spurring towards us.

The enemy's emissary was a tall man who rode well. He had an iron helmet crested with swan feathers, a lance and sword, but no shield. He wore a breastplate and his saddle was a sheepskin. He was a striking-looking man, dark-eyed and black-bearded, and there was something familiar in his face, but it was not till he had reined in above me that I recognized him. It was Valerin, the chieftain to whom Guinevere had been betrothed when she had first met Arthur. He stared down at me, then slowly raised his spearhead until it was pointed at my throat. 'I had hoped,' he said, 'that you would be Arthur.'

'My Lord sends you his greetings, Lord Valerin,' I said.

Valerin spat towards my shield that again carried the symbol of Arthur's bear. 'Return my greetings to him,' he said, 'and to the whore he married.' He paused, raising the spear-point so that it was close to my eyes. 'You're a long way from home, little boy,' he said, 'does your mother know you're out of bed?'

'My mother,' I answered, 'is readying a cauldron for your bones, Lord Valerin. We have need of glue, and the bones of sheep, we hear, make the best.'

He seemed pleased that I knew him, mistaking my recognition for fame and not realizing that I had been one of the guards who had come to Caer Sws with Arthur so many years before. He raised his spear-point clear of my face and stared at my men. 'Not many of you,' he said, 'but many of us. Would you like to surrender now?'

'There are many of you,' I said, 'but my men are starved for battle, so will welcome a large helping of enemies.' A leader was expected to be good at these ritual insults before battle and I always rather enjoyed them. Arthur was never good at such exchanges, for even at the last moment before the killing began he was still trying to make his enemies like him.

Valerin half turned his horse. 'Your name?' he asked before riding away.

'Lord Derfel Cadarn,' I said proudly, and I thought I saw, or maybe I hoped I saw, a flicker of recognition before he kicked his heels back to drive his horse north.

If Arthur did not come, I thought, then we were all dead men, but by the time I rejoined my spearmen beside the barricade I found Culhwch, who once again rode with Arthur, waiting for me. His big horse was noisily cropping the grass nearby. 'We're not far away, Derfel,' he reassured me, 'and when those vermin attack, you're to run away. Understand? Make them chase you. That'll scatter them, and when you see us coming get out of the way.' He grasped my hand, then enfolded me in a bear hug. 'This is better than talking peace, eh?' he said, then walked back to his horse and heaved himself up into its saddle. 'Be cowards for a few moments!' he called to my men, then raised a hand and spurred away southwards.

I explained to my men what Culhwch's parting words had meant, then I took my place in the centre of the shield-wall that stretched across the gap we had made in the felled trees. Nimue stood behind me, still holding her bloody sword. 'We'll pretend to panic,' I called to the shield-wall, 'when they make their first attack. And don't trip over when you run, and make sure you get out of the way of the horses.' I ordered four of my men to help the two with broken ankles to a thicket behind the fence where they could hide.

We waited. I glanced behind once, but could not see Arthur's men who I presumed were hidden where the road entered a patch of trees a quarter-mile to the south. To my right the river ran in dark shining swirls on which two swans drifted. A heron fished the river's edge, but then lazily spread its wings and flapped away northwards, a direction Nimue took to be a good augury because the bird was taking its bad luck towards the enemy.

Valerin's spearmen came on slowly. They had been woken to battle and were still sluggish. Some were bare-headed and I guessed their leaders had rousted them from their straw beds in such haste that not all had been given time to gather their armour. They had no Druid, so at least we were free of spells, though like my men I muttered swift prayers. Mine were to Mithras and to Bel. Nimue was calling to Andraste, the Goddess of Slaughter, while Cavan called on his Irish Gods to give his spear a good day's killing. I saw that Valerin had dismounted and was leading his men from the line's centre, though I noted a servant was leading the chieftain's horse close behind the advancing line.

A heavy gust of damp wind blew the smoke of the burning huts across the road, half hiding the enemy line. The bodies of their dead comrades would wake these advancing spearmen, I thought, and sure enough I heard the shouts of anger as they encountered the newly made corpses, and when a gust of wind cleared the smoke away the attacking line was coming on faster and shouting insults. We waited in silence as the grey early light seeped down to the valley's damp floor.

The enemy spearmen stopped fifty paces from us. All of them carried Powys's eagle on their shields, so none were from Siluria or from the other contingents gathering with Gorfyddyd. These spearmen, I assumed, were among Powys's best, so any we killed now would be a help later, and the Gods knew how we needed help. Thus far we were having the best of the day, and I had to keep reminding myself that these easy moments were designed only to bring the full might of Gorfyddyd and his allies on to Arthur's few loyal men.

Two men raced out from Valerin's line and hurled spears that went high over our heads to bury themselves in the turf behind. My men jeered, and some deliberately took the shields away from their bodies as though inviting the enemy to try again. I thanked Mithras that Valerin had no archers. Few warriors carried bows for no arrow can pierce a shield or a leather breastplate. The bow was a hunter's weapon, best for use against wildfowl or small game, but a mass of levied countrymen carrying light bows could still make themselves a nuisance by forcing warriors to crouch behind their shield-walls.

Two more men hurled spears. One weapon thumped into a shield and stuck there, the other flew high again. Valerin was watching us, judging our resolve, and perhaps because we did not hurl spears back he decided we were already beaten men. He raised his arms, clashed his spear on his shield, and shouted at his men to charge.

They roared their challenge and we, just as Arthur had ordered, broke and fled. For a second there was confusion as men in the shield-line impeded each other, but then we scattered apart and pounded away down the road. Nimue, her black cloak flying, ran ahead of us, but always looking back to see what happened behind her. The enemy cheered their victory and raced to catch us while Valerin, seeing a chance to ride his horse among a broken rabble, shouted at his servant to bring the beast.

We ran clumsily, cumbered by cloaks, shields and spears. I was tired and the breath pounded in my chest as I followed my men southwards. I could hear the enemy behind and twice looked over my shoulder to see a tall, red-headed man grimacing as he strained to catch me. He was a faster runner than I, and I was beginning to think I would need to stop, turn and deal with him when I heard that blessed sweet sound of Arthur's horn. It sounded twice and then, out of the dawn-dulled trees ahead of us, Arthur's might erupted.

First came white-plumed Arthur himself, in shining armour and carrying his mirror-bright shield and with his white cloak spread behind like wings. His spearhead dipped as his fifty men came into sight on armoured horses, their faces wrapped in iron and their spear-points glittering. The banners of the dragon and the bear flew bright and the earth shook beneath those ponderous hooves that slung water and mud high into the air as the big horses gathered speed. My men were running aside, forming two groups that swiftly gathered into defensive circles with shields and spears outermost. I went left and turned around in time to see Valerin's men desperately trying to form a shield-wall. Valerin, mounted on his horse, shouted at them to retreat to the barricade, but it was already too late. Our trap was sprung and Lugg Vale's defenders were doomed.

Arthur pounded past me on Llamrei, his favourite mare. The skirts of his horse blanket and the ends of his cloak were already soaked in mud. A man threw a spear that glanced off Llamrei's breast armour, then Arthur thrust his spear home into the first enemy soldier, abandoned the weapon and scraped Excalibur into the dawn. The rest of the horse crashed past in a welter of water and noise. Valerin's men screamed as the big brutes hurtled into their broken ranks. Swords slashed down to leave men reeling and bloody while the horses ploughed on, some driving panicked men down beneath their heavy iron-plated hooves. Broken spearmen had no defence against horses, and these warriors of Powys had no chance to form even the smallest shield-walls. They could only run and Valerin, seeing there was no salvation, turned his light horse and galloped northwards.

Some of his men followed, but any man on foot was doomed to be ridden down by the horses. Others turned aside and ran for the river or the hill, and those we hunted down in spear-bands. A few threw down spears and shields and raised their arms, and those we let live, but any man who offered resistance was surrounded like a boar trapped in a thicket and speared to death. Arthur's horse had disappeared into the vale, leaving behind a horrid trail of men with heads cut to the brain by sword-blows. Other enemies were limping and falling, and Nimue, seeing the destruction, screeched in triumph.

We took close to fifty prisoners. At least as many others were dead or dying. A few escaped up the hill we had come down in the grey light, and some had drowned trying to cross the

Lugg, but the rest were bleeding, staggering, vomiting and defeated. Sagramor's men, a hundred and fifty prime spearmen, marched into sight as we finished rounding up the last of Valerin's survivors. 'We can't spare men to guard prisoners,' Sagramor greeted me.

'I know.'

'Then kill them,' he ordered me, and Nimue echoed her approval.

'No,' I insisted. Sagramor was my commander for the rest of this day and I did not enjoy disagreeing with him, but Arthur wanted to bring peace to the Britons and killing helpless prisoners was no way to bind Powys to his peace. Besides, my men had taken the prisoners, so their fate was my responsibility and, instead of killing them, I ordered them stripped naked, then they were taken one by one to where Cavan waited with a heavy stone for his hammer and a boulder for an anvil. We placed each man's spear hand on the boulder, held it there, then crushed the two smallest fingers with the stone. A man with two shattered fingers would live and he might even wield a spear again, but not on this day. Not for many a day. Then we sent them southwards, naked and bleeding, and told them that if we saw their faces again before nightfall they would surely die. Sagramor scoffed at me for displaying such leniency, but did not countermand the orders. My men took the enemy's best clothes and boots, searched the discarded clothing for coins, then tossed the garments on to the still burning huts. We piled the captured weapons by the road.

Then we marched north to discover that Arthur had ended his pursuit at the ford, then returned to the village that lay about the substantial Roman building which Arthur reckoned had once been a resthouse for travellers going into the northern hills. A crowd of women cowered under guard beside the house, clutching their children and paltry belongings.

'Your enemy,' I told Arthur, 'was Valerin.'

It took him a few seconds to place the name, then he smiled. He had removed his helmet and dismounted to greet us. 'Poor

Valerin,' he said, 'twice a loser,' then he embraced me and thanked my men. 'The night was so dark,' he said, 'I doubted you would find the vale.'

'I didn't. Nimue did.'

'Then I owe you thanks,' he said to Nimue.

'Thank me,' she said, 'by bringing victory this day.'

'With the Gods' help, I shall.' He turned and looked at Galahad who had ridden in the charge. 'Go south, Lord Prince, and give Tewdric my greetings and beg his men's spears to our side. May God give your tongue eloquence.' Galahad kicked his horse and rode back through the blood-stinking vale.

Arthur turned and stared at a hilltop a mile north of the ford. There was an old earth fort there, a legacy of the Old People, but it seemed to be deserted. 'It would go ill with us,' he said with a smile, 'if anyone was to see where we hide.' He wanted to find his hiding place and leave the heavy horse armour there before he rode north to roust Gorfyddyd's men out of their camps at Branogenium.

'Nimue will work you a spell of concealment,' I said.

'Will you, Lady?' he asked earnestly.

She went to find a skull. Arthur clasped me again, then called for his servant Hygwydd to help him tug off the suit of heavy scale armour. It came off over his head, leaving his short-cut hair tousled. 'Would you wear it?' he asked me.

'Me?' I was astonished.

'When the enemy attack,' he said, 'they'll expect to find me here and if I'm not here they'll suspect a trap.' He smiled. 'I'd ask Sagramor, but his face is somewhat more distinctive than yours, Lord Derfel. You'll have to cut off some of that long hair, though.' My fair hair showing beneath the helmet's rim would be a sure sign I was not Arthur, 'and maybe trim the beard a little,' he added.

I took the armour from Hygwydd and was shocked by its weight. 'I should be honoured,' I said.

'It is heavy,' he warned me. 'You'll get hot, and you can't see to your sides when you're wearing the helmet so you'll need two good men to flank you.' He sensed my hesitation. 'Should I ask someone else to wear it?'

'No, no, Lord,' I said. 'I'll wear it.'

'It'll mean danger,' he warned me.

'I wasn't expecting a safe day, Lord,' I answered.

'I shall leave you the banners,' he said. 'When Gorfyddyd comes he must be convinced that all his enemies are in one place. It will be a hard fight, Derfel.'

'Galahad will bring help,' I assured him.

He took my breastplate and shield, gave me his own brighter shield and white cloak, then turned and grasped Llamrei's bridle. 'That,' he told me once he had been helped into the saddle, 'was the easy part of the day.' He beckoned to Sagramor, then spoke to both of us. 'The enemy will be here by noon. Do what you can to make ready, then fight as you have never fought before. If I see you again then we shall be victorious. If not, then I thank you, salute you, and will wait to feast with you in the Otherworld.' He shouted for his men to mount up, then rode north.

And we waited for the real battle to begin.

The scale armour was appallingly heavy, bearing down on my shoulders like the water yokes women carry to their houses each morning. Even lifting my sword arm was hard, though it became easier when I cinched my sword belt tight around the iron scales and so took the suit's lower weight away from my shoulders.

Nimue, her spell of concealment finished, cut my hair with a knife. She burned all the loose hair lest an enemy should find the scraps and work an enchantment, and then I used Arthur's shield as a mirror to hack my long beard short enough so that it would be concealed behind the helmet's deep cheek pieces. Then I pulled the helmet on, forcing its leather padding over my skull and tugging it down until it enclosed my head like a shell. My voice seemed muffled despite the perforations over the ears in the shining metal. I hefted the heavy shield, let Nimue fasten the mud-spattered white cloak around my shoulders, then I tried to get used to the armour's awkward weight. I made Issa fight me with a spear-shaft as a single-stick and found myself much slower than usual. 'Fear will quicken you, Lord,' Issa said when he had rounded my guard for the tenth time and whacked me an echoing blow on the head.

'Don't knock the plume off,' I said. Secretly I was wishing I had never accepted the heavy armour. It was horseman's gear, designed to add weight and awe to a mounted man who had to batter his way through the enemy's ranks, but we spearmen depended on agility and quickness when we were not locked shoulder to shoulder in the shield-wall.

'But you look wonderful, Lord,' Issa told me admiringly.

'I'll be a wonderful-looking corpse if you don't guard my flank,' I told him. 'It's like fighting inside a bucket.' I tugged the helmet off, relieved when its constricting pressure was gone from my skull. 'When I first saw this armour,' I told Issa, 'I wanted it more than anything in the world. Now I'd give it away for a decent leather breastplate.'

'You'll be all right, Lord,' he told me with a grin.

We had work to do. The women and children abandoned by Valerin's defeated men had to be driven south away from the vale, then we prepared defences close to the remnants of the tree fence. Sagramor feared that the overwhelming weight of the enemy could drive us clear out of the vale before Arthur's horsemen arrived to our rescue and so he prepared the ground as best he could. My men wanted to sleep, but instead we dug a shallow ditch across the vale. The ditch was nowhere near deep enough to stop a man, but it would force the attacking spear-men to break step and maybe stumble as they closed on our spear-line. The tree barricade lay just behind the ditch and marked the southern limit to which we could retreat and the place we must defend to the death. Sagramor anchored the felled trees with some of Valerin's abandoned spears that he ordered driven deep into the earth to make a hedge of angled spear-points inside the pine branches. We left the gap where the road ran through the centre of the fence so we could retreat behind the fragile barrier before we defended it.

My worry was the steep and open hillside down which my men had attacked in the dawn. Gorfyddyd's warriors would doubtless attack straight up the vale, but his levies would probably be sent to the high ground to threaten our left flank and Sagramor could spare no men to hold that high ground, but Nimue insisted there was no need. She took ten of the captured spears and then, with the help of a half-dozen of my men, she cut the heads from ten of Valerin's dead spearmen and carried the spears and bloody heads up the hill where she had the spear-shafts driven butt-first into the ground, then she rammed the bloody heads on to the spears' iron points and draped the dead heads with ghastly wigs of knotted grass, each knot an enchantment, before scattering branches of yew between the widely spaced posts. She had made a ghost-fence: a line of human scarecrows imbued with charms and spells that no man would dare pass without a Druid's help. Sagramor wanted her to make another such fence on the ground north of the ford, but Nimue refused. 'Their warriors will come with Druids,' she explained, 'and a ghost-fence is laughable to a Druid. But the levy won't have a Druid.' She had fetched an armful of vervain down from the hill and now she distributed its small purple flowers among the spearmen who all knew that vervain gave protection in battle. She pushed a whole sprig inside my armour.

The Christians gathered to say their prayers, while we pagans sought the Gods' help. Men tossed coins into the river, then brought out their talismans for Nimue to touch. Most carried a hare's foot, but some brought her elf bolts or snake stones. Elf bolts were tiny flint arrowheads shot by the spirits and much prized by soldiers, while snake stones had bright colours that Nimue enriched by dipping the stones in the river before touching them to her good eye. I pressed the scale armour until I could feel Ceinwyn's brooch pricking against my chest, then I knelt and kissed the earth. I kept my forehead on the damp ground as I beseeched Mithras to give me strength, courage and, if it was His will, a good death. Some of our men were drinking the mead we had discovered in the village, but I drank nothing but water. We ate the food Valerin's men had thought would be their breakfast, and afterwards a group of spearmen helped Nimue catch toads and shrews that she killed and placed on the road beyond the ford to give the approaching enemy ill omens. Then we sharpened our weapons again and waited. Sagramor had found a man hiding in the woods behind the village. The man was a shepherd and Sagramor questioned him about the local countryside and learned there was a second ford upstream where the enemy could outflank us if we tried to defend the river bank at the vale's northern end. The second ford's existence did not trouble us now, but we needed to remember that it existed for it gave the enemy a way of outflanking our northernmost defence line.

I was nervous of the coming fight, but Nimue seemed un-afraid. 'I have nothing to fear,' she told me. 'I've taken the Three Wounds, so what can hurt me?' She was sitting beside me, close to the ford at the vale's northern end. This would be our first defence line, the place where we would begin the slow retreat that would suck the enemy into the vale and Arthur's trap. 'Besides,' she added, 'I am under Merlin's protection.'

'Does he know we're here?' I asked her.

She paused, then nodded. 'He knows.'

'Will he come?'

She frowned as though my question was crass. 'He will do,' she said slowly, 'whatever he needs to do.'

'Then he will come,' I said in fervent hope.

Nimue shook her head impatiently. 'Merlin cares only for Britain. He believes Arthur could help restore the Knowledge of Britain, but if he decides that Gorfyddyd would do it better, then believe me, Derfel, Merlin will side with Gorfyddyd.'

Merlin had hinted as much to me at Caer Sws, but I still found it hard to believe that his ambitions were so far from my own allegiances and hopes. 'What about you?' I asked Nimue.

'I have one burden that ties me to this army,' she said, 'and after that I shall be free to help Merlin.'

'Gundleus,' I said.

She nodded. 'Give me Gundleus alive, Derfel,' she said, looking into my eyes, 'give him to me alive, I beg you.' She touched the leather eyepatch and went silent as she summoned her energy for the revenge she craved. Her face was still bone pale and her black hair hung lank against her cheeks. The softness she had revealed at Lughnasa had been replaced by a chill bleakness that made me think I would never understand her. I loved her, not as I believed I loved Ceinwyn, but as a man can love a fine wild creature, an eagle or a wildcat, for I knew I would never comprehend her life or dreams. She grimaced suddenly. 'I shall make Gundleus's soul scream through the rest of time,' she said softly, 'I shall send it through the abyss into nothingness, but he will never reach nothingness, Derfel, he will always suffer on its edge, screaming.'

I shuddered for Gundleus.

A shout made me look across the river. Six horsemen were galloping towards us. Our shield-wall stood and thrust their arms into their shield-loops, but then I saw the leading man was Morfans. He rode desperately, kicking at his tired sweat-whitened horse, and I feared those six men were all that remained of Arthur's troop.

The horses splashed through the ford as Sagramor and I went forward. Morfans reined in on the river bank. 'Two miles away,' he panted. 'Arthur sent us to help you. Gods, there are hundreds of the bastards!' He wiped sweat off his forehead, then grinned. 'There's plunder enough for a thousand of us!' He slid heavily from his horse and I saw he was carrying the silver horn and guessed he would use it to summon Arthur when the moment was right.

'Where is Arthur?' Sagramor asked.

'Safely hid,' Morfans assured us, then looked at my armour and his ugly face split into a lopsided grin. 'Weighs you down, that armour, doesn't it?'

'How does he ever fight in it?' I asked.

'Very well, Derfel, very well. And so will you.' He clapped my shoulder. 'Any news from Galahad?'

'None.'

450

'Agricola won't let us fight alone, whatever that Christian King and his gutless son might want,' Morfans said, then he led his five horsemen back through the shield-wall. 'Give us a few minutes to rest the horses,' he called.

Sagramor pulled his helmet over his head. The Numidian wore a coat of mail, a black cloak and tall boots. His iron helmet was painted black with pitch and rose to a sharp point that gave it an exotic appearance. Usually he fought on horseback, but he showed no regret at being an infantryman this day. Nor did he display any nervousness as he prowled long-legged up and down our shield-wall and growled encouragement to his men.

I pulled Arthur's stifling helmet over my head and buckled its strap under my chin. Then, arrayed as my Lord, I also walked along the line of spears and warned my men that the fight would be hard, but victory certain so long as our shield-wall held. It was a perilously thin wall, in some places just three men deep, but those in the wall were all good men. One of them stepped out of the line as I approached the place where Sagramor's spearmen bordered mine. 'Remember me, Lord?' he called.

I thought for a moment he had mistaken me for Arthur and I pulled the hinged cheek pieces aside so he could see my face, then at last I recognized him. It was Griffid, Owain's captain and the man who had tried to kill me at Lindinis before Nimue intervened to save my life. 'Griffid ap Annan,' I greeted him.

'There's bad blood between us, Lord,' he said, and fell to his knees. 'Forgive me.'

I pulled him to his feet and embraced him. His beard had gone grey, but he was still the same long-boned, sad-faced man I remembered. 'My soul is in your keeping,' I told him, 'and I am glad to put it there.'

'And mine yours, Lord,' he said.

'Minac!' I recognized another of my old comrades. 'Am I forgiven?'

'Was there anything to forgive, Lord?' he asked, embarrassed at the question.

'There was nothing to forgive,' I promised him. 'No oath was broken, I swear it.'

Minac stepped forward and embraced me. All along the shield-wall other such quarrels were being resolved. 'How have you been?' I asked Griffid.

'Fighting hard, Lord. Mostly against Cerdic's Saxons. Today will be easy compared with those bastards, except for one thing.' He hesitated.

'Well?' I prompted him.

'Will she give us back our souls, Lord?' Griffid asked, glancing at Nimue. He was remembering the awful curse she had laid on him and his men.

'Of course she will,' I said, and summoned Nimue who touched Griffid's forehead, and the foreheads of all the other surviving men who had threatened my life on that distant day in Lindinis. Thus was her curse lifted and they thanked her by kissing her hand. I embraced Griffid again, then raised my voice so that all my men could hear me. 'Today,' I said, 'we shall give the bards enough songs to sing for a thousand years! And today we become rich men again!'

They cheered. The emotion in that shield-line was so rich that some men wept for happiness. I know now that there is no joy like the joy of serving Christ Jesus, but how I do miss the company of warriors. There were no barriers between us that morning, nothing but a great, swelling love for each other as we waited for the enemy. We were brothers, we were invincible and even the laconic Sagramor had tears in his eyes. A spearman began singing the War Song of Beli Mawr, Britain's great battle song, and the strong male voices swelled in instinctive harmony all along the line. Other men danced across their swords, capering awkwardly in their leather armour as they made the intricate steps either side of the blade. Our Christians had their arms spread wide as they sang, almost as though the song was a pagan prayer to their own God while other men clashed their spears against their shields in time to the music.

We were still singing of pouring our enemies' blood on to our land when that enemy appeared. We sang defiantly on as spear-band after spear-band came into view and spread across the far fields beneath kingly banners that showed bright in the day's cloudy gloom. And on we sang, a great torrent of song to defy the army of Gorfyddyd, the army of the father of the woman I was convinced I loved. That was why I was fighting, not just for Arthur, but because only by victory could I make my way back to Caer Sws and thus see Ceinwyn again. I had no claim on her, and no hopes either for I was slave-born and she a princess, yet somehow I felt that day as though I had more to lose than I had ever possessed in all my life.

It took over an hour for that cumbersome horde to make a battle line on the river's far bank. The river could only be crossed at the ford, which meant we would be given time to retreat when the moment came, but for now the enemy must have assumed that we planned to defend the ford all day for they massed their best men in the centre of the line. Gorfyddyd himself was there, his eagle banner stained by its dye that had run in the rain so that the flag looked as though it had already been dipped in our blood. Arthur's banners, the black bear and the red dragon, flew at our line's centre where I stood facing the ford. Sagramor stood beside me, counting the enemy banners. Gundleus's fox was there, and the red horse of Elmet, and several others we did not recognize. 'Six hundred men?' Sagramor guessed.

'And more still coming,' I added.

'Like as not.' He spat towards the ford. 'And they'll have seen that Tewdric's bull is missing.' He gave one of his rare smiles. 'It'll be a fight worth remembering, Lord Derfel.'

'I'm glad to share it with you, Lord,' I said fervently, and so I was. There was no warrior greater than Sagramor, no man more feared by his enemies. Even Arthur's presence did not raise the same dread as the Numidian's impassive face and ghastly sword. It was a curved sword of strange foreign make and Sagramor wielded it with a terrible quickness. I once asked Sagramor why he had first sworn loyalty to Arthur. 'Because when I had nothing,' he explained curtly, 'Arthur gave me everything.'

Our spearmen at last stopped singing as two Druids advanced from Gorfyddyd's army. We only had Nimue to counter their enchantments and she now waded through the ford to meet the advancing men who were both hopping down the road with one arm raised and one eye closed. The Druids were Iorweth, Gorfyddyd's wizard, and Tanaburs in his long robe embroidered with moons and hares. The two men exchanged kisses with Nimue, talked with her for a short while and then she returned to our side of the ford. 'They wanted us to surrender,' she said scornfully, 'and I invited them to do the same.'

'Good,' Sagramor growled.

Iorweth hopped awkwardly to the ford's farther side. 'The Gods bring you greeting!' he shouted at us, though none of us answered. I had closed my cheek pieces so that I could not be recognized. Tanaburs was hopping up the river, using his staff to keep his balance. Iorweth raised his own staff level above his head to show that he wished to speak further. 'My King, the King of Powys and High King of Britain, King Gorfyddyd ap Cadell ap Brychan ap Laganis ap Coel ap Beli Mawr, will spare your bold souls a journey to the Otherworld. All you need do, brave warriors, is give us Arthur!' He levelled the staff at me and Nimue immediately hissed a protective prayer and tossed two handfuls of soil into the air.

I said nothing and silence was my refusal. Iorweth whirled the staff and spat three times towards us, then he began hopping down the river's bank to add his curses to Tanaburs's spells. King Gorfyddyd, accompanied by his son Cuneglas and his ally Gundleus, had ridden halfway to the river to watch their Druids working, and work they did. They cursed our lives by the day and our souls by night. They gave our blood to the worms, our flesh to the beasts and our bones to agony. They cursed our women, our children, our fields and our livestock. Nimue countered the charms, but still our men shivered. The Christians called out that there was nothing to fear, but even they were making the sign of the cross as the curses flew across the river on wings of darkness.

The Druids cursed for a whole hour and left us shaking. Nimue walked the shield-line touching spearheads and assuring men that the curses had not worked, but our men were nervous of the Gods' anger as the enemy spear-line at last advanced. 'Shields up!' Sagramor shouted harshly. 'Spears up!'

The enemy halted fifty paces from the river while one man alone advanced on foot. It was Valerin, the chief whom we had driven from the vale in the dawn, and who now advanced to the ford's northern edge with shield and spear. He had suffered defeat in the dawn and his pride had forced him to this moment when he could retrieve his reputation. 'Arthur!' he shouted at me. 'You married a whore!'

'Keep silent, Derfel,' Sagramor warned me.

'A whore!' Valerin shouted. 'She was used when she came to me. You want the list of her lovers? An hour, Arthur, would not be time enough to give that list! And who's she whoring with now while you're waiting to die? You think she's waiting for you? I know that whore! She's tangling her legs with a man or two!' He spread his arms and jerked his hips obscenely and my spearmen jeered back, but Valerin ignored their shouted insults. 'A whore!' he called, 'a rancid, used-up whore! You'd fight for your whore, Arthur? Or have you lost your belly for fighting? Defend your whore, you worm!' He walked through the ford that came up to his thighs and stopped on our bank, his cloak dripping, just a dozen paces away from me. He stared into the dark shadow of my helmet's eye-hole. 'A whore, Arthur,' he repeated, 'your wife is a whore.' He spat. He was bare-headed and had woven sprigs of protective mistletoe into his long black hair. He had a breastplate, but no other body armour, while his shield was painted with Gorfyddyd's spread-winged eagle. He laughed at me, then raised his voice to call to all our men. 'Your leader won't fight for his whore, so why should you fight for him?'

Sagramor growled at me to ignore the taunts, but Valerin's defiance was unsettling our men whose souls were already chilled by the Druids' curses. I waited for Valerin to call Guinevere a whore one more time and when he did I hurled my spear at him. It was a clumsy throw, made awkward by the scale armour's constriction, and the spear tumbled past him to splash into the river. 'A whore,' he shouted and ran at me with his war spear levelled as I scraped Hywelbane out of her scabbard. I stepped towards him and had time to take just two paces before he thrust the spear at me with a great shout of rage.

I dropped to one knee and raised the polished shield at an angle so that the spear-point was deflected over my head. I could see Valerin's feet and hear his roar of rage as I stabbed Hywelbane under my shield's edge. I lunged upwards with the blade, feeling it strike just before his charging body struck my shield and drove me down to the ground. He was screaming instead of roaring now, for that sword thrust beneath the shield was a wicked cut that came up from the ground to pierce a man's bowels and I knew Hywelbane had plunged deep into Valerin, for I could feel his body's weight pulling the sword blade down as he collapsed on to the shield. I heaved up with all my strength to throw him off the shield and gave a grunt as I jerked the sword back from his flesh's grip. Blood spilt foul beside his spear that had fallen to the ground where he now lay bleeding and twitching in awful pain. Even so he tried to draw his sword as I clambered to my feet and put my boot on to his chest. His face was going yellow, he shuddered and his eyes were already clouding in death. 'Guinevere is a lady,' I told him, 'and your soul is mine if you deny it.'

'She's a whore,' he somehow managed to say between clenched teeth, then he choked and shook his head feebly. 'The bull guards me,' he managed to add, and I knew he was of Mithras and so I thrust Hywelbane hard down. The blade met the resistance of his throat, then swiftly cut to end his life. Blood fountained up the blade, and I do not think Valerin ever knew it was not Arthur who sent his soul to the bridge of swords in Cruachan's Cave.

Our men cheered. Their spirits, so abraded by the Druids and chilled by Valerin's foul insults, were instantly restored for we had drawn the first blood. I walked to the river's edge where I danced a victor's steps as I showed the dispirited enemy Hywelbane's bloodstained blade. Gorfyddyd, Cuneglas and Gundleus, their champion defeated, turned their horses away and my men taunted them as cowards and weaklings.

Sagramor nodded as I returned to the shield-wall. The nod was evidently his way of offering praise for a well-fought fight. 'What do you want done with him?' He gestured to Valerin's fallen body.

I had Issa strip the corpse of its jewellery, then two other men heaved it into the river and I prayed that the spirits of the water would carry my brother of Mithras to his reward. Issa brought me Valerin's weapons, his golden torque, two brooches and a ring. 'Yours, Lord,' he said, offering me the plunder. He had also retrieved my spear from the river.

I took the spear and Valerin's weapons, but nothing else. 'The gold is yours, Issa,' I said, remembering how he had tried to give me his own torque when we had returned from Ynys Trebes.

'Not this, Lord,' he said, and he showed me Valerin's ring. It was a piece of heavy gold, beautifully made and embossed with the figure of a stag running beneath a crescent moon. It was Guinevere's badge, and at the back of the ring, crudely but deeply cut into the thick gold, was a cross. It was a lover's ring and Issa, I thought, had been clever to spot it.

I took the ring and thought of Valerin wearing it through all the hurt years. Or maybe, I dared to hope, he had tried to re-venge his pain on her reputation by cutting a false cross into the ring so that men would think he had been her lover. 'Arthur must never know,' I warned Issa and then I hurled the heavy ring into the river.

'What was that?' Sagramor asked as I rejoined him.

'Nothing,' I said, 'nothing. Just a charm that might have brought us ill luck.'

Then a ram's horn sounded across the river and I was spared the need to think about the ring's message.

The enemy was coming.

THE BARDS STILL SING of that battle, though the Gods only know how they invent the details they embroider into the tale because to hear their songs you would think none of us could have survived Lugg Vale and maybe none of us should. It was desperate. It was also, though the bards do not admit as much, a defeat for Arthur.

Gorfyddyd's first attack was a howling rush of maddened spearmen who charged into the ford. Sagramor ordered us forward and we met them in the river where the clash of the shields was like a crack of thunder exploding in the valley's mouth. The enemy had the advantage of numbers, but their attack was channelled by the ford's margins and we could afford to bring men from our flanks to thicken our centre.

We in the front rank had time to thrust once, then we crouched behind our shields and simply shoved at the enemy line while the men in our second rank fought across our heads. The ring of sword blades and clatter of shield-bosses and clashing of spear-shafts was deafening, but remarkably few men died for it is hard to kill in the crush as two locked shield-walls grind against each other. Instead it becomes a pushing match. The enemy grasps your spearhead so you cannot pull it back, there is hardly room to draw a sword, and all the time the enemy's second rank are raining sword, axe and spear blows on helmets and shield-edges. The worst injuries are caused by men thrusting blades beneath the shields and gradually a barrier of crippled men builds at the front to make the slaughter even more difficult. Only when one side pulls back can the other then kill the crippled enemies stranded at the battle's tide line. We prevailed on that first attack, not so much out of

458

valour but because Morfans pushed his six horsemen through the crush of our men and used his long horse spears to thrust down on the crouching enemy front line. 'Shields! Shields!' I heard Morfans shouting as the six horses' vast weight buckled our shield-line forward. Our rear-rank men hoisted their shields high to protect the big war horses from the rain of enemy spears, while we in the front rank crouched in the river and tried to finish off the men who recoiled from the horsemen's thrusts. I sheltered behind Arthur's polished shield and stabbed with Hywelbane whenever a gap offered in the enemy's line. I took two mighty blows to the head, but the helmet cushioned both even if my skull did ring for an hour afterwards. One spear struck my scale armour but could not pierce it. The man who launched that spear lunge was killed by Morfans, and after his death the enemy lost heart and splashed back to the river's northern bank. They took their wounded, all but for a handful who were too close to our line and that handful we killed before we retreated to our own bank. We had lost six men to the Otherworld and twice that many to wounds. 'You shouldn't be in the front line,' Sagramor told me as he watched our wounded being carried away. 'They'll see you're not Arthur.'

'They're seeing that Arthur fights,' I said, 'unlike Gorfyddyd or Gundleus.' The enemy Kings had been close to the fight, but never close enough to use their weapons.

Iorweth and Tanaburs were screaming at Gorfyddyd's men, encouraging them to the slaughter and promising them the rewards of the Gods, but while Gorfyddyd reorganized his spearmen a group of masterless men waded the river to attack on their own. Such warriors relied on a display of bravery to bring them riches and rank, and these thirty desperate men charged in a screaming rage once they were through the deepest part of the river. They were either drunk or battle-mad, for thirty alone attacked our whole force. The reward for their success would have been land, gold, forgiveness of their crimes and lordly status in Gorfyddyd's court, but thirty men were not enough. They hurt us, but died doing it. They were all fine spearmen with shield hands thick with warrior rings, but each now faced three or four enemies. A whole group rushed towards me, seeing in my armour and white plume the fastest route to glory, but Sagramor and my wolf-tailed spearmen met and matched them. One huge man was wielding a Saxon axe. Sagramor killed him with his dark curved blade, then plucked the axe from the dying hand and hurled it at another spearman, and all the while he was chanting his own weird battle song in his native tongue. A last swordsman attacked me and I parried his scything blow with the iron boss of Arthur's shield, knocked his own shield aside with Hywelbane, then kicked him in the groin. He doubled over, too hurt to cry out, and Issa rammed a spear into his neck. We stripped the dead attackers of their armour, their weapons and their jewellery and left their bodies at the ford's edge as a barrier to the next attack.

That attack came soon and came hard. Like the first this third assault was made by a mass of spearmen, only this time we met them at the near river bank where the press of men behind the enemy's front rank forced their leading spearmen to stumble on the piled bodies. Their stumbling opened them to our counter-attack and we shouted in triumph as we slashed our red spears forward. Then the shields cracked together again, dying men screamed and called on their Gods, and the swords rang loud as the anvils in Magnis. I was again in the front rank, crammed so close to the enemy line that I could smell the mead on their breath. One man tried to snatch the helmet from my head and lost his hand to a sword stroke. The pushing match started again and again it seemed that the enemy must force us back by sheer weight, but again Morfans brought his heavy horses through the crush, and again the enemy hurled spears that clattered on our shields, and once again Morfans's men thrust down with their long horsemen's spears and once again the enemy pulled back. The bards say the river ran red, which is not true, though I did see tendrils of blood fading downstream from the wounded who tried and failed to get back through the ford.

'We could fight the bastards here all day,' Morfans said. His horse was bleeding and he had dismounted to treat the animal's wound.

I shook my head. 'There's another ford upriver.' I pointed westwards. 'They'll have spearmen on this bank soon enough.'

Those outflanking enemy came sooner than I thought, for ten minutes later a shout from our left flank warned us that a group of enemy had indeed crossed the river to the west and was now advancing along our bank.

'Time to go back,' Sagramor told me. His clean-shaven black face was smeared with blood and sweat, but there was joy in his eyes for this was proving to be a fight that would make the poets struggle for new words to describe a battle, a fight that men would remember in smoky halls for winters to come, a fight that, even lost, would send a man in honour to the warrior halls of the Otherworld. 'Time to draw them in,' Sagramor said, then shouted the order to withdraw so that slowly and cumbersomely our whole force retreated past the village with its Roman building and stopped a hundred paces beyond. Our left flank was now anchored on the vale's steep western side while our right was protected by the marshy ground that stretched towards the river. Even so we were much more vulnerable than we had been at the ford for our shield-wall was now desperately thin and the enemy could attack all along its length.

It took Gorfyddyd a whole hour to bring his men across the river and array them in a new shield-line. I guessed it was already afternoon and I glanced behind me for some sign of Galahad or Tewdric's men, but I saw no one approaching. Nor, I was glad to see, were there any men on the western hill where Nimue's ghost-fence guarded our flank, but Gorfyddyd hardly needed men there for his army was now bigger than ever. New contingents had come from Branogenium and Gorfyddyd's commanders were tugging and shoving those newcomers into the shield-wall. We watched the captains using their long spears to straighten the enemy's line and all of us, despite the defiance we shouted, knew that for every man we had killed at the river ten more had come across the ford. 'We'll never hold them here,' Sagramor said as he watched the enemy forces grow. 'We'll have to go back to the tree fence.'

But then, before Sagramor could give the order to retreat, Gorfyddyd himself rode forward to challenge us. He came alone, without even his son, and he came with just a sheathed sword and a spear for he had no arm to hold a shield. Gorfyddyd's gold-trimmed helmet, that Arthur had returned the week of his betrothal to Ceinwyn, was crowned with the spread wings of a golden eagle, and his black cloak was spread across his horse's rump. Sagramor growled at me to stay where I was and strode forward to meet the King.

Gorfyddyd used no reins, but spoke to his horse that obediently stopped two paces away from Sagramor. Gorfyddyd rested his spear-butt on the ground, then forced his helmet's cheek pieces aside so that his sour face showed. 'You're Arthur's black demon,' he accused Sagramor, spitting to avert any evil, 'and your whore-loving Lord shelters behind your sword.' Gorfyddyd spat again, this time towards me. 'Why don't you talk to me, Arthur?' he shouted. 'Lost your tongue?'

'My Lord Arthur,' Sagramor answered in his heavily accented British, 'is saving his breath to sing his victory song.'

Gorfyddyd hefted his long spear. 'I'm one-handed,' he shouted at me, 'but I'll fight you!'

I said nothing, nor did I move. Arthur, I knew, would never fight in single battle against a crippled man, though Arthur would never have stayed silent either. By now he would have been pleading with Gorfyddyd for peace.

Gorfyddyd did not want peace. He wanted slaughter. He rode up and down our line, controlling his horse with his knees and shouting at our men. 'You're dying because your Lord can't keep his hands off a whore! You're dying for a bitch with a wet rump! For a bitch in perpetual heat! Your souls will be cursed. My dead are already feasting in the Otherworld, but your souls will become their throwpieces. And why will you die? For his red-headed whore?' He pointed his spear at me, then rode his horse directly at me. I pulled back lest he saw through the helmet's eyeslit that I was not Arthur and my spearmen closed protectively around me. Gorfyddyd laughed at my apparent timidity. His horse was close enough for my men to touch, but Gorfyddyd showed no fear of their spears as he spat at me. 'Woman!' he called out, his worst insult, then touched his horse with his left foot and the beast turned and galloped back towards his army.

Sagramor turned to us and raised his arms. 'Back!' he shouted. 'Back to the fence! Quick now! Back!'

We turned our backs on the enemy and hurried away and a great shout went up as they saw our twin banners retreat. They thought we were running and they broke their ranks to pursue us, but we had too great a start on them and we had streamed through the gap in the barricade long before any of Gorfyddyd's men could reach us. Our line spread behind the fence while I took Arthur's proper place in the very centre of the line where the road ran through the empty gap between the felled trees. We deliberately left the gap without any obstacles in the hope that it would draw Gorfyddyd's attacks and thus give our flanks time to rest. I raised Arthur's two banners there and waited for the assault.

Gorfyddyd roared at his disordered spearmen to make a new shield-wall. King Gundleus commanded the enemy's right flank and Prince Cuneglas the left. That arrangement suggested that Gorfyddyd was not going to take our bait of the open gap, but intended to assault all along the line. 'You stay here!' Sagramor shouted at our spearmen. 'You're warriors! You're going to prove it now! You stay here, you kill here and you win here!' Morfans had forced his wounded horse a small way up the western hill from where he looked north up the vale, judging whether this was the moment to sound the horn and summon Arthur, but enemy reinforcements were still crossing the ford and he came back without putting the silver to his lips.

Gorfyddyd's horn sounded instead. It was a raucous ram's horn that did not send his shield-line forward, but instead provoked a dozen naked madmen to burst out of the enemy's line and rush on our centre. Such men have put their souls in the

Gods' keeping, then fuddled their senses with a mixture of mead, thorn-apple juice, mandrake and belladonna, which can give a man waking nightmares even as it takes away his fears. Such men might be mad, drunk and naked, but they were also dangerous for they had only one aim and that was to bring down the enemy commanders. They rushed at me, mouths foaming from the magical herbs they had been chewing and with their spears held overhead ready to drive down.

My wolf-tailed spearmen advanced to meet them. The naked men did not care about death, they threw themselves on my spearmen as if they welcomed their spear-points. One of my men was driven backwards with a naked brute clawing at his eyes and spitting into his face. Issa killed that fiend, but another managed to kill one of my best men and then screamed his victory, legs apart, arms upheld and bloody spear in bloody hand, and all my men thought the Gods must have deserted us, but Sagramor ripped the naked man's belly open, then half severed his head before the corpse had even fallen to the ground. Sagramor spat on to the naked, eviscerated corpse, then spat again towards the enemy shield-wall. That wall, seeing the centre of our line was disordered, charged.

Our hastily realigned centre buckled when the mass of spearmen slammed home. The thin line of men stretched across the road bent like a sapling, but somehow we held. We were cheering each other, calling on the Gods, stabbing and cutting while Morfans and his horsemen rode all along the shield-wall and threw themselves into the fight wherever the enemy seemed about to break through. The flanks of our shield-wall were protected by the barricade and so had an easier time, but in the centre our fight was desperate. I was maddened by now, lost in the weltering joy of battle. I lost my spear to an enemy's grip, drew Hywelbane, but held back her first stroke to let an enemy's shield hammer into Arthur's polished silver. The shields banged together, then the enemy's face showed for an instant and I lanced Hywelbane forward and felt the pressure vanish from the shield. The man fell, his body making a barrier over which his comrades had to climb.

Issa killed one man, then took a spear thrust to his shield arm that soaked his sleeve in blood. He kept fighting. I was hacking madly in the space made by my fallen enemy to carve a hole in Gorfyddyd's shield-wall. I saw the enemy King once, staring from his horse to where I screamed and slashed and dared his men to come and take my soul. Some did dare, thinking to make themselves the stuff of songs, but instead they made themselves into corpses. Hywelbane was soaked in blood, my right hand was sticky with it and the sleeve of the heavy scale coat was smeared with it, but none of it was mine.

The centre of our line, unprotected by the tangling trees, very nearly did break once, but two of Morfans's horsemen used their beasts to plug the gap. One of the horses died, screaming and thrashing its hooves as it bled to death on the road. Then our shield-wall mended itself and we shoved back at the enemy who slowly, slowly were being choked by the press of dead and dying bodies that lay between the two front ranks. Nimue was behind us, shrieking and hurling curses.

The enemy pulled away and at last we could rest. All of us were bloody and mudstained, and our breath came in huge gasps. Our sword and spear arms were weary. News of comrades was passed along the ranks. Minac was dead, this man wounded, another man dying. Men bandaged their neighbours' wounds, then swore oaths to defend each other to the death. I tried to ease the galling pressure of Arthur's armour that had rubbed great sores on my shoulders.

The enemy was wary now. The tired men who faced us had felt our swords and learned to fear us, yet still they attacked again. This time it was Gundleus's royal guard that assaulted our centre and we met them at the bloody pile of dead and dying that was left from the last attack, and that gory ridge saved us, for the enemy spearmen could not clamber over the bodies and protect themselves at the same time. We broke their ankles, cut open their legs, then speared them as they fell to make the bloody ridge higher. Black ravens circled the ford, their wings ragged against the dun sky. I saw Ligessac, the traitor who had yielded Norwenna to Gundleus's sword, and I tried to cut my way through to him, but the tide of battle swept him away from Hywelbane. Then the enemy pulled back again and I hoarsely ordered some of my men to fetch skins of water from the river. We were all thirsty for the sweat had poured off us, mingling with blood. I had one scratch on my sword hand, but nothing else. I had been to the death-pit and always reckoned that was why I was lucky in battle.

The enemy began putting new troops in their front line. Some carried Cuneglas's eagle, some Gundleus's fox and a few had emblems of their own. Then a cheer sounded behind me and I turned, expecting to see Tewdric's men arriving in their Roman uniforms, but instead it was Galahad who came alone on a sweating horse. He slid to a halt behind our line and half fell off the horse in his haste to reach us. 'I thought I'd be too late,' he said.

'Are they coming?' I asked.

He paused and even before he spoke I knew that we had been abandoned. 'No,' he said at last.

I swore and looked back to the enemy. It was the Gods alone who had saved us in the last attack, but the Gods alone knew how long we could hold now. 'No one is coming?' I asked bitterly.

'A few maybe.' Galahad gave the bad news in a low voice. 'Tewdric believes we're doomed, Agricola says they should help us, but Meurig says we must be left to die. They're all arguing, but Tewdric did say that any man who wants to die here could follow me. Maybe some are on the way?'

I prayed there were, for some of Gorfyddyd's levy had arrived on the western hill now, though none of that ragged horde had yet dared to cross Nimue's ghost-fence. We could hold for two more hours, I thought, and after that we were doomed, though Arthur would surely come first. 'No sign of the Blackshield Irish?' I asked Galahad.

'No, thank God,' he said, and it was one small blessing on a day almost bereft of blessings, though a half-hour after Galahad came, we did at last receive some reinforcements. Seven men walked north towards our battered shield-wall, seven men in war gear carrying spears, shields and swords, and the symbol on the shields was the hawk of Kernow, our enemy. Yet these men were no enemies. They were six scarred and hardened fighters led by their Edling, Prince Tristan.

He explained his presence when the excitement of greeting was over. 'Arthur fought for me once, and I have long wanted to repay the debt.'

'With your life?' Sagramor asked grimly.

'He risked his,' Tristan said simply. I remembered him as a tall handsome man, and so he still was, but the years had added a wary and tired look to his face as though he had suffered too many disappointments. 'My father,' he added ruefully, 'may never forgive my coming here, but I could never have forgiven my absence.'

'How's Sarlinna?' I asked him.

'Sarlinna?' He took a few seconds to remember the small girl who had come to accuse Owain at Caer Cadarn. 'Oh, Sarlinna! Married now. To a fisherman.' He smiled. 'You gave her the kitten, didn't you?'

We put Tristan and his men in our centre, the place of honour on this battlefield, yet when the enemy's next assault came it was not against the centre, but against the tree fence protecting our flanks. For a time the shallow trench and the fence's tangling branches caused them havoc, but they learned swiftly enough to use the felled trees to protect themselves and in some places they burst clean through and bent our line backwards again. But again we held them, and Griffid, my erstwhile enemy, made a name for himself by cutting down Nasiens, Gundleus's champion. The shields crashed incessantly. Spears broke, swords shattered and shields split as the exhausted fought the weary. On the hilltop the enemy levy gathered to watch from beyond Nimue's ghost-fence as Morfans once again forced his tired horse up the perilously steep slope. He stared northwards and we watched him and prayed that he would blow the horn. He stared for a long time, but he must have been satisfied that all the enemy forces were now trapped in the vale for he put the silver horn to his lips and blew the blessed summons across the din of battle.

Never was a horn call more welcome. Our whole line surged forward and scarred swords hammered at the enemy with a new energy. The silver horn, so pure and clear, called again and again, a hunting call to the slaughter, and each time it sounded our men pressed forward into the branches of the felled trees to cut and stab and scream at the enemy who, suspecting some trickery, glanced nervously around the vale as they defended themselves. Gorfyddyd shouted at his men to break us now, and his royal guard led the attack on our centre. I heard Kernow's men screaming their war cry as they paid their Edling's debt. Nimue was among our spearmen and wielding a sword with both hands. I shouted at her to get back, but the bloodlust had swamped her soul and she fought like a fiend. The enemy was scared of her, knowing that she was of the Gods, and men tried to evade rather than fight her, but all the same I was glad when Galahad thrust her away from the fight. Galahad might have come late to the battle, but he fought with a savage glee that drove the enemy back from the twitching pile of dead and dying men.

The horn sounded a last time. And Arthur, at last, charged.

His armoured spearmen had come from their hiding place north of the river and now their horses foamed through the ford like a tide of thunder. They crashed over the bodies left by the early fighting and brought their bright spears down into the charge as they seared into the enemy's rearward units. Men scattered like chaff as the iron-shod horses drove deep into Gorfyddyd's army. Arthur's men divided into two groups that cut deep channels through that press of spearmen. They charged, they left their spears fixed in the dead and then made more dead with their swords.

And for a moment, for a glorious moment, I thought the enemy would break, but then Gorfyddyd saw the same danger and he shouted at his men to form a new shield-wall facing north. He would sacrifice his rearward men and instead make a new line of spears from the backmost ranks of his forward

468

troops. And that new line held. Owain, so long ago, had been right when he told me that not even Arthur's horses would charge home against a well-made shield-wall. Nor would they. Arthur had brought panic and death to a third of Cuneglas's army, but the rest were now formed properly and they defied his handful of cavalry.

And still the enemy outnumbered us.

Behind the tree fence our line was nowhere more than two men deep and in places it was just one. Arthur had failed to cut through to us, and Gorfyddyd knew that Arthur never would cut through so long as he kept a shield-wall facing the horses. He planted that shield-wall, abandoning the lost third of his army to Arthur's mercy, then turned the rest of his men to face Sagramor's shield-wall again. Gorfyddyd now knew Arthur's tactics, and he had defeated them, so he could hurl his spearmen into battle with a new confidence, though this time, instead of assaulting all along our line, he concentrated his attack along the vale's western edge in an attempt to turn our left flank.

The men on that flank fought, they killed and they died, but few men could have held the line for long, and none could have held it once Gundleus's Silurians outflanked us by climbing the lower slopes of the hill beneath the ghastly ghost-fence. The attack was brutal and the defence just as horrid. Morfans's surviving horsemen hurled themselves at the Silurians, Nimue spat curses at them and Tristan's fresh men fought there like champions, but if we had possessed double our numbers we could not have stopped the enemy from outflanking us and so our shield-wall, like a snake recoiling, collapsed on to the river bank where we made a defensive half-circle about two banners and the few wounded men we had managed to carry back with us. It was a terrible moment. I saw our shield-wall break, saw the enemy begin the slaughter of scattered men, and then I ran with the rest into the desperate huddle of survivors. We just had time to make a crude shield-wall, then we could only watch as Gorfyddyd's triumphant forces pursued and killed our fugitives. Tristan survived, as did Galahad and Sagramor, but that was small consolation for we had lost the battle and all that remained for us now was to die like heroes. In the northern half of the vale Arthur was still held by the shield-wall, while to the south our wall, that had resisted its enemies all that long day, had been broken and its remnant surrounded. We had gone into battle two hundred strong and now we numbered just over a hundred men.

Prince Cuneglas rode forward to ask for our surrender. His father was commanding the men facing Arthur and the King of Powys was content to leave the destruction of Sagramor's remaining spearmen to his son and to King Gundleus. Cuneglas, at least, did not insult my men. He curbed his horse a dozen paces from our line and raised an empty right hand to show he came in truce. 'Men of Dumnonia!' Cuneglas called. 'You have fought well, but to fight further is to die. I offer you life.'

'Use your sword once before you ask brave men to surrender,' I shouted at him.

'Afraid to fight, are you?' Sagramor jeered for so far none of us had seen Gorfyddyd, Cuncglas or Gundleus in the front of the enemy shield-wall. King Gundleus sat on his horse a few paces behind Prince Cuneglas. Nimue was cursing him, but whether or not he was aware of her I could not tell. If he was he could not have been worried, for we were all now trapped and surely doomed.

'Or fight me now!' I shouted at Cuneglas. 'Man to man, if you dare.'

Cuneglas gazed at me sadly. I was bloodstained, mud-covered, sweaty, bruised and hurting, while he was elegant in a short suit of scale armour and with a helmet surmounted by eagle feathers. He half smiled at me. 'I know you're not Arthur,' he said, 'for I saw him on horseback, but whoever you are, you have fought nobly. I offer you life.'

I pulled the sweaty, confining helmet off my head and tossed it into the centre of our half-circle. 'You know me, Lord Prince,' I said.

'Lord Derfel.' He named me, then did me honour. 'Lord Derfel Cadarn,' he said, 'if I stand surety for your life and for the lives of your men, will you surrender?'

'Lord Prince,' I said, 'I do not command here. You must speak to Lord Sagramor.'

Sagramor stepped up beside me and took off his black spired helmet that had been pierced by a spear so that his black curly hair was matted with blood. 'Lord Prince,' he said warily.

'I offer you life,' Cuneglas said, 'so long as you surrender.'

Sagramor pointed his curved sword to where Arthur's horsemen dominated the northern part of the vale. 'My Lord has not surrendered,' he told Cuneglas, 'so I cannot. But nevertheless' – he raised his voice – 'I release my men from their oaths.'

'I also,' I called to my men.

I am sure some were tempted to leave the ranks, but their comrades growled at them to stay, or perhaps the growl was simply the sound of tired men's defiance. Prince Cuneglas waited a few seconds, then took two thin gold torques from a pouch at his belt. He smiled at us. 'I salute your bravery, Lord Sagramor. I salute you, Lord Derfel.' He threw the gold so that it landed at our feet. I picked mine up and bent the ends apart so that it would fit around my neck. 'And Derfel Cadarn?' Cuneglas added. His round, friendly face was smiling.

'Lord Prince?'

'My sister asked that I should greet you. And so I do.'

My soul, so close to death, seemed to leap with joy at the greeting. 'Give her my greetings, Lord Prince,' I answered, 'and tell her I shall look forward to her company in the Other-world.' Then the thought of never seeing Ceinwyn again in this world overcame my joy and suddenly I wanted to weep.

Cuneglas saw my sadness. 'You need not die, Lord Derfel,' he said. 'I offer you life, and I stand surety for you. I offer you my friendship too, if you will have it.'

'I would honour it, Lord Prince,' I said, 'but while my Lord fights, I fight.'

Sagramor pulled his helmet on, wincing as the metal slid

over the spear wound on his scalp. 'I thank you, Lord Prince,' he told Cuneglas, 'and choose to fight you.'

Cuneglas turned his horse away. I looked at my sword, so battered and sticky, then I looked at my surviving men. 'If we did nothing else,' I told them, 'we made sure Gorfyddyd's army can't march on Dumnonia for many a long day. And maybe never! Who'd want to fight men like us twice?'

'The Blackshield Irish would,' Sagramor growled and he jerked his head towards the hillside where the ghost-fence had held our flank all day. And there, beyond the magic-ridden posts, was a war-band with round, black shields and the wicked long spears of Ireland. It was the garrison of Coel's Hill, Oengus Mac Airem's Blackshield Irish, who had come to join the killing.

Arthur was still fighting. He had torn one-third of his enemy's army into red ruin, but the rest now held him checked. He charged again and again in his efforts to break that shield-line but no horse on earth would ride through a thicket of men, shields and spears. Even Llamrei failed him and all that was left for him to do, I thought, was to thrust Excalibur deep into the blood-reddened soil and hope that the God Gofannon would come from the darkest abyss of the Otherworld to his rescue.

But no God came, nor did any man come from Magnis. We later learned that some volunteers had set out, but they arrived too late.

Powys's levy stayed on the hill, too scared to cross the ghost-fence, while beside them were gathered more than a hundred Irish warriors. Those men began to walk south, aiming to walk around the fence's vengeful ghosts. In a half-hour, I thought, those Blackshield Irish would be joining Cuneglas's final attack and so I went to Nimue. 'Swim the river,' I urged her. 'You can swim, can't you?'

She held up her left hand with its scar. 'You die here, Derfel,' she said, 'then I die here.'

'You must –'

472

'Hold your tongue,' she said, 'that's what you must do,' and then stood on tiptoe and kissed me on the mouth. 'Kill Gundleus for me before you die,' she pleaded.

One of our spearmen began singing the Death Song of Werlinna and the rest of them took up the slow, sad melody. Cavan, his cloak blackened by blood, was hammering the socket of his spearhead with a stone, trying to tighten the shaft's fit. 'I never thought it would come to this,' I said to him.

'Nor me, Lord,' he said, looking up from his work. His wolf-tail plume was bloodsoaked too, his helmet dented and there was a rag bandaged about his left thigh.

'I thought I was lucky,' I said. 'I always thought that, but perhaps every man does.'

'Not every man, Lord, no, but the best leaders do.'

I smiled my thanks. 'I would have liked to have seen Arthur's dream come true,' I said.

'There'd be no work for warriors if it did,' Cavan said dourly. 'We'd all be clerks or farmers. Maybe it's better this way. One last fight, then down to the Otherworld and into Mithras's service. We'll have a good time there, Lord. Plump women, good fighting, strong mead and rich gold for ever.'

'I shall be glad of your company there,' I told him, but in truth I was utterly bereft of joy. I did not want to go to the Otherworld yet, not while Ceinwyn still lived in this one. I pressed the armour at my chest to feel her small brooch and I thought of the madness that would never now run its course. I said her name aloud, puzzling Cavan. I was in love, but I would die without ever holding my love's hand or seeing her face again.

Then I was forced to forget Ceinwyn for the Blackshield Irish of Demetia, instead of walking around the fence, had decided to risk the ghosts and cross it. Then I saw why. A Druid had appeared on the hill to lead them through the spirit line. Nimue came to stand beside me and stared up the hill to where the tall, white-cowled and white-robed figure strode long-legged down the steep slope. The Irish followed him, and behind their black shields and long spears came Powys's levy with its mixed weaponry of bows, mattocks, axes, spears, single-sticks and hayforks.

My men's singing faded away. They hefted spears and touched their shield-edges on each other to make sure the wall was tight. The enemy, who had been readying their own shield-wall to attack ours, now turned to watch as the Druid brought the Irish down to the valley. Iorweth and Tanaburs ran to meet him, but the newly come Druid waved his long staff to order them out of his path and then he pushed his robe's hood back and we saw the long, plaited white beard and the swinging pigtail of his black-wrapped hair. It was Merlin.

Nimue cried when she saw Merlin, then she ran towards him. The enemy moved aside to let her pass, just as they parted to let Merlin walk towards her. Even on a battlefield a Druid could walk wherever he wanted, and this Druid was the most famed and powerful in all the land. Nimue ran and Merlin spread his arms to welcome her and she was still sobbing as at last she found him again and threw her thin white arms around his body. And suddenly I was glad for her.

Merlin kept one arm around Nimue as he strode towards us. Gorfyddyd had seen the Druid's arrival and now galloped his horse towards our part of the battlefield. Merlin raised his staff in greeting to the King, but ignored his questions. The Irish war-band had stopped at the hill's foot where they formed their grim black wall of shields.

Merlin walked towards me and, just as on the day when he had saved my life at Caer Sws, he came in stark, cold majesty. There was no smile on his dark face, no hint of joy in his deep eyes, just a look of such fierce anger that I sank to my knees and bowed my head as he came close. Sagramor did the same, then suddenly our whole battered band of spearmen was kneeling to the Druid.

He reached out with his black staff and touched first Sagramor and then me on the shoulders. 'Get up,' he said in a low, hard voice before turning to face the enemy. He took his arm from around Nimue's shoulders and held his black staff level above his tonsured head with both hands. He stared at

Gorfyddyd's army, then slowly lowered the staff, and such was the authority in that long, ancient, angry face and in that slow, sure gesture that the enemy all knelt to him. Only the two Druids stayed standing and the few horsemen remained in their saddles.

'For seven years,' Merlin said in a voice that reached clear across the vale and right up its deep centre so that even Arthur and his men could hear him, 'I have searched for the Knowledge of Britain. I have searched for the power of our ancestors that we abandoned when the Romans came. I have searched for those things that will restore this land to its rightful Gods, its own Gods, our Gods, the Gods who made us and who can be persuaded to come back to help us.' He spoke slowly and simply so that every man could hear and understand. 'Now,' he went on, 'I need help. I need men with swords, men with spears, men with hearts unafraid, to go with me to an enemy place to find the last Treasure of Britain. I seek the Cauldron of Clyddno Eiddyn. The Cauldron is our power, our lost power, our last hope to make Britain once again into the island of the Gods. I promise you nothing but hardship, I will give you no reward but death, I shall feed you nothing but bitterness, and will give you only gall to drink, but in return I ask for your swords and your lives. Who will come with me to find the Cauldron?'

He asked the question abruptly. We had expected him to talk of this sprawling blood-letting that had turned a green vale red, but instead he had ignored the fight as though it was irrelevant, almost as if he had not even noticed that he had strayed on to a battlefield. 'Who?' he asked again.

'Lord Merlin!' Gorfyddyd shouted before any man could respond. The enemy King pushed his horse through the ranks of his kneeling spearmen. 'Lord Merlin!' His voice was angry and his face bitter.

'Gorfyddyd,' Merlin acknowledged him.

'Your quest for the Cauldron can wait one short hour?' Gorfyddyd asked the question sarcastically.

'It can wait a year, Gorfyddyd ap Cadell. It can wait five years. It can wait for ever, but it should not.'

Gorfyddyd rode his horse into the open space between the spear-walls. He was seeing his great victory jeopardized and his claim to be the High King threatened by a Druid, and so he turned his horse towards his men, pushed back the cheek pieces of his winged helmet and raised his voice. 'There will be time to pledge spears to the Cauldron's quest,' he called to his men, 'but only when you have punished the whoremonger and drowned your spears in his men's souls. I have an oath to fulfil, and I will not let any man, even my Lord Merlin, deflect that oath's keeping. There can be no peace, no Cauldron, while the whore's lover lives.' He turned and stared at the wizard. 'You would save the whore-lover by this appeal?'

'I would not care, Gorfyddyd ap Cadell,' Merlin said, 'if the land opened and swallowed Arthur and his army. Nor if it engulfed yours as well.'

'Then we fight!' Gorfyddyd shouted, and he used his one arm to drag his sword free of its scabbard. 'These men' – he spoke to his army, but pointed the sword towards our banners – 'are yours. Their lands, their flocks, their gold and their homes are yours. Their wives and daughters are now your whores. You have fought them this far, would you now let them walk away? The Cauldron will not vanish with their lives, but your victory will vanish if we do not finish what we came here to do. We fight!'

There was a heartbeat of silence, then Gorfyddyd's men stood and began to beat their spear-shafts against their shields. Gorfyddyd gave Merlin a triumphant look, then kicked his horse back into his men's clamorous ranks.

Merlin turned to Sagramor and me. 'The Blackshield Irish,' he said in a casual voice, 'are on your side. I talked with them. They will attack Gorfyddyd's men and you shall have a great victory. May the Gods give you strength.' He turned again, put an arm around Nimue's shoulders and strode away through the enemy ranks that opened to let him through.

'It was a good try!' Gundleus called to Merlin. The King of

Powys was on the threshold of his great victory and that giddy prospect had filled him with the confidence to defy the Druid, but Merlin ignored the crowing insult and just walked away with Tanaburs and Iorweth.

Issa brought me Arthur's helmet. I crammed it back on my head, glad of its protection in these last few moments of battle.

The enemy re-formed its shield-wall. Few insults were shouted now, for few men had energy for anything other than the grim slaughter that loomed on the river's bank. Gorfyddyd, for the first time all day, dismounted and took his place in the wall. He had no shield, but he would still lead this last attack that would crush his hated enemy's power. He raised his sword, held it aloft for a few heartbeats, then brought it down.

The enemy charged.

We thrust spears and shields forward to meet them and the two walls crashed with a terrible sound. Gorfyddyd tried to thrust his sword past Arthur's shield, but I parried it and cut at him with Hywelbane. The sword glanced off his helmet, severing an eagle wing, then we were locked together by the pressure of the men thrusting from behind.

'Push them!' Gorfyddyd shouted at his men, then he spat at me over the shield. 'Your whore-lover,' he told me over the battle's din, 'hid while you fought.'

'She is no whore, Lord King,' I said, and tried to free Hywelbane from the crush to give him a blow, but the sword was trapped fast by the pressure of shields and men.

'She took enough gold from me,' Gorfyddyd said, 'and I don't pay women whose legs don't part.'

I heaved at Hywelbane and tried to stab at Gorfyddyd's feet, but the sword just glanced off the skirts of his armour. He laughed at my failure, spat at me again, then raised his head as he heard a dreadful screaming battle cry.

It was the attack of the Irish. The Blackshields of Oengus Mac Airem always charged with a ululating scream; a terrible battle-cry that seemed to suggest an inhuman delight in slaughter. Gorfyddyd shouted at his men to heave and cleave, to break our tiny shield-wall, and for a few seconds the men of

Powys and Siluria struck at us with a new frenzy in the belief that the Blackshields were coming to their aid, but then new screams from the rearward ranks made them realize that treachery had changed the Blackshields' allegiance. The Irish sliced into Gorfyddyd's ranks, their long spears finding easy targets, and suddenly, swiftly, Gorfyddyd's men collapsed like a pricked waterskin.

I saw the rage and panic cross Gorfyddyd's face. 'Surrender, Lord King!' I shouted to him, but his bodyguard found space to hack down with their swords and for a few desperate seconds I was defending myself too hard to see what happened to the King, though Issa did shout that he saw Gorfyddyd wounded. Galahad was beside me, thrusting and parrying, and then, magically it seemed, the enemy was fleeing. Our men pursued, joining with the Blackshields to drive the men of Powys and Siluria like a flock of sheep to where Arthur's horsemen waited to kill. I looked for Gundleus and saw him once among a mass of running, mud-covered, bloody men, and then I lost sight of him.

The vale had seen much death that day, but now it saw outright massacre for nothing makes for easy killing like a broken shield-wall. Arthur tried to stop the slaughter, but nothing could have checked that pent-up release of savagery, and his horsemen rode like avenging Gods among the panicked mass while we pursued and cut the fugitives down in an orgy of blood. Scores of the enemy succeeded in fleeing past the horsemen and crossing the ford to safety, but scores more were forced to take refuge in the village where at last they found the time and space to make a new shield-wall. Now it was their turn to be surrounded. The evening light was stretching across the vale, touching the trees with the first faint yellow sunlight of that long and bloody day as we stopped around the village. We were panting and our swords and spears were thick with blood.

Arthur, his sword as red as mine, slid heavily from Llamrei's back. The black mare was white with sweat, trembling, her pale eyes wide, while Arthur himself was bone-weary from his desperate fight. He had tried and tried again to break through to us; he had fought, his men told us, like a man possessed by the Gods even though it had seemed, all that long afternoon, as if the Gods had deserted him. Now, despite being victor of the day, he was in distress as he embraced Sagramor and then hugged me. 'I failed you, Derfel,' he said, 'I failed you.'

'No, Lord,' I said, 'we won,' and I pointed with my battered, reddened sword at Gorfyddyd's survivors who had rallied around the eagle banner of their trapped King. Gundleus's fox banner also showed there, though neither of the enemy Kings was in view.

'I failed,' Arthur said. 'I never broke through. There were too many.' That failure galled him, for he knew only too well how close we had come to utter defeat. Indeed, he felt he had been defeated, for his vaunted horsemen had been held and all he had been able to do was watch as we were cut down, but he was wrong. The victory was his, all his, for Arthur, alone of all the men of Dumnonia and Gwent, had possessed the confidence to offer battle. That battle had not gone as Arthur had planned; Tewdric had not marched to help us and Arthur's war horses had been checked by Gundleus's shield-wall; but it was still a victory and it had been brought about by one thing only: Arthur's courage in fighting at all. Merlin had intervened, of course, but Merlin never claimed the victory. That was Arthur's and though, at the time, Arthur was full of self-recrimination it was Lugg Vale, the one victory Arthur always despised, that turned him into the eventual ruler of Britain. The Arthur of the poets, the Arthur who wearies the tongues of the bards, the Arthur for whose return all men pray in these dark days, was made great by that stumbling shambles of a fight. Nowadays, of course, the poets do not sing the truth about Lugg Vale. They make it sound like a victory as complete as the later battles, and perhaps they are right to shape their story thus for in these hard times we need Arthur to have been a great hero from the very first, but the truth is that in those early years Arthur was vulnerable. He ruled Dumnonia by virtue of Owain's death and Bedwin's support, but as the

479

years of war ground on there were many who wished him gone. Gorfyddyd had his supporters in Dumnonia and, God forgive me, too many Christians were praying for Arthur's defeat. And that was why he fought, because he knew he was too weak not to fight. Arthur had to provide victory or lose everything, and in the end he did win, but only after coming within a blade's edge of disaster.

Arthur crossed to embrace Tristan, then to greet Oengus Mac Airem, the Irish King of Demetia, whose contingent had saved the battle. Arthur, as ever, went to his knees before a king, but Oengus lifted him up and gave him a bear hug. I turned and stared at the vale as the two men talked. It was foul with broken men, pitiful with dying horses, and glutted with corpses and littered weapons. Blood stank and the wounded cried. I felt more weary than I had ever felt in my life and so did my men, but I saw that Gorfyddyd's levy had come down from the hill to start plundering the dead and wounded and so I sent Cavan and a score of spearmen to drive them away. Ravens flapped black across the river to tear at dead men's bowels. I saw that the huts we had fired that morning still smoked. Then I thought of Ceinwyn, and amid all that bestial horror, my soul suddenly lifted as though on great white wings.

I turned back in time to see Merlin and Arthur embrace. Arthur almost seemed to collapse in the Druid's arms, but Merlin lifted and clasped him. Then the two of them walked towards the enemy's shields.

Prince Cuneglas and the Druid Iorweth came from the en-circled shield-wall. Cuneglas carried a spear, but no shield, while Arthur had Excalibur in its scabbard, but no other weapon. He paced ahead of Merlin and, as he drew near to Cuneglas, he dropped to one knee and bowed his head. 'Lord Prince,' he said.

'My father is dying,' Cuneglas said. 'A spear thrust took him in the back.' He made it sound like an accusation, though everyone knew that once a shield-wall broke many men would die with their wounds behind.

Arthur stayed on one knee. For a moment he did not seem to know what to say, then he looked up at Cuneglas. 'May I see him?' he asked. 'I offended your house, Lord Prince, and insulted its honour, and though no insult was meant, I would still beg your father's forgiveness.'

It was Cuneglas's turn to seem bemused, then he shrugged as though he was not certain he was making the right decision, but at last he gestured towards his shield-wall. Arthur stood and, side by side with the Prince, went to see the dying King Gorfyddyd.

I wanted to call out to Arthur not to go, but he was swallowed in the enemy's ranks before my muddled wits recovered. I cringed to think what Gorfyddyd would say to Arthur, and I knew Gorfyddyd would say those things, the same filthy things that he had spat at me across the rim of his spear-scarred shield. King Gorfyddyd was not a man to forgive his enemies, nor one to spare an enemy hurt, even if he was dying. Especially if he was dying. It would be Gorfyddyd's final pleasure in this world to know that he had hurt his foe. Sagramor shared my fears, and both of us watched in anguish as, after a few moments, Arthur emerged from the defeated ranks with a face as dark as Cruachan's Cave. Sagramor stepped towards him. 'He lied, Lord,' Sagramor said softly. 'He always lied.'

'I know he lied,' Arthur said, then shuddered. 'But some untruths are hard to hear and impossible to forgive.' Anger suddenly swelled up inside him and he drew Excalibur and turned fiercely on the trapped enemy. 'Does any man of you want to fight for your King's lies?' he shouted as he paced up and down their line. 'Is there one of you? Just one man willing to fight for that evil thing that dies with you? Just one? Or else I'll have your King's soul cursed to the last darkness! Come on, fight!' He flailed Excalibur at their raised shields. 'Fight! You scum!' His rage was as terrible as anything the vale had seen that whole day. 'In the name of the Gods,' he called, 'I declare your King a liar, a bastard, a thing without honour, a nothing!' He spat at them, then fumbled one-handed at the buckles of my leather breastplate that he still wore. He succeeded in freeing the shoulder straps, but not the waist, so that the breastplate hung in front of him like a blacksmith's apron. 'I'll make it easy for you!' he yelled. 'No armour. No shield. Come and fight me! Prove to me that your bastard whore-mongering King speaks truth! Not one of you?' His rage was out of control for he was in the Gods' hands now and spattering his anger at a world that cowered from his dreadful force. He spat again. 'You rancid whores!' He whirled around as Cuneglas reappeared in the shield-wall. 'You, whelp?' He pointed Excalibur at Cuneglas. 'You'd fight for that lump of dying filth?'

Cuneglas, like every man there, was shaken by Arthur's fury, but he walked weaponless from the shield-wall and then, just feet from Arthur, he sank to his knees. 'We are at your mercy, Lord Arthur,' he said and Arthur stared at him. His body was tense for all the rage and frustration of a day's fighting was boiling inside him and for a second I thought that Excalibur would hiss in the dusk to strike Cuneglas's head from his shoulders, but then Cuneglas looked up. 'I am now King of Powys, Lord Arthur, but at your mercy.'

Arthur closed his eyes. Then, still with his eyes shut, he felt for Excalibur's scabbard and thrust the long sword home. He turned away from Cuneglas, opened his eyes and stared at us, his spearmen, and I saw the madness pass away from him. He was still seething with anger, but the uncontrollable rage had passed and his voice was calm as he begged Cuneglas to stand. Then Arthur summoned his banner holders so that the twin standards of the dragon and the bear would add dignity to his words. 'My terms are these,' he said so that everyone in the darkening vale could hear him. 'I demand King Gundleus's head. He has kept it too long and the murderer of my King's mother must be brought to justice. That granted, I ask only for peace between King Cuneglas and my King and between King Cuneglas and King Tewdric. I ask for peace between all the Britons.'

There was an astonished silence. Arthur was the winner on this field. His forces had killed the enemy's king and captured Powys's heir, and every man in the vale expected Arthur to demand a royal ransom for Cuneglas's life. Instead he was asking for nothing but peace.

Cuneglas frowned. 'What of my throne?' he managed to ask.

'Your throne is yours, Lord King,' Arthur said. 'Whose else can it be? Accept my terms, Lord King, and you are free to return to it.'

'And Gundleus's throne?' Cuneglas asked, perhaps suspecting that Arthur wanted Siluria for himself.

'Is not yours,' Arthur replied firmly, 'nor mine. Together we shall find someone to keep it warm. Once Gundleus is dead,' he added ominously. 'Where is he?'

Cuneglas gestured towards the village. 'In one of the buildings, Lord.'

Arthur turned towards Powys's defeated spearmen and raised his voice so that each man could hear him. 'This war should never have been fought!' he called. 'That it was fought is my fault, and I accept that fault and shall pay for it in any coin other than my life. To the Princess Ceinwyn I owe more than apology and shall pay whatever she demands, but all I now ask is that we should be allies. New Saxons come daily to take our land and enslave our women. We should fight them, not amongst ourselves. I ask for your friendship, and as a token of that desire I leave you your land, your weapons and your gold. This is neither victory nor defeat' – he gestured at the bloody, smoke-palled valley – 'it is a peace. All I ask is peace and one life. That of Gundleus.' He looked back to Cuneglas and lowered his voice. 'I wait your decision, Lord King.'

The Druid Iorweth hurried to Cuneglas's side and the two men spoke together. Neither seemed to believe Arthur's offer, for warlords were not usually magnanimous in victory. Battle winners demanded ransom, gold, slaves and land; Arthur wanted only friendship. 'What of Gwent?' Cuneglas asked Arthur. 'What will Tewdric want?'

Arthur made a show of looking about the darkening valley. 'I see no men of Gwent, Lord King. If a man is not party to a fight then he cannot be party to the settlement afterward. But I can tell you, Lord King, that Gwent craves for peace. King

483

Tewdric will ask for nothing except your friendship and the friendship of my King. A friendship we shall mutually pledge never to break.'

'And I am free to go if I give you that pledge?' Cuneglas asked suspiciously.

'Wherever you wish, Lord King, though I ask your permission to come to you at Caer Sws to talk further.'

'And my men are free to go?' Cuneglas asked.

'With their weapons, their gold, their lives and my friendship,' Arthur answered. He was at his most earnest, desperate to ensure that this was the last battle ever to be fought among the Britons, though he had taken good care, I noticed, to mention nothing of Ratae. That surprise could wait.

Cuneglas still seemed to find the offer too good to be true, but then, perhaps remembering his former friendship with Arthur, he smiled. 'You shall have your peace, Lord Arthur.'

'On one last condition,' Arthur said unexpectedly and harshly, yet not loudly, so that only a few of us could hear his words. Cuneglas looked wary, but waited. 'Promise me, Lord King,' Arthur said, 'upon your oath and upon your honour, that at his death your father lied to me.'

Peace hung on Cuneglas's answer. He momentarily closed his eyes as though he was hurt; then he spoke. 'My father never cared for truth, Lord Arthur, but only for those words that would achieve his ambitions. My father was a liar, upon my oath.'

'Then we have peace!' Arthur exclaimed. I had only seen him happier once, and that was when he had wed his Guinevere, but now, amidst the smoke and reek of a battle won, he looked almost as joyful as he had in that flowered glade beside the river. Indeed, he could hardly speak for joy for he had gained what he wanted more than anything in all the world. He had made peace.

Messengers went north and south, to Caer Sws and to Durnovaria, to Magnis and into Siluria. Lugg Vale stank of blood and smoke. Many of the wounded were dying where they had fallen and their cries were pitiful in the night while the living huddled round fires and talked of wolves coming from the hills to feast on the battle's dead.

Arthur seemed almost bewildered by the size of his victory. He was now, though he could scarcely comprehend it, the effective ruler of southern Britain, for there were no other men who would dare stand against his army, battered though it was. He needed to talk with Tewdric, he needed to send spearmen back to the Saxon frontier, he desperately wanted his good news to reach Guinevere, and all the while men begged him for favours and land, for gold and rank. Merlin was telling him about the Cauldron, Cuneglas wanted to discuss Aelle's Saxons, while Arthur wanted to talk of Lancelot and Ceinwyn, and Oengus Mac Airem was demanding land, women, gold and slaves from Siluria.

I demanded only one thing on that night, and that one thing Arthur granted me.

He gave me Gundleus.

The King of Siluria had taken refuge in a small Roman-built temple that was attached to the larger Roman house in the small village. The temple was made of stone and had no windows except for a crude hole let into its high gable to let smoke out, and only one door which opened on to the house's stableyard. Gundleus had tried to escape from the vale, but his horse had been cut down by one of Arthur's horsemen and now, like a rat in its last hole, the King waited his doom. A handful of loyal Silurian spearmen guarded the temple door, but they deserted when they saw my warriors advance out of the dark.

Tanaburs alone was left to guard the firelit temple where he had made a small ghost-fence by placing two newly severed heads at the foot of the door's twin posts. He saw our spearheads glitter in the stableyard gate and he raised his moon-tipped staff as he spat curses at us. He was calling on the Gods to shrivel our souls when, quite suddenly, his screeching stopped.

It stopped when he heard Hywelbane scraping from her scabbard. At that sound he peered into the dark yard as Nimue and I advanced together and, recognizing me, he gave a small frightened cry like the sound of a hare trapped by a wildcat. He knew that I owned his soul and so he scuttled in terror through the temple door. Nimue kicked the two heads scornfully aside then followed me inside. She was carrying a sword. My men waited outside.

The temple had once been dedicated to some Roman God, though now it was the British Gods for whom the skulls were stacked so high against its bare stone walls. The skulls' dark eye-sockets gazed blankly towards the twin fires that lit the high narrow chamber where Tanaburs had made himself a circle of power with a ring of yellowing skulls. He now stood in that circle chanting spells, while behind him, against the far wall where a low stone altar was stained black with sacrificial blood, Gundleus waited with his drawn sword.

Tanaburs, his embroidered robe spattered with mud and blood, raised his staff and hurled foul curses at me. He cursed me by water and by fire, by earth and by air, by stone and by flesh, by dewfall and by moonlight, by life and by death, and not one of the curses stopped me as I slowly walked towards him with Nimue in her stained white robe beside me. Tanaburs spat a final curse, then pointed the staff straight at my face. 'Your mother lives, Saxon!' he cried. 'Your mother lives and her life is mine. You hear me, Saxon?' He leered at me from inside his circle and his ancient face was shadowed by the temple's twin fires, which gave his eyes a red, feral threat. 'You hear me?' he cried again. 'Your mother's soul is mine! I coupled with her to make it so! I made the two-backed beast with her and drew her blood to make her soul mine. Touch me, Saxon, and your mother's soul goes to the fire-dragons. She will be crushed by the ground, burned by the air, choked by the water and thrust into pain for evermore. And not just her soul, Saxon, but the soul of every living thing that ever slithered from her loins. I put her blood into the ground, Saxon, and slid my power into her belly.' He laughed and raised his staff high towards the temple's beamed roof. 'Touch me, Saxon, and the curse will take her life and through her life

486

yours.' He lowered the staff so it pointed at me again. 'But let me go, and you and she will live.'

I stopped at the circle's edge. The skulls did not make a ghost-fence, but there was still a dreadful power in their array. I could feel that power like unseen wings battering great strokes to baffle me. Cross the skull-circle, I thought, and I would enter the Gods' playground to contend against things I could not imagine, let alone understand. Tanaburs saw my uncertainty and smiled in triumph. 'Your mother is mine, Saxon,' he crooned, 'made mine, all mine, her blood and soul and body are mine, and that makes you mine for you were born in blood and pain from my body.' He moved his staff so that its moon tip touched my breast. 'Shall I take you to her, Saxon? She knows you live and a two-day journey will bring you back to her.' He smiled wickedly. 'You are mine,' he cried, 'all mine! I am your mother and your father, your soul and your life. I made the charm of oneness on your mother's womb and you are now my son! Ask her!' He twitched his staff towards Nimue. 'She knows that charm.'

Nimue said nothing, but just stared balefully at Gundleus while I looked into the Druid's horrid eyes. I was frightened to cross his circle, terrified by his threats, but then, in a sickening rush, the events of that long-ago night came back to me as if they had happened just yesterday. I remembered my mother's cries and I remembered her pleading with the soldiers to leave me at her side and I remembered the spearmen laughing and striking her head with their spear-staves, and I remembered this cackling Druid with the hares and moons on his robe and the bones in his hair and I remembered how he had lifted me and fondled me and said what a fine gift for the Gods I would make. All that I remembered, just as I remembered being lifted up, screaming for my mother who could not help me, and I remembered being carried through the twin lines of fire where the warriors danced and the women moaned, and I remembered Tanaburs holding me high above his tonsured head as he walked to the edge of a pit that was a black circle in the earth surrounded by fires whose flames burned bright enough to illuminate the blood-smeared tip of a sharpened stake that protruded from the bowels of the round dark pit. The memories were like pain serpents biting at my soul as I remembered the bloody scraps of flesh and skin hanging from the firelit stake and the half-comprehended horror of the broken bodies that writhed in slow pitiful agony as they died in the bloody darkness of this Druid's death-pit. And I remembered how I still screamed for my mother as Tanaburs lifted me to the stars and prepared to give me to his Gods. 'To Gofannon,' he had shouted, and my mother screamed as she was raped and I screamed because I knew I was going to die, 'to Lleullaw,' Tanaburs shouted, 'to Cernunnos, to Taranis, to Sucellos, to Bel!' And on that last great name he had hurled me down on to the killing stake.

And he had missed.

My mother had been screaming, and I still heard her screams as I kicked my way through Tanaburs's circle of skulls, and her screams melded into the Druid's shriek as I echoed his long-ago cry of death. 'To Bel!' I shouted.

Hywelbane cut down. And I did not miss. Hywelbane cut Tanaburs down through the shoulder, down through the ribs and such was the sheer blood-sodden anger in my soul that Hywelbane cut on down through his scrawny belly and deep into his stinking bowels so that his body burst apart like a rotted corpse, and all the time I screamed the awful scream of a little child being given to the death-pit.

The skull circle filled with blood and my eyes with tears as I looked up at the King who had slain Ralla's child and Mordred's mother. The King who had raped Nimue and taken her eye, and remembering that pain I took Hywelbane's hilt in both my hands and wrenched the blade free of the dirty offal at my feet and stepped across the Druid's body to carry death to Gundleus.

'He's mine,' Nimue shouted at me. She had taken off her eye-patch so that her empty socket leered red in the flamelight. She walked past me, smiling. 'You're mine,' she crooned, 'all mine,' and Gundleus screamed.

And perhaps, in the Otherworld, Norwenna heard that scream and knew that her son, her little winter-born son, was still the King.

Author's Note

It is hardly surprising that the Arthurian period of British history is known as the Dark Ages for we know almost nothing about the events and personalities of those years. We cannot even be certain that Arthur existed, though on balance it does seem likely that a great British hero called Arthur (or Artur or Artorius) temporarily checked the invading Saxons sometime during the early years of the sixth century AD. One history of that conflict was written during the 540s, Gildas's *De Excidio et Conquestu Britanniae*, and we might expect such a work to be an authoritative source on Arthur's achievements, but Gildas does not even mention Arthur, a fact much relished by those who dispute his existence.

Yet there is some early evidence for Arthur. Around the middle years of the sixth century, just when Gildas was writing his history, the surviving records show a surprising and atypical number of men called Arthur which suggests a sudden fashion for sons being named after a famous and powerful man. Such evidence is hardly conclusive, any more than is the earliest literary reference to Arthur, a glancing mention in the great epic poem *Y Gododdin* that was written around AD 600 to celebrate a battle between the northern British ('a mead-nourished host') and the Saxons, but many scholars believe that reference to Arthur is a much later interpolation.

After that one dubious mention in *Y Gododdin* we have to wait another two hundred years for Arthur's existence to be chronicled by an historian, a gap that weakens the authority of the evidence, yet nevertheless Nennius, who compiled his history of the Britons in the very last years of the eighth century, does make much of Arthur. Significantly Nennius never calls him a king, but rather describes Arthur as the *Dux Bellorum*, the Leader of Battles, a title I have translated as Warlord. Nennius was surely drawing on ancient folktales, which were a fertile source feeding the increasingly frequent retellings of the Arthur story that reached their zenith in the twelfth century when two writers in separate countries made Arthur into a hero for all times. In Britain Geoffrey of Monmouth wrote his wonderful and mythical *Historia Regum Britanniae* while in France the poet Chrétien de Troyes introduced, among other things, Lancelot and Camelot to the royal mix. The name Camelot might have been pure invention (or else arbitrarily adapted from Colchester's Roman name, Camulodunum), but otherwise Chrétien de Troyes was almost certainly drawing on Breton myths which might have preserved, like the Welsh folktales that fed Geoffrey's history, genuine memories of an ancient hero. Then, in the fifteenth century, Sir Thomas Malory wrote *Le Morte d'Arthur* which is the proto-version of our flamboyant Arthur legend with its Holy Grail, round table, lissom maidens, questing beasts, mighty wizards and enchanted swords.

It is probably impossible to disentangle this rich tradition to find the truth of Arthur, though many have tried and doubtless many will try again. Arthur is said to be a man of northern Britain, an Essex man, as well as a West Countryman. One recent work positively identifies Arthur as a sixth-century Welsh ruler called Owain Ddantgwyn, but as the authors then note that 'nothing is recorded of Owain Ddantgwyn' it does not prove very helpful. Camelot has been variously placed at Carlisle, Winchester, South Cadbury, Colchester and a dozen other places. My choice in this matter is capricious at best and fortified by the certainty that no real answer exists. I have given Camelot the invented name of Caer Cadarn and set it at South Cadbury in Somerset, not because I think it the likeliest site (though I do not think it the least likely), but because I know and love that part of Britain. Delve as we like, all we can safely deduce from history is that a man called Arthur probably lived in the fifth and sixth centuries, that he was a great warlord even if he was never a king, and that his greatest battles were fought against the hated Saxon invaders.

We might know very little about Arthur, but we can infer a lot from the times in which he probably lived. Fifth- and sixth-century Britain must have been a horrid place. The protective Romans left early in the fifth century and the Romanized Britons were thus abandoned to a ring of fearsome enemies. From the west came the marauding Irish who were close Celtic relatives to the British, but invaders, colonizers and slavers all the same. To the north were the strange people of the Scottish Highlands who were ever ready to come south on destructive raids, but neither of these enemies was so feared as the hated Saxons who first raided, then colonized, and afterwards captured eastern Britain, and who, in time, went on to capture Britain's heartland and rename it England.

The Britons who faced these enemies were far from united. Their kingdoms seemed to spend as much energy fighting each other as opposing the invaders, and they were doubtless divided ideologically as well. The Romans left a legacy of law, industry, learning and religion, but that legacy must have been opposed by many native traditions that had been violently suppressed in the long Roman occupation, but which had never entirely disappeared, and chief amongst those traditions is Druidism. The Romans crushed Druidism because of its associations with British (and thus anti-Roman) nationalism, and in its place introduced a welter of other religions including, of course, Christianity. Scholarly opinion suggests that Christianity was widespread in post-Roman Britain (though it would be an unfamiliar Christianity to modern minds), but undoubtedly paganism also existed, especially in the countryside (pagan comes from the Latin word for country people) and, as the post-Roman state crumbled, men and women must have clutched at whatever supernatural straws offered themselves. At least one modern scholar has suggested that Christianity was sympathetic to the remnants of British Druidism and that the two creeds existed in peaceful cooperation, but toleration has never been the strongest suit of the church and I doubt his

493

conclusions. My belief is that Arthur's Britain was a place as racked by religious dissent as it was by invasion and politics. In time, of course, the Arthur stories became heavily Christianized, especially in their obsession with the Holy Grail, though we might doubt whether any such chalice was known to Arthur. Yet the Grail Quest legends might not be wholly later fabrications for they bear a striking resemblance to popular Celtic folktales of warriors seeking magic cauldrons; heathen tales on to which, like so much else in Arthurian mythology, later Christian authors put their own pious gloss, thus burying a much earlier Arthurian tradition which now exists only in some very ancient and obscure lives of Celtic saints. That tradition, surprisingly, depicts Arthur as a villain and as an enemy of Christianity. The Celtic church, it seems, was not fond of Arthur and the saints' lives suggest that it was because he sequestered the church's money to fund his wars, which could explain why Gildas, a churchman and the closest contemporary historian to Arthur, refuses to give him credit for the British victories which temporarily checked the Saxon advance.

The Holy Thorn, of course, would have existed at Ynys Wydryn (Glastonbury) if we believe the legend that Joseph of Arimathaea brought the Holy Grail to Glastonbury in AD 63, though that story only really emerges in the twelfth century so I suspect my inclusion of the Thorn in *The Winter King* is one of my many deliberate anachronisms. When I began the book I was determined to exclude every anachronism, including the embellishments of Chrétien de Troyes, but such purity would have excluded Lancelot, Galahad, Excalibur and Camelot, let alone such figures as Merlin, Morgan and Nimue. Did Merlin exist? The evidence for his life is even less compelling than that for Arthur, and it is highly improbable that the two co-existed, yet they are inseparable and I found it impossible to leave Merlin out. Much anachronism could, however, happily be jettisoned, thus the fifth-century Arthur does not wear plate armour nor carry a mediaeval lance. He has no round table, though his warriors (not knights) would, in Celtic fashion, often have feasted in a circle on the ground. His castles would have been made of earth and wood, not from towering and turreted stone, and I doubt, sadly, that any arm clad in white samite, mystic and wonderful, rose from a misty mere to snatch his sword into eternity, though it is almost certain that the personal treasures of a great leader would, on his death, be cast into a lake as an offering to the Gods.

Most of the characters' names in the book are drawn from records of the fifth and sixth centuries, but about the people attached to those names we know next to nothing, just as we know very little about the post-Roman kingdoms of Britain – indeed modern histories even disagree on the number of kingdoms and their names. Dumnonia existed, as did Powys, while the narrator of the tale, Derfel (pronounced, in Welsh fashion, Dervel) is identified in some of the early tales as one of Arthur's warriors and it is noted that he later became a monk, but we know nothing else about him. Others, like Bishop Sansum, undoubtedly existed and remain known today as saints, though it seems precious little virtue was required of those early holy men.

The Winter King is, then, a tale of the Dark Ages in which legend and imagination must compensate for the dearth of historical records. About the only thing of which we can be fairly certain is the broad historical background: a Britain in which Roman towns, Roman roads, Roman villas and some Roman manners are still present, but also a Britain fast being destroyed by invasion and civil strife. Some of the Britons had already abandoned the fight and settled in Armorica, Brittany, which explains the persistence of the Arthurian tales in that part of France. But for those Britons who remained in their beloved island it was a time when they desperately sought salvation, both spiritual and military, and into that unhappy place came a man who, at least for a time, repelled the enemy. That man is my Arthur, a great warlord and a hero who fought against impossible odds to such effect that even fifteen hundred years later his enemies love and revere his memory.

BERNARD CORNWELL

ENEMY OF GOD

The Warrior king has brought peace to Britain – but for how long?

Following a hard fought victory, Arthur appears to have at last won the unity of the British kingdoms. He turns his attention to face the invading Saxons, while Merlin begins a quest to uncover the sacred Treasures of Britain, believing they will bring the might of the old Gods behind Arthur for one last decisive battle. But the quest soon unravels the fragile peace, as bitter rivalries come to the fore and threaten to undo Arthur's successes, while those closest to him move to betrayal.

In the second book of the Warlord Chronicles, Bernard Cornwell once again brings new life to Arthurian legend, weaving together historical fact, intense battles and the old-world magic of Merlin.

BERNARD CORNWELL

EXCALIBUR

Arthur's final test of courage is upon him ...

Arthur has crushed Lancelot's rebellion, but at a cost. Guinevere's betrayal has left him reeling, and his Saxon enemies seek to destroy him while he is weak. Chaos threatens to engulf Britain. Yet Arthur is a military genius and noble leader. As the last battle draws close, he prepares to fight his way to victory at Mount Badon and also win back the woman he lost. But in this final journey of the warlord, the intrigues of Mordred, now the adult heir to the throne of Britain, and the magics of the priestess Nimue could prove to be Arthur's downfall.

Bernard Cornwell concludes The Warlord Chronicles, bringing new life to Arthurian legend, successfully marrying myth with historical fact.

'A powerful and dramatic retelling of the Arthurian legend' Sharon Penman

BERNARD CORNWELL

SCOUNDREL

Bad to the bone – and then some ...

Paul Shanahan – part-time surveyor, erstwhile IRA arms dealer and some-time suspected CIA agent – is a full-time scoundrel. But he's the perfect man if you need an illicit operation done – and done well.

So when five million dollars worth of gold smuggled out of occupied Kuwait needs to get from Morocco to Miami by boat with no questions asked, Paul Shanahan is the name on everyone's lips.

Except this time Paul has other, more personal plans for the money. But first he must outwit the IRA, the CIA, British Intelligence and Palestinian terrorist Il Hayaween in order to prove just how big a scoundrel he really is ...

'Convincing, fast moving and extremely readable' *Today*

He just wanted a decent book to read ...

Not too much to ask, is it? It was in 1935 when Allen Lane, Managing Director of Bodley Head Publishers, stood on a platform at Exeter railway station looking for something good to read on his journey back to London. His choice was limited to popular magazines and poor-quality paperbacks – the same choice faced every day by the vast majority of readers, few of whom could afford hardbacks. Lane's disappointment and subsequent anger at the range of books generally available led him to found a company – and change the world.

'We believed in the existence in this country of a vast reading public for intelligent books at a low price, and staked everything on it'
Sir Allen Lane, 1902–1970, founder of Penguin Books

The quality paperback had arrived – and not just in bookshops. Lane was adamant that his Penguins should appear in chain stores and tobacconists, and should cost no more than a packet of cigarettes.

Reading habits (and cigarette prices) have changed since 1935, but Penguin still believes in publishing the best books for everybody to enjoy. We still believe that good design costs no more than bad design, and we still believe that quality books published passionately and responsibly make the world a better place.

So wherever you see the little bird – whether it's on a piece of prize-winning literary fiction or a celebrity autobiography, political tour de force or historical masterpiece, a serial-killer thriller, reference book, world classic or a piece of pure escapism – you can bet that it represents the very best that the genre has to offer.

Whatever you like to read – trust Penguin.